CAPTAIN COOK, THE CIRCUMNAVIGATOR

(Carefully copied from the Original Painting in Greenwich Hospital).

Presented to every purchaser of No. 3 of "The Adventures and Vicissitudes of Captain Cook, Mariner."

LONDON: E. HARRISON, MERTON HOUSE, SALISBURY SQUARE

THE
ADVENTURES AND VICISSITUDES
OF
CAPTAIN COOK,
MARINER.

Showing how by Honesty, Truth, and
Perseverance, a Poor, Friendless Orphan Boy
became a Great Man.

WITH ILLUSTRATIONS.

LONDON:

E. HARRISON, SALISBURY SQUARE, FLEET STREET.

1870.

THE
ADVENTURES AND VICISSITUDES
OF
CAPTAIN COOK,
MARINER.

Showing how by Honesty, Truth, and Perseverance, a Poor, Friendless Orphan Boy became a Great Man.

[JAMES COOK ATTACKED BY THE FARMER'S DOG.]

Chapter I.

HARD TIMES—HARD WEATHER—AND HARD HEARTS.

IT was the month of January: cold—bitter cold! Ice and snow had bound up the earth in their frozen mantles for many long weeks.

Even the robins—those cheerful, hardy little companions of the English homestead—couldn't bear up against the freezing blast, but ceased their sociable twitterings, drooped, and died, and were found by scores stiff and frozen under the snowclad hedges.

The hawthorn and the holly were the only things that looked healthy, and they seemed to flourish amid the surrounding desolation, the latter putting forth its bright red berries in rich profusion, as though anxious to throw a little warmth over the dreary face of nature.

In no part of the country was the cold more intense than in the North Riding of Yorkshire, where was situate the obscure village of Marton; and to none did the sting of poverty come with a keener edge than to the sick widow of James Cook, who, confined to her bed by a lingering and wasting disease, could do nothing to keep the hungry wolf from the door—that came to it in the shape of starvation for herself and her boy, who was dearer to her than life.

It was, then, a bitter morning in January, when Mary Cook, after a sleepless night, lay on her scantily-covered bed of wearisome pain, sadly watching her little James, then a boy of ten years old, as, with a few sticks gathered from the hedges, he strove to kindle a fire in their humble dwelling.

The poor mother, who required good living and nourishment, was slowly starving: disease and hunger were battling together to bring her to the grave.

She suffered intensely from bodily weakness, but she was compelled to endure a sharper pang than any bodily pain could inflict, as she thought what would become of her poor orphan when she was taken from him.

As she looked upon him, with his pale, patient face, and dark, sad eyes, made melancholy by long privations, as he performed his task of making the fire, the bitter tears trickled from her eyes, as she sent up from the depths of her heart a silent prayer, that He who feeds the young ravens that cry to Him would have mercy on her boy.

Little James, however, did not cry—that is, he uttered no complaint—but went about his work with a serious earnestness which, but for the miserable poverty that surrounded him, would have had in it something almost cheering.

Neither mother nor son had tasted food since the morning of the previous day—and that had been no more than a dry crust—and the hearts of both were sick and faint with the pangs of hunger.

But neither complained.

James having at length induced the fire to burn, rose from his knees and went to the bedside.

His mother's heart ached as she noticed how ghastly white he looked, and as she contemplated his sunken cheek and hollow eye, that ought to have been full of the roundness of youth and health, she seemed to drink the bitter cup of poverty to the very dregs.

She dared not trust herself to speak; but gently putting aside the brown, clustering curls from her boy's marble forehead, she drew him to her loving embrace, which was all her yearning heart could give him.

James returned her caress, and then looking thoughtfully at his mother, said:

"Ain't you hungry, mother dear?"

"No, darling," she replied, in a faltering voice; "I have no appetite for food, even if I had it. I am very ill, Jemmy dear."

"No wonder either," said the poor boy, the tears starting to his eyes, "and nothing to eat since yesterday!"

"Food would do me no good; but you—my poor dear—you need it!" cried the sick woman, in a voice of anguish. "Oh, pray God! send me food for my poor boy!" she earnestly exclaimed.

"And for my dear mother!" added James, no less fervently. "And you shall have it, too!" he continued. "I'm big enough to work, and I will work, too! I'll go down to Farmer Gripman's, where father was employed when he fell off the stack——"

"That killed him!" sighed the widow.

"Ah, poor father!" said James. "If he'd been alive, we shouldn't be like this—should we, mother?"

"No, my dear; nor should we if I were well enough to rise from my bed," moaned the poor woman.

"Well, mother, don't fret!" cried James, in a voice as cheerful as he could command, laying his pale cheek against the equally pallid face of his beloved relative. "Mr. Gripman will be more likely to give me work when he knows that poor father was killed on his farm."

Mrs. Cook sighed.

"He gave him no help when he lay on his sick-bed, James," she replied, sadly; "but perhaps he may be kinder to his son."

"At least, I'll go and try," said the boy. "I'll tell him I'm strong and willing: and you'll see, dear mother, if I don't get him to employ me—you'll see!"

James spoke hopefully, and his eye brightened up, and communicated a ray of hope even to the sad heart of the sick woman.

"Pray Heaven you may succeed, my love!" she exclaimed, fervently.

"I feel as if I should. And see how nicely the fire is burning up; it will be quite warm and cheerful presently. Good-bye, dear! I'll be back as soon as ever I can, and, I hope, with good news."

James kissed his mother affectionately, and after raking the wood on the fire, he threw a parting smile, that was like a gleam of sunshine, over the sick-bed, and went out.

The wintry wind blew keenly, and poor James's clothes were ill calculated to repel the keen blast.

While his mother was in health, she had been always careful to keep her boy free from rags; but now, alas! several rents in his garments told the tale that she was no longer able even to hold her needle, that was wont to be so busily employed by her industrious fingers.

The poor boy shivered from head to foot as the keen element pierced him, like a knife, to the very marrow. A good breakfast, or a basin of warm bread-and-milk, would have seemed delicious to him; but, alas! there was no such luxury awaiting him.

Still he did not despair; he was thinking of his mother—not himself—and that thought cheered him.

"I should be so glad if Farmer Gripman would take me on to work; then dear mother could have plenty to eat, and she'd soon get well, I know. Oh, I hope he'll give me something to do!"

With such thoughts in his mind, and such soliloquies on his tongue, the little hero of ten years trudged along—sometimes running, sometimes walking, and occasionally breathing on his blue knuckles to keep a little life in his frozen hands.

At length he reached Mr. Gripman's farm.

It was only when he reached the gate that his heart began to sink a little.

Like people going to the dentist's to have a tooth extracted, who suddenly feel the torture cease as they reach the door, poor James felt quite full as he laid his hand on Farmer Gripman's gate.

"I wonder what he'll say to me?" he thought.

There was a large dog in the garden before the house, whose nose and paws were just visible protruding from his kennel.

"P'rhaps he'll set his dog at me," James said to himself.

He stood thus irresolutely at the gate, imagining all sorts of dangers and difficulties; and having come, as it were, to the point, he felt strongly inclined to "right about face" and run back again.

But pray do not let this hesitation lessen my hero in the eyes of my readers.

Remember, he was only a little boy—ten years old—and that he had had nothing to eat for a day and a half.

Everyone knows how courageous a good dinner makes a fellow, and what a sinking, prostrating thing the want of it is! I am not speaking of the agonies of absolute starvation—they, of course, are desperate, like everything else in its extremity.

But poor James did not linger long in this state of indecision.

The thought of his mother once more flashed across him, and that thought decided him.

"She shall not die for want of food through me!" he said to himself, boldly. "I won't be a coward!"

As he gave utterance to this sentiment, he pushed open the gate, that creaked on its hinges, and entered the garden.

The sound aroused the dog, who darted out, and, of course—as dogs have a habit of doing—seeing a small, shabbily-dressed object of a somewhat shrinking demeanour, made a desperate rush towards it so far as his chain would allow, and set up a furious barking.

It so happened that Farmer Gripman was at that moment indoors, seated by the side of a blazing fire, having his lunch (a "snack," he called it), which consisted of a large lump of bacon, a monster loaf, and a large can of strong ale.

He was paying particular attention to these luxuries, when the loud barking of the dog arrested his attention.

At first he took no notice; but as the dog still continued his alarum, and as Farmer Gripman, never remarkable for good temper, was on that particular day exceedingly ill-humoured, he at last dashed the can on the table, and roared out:

"What be that dorg makin' that row about?"

No one answered, for the simple reason that no one happened to be near; therefore, as the row continued without the slightest mitigation, Farmer Gripman started from his seat, rushed to the door, and threw it open with a bang.

He had, of course, expected to encounter a tattered beggar; but when he saw a little, half-starved-looking boy, with distended eyes and nervously-agitated limbs, looking apprehensively at the dog without daring to pass him, he called out, in a gruff voice:

"Noo, then, come on! What bee'st thee afeard on?"

"I'm afraid the dog'll bite me!" faltered James, glancing with a terrified look at the open, hungry jaws and formidable fangs of the bullying brute.

"Doan't yer see 'e be chained oop?" roared the farmer. "Come on! If thou doan't, Oi'll set 'un at thee!"

At this threat, poor James, coming to the desperate conclusion that he could only be devoured once, and that then there would be an end of him altogether, went on.

He held his breath as he passed the savage animal, who howled and plunged and dragged at his chain in a most appalling manner.

The farmer, who was somewhat bewildered by the noise, shouted out:

"Lie down, durn thee!—lie down, Snap!"

Snap, finding his prey was beyond his reach, ceased his barking, and contented himself with growling out his indignation in a more private and confidential manner; still, however, keeping his eye savagely upon the slight form, that slowly drew near the burly farmer, who, with his mouth full, stood looking down upon him like a giant on a pigmy.

After contemplating him till he had got rid of the food he was chewing, he said, at length:

"Well, an' who be yow?"

"I'm James Cook, sir," answered the boy, timidly, "and I've made so bold as to come——"

"Well, then, p'raps you'll make a little bolder," interrupted the farmer, impatiently, "an' coom inside t' door: it be rather too coald out 'ere."

James crept in submissively; and Farmer Gripman, having slammed the door to, re-seated himself at the table, and continued his "snack" without seeming to take any notice of the poor famished boy, who stood cowering before him, almost like a culprit before the judge.

The fire looked very warm and cosy, the bacon and bread smelt very tempting, and the ale, as it gurgled down the farmer's capacious throat, sounded very inspiring; but poor James was not invited to partake.

At length, coming to a pause, Mr. Gripman took a long breath, and, resting both his arms on the table and leaning forward, asked him, in a dictatorial manner, what he wanted.

"Please, sir, I want something to do," faltered James.

"Oah! You be Jeames Cook's son, bean't thee?" asked the farmer.

"Yes, sir. Father broke his leg by falling from one of your stacks."

"Well, what be that to do wi' me?"

"Nothing, sir; only he died, and poor mother's so ill she can't get up from her bed, and we've got nothing to eat, and I thought p'r'aps you would give me a job of work."

"Work?" grunted the farmer, impatiently.

"Yes, sir; I'm very strong."

"Hoa—hoa! Strong! Yow look strong—very!" And the coarse, well-fed man gave a horse-laugh. "Strong!" he continued. "Why, yow look as though a poof o' wind 'ud blow 'ee from 'ere to Jericho!"

"I haven't had much to eat lately, sir," said the poor little boy, glancing wistfully at the bacon, "no more has mother; but I could get something for us both if you'd kindly give me some work to do."

"Work!" growled the farmer. "I've got noa work to do mysen wi' this weather; an' if yow coom 'ere for

work, yow've coom to the wrong pleace, an' soa I tell 'ee! Yow mun wait till t' froast breaks, an' then we'll see aboot it! I doan't pay boys to do nout!"

Poor James's heart sank within him, but he ventured on another appeal.

"Couldn't you give me a job of some kind, sir?" he asked, in a pleading, mournful voice. "I don't care what it is."

"Noa!" gruffly answered the farmer. "Doan't I tell 'ee soa?"

"But mother's almost starving, sir!" faltered the poor boy.

"I can't 'elp it!"

"But she'll die, sir; and then—then——"

The lad's heart was too full to utter another syllable, and he burst into tears.

"Why, then she'll be dead, an' there'll be an end of 'er!" said the unfeeling man, finishing in this rude manner the sentence the poor boy's grief had interrupted.

But James suddenly stopped the tears the coarse brutality of Farmer Gripman could never have caused to flow, and dashed them away with his hand.

"All hearts are not so hard as his," he thought. "I'll try somewhere else. Mother sha'n't die—I won't let her!"

It was, however, rather a forlorn hope, for there were no other farmers for some miles, and the inclement weather had brought everything to a standstill.

He was roused from his momentary reverie by the harsh voice of Mr. Gripman.

"Now, then, be 'ee goin' to stay 'ere all day?" he cried. "Yow've 'eerd what I say, an' now yow can go!"

"I'm going, sir," said James, faintly.

He turned towards the door, but a sudden weakness passed over him, and he staggered as though he would have fallen.

"Why, what be th' matter wi' yow!" exclaimed the farmer. "Yow look as if yow'd been drinkin'."

And with this mockery of a jest, he held out the can of ale.

James, who felt ready to faint with exhaustion, eagerly grasped it, and drank some of the sturdy beverage.

It revived him, and enabled him to open the door.

"Here!" cried the farmer. "'Ere be summat for thee to chaw."

As he spoke, he cut off a lump of bacon and bread, and threw them down on the table in much the same manner as he would have cast them to his dog.

But James was too hungry to be particular—besides, he would have endured any ill-treatment that purchased food for his mother.

He murmured his thanks, and, taking up the food, went slowly out at the door.

"Mind t' dorg—'e be moartal fond o' beacon!" bawled Mr. Gripman, facetiously, as James disappeared.

The animal in question, who had never removed his keen eyes from the door, renewed his barking and strugglings with more violence than ever as the boy drew near him.

It seemed as though the remark of the farmer was true, and that Snap was highly excited by either the sight or the smell of the meat the lad carried in his hand.

So fierce were his efforts to burst his bonds that he dragged his kennel from its resting-place.

James passed by him with considerable apprehension as hastily as possible, and made towards the gate.

He had nearly reached it, followed by the fierce baying of the savage brute behind him, when a sudden yell and clanking of the chain on the ground informed him that his enemy had burst his bonds, and was rapidly advancing towards him.

He uttered a startled cry as the animal came tearing madly along, and rushed towards the gate.

Unfortunately, however, the latch stuck fast, and before he could climb over, the mastiff's heavy paws were on his shoulders, and his hot breath puffing out, with unpleasant and ominous warmth, against the boy's neck and ears.

At the same moment Mr. Gripman appeared at the door, evidently delighted at his dog's prowess, and as evidently reckless as to its results.

"I told 'ee 'e wur fond o' beacon!" he cried. "Coom

off, drat thee!" he added, calling to the animal, and laughing at the same time.

But the dog had no such intentions.

Growling fiercely, he dragged his half-starved, weak victim backwards with his strong paws, and then made a dash at his throat.

The animal's intentions were frustrated by the sudden lifting of the boy's arm, which act for a moment disconcerted the dog.

But the next instant the brute was on him again, and by a sudden snap had gripped—not his throat, but the handkerchief that was loosely knotted round it, and, having now got a hold, he shook the poor fellow with savage violence, growling all the time like a tiger over his prey.

The position of James Cook was critical in the extreme.

He had no weapon of any kind, and he was very weak, his only strength at that moment being the strength of sheer desperation.

He could feel the nose of the dog pressing against his throat, and every now and then the grazing of the sharp teeth against the flesh, as the animal tried to gain a hold with his fangs.

The boy desperately seized his assailant by the ears, and endeavoured to hold him back, but he might as well have tried to repel the rush of a torrent.

The dog, irritated at being thus retained, grew more furious and vindictive every moment.

The attacker and the attacked rolled over on the ground together.

Even the admiring Gripman began to think the affair was getting a little past a joke, and came rolling down the path at a jog-trot.

Suddenly, with a savage jerk of his head, the mastiff tore the handkerchief completely away from the boy's neck, and again flew like a panther at his victim's throat.

Poor James was exhausted; he could just see the angry, widely-extended jaws and the cruel fangs of his adversary, but he had no longer strength to resist.

Uttering a faint cry for help, he closed his eyes with a shudder of horrible apprehension, expecting every moment to feel the sharp fangs buried in his flesh, when a loud report was suddenly heard, and, with a yell of agony, the ferocious animal fell mortally wounded to the earth.

Farmer Gripman uttered a corresponding yell as he arrived at the spot and knelt by the side of his dying favourite, not troubling himself about poor James Cook, who, scarcely conscious of what he was doing, staggered to his feet, dragged the gate open desperately, and ran along the snowy road, until, utterly exhausted, he dropped down senseless by the wayside.

Chapter II.

COMPANIONS IN MISFORTUNE.

WHEN James Cook came at length to his senses and opened his eyes, he saw a face bent down over him, and a pair of large, round, black eyes watching him with a great deal of anxiety.

James recognised the face immediately.

"Ah! Ikey," he said, faintly. "Is it you?"

"Yes," returned the individual addressed—"it's me; an' ain't I glad to see yer open yer heyes an' yer mouth, an' speak to a cove! Blest if I didn't think yer vas gone for good!"

He who uttered these words was a boy of about the same age as James—perhaps a little older; but between the two lads there was a great difference.

On the pale faces of both the gaunt hand of Famine had laid its unmistakable marks.

Ghastly, wan, and sickly, their very smiles seemed sad and unnatural, like a hollow jest coming from dying lips.

Both were poorly clad; but whilst James was only partially ragged, Ikey was such a bundle of tatters that he looked more like a scarecrow than a human being.

There was, besides, a look of cunning in the black eyes—seeming, from the hollowness of their sockets, preternaturally large—that was apt to produce an unfavourable impression.

His head altogether seemed to possess a similar disproportion, and presented an appearance as though it might have belonged originally to some other individual of much larger proportions, and had somehow been stuck on to the trunk of its present owner by mistake.

But this peculiarity might have owed its existence to a long course of bad feeding.

Continual hunger and privation had stunted the poor boy's growth, and stamped his young face with the marks of premature age, whilst his attenuated limbs, like those of a skeleton, made all the extremities by contrast look disproportionately large.

Ichabod—or Ikey Mangles, as he was called—was one of those unfortunate waifs who seemed to belong to nobody.

When or where he came into the world nobody seemed to know or care.

All that appeared evident was, that he *was in the* world, and that he must scramble through it in the best way he could.

In better times, before his father's death, little James Cook had pitied the forlorn condition of this poor boy, and had many a time given him portions of his meals and many a good warm by his fireside; and now adversity had spread its dark pinions over the once happy roof, Ikey did not forget these kindnesses, but tried to repay them by the only means in his power—sympathy.

He was now kneeling down on the cold ground, supporting his friend's head, and looking at him with much such solicitude as a mother or a nurse might contemplate the features of a sick child.

He was greatly rejoiced to hear James speak, and endeavoured to administer all the consolation in his power.

"Ye're all right now, Jem; that theer dorg 'll never trouble you nor anyvun helse agin," he said.

"Ah, that dog!" reiterated James, in rather a wandering tone, as though he had not quite come to his senses. "I remember the dog—yes—yes!"

"Vell, Hi should think yer hought to remember 'im, considerin' as 'e as near as a toucher strangilated yer."

"Where is he?" cried James, with a shudder, glancing round apprehensively, as though he almost expected the brute at his elbow.

"Don't be afear'd! 'e ain't 'ere," said Ikey, soothingly.

"Where is he, then?"

"Wheer Hi left 'im—lyin' on the ground in his own garding—with a bullet in 'is nob."

Ikey grinned as he spoke, and produced a curious kind of apology for a pistol, which looked as though it would do anything but fire.

"Did you kill that great dog with this?" asked James, in a tone of wonder.

"Hi jest did," answered Ikey; "though anyvun 'd 'ardly believe it unless they see it. This 'ere pistol's summat like me, it's a rum 'un to look at but a good 'un to go."

James stretched forth his thin hand, and grasped the tremendous weapon, looking at it admiringly.

"Don't touch the trigger, Jem; and don't pint th' muzzle agin my nut, 'cos it's loaded," remarked Ikey, gently guiding the barrel with his hand from too dangerous a proximity to the member alluded to.

"Are you going to shoot another dog?" inquired James.

"No; Hi'm a goin' to try to shoot an 'are," returned Ikey; "this 'ere's loaded wi' powder an' shot, an' the fust pussy as Hi sees, 'as th' lot!"

"But they call that poaching, don't they?"

"Hi don't care vot they calls it," said Ikey, doggedly; "but Hi calls vot Hi be doin' now starvin' by hinches, an' Hi von't starve while theers 'ares a runnin' in th' woods an' across th' roads, right hunder yer nose, a askin' yer to shoot 'em."

"Oh, Ikey," cried James, reprovingly, "don't turn poacher!"

"Vhy not, vhen it's to keep yer alive?"

"Mother says it's wrong. She knows what it is to be hungry, but I've often heard her say it was better to starve than to take what doesn't belong to us."

"Vell, that's all werry vell, Jem, for people as can't heat; but when a cove gets so rawenous as 'e feels inclined to swaller 'is boots—if 'e'd got any—vot's 'e to do?"

Poor James felt inclined to reply, "swallow his boots;" but it struck him as somewhat absurd, and he was silent.

"Vhy, now, there's your poor mother," Ikey continued, "as a good basin o' 'are soup, sich as I can make when I've got the 'are, 'ud set upon 'er legs direckly."

"D'ye think so, Ikey?" exclaimed James, eagerly.

"Hi'm sure on it!" affirmed his companion, positively. "An' do you mean to say if an 'are vos to come an' jump slap into yer arms, an' say 'make me into soup,' as yer vouldn't?"

James could not help smiling at Ikey's rhetoric, but it was but a faint shadow of a smile, and he replied:

"It wouldn't be any use my taking home a hare I hadn't come by honestly. Mother 'd be sure to ask me where I got it, and I couldn't tell a lie about it; and when she knew I'd shot it, she wouldn't touch it—no, not to save her life!"

James spoke warmly, and Ikey gave up—or seemed to give up—his point; but he had, nevertheless, made up his mind that by hook or by crook Mrs. Cook should taste some of his hare soup that very day.

"Vell," he said, "yer looks better than yer did, Jem. I s'pose ye're a goin' 'ome, ain't yer?"

"Yes," replied James, sadly, "and I've only bad news to tell poor mother when I get there. I thought Farmer Gripman would have given me a job, as father worked on his farm——"

"What! 'e give yer a job?" exclaimed Ikey, with an explosion of disgust and indignation. "Not 'e! If yer expecks anythink out o' 'im, yer'll be disappointed. 'E ain't got no 'eart, nor bowels neither. Hi vent vonce an' axed 'im for a job, an' 'e set 'is dorg at me, but Hi've paid 'im out for tearin' my linnin."

Ikey glanced at his rags with a peculiar smile at this joke against himself, and then seeing his companion rise, he followed his example, thrusting his pistol in some mysterious manner into a place of concealment in his ragged breeches.

"Well, good-bye, Jem," he said; "an' if Hi finds an' 'are vot's dead in th' path—an' Hi hoften does—Hi shall bring it over to your cottage an' make a prime drop o' soup; so don't be surprised if yer sees me."

He sprang over the hedge at these words, and disappeared.

James stood still, as though lost in thought.

Suddenly he started from his reverie.

"How can I go home and make dear mother miserable with the bad news I have to tell her?" he sadly soliloquised. "And I have lost the food I hoped to carry her. Oh, what shall I do?" he cried, in despair, as he leant disconsolately against a gate at the roadside, and buried his face in his hands—"what shall I do?"

"Why, stand out of my way, you young ragamuffin!" cried a harsh, unfeeling voice, and immediately he felt the sharp cut of a whip.

The poor boy, thus rudely startled from his troubled meditations, looked up in a scared manner and encountered the supercilious, but otherwise handsome countenance of Octavius Challoner, the nephew of Squire Markham, who owned a large estate in the neighbourhood, and who, with his cousin Augustus, the squire's only son—a boy of about James's age—was making his way to the Hall.

James was so taken aback by this sudden assault, that he only looked, without moving.

"What are you gaping at, idiot?" he exclaimed, sternly. "Get out of the way!" He accompanied these words with a cruel stripe across the poor child's knuckles, already blue and aching with the cold.

"Oh, Otty—don't!" cried his young cousin, in a tone of sympathy. "See, you've made his knuckles bleed!"

"Oh, psha!" returned the amiable Octavius. "It will teach him to move a little quicker when he's ordered. Here, you boy," he cried, in the same brutal tone, "don't stand wriggling there! Open the gate!"

The poor boy was indeed writhing with the pain of the unfeeling blow, and had buried his swollen knuckles under his folded arms, to endeavour by the pressure to lessen the anguish he endured; but there was not the vestige of a tear.

"Do you hear me, you whelp?" shouted the infuriated coward, who looked upon James's conduct as dogged obstinacy.

"Yes, sir," said the boy, looking up at him with the quiet firmness of a martyr, "I hear you."

"Then why don't you obey me?"

"I'll open the gate if you ask me civilly, and don't call me names," replied James, quietly.

"I tell you what!" cried the squire's nephew, more irritated than ever, "if you stand there talking such stuff to me, I'll break your back for you!"

He raised his whip as he spoke.

"Oh! no—no, cousin!" interposed Augustus, whose pity was strongly excited by the sufferings and the heroism of the poor pale-faced boy he gazed upon. "Don't hit him again!"

He clung to his cousin as he spoke.

"But I will hit him again!" shouted Octavius, putting his boy-cousin roughly aside. "I'll cut the obstinacy out of the young beggar!"

He advanced to where James stood, and seized him by the collar, as though he would have wrenched his poor garments from off his back.

"Now," he said, in a brutal tone, raising the cruel whip, "do you mean to open that gate?"

"Yes," answered the poor boy, in the same quiet tone as before, "if you ask me civilly: I told you I would."

"You'll open it without! What does a cur like you know, or deserve to know, about civility?"

"I won't open it, unless you do ask me civilly," said the boy.

"You won't?"

"No!"

"I warn you!—will you open it?"

"No!"

"Will you open that gate, I say?"

The cowardly wretch accompanied these words by a shake that threatened destruction to the poor boy's threadbare garments, and made his teeth chatter and his brain reel.

"For the last time?"

"No!" cried James, in a voice as loud as his weakness would permit, and that, alas! was anything but stoutly. "I will not!"

"Then, you obstinate whelp, I'll——"

The unfeeling scoundrel raised the whip to the full extent of his arm, and his malignant and unreasonable rage would have probably finished his poor victim's earthly career, when a grasp like an iron vice falling on his wrist suddenly arrested the threatened blow, whilst a hand seizing the whip, wrenched it from his grasp.

He turned with an angry imprecation, and found himself face to face with an old man, whose reverend appearance and suit of sober black seemed to proclaim him a minister, but whose strength of limb was a strange contradiction to his snow-white locks and calm, pacific looks.

The squire's nephew was astounded, as well he might be, and glared at the intruder utterly unable to speak.

"How long has it been the custom for Englishmen to raise their hands against children, armed with such weapons as this?" said the old man, turning the whip over in his hand as he spoke.

"He's an obstinate, insolent cub!" exclaimed the discomfited castigator, "and richly deserves——"

"Tut, tut!—say no more," interrupted the old gentleman, abruptly, "or I may be induced to call you an unfeeling brute, or an unmanly villain, or some other impertinent name; and as you seem so sensitive, perhaps it might offend you."

"Who are you, sir?" fiercely demanded Octavius.

"Don't speak so loud, Mr. Challoner!" said the old gentleman, with the utmost calmness. "We don't want the whole county to hear us. Lend me your ear!"

Bending forward as he spoke, he whispered a word to him.

What it was the old man breathed was not audible, but the change it produced in the man to whose ear it was conveyed was sudden and marvellous.

His wrath and fierceness vanished in a moment: the lion became a lamb.

"Come with me," said the old gentleman, "I will only detain you a few moments."

He led the way into a kind of plantation, the fierce Octavius following mechanically. His young cousin, glancing round and seeing his relative occupied with his own thoughts, hastily approached James

"I'm very sorry for this," said the kind-hearted boy, hastily; "I would have prevented it if I could; but don't think anything of it: my cousin is out of temper. You'll try to forgive him, won't you?"

The young gentleman spoke in a kind, gentle tone, and, as he uttered these words, threw one arm round the poor ragged boy he addressed, and placed the hand that was at liberty tenderly on his bruised knuckles.

The voice and manner of the young speaker were so thoroughly kind and earnest that poor James, who had remained utterly impervious to the violent threats he had so lately endured, gave in at once to this tender sympathy, and burst into a flood of tears that relieved his overcharged heart.

"You will forgive my cousin, won't you?" asked Augustus.

"I will," answered James, "for your sake."

"Thank you!" returned the young peacemaker.

The boys shook hands warmly, to the great distress of poor James's bruised knuckles; and then they parted, each with a lighter heart than they had known that day.

Chapter III.

THE WOUNDED HARE.

JAMES COOK hurried along the road in a somewhat complicated state of mind.

He was somewhat astonished at his own firmness, and could hardly understand how it was that he, who was so alarmed at a brute with four legs, could have been so resolute when in the grasp of a brute with two.

Young as he was, he was becoming conscious of the possession of a power of which hitherto he had known nothing.

This was the first development of his future character.

Then he was greatly cheered by the kind words of the squire's son.

They warmed his young heart, and made him forget the pain of the blows he had endured.

And then came the cloud over all these pleasant sensations as he thought of his sick mother.

"Poor dear mother!" he cried, sadly.

He had hardly uttered this ejaculation when the report of a gun at some distance made him start.

He recovered himself, however, and went on, his thoughts again reverting to the pallid but beloved form, from which the very life was oozing away, and he powerless to preserve it.

"How I do wish I could get some work to do!" he exclaimed, pausing, and giving utterance to his thoughts aloud. "I shouldn't care how hard it was; I'd toil night and day for her! If I could only get her something to make her strong and well as she used to be, I should be quite happy!"

Alas! the poor boy little knew that her hours of whom he spoke were numbered.

He little deemed that at that moment the Angel of Death was preparing to spread his dark wings over the poor dwelling-place he called his home.

He felt that if he could only procure food for his mother she would recover rapidly.

He was regardless of his own cravings, though they now were becoming almost unendurable.

But he threw them aside with a strong effort beyond his years, and once more fastened his thoughts upon his mother.

"Oh, pray God help us!" he cried, clasping his hands fervently—"pray God send food to save my dear mother's life!"

The prayer had hardly passed his lips when a slight rustling was heard in the hedge at one side of the road.

He looked in the direction from whence the sound proceeded, and perceived a wounded hare that had been shot in the loins, painfully dragging itself through the hedge.

With much effort it slowly crossed to the middle of the road, marking its course over the snow-clad ground by a trail of blood.

"Poor thing!" cried James, piteously: "some one has shot it."

The wounded animal stopped at the feet of the young speaker, unable to proceed further, and falling over on its side, gave a few convulsive struggles and lay dead before him.

It seemed as though Heaven had heard and answered his prayer for food.

"Oh yes!" he cried, after looking at the hare thoughtfully for a moment. "I do believe this is sent for us!

I know it's wrong to kill a hare; but I don't think it is to take one that we find dead in the road, when we're starving, too, for want of food."

With a conscience clear from any sense of guilt, James picked up the hare, and putting it inside his tattered coat, buttoned it up as closely as he could, the warmth of the animal's body communicating a comfortable sensation of heat to his own.

He had hardly accomplished this when a man of stern visage burst through the hedge, and hastily advancing to the centre of the road, seized the lad by the collar.

The attire of the man, consisting of shooting-coat, breeches, and gaiters, left no doubt as to his calling.

He was evidently one of the squire's gamekeepers.

"So I've caught you at last, my fine feller!" cried the man, gruffly. "I thought I should drop upon you one of these fine days!"

The tightness of the man's grasp, and the strain upon the buttons of the coat, were more than they could bear; the consequence was, they parted company with the cloth simultaneously, and the dead hare, released from its confinement, fell to the ground.

"You're a pretty fellow!" exclaimed the gamekeeper, "upon my word!"

"I didn't kill it, sir—indeed I didn't!" affirmed James.

"Of course not!" said the man, ironically—"oh, no! And pray who did kill it, then?" he asked.

"I don't know, sir. It crawled out, wounded and bleeding, from the hedge yonder—you can see the way it came by the blood—and died at my feet; and as my mother's ill and starving at home, I thought I might take it."

"A very likely story!" sneered the keeper; "but it won't do for me. I've watched you sneaking about for some time, and, now I've caught you, off you go before his honour the squire!"

The man gave the small form he grasped a rough shake, and was about to drag him away, when another form, equally diminutive and shadowy, looked over the hedge.

"'Ere, old 'ard, Mr. Keeper!" it cried. "Ye're hon th' wrong tack! It ain't 'e as yer vants: it's me!"

The boy crept through the hedge as he spoke and came forward, looking the astonished keeper full in the face as bold as brass.

"Who are you?" he growled.

"Hi'm Hikey Mangles! It wur me as shot that 'ere 'are! Hi shot 'un wi' this pistol!"

He produced the weapon as he spoke.

"An' now yer knows the rights on it, yer can take me, and let Jem go!"

The keeper looked aghast at the assurance of the cadaverous little atom with the large head and eyes, but he did not release his prisoner.

"You're confederates!" he cried, making a grab at Ikey and seizing him by the arm, that was mere skin and bone. "I shall take yer both!"

"Yer may as vell carry us, then," remarked Ikey, facetiously. "Ve don't veigh more than a few hounces, vith all the fattenin' ve gets out o' th' 'ares."

"I'll horsewhip yer, if yer talk to me!" threatened the indignant keeper. "Come along!"

He was about to drag the boys away very unceremoniously, when a voice at his elbow made him stop suddenly.

James immediately recognised the speaker as the old white-haired gentleman in the black suit who had a little while before interposed in his behalf.

The keeper, still grasping the boys by the collars of their tattered coats, stood gazing with open eyes and mouth at the reverend old gentleman.

"Stay!" said the latter, in a calm tone. "I've a word to say to you."

These words were addressed to the gamekeeper, who did not appear to relish the interruption.

However, as the speaker appeared to be a minister, the man could not very well refuse.

But he obeyed with a bad grace, as he said, in an impatient manner:

"I hope you won't keep me long, sir. I've got to take these two young vagrants up to the Hall."

"It is of these boys I would speak," continued the stranger. "I've been listening to your conversation for some time, and I think the best thing you can do is to set them both at liberty."

"Well, then, yer'll excuse me, sir," returned the gamekeeper, "I don't! I know my business, sir, p'r'aps a little better than you can teach me; and now I've got 'em I mean to keep 'em!"

"Come, now, don't be hard! The offence these poor boys have committed, if it be an offence at all, is a very trifling one, and——"

"It's all very well," interrupted Burnley, who was Squire Markham's head gamekeeper, and who considered himself a very important personage, "for you to talk, sir; gentlemen of your cloth are bound to believe in the good o' human natur'; but I say it's all 'umbug! There's no good about it at all, 'specially in boys. They're a compound o' depravity an' everything that's bad!"

"I deny that they have done anything that's *bad!*" said the old gentleman.

"I haven't, sir," pleaded James, with an imploring look towards his advocate.

"No more 'a Hi," added Ikey, "'xcep shootin' an 'are by haccident, as run across the path jest as I vos a firin' off my pistol."

This assertion roused the gamekeeper's ire wonderfully.

"There! did yer ever hear the likes o' that?" he exclaimed, giving the boy a vicious shake. "The fact is, these boys are as artful as Old Nick himself, and now they see you take their part, they'll pitch you in lies by the cartload, and stick to 'em till they're black in the face!"

"Listen to me, my friend," said the old gentleman, in the same quiet tone as before, "and I'll give you a reason why these lads should be allowed to go free."

The eyes of the boys brightened up with the hope of speedy release; but the incredulous Burnley, with an ironical laugh and an ominous shake of the head, only demanded:

"Why—why should they be allowed to go free?"

"This lad," answered the old gentleman, placing his hand on James Cook's curly head, "I know to be perfectly innocent, for I was watching him, when I saw the hare crawl from the hedge towards him and fall dead at his feet."

"Oh!" ejaculated Burnley, in a tone of ironical conviction, "that was it, was it? An' what o' this one?" he inquired, giving Ikey another shake up that made his rags flutter like so many live things—"what of him?"

"He deserves liberty for the straightforward manner in which he came forward to rescue his companion by taking his fault upon his own shoulders," answered the old gentleman.

"That may be your opinion, but it ain't mine," said the imperious gamekeeper, who was neither to be mollified nor convinced. "I shall take 'em both. If the squire likes to let 'em off, he can! Come on!"

"Stop! It seems, then, you're determined not to let these boys go?"

"Yes."

"You're quite resolved?"

"Quite!" was the dogged answer.

"Then," replied the old gentleman, "I am equally resolved that you shall!"

"What?" shouted the indignant Burnley, whose face was crimson at this daring announcement.

"I say," continued the veteran defender, "if you deny those boys liberty at my intercession, I'll try what force can do!"

As he spoke he threw his arms round the gamekeeper and pinioned him.

Ikey took an immediate advantage of this act to give himself a jerk that set him free with the loss of the collar of his coat, which remained in Mr. Burnley's grasp.

The latter, who in his own mind laughed to scorn the idea of an old white-haired man detaining him by main force, gave himself an indignant shake to dislodge his venerable opponent.

But, to his great surprise, his effort was not attended with the success he anticipated.

The old gentleman not only was not to be dislodged, but held him rooted to the spot as though he had been screwed up in a vice.

He became furious and struggled violently, and in order to be more at liberty for an encounter that appeared inevitable, he released James, who, with his companion, Ikey, looked on in breathless amazement at the strange sight that presented itself:

An old white-haired man holding a stalwart, burly gamekeeper in his arms as firmly and as calmly as he would have detained a refractory child.

"Let me go!" shouted the man, with an angry imprecation.

"You must get away first!" quietly answered his captor.

"If you interfere wi' me in my duty," shouted the gamekeeper, in a voice hoarse with passion, the veins in his purple forehead swelling almost to bursting as he struggled to get free, "I'll brain thee!"

The old gentleman, in reply to this, raised him in his arms and dashed him to the ground.

John Burnley was as tough as iron, and, springing up, rushed upon the old gentleman with his brawny fist clenched, and delivered a blow that would almost have felled an ox.

But the veteran guarded it, as an experienced prize-fighter would have done, and returned the compliment by a left-hander that lifted Mr. Burnley completely off his legs, and laid him sprawling in the middle of the road.

"Hooray!" shouted Ikey Mangles, with an involuntary burst of admiration—"hooray!"

But the contest was not yet over.

The evil passions of the gamekeeper were aroused, and staggering to his feet before the old gentleman was aware of his intention, he seized his gun from the gate against which it was resting and cocked it.

"You've interfered wi' me in my duty," he cried, in a voice almost inarticulate with passion, "an' this shall pay thee!"

He levelled the gun at the old gentleman and pulled the trigger.

There was a loud report and a cloud of smoke in the air. But the result was very different from what might have been anticipated.

The indomitable old gentleman still stood calmly erect, while, for the third time, the evil-intentioned Burnley lay prostrate on his back, but now stunned and unable to move. This result had been brought about—not by magic—but by the united efforts of the two boys.

Little James, seeing the gamekeeper about to fire at his defender, rushed quickly forward, and as the man pulled the trigger, sprang up, desperately regardless of consequences, and knocked up the weapon, the contents of which were discharged on the air; whilst at the same moment Ikey made a plunge with all his might at Mr. B.'s heels, like a sort of human skittle-ball, and knocked his legs clean from under him.

The result of this was a back fall that almost shook the life out of him, and left him completely *hors de combat.*

The boys having performed this feat, ran off as fast as they could, terrified at their own audacity.

Ikey, however, was not so frightened as to forget the hare.

He darted upon it as his lawful prey, and carried it away huddled close to him under his rags.

After running some time, they paused from exhaustion. They listened, but hearing no sounds of pursuit, they thought they might venture to breathe a little.

"See 'ere!" cried Ikey, as they sank down on an old trunk in a secluded little nook in the road, "Hi've got the 'are—Hi warn't a goin' to leave that be'ind."

The boy held it up triumphantly as he spoke.

"Don't you think it would have been better to have left it where it was?" asked James.

"Vot! arter all th' trouble we ud 'ad about it?" exclaimed Ikey. "Hi should think not! 'Ow could ve make hany soup vithout an 'are to make it vith?"

"It was the hare that got us into the trouble," responded James; "and if it hadn't been for that gentleman, the gamekeeper would have locked us both up."

"Ah, vell," said Ikey, in a tone of much consolation, "it's a good deal better as it is. Instead o' lockin' us up, e's got 'isself knocked down."

"I wonder whether he's much hurt?" asked James, apprehensively.

"Vell, Hi don't think it could 'a done 'is nut much good, 'a comin' bosh on th' ground as it did," remarked Ikey.

"P'r'aps he's dead," returned James, his face growing whiter than it was, at the terrible thought.

"All the better if 'e is," returned his less sensitive companion—"a big brute! 'E von't tear no more collars. Look'ee 'ere!" he continued, displaying the jagged edge from which the collar had been ripped.

James looked at the miserable apology for a coat with a sorrowful expression, and then said:

"When we get home, I'll ask mother for a needle, and you must take it off, and we'll try and mend it."

"Take it horff?" echoed Ikey, with a look of comic surprise at the absurdity of the idea. "Hi should like to ketch myself a takin' horff any o' my toggery!"

"But you do take it off sometimes, don't you?" asked James.

"No, it's a hunposserbility!" replied Ikey, decidedly. "My clo'es is so precious ragged, that if Hi vos vonce to get hout on 'em, Hi should never be hable to find my vay hinto 'em agin. So Hi never takes 'em horff at all."

This seemed tolerably explanatory, so James said no more on the subject, but proposed that, having rested, they should continue their way homeward.

"Hi'm ready," said Ikey, "an' th' sooner ve gits theer th' better. Hi longs to get my teeth into this ere 'are: blest if Hi ain't reg'lar starvin'!"

Both the poor lads felt bitterly the excruciating pangs of hunger at that moment, and the very idea of food seemed to inspire them with renewed strength.

"Can you run, Jem?" asked Ikey.

"I'll try!" answered James, feeling ready to faint with exhaustion.

"Come on, then, ole chap, give us yer 'and!" cried his companion.

James languidly placed his hand in Ikey's as requested, and the two friends were about to continue their journey, when a voice cried:

"Stop, my lads!"

"It's the old gen'l'man!" hastily whispered Ikey.

There was no doubt about the voice, but when the boys turned to look at the speaker, they nearly dropped with astonishment.

It was no old gentleman that met their sight, but a very handsome-looking young one, whose dark eyes beamed kindly on them, and whose friendly smile was mingled with an expression of enjoyment at the evident surprise his appearance excited.

After gazing at them a moment, the stranger thrust his hands in his pockets, and drew forth a biscuit between each thumb and finger.

"You are hungry, my boys!" he exclaimed.

"Yes, yes!" they cried, eagerly, in a breath.

"Then eat!" answered the gentleman, with a kind smile.

The poor famished lads darted eagerly upon the biscuits, and two sets of sharp teeth were instantly in active employment.

"It's all I have eatable about me at present," said the handsome stranger, as he watched the hungry boys as they devoured the food with almost desperate eagerness.

No answer was returned. The lads were too hungry to do anything but eat.

"Poor fellows!" murmured the gentleman to himself, in a pitying tone, "how glad I am I had those two biscuits, anyhow. Would they had been two pounds of roast beef! How the young rascals seem to enjoy them; they look as ravenous as two young foxes! And that rascally gamekeeper to talk of locking them up! I wonder whether he ever knew what it was to be hungry? I should like to give him a few days' confinement, during this cold weather, in the cage to which he would consign these poor children, until he learnt the painful sensation from experience."

"Here, my boys," cried the stranger, as they were devouring their last mouthful of biscuit, "take a pull at this."

He handed them a pocket-flask as he spoke, in which was some excellent sherry.

The lads drank, and the demon Hunger was for a time held in abeyance.

The prostrating sense of sick faintness they had before experienced was gone—they felt revived.

"You seem in a pitiful plight, my boys," said their benefactor, in a tone and with a look full of sympathy.

"We jest are, sir!" answered Ikey, who was always the first to speak.

"Have you no parents or friends?" inquired the gentleman.

"Hi ain't got none," said Ikey again—"Hi never 'ad none. Jemmy 'ad; but 'is father be dead, an' 'is mother——"

The boy paused instinctively, and glanced at his companion, who, with tears in his eyes and quivering lips, was trying to speak.

"And your mother?" inquired the stranger, kindly, advancing towards James, and taking his thin, wan hand in his, "what of her?"

"She's very ill, sir!" cried James, at length, with a burst of grief—"she's dying for want of food!"

"Good Heaven! is it possible?" exclaimed the gentleman, turning away and performing a significant action with his handkerchief that looked very much like wiping away the tears caused by this affecting revelation. "Dying?" he echoed.

"Yes, sir, I'm afraid so," said James.

"Here, take this; and let her drink a cupful the moment you reach home."

He drew from his pocket a larger flask of wine than he had previously produced, and gave it to James.

"Oh, thank you, sir!" he exclaimed, with grateful eagerness, as he grasped the welcome gift, "it will save poor mother's life!"

"Now, if you had but that hare," remarked the gentleman, "you could——"

"Hi've got that, sir!" grinned Ikey, as he produced the animal from under his rags; "an' Hi'm a goin' to make it hinto soup; but Hi'm afraid as Mrs. Cook won't eat none, 'cos she'll think Hi've been a stealin' it."

"I can relieve her conscience and yours from any such idea. I make you a present of that hare," said the stranger. "So you can tell your mother a gentleman gave it you."

This seemed to be a great relief to James, whose conscience had not been quite clear as to whether he was entitled to the disputed animal.

"And now," said the gentleman, "I must be journeying onwards. Here! here's a trifle each for you."

As he spoke, he pressed a guinea a piece into their hands.

"There!" he cried, cheerfully, "go and get something to comfort the invalid; and if you can, meet me, both of you, to-night, at nine o'clock, at the cross-roads down the road yonder. Can you come?"

"Y—yes, sir!" gasped the boys, who were literally rendered breathless at the sight of so much wealth.

"Very well, then; I shall expect you," cried the stranger; "I may be able to do something for you," he called out as he walked briskly off.

The two lads were well-nigh bewildered with joy. Cold, hunger, rags—all were forgotten; and with hearts lighter than they had known for many a day, they passed quickly through the narrow turnstile that led into the path to Mrs. Cook's cottage, and in a short time were safe within its walls.

JAMES COOK ESCAPING FROM THE COTTAGE.

Chapter IV.

DEATH IN THE COTTAGE.

WHEN they entered the cottage, very softly, James found his mother asleep.

Though anxious to administer the restorative with which the kind stranger had furnished him, he would not rouse her, but helped Ikey to prepare the hare. The latter was more experienced in this matter than James.

He skinned, cleaned, and disjointed the animal with considerable dexterity.

"I've seed this done afoor," he said, in a whisper, to his companion. "And now wheere's th' pot!"

Amongst the few relics of better days was an iron kettle, in which James remembered many a good dinner to have been cooked.

This was disinterred from its place in the cupboard, and placed upon the fire.

"Now then, the water," said Ikey, as he poured into it some of the cold liquid from a jug that stood near.

"And now the hare," added James.

These preliminaries having been completed, the boys piled some more branches on the fire, and sat down to watch the progress of their undertaking.

Their thoughts naturally reverted to their recent adventures, foremost amongst which stood forth the form of the generous stranger.

"I wonder who that gentleman was?" said James, thoughtfully.

"I dun'no," replied Ikey. "'E wur a rare sort, though, to gi'e us a guinea each, warn't 'e?"

"Didn't his voice seem to you very much like that of the old gentleman who wouldn't let the keeper take us?" asked James.

" Werry like !—uncommon like !—vonderful like !" cried Ikey ; " only it couldn't a bin 'e, 'cos the hold gen'l'man 'ad got white 'air, an' t'other gen'l'man 'ad got black."

" I can't make it out," James replied, with a perplexed expression in his face; " it seems to me as if they must be the same persons."

" Vell, never mind ; it's no good a vorritin' yerself about it ; ve'll go to th' cross-roads to-night, an' then, p'r'aps ve shall know summat more about it."

James found it difficult to settle the point so easily in his mind ; but a weak voice arrested his thoughts.

" Jemmy, darling !" called his mother, from the bed.

She had woke from her transient slumber, and was rather surprised at the preparations she observed.

" Yes, dear mother," said James, starting up and going to the bedside.

" Any good news ?"

" No, mother ; none from Farmer Gripman's."

The faint ray of hope died out in the poor woman's face, and she sighed.

Her son's quick eye noted this, and he hastened to cheer her.

" Don't be cast down on that account, dear mother," said the affectionate boy; " though Mr. Gripman couldn't give me any work, I met a kind gentleman who gave me a guinea, and some wine for you, and a hare ; didn't he, Ikey ?"

" That 'e did," responded Ikey, rising up from the operation of stirring the hare, which manœuvre he had accomplished with a piece of green branch. " 'E gave me a guinea, too ; an' 'ere it is," he added, diving into a pocket that seemed to descend almost to the bottom of his leg, and fishing up the golden coin.

The poor invalid's eyes beamed gratefully, and her lips murmured a heartfelt thanksgiving.

James, in the meantime, had poured out a half-cupful of wine, and brought it to his mother.

The very odour of the grateful stimulant seemed to revive the fainting spirit of the sick woman.

She took the proferred cordial eagerly, and then sank back upon the bed.

" We shall 'ave a prime cup o' soup for yer afoor long, Mrs. Cook," said Ikey, who was anxiously watching the seething hare.

The invalid made a faint attempt at a smile, and shook her head mournfully.

The act seemed to imply that it was little more she should require in this world.

" Poor children !—poor outcasts !" she murmured. " One an orphan, and the other soon to be one. God help them !" She clasped her hands together and closed her eyes.

The motion of her lips told only that she was praying for them.

She was aroused by feeling the lips of her boy pressed upon her pale cheek.

She turned towards him, and with a glance of motherly love that even death itself could not dispel, threw her wasted arms round him, and drew him towards her. At the same moment there came a sharp rap at the door.

Ikey started up and nearly overturned the soup-kettle. James also released himself quickly from his mother's embrace.

The two boys looked at one another with apprehension.

Could it be the cruel gamekeeper come to take them ? they thought.

It was a moment of terrible suspense.

" Now, then," cried a fat, wheezy voice outside " is anyone coming to open the door or not ?"

The tapping was repeated.

" Open the door, my dear," said Mrs. Cook to her son.

James, with his heart beating rapidly, went to the door and opened it, fully expecting to see a body of constables, with handcuffs and fetters, standing outside ready to arrest him.

No such formidable sight appeared ; but instead, a short, stout, little man, in a suit of shining black, with a round, red face, well sprinkled with port-wine blossoms, a voluminous white cravat, an equally voluminous shirt-frill, and an imposing bunch of gold seals dangling from beneath his vest.

" I'm glad to find there's somebody alive," he said, as he marched in.

The little gentleman with the seals stood still for a moment sucking the top of his cane, taking a kind of mental inventory of the poor chamber, the ragged boys, and the soup-kettle.

The head of the bedstead interposing prevented his including the invalid in this scrutiny.

" Ahem !" he ejaculated, at length ; " somebody ill here, isn't there ?"

" Yes, sir," said James—" mother is."

" Who is it ?" asked Mrs. Cook, feebly, of her son.

" It's a gentleman, mother, but——"

" I'm Dr. Julep, M.D., M.R.C.S. and F.R.S.," interrupted the red-faced individual.

Poor James, who was quite overwhelmed by the doctor's shirt-frill, and his seals, and the quantity of letters he laid claim to, could only open his eyes and look at him.

" Where's the patient ?" asked the M.D., abruptly, advancing. " Oh, I see !" he exclaimed, as he caught sight of the pale, worn sufferer. " Stand out of the way, little boy," he added, with a magnificent wave of the hand that nearly swept poor James into the soup-kettle. " Let me have room."

He approached the bed and looked through his gold-rimmed spectacles at the sick woman in a profound and professional manner.

" Um—ah—just so !" he ejaculated.

The boys looked on without being much enlightened by these ejaculations.

Dr. Julep then took hold of the sick woman's wrist with one hand and pulled out his gold watch with the other, while he counted as he felt his patient's pulse.

" Um—ah—um !" he exclaimed : " weak—very weak—utter prostration ! You ought to have sent for me before ! Why didn't you send for me before, eh ?"

He turned and looked sternly at James as he spoke.

The lad, feeling himself called upon to reply, was about to explain as well as he could, when his mother relieved him by saying, in a weak voice :

" I could not send for advice and medicine that I could not afford to pay for, sir."

" Advice and medicine—bosh !" echoed the portly little doctor, in a tone of disgust. " The medicine you want ought to come from the butcher, not from me. You require nourishment—good living. You must see that your mother has good living, little boy ! How is it she hasn't had good living, eh ?"

The M.D., in his indignation, turned once more with startling suddenness upon poor James, who felt quite guilty.

" I can't get any work to do, sir," he said. " I have tried. I asked Farmer Gripman, but he couldn't give me any."

" Farmer Gripman !" echoed the doctor—" Farmer Gripman ! Oh, yes—just so ! Sent for me to his dog this morning ; the brute had a bullet in his brain."

Ikey might have been observed to disappear suddenly into the cupboard.

" The idea of any man sending for an M.D. to prescribe for a dead dog ! It's an insult to the profession !"

The doctor, having thus vented his indignation, pocketed his watch, and adjusted his vest.

" I'll make you up a draught," he said, turning to Mrs. Cook, " and one of your boys can come for it. You know my residence, of course—Dr. Julep, in the Valley."

It is possible the poor sick woman did not hear his words.

At all events, she did not answer.

" Mind and take plenty of nourishment ; a basin of soup now would——"

The doctor paused suddenly and sniffed.

Ikey, finding the subject of Farmer Gripman's dog discontinued, had emerged from the cupboard, and just at that moment had given the soup a vigorous stir with the branch.

The savoury odour had mounted in the air and reached the nostrils of Dr. Julep.

" Eh—eh ?" he ejaculated, sniffing violently. " What's that ? Why, surely——"

He turned round, and following his nose, came at length to the soup-kettle.

He looked at it a moment, and then, transferring his gaze to Ikey, said, pointing to the iron pot :

" What's in there ?"

"Soup," answered the boy.

"Let me taste it," returned the doctor. "Or stay," he added, "give me a fork—I'll help myself."

Ikey looked round somewhat vaguely in search of such a thing; and encountering a toasting fork hanging on the wall, handed it to the doctor.

The M.D. fished about in the kettle for a few moments as though he had been spearing eels, and at last brought up a delicious piece of hare.

He contemplated it for an instant through his spectacles.

"Um—ah—yes—just so!" he exclaimed, and immediately began to devour it with evident relish.

"Well, if that hain't himperence!" muttered Ikey to himself, "Hi don't know what his!"

"I hope," remarked Dr. Julep, "you came by this honestly, eh? Hares are expensive things, eh—eh?"

He looked searchingly at the lads through his spectacles, smacking his lips and chewing hard as he spoke:

"Yes, sir," answered James, boldly, "a kind gentleman gave it us."

"Ah, that's right!" returned the M.D.; "so long as you came by it honestly: honesty's everything."

He glanced round as he spoke, and his eye fell on the bottle of sherry.

"Eh—eh?" he exclaimed, smacking his lips in a thirsty manner—"what's that?"

"That's vine!" cried Ikey, making a sudden rush at the bottle just as the doctor was about to seize upon it, no doubt for the purpose of testing its excellence in the same manner as he had previously done the hare.

"Ah yes—just so!" growled the disappointed physician; but swallowing his chagrin, he said to James: "Let your mother have a table-spoonful in a little water every hour." Then, turning to Ikey, he exclaimed, in a venomous tone: "You, boy, come with me for the medicine."

Having issued the order, he pulled his coat to with an angry jerk, arranged his shirt-frill, and waddled out.

Ikey whispered to James to look after the soup, and followed.

James was left alone.

He sat for a few moments watching the liquor as it bubbled in the kettle, and became rather absorbed in the contemplation, when a movement of the invalid, causing the rickety old bedstead to creak, made him turn quickly.

He uttered a startled cry as he did so.

His mother had turned herself in the bed, and now lay motionless, with her face towards him.

She was evidently not asleep, for her eyes were open, but they appeared to be perfectly unconscious.

The light of the fire played full upon her features, but she heeded it not.

There was no expression of pain in the rigid features.

What was it, then, that made him cry out?

Was it that awful, indescribable change that warns the watcher by the sick-bed that the time of dissolution is approaching, was passing over the face of his beloved mother?

Alas! yes.

Her complexion was no longer white, but a dull hue, that might have been almost described as gray, had settled upon her features—an ashy, leaden paleness that those who have once witnessed in the face of the dying will recognise at once.

She was—to use an expression generally understood—

Struck for death!

But the poor boy who gazed upon her as she lay in that mysterious and awful lethargy, knew nothing of this.

He only noticed something unnatural in the dear, familiar face, and felt frightened.

"Oh, mother—mother!" he cried, "what's the matter?"

He suddenly bethought him of the wine and the doctor's orders, and he hastily dashed some into the cup, omitting the water.

He went to the bedside with the stimulant, and, to his great joy, his mother was again conscious; her features had lost the awful tint that had so lately overshadowed them.

She looked, though very pale, like herself once more.

But, nevertheless, the Angel of Death had planted his standard on her pale brow.

The dying woman had awoke to consciousness in time to hear the boy's anguished cry, and she said soothingly:

"What's the matter, love?"

"Oh, nothing, mother," he answered, in an agitated tone—"nothing now; but a moment since, you—you looked so—so dreadful——"

"Did I, my dear?"

"Yes, mother—I thought you were—were—dead!"

The poor woman held out her drooping hand, and faintly pressed her child's, to endeavour to reassure him.

James held forth the cup of wine.

"Drink, dear mother," he said; "the doctor says you're to drink this every hour."

He guided the cup to her lips.

She tried to swallow, but the power was gone.

"I can't drink it, darling," she cried.

"Oh, try, mother dear—do try!" urged the anxious boy.

"Set it down, love—I'll drink it presently," replied his mother.

James placed the cup upon the table, and then took up his position by the side of her he loved so fondly, gliding his arm under her neck, and nestling close to her.

His mother lay for a few moments, with her eyes fixed upon him, and then, in a calm clear tone, stronger and more distinct than she had used of late, said:

"Jemmy, my own love, don't be frightened—but I'm dying!"

"Oh, mother!" cried the poor boy, starting up, "let me go for the doctor!"

"No, darling—no: all the doctors in the world could do me no good now. Come to me, and hear the last words I shall ever be able to speak."

Poor James rushed to the bedside.

"Oh, mother—mother!" was all he could reply.

"Don't weep, darling," said the dying woman, in a voice strangely calm, "but try and fix the words I utter in your mind."

"I listen, mother," answered the broken-hearted child, as firmly as he could.

"You will be soon alone in this cold world, with no one to guide you but God, and the memory of your mother."

A stifled sob burst from the lips of the listener.

"Let that memory be your guide. Hear me, darling," she continued, "be honest—be kind—always speak the truth—avoid bad companions—and if ever you are tempted to forget my last admonitions and to go in the wrong path, remember your mother's dying words, that that path will lead you to shame and misery."

"I won't go in it," cried the weeping boy; "I will remember your words—I will!" he almost shrieked.

But the wail of anguish came faintly on the dying ear.

The sufferer scarcely felt the clinging arms of her beloved child around her.

"Oh, mother, speak to me—look at me!" he cried.

"I hear your voice, darling, but I can no longer see you," she murmured, faintly.

"Oh, you are dying, mother—I know you are!" groaned James.

"Y-es—y-es darling," she gasped. "Your arms are round my neck!"

"They are, dearest mother!" he cried.

The dying woman smiled—a smile of unearthly sweetness, such as none but those who die in peace can smile.

"Kiss me, love," she murmured, so faintly that it seemed like a distant echo.

The poor boy, choked with sobs, pressed his trembling lips to his mother's.

"God bless you, my darling!" she cried, with a last expiring effort—"God bl——"

The blessing was never finished: in that parting, uncompleted prayer, the mother's spirit passed away, the powerless clay lay lifeless on the humble bed, and James Cook, young as he was, knew that he was an orphan.

Chapter V.

THE PURSUIT.—THE CAPTURE.

A POOR neighbour came and performed the last offices towards the dead woman.

The body was laid out, and covered with a coarse but clean sheet, which Mrs. Cook, conscious of her approaching end, had reserved for that purpose.

But where was the coffin in which to deposit her remains?

Who was to bury her?

The silence of death reigned in that poor cottage, broken only by the sobs of the chief mourner.

Ikey had returned with the medicine after the patient was dead.

He also brought with him some medicine of another description, in the shape of a quartern loaf, which he purchased at the little shop—the only one, save the ale-house, in the village—as he came along.

To pay for this, it was necessary he should change the guinea the stranger had given him.

The sight of the coin threw the shopkeeper—who could hardly conceive the idea of such a sum as a guinea all at once—into a perfect consternation.

She had to go to the ale-house for change, and the general impression seemed to be that Ikey Mangles had been committing either burglary or highway robbery.

The latter on his return, seeing the ghostly white sheet spread over the bed, and his friend James sobbing as though his heart would burst, at the loss of his only earthly protector, comprehended at once what had occurred.

The lad, prematurely sharp and cunning for his years as he seemed to be, had still a heart to feel.

Ikey was fond of James, and he now sympathised with his sorrowing friend very much indeed.

But he remained silent, and wisely allowed the first flood of grief to continue its course unchecked.

"It's no good a sayin' hanythin' to 'im jest now," he thought; "e'll be better presently."

So instead of attempting ineffectual consolation, he turned his attention to the soup, which was now finished, and into which he threw certain mysterious herbs, that he had either bought, gathered, or begged, when he fetched the medicine.

The savoury odours steamed upwards to the very roof of the cottage.

Ikey was awfully hungry, and the same remark might have applied to James, save that his recent loss had rendered him almost indifferent to such feelings.

But grief for the dead, however intense, cannot altogether destroy the imperative necessity for supplying the wants of the living; and Ikey, having by a great effort of self-control, sat patiently watching his sorrowing friend till he perceived his grief had well-nigh expended itself, at last ventured to suggest the propriety of his partaking of some of the soup on which he had been exercising his culinary skill.

"Come on, Jem, 'ole chap," he said, kindly, to his weeping friend, laying his arm on his shoulder coaxingly—"come an' 'ave summat to eat. The soup's ready, an' Hi've got a loaf o' bread. Don't yer go on a cryin' yer heyes out o' yer 'ead—don't!"

But James still wept.

"Come, Jemmy," he continued, pleadingly, "now yer poor mother's gorn, yer knows, if yer vos to cry from now till nex' year it vouldn't bring 'er back agin."

"I know that," sobbed James; "but she was my only friend. Now she's gone, I've no one to care for me —no one!"

"Oh, don't say that!" exclaimed Ikey, in an earnest, reproachful manner—"don't go sayin' that, Jemmy: Hi cares for yer!"

There was something so from the heart in the tone in which the boy spoke, that James could not help feeling his words.

He immediately stretched forth his hand and grasped that of his friend.

"That's right!" said Ikey, who was much cheered by this fraternal squeeze. "Never say as Hi doesn't care for yer, 'cos Hi does!—ye're th' honly vun in th' vorld as Hi've got to care for."

There was something so sad and forlorn, and yet so true, in this, that it caused James to think that he was not the *only orphan* in existence.

This thought did him good, and helped him to overcome his grief.

He wiped his eyes, and tried to look more cheerful.

"There, that's right—yer looks better now," said Ikey. "'Ere!"

As he spoke, he poured out a basin of soup, and gave it to James, with a large slice of bread.

It was not refused. And having then helped himself, the two famished boys were for a time fully occupied in filling the painful vacuum that hunger had caused in their insides.

It was evident they thoroughly enjoyed it.

There seemed life in every mouthful.

Ikey poured out some more wine in the cup, and they drank.

They had not had such a feast since—they could not remember when.

Their souls revived within them.

So intimately are the mental and bodily feelings connected with each other, that being relieved from the torturing pangs of hunger, and cheered by the sip of generous wine they had tasted, they felt, in spite of their forlorn situation, comparatively happy.

The fire glowed brightly on the hearth, and their limbs, that had been half-frozen, were warm again. Their blood once more circulated briskly in their young veins.

Pleasant images and visions of the future seemed to start, as it were, out of the cheering rays of the fire.

"I say, Jem," said Ikey, as he sat by his companion's side, with his arm thrown over his shoulder in a brotherly manner, "ve're both alone in the vorld now, hain't ve?"

"Yes, Ikey," answered James, more thoughtfully than sadly.

"Then vhy shouldn't ve stick together, eh?"

"I should like to if we could; it's so nice to have a friend."

"That's jest wot Hi thinks. Vun chap can often 'elp th' hother, vhen th' hother can't 'elp 'imself."

"That's very true!" said James, meditatively.

"Vell, then, let's make up our minds to stick together through thick an' thin. Two can allus get along better nor vun. Shall us?"

"I'm willing," replied James.

"Then there's my 'and upon it!" Ikey exclaimed, holding his hand out.

"And there's mine!" returned James, grasping it; "and as long as we can go along honestly we'll keep together."

"That's right! Vhen shall we make a start?"

"A start?" echoed James. "Do you mean to go away from here?"

"O' course! Vot's the good o' stayin' 'ere?"

"Not much, I think," said James, sadly.

"There's not a bit o' good in this 'ere place!—not a little bit—nothin' but starvation 'ere!" affirmed Ikey, decidedly.

"And where are we to go?" asked James.

"Ah, that's the pint! Wheer are ve? Hi dun no— there's so many places."

"And we've no one to tell us, or to put us in the right road," remarked James.

"Hi tell yer vot ve'll do," suddenly exclaimed Ikey; "ve'll blow a feather hup in the hair, and vhichever vay th' feather goes ve'll go—shall ve?"

"We can't go up in the air, though, after the feather, can we?" said James, with a faint smile.

"O' coorse not; Hi didn't mean that—Hi meant that ve should take th' same course on th' ground as th' feather took in the hair: that's vot Hi meant," exclaimed Ikey.

"So I understood; what I said was only in fun," James answered; "though I think our road would be very much which way the wind blew us."

"Talkin' o' th' vind, though," remarked Ikey, thoughtfully, "I vishes as our clo'es vos a little varmer. Mine's so full o' oles that the vind comes hin a vun side an' hout o' th' hother, an' almost freezes me."

"You must be cold, poor fellow," said his com-

panion, pitifully; "your clothes are worse than mine."

"A good deal," continued Ikey. "Yer've got six buttons on yer coat an' veskitt alone, an' Hi've only got two haltogether, breeches included."

"How d'ye keep your clothes on, then?" asked James.

"I pegs 'em," answered Ikey, with a grin at his own cleverness.

His friend looked at him a little mystified.

Ikey hastened to explain his plan.

"Look'ee 'ere," he said.

James bent his gaze upon the confused heap of tatters that constituted his companion's garments, and at length perceived, as they were pointed out to him, numerous small pieces of stick sharpened at one end, with which the rags were actually skewered together in different places, and in this manner kept from dropping off the spider-like limbs they covered.

"Well, Ikey," said James, "I don't think I should ever have thought of doing that."

"Hi don't think Hi should hever a thought on it myself if Hi 'adn't a bin obligated by nercess'ty; an' they says nercess'ty's th' mother o' hinwenshun," explained the poor boy.

"Well, never mind, Ikey!" James remarked, cheeringly. "P'r'aps we shall get on, and then we shall be able to buy some new clothes, sha'n't we?"

"O' course we shall!" returned the hopeful little scarecrow, briskly. "Hi means to 'ave a blue coat an' a canary-coloured veskitt, like th' squire, some days. Vouldn't it be prime to 'ave vun good soot? Ve could take it in turns to vear it then, couldn't ve?"

James could not forbear smiling.

Ikey had such a strange way of representing things that it was impossible to avoid it.

He replied, however:

"I hope the day will come when we shall have a new suit apiece; I don't care what colour, if it is only warm."

"Ah, that's the princerpal thing, Jem, hain't it?" assented Ikey. "It's so long since Hi've been varm, that Hi'm almost afeard if Hi vos to 'ave a proper soot on my back hall at vonce, Hi should melt avay hinto drippin'."

James was again compelled to smile at Ikey's strange imaginings; but he said:

"I don't think there's much fear of either of us melting at present."

"No; nor bustin' heither," added Ikey, grinning; but he stopped suddenly.

"Oh, ve forgot th' gen'l'man as ve're to meet at nine o'clock!" he exclaimed.

"I haven't forgotten him," returned James. "I was just thinking of him."

"Ah, ve mustn't forget 'im! It strikes me as e'll be a friend to us."

The two lads seemed to grow thoughtful and silent after this; they spoke no more.

Probably they were reflecting on the handsome stranger, and trying to reconcile the strange anomaly of two different persons possessing the same voice.

The truth was that the combined effects of the good dinner, the wine, and the genial warmth of the fire had gradually lulled them off to sleep, and they were now in a happy slumber, in which, for a time, past, present, and future, were alike forgotten.

While the poor lads were thus in a state of happy unconsciousness within doors, let us return to John Burnley, who, having recovered from his stunning fall, had risen from the ground in a state of the most bitter wrath.

He anathematised all white-haired old men and ragged, half-starved boys, with a fierceness that augured ill for any such should he happen to light upon them in his present mood.

He had plenty of opportunity to give undisturbed vent to his spleen, the spot being entirely deserted.

After, therefore, disburdening himself of a volley of oaths, he proceeded to seek Matthew Jorrocks, his brother keeper, to secure his assistance in endeavouring to discover the retreat of the authors of his annoyance. Mat was, of course, indignant at the account —exaggerated, of course—given by his fellow-servant, and proffered his assistance willingly.

They accordingly, having first fortified themselves with a flagon of the worthy squire's strong ale, proceeded towards the village.

Not a soul, however, answering to the description of a white-haired old man and two ragged boys did they see.

When they reached the small knot of poor, straggling tenements that went by the name of the village, they called at the small chandler's shop at which Ikey had purchased the loaf.

The owner of the shop, who was literally bursting to communicate the extraordinary history of the guinea to some one besides the landlord of the Jolly Haymaker and the few loiterers round his bar, rejoiced at the sight of two gamekeepers from the Hall.

In a very few minutes, Messrs. Burnley and Jorrocks were in possession of the important facts of the case, and a full description of poor Ikey Mangles and his rags.

"'E be no good, sir!" said the benevolent shopwoman, giving poor Ikey a lift the wrong way with the gamekeeper. "'E be th' dirtiest, raggedest yoong scamp i' t' pleace!"

But Mr. Burnley, having got a clue as to where this monster of iniquity was likely to be found, waited to hear no more, but started off abruptly in the midst of the woman's graphic description.

"The poachin' scamp!" growled Burnley. "I'll teach 'em to shoot hares, and resist the law afterwards!"

Full of venomous and angry thoughts, he, accompanied by his companion, Jorrocks, made his way to Mrs. Cook's humble cottage.

They say that there is within us a certain instinct that warns us when we stand in the presence of an enemy.

May we not go a step further and say that the same instinct may give us an intimation of the approach of a foe, even before he comes in sight?

Be this as it may, Ikey suddenly started from his slumbers before the fire, as if from an unpleasant dream, opened his eyes, and listened.

His countenance changed as the sound of heavy footsteps fell upon his ear.

He rushed to the door, and dropping the heavy wooden bar across it to secure it, peeped through the keyhole.

That one glance was sufficient.

With a gasp of terror, he hastily approached James, who still slumbered on calmly.

"Jemmy!—Jemmy!" he cried, in a hurried whisper, "vake hup! 'ere's the keepers!"

That name was sufficient. James was instantly wide awake.

"The keepers!" he echoed, in a terrified voice, looking very white and scared. "Where?"

"Out theer!" said Ikey, pointing to the door. "Hi seed 'em through th' keyhole. They can't get in, though, 'cos Hi've dropped th' bar acrost."

"Is it us they want?" inquired James, in a tone of alarm.

"You may be sure o' that!" exclaimed Ikey. "They vants to lock us up."

"What can we do?" cried James.

"Ve must get hout—that's th' only vay," Ikey answered.

"But how can we, when they're coming in? They'd be sure to see us," said James, nervously. "It's very cruel," he continued; "and poor mother lying dead there."

"They knows nout about feelin's," said Ikey.

At this moment there came several loud knocks at the door.

"Hush!" whispered Ikey. "Let's come hupstairs."

"I don't like to leave her," James replied, looking with a gaze of lingering sadness at his mother's shrouded form.

"Yer must for a bit, or yer'll be collard, and then p'r'aps yer'll never see 'er no more."

The tears started into the poor boy's eyes at such a prospect.

The knocking was repeated, and at the same time the harsh voice of Burnley was heard.

"Open th' door you, inside, will yer?" he growled.

"Come on hupstairs!" whispered Ikey, seeing James still lingered, with his eyes turned towards the bed. "Yer can come back to-night," he continued.

"And how do you mean to escape?" asked James.

"By the vinder. Theer sure to bust hopen the door in a minnit, an' as they comes in below ve must drop hout above."

"D'ye hear?" shouted Burnley, without.

"Come, now, it's no good a vaitin' hany longer," said Ikey.

He grasped his companion's arm as he spoke, and the two boys quietly crept up the narrow staircase.

"Will you open the door?" once more roared the gamekeeper. "It's no use pretendin' there's no one at home, 'cos I can see th' light o' th' fire!"

Still no one answered.

"If thee don't open th' door, I'll boorst it open!" shouted the keeper, furious at this contemptuous silence and delay.

"D'yo 'ear?" whispered Ikey, who distinctly heard these words, to his companion.

"Yes, I hear," was the quiet reply.

Then came a loud and prolonged battering at the door.

"'E's a breakin' it open! Hi said 'e vould," Ikey remarked, peeping from the upper window.

Burnley was close to the door, hammering against it.

Jorrocks stood at some distance, looking on, but in such a position as to command a full view of the window, and consequently to frustrate their idea of getting out that way.

"Cuss 'im!" muttered Ikey. "Hi vish 'e'd go an' 'ammer at the door as vell as t'other; ve shall never be hable to get avay."

Just as he spoke there was a loud crash below.

"There goes th' hold door!" cried Ikey.

He was perfectly correct; the gamekeeper's foot had just burst in one of the planks.

Crash!—crash! followed in rapid succession.

The lower half of the door was demolished.

Burnley stooped and went in.

"Stay there, Mat, till I call you," said he, speaking to his companion.

James and Ikey, seeing their anticipated escape cut off, were in a fever of anxiety.

They knew the gamekeeper was in the room beneath.

"If 'o comes hupstairs," whispered Ikey, in a voice that trembled with excitement—"oh, lor'! if he does—vot is theer as Hi can get to 'it 'im on th' 'ead vith?"

The boy looked round quite savagely; but there was nothing in the shape of an offensive weapon near.

"Is the other man there still?" asked James, as he stepped cautiously to the window.

"Yes, cuss 'im—there 'e is!" muttered Ikey, through his teeth. "Vun 'ud almost think as 'e know'd ve vos 'ere, an' vos a stoppin' theer o' purpose to perwent us from gettin' hout."

"Hark!" said James, suddenly.

The boys listened at the top of the stairs.

They could hear Burnley looking about and swearing to himself at his want of success.

He could find nothing.

Presently there was a clatter of iron.

"'E's kicked ower th' soup-kettle!" growled Ikey, indignantly—"the great pig!"

This was a fact: the gamekeeper's wrath was trebly excited at the sight of the fragrant concoction, and he furiously hurled the iron pot and its contents to the other end of the room.

Then a door was violently banged, as though it had been wrenched off its hinges.

"That's the cupboard door," whispered James.

"Theer's no hother place to look in!" cried Ikey, working his fingers nervously. "The next t'ing 'e'll do 'll be to come hupstairs! Oh, lor'!—oh, lor'! Ve'll both pitch into 'im, if 'e does, an' chuck 'im hout o' vinder, shall ve?"

This was rather a bold idea for one boy of ten to propose to another of the same age.

But poor Ikey was desperate, and did not at that moment quite know what he was talking about.

James was very pale; but though he shared the excitement of his companion, he did not show it so plainly.

Burnley, having looked into the cupboard and finding no one concealed there, came to a pause.

"Where have they all gone to?" he growled.

Suddenly his eye fell on the bed on which the corpse lay, covered with a sheet.

"Ha!" he exclaimed, as he dragged it off, "are they here?"

He started back as his eyes fell upon the pale, rigid features, and the perspiration started to his forehead.

"Why, what's this? Here, Mat!" he called to his companion—"look here!"

Mr. Jorrocks squeezed his portly form through the aperture in the door, and advanced to the bed.

"What's this mean?" asked Burnley.

"It's a corpse," answered Mat.

"I can see that. But whose corpse?"

"Why, it must be Mrs. Cook; the poor woman has been bad for a long time."

"But where's the boy?"

"That's more than I can say," returned Jorrocks. "There were two; one was Ikey Mangles."

"Ikey Mangles!" echoed Jorrocks. "He's a pretty imp of mischief, he is—accordin' to accounts."

"I must find 'em," cried Burnley, determinately; "and I feel pretty sure that wherever one is, the other isn't far off."

"Have yer searched upstairs?" inquired Jorrocks.

"Upstairs? No!" said Burnley. "I'd almost forgotten there was an upper floor; and here I've been losing all this time."

"I should say it was most likely they was upstairs."

At this moment a sound in the upper room reached their ears.

"There they are!" cried Burnley. "Let's come on."

The two keepers disappeared up the staircase.

At the same instant Ikey's round head appeared through the breach caused by Mr. Burnley's foot, with a grin of triumph on his features.

The sound they had heard had been caused by him as he lowered himself from the window to the ground, by a piece of clothes-line.

"Ha, ha!" he laughed, as he sprang in and turned the key in the lock of the door at the bottom of the staircase by which the unsuspecting keepers were ascending.

"Theer!" he ejaculated with a chuckle, as though addressing himself to them, "yer can't get hout this vay, no more yer can by the vinder hupstairs, 'cos it's too small."

This delightful state of things seemed to give the little urchin unbounded pleasure.

There was a trap-door in the floor, exactly at the foot of the stairs.

His quick eye fell upon it, and an idea appeared to strike him as he darted upon it and dragged it open.

"Theer!" he cried, exultingly. "Now, if yer busts the door open, Hi knows wheer yer'll go to!" And with another grin at his precautions, he hastened out.

In the meantime, the two keepers, who had no idea what was going on above, had entered the room just in time to see James, who was in the act of following his companion, disappear through the window.

Burnley, with a shout, rushed to it, and made a grab at the boy.

He was clinging to the rope within reach, and as he saw the large hand of the gamekeeper descending as though he would have seized him by the hair of his head, he gave himself up for lost.

"You 'owdacious young scamp, I've got you this time!" he cried.

But he was mistaken: he had *not* got him, for just as his hand was within an inch of the boy's head, the frail old clothes-line broke, and James, to his great joy, came to the ground with a run.

At another time he would have been horrified at such a fall—now he looked upon it as the most fortunate event that could have happened.

"Curse the rope!" growled Burnley.

"Bless the rope!" shouted Ikey, who picked up his companion.

Burnley was furious.

As for Jorrocks, he seemed to have a desire to throw himself from the window after the boys.

But, as Ikey remarked, it was too small to allow his broad shoulders to pass.

This increased the irritation of the gamekeepers.

Ikey laughed and put his thumb to his nose and worked his fingers at Jorrocks, as though he were performing on an imaginary flageolet, and this made his irritation all the greater.

"Never mind!" shouted Burnley. "I'll pay you both out when I come down!"

"We'll break the young scamps' necks when we lay hold on 'em!" cried Jorrocks, as he tramped down the dark, narrow staircase, and nearly trod on his comrade, Burnley, at the bottom.

"Go on!" he cried, excitedly.

"I can't get out!" grumbled Burnley, who was twisting the handle round and round furiously.

"Why not?"

"The door's locked!"

"Bust it open!" cried Jorrocks, kicking out vigorously, and saluting his comrade with the toe of his heavy boot in such a startling manner from behind, that Burnley howled piteously.

"Wur that you?" asked Jorrocks. "I thought I wur kickin' th' door," he added. "Who could 'a' fastened it?"

"One o' them imps, I suppose!" growled Burnley.

"Well, it's no good our stoppin' 'ere a supposin'," his companion observed. "Put your foot through the panel!"

But this was not so easy.

The staircase at the bottom turned round suddenly at a very abrupt angle.

They were, therefore—being both stout, burly men—jammed up together in close quarters, and had little room for an effectual kick.

They were both getting into a fever of rage.

They felt inclined, for the turn of a hair, to abuse one another.

"This is your fault, Jorrocks!" grumbled Burnley. "You ought to have kept your eyes open!"

"My fault!" growled Jorrocks. "Well, I like that! Where was yer own eyes?"

"Bah!" exclaimed the former, aiming a venomous blow at the door with his fist, but hitting Jorrocks, whose head was in the way, under his ear.

Jorrocks, who thought the blow was intentional, uttered an imprecation, shot out in the dark with his right, missed his mark, and nearly smashed his knuckles against the upright post at the bottom of the stairs.

A fierce scuffle now took place in this confined space between the gamekeepers, in which their knuckles and elbows were the principal sufferers.

But it had one effect, and that was to burst open the door suddenly.

Just at that moment it chanced, in the fortune of war, Burnley had laid violent hands on Jorrocks's nose, whilst Jorrocks had fastened his teeth in Burnley's ear.

They both, of course, shot out of the open door, and, as a natural consequence, went plump into the trap that was yawning to receive them.

After much struggling and growling, however, they contrived to extricate themselves; their tempers began to cool, and then feeling that they had been making great fools of themselves, they shook hands and departed in search of the fugitives, whom, by their quarrel, they had so materially assisted to escape.

And what had become of James Cook and Ikey Mangles all this time?

Of course, as our readers will suppose, they lost no time in making the best use of their legs.

They felt quite strong from the influence of excitement and the hearty meal they had taken.

"This 'ere's prime!" cried Ikey, as they ran along. "It's vorth hanythin' to get avay from them keepers!"

They had reached the lane, at the bottom of which was the turnstile.

"There's the turnstile!" said James, cheeringly.

"Yes, there it is!" echoed Ikey. "Ve've only got to get through that, an' then ve're hin the 'igh-road."

They increased their speed, congratulating themselves on the start they had of their pursuers; their hands were almost on the turnstile, when suddenly, as though he had dropped from the clouds, to their horror and dismay, Farmer Gripman gave the machine a turn, and stood right before them in the narrow path.

This was a stopper, and a very serious one.

The farmer, brooding over the loss of his dog, looked flushed and angry.

His eye fell savagely on James, whom he looked upon as specially concerned in the loss of his favourite.

He did not for a moment consider how nearly the ferocious brute had cost the poor boy his life.

"Soa," he exclaimed, folding his arms, and scowling at James, "it's thee, is it?"

"Yes, sir," replied James, meekly, "it's me."

"Soa you killed my dorg, did yow?" he said.

"No, sir," answered the boy, with much simplicity, "your dog nearly killed me."

"Doan't stand there an' tell me them loies!" cried the savage man, who was of much the same breed as his dog. "Didn't Oi see thee strooglin' wi' 'un on t' ground, an' didn't Oi see t' pistol go off, an' yow mean to say it warn't yow?"

"No, sir, it wasn't indeed!" said James.

"Look 'ere!" continued Mr. Gripman, looking more stern and ferocious as he proceeded; "my dorg wur shot when yow wur a strooglin' wi' 'un, an' if yow didn't shoot 'un, soomun' else did!"

This was a fact poor James couldn't dispute.

It was also a fact that made Ikey Mangles feel particularly uncomfortable, especially as he observed the farmer had a heavy whip in his hand.

Both the boys were silent.

"Oi wants to know from yow," Mr. G. continued, still addressing himself to James, "without any more o' your 'umbuggin' loies, who that soomun' else was?"

There was a pause—a pause that was almost terrible.

Our young readers will readily see that our hero, James, was in a position that was to test his *moral* courage to the utmost.

James was silent.

"Be yow goin' to speak?" asked the farmer, savagely. "An', mark me, doan't thee say thee doan't know, mind thee, 'cos I believe yow do know! Answer me!" he shouted, suddenly raising his whip. "*Do yow know who shot my dorg?*"

Ikey drew up quietly close to his friend, and both the poor lads kept their eyes fixed on the formidable whip.

"Do yow know?" repeated the farmer.

"Yes, sir," answered James, with desperate calmness.

"Then tell me, or I'll cut you into mincemeat wi' this whip!"

Still James was silent.

He remembered the advice of his dead mother, and his lips were sealed.

"Aren't thee goin' to speak?" shouted the brutal man.

There was no reply.

If he spoke, James felt he must tell the truth, and if he told the truth he must betray his friend; and he scorned to do that, so he said, with innocent candour:

"You may cut me into mincemeat, sir—I can't tell you!"

"Yow mean yow woan't!" blared out Mr. Gripman, pale with rage. "Then Oi'll thrash thee within an inch o' thy life! Stand out o' th' way, yow boy!" he shouted to Ikey, as he raised the terrible whip.

"No, Hi sha'n't!" answered Ikey, bluntly.

"If yow doan't, Oi'll cut thee up as well!" roared the farmer.

"Vell, if yer does, yer'll cut hup the right vun, 'cos it vos me as shot your dorg," said the boy, boldly.

Farmer Gripman's face flushed crimson, and then turned pale at this daring avowal.

But he had found the right culprit, and he resolved to wreak his vengeance upon him.

Grasping the poor boy's arm with one of his strong hands, he raised the whip with the other, and was about to commence his cruel work, when his attention was arrested by the sound of hasty footsteps.

Looking up, he saw two men running towards him.

These were no other than Burnley and Jorrocks in pursuit of our little heroes.

They were now like a forlorn hope, hemmed in on every side by their enemies.

The poor lads' hearts sunk within them as they caught sight of the gamekeepers.

The latter seemed more terrible than the farmer's whip, for they threatened to deprive them of liberty.

But as there was no escape, there was no resource but to resign themselves to circumstances and submit.

But it often happens in the course of events that those circumstances which appear most against us, sometimes turn out to our advantage. So it was in this case.

The arrival of the keepers preserved the boys from a brutal attack that would, in all probability, have ruined them for life.

The reason was this: that the keepers were not friendly with Farmer Gripman; and as they claimed the lads as their prisoners, they would not allow him to take the law out of their hands.

"This young rooffian ha' killed my dorg!" growled the farmer, pointing to Ikey.

"Blow your dorg !" politely returned Burnley.

"What's your dorg to the squire's hares ?" added Jorrocks. "The vagabones has been a killin' them."

Mr. Gripman looked terribly revengeful, and gripped his whip and clenched his teeth, and would have given anything to have been allowed quietly to smash every bone in poor Ikey's attenuated body, but he dared not lay a finger on him.

The gamekeepers, too, having exhausted their wrath to a great extent in pummelling each other, had no longer any desire to pay off small scores of private spite upon the backs or limbs of their prisoners.

They therefore contented themselves by giving them a "jerk up," as they called it, which made the very teeth chatter in their victims' heads; and then handcuffing their wrists together, ordered them to march before them to the cage, leaving Farmer Gripman to chew the cud of his disappointed revenge, and to lament the untimely death of his "dorg."

Chapter VI.

THE CAGE—INSIDE AND OUT.

THE cage was some distance from the spot on which the events recorded in the last chapter had taken place, but they reached it much sooner than James and Ikey liked.

They would have preferred walking all night, till they had dropped from fatigue, rather than have entered its dreary walls.

It was, like most cages, a brick building, with a strong door, and a small window with iron bars, that prevented the prisoners from getting out; but did not prevent the cold air from getting in.

It was getting dark when they reached their temporary prison.

The arrangements were exceedingly simple.

The door was unlocked by Burnley.

Jorrocks, standing close behind the boys, cried:

"Go in, yer scamps !" assisting them in their progress by a lift from his foot that sent them flying in as though they had been propelled from a cannon.

They were stopped in their impetuous career by the wall of the cage, against which they dashed, and rebounding, fell in a heap on the ground.

Burnley then, holding up his lantern to be quite sure they actually were there, said:

"You two young vagabones 'll stop here to-night, an' to-morrer you'll be brought up before th' squire to be dealt with according to law."

He then walked out, taking his lantern with him, locked the door, and departed with Jorrocks; leaving the two poor little ten-year-old culprits in darkness, exposed to the bitter cold, and handcuffed together, to linger out the dreary hours of the night, and to escape freezing in the best way they could.

Had it been Jack Sheppard or Dick Turpin that was confined there, we know very well that they would have laughed to scorn the gamekeepers, the handcuffs, and the cage, with its brick walls and iron-barred windows, and have been on the outside in no time.

But it was a very different matter in the case of these two young boys.

They were not yet sufficiently familiar with crime to laugh at bars and bolts, or skilled enough to effect a breach in a brick wall.

They seemed to have been suddenly consigned to the regions of despair, and their hearts sunk within them.

"Oh, lor !" exclaimed Ikey, after they had sat in melancholy silence for nearly ten minutes, "'ere's a horful place to put two poor boys hin !"

Poor James thought of the humble cottage that had been his home, and the silent form sleeping on the bed beneath its roof, and he wept silently in the dark.

But before long the cold damp of the cell struck home to their young hearts.

"Ain't it dreadful cold !" said Ikey, at length.

"Yes," answered James, with a shiver.

"Hi can't count 'ow many fingers Hi've got; an' as for my toes, Hi don't seem as hif Hi'd got hany at hall," Ikey murmured. "Ugh! ouf !" he shuddered, breathing on his fingers to try to impart a little warmth.

"Did you ever hear of boys being frozen to death ?" asked James, in a calm, quiet voice.

"Yes, Hi 'ave," answered Ikey, in an uneasy tone. "But don't talk in that vay, that's a good chap; it makes me feel as though ve vos a goin' to be friz. Blest if Hi can stand it !" he exclaimed, suddenly. "Let's git hup an' 'ave a dance, jest to varm us !"

"You can dance if you like, Ikey," said James, in a dull tone of despair: "I shall sit here and die. What have I got to live for ?"

"Not much," answered his companion; "no more 'a Hi, but somehows Hi don't vornt to die—Hi vornts to dance; but as ve're fastened together, Hi can't unless you dances too."

James, at this appeal, rose at once from his seat, and the boys went through a slight series of muscular feats to endeavour to keep their blood from becoming stagnant.

But it was very hard work.

Never was a dance performed under less jovial circumstances.

"Don't Hi vish as ve'd got a drop o' that soup 'ere, an' a drop o' that vine !" remarked Ikey.

"I do," answered James: "it was nice, wasn't it ?"

"Hi believe yer, it vos too !" replied his friend, smacking his lips. "Ve sha'n't get hany sich soup as that 'ere—Hi knows !"

"I'm afraid not," returned James.

"Sure not," continued Ikey. "Vhy, if they vos to feed pris'ners with soup like that, this 'ere place vouldn't be 'alf big enough to 'old 'em. Besides, it vouldn't do; 'cos hif a cove as vos 'ungry vornted a good dinner, all 'e'd 'ave to do 'ud be to go an' murder somebody, an' e'd be sure to get it."

"I don't see what harm we've done, that we should be locked up here," said James.

"You 'aven't done nothin' at all," replied Ikey, "an' Hi hain't done much—honly shot an 'are. But vot frets one most his that ve sha'n't be hable to meet that kind gen'l'man as give us the guineas !"

"Ah !" sighed James.

"D'ye think ve might manage to get hout ?" asked Ikey.

"How could we ?"

"Hi can't say, but Hi thinks ve might get rid o' these 'an'cuffs; it's preshus huncomfortable a bein' fastened together in this vay. Hi shall try."

Ikey accordingly squeezed his thin hand together tightly till the bones cracked again, and then without any great effort drew them through the steel band of the handcuff in a manner that would have gained applause from Jack Sheppard himself.

"Now you try, Jem," he said to his comrade. "Straighten yer fingers till theer as stiff as pokers, an' then sqveedge 'em together, till they hall sticks together, an' then pull avay like vinkin'—theer sure to come through."

James followed this graphic advice, and succeeded.

The boys had got rid of one unpleasant companion at least.

Ikey then looked up at the small grated window with its iron bars.

"Hi don't think ve could sqveedge through them bars, could ve, Jem ?" he said. "The soup's made us too fat, hain't it ?"

James gave a melancholy smile at this ludicrous idea under such depressing circumstances.

At that moment the clock from the old church struck nine.

The sounds seemed to peal forth with startling clearness in the clear, frosty air.

"Theere's the clock a strikin' nine !" Ikey exclaimed, fretfully. "It's hall hover vith hus now, an' ve shall never see the gen'l'man agin ! Oh, cuss it !" he cried, in a vexed, impatient tone. "Ain't it a shame ?"

The boy was quite excited, and walked rapidly to and fro in the cell like a young tiger caged.

"If Hi hever meets with them gamekeepers vhen Hi'm a man, von't Hi drop hinto 'em !" he cried.

"I don't think I shall ever live to be a man," said James, gloomily.

"Oh yes, yer vill ! An' ve'll 'ave the blue coats and veskitts yet !" predicted Ikey, in a cheering voice.

[JAMES COOK AND HIS COMPANION ARE INTRODUCED TO THE PIRATES.]

" I fancy," continued James, as though talking to himself, " I can see her looking down upon me—I seem as though I heard her speaking to me."

" Vot does she say ?" asked Ikey, in a low voice, as though he fully believed the words of his companion.

" She bids me hope !"

" Vell, that's wery good adwice, an' Hi hopes yer'll do vot she tells yer !"

" I will—I will !" cried James. " Since she tells me, I feel as though I could hope—— Hark !" he exclaimed, suddenly. " What's that ?"

" Vot ?" inquired Ikey.

" I fancy I heard the sound of a horse's feet."

" Does yer ?"

" Yes—listen !"

Both strained their ears to catch the sound.

There was no mistake about it—it was not imagination.

It was a horse galloping, coming towards them evidently, since the sounds became every moment more distinct.

" Hi 'opes it someuns a comin' for us !" said Ikey.

Suddenly, however, to their great disappointment, the horse was no longer heard.

This incident depressed the lads greatly.

" It hain't a comin' 'ere," Ikey grumbled. " Hi don't think it was an 'orse at hall : it couldn't a stopped dead in a hinstant like that."

" I believe it *was* a horse, and I believe it has stopped," persisted James, confidently.

He had hardly uttered these words when a footstep, so light as to be hardly discernible, arrested their attention.

" Isn't that it agin ?" asked Ikey.

" Hi think so !" answered James ; " but it is the footstep of a man, not a horse."

" Ve shall know presently," said his companion.

They listened, and the footstep was distinctly audible.

" Hi vonder 'oo it his ?" Ikey remarked.

" It might be the gamekeepers returning," suggested James.

The steps now seemed to move round the cage.

"I think they are the steps of a friend," said James, hopefully.

Suddenly the footsteps ceased.

And then immediately after a voice without ejaculated, in a cautious whisper:

"Hist—hist!"

"Ha!—the gentleman!" cried both the boys together, with delighted eagerness.

"Are you there?" inquired the voice, in the same cautious tone.

"Yes, sir," the lads answered.

"How is it you didn't keep your appointment with me at the cross-roads, eh?"

Could the lads have seen the stranger's face, they would have observed on it a smile almost of pity, as he glanced at the grated window, that was more than a sufficient answer to his question.

"Because the gamekeepers locked us up in here, sir," said Ikey.

"Well, never mind: I've come to let you out."

A thrill of joy passed through the hearts of the young prisoners and cheered them.

There was a prospect of deliverance now their friend was near them.

"Do either of you boys know how to use a file?" he cried.

"I do, sir," answered Ikey.

"Take this, then," said the stranger, throwing a file through the grating as he spoke. "Be speedy: file low down—two bars will be sufficient to remove."

"Come on, Jemmy!" cried Ikey, eagerly, as he stooped down and scraped the ground with his hand till he found the file.

"You must stand on my shoulders," James said.

"Hi'm ready!" answered Ikey.

The former placed himself against the wall of the cell, and his companion clambered up, and commenced filing the rusty bars near the bottom.

"Quick—quick!" cried James.

"So Hi ham—Hi'm a cuttin' avay like a razor!"

The bars were old and rusty, and not very thick—the file was new and keen.

In an incredibly short space of time the boy had cut through two bars at their lower ends.

"Hi've cut 'em through, sir," he said.

"Now, then, try if you can snap them off," directed the stranger from without.

Ikey grasped the bars near the bottom, and tugged at them so vigorously that they suddenly snapped, and Ikey flew, bars in hand, against the opposite wall of the cell.

"Are you hurt?" cried James, hastily, going to him.

"Hi've give my nob a scrape, but that hain't nothin'," said Ikey, with great cheerfulness. "Let's get out. You'd better go fast."

He hoisted up his friend as he spoke.

James's slight, ductile frame easily squeezed through the narrow aperture, and the stranger received him in his arms.

He did the same also for Ikey, who clambered up to the grating by means of the file, and the two lads were once more at liberty.

"So, then, you hadn't forgotten me?" said the stranger, as he shook them by the hand in a friendly manner.

"Oh no, sir!" they answered, warmly.

"And now are you ready to come with me?" asked the gentleman.

"Where to, sir?" James asked, in return—"home?"

"Not to your home. I am going to take you with me to see some friends of mine," the stranger remarked.

"Oh, sir, thank you! But my poor mother——"

"Ah! true—your mother! Did the doctor I sent come to her?" inquired the gentleman.

"Yes, sir. Was it you who sent him?" James asked, in a tone of surprise.

"Yes, my boy. Is your mother better?" continued the stranger.

"Alas! sir, she's dead!" replied James, tearfully. "She died this afternoon, soon after the doctor left; and though I should like to go with you, I can't bear to leave her in the cottage all by herself. It seems to me as if she'd miss me."

The stranger looked moved with compassion.

"My poor boy," he said, patting James's curly locks, that were crisp with the frost, "your feelings do you honour, but you must consider two things: In the first place, your mother, being dead, cannot possibly be benefited by your presence or grieved at your absence."

"No, sir, I know that; but it seems unkind to leave her."

"Then," the gentleman continued, "you must remember also that as soon as your flight from this cage is discovered your mother's cottage would be the first place to which the keepers would direct their search."

"So they would," said the boy, thoughtfully, but in a tone that proved he was convinced by the stranger's words. "Well, then, sir, I'll go with you."

"So'll Hi, sir," cried Ikey, eagerly—"hall the vay there an' back agin!"

"We'll start, then, in a moment."

The stranger whistled softly, and in answer to his call a beautiful gray steed trotted up to him, and stood motionless by his side.

And now the gentleman made certain preparations that struck the boys—James especially—as somewhat strange.

He unbuckled from the saddle a large cloak, in which he enveloped himself.

He then drew from his pocket a snow-white wig, which he put on over his own dark ringlets.

The mystery of the two men with one voice between them was at once made clear to the two astonished boys, for, as the white locks fell over the sable cloak, they recognised at once that the old man and the handsome young gentleman were one and the same person.

The stranger saw surprise written on the youngsters' features, and he remarked, with a smile:

"I do this in order to disguise myself."

He then drew a pair of pistols from his saddle-holsters, carefully examined their primings, and replaced them, adding, at the same time:

"I carry these in order to protect myself—and you, too, if necessary."

He noticed as he uttered these words a slight cloud of something very like suspicion pass over the features of young James Cook.

The boy said nothing, but he was evidently reflecting.

Ikey, however, was not so modest.

He was highly interested in the whole proceedings, and being, moreover, somewhat curious, said:

"Vhy do you vont to disguise yerself, sir: 'ave you bin shootin' 'ares?"

The stranger gave a curious smile as he answered:

"Little boys shouldn't be too inquisitive! You want to know a trifle too much, my lad."

Having thus quietly bottled up Ikey Mangles for the present, the gentleman mounted his horse, hoisted up the lads before him on his saddle, pulled his cloak round them, and telling them to "hold tight," trotted off.

Chapter VII.

THE RIDE TO THE CLIFFS.

JAMES and Ikey soon grew accustomed to the jolting of the horse, and after the first apprehensions of a tumble had subsided, began rather to enjoy the novelty of their position. The steed was a powerful animal, and, being rough-shod, he stepped confidently on the frozen, slippery road, and progressed rapidly.

Nestled closely to the stranger's side, and protected from the keen blast by the thick folds of the cloak that enveloped them, the lads gradually became warm and comfortable.

"I say, Jem," said Ikey, "it's a good deal varmer 'ere than it vos in th' cage, ain't it?"

"Yes," replied James; "I'm quite warm now."

These words were spoken in a tone somewhat of abstraction.

The boys had not yet got over the mystery of the white wig, or why it was necessary for the gentleman to disguise himself.

There was something in the very necessity that seemed to his young mind suspicious.

"I don't remember father ever disguising himself when he was alive," he said to himself; and then he went on to wonder if disguises were necessary for *good* people, and whether they ever wore white wigs at all.

While James was pondering on these matters, Ikey was wondering how the stranger had discovered their retreat; and, being less reserved than his companion, was half inclined to assure himself on this point by asking.

Certainly the gentleman had previously reproved his curiosity, but Ikey could stand a good deal of reproving, and had recovered himself.

"'E won't chuck me hoff th' 'oss if Hi askes," he reasoned with himself.

It was an awkward circumstance to contemplate, but the lad's curiosity triumphed over probable results, and, thrusting his head through the opening of the cloak, he looked up in the horseman's face and said:

"Please, sir, may Hi ax yer a question?"

"As many as you please," replied the stranger, "but I don't promise to answer them all."

This was encouraging—especially as the speaker's tone was kind; therefore, without further delay, Ikey continued:

"Hi vos a vonderin' 'ow you come to know as ve vos locked hup in that ere cage."

"I can easily set your wonder at rest," answered the gentleman, smiling. "I was going to the cross-roads to meet you, when I passed two men who were speaking of some prisoners they had evidently taken a short time previous."

"They vos the gamekeepers, an' ve vos th' prisoners," interposed Ikey.

"I went straight to the place of appointment," continued the stranger, "and, finding you did not come, I concluded that it was you the men were speaking of, and I went at once to ascertain."

"It vos werry kind on yer, sir," returned Ikey. "Hif yer 'adn't 'a come, ve should a been froze as stiff as pokers afore th' mornin'—Hi knows ve should."

The horse at this moment, urged by the rider's heel, gave a bound forward and increased his speed.

Ikey, who had an idea he was going to fall, drew suddenly back into the folds of the cloak like a snail into its shell, and asked no more questions.

After a sharp gallop, the horseman gradually checked the speed of his steed to a walk, and presently the grating of a gate on its hinges, and the noise of its slamming, together with the cessation of any sound from the horse's hoofs, proved they had entered a field.

They had now altered their course, and were taking a cross cut towards the coast.

It was evident, from the quietness with which they travelled, and from the frequent pauses to open gates, they were journeying across fields.

At length the increased keenness of the breeze, and the saline odours it wafted on its bosom, proved they were near the sea.

Ikey was the first to notice this fact, and he expressed his conviction by frequent sniffings.

"Jem," he whispered, "ve're near th' sea; Hi can smell th' salt water."

He had hardly made this remark when the gentleman reined-in his steed.

"We are now almost at our journey's end, and are going to alight," he said, as the horse came to a stop.

In a moment he had thrown open his cloak, and lowered the boys to the ground.

The difference in the temperature made them shiver as though they had been suddenly thrown into a cold bath.

"It won't be for long," remarked the stranger, kindly, as he noticed their rags fluttering in the night breeze; "you'll soon be where you will be warm."

He then dismounted himself, and led his horse towards a small, desolate-looking hut, in which he left him. A cold, fitful-looking moon shone in the sky, and cast her pale rays on to the snowy ground.

On their right rose the white, giant cliffs, towering over the angry-looking German Ocean.

The tide was coming in, and dashed with its harsh murmur against the rocks at their base.

"Now, then, my boys," said the stranger, after housing his steed in the little hut and closing the door, "give me your hands."

This request being instantly complied with, the gentleman led his charges, who were full of wonderment as to whither they were going, up the ascent that led to the summit of the cliffs.

They went on in silence; the stranger made no remark, and the boys forbore questioning.

"Ve shall see vheer ve're a goin' vhen ve gets theer," thought Ikey, and in that philosophical state of resignation, he trudged along by the side of his conductor.

After walking for some little time, they stood on the top of the dizzy height, where they could look down upon the surging waters beneath.

They continued their journey till they came to a wide fissure in the cliff.

Here the stranger paused, and, drawing a small whistle from his breast, blew a prolonged note—not loud, but peculiar.

This act again excited the suspicions of young James Cook. What with the disguise, the white whig, and the whistle, he was almost bewildered.

While, however, he was reflecting, the gentleman's signal was answered by another exactly similar.

It had hardly died away when a figure appeared in the fissure—scarcely visible in the dim light—and a voice exclaimed, in a low tone:

"What name?"

"Carew!" replied the stranger, under his breath.

"Right!" said the voice.

The man then advanced, as they went forward to meet him, and the lads then distinguished a rough-looking individual in a coarse pilot coat, dreadnought hat, and a pair of strong sea-boots.

"I've been waitin' for you, sir, some time," he said.

"I'm rather later than I had anticipated," answered the stranger; "but it is of no great consequence. Will you take charge of these boys?" he added.

"I'll look after 'em," said the man. "Come along, youngsters."

As he spoke, he grasped their hands, and led them to a fissure in the cliff.

The boys hung back as they looked down the steep declivity.

"Are ve a goin' down theer?" asked Ikey, in a tone of considerable apprehension.

"O' course you are," answered their guide. "Don't be afraid: the path's rather steep, but it's safe enough to tread."

Assured by this piece of information, they went forwards, or rather downwards, the stranger following.

After proceeding in this manner for some distance, occasionally slipping, and as often kept from falling by the strong hands that grasped them they heard the murmuring of voices.

The path that had hitherto been almost perpendicular, now seemed to be horizontal.

The man paused and kindled a torch, and by its light they found themselves in a narrow passage that appeared to have been scooped out of the chalky cliff.

Along this they went, until they reached an opening, across which a crimson curtain was stretched, but through which a bright light beyond could be distinctly seen.

On one side of this opening rested a large mass of chalky rock, and Ikey was much surprised on pressing his hand against it to find that it moved. He drew back with a start, having an indistinct apprehension that he was pulling down the rocks on the top of them, and had hardly time to wonder at his own gigantic strength when the crimson veil was drawn aside, and the interior of the cavern disclosed to their view.

"Go forward!" said the guide to the boys, who, in open-mouthed astonishment, were taking in the scene before them.

At these orders, James and Ikey descended some dozen steps cut in the rock.

The stranger followed, whilst the man who had conducted them remained behind.

On looking back, as they reached the floor of the cave, the red curtain had fallen and concealed the entrance.

But, oh the wonders of that rocky chamber!

In the centre blazed a large fire, whose rays cast a

bright and cheerful light throughout the whole interior.

In addition to this, lamps were placed in various directions in niches in the rocks, the reflection from which added to the cheerfulness of the scene.

A number of men, evidently sailors, of different ages and climates—from the white hue of Europe to the dusky black of Africa—were stretched upon the ground in all the *abandon* of perfect non-restraint.

Some of these were smoking and drinking; some playing at cards, or with dice; whilst some were gathered in knots, rehearsing past exploits, or anticipating before-hand fresh adventures.

On the arrival of the strangers, they looked up lazily, and then continued their various pastimes, without taking further notice.

The gentleman, beckoning to the boys, went forward towards the end of the cavern, which was very spacious. And here a new surprise awaited them.

In a recess hollowed out of the wall, reclining on a pile of costly furs placed promiscuously one upon the other, were two persons, entirely different from those to whom they were in such close proximity. This recess was festooned round the upper portion of the interior with a drapery, that had the appearance of a mixture of colours—half being crimson and half black.

This parti-coloured material extended over the roof of the rocky alcove, and formed a kind of canopy, changing the appearance of the recess from a cave to that of an elegant boudoir.

To add to the peculiarity of the effect, lamps shaded with curious gauze globes of crimson, orange, and purple, threw forth their prismatic hues upon the snow-white walls, giving to the whole a rich beauty that was almost fairy-like.

The boys could only look their admiration; they were too surprised to speak.

The stranger advanced to the occupants of the alcove, who rose to welcome him.

They were both enveloped in loose robes, with sleeves trimmed with fur, that had much the appearance of dressing-gowns, being fastened by a girdle round the waist.

Each wore on his head a round fur cap, from which depended a long tassel of golden threads.

It would seem that the wearers of these garments had been accustomed to warm climates, and adopted them as a defence against the cold.

They held forth their hands simultaneously to the stranger as he advanced; and a mutually cordial welcome and shake of the hand was given and returned by the trio.

"Welcome, George!"

"Welcome, Paul!"

"Welcome, Jack!"

These were the first salutations, uttered with much warmth and sincerity.

Of course, James and Ikey, being quite in the dark as to who these persons might be, remained at a respectful distance, looking and listening, and, as usual, wondering profoundly.

The appearance of the individuals designated as "Paul" and "Jack," was very different from what such common-place terms would seem to have implied, and deserve some particular notice.

Paul was a man of youthful appearance, and apparently slight figure, which was almost entirely concealed by the voluminous robe he wore.

It was only while speaking, an occasional rapid action—a casual movement of the arm—attested the energy that reposed within him.

His face was oval, shaded by locks of light wavy hair; his features delicate and aquiline—so much so, as to be almost effeminate but for the sun tan, which exposure to the weather had spread over them.

But his mouth and chin expressed great decision.

The thin lips at times, either firmly compressed or curled into a sneer, expressed somewhat of cruelty and sarcasm.

His eyes were of a pale gray, full of sweetness and gentleness when he smiled, but deadly and terrible in their sterner glances.

His companion, "Jack," was altogether the reverse, being dark as night, tall, thick-set, strong-limbed, looking like a good-humoured giant in his flowing robes, with a florid complexion, a prolific beard, and a jovial

voice, that seemed to do the boys good whenever he spoke.

In fact, as Ikey and James gazed admiringly at his commanding figure, his jet black hair and eyes, and the vivid crimson colour of his cheek that caused the latter by contrast to sparkle like diamonds, they felt strongly inclined to like him the best of the three.

"I see," said the stranger, whom we shall henceforth call George Carew, "you fortify yourselves against the bleak air of our northern climate"

This remark was an allusion to the furred robes his companions wore.

"Yes," replied Jack, laughing, "after floating about so long between the tropics, we did not wish to be frozen to death, if we escaped other dangers, on this our first visit to the shores of Britain."

"And so, captain, you really have trusted your precious necks on our coast when such necks as yours would be so highly prized. You're a couple of bold fellows."

"Our worst enemies," rejoined Paul, "pay us the compliment of admitting that we are bold enough."

"And might they not add, captain, in this case—a little over rash?" inquired George.

Ikey and James noticed that their friend called his two companions by the title of captain, and it increased the respect of the former for them immensely.

"They're captings," he whispered, nudging his companion, excitedly. "Hain't they grand folks?"

Before James had time to reply, Captain Paul answered:

"Rashness and courage generally go together; only when a bold stroke happens to be successful, it is called skill: it is only called rashness when it fails."

"There is much truth in that," said George Carew.

"I have performed the greater part of my most successful exploits," continued Captain Paul, "under circumstances that one-half the world would call rashness, and the other half insanity; but those are just the very actions that make me what I am."

"I suppose," inquired George, "you have some motive in visiting our coast?"

"None in the world," returned Captain Paul, with a light laugh. "We are here partly out of bravado, to prove how we could dodge the English and French cruisers, and partly to see you."

"Well, I'm glad to see you both," said George Carew, heartily. "When first we met, ten years ago, in the Gulf of Mexico, I little thought I should have the opportunity of welcoming you so near home."

"You received our letter?" inquired Captain Jack.

"Yes, or I should not be here," answered George. "It is strange, though, that business required my presence in this part of the country, so that I am able to kill two birds with one stone."

"You still belong to the Secret Society of the Confederate Brothers?"

"Yes; that society, when we first met, was in its infancy. I enrolled you then as members before I knew your names, or the avocation you pursue."

"Yes," replied the captains, glancing simultaneously at the palms of their hands, on which were indelibly imprinted the initial letters of the order, "C. B."

"Probably, had you been more intimately acquainted with us, you would have declined two such daring associates," remarked Captain Paul.

"Possibly I might," returned the other, candidly; "but once members, you become Brothers of that society, which now extends its influence over half the world, and of which I am President."

"It is a grand establishment!" exclaimed Captain Jack.

"It is," replied George Carew. "There is not one member out of the thousands who compose it who is not bound, by virtue of the oath of membership, to assist his brother and stand by him to the death."

"We have both tested the virtues of this bond of brotherhood, even on the far-distant shores of the Pacific," said Captain Jack. "We are indebted to it for being able to stand before you alive at this moment; but," he added, fastening his eyes with a smile on the President's snow-white wig, "are the cares of the Confederacy so weighty as to have blanched the locks that were ten years ago as dark as my own?"

George Carew replied by gaily whisking off the wig, and converting himself in an instant from an old to a young man.

The captains burst into an exultant laugh.

"Ah," they cried, "now you're yourself again!"

"The affairs of our society are conducted with the utmost privacy; but here there is no need of concealment," the President remarked, as he passed his hand through his wavy hair, as though relieved by the removal of the wig.

"But come," exclaimed Captain Paul, "this is poor cheer. The pleasure of meeting you, worthy President, has made us forget the duties of hospitality. Here, Erebus!" he called.

A deformed negro dwarf limped forward, passing close by James and Ikey, who shrank from him and huddled close together at the strange object.

"What's that?" whispered James.

"Hi dunno; Hi think it's a beer, or a monkey," returned Ikey.

"Let us have refreshments quickly," cried Captain Paul.

The dwarf bowed his head and disappeared, but in a few moments returned laden with bottles of various shapes, dried meats, and curious foreign fruits.

These were placed on silver trays upon the ground.

The wine, being uncorked, was transferred by Erebus into flagons of silver, and poured by him into cups of the same metal.

Having done this, he retired, with a profound salam.

The boys looked on in silent admiration at these magnificent preparations.

The hare was long since digested, and their mouths were watering for some of the delicacies they could only devour with their eyes.

"Shouldn't Hi like some o' them!" whispered Ikey, smacking his lips.

"They do look nice, don't they?" James said, wistfully.

"Hi thinks as the gen'l'man's forgot all about us," his companion observed.

This opinion was perfectly correct.

In the temporary excitement of the scene, George Carew had for the moment forgotten his young charges.

"Healths round!" cried Captain Paul, raising his goblet.

The toast was duly honoured, and the three cups were returned empty.

For a few moments there was little said: the repast continued in silence.

This was broken by George Carew, who, having replenished his cup, exclaimed:

"Charge your goblets, gentlemen!"

This injunction being instantly complied with, the President proposed:

"The Confederate Brothers! May their motto, 'Unity is strength,' never be changed! May the bonds that unite them never be broken!"

This was received with a shout by his companions, as they drained their cups.

"Ha, ha!" laughed Captain Paul; "who would think now that the two most renowned pirates of the age—whose flags are the terror of the seas—and the President of the Secret Society of the Confederate Brothers, should so meet together, like Macbeth's witches, in this old cavern!"

George Carew smiled, and said, simply, in reply:

"We are, by the rules of the society, *Brothers*."

The last speech of Captain Paul, however, had caused considerable emotion in the minds of James and Ikey.

They had both heard of pirates, and James had read an extraordinary account of a certain bloodthirsty monster called Blackbeard, whose adventures he had over and over again related to Ikey as they sat by the cottage fire; and now, to find themselves all of a sudden in company with (for anything they knew to the contrary) some of his relations, was rather startling.

James thought of his dead mother, and glanced hurriedly round, as though more than half inclined to steal away from such disreputable company.

Ikey, though slightly scared at what he had heard, was by no means anxious to be gone.

The men before him appeared such handsome, daring, jovial fellows, that he was rather inclined to regard them with a species of admiration than with a feeling of dread.

The boy looked at them eagerly from out his large, gaunt eyes, and various ideas presented themselves to his crude imagination.

Captain Jack seemed to be the most absorbing of the party.

"E's got a black beard," he ruminated—"werry black! Hi vunder vhether e's hany relation to th' Blackbeard as Jem told me hof? 'E used to heat vimen an' child'en, 'e did. P'r'aps this vun's his brother—Hi vunder vhether 'e eats vimen an' childen?"

This idea was very unpleasant to contemplate, so he turned to his companion, and said, in a whisper:

"I say, Jem"

"What, Ikey?"

"If they vos to ax yer, vould yer be a pirate?"

"No!" said James, decidedly. "You wouldn't either, would you?"

"Vell," replied Ikey, somewhat apologetically, "Hi don't know as Hi should mind bein' a pirate; but o' coorse Hi shouldn't like to heat vimen an' childen," he added.

"But pirates are not good people—they steal!" returned James.

"They seems rayther a good sort, though," pleaded Ikey. "They don't look as if they vos bad. Blest if Hi thinks they his bad heither," he muttered to himself.

"But if they steal, and kill people, they *must* be bad!" James argued.

"Vell, vatever they his, they seems to get on werry vell," said Ikey, rather doggedly; "an' they don't varnt for nothin'; see 'em: they're a tuckin' hinto the purwisions, an' 'ere are ve as 'ungry an' hempty as hever ve can be!" The boy rubbed his stomach expressively as he spoke.

"Better be hungry and empty as we are," James replied, "than be filled with the food that's got by dishonesty"

"Hi'm tired o' starwation, an' that's the truth," exclaimed Ikey.

"So am I," returned his companion, firmly; "but for all that, I'd rather starve to death than be dishonest!"

"Hi don't think as Hi vould," muttered Ikey. "Hi honly vishes as Hi'd got summat to heat."

It would rather have surprised the two captains and the President, could they have heard the argument of these two poor hungry boys, but they were too much engrossed to notice them.

In fact, neither Captain Paul nor Captain Jack had observed them at all from the first moment of their entrance.

Their shadowy, thin forms might easily be overlooked; and as they sat squatted down on the ground, they had disappeared altogether from the eyes of the revellers.

Suddenly, however, Captain Paul, having shifted his position slightly, caught sight of them.

"Hallo!" he cried, "what have we there?"

He leant forward, and fixed his keen gray eyes on the boys as he spoke, till they felt pierced through and through.

"Oh lor! 'e's a goin' to heat us!" groaned Ikey, inwardly.

George Carew started up with an expression of self-reproach on his handsome features.

"Those poor boys!" he exclaimed. "I declare I had quite forgotten them!"

"Are they two young Confederates?" asked Captain Jack, smiling, as he turned his bright black eyes upon the quailing youngsters, who were quite overpowered at such close scrutiny.

"Oh no!" answered George, "they're two poor lads I picked up to-day. They were in trouble, and I helped them out of it. Come here, my boys!" he cried, in a kind, encouraging voice; "don't be afraid!" he added, as he observed their hesitation.

"No, don't fear!" exclaimed Captain Jack, in a round, jovial tone, "we won't bite you!"

On this comforting assurance, James and Ikey came forward, and stood face to face with the formidable captains.

Chapter VIII.

THE CAPTAINS AND THE BOYS.

GEORGE CAREW bent down to his friends, and said, in a low tone—not so low, however, but that the boys heard his words:

"These two poor lads seem as near starvation as they possibly can be to stand on their legs at all."

The two captains opened their eyes at this, and glanced at James and Ikey.

George Carew continued:

"That one," pointing to James, "had the misfortune to lose his mother this very day. She now lies dead in her poor cottage. I think I should not be wrong if I were to say she was *starved to death!*"

"Poor woman! Poor boys!" murmured the captains, in a tone of deep sympathy.

Ikey's quick ears caught up these exclamations, and his equally quick eyes recognised pity in the looks that accompanied them.

"D'ye 'ear that, Jem?" he whispered to his companion. "They calls us poor boys—they pities us—they'll give us somethin' to heat, you see if they don't. Blest if they han't kinder by chalks than anyvun as Hi hever met, pirates or no pirates!"

For some time George Carew continued speaking in a low tone to the captains; but from occasional words that reached their ears, the boys knew he was speaking about them. At length he paused; and, rising up, said, in a louder tone:

"I shall leave my young protégés to your care for a short time."

"Are you going to leave us?" inquired his friends.

"Only for a short time," answered George. "The society's business calls me away. I have to meet a person by appointment not far from hence; and as it is to receive money, I must not miss him. I shall not be long." Then turning to the boys, he observed:

"You will wait for me here."

He then reassumed the white wig, put on his hat, and left the cave. The boys looked after their friend wistfully, and felt considerable misgivings as he disappeared behind the crimson drapery that masked the entrance.

They were now entirely in the power of the child-eaters. There would be plenty of time for these cannibal pirates to devour them before their friend's return, if they felt so disposed.

These apprehensions were not diminished by their observing that both the captains fixed their eyes upon them with peculiar earnestness.

"Well, my lads," asked Captain Jack, at length, "what are your names?"

"James Cook—"

"Ikey Mangles," they answered, one after the other.

"Um!" continued the captain, running his eye over them. "You both look as though you wanted a little fattening."

This remark was an immense relief to Ikey.

"It's all right!" he said to himself. "They won't heat us yet—they'll fatten us first."

"You haven't, either of you, had much over-feeding of late, I should imagine, from your appearance," Captain Jack went on.

"No, sir," answered James; "we've had very little indeed to eat."

"Ve've been fattenin' on nothin', sir," said Ikey, "an' Hi feels ready to bust, but it's wi' wind, not wi' grub."

"Well, then, if that's the case, my boys, sit down and eat and drink."

As he spoke, the good-natured captain pointed to the provisions on the ground.

James and Ikey immediately dropped down.

"There," Captain Jack continued, "you can peck away there till you're satisfied. Don't be shy; eat and drink to your hearts' content."

Whatever latent motive the captain might have had in pressing the boys to partake of the luxuries before them, they were too hungry to decline his friendly offer.

They accordingly set to work tooth and nail.

They ate whatever came first.

They had never before seen anything like the dried meats they were devouring; they had never tasted anything half so delicious.

After eating for some time, they began to grow thirsty.

Ikey peeped furtively into the wine flagon.

"Hi vonder vhether ve may?" he whispered.

"Of course you may," cried Captain Jack, who was watching the famished youngsters with great enjoyment.

Thus encouraged, Ikey poured out wine for his companion and himself.

"You'd better mix it," said his supervisor, handing him a crystal flask of water: "that wine alone would be too strong for you."

James took upon himself the task of diluting the generous liquor, and the boys then took a prolonged draught. The poor little fellows, under the influence of such good cheer, couldn't help feeling a strange and unusual sensation of comfort stealing over them.

The wine revived them; the cavern looked light and cheerful, and felt warm.

It was hardly possible to resist such agreeable associations.

Even James, for the moment, forgot his mother's oft-repeated admonition not to be led away by evil companions, and began to feel that he was among friends.

Their meal being finished, Captain Jack turned towards them.

"Well, my boys, do you feel better?" he asked.

"A great deal!" they both replied.

"That's right," answered the captain, smiling across at his comrade, who sat watching the boys, though he said nothing.

"And what are you two lads going to do with yourselves?" he inquired, after a pause.

"I don't know, sir," answered James, sadly. "I wish I did."

"So do Hi," dropped in Ikey. "But theer seems to be nout to be done."

"Oh yes! there's always something for boys to do if they're willing to work," replied the captain. "Not that either of you appear to be much fitted for labour. How old are you?"

"I was ten years old the twenty-third of last October," answered James.

"Hi don't know 'ow hold Hi am," said Ikey; "Hi dunno as Hi've got hany birthday at all, but as Jem an' me's about th' same size, Hi s'pose we're about th' same hage as each hother."

The captain smiled at Ikey's process of reasoning.

"I suppose you'd both like to be doing something, wouldn't you?" asked Captain Jack.

"Hi should!" answered Ikey, eagerly. "An' Hi don't care much vot it his as long as it's somethink."

"But wouldn't you like to be employed?" said Captain Jack, addressing himself particularly to James, seeing that he remained silent.

"Yes, sir, very much indeed—that is," he added, in a lower tone, "in anything that's *honest!*"

"You seem to lay great stress on that word *honest*, my lad," remarked Captain Paul, joining for the first time in the conversation.

"Yes, sir," said James, sadly, "it was one of the last commands my mother gave me before she died, to be honest."

The two captains gazed for a moment at the pale face of the speaker, and then looked at each other. Accustomed to study the human character in almost every clime, and under all kinds of aspects, they had already formed their estimates of the dispositions of the two lads before them.

In Ikey Mangles they saw a neglected urchin, who was ready to take any path, right or wrong, that promised him relief from the privations he was enduring; whilst in James Cook, young as he was, they discovered strong principles of right, that would struggle to resist those hard tempters to evil—poverty, hunger, and contempt—and probably die rather than yield.

"Well, then," said Captain Paul, at length, "come with us: we'll find you employment. Will you?"

"Hi vill," eagerly exclaimed Ikey, who was quite

excited at the prospects that seemed to be dawning upon them.

"All in good time, my young friend," answered Captain Paul, reprovingly. "I was speaking to your companion; as for you, you seem ready for anything."

"So Hi are, sir," returned Ikey, boldly, determined to get a hearing somehow.

"Ah, well; we'll talk to you presently." Then addressing himself once more to James, he said: "And you, my lad—are you *ready for anything?*"

"No, sir," answered James, firmly.

It cost him some effort to deliver these two little words, but he triumphed over his hesitation.

"Am I, then, to understand that you will not go with us?" Captain Paul inquired.

"Yes, sir," James answered, "I would rather not."

Ikey was aghast at this unexpected reply.

It seemed like a wilful rejection of Fortune's favours.

"Oh don't—don't be foolish!" he whispered, nudging James sharply in the ribs with his elbow; "don't go for to say as yer won't go—don't!"

Poor James's ribs being covered with nothing thicker than bare skin, ached under the application of his companion's elbow-joint, which was as sharp as a spike.

But though he winced under the infliction, he turned a deaf ear to his entreaties, and quietly edged away from him a little.

Captain Paul was rather surprised at James's answer, and after a moment said:

"Why—why will you not go with us?"

The poor boy coloured and faltered, as though he could not make up his mind to reply.

"Say as you'll go!" whispered the persevering Ikey, who had crept up closely to his friend, and gliding his hand upwards, enforced his persuasion by giving him a sharp nip on his arm. But James, beyond a slight compression of the lip, took no notice.

He could bear pain wonderfully well.

Captain Paul, who was ignorant of the mysterious torture Ikey was privately administering, put down the pained expression on James's face to embarrassment, as, indeed, it partly was; therefore, to encourage him, he said:

"Don't be afraid to speak—you won't offend me; I like boys who are brave enough to speak the truth, though I may not always do so myself."

These words encouraged the young trembler, who, in a low but distinct tone, thus explained himself:

"I heard you say, sir, not long ago, that you and that gentleman," pointing to Captain Jack—who, by a strong effort, had succeeded in screwing his features into an expression about as serious as might be supposed to belong to a good-natured owl—"were pirates; and from what I've read about them, I'm afraid they're not good men, and I shouldn't like to go with men who are not good."

It must not be supposed that this innocent and simple explanation was given without much internal struggle and many misgivings as to how it would be received. Quite the contrary. Child as James Cook was, he felt perfectly conscious that the words he was uttering were calculated to give offence.

Having, therefore, made a clean breast of it, he stood in a meek, submissive, but not cringing, manner before his listeners.

He expected, and was prepared to receive, some punishment at least at their hands.

As for Ikey, he was perfectly paralysed at James's boldness. As he afterwards expressed himself to his companion, he "felt as though cold vater vas a bein' poured down 'is back by pailfuls."

He expected nothing less than immediate and summary vengeance on the part of the captains.

Had Captain Paul beheaded James on the spot, and Blackbeard's big brother bolted the savoury morsel, he would not have been in the least surprised.

In fact, he shut his eyes immediately, and clenched his hands, in a desperate effort not to shriek; and when he did venture to look again, he could scarcely believe his senses at beholding his friend still in possession of his "nob."

As for the captains themselves, they looked at one another for an instant, and then, unable longer to restrain themselves, burst into a violent fit of laughter.

This proceeding, whilst it disconcerted poor James, restored the less sensitive Ikey quite to himself again.

After their laughter had somewhat subsided, Captain Paul turned again to James.

"So you've read about pirates, have you?" he asked, in a voice much more expressive of suppressed mirth than of anger.

"Yes, sir," replied James.

"What pirates?"

"Blackbeard, sir."

"Any others?"

He glanced at Ikey as he spoke, who was ready for him on the instant with an answer.

"Yes, sir," he burst out. He had been bottled up for some time, and went off with a kind of verbal pop. "Theer vos two hothers as Jemmy read to me about hout of 'is book."

"Who were they?"

"Von vas Paul Jones."

Captain Jack raised his eyebrows with a comical expression, and looked at his companion.

"Indeed!" he said. "And the other?"

"Th' hother vas Capting Kyd."

It was now Captain Paul's turn to glance slily at Captain Jack.

"Well," asked the last-named personage, in a good-natured, jolly tone, "and what did they do?"

"They gobbled up vimen an' childen, they did," said Ikey, in a tone of strong reprobation; "they vos vicked! they vos! but ve don't think as you does sich things," he added, in an insinuating manner; "yer don't look as hif yer could."

"We feel flattered by your opinion," replied Captain Paul, in a tone of mock suavity; "and though I am not aware that I ever devoured a child, still there is no knowing to what hunger or curiosity might tempt me; and should I at any time be induced to indulge in such a luxury, I promise, as a particular favour, that *you* shall be the first I eat."

The speaker eyed Ikey in such a peculiarly sardonic manner, that the latter gave himself up for lost, and had serious thoughts of falling on his knees and praying to be released from such a distinguished honour, when a sudden and startling cry fell upon the ears of all within the cavern.

"What was that?" exclaimed Captain Paul, hastily.

Everyone listened, but the cry was not repeated.

"It must have been the shrieking of the wind—nothing more," said Captain Jack.

"Perhaps so," returned his comrade: "it howls to-night like a wild demon!"

These words were hardly spoken, when the whistle of the man on the look-out was heard.

"It is the worthy President returning," said Captain Paul; then turning to the lads, he added. "We'll consult with our friend what to do with you; and in the meantime you can amuse yourselves as you please."

The boys thus dismissed, crept away in a somewhat doubtful state of mind, and ensconced themselves in a small cavity in the rock, that was, however, large enough to admit their small persons.

At the same moment, the red drapery at the entrance was raised, and footsteps were heard approaching.

Chapter IX.

THROWN FROM THE CLIFF.

WHEN George Carew left the cavern, he retraced the rocky path to the summit of the cliff.

Near the top of the acclivity sat the scout, with his arms folded, out of reach of the wind.

"Mr. Carew?" he inquired, drowsily, as the President passed him.

"Yes!" was the answer. "I shall not be long."

"Right, sir!" said the scout.

The night wind blew in keen, fitful gusts from the

stormy bosom of the German Ocean, and the thickly gathering clouds had obscured the sickly moon, shrouding the scene in darkness.

The President listened, but no footstep reached his ear.

Nothing but the tempestuous breeze and the dashing of the waves beneath the cliff.

"He will surely come!" he soliloquized. "If not, he will rue the day on which he broke his appointment with a Confederate Brother."

He walked forward towards the hut in which he had left his horse.

Opening the door, he entered, and kindled a small lantern.

Hardly had he done so when a mounted horseman approached the hovel.

The footsteps of the steed reached the expectant ears within.

George Carew instantly appeared at the door, as the rider reined in his horse.

"Is that you, Mr. Challoner?" he inquired.

"Yes!" replied Octavius, in a manner disagreeably abrupt.

The President, not appearing to notice this peculiarity, said:

"You have some one with you in front of your saddle?"

"Only my cousin," answered Octavius. "The young rascal wanted a night ramble, so I brought him with me. Now, then, Gus, I'm going to place you once more on *terra firma*," he cried, as he lowered the boy to the ground, and immediately followed.

"Rather a rough night for a lad like that to be out in," remarked the President. "I should have thought bed would have been the more fitting place."

"Oh, I like it!" said Augustus, his fair cheek flushed with the excitement of his ride and the warm folds of his cousin's cloak, that had been wrapped round him.

"Well, we need not delay our business," Octavius observed, still in a tone of irritable abruptness; "it is a strange hour you have chosen for this meeting, and the sooner it is over the better."

"Decidedly! It will not occupy us long—that is, if you have brought the money. Shall we enter the hut?" inquired the President.

"No; the boy can remain there with the horses—it will be warmer for him than out here," returned Octavius; "besides, his ears are quick, young as he is, and I do not wish our business to be known to any but ourselves."

"A wise precaution. We can always keep our own secrets securely!" answered George Carew.

"Come, then, let us move a little from this place; the wind will not blow us away," said Mr. Challoner, in a tone of ill-concealed impatience. "Gus!" he cried to his young cousin, "you will remain in the hut for a few moments with Dapple; I shall be back presently."

"Very well, cousin," answered the boy, cheerfully. "And then," he whispered, coaxingly, "you'll show me the smugglers' cave—won't you?"

"Yes!" returned his cousin, also in a whisper.

The gray steed was led into the hovel; Augustus followed, and the door was closed.

"Now," said Octavius, "I am ready."

The two men walked some distance towards the edge of the cliff, and then stopped.

Octavius was the first to speak.

"It appears," he said, "you make a demand upon me, in the name of the Society of the Confederate Brothers, for the sum of five hundred pounds?"

"Yes—a demand with which you will do well to comply."

"On what grounds do you make this claim?"

"It is simply a just demand that you must pay!"

"Must?"

"Yes, *must*!"

"By what authority?"

"The claim of your creditor—Eustace Mortimer—and that is using a very mild term. Look!" continued the President, holding forth a strip of paper, on which he directed the rays of his lantern, "you know his hand?"

Octavius glanced at it, frowned, and bit his lip; and then his lip curled into a sneering smile.

"How do I know that this is not a forgery?" he asked.

"At all events," answered the President, sternly, "you will know *this* is not."

As he spoke, he placed before him another paper, on which, as his eye fell, Octavius started; and his face never bearing much colour, turned ashy pale.

He uttered at the same time a stifled imprecation.

"I see," remarked George Carew, coolly, "you understand *this*. I preferred at first showing you simply the commercial demand to pay; as you dispute that, I now show you the written accusation of murder!"

"Murder!" echoed Octavius, glaring at the speaker from under his contracted brows, with eyes that gleamed like evil meteors.

"Yes," replied the President, calmly, "you know very well that twelve months since you were in Paris; that there you became acquainted with Eustace Mortimer; that in a gambling house you drugged his wine and robbed him of five hundred pounds!"

Octavius started, and clenched his hands fiercely.

The President continued, in the same unmoved tone:

"The narcotic you administered was not quite sufficient to lull your victim; he resisted, struggled, and you stabbed him! See, here is the knife you left with the blade buried in his breast."

As he spoke, the President displayed the weapon.

Octavius, with a face more ghastly and convulsed than ever, gazed upon the knife speechless.

At length, after a pause, he gasped forth:

"Does he live?"

"He does; and if you refuse to pay, he will stand forth as your accuser at the bar of justice! If that fails to reach you, ten thousand Confederate Brothers are pledged to perform the act of retribution."

There was a silence of some moments, during which Octavius stood murmuring inwardly and incoherently to himself.

"Come!" said the President, at length, "we waste time. Do you intend to pay?"

"Yes—yes!" muttered the culprit, in a broken, excited manner, as though communing with himself rather than answering a question—"I must—I must! —there is no escape!"

His hand gradually wandered into his breast pocket, but he continued murmuring:

"Five hundred pounds!—five hundred! But then murder——"

Suddenly there was a crash, and the lantern was extinguished.

Then came a struggle—a fall—and a shriek (it was this cry that reached the ears of the pirates in the cavern), and then silence; whilst through the gloom a cloaked form might have been seen desperately dragging some dark object towards the edge of the cliff. Nearer and nearer it approached, till it reached the brink; an instant's pause, and a fluttering black mass descended like lead into the blacker darkness beneath.

* * * * * * *

The scout, who was dozing at his post, opened his eyes lazily at the sound of footsteps, but closed them again as the President's white hair flashed before him in the darkness.

"You've got back again, sir," he remarked, as the cloaked figure passed, and continued his nap.

Ikey and James had fastened their eyes eagerly at the sound of the footsteps upon the entrance to the cave, fully expecting to see their friend, the President.

They had not long to wait.

The cloak and the white wig came in sight; but, to their great astonishment, they beheld at the side of their friend, and grasping his hand, a well-dressed young gentleman about their own age.

At this sight, the most horrible suspicions rushed into Ikey's brain.

"Oh, lor!" he said to James, in a terrified whisper, "there's another poor boy! Hi sees vot it is now: that 'ere gen'l'man in th' white vig goes hout a collectin' of 'em. 'E's kind to the boys, an' gives 'em nice things to heat, an' then they follers 'im jest as ve did. 'E brings 'em to this ere cave, an' then he heats 'em! Ho, ho, ho!"

His agitation was becoming so noticeable, that James checked him.

"Sh!" he exclaimed, softly, "be quiet! If we make a noise, or seem to be afraid, perhaps the gentleman will keep his promise and *eat us first*."

This reminder had the effect of rendering Ikey perfectly mute. The two boys fastened their eyes upon

[JAMES COOK AND HIS COMPANIONS ESCAPING FROM THE PIRATES' HAUNT.]

the cloaked figure as it slowly advanced, leading the lad by the hand.

James suddenly uttered an exclamation.

"Why, it's young Master Markham, the squire's son!" he said.

"So it are!" asserted Ikey. "Poor boy! it's all hup vith 'im."

"Let's hear what they say," said James.

"Well," cried Captain Jack, who, with his companion, had been taking forty winks, but who now roused himself; "so you've got back again!"

Instead of replying, the figure deliberately threw off its cloak, hat, and wig.

And now a new surprise awaited the boys.

It was not their friend, George Carew, who stood revealed, but the pale-featured Octavius Challoner. By both Ikey and James he was well known and remembered, from reasons too obvious to mention.

In fact, all the *poor boys knew* him as a plague to be avoided, since he never passed one without bestowing

upon him an expression of contempt and a stripe from his whip.

"What could he possibly want there?" was the first thought that passed through their minds.

A similar thought seemed to seize upon Captains Jack and Paul, who, finding themselves suddenly confronted by a stranger, started up fiercely.

"Who are you?"

"What seek you here?" they inquired, simultaneously.

"Your patience for a moment, and I will explain," said Octavius, coolly.

But neither of the persons he addressed seemed disposed to patience.

"Is there no man on the look-out, that strangers are allowed to enter without warning?" cried Captain Paul, angrily.

"There is a man on the watch now, but he is not to blame," explained Octavius; "the fact is, I was on my way hither, when I met my friend, George Carew, who, when I informed him that my business with you was of a strictly private nature, proffered me the use of the wig he wore, as a disguise. This deceived your scout, who, in the dark, did not notice the change, or the difference in our persons, and enabled me to come into your very midst entirely unsuspected."

This explanation seemed to satisfy Captain Paul, who, in a calmer voice, inquired of the stranger what business he had to transact with them.

Octavius, after glancing at his cousin, who, boy-like, was eagerly examining the numerous objects that met his eye, in the shape of flags, weapons, &c., and satisfied that he could not overhear his words, turned once more to the captains.

He little suspected that there were two other pairs of ears and eyes busily engaged in listening to his words and watching his actions.

"I had heard," he commenced, "that this cave was the haunt of smugglers, and, knowing that men of your profession are not over scrupulous as to what they do, providing they are paid well for it, I have sought you for the purpose of entrusting you with a very important commission."

Octavius had commenced his address to the captains in a careless, indifferent tone, as though wishing by that to convince them of his great superiority; but finding that his listeners seemed to treat him with equal indifference, he gradually became more earnest.

"What commission?" asked the captains.

Octavius Challoner glanced round, and pointing to where his young cousin stood, absorbed in admiration at a pistol of foreign workmanship in the belt of a stalwart sailor, said, in a low tone:

"_The removal of that boy!_"

Captain Paul fixed his cold gray eyes searchingly upon him as he inquired:

"What do you mean by the term _removal?_"

"I mean _his death!_" was the cold-blooded answer.

Could the villain who made this proposal have seen the horror depicted on the features of James and Ikey, it would, perhaps, have awakened in his breast a sense of the enormity of his crime.

The poor lads seemed too much appalled to speak. They seemed so surrounded by fearful images in the cave of horrors into which they had been lured, that they could at that moment only cling closer together in silent consternation, and, from their place of retreat, look and listen.

"Why do you wish his death?" asked Captain Paul, after a pause.

"Because he stands between me and a fortune."

"Have the goodness to be a little more explicit!"

"Have I not told you sufficient?"

"Not to satisfy us. If you wish to be served, we expect to be trusted!"

The young man paused irresolutely for a moment, and then continued:

"I have been brought up under the supposition that I should be my uncle's heir."

"He is rich, I presume?"

"Yes. He was a widower, but childless, and being much attached to me——"

"You counted, of course, upon succeeding to all his wealth?"

"I did. However, when advanced in life, he thought fit to commit the folly of marrying again—a woman much younger than himself."

"Umph! that was very unkind of him."

"His second wife died in giving birth to my cousin, that boy yonder!" exclaimed Octavius, bitterly.

"And he, then, is the rock on which your hopes founder?" added Captain Paul.

"Yes," continued the young man, frowning darkly. "The squire dotes upon the brat; and though he assures me I shall not be forgotten in his will, I am fully convinced that if that boy lives, I must make up my mind to receive a few paltry thousands, instead of the whole of my uncle's property and estates."

"And therefore you wish him dead?"

"I do! Is it not natural?"

"Very _unnatural_, I think; but that's not the point in question. Your object in seeking us is to induce us to remove the _trifling obstacle_ that stands between you and your uncle's wealth."

"It is. Will you undertake the task?"

"Well, in the first place, it's murder!"

"But that's nothing—to _you_, at least!"

"Oh, nothing!" said Captain Paul, drily—"nothing but the risk, and that's something."

"There is no risk," eagerly interposed Octavius—"none in the world."

"The boy would be missed!"

"Yes; but for all that, detection is impossible!"

"How impossible?"

"He is supposed at this moment to be fast asleep in bed. I have humoured the brat from his infancy, till I can lead him where and how I please."

"I suppose the child is fond of you?"

"Yes, I can do anything with him."

Captain Paul muttered something between his teeth perfectly unintelligible and highly uncomplimentary to Octavius could he have heard it.

The latter continued:

"It was easy for me to steal to his bedroom, and tempt him out with the idea that I was going to take him on board a vessel, especially as he is fond of the sea, while at the same time his absence from home is entirely unsuspected."

"Then, of course, if the boy were missing, you would know nothing about him?"

"Nothing!"

"And his father—the squire?"

"Would fret himself into his grave at the loss of him, in less than a twelvemonth."

"You have forgotten one thing."

"What?"

"That without good proof of the boy's death, the old man—his father—would cling to the hope, however delusive, that he still lived, and would naturally hesitate to make a will in your favour, that would leave his own son a beggar, should he happen to turn up at any future period."

This probability certainly had not struck Octavius, and for a moment it seemed to disconcert him; but his evil scheming brain speedily recovered itself, and he said:

"The boy once got rid of, it will not be difficult to procure proofs—of some kind at least. I will see to that; or stay," he exclaimed, suddenly. "The best plan of all would be, if you could throw him overboard, and so contrive it that his lifeless body should drift ashore."

The captains interchanged glances, and there was a pause, during which each seemed occupied with his own reflections.

In the meantime, we may return to James Cook and Ikey Mangles.

Terror at first had utterly unnerved them.

It was the first time in their young lives that human nature had been presented to them in such a revolting aspect.

The result of this dire spectacle, and the apprehensions of what might possibly occur to themselves in that den of terrors, had been to prostrate their bodily and mental faculties, as though they had received some violent shock that had stunned them.

However, by slow degrees they partially recovered themselves; and as the designs of the villain Octavius, to which they were compelled to listen, gradually developed themselves in all their cold-blooded atrocity, as they heard him coolly talking over the murder of an innocent child no older than themselves—that child, too, his own relation and the son of his benefactor—terror gave place to indignation, and, boys as they were, they felt their young blood stirred within them.

Loathing and disgust triumphed over their own personal fears.

"Vell," said Ikey, at last, bursting out with an aspiration too powerful to be restrained, "vot d'yer think o' 'im Jem?"

He, of course, alluded to Octavius.

"I think he's a dreadful, cruel, wicked man!" answered James, unhesitatingly, in a tone of vehement indignation.

"'E's wus nor a wolf or a beer, ain't 'e, Jemmy?" continued Ikey—"a vantin' to kill that poor boy!"

"He sha'n't kill him—he sha'n't! I won't let him!" exclaimed little James, in a tone that sounded all the more intense because it was under his breath; whilst his pale features flushed, and his thin, delicate fingers trembled with nervous energy, as though they longed to grip the cowardly murderer by the throat. "He sha'n't kill him!" he repeated.

"But if they settles among 'em as 'e his to be killed, 'ow can us two boys 'elp 'im?" asked Ikey, anxiously.

"I don't know—I don't know!" replied his excited companion; "but I'll try with all my might! If it's wicked to murder, it's good to try and prevent it, and I will, too, though they kill me instead!"

"So'll Hi!" protested Ikey, warmly. "Hi'll stick to yer, Jem; there's my 'and upon it!"

The two little fellows clasped each other's hands with the utmost sincerity, and at that moment felt almost ready to rush out at once and upset the captains and Octavius.

The voice of Captain Paul, however, put these last ideas to flight at once.

"Well, sir," said he, to Octavius, "as this is entirely a matter of business, what price do you offer in return for the service you wish us to perform?"

"What do you demand?"

"Nay, I don't buy and sell at the same time. Name your price."

"Five hundred pounds."

The captains looked up in the speaker's face and laughed derisively.

Octavius frowned and bit his lip, whilst an angry flush passed over his pale cheek.

"Is not that sufficient?" he inquired.

"No. Multiply it by ten," was the answer.

"Five thousand!" exclaimed Octavius, recoiling with surprise.

"Yes, five thousand! and very cheap too," replied Captain Paul. "Murder, like many other luxuries, is costly, and must me paid for handsomely."

"It is too much," replied the scoundrel, angrily; "your terms are exorbitant, and I shall not comply!"

"Very well, then, find some other agent to perform your dirty work; or, what would be still cheaper, suppose you were to do it yourself!"

"Psha!" growled Octavius, "I'm in no mood to enjoy your sarcasms. You refuse my offer, and our business is ended."

"Not quite," remarked Captain Paul, quietly; "you must remember we are acquainted with your kind intentions towards your cousin, and might, if we felt so disposed, frustrate them."

"What!" exclaimed Octavius, with surprise; then, recovering himself, he said, sneeringly: "I understand—you must be paid for your silence. Here!" he added, taking out his purse and throwing it at the captain's feet, "that will purchase it."

Captain Paul's eye dilated suddenly, and blazed up like the flash of an explosion, whilst his comrade's face was suffused with a blush of indignation.

But they restrained themselves.

"Harkye, sir gentleman!" said Captain Paul, in a tone of forced calmness, "you are in the presence of men whose very element is danger; perils by land and wave—in storm and tempest—by lightning and thunder. To pursue the path we wish to follow we should not scruple in the heat of battle to destroy a town or a fleet, with its hecatomb of living souls; but when you ask us to murder in cold blood an innocent child, now amusing himself in unsuspecting confidence in this cavern——"

"You decline—you said so!" interrupted Octavius.

"More than that," continued Captain Paul, "for at the same time that we despise and loathe the cowardly butcher who could propose so vile a deed, we are resolved to rescue the lamb from his grasp!"

"Rescue!" gasped Octavius.

"Yes!" shouted Captain Paul, with flashing eyes. "In other words, we intend to preserve the boy you seek to destroy from the cruel hand of his unnatural cousin!"

What a profound relief it would have been to James and Ikey could they have heard these words!

How they would have altered their opinions of these bloodthirsty pirates!

But the boys had disappeared some time before, and had shifted their quarters, still under the conviction that all within the precincts of that dreadful cave were ravenous monsters, craving for their destruction. Whither they had gone will presently appear.

To continue—

Octavius glared apprehensively at the pirates.

"You mean, then, that you would make my designs known?" he said.

"We do! Pick up the trash with which you would bribe us to silence!"

As he spoke, Captain Paul contemptuously kicked the purse, that had lain untouched on the ground where it fell, towards Octavius.

He hastily snatched it up, and with features distorted with vindictive fury, exclaimed, in a hoarse voice:

"Then, mark me! not a hundred yards from the summit of the cliff over your heads are posted a strong body of the Coastguard Blockade!"

A scornful smile passed over the faces of the captains as the speaker drew a small horn from his breast.

"I have only to sound this horn," he continued, fiercely, "and in an instant the beacon light would be kindled, the glare of which would illumine the bay to its utmost extent, and you would be surrounded by those at the hands of whom you know what mercy to expect!"

"Do you threaten us?" cried Captain Paul, whose eyes, now that he was thoroughly aroused, gleamed with the concentrated deadly power of a basilisk. "Fool! braggart! traitor!" he hissed between his teeth, "before you could raise your craven hand to give the signal your brains would bespatter the ground on which you stand!"

As he rapidly uttered these words, he drew a pistol from beneath his robe, and stood with his finger resting on the trigger glaring his scorn upon Octavius Challoner, who stood irresolute, apparently at a loss what course to take.

"Come, comrade," cried Captain Paul, with a contemptuous laugh at the indecision of the man who had been just before so forward to threaten, "it's time this poor land-rat should know with whom he has to deal!"

As he spoke, he struck a small gong at one side of the recess, that resounded with a sonorous clang.

At the same moment he and his companion threw off their furred robes, and appeared in the imposing costumes they wore beneath.

Captain Paul's was a magnificent coat, and short under-skirt of crimson, with richly embroidered buskins of the same hue, whilst from his shoulders depended a pair of massive gold epaulettes.

That of his companion was entirely different, being composed of sombre black, relieved only by a skull and crossbones of dead silver embroidered on the breast. The festooned drapery detached itself, and fell waving in massive folds—half crimson, like his own dress, and the remainder black, like his comrade's —to the ground.

Then, snatching up their respective flags—crimson, with a flaming torch emblazoned in gold; and sable, with the skull and crossbones in white—they held them aloft, whilst the entire crew having started from their recumbent positions, stood with expectant eyes, and polished weapons, that flashed like diamonds in the light, motionless as statues, awaiting the signal of their leaders.

Octavius Challoner at this unexpected transformation, stood riveted to the spot in mute surprise.

"You honoured us not long since," cried Captain Paul, "with the title of 'smugglers;' it is fit you should now know us better. I am PAUL JONES, THE PIRATE!"

"And I," exclaimed his comrade, "am CAPTAIN KYD, THE WIZARD OF THE WAVE!"

Chapter X.

THE THREE BOYS IN THE BOAT.

A DEAD pause followed this announcement. This the baffled Octavius was the first to break. A glance hastily thrown around told him it was no time to trifle.

He came to a rapid conclusion that his position was extremely critical—

That he was completely at the pirates' mercy.

He fell back, therefore, upon the usual refuge of the coward—a lie.

"Ha, ha!" he cried, forcing a laugh, which was after all a very melancholy imitation, "I suspected you were here under a mask, and I resolved, if possible, to draw you forth from your concealment, and I think I have succeeded."

"You were not in earnest, then?" said Captain Paul, waving his hand to his crew, who sank once more on the ground.

"Certainly not!"

"Then the proposed murder of your cousin?"

"Merely a trial of your moral principles."

"And the beacon light, and the Coastguard Blockade?"

"Jests—nothing more!"

"If so, then, allow me to saw you jest on perilous subjects; many a more valuable life than yours has been sacrificed by such folly."

"I am ready to admit my rashness."

"Are you also willing to admit that the words you have just uttered are *deliberate lies?*"

Octavius Challoner was not proof against the searching tone in which this accusation was delivered. He turned pale, and his eyes wandered uneasily, as though to escape the piercing glance of his inquisitor. But it was necessary he should cover his deceit with some attempt at least at candour.

"I assure you," he at length exclaimed, "you are mistaken. And, with respect to my cousin Augustus, I wish the boy no harm; I merely wished to see to what extent money could influence such wild and daring natures as yours must necessarily be."

"I trust, then," replied Captain Paul, "you are satisfactorily convinced that there may exist a sense of honour even amongst *pirates?*"

"Most agreeably so!" returned Octavius, with as much sarcasm in his tone as he dared to use—"the idea is most delightful to contemplate."

But his listeners were not to be hoodwinked or deceived.

"Enough of this balderdash!" Captain Paul suddenly burst out in a tone of profound contempt. "You are mistaken if you think you can so impose upon us. *You* know, and *we* know, full well you mean harm to the son of your benefactor. But, mark me, if you raise a hand to injure that innocent boy, you are doomed! The avenging blow may fall sooner or later, according to circumstances; but that it *will* fall is as certain as that I now stand here to warn you; therefore beware! I have done—now you can go!"

With a contemptuous wave of the hand Captain Paul turned his back upon his listener, and conversed in low tones with his comrade.

Bitterly chagrined and perplexed, baffled in his vile proposal, Octavius Challoner looked round for his cousin Augustus.

Not seeing him, and endeavouring to put as good a face upon the matter as possible, he called in as amicable a voice as he could assume:

"Gus, where are you? I am going."

"I think," said Captain Kyd, satirically, "the youngster suspects foul play, and has stolen a march upon his loving cousin. You had better call again."

Forcing himself to smile outwardly, but full of bitter wrath within, the baffled villain searched every nook and recess, but no signs of his cousin's presence were visible.

He began to think he had been duped, and that his prey had slipped through his fingers.

At the extreme end of the cavern was a narrow opening that appeared to lead into another.

Towards this, Octavius, biting his lips and frowning heavily, bent his steps.

He looked in at the entrance, but all was profoundly dark.

He called, but there was no answer.

"Where can the brat be?" he muttered between his teeth.

Returning a few steps, he seized a torch, and hastily passed through the aperture.

He found himself in another cave of much smaller dimensions, but he did not discover the object of his search.

As the rays of the torch fell around, they lighted on a dark mass at a little distance from him.

He approached and raised the drapery that covered it, and started back as he gazed on the dead body of a boy, apparently about his cousin's age.

He bent down and gazed eagerly at the pale, delicate features, calm and composed, in their death sleep, and withdrew, after an earnest scrutiny, with a frown of disappointment.

"It is not he!" he muttered. "Would that it were!"

The wind suddenly blowing upon the torch, caused the flame to dance and flicker.

In the fitful light the dead boy's face appeared to smile derisively.

"Psha!" he exclaimed, as he drew the covering hastily over the features of the corpse.

He proceeded to examine the cave, and found at the extremity a large opening leading on to the rocks, in which a channel had been cut by the waves, that dashed their spray into the very entrance.

He went out on to the slippery boulders, that were covered with slimy weeds, and holding the torch aloft over the dark waters, called:

"Augustus!—Gus!"

But there was no reply but the hoarse moaning of the wind and waves.

"Where can he be?" he ejaculated.

"Well, have you found him?" cried a voice at his elbow.

Turning round with a start, he beheld the features of Paul Jones.

"No, I have not," he replied, "and I feel anxious!"

"Lest he should be drowned, or have escaped—which?" inquired Paul, sarcastically. "Make way for me!" he continued, abruptly, as he stepped forward on the boulders.

He knelt down and examined the side of the rocky channel.

He passed his hand over the spot where a boat was usually fastened to an iron ring in the rock.

There was the ring, but neither rope nor boat.

He paused for a moment, and then sprang up with a sudden exclamation.

"What is the matter?" eagerly inquired Octavius.

"Why," exclaimed Paul, with an exulting laugh, "the boat's gone, and it's my belief the boys are gone in her!"

*   *   *   *   *   *   *

The terrible revelations that reached the ears of James Cook and Ikey Mangles, as they sat crouched in the hole in the rock, filled them with but one idea.

This was to get out of the cavern as quickly as possible, and to take Augustus, whom they looked upon as doomed if he remained in the clutches of his cousin, with them.

The difficulty was how to accomplish their design.

They kept their eyes fixed upon Augustus, as though they dreaded letting him go out of their sight.

The unconscious boy, delighted with the novelty of the scene, and unsuspicious of any danger, rambled about in all directions, and at last arrived at the aperture leading to the small cavern previously spoken of.

With a kind of timid curiosity, he peered in, as though desirous to explore its recesses, but he seemed irresolute.

Ikey, who was watching him anxiously, said:]

"Hi vishes 'e'd go in theer; ve could slip in arter 'im, an' varn 'im—couldn't ve?"

His wishes were gratified; for after lingering at the entrance for a moment or two, as if undecided, the curiosity of Augustus overcame his doubts, and he went in.

Ikey and James instantly glided from their place of concealment like two little white mice, and without attracting any attention, followed him.

The small cavern was dimly lighted by a solitary lamp fixed in a hole in the rock.

When they entered, they found Augustus looking around him with a kind of timid amazement.

The sight of them did not appear to alarm him—rather the contrary.

He did not seem surprised that there should be other boys besides himself in the cave.

But when, upon closer inspection, he recognised James and Ikey as two poor ragged boys that he was often accustomed to meet in his walks, he opened his eyes with astonishment.

"What, is it you?" he exclaimed, in a tone of wonder.

"Sh!" said James, hastily, in a whisper, putting his finger on his lip to enjoin caution—"speak low, or they'll hear us!"

Naturally enough, the thoughts of Augustus reverted to the cruel blow James had received from his cousin that morning.

"Is your hand better?" he asked.

"Yes, thank you," answered James, "but that's nothing—never mind that!"

"Oh, but I do mind it!" said the generous little fellow. "I think it was very cruel of my cousin; he ought not to have hurt you; but never mind, if you'll come up to the Hall I'll ask my father to help you."

"Before ve can go hup theer, ve must get out o' 'ere," thought Ikey—"that's the fust thing to do."

"How did you come here?" inquired Augustus of James.

"The gentleman brought us," he answered.

"I came with cousin Otty," said Augustus.

"But 'ow's yer goin' to get avay?" asked Ikey, in an ominous tone.

"Get away?" repeated Augustus, as if surprised at the question. "I shall go with my cousin, of course."

Ikey's jaw dropped with dismay at what appeared to him the credulous confidence of the speaker.

"Oh don't!—don't go with him!" exclaimed James, in an earnest, pleading tone, clasping his hand as he spoke.

"Why not?" asked Augustus, looking very much astonished at his agitated countenance.

"Why! Because—because it's not safe for you to go with him!" said James, earnestly.

"Not safe with cousin Otty?" repeated Augustus, with increased astonishment. "Why not safe?"

"Becos' it hain't!" replied Ikey, forcibly, but by no means convincingly to the mind of the young gentleman.

Ikey noticed this, and continued, with a mixture of warmth and impatience:

"If yer goes vith yer cous'n Hotty, yer'll be cold enough afore yer gets 'ome."

"No, I sha'n't!" returned Gus. "My cousin keeps me warm under his cloak."

"Take care 'e don't keep yer too varm, an' smother yer!" returned Ikey, forebodingly.

"What do you mean?" inquired Augustus Markham.

"Vhy, Hi means as your cous'n's a reg'lar bad 'un—'e's a werry vicked man!"

"I'm sure he isn't!" retorted Gus, indignantly.

"Hi'm sure 'e his!" cried Ikey, decidedly. "Hi 'eerd 'im a hoffering them pirates 'undreds o' poun's to put you hout o' th' vay, so as 'e might 'ave all yer father's money."

Augustus looked earnestly at the excited face of the speaker, and noticed the nervous twitching of his pale features as he detailed these horrors.

"Where did my cousin want the pirates to put me?" he asked; "and what does it mean by putting anyone 'out of the way'?"

"Don't yer know?" said Ikey, in a most impressive tone of surprise.

"No."

The boy bent forward, and placing his mouth close to the ear of Augustus, answered, in a terrified whisper:

"It means murd'rin' 'em!"

The young gentleman recoiled with horror.

"I can't believe this!" he said, in a troubled tone.

"It's true—it's true!" cried James, who had been a silent listener for some time, but who now, with clasped hands and agitated countenance, added these words of earnest affirmation.

"I heard your cousin ask the men to kill you, as well as Ikey," he continued. "Oh, this is a dreadful place, and they are all wicked men here!"

"Hi thinks as they 'tices poor boys 'ere o' purpose to m-murder 'em, and heat 'em artervards," faltered Ikey. "Oh, lor!" he groaned, in the extremity of his fears, "hit's all hup vith us!"

Augustus, though evidently impressed by the manifest terror of his companions, was slow to believe that his cousin Octavius could be guilty of the designs of which he was accused.

The boys stood huddled together in the semi-obscurity of the cavern, when suddenly young Markham's attention was arrested by a face that was partly covered with a dark drapery, at a little distance off.

"What's that?" he asked, in a tone of more apprehension than he had hitherto exhibited.

"What?" inquired his companions, tremulously.

"That white face there!" he exclaimed, pointing to the spot where the dead body of the boy laid, and which came out in sombre distinctness through the gloom.

They all turned, and stood riveted to the spot as they gazed upon it in awe-struck silence.

Ikey was the first to speak.

"It's a dead b—o—oy, Hi thinks!" he gasped.

A shudder ran through their young veins, and made the poor .... cold from head to foot.

"Let us go u..... and see what it is," proposed James, who was the first to recover from the shock.

"Hi don't like!" said Ikey.

"Nor I!" added Augustus.

"Let's come," urged James. "Whatever it is, if it's dead, it can't hurt us."

But the boys could not be induced to approach.

"Then I will go by myself," said James.

"No you sha'n't, Jem—Hi'll go vith yer!" Ikey burst out, as if ashamed of his cowardice.

"So will I!" chimed in Augustus, stimulated by his example.

The boys then drew near the body, and James, drawing aside the drapery that covered it, revealed the lifeless form.

The boys gazed at it for a moment with a complication of feelings.

It was evidently that of a lad about their own age.

This fact greatly increased their interest, and—their fears.

To their minds, he was undoubtedly one of the victims of the remorseless wretches in the adjoining cavern.

"Hi vonders 'ow they killed 'im?" murmured Ikey, under his breath, as he peered curiously at the silent clay, expecting to behold some gaping wound or hideous gash from whence life's stream had departed.

The boys' imaginations were overcharged and distempered with what they had heard; or they might have guessed that the dead boy on which they gazed belonged to the crew, and, having died, was placed where it lay until the time arrived for its interment, either in the cave or the ocean depths.

But anything so probable would not have been listened to at that moment.

Their apprehensions were strung up to the highest pitch of endurance, and their only desire was, by any means, to get clear of the dreadful place that held them in its rocky confines.

Even Augustus at last shared in this anxiety.

The giant difficulty was how to get away.

If they crept through the large cavern, it was a thousand chances to one they would be seen.

If even they could evade the glances of some fifty or sixty eyes, and gain the entrance, and pass behind the red drapery, how could they pass the man stationed at the top of the narrow rocky ascent?

He would be sure to see them, and bring them back in triumph as runaway captives.

Then as a punishment for trying to escape, they would be sure to be eaten at once.

These thoughts passed rapidly through the minds of James and Ikey; and while they filled them with horrors, at the same time added to their desperation and determination at any risk to escape somehow.

Augustus suddenly noticed the opening at the end of the cave.

"We can go out there!" he cried, eagerly.

"So ve can!" said Ikey, with reciprocal wamth. "Hi sees a hopenin'."

This was enough to cause in his breast unbounded exultation.

That there was a *way out* of the horrid den, no matter where it led to, was a sufficient cause of congratulation.

The boys hastened forward.

How they welcomed the cold wind as it came rushing in their faces!

How delightful it was to feel the spray dashing over them!

"Come hon!" cried Ikey, with eager impetuosity, rushing out on to the slippery boulders and instantly falling on his back.

"Oh!" he exclaimed, rubbing his head, which had come into sudden and sharp contact with the rock, "if it hain't as slippery as hice!"

His companions, warned by his example, were more cautious; and having helped him on to his feet, the trio began to look about for a path that would lead them to the top of the cliffs that towered above their heads.

No such path, however, appeared, and to their great dismay they found themselves cut off from any hope of escape, at the very point where they had a moment before most confidently expected it.

"It's all hover vith us!" groaned Ikey; "vo may make hup our minds to be heat alive."

Suddenly his feet slipped once more from under him, and, with a cry, he disappeared over the side of the rocky channel, in which the seething waves swelled fiercely.

"He's drowned!—he's drowned!" shrieked James, in a voice of agony.

"No, Hi hain't!" cried Ikey, who was at that moment audible, though not visible.

"Where are you, then?" asked his anxious companions.

"Hi'm hin th' boat," answered Ikey.

Fortunately for him, a boat moored by a rope to an iron ring floated in the narrow creek, but for which the boy, when he slipped, would have been precipitated into the foaming waters.

As it was, however, he fell on his back in the boat instead.

He lost no time in getting on to his legs, when the first words he uttered were:

"Hain't yer coming?"

"Where?" inquired James.

"Why, hin th' boat, o' course," answered Ikey.

"Oh, yes! do let's come!" urged Gus, who was fond of the sea.

James, who had a similar predilection, had no objection to offer.

Certainly it seemed rather a rash step for three boys to take on a dark night.

It struck James as such, and he said to his companions:

"Have you ever been on the sea before?"

"Never," they replied.

"We sha'n't know where we're going, shall we?" James continued.

"Yes, ve shall—ve shall know ve're a goin' avay from these vicked boy-heaters," Ikey remarked.

"But how can we manage the boat?"

"The boat must manage isself; come hon!"

No better alternative appearing, and the prospect of being swallowed up by the waves seeming less terrible than being devoured by the pirates, James helped Augustus into the boat, and then jumped in himself.

"That's hall right!" cried Ikey, who felt, now they were all on board, that their perils were at an end.

All that was necessary now to do, was to detach the rope. This Ikey accomplished.

"Now, then," he cried, exultingly, "hoff ve goes!"

The boat rose and fell, and swayed from side to side in the narrow channel, scraping its sides against the rocks.

James seized an oar, and contrived, by digging the end into the sand at the bottom—the water not being deep—and leaning his weight upon it, to propel the boat to the end of the channel.

He then made use of the same implement to push off from the rocks, and gradually they found themselves in almost total darkness, tossing about at the mercy of the winds and waves.

But presently there came a change. The moon made a temporary appearance from behind a mass of dark clouds, as if for the express purpose of showing the young adventurers where they were, and what they might have to expect.

The giant cliffs sweeping round in a vast curve, looked quite ghastly in the moonlight, whilst the waves dashing against the beach at their base, and showering up masses of white spray, suggested unseen perils from rocks beneath.

There was a strong ground-swell, and the small boat rose and fell, pitched and tumbled, and rolled from side to side in such a manner, that the boys were not quite decided whether it was "good fun" or great danger.

Suddenly James pointed to an object at some little distance ahead.

"What is it?" asked Augustus.

"P'r'aps hit's a fish," suggested Ikey.

Whatever it was, it was nearing the boat.

"It looks more like a face," said James, as it approached.

There was no doubt about it. It was a human body, borne upon the waves' bosom.

"Is it alive, or dead?" they wondered.

The floating form, rising and falling, now came in its onward progress close to the boat.

The features were distinctly visible.

Both James and Ikey uttered a shriek of horror.

"It's the *face of the gentleman!*" they cried.

The body swept rapidly by.

The moon went suddenly out, and they were once more in total darkness.

Chapter XI.

THE EXPLOSION.

IT was with mingled feelings that Octavius Challoner listened to the pirate's assertion that the boys had departed in the boat.

He was not troubled with any anxiety for their preservation, but the term *boys* somewhat puzzled him. Had Captain Paul said *boy*, he would have understood him to mean his cousin, who might, perhaps, in a boyish freak, have unmoored the boat, and have paid the penalty of his rashness with the loss of his life.

Such an event would have been joyfully welcomed by the cruel Octavius.

But the word "boys" implied more than one, and excited his curiosity.

"I was not aware you had any boys in the cavern beside my cousin!" he said to Captain Paul.

"Oh yes, there were two others," answered the pirate.

"Two of your own boys, you mean, of course—two young sailors who understand the management of a boat?" Octavius continued to inquire, with evident anxiety.

"Nothing of the sort," said the captain. "These are a couple of poor, half-starved little wretches whom my friend George Carew brought here with him. I understand from him, one of them was dragged away almost from his mother's death-bed, by Squire Somebody's gamekeepers, and locked up in the cage, from which he rescued them."

"And is it they with whom my cousin is gone?" eagerly asked Octavius.

"I suspect so; boys are all alike when they get together; and, what more likely than that they should have found out this boat, got on board her, and have loosed the rope and let her float out to sea?"

A peculiarly fiendish expression stole over the features of Octavius at this suggestion of the pirate.

It was a rough, bitter night; the wind, gradually increasing, as it howled across the dark waters, lashed them into a fury.

What could three children, neither much over ten years old, do in a small boat at such a time?

His cruel heart warmed as the thought flashed across him that destruction was inevitable, and that his cousin's death, which he so ardently desired, and which he would have sought by such desperate measures, would, in all probability, be brought about by the hand of fate itself.

The fierce light that gleamed in his eyes was but a reflection of the fiendish thoughts within him.

Captain Paul, who had been watching him intently for some time, said at length:

"Your face is like a book, sir child-slayer: in it I can read your thoughts distinctly."

"Psha!" exclaimed Octavius, angrily; "you assume to know too much!"

"Oh, no! You think it impossible for a small boat manned by three children to live in such a dark and stormy night."

"It seems so to me," remarked Octavius, gruffly.

"Ay, to you; but a cargo of innocence such as that has on board, will make a craft lighter than cork and stronger than iron! They'll get safe to land, depend on't."

"I doubt it."

"You are unwilling to believe it—you wish your cousin dead!"

"Psha! I wish the boy no harm, and hope he may escape. I am sorry you have formed so bad an opinion of me; but since it is so, the sooner I depart the better."

"You are at liberty to go," said Captain Paul, coolly; "but do not slight the warning I have given you—lift not your hand against your cousin's life—remember!"

Octavius Challoner, with a compressed lip and moody brow, passed through the caverns, and paused not till he reached the top of the cliff.

He went to the hut and led out his gray steed, which, having mounted, he galloped off, not by the road he had come, but in an exactly opposite direction.

No sooner had he departed than Captain Paul, having informed his comrade what had occurred, said:

"We must go in search of this boat, Jack!"

"With all my heart! and the sooner we start the better," replied Captain Kyd, "or the poor boys will stand but a small chance of reaching the shore alive."

Captain Paul hailed one of the crew.

The man approached.

"Run a boat down to the creek, and launch her, instantly. Rig up a sail—let two men be ready to start with us."

"Ay, ay, captain!" answered the sailor, as he departed to obey the order.

"What madness could have tempted these youngsters to venture out on such a stormy night as this?" mused Captain Kyd, as he looked across the troubled waters.

"I rather think they were suspicious of us, Jack," returned his comrade. "But who would have thought my young *Honesty*, with his pale, sad face, and melancholy eyes, would have had pluck enough in him to make one in such an attempt?"

"Nay, if I am any judge of character," answered Captain Jack, "he seems to me just the sort of lad that would have courage enough to attempt anything. Don't be deceived, Paul: a pale face and a melancholy eye are no signs of cowardice."

"By no means," his comrade assented.

"Besides, the poor little fellow had reason enough to be sad; he had only just lost his mother—his only friend—and was almost broken-hearted."

"True—true, Jack!" cried Captain Paul—"I forgot that!"

"I thought you had," said his comrade. "Depend upon it young James Cook is a brave boy, and will make a stir in the world yet, who ever lives to see it."

"What makes you think so highly of his courage, Jack? He seemed to me timid and trembling."

"The boy is of a highly delicate and nervous temperament; but that is not uncommon amongst persons of the highest courage. Such, though they feel acutely before the decisive moment for action arrives, still, when it does arrive, are firm as iron or rock."

"And do you think this lad you speak of belongs to this class?"

"I am sure of it!" warmly asserted Captain Kyd.

"Why?"

"Because he had the courage to act conscientiously, and dared to refuse to do what he believed to be wrong. He who can act thus as a boy, is sure, if he lives, to turn out a brave man."

"Then, Jack," laughed Paul Jones, "by Neptune with the sea-green beard, he's braver than any of us!"

"You're right, he is," returned Captain Jack; "though it's no compliment to ourselves to say so."

A party of men now came into the cavern dragging the boat, which in a few moments was rising and falling with the waves in the creek.

Some of the sailors jumped into it, and proceeded to run up a mast and small square sail.

The two captains stood by watching them.

Captain Paul seemed to have fallen into a reverie. Suddenly he started, and turning towards the entrance of the cavern, remained a moment gazing earnestly, as though some object riveted his attention.

"What, George!" he said, "is it you returned? You're just in time to make one in an expedition! Why, what's the matter?" he suddenly exclaimed; "you look as pale as death!"

Captain Kyd hearing his comrade thus address a person that was invisible, said:

"To whom do you speak?"

"To our worthy President, George Carew," returned Paul. "You know he promised to return—do you not see him?"

"Where?"

"There!" pointing as he spoke to the cave's mouth.

"My dear fellow," cried Captain Kyd, "you're dreaming! I see nothing."

"I tell you he stands there!" persisted Paul Jones. "There," he repeated—"in the entrance of the cave! Look at his pale face—he is ill. Why, what is this?" he cried, with sudden surprise, pressing his hands to his eyes, as though he began to doubt his powers of vision. "He is gone!—vanished!—melted into thin air!"

Captain Jack, who began to think his comrade was a little demented, laid his hand on his shoulder.

"My dear Paul," he said, "are you taking leave of your senses?"

"Not the least in the world, Jack!" replied his comrade; "but as surely as we now stand together here, so surely I saw George Carew distinctly standing there, on the spot to which I pointed."

Captain Kyd looked at his friend with an incredulous smile.

"You do not believe me," continued Paul Jones, seriously, "but I am possessed of the gift of *second sight*. I have seen people before now whom I knew to be thousands of miles away appear suddenly before me, and a few days after I have *heard of their death!*"

"But surely," said Captain Jack, impressed by the serious tone of his comrade, "you do not mean to infer that George Carew is dead?"

"I believe," replied Paul Jones, "that if he is not dead, he has met with some serious calamity."

One of the sailors in the fore part of the boat cried out:

"Look, captain!"

The sudden exclamation of the man at that particular moment caused them both to start.

"What say you?" exclaimed the pirates, simultaneously.

"A man in the sea floating this way!" answered the sailor. "Whether alive or dead, I can't say!"

"Give me a torch!" said Paul Jones, as he snatched a blazing link from the outstretched hand of one of the men.

Hastily leaping into the boat, he raised the torch and looked out eagerly in the direction pointed out to him.

Tossed hither and thither by the swelling tide, now covered by a foaming wave, and the next moment raised aloft upon its mounting crest, the body gradually drifted towards the boat.

The eyes of all were riveted upon it.

Slowly but certainly it came nearer.

Its face was upturned, and as the rays of the torch shone down upon it, the features were at once recognised.

"Jack!" cried Captain Paul, in a deep whisper, grasping his companion—who had followed him into the boat—by the arm, "do you believe me now? Whose face is that?"

"The face of our President, George Carew!" replied Captain Kyd, in a tone that proved how greatly he was impressed.

It was certainly one of those incidents calculated to affect a mind under ordinary circumstances unimpressible.

A moment before, his comrade, Captain Paul, had distinctly declared that he saw the President, who had mysteriously disappeared, even whilst he was addressing him.

From this mysterious disappearance, his friend had prophesied some serious calamity, and lo! with the prediction almost on his lips, came its fulfilment.

The senseless, and apparently lifeless, body of George Carew floated before them.

The body was quickly lifted into the boat, and from thence conveyed to the cavern.

It was soon perceptible to the experienced eyes of the pirates that the President had been wounded in the breast—by whom they were of course ignorant.

It appeared to them that the assassin, having delivered the blow, had dragged his victim to the edge of the cliff, and plunged the body into the waves beneath.

Thus far their surmises were perfectly correct.

The sudden shock of the immersion appeared to have checked the effusion of blood; if, therefore, the wound had not bled inwardly, the general opinion was that life might still hold its seat in the victim's breast.

Placing his hand upon the heart of the wounded man, Captain Paul was rejoiced to find that that all-important vital organ still beat, though faintly.

How it happened that it was so, that its pulsations had not long since been hushed in death, was one of those almost miraculous interpositions of Providence that often occur to deprive the grim monster of his prey at the very moment when it appears ready to sink into his jaws.

But so it was: George Carew still lived, though the spark of life glimmered so feebly that it seemed as if the slightest breath would extinguish it for ever.

Captain Paul bound up the wound, and, having removed the brine-saturated garments from the body of the patient, enveloped him in warm furs, and administered a restorative cordial that appeared to have a favourable effect.

Though still unconscious, the pulse gradually became stronger, and the pirates began to hope that their efforts would be ultimately successful.

As they gazed down upon the sufferer, each pondering in his own mind as to whose hand it was that had perpetrated the deed, a lightning thought rushed into their breasts simultaneously.

They remembered that Octavius Challoner had mentioned his having met the President on his way to the cavern, that he came also wearing the same disguise as their friend, which he affirmed he had borrowed.

From the exhibition they had had of his character, they were both impressed with the idea that his hand had struck the blow.

On this suspicion they vented their indignation freely.

They could not leave their friend at such a crisis, and yet to delay their departure in search of the boys would be to ensure their destruction.

After a brief consultation, it was arranged that Captain Kyd should remain with the wounded man, while Paul Jones, with a few men, undertook the expedition for the recovery of the missing boat.

This being determined, Captain Paul, hastily collecting a few necessaries for a voyage, that might extend over the succeeding day, shouted to the men:

"Now, my lads, are you ready?"

"Ay, ay, captain!" was the prompt reply.

"Forward, then!" he cried. "Good-bye, Jack!"

"Good-bye, Paul! Success attend you!" his comrade exclaimed, warmly, as he grasped the hand extended to him.

Captain Paul hastened to the boat, and was in the act of leaping on board, when a bright light suddenly shot up on the summit of the cliff over his head, casting its glare over the dark waters.

"Hallo!" cried he, "what is the meaning of that? Ha!" he exclaimed, in the same breath, "I understand—treachery! That murderous villain has kept his word: he has alarmed the Coastguard, and they have fired the beacon-light! Well, we shall see, though there's no time to be lost! Follow me, men!" he shouted, as he retreated hastily to the cavern.

Captain Kyd was surprised to see him return, but ere he could ask the reason of that, and the excited look his comrade wore, a shrill whistle was heard without.

"Hark!—the alarm whistle!" cried Captain Jack, starting up.

"We are betrayed!" said Paul Jones, hastily.

At the same moment the scout rushed into the cavern.

"The Coastguard are alarmed, captain!" he exclaimed, breathlessly. "They're coming down upon us fifty strong!"

"Let them come, a hundred strong, if they like!" returned Captain Paul, coolly.

His excitement had vanished, and he was as calm and rigid as a block of stone.

"How near are they?" he inquired.

"Not a hundred yards off."

"Good!" exclaimed the captain. "Now, my lads, bear a hand—quick! Roll a barrel of gunpowder to the top of yonder steps!"

He pointed to the entrance as he spoke.

His orders were obeyed in an instant.

"Place it beneath the overhanging rock!"

"'Tis done, captain!"

"Now stave in the head, and introduce the end of the fusee you will see on the left of the entrance!"

"Right, captain!"

"Is it done?"

"Yes, captain."

"Then come to me here!" cried Captain Paul, seizing a flaming torch. "All hands around me, and dead silence! We'll soon have noise enough!"

The crew gathered round him, and remained motionless as statues.

Their leader stood with the blazing firebrand in his hand, and a grim smile passed over his features as the hurried tread of advancing footsteps reached his ear.

Near him, and just peeping out from a crevice in the rock, was the head of the fusee, the other end of which rested in the powder-barrel at the entrance.

The previous preparations had occupied scarcely a minute.

The sounds of the advancing guard as they hastily descended the rocky path grew more and more distinct; the hum of murmuring voices was heard.

It was one of those moments of terrible intense excitement which once experienced is never forgotten.

Like the rush of many waters, the living stream poured on.

They were almost at the cavern's mouth, and a ringing shout was raised by the Coastguard-men at their anticipated triumph.

The cheer was answered from within, and at the same moment the captain applied his torch to the fatal quick match.

There was a loud whizzing hiss as the explosive material rushed like a fiery serpent along the sides of the cavern, till it reached the powder barrel.

Then came a blinding flash of light, and a report like a violent thunderclap, as the massive rock, dislodged from its oscillating basis, was propelled forwards, and fell, completely blocking up the entrance to the cavern.

"That will do!" remarked Paul Jones, freezingly, as the hollow reverberations died away. "'Tis an excellent English proverb, 'There's many a slip between the cup and the lip.'"

After the explosion there was a momentary pause of dead silence, and then came sounds even more terrible than any that had yet been heard—

The revengeful execrations of the barricaded foe and the groans of the wounded and dying.

"To the boats!" cried Captain Paul. "Clear off all, and away; we sail under cover of the darkness!"

The preparations for departure were promptly and rapidly made.

Boat after boat was hurried down to the narrow channel, loaded, and guided forth on to the stormy ocean.

[OUT OF THE FIRE INTO THE WATER.]

The pirates' vessel lay at some distance from the land, and towards this the small craft made their way, urged onwards by the strong arms of the oarsmen, and lighted on their dangerous track by the blazing pile on the summit of the cliff, whilst ever and anon, higher than the fierce wind and the dashing waves, came the shriek of some poor sufferer who had been mutilated by the late terrible discharge.

Long after all the boats were out of sight, one solitary craft cruised hither and thither, searching vainly in the dark for some object that could not be found.

Ever and anon rang out the cheering "Halloo!" across the stormy main, but no voice answered!

Nothing seemed to be abroad there but the demons of darkness and destruction.

Chapter XII.

PERILS IN THE DEEP.

URGED on by their fears, which had received an additional impetus from the discovery of the dead body of the boy, our three little friends —James, Ikey, and Augustus—had welcomed the boat as a haven of safety, and joyfully launched forth upon the stormy deep as they would have fled to the bosom of a friend.

But a little experience speedily changed their opinions, and convinced them that in endeavouring to avoid one danger on land they had plunged into a host of perils afloat.

The sudden appearance of the ghastly, drenched countenance of their kind protector—to all appearance dead—as his body drifted past them on its way to the rocks, filled them with gloomy presentiments, and they felt inclined to look upon it in some way as a warning of their own fate.

The ground-swell had broken up, and the angry waters, stirred to their very depths, and boiling up like a huge cauldron, had burst through the foaming, bubbling surface, dashing its spray in fierce torrents against the advancing blast that scattered and drove it back in its fury.

Ikey, who felt himself condemned to a state of perpetual motion, being at one moment standing on his head, the next on his heels, and then on his head again, varied with occasional lurches from side to side, looked ominously at the prospect before him. He began to feel he had been rash.

" Hi dunno what to make o' this 'ere," he gasped to Augustus, just after a wave had dashed its spray over them and wetted them through. " Hi halmost vishes as Hi'd stayed on dry land."

" I'm sure I do !" cried his more delicate companion, shivering with cold. " I don't believe they'd have murdered us."

" It's horful 'ere, ain't it ?" he exclaimed, dolefully, his teeth chattering so forcibly that he could hardly articulate.

" Oh !" shrieked Augustus, as the boat rose upon a wave, and pitched downwards so abruptly that it seemed as if they were all going at once to the bottom.

The poor little fellow began to cry : a terrible death seemed to him from that moment inevitable.

It was very awful to drown in those dark waters on such a bitter night.

He thought—strange thoughts pass through the mind in such terrible moments—that death would have been less frightful if it had been daylight and the sun had been shining.

But to sink into the angry, foaming, boiling depths that surrounded them on every side seemed to invest the approaching crisis with tenfold terrors.

The childish faults he had committed rose up before him till they were magnified to glaring crimes. Angry tempers he had shown ; hasty words he had spoken ; acts of disobedience he had committed and long since forgotten, seemed to start into vivid remembrance as though the thick darkness made them more visible.

Ikey, too, thought of the hare he had shot, and was half inclined to look upon his present position in the light of retributive judgment.

" Vot right 'ad Hi got to go an' shoot th' poor 'are as 'ad never done me no 'arm ?" he whispered to himself. " Oh ! vot a vicked boy Hi ham !"

After a few sobs he continued :

" Hi vonder 'ow Jemmy feels ? E's a good boy, 'e is —Hi vishes Hi vos as good as 'im !"

He heard Augustus crying nearer him, and his heart was touched.

" Hi'm wery sorry as Hi axed yer to come in the boat, Master Gus," he said ; " but Hi thought ve should be safer theer than in th' cave ; Hi 'opes as yer'll forgive me."

" I forgive you," replied Augustus, in a voice that, between sobbing and shivering, was almost inaudible. " Where's James Cook ?" he asked, presently. " I should like to be near him."

" 'E's at t'other end o' th' boat," answered Ikey. " I should like 'im to be a little nearer to us myself."

It was strange that both boys seemed to look upon James as a being in some way superior to themselves ; and to have an idea, however fallacious that idea might be, that they were safer when he was close at their side.

And where was James all this time ?

Seated in the prow of the boat, silent, absorbed ; the fierce wind and the raging waters howled around him, and he heeded them not.

His pale face was upturned, and his dark eyes fixed on the firmament above his head, in which here and there a solitary star twinkled as though trying to pierce beyond that veil to those bright regions to which, he believed, his mother's spirit had taken her departure.

The longer he gazed the deeper was the calm that stole over him.

The distance between the sea and sky seemed to lessen, and once more he fancied he heard the dear familiar voice of that mother he had loved so fondly, and he felt no longer alone.

He was aroused from his reverie by the piteous voice of his friend Ikey.

" Hi say, Jem—Jemmy dear !" he cried, appealingly, " wheer are yer ?"

" I'm here," answered James, starting from his absorption to a sense of his real position, that may be summed up briefly in a few words :

Drenched to the skin and half-frozen with cold.

" Say summat to us, that's a good chap," pleaded Ikey. " 'Ere's Master Gus a cryin' 'cos 'e thinks we're a goin' to th' bottom o' th' sea, an' it's no good me a sayin' anythin' to 'im, 'cos 'e knows Hi'm as frittened as 'e his."

James was not selfish.

In that moment of peril, when his companions were in agonies of fear, he was calm and unmoved. But he did not on that account turn a deaf ear to their complaints.

He felt in his own mind that they would never survive that tempestuous night, but he resolved nevertheless to try and cheer them.

With this intent, then, he crawled along, feeling his way over the seats of the boat till he reached his young friends, who were huddled together almost at the other extremity.

" Here I am," he said, in as comforting a voice as the intense cold he suffered would allow him.

No sooner did Ikey and Augustus feel him close to them, than the poor boys flung their dripping arms round him, and clung to him tenaciously.

It was very cold comfort for all of them, for each one was as wet as his fellow, and there was little warmth imparted from their chilled bodies.

" Oh, Jemmy !" said Ikey, shivering between each letter, " Hi'm glad to be alongside o' you again."

" Do you think we shall meet anyone to help us ?" asked poor little Gus, in a melancholy voice.

" I hope we shall," answered James, not daring to say how slight he thought that hope was.

" But do you *think* we shall ?" repeated Gus, with nervous anxiety.

" P'raps we shall pass a ship presently," returned the young comforter, " and they'll take us in, and then we shall be safe."

" But it's so dark they wouldn't see us," murmured Gus, " and they might run against us, and upset the boat, and then we should be all drowned just the same."

At this dismal prospect the tears of the poor boy, who was full of dire forebodings, began to flow afresh.

" Can't we get to the shore somehow ?" he asked, with the faintest possible glimpse of hope in his tone.

" We must try !" said James, cheeringly.

" Hi can't make hout vich vay th' shore his—it's so orful dark !" whimpered Ikey.

" Let's see," said James, reflectively, turning his head, as though seeking the point from which they had started, in order to guess at their present position.

A sailor might have called it taking their bearings.

But Ikey did not seem to see the utility of this proceeding.

Perhaps James did not either ; but only performed the act for the purpose of encouraging his drooping companions.

" We started from there, I think," he said, thoughtfully.

" Hi'm sure yer can't tell, Jemmy," remarked Ikey ; " th' boat's been a doin' nothin' but turn round 'an round, an' stand fust on vun hend an' then on t'other, till it's qvite hemposs'ble to know vheer ve come from or vheer ve're goin,' 'xcept vun place, an' that's th' bottom—oh ! oh !"

" Sh !" whispered James to him, " don't make the worst of it. We must try and cheer up poor Gus ; and if he hears you crying, he'll be all the more frightened."

Ikey felt the reproof, and endeavoured to compose himself.

" Hi von't cry hany more if Hi can 'elp it," he murmured to his friend ; " but Hi feels so fritted, an' Hi'm so dreadful cold an' vet !"

" So am I," answered James, quickly, " but crying will neither make me drier nor warmer."

" No, more it von't," remarked Ikey, " but you can bear things better than ve can."

Augustus now spoke.

"Have you found out where the shore is?" he asked, anxiously.

"I think it must be there," replied James, pointing vaguely anywhere—as it happened—right away from the land, far out across the ocean.

"I hope we shall be able to get to it," Gus continued.

"We must try," again remarked James.

"'Ere's summat at th' bottom o' th' boat that feels like a sail," said Ikey.

Augustus smiled with delight.

Deliverance seemed to his young mind certain.

"Let's put it up; we shall soon get to shore then!" he cried, eagerly.

James, willing to humour the child, though much perplexed how to comply with his request, being only a child himself, said in reply:

"We'll see." Then addressing himself to Ikey, he asked: "Is it a sail?"

"Hi dun'no for certain," answered the boy, tugging at a piece of canvas that was rolled up at the bottom of the boat, "but it feels somethin' like it."

After some efforts, in which James assisted, the drenched material was dragged from under the seats.

"Make haste!" cried Augustus, who was nervously anxious to see, or rather to hear, the sail that was to waft them to land fluttering in the wind—"do make haste!"

This was easier to say than to do.

The poor boy's hands were numbed with the cold, and it was with the utmost difficulty they could unroll it.

This, however, was at last accomplished.

But now came other difficulties.

One of these Ikey recognised at once.

"'Ere's th' sail," he said, "but where's th' *mask* to fix it to?"

He should have said "mast;" but Ikey's grammar, as our readers will by this time have discovered, was, alas! like his garments, sadly open to criticism.

There was a slight pause after this question; but Augustus, whose heart was set upon the sail, felt about with his hands at the bottom of the boat, in search of a mast, and presently came in contact with a pair of oars.

"Here are two!" he cried, excitedly.

"Masks?" inquired Ikey.

"I think so," answered Augustus.

Ikey corrected him in most incorrect grammar.

"They hain't masks, but hoars," he said.

"Never mind," urged Gus—"one of them will do; here are some strings on the sail to tie it with: I can feel them!" he cried.

But now came another embarrassment: there was nothing in the shape of a yard, or crossbar, to tie it to.

James and Ikey had often watched the fishermen on the coast, and they knew that this was necessary to rig up the smallest sail.

But Augustus was not so well informed on this point, and was impatient at the delay.

"Oh, do fasten it up!" he cried—"we shall never get to land if you don't."

"Vot are ve to do?" shivered Ikey, between his teeth, into James's ear.

"We can't do anything," was the quiet reply; "only to please the young gentleman, let us try and fasten the sail to one of the oars."

This act, kind in its intention, though useless in its effects, was with some difficulty performed.

The appearance it presented, when finished, could it have been seen, was that of an unwieldy canvas flag.

But it satisfied Augustus.

"Now we'll stick it up!" he cried.

The canvas, being drenched with wet, was very heavy, and this, added to the weight of the oar, made it as much as the united strength of the three half-frozen children could effect to raise it to an upright position; and then came a gust of wind and a lurch of the boat, and away went the mast—not overboard, for they all clung to it to save themselves, but it lay prostrate once more, and they were too benumbed and disheartened to attempt such an impossibility as raising it again.

Augustus was sorely disappointed.

James, still willing to comfort him if possible, suggested to Ikey that they should thrust the oar with the sail attached, out at the boat's head.

"It won't do any good," he whispered to his friend; "but it will satisfy him, p'r'aps."

Accordingly they pushed it forward over the prow, till the sail fell over and draggled in the water.

"Will it do like that?" asked Augustus, who had a strong suspicion that it was in the wrong place for a mast.

"It must do," answered James, in a coaxing tone "because we can't put it anywhere else."

On this assurance, the young gentleman became more resigned, and began to comfort himself that the motion of the boat was less violent, and they were moving towards the shore.

But James and Ikey by no means shared in his satisfaction.

In fact, the latter had strong misgivings with respect to the sail, and whispered his fears to his comrade.

"I say, Jemmy," he said, "don't you think that 'ere sail hout in front o' th' boat makes it pitch down 'ead forrards more than hever?"

"I think it does," acquiesced James. "We'll draw it in."

They accordingly dragged the oar, with its drenched appurtenance, back into the boat, to the great chagrin of Augustus.

But James endeavoured to explain to him that in the position it had occupied, it could not assist them to get to the land, and might possibly tend to overturn the boat. To arrest his attention and inspire him with hope, James proposed that they should hallo for help.

This suggestion was acted upon immediately, and three small voices, weak with cold and exhaustion, though rendered shrill by fear, cried out:

"Help—help—help!"

But the mighty wind, as though it scorned their feeble efforts, came howling past them in derision, and drowned their supplications utterly.

The waves, too, dashed over them, and froze them to the marrow.

The small boat was half full of water.

The poor victims groaned inwardly, and cast up their imploring eyes to Heaven, huddling closer to each other as the keen north-easterly blast pierced them to the marrow.

They spoke not a word.

Their sufferings were too intense

Despair had laid its deadening hand on their sinking hearts.

Silently they succumbed to a destiny that seemed inevitable.

Augustus, the delicately-nurtured boy, murmured his father's name.

The one word "mother!" oozed out from James's icy lips.

As for poor Ikey, he had no recollections of either father or mother, and he only muttered something in a wandering manner about "that poor 'are."

Suddenly there arose a startling cry—a wild shriek of terror, as the impending fate they had been dreading reached a terrible crisis.

A giant wave had burst over them—the boat had capsized, and the three poor boys were struggling for life in the cruel waters.

An instant of silence followed this catastrophe, and then might have been heard the convulsive, quick gasps for breath as the poor boys rose to the surface, and with outstretched arms, clutched frantically at the first object that offered itself.

This, fortunately for them, happened to be the boat itself, which, after being overturned, floated bottom upwards. Borne upwards by the swelling waves, they were enabled to grasp the keel, and to this uncertain support they clung with a tenacity, prompted by the desperation that the love of life alone can give, and which first induced them to hazard their perilous journey. The shock of their immersion, the terrible apprehension that the motion of the waves would dash them from their hold into the dark vortex that yawned around them, for a time absorbed all their thoughts.

But by degrees their senses, already somewhat inured to terrors, began to collect themselves, and Ikey then asked, in a doleful, gasping manner:

"Jemmy, are you there?"

To the poor boy's unspeakable delight, James's voice replied:

"Yes, Ikey, I'm here."

"Oh, Hi'm so glad!" exclaimed Ikey, with a kind of shuddering joy; "Hi thought yer vos drownded."

"No, I'm safe at present."

"Vheer abouts are yer? Hi can't see yer."

"Here," cried James, "opposite to you, I think, from the sound of your voice."

"Let's feel yer 'and if yer can, though mine's so cold Hi don't think Hi can feel hanythink," chattered Ikey.

A wet cold hand was placed on his in answer to this request, and its slight pressure told him it was his friend's, and served in some measure to reassure him.

"But where's poor Augustus Markham?" asked James, "I don't hear his voice. Augustus!" he called.

There was no answer.

"'E hain't o' my side o' th' boat," said Ikey. "Hi'm afeard 'e's drownded."

At this melancholy supposition the poor boy's voice faltered. This was not strange, since every circumstance seemed to render it highly probable that a short time would bring with it a similar fate for himself and his companion.

The waves dashed over them constantly.

If they had been very cold before they were now completely benumbed.

They had lost all sense of feeling in their hands; but still they clung to the boat's keel with a kind of tenacious instinct, as the last expiring effort of self-preservation.

But even this was becoming gradually fainter, and their minds began to wander.

"Ikey," said James at length, in a voice dreamy, though calm in its tone, "I can't hold on much longer—I shall be with dear mother before long."

Already the frozen fingers were relaxing.

Strange lights seemed to flash in the boys' eyes through the darkness.

In another moment or two all would be over.

"Pray God help us!" murmured James.

At the same moment a huge wave dashed over them, and then came a shock, and a grinding sound as though the boat were grating against the beach.

This aroused them both.

"Ve're hon th' ground!" shouted Ikey. "Hi can feel it!"

"So can I!" returned James.

Once more a tremendous wave propelled the boat forward with its exhausted hangers-on, and then retiring, left them high and dry on the beach.

Numb and frozen as they were, they instinctively staggered forward, and then when they felt they were beyond the reach of danger, gave in at once, and fell exhausted and senseless on the stony beach.

Thus two out of the number who ventured forth in the boat had escaped a watery grave; but the *third*—Augustus Markham—where was he?

Chapter XIII.

ALONE IN THE PIRATES' CAVE.

THE half-drowned boys remained oblivious for a long time on the spot where they fell.

The thunder of the explosion had not reached their ears, nor the glare of the beacon fire attracted their eyes.

They were dead alike to sight and sound.

It was intensely cold, but this, instead of killing them, restored them by slow degrees to consciousness.

The symptoms of returning animation betrayed themselves in long-drawn sighs and faint moans.

James was the first to recover his senses.

He heard the murmured exclamations of his still unconscious companion, and staggering to his feet, did all he could to help him.

He raised his head, and whispered hopeful words in his ear.

"Come, Ikey, cheer up!" he cried, "we're no longer tossed about by the waves—we're on dry land once more."

"Are ve?" exclaimed his comrade, piteously, faintly opening his eyes, but seeing nothing but darkness, and feeling terribly cold.

"Yes, Ikey; don't you feel you are?"

"No Hi don't," he murmured, fretfully. "Hi doesn't feel dry at hall: Hi feels werry vet an' cold—oh. so bad!" he cried, with a shudder.

"Try and walk," said James, in an encouraging tone. "Can you stand?"

"Hi dunno, Jem," answered Ikey, "till Hi try."

With James's assistance, he managed to get on to his feet, but he felt very shaky, and as the gusty wind came rushing against him, he clung to his companion, as though he almost feared he should be blown away.

"Vheer are ve?" he asked at length.

"I don't know where," answered James.

"Ve hain't hin foreign countries, are ve?" he continued.

"I should think not," returned his comrade.

"Ve might be," Ikey went on; "'ow d'ye know as ve hain't been throw'd hon a deserlate hisland full o' savages?"

"I don't think that," said James, almost inclined to smile at his companion's fears, only he was too cold and miserable: "we haven't been on the sea long enough to get so far."

"Ve've been long enough, though," groaned Ikey, "to get soaked; Hi'm vet an' almost friz wi' cold."

Here a prolonged shudder put a stop to further conversation.

"Come, Ikey," said James, who began to feel like a human icicle, "let's try and walk, or we shall be frozen outright, and it would be hard to die of cold, after escaping being drowned."

"Hi'm ready," gasped Ikey—"Hi'll try. Hi don't vant to be friz, any more than Hi vanted to be drownded, an' Hi feels as hif Hi should be, hif Hi stops 'ere much longer."

"Come, then, let's walk," said James, as he drew his companion's arm through his own.

Clinging to each other, slipping, staggering over the loose shingles of the beach, they proceeded along the gloomy shore, utterly ignorant whither they were going, or where they would arrive at.

Ikey in his own mind had a strong presentiment that they should find themselves in the morning at Botany Bay, or the Cape of Good Hope, or some other distant locality.

They continued to progress until they found themselves stopped by rocks.

Over these they clambered with much difficulty.

Both were wondering what part of the coast they had reached when the moon, emerging from behind a cloud, at once solved their difficulties.

They had travelled back to the very point from which they had started, and were now standing almost at the brink of the narrow channel where the boat had been moored, and—oh, horror!—once more in close proximity to the retreat of the terrible pirates.

At this discovery, the first impulse of the exhausted boys was to make a precipitate retreat; but, alas! though the will was present, they lacked the power: their stiff and frozen limbs refused to support them over the slippery rocks.

They were, therefore, obliged to resign themselves to the prospect of remaining where they were.

They dragged themselves with slow and painful steps towards the entrance of the outer cavern.

It seemed strange to them, as they approached, all was profoundly silent; the hum of voices that had formerly reached their ears was hushed.

They crept cautiously into the cavern and listened.

All was dark and still as death itself.

"P'r'aps theer hall asleep," said Ikey.

"Let us draw near to the entrance—we shall be able to see," proposed James.

Acting upon this advice, they advanced, and looked in.

The large cavern, like the outer one, was dark. The boys were at a loss how to understand this. But as their eyes became accustomed to the gloom, they became conscious that a dim light was burning somewhere.

Presently they were able to discern that the cavern was tenantless.

This was a joyful discovery.

"Hit's hempty!" cried Ikey; "they're all gone—gone

to look arter us, p'r'aps," he added, with sudden apprehension.

"I don't think that," remarked James; "for, see, they have taken away everything—all the guns, swords, and tubs, that were scattered about when we were here before."

"So they 'as," returned Ikey; "dy'e think we might wentur hin ?"

"I think so," answered James. "If they come back they can only kill us, and there's not much difference between being killed and freezing to death."

"Not much," said Ikey: "it comes to th' same thing in th' hend, don't it ?"

"Then suppose we go in and chance it ?"

"Come on, Jem," his comrade exclaimed, with considerable vehemence, "let's chance it! I can't stand these 'ere vet rags o' mine hany longer."

The boys then went into the cavern, that had so recently been full of life, light, and warmth.

The life and light had departed; the warmth, or at least a great portion of it, remained.

The remains of the fire that had burnt so cheerfully when James and Ikey had first been introduced to the interior of the cavern, still lingered in the form of hot embers.

These smouldering fragments caught the quick eyes of Ikey Mangles, who was creeping about ruefully, in a state of great indecision what to do with his rags and himself.

He shouted with delight:

"Look, Jemmy—look: the fire's alight !"

All his caution was forgotten in the ecstasy of happiness the sight of the red-hot embers plunged the poor, half-frozen boy.

Had the cavern teemed with pirates, he would have rushed to the genial ashes, and, throwing himself prostrate on the warm ground, have defied them at that moment to move him.

Nor was James less affected by the sight.

Both the boys hastily approached, and crouched down to get all the warmth possible from that element they had never before felt the want of so greatly as now.

But it was still insufficient to *thaw* them.

James, on casting his eyes around, saw here and there a stray barrel that the pirates, in their hurried departure, had forgotten.

Ikey, too, between the pauses of his ague-like shivering fits, had made similar observations.

"I think," remarked James, at length, "if we were to drag those tubs here and put them on the ashes, we might make a better fire."

"So do Hi !" exclaimed Ikey, rising with considerable alacrity, and steaming like a wet blanket. "Ve vants a good blaze, that's vot ve vants."

James rose from his recumbent position, and by the united efforts of himself and his companion, several empty barrels were rolled towards the embers and placed upon them.

In a short time they began to ignite, and one being impregnated with tar, the effects were speedily manifest in the bright flame that shot up, and communicated itself to the rest.

"Hain't it prime ?" exclaimed Ikey, as he turned himself round and round in the effort to roast himself thoroughly, revelling in the grateful warmth that appealed so delightfully to his frozen limbs.

"It is beautiful !" joined in James, who, less demonstrative than his companion in his expressions of satisfaction, was as equally alive to the sensations that evoked them.

It was not long before the eyes of our young adventurers, roaming as they did through the cave, lighted upon sundry miscellaneous articles of wearing apparel.

In one place was a woollen shirt, in another a frieze jacket, whilst scattered about promiscuously were pieces of rug, boots and shoes, and other relics that had not departed with their owners.

"Hi say, Jem," said Ikey, as his eye wandered over these corporeal luxuries, "if the pirates is gorn, an' left them clo'se be'ind 'em, ve might as vell 'ave 'em, mightn't ve, specially as hours is so ragged an' vet ?"

James considered for a moment, and then replied :

"They don't belong to us, certainly; but as they seem to be all odd things that wouldn't be of much use to anybody, and as we're so starved with cold, and

drenched with the sea water, I don't think it would be wrong for us to take them."

"No more do Hi," said Ikey; "an' vot's more, Hi don't think as Capting Jack 'd mind our 'avin' 'em. Vasn't 'e werry good-natur'd to us, an' didn't 'e give us summat to heat ?"

There was no denying this fact.

"Besides," remarked James, "if these men should come back, we can tell them why we took the things, and if they want them, we can give them up then can't we ?"

"Oi course ve can," returned Ikey.

This point being settled, the boys made a grand foray upon everything in the shape of wearing apparel that was to be found.

In a short time they had collected quite a heap of odds and ends.

"Now," said Ikey, as he surveyed the pile of clothes with unbounded satisfaction, "th' next thing is to divide 'em."

James smiled.

"We sha'n't quarrel about that," he said.

"Hi should think not," answered Ikey. "Ve shall never quarrel, ve sha'n't."

And, as if to prove his desire that the distribution of the property should be conducted on the fairest and most amicable principles, he picked up a warm jacket that must have belonged to one of the crew's lads, and threw it at James's feet.

"There's a nice varm coat for you, Jem, to begin vith !" he cried.

"And there's another for you, Ikey," said James, as he disentangled a jacket from the heap.

"Ah, this'll do prime !" cried Ikey, taking possession of the proffered garment. "An' 'ere's some stockings big enough to sleep hin, an' 'ere's a veskitt !"

"And here's a boot !" exclaimed James.

"An' 'ere's another, an' two shoes besides, and an 'at," burst out Ikey, as he picked out the several articles.

The poor boys became quite excited over their treasures. It seemed so long since they had had warm clothing on their limbs that the prospect was more than they could contemplate quietly.

"I think," said James, "we had better spread some of these pieces of rug on the ground to lie upon, and then we can take off our wet clothes and hang them near the fire to dry."

"That's jest vot Hi'm a goin' to do," returned Ikey, proceeding to disrobe, which operation was performed by the simplest possible means, and much quicker than any pantomimic transformation of more modern days could possibly have been accomplished.

He had only to remove about three of the small wooden skewers with which his garments were fastened together, and the tattered mass fell in a heap upon the ground, leaving their owner in his original state of nature.

James followed his example, and threw off his wet clothes.

It was a pitiful sight to see those two poor homeless, friendless children, as they stood basking in the warm blaze of the fire.

It was painful to observe the delicate framework of the frail machine they called their bodies.

So poorly had they been fed that every bone and joint was painfully prominent and perceptible.

Where was the roundness, the plumpness, the rosy, healthy hue of youth ?

Alas ! save from the childish expression of their features their attenuated limbs more resembled the emaciation of old age.

After they had stood by the fire for some little time, James suggested that they should dress themselves in the most available garments they could select from their stock.

In this proposal Ikey readily acquiesced.

This operation, even under the somewhat critical circumstances in which they were placed, afforded them some little merriment.

It is happily one of the tendencies of our nature to catch at a gleam of sunshine if possible in the most depressing vicissitudes, and it was so with our poor little friends.

Ikey nearly lost his way in the depths of a large worsted stocking that had been originally intended for some stalwart, muscular leg; whilst James struggled

manfully to thrust his head from out the collar of the pilot coat he had crept into, and catch a glimpse of the tips of his fingers from the bottom of the sleeves. At length, however, by mutual assistance, turning down a bit here and tearing off a bit there, they managed to catch a glimpse of one another from out the thick barricade of garments in which they had enveloped themselves.

And then they laughed at the droll aspect they each presented.

It was not possible to avoid it, neither was there any particular reason why they should have avoided it.

It did no one any harm, and it did them good, as it helped to circulate their blood.

"Vot *do* ye look like, Jem?" said Ikey, with a grin on his gaunt little features, that gave him something the resemblance of one of those small monkeys we occasionally see on the top of an Italian boy's organ in the streets.

"I hardly know," answered James, laughingly. "Do you think we look anything like pirates?"

"More like guys, Hi thinks," returned Ikey, complimentarily.

"Well, never mind what we look like," James remarked, "the things are beautiful and warm, and that's of most consequence, isn't it?"

"Certingly it his," warmly assented Ikey; "Hi hain't felt so varm Hi dunno vhen."

They then, by means of some pieces of wood they found, erected a kind of framework, on which they hung their wet clothes, as close to the fire as possible.

After this was done they became conscious of another necessity.

They were both very hungry.

This was a good sign that neither the salt water nor the cold had done them any material injury.

"P'r'aps," said Ikey, "if ve looks about ve shall find summat to heat."

Such a prospect was too inviting to be unheeded, and in a moment four eyes were using the most scrutinising efforts to discover, and two noses sniffing vigorously to detect the earliest signs of anything eatable.

A few lamps still burnt dimly, and they, in addition to the light from the fire, materially assisted them in their search.

After a short time their efforts were rewarded with success.

Ikey came upon a small cask full of preserved meat.

James overhauled a basket of raisins and other dried fruits.

But there was another treasure yet in store; for in the recess which the captains had previously occupied, they came upon a case containing bread and wine.

"'Ooray!" shouted Ikey, with irrepressible delight, "vine an' bread! Ooray! Ve sha'n't vant for nothink now, shall ve?"

Eagerly dragging their provisions to the fire, they sat down on the pieces of rug, and commenced their repast.

They had neither knives nor forks, but they did not miss them, inasmuch as they had excellent teeth.

How they wished poor Augustus had been with them! Everything seemed delicious.

The wine was nectar.

They would have mixed water with the latter as Captain Jack had recommended; but as they had none, they drank it pure as it was.

The result of the food, the wine, and the warmth will easily be imagined.

The poor tired boys, now that their bodily necessities were provided for, sank down side by side in a state of drowsy, dreamy, delightful comfort, with which the sensations of the Sybarite or the opium eater could offer no comparison, and pulling a piece of rug over them, fell immediately into a sweet and profound sleep.

Chapter XIV.

ROUSED FROM SLUMBER.

WHEN Octavius Challoner, baffled in his schemes against the life of his young cousin, quitted the pirates' cave, he directed his course at once to the station of the Coastguard.

Full of vindictive spite at the failure of plans he had flattered himself would be so successful, he sought to revenge himself by giving information of the proximity of the freebooters.

This was sufficient to arouse the guard to go forth to the attack.

The dire result of the expedition has been already alluded to.

Several of the men were blown to atoms, whilst numbers were more or less injured by the violence of the explosion.

The pirates alone remained unscathed.

They all effected their retreat by the boats in safety.

Octavius, however, having given the alarm, was not sufficiently heroic to head the expedition.

On the contrary, he made the best of his way homewards, little reckoning the result of what he had done, or what loss of life it might occasion.

But though he entered the Hall long after midnight, and retired unseen to his chamber, he could not rest.

How was it possible he should?

His breast was full of murderous thoughts, and that sweet, peaceful sleep that waits only at the couch of innocence, fled from his bloodshot eyes.

He tossed and tumbled restlessly upon his bed, and heard the hours strike successively until the cold gray dawn of morning stole once more over the landscape.

Then he sank into a fitful, troubled slumber, that was not repose, but merely a dreamy repetition of the events of the past night.

There was great consternation when it was discovered that young Master Augustus was not in his bed.

When his nurse went at the usual hour to dress the prospective heir, she found his cot empty.

The news ran like wildfire through the Hall. Everyone was, or pretended to be, in a fever of anxiety.

No one more so than Octavius himself.

He interrogated Mrs. Wilson, the nurse, searchingly, but the good woman vehemently protested that she had put her dear boy to bed at the usual hour, as she always did, and seemed very much aggrieved at even the shadow of a doubt being cast over her well-known solicitude for the welfare of the young heir.

Octavius examined and cross-examined the servants, but elicited nothing to account for his mysterious disappearance.

The old squire, whose heart and hopes seemed to be bound up in the child, was well-nigh distracted at his loss. Opinions as to the cause were, as usual in such cases, numerous.

Everyone had his, or her, own and particular ideas on the subject.

The boy had been carried off by gipsies, or lured away by smugglers—or he had fallen into the well in the garden—or into the pond—or he had been shot by a poacher.

But to set two of these opinions at least at rest, the depths of the well were explored and the pond was dragged, but no Augustus was found.

The wood was vigilantly explored, but still no signs of the boy.

The matter grew more and more mysterious every moment to all—but one.

While the poor old squire was breaking his heart, and offering up earnest prayers to Heaven for the preservation and restoration of his darling child, and while every member of his household was earnestly desirous that the young heir, who was generally beloved, might be restored, the ungrateful and unnatural Octavius was yearning with malignant eagerness for some proof that he had perished.

He could not believe it probable that a small boat should live through the storm of the preceding night, but at the same time it was within the bounds of possibility, and being so, he longed for proof.

He felt he would have given almost anything could he but have seen his boy cousin, with his soft, silky curls drenched with brine, silent, pale, and lifeless at his feet.

He could not endure the thought, that would ever and anon intrude itself, that the child by some interposition of Providence have escaped.

To so great a pitch did his anxiety rise, that it became at length unbearable, and he resolved to go at once, and search along the shore, if by chance he might catch a glimpse of what he so ardently longed to see.

Accordingly, under an assumption of real and intense grief, he announced to the distracted parent his determination to go forth in search of the poor boy.

The squire received this intelligence with tears of gratitude, and the snake in the grass, Octavius, hoping the worst, but, hypocrite like, praying the best for his cousin, departed for the purpose of seeking him.

He took exactly the same route as he had taken the previous night, till he drew near the cliffs, when instead of ascending to the summit, he made his way to the beach.

Along this he proceeded, the giant rocks towering high above his head, towards the pirates' cave.

He had taken care to possess himself of the facts that its former occupants had vacated their post, or he would not have dared to approach those precincts.

As it was, he expected to encounter at every step the mangled, lifeless body of the President George Carew, whom he had hurled from the cliff on the preceding night. This would also have been a welcome sight to him. In fact, his anxiety proceeded not from any remorse at his deeds, but from fears that they might have miscarried.

It was nothing to him to strike the coward's blow in the dark, but it would have been terrible had the victim started up in broad daylight and confronted him face to face.

The tide was receding, and as he rode slowly along his eyes looked anxiously on every side in the hope of beholding the lifeless bodies of those he sought.

No such sight, however, greeted him.

He gazed out upon the angry ocean, that looked dark and threatening on that chill, misty January morning, with its overhanging canopy of gloomy clouds, that seemed as if they had caught the hue of the sullen waters that chafed beneath.

But nothing floated on its surging bosom.

No lifeless body rose and fell with its restless motion, neither did the receding tide bring anything to light but masses of weedy rock.

Muttering to himself, with moody brow and compressed lips, he continued his course.

"The tide must have carried them all away," he argued; "and if so, they lie securely buried in the ocean depths."

Thus meditating, he drew near the cavern.

He had his dog with him, and as he approached, he motioned the animal towards the entrance.

The dog understood his master's sign, and ran forward, sniffing the air as he went.

* * * * *

James and Ikey at length awoke from their slumbers. How long they had slept they, of course, had not the slightest idea.

But when they opened their eyes they were conscious of a pleasant sensation of warmth and comfort, that induced them to close them again, and continue to doze on.

"'Ow do you feel, Jemmy?" was the first question Ikey asked on waking.

"So nice and warm!" answered James.

The youngsters were cuddled as closely together as possible, and did not seem at all inclined to rouse themselves.

"There don't seem no signs o' hany pirates comin' back, does theer?" said Ikey.

"No," answered James, "I don't think they'll come any more."

Just at this moment they heard a pattering of feet close to them, and then the quick pantings of an animal.

"Vot's that?" whispered Ikey, in a tone of alarm.

"I don't know," replied James, whose heart began to beat with apprehension.

The two poor outcasts felt so utterly friendless, that they were inclined to look upon themselves in the light of two small targets, at which every passer-by might fire a shot.

The pattering and sniffing still continued, and, the worst of it was, these sounds came nearer and nearer, till at last they could feel a stream of warm breath puffing down upon them.

"It's a hanimal!" whispered Ikey, in a perturbed tone, trying hard at the same time to poke his head in his pocket for safety.

"What animal can there be here?" asked James, softly—"I didn't see any."

The reply to this question was a succession of short, quick barks.

"Oh, lor! it's a dorg!" cried Ikey.

The animal having discovered the sleepers, ran back to his master.

This they discovered from the barking growing more indistinct.

James and Ikey started up.

"Vot shall ve do?" asked the latter, looking, in his peculiar costume, like a small specimen of a frightened Esquimaux. "Hi thinks hit's th' pirates comin' back!"

"Hush!" exclaimed James; "let's listen."

The boys strained their ears intently.

They distinctly heard the barking of the dog outside the cavern, and the voice of his master ordering him to be silent.

But oh, that voice!

It carried with it a thousand times more terror in its sound than a whole legion of dogs, had they been ever so ravenous.

The faces of the poor boys lost the flush the heat of the fire and the rug had imparted to their wan cheeks, and became white as the walls that surrounded them.

"It's 'im!" cried Ikey, in a rigid tone of terror.

"Mr. Octavius Challoner!" said James, in a blank voice.

"Him as wanted to drownd 'is poor little cous'n," continued Ikey, with a mixture of horror and disgust. "If 'e comes in 'ere, 'e'll be sure to set 'is dorg on us."

"Perhaps he won't find us—we must hide ourselves."

"Vheer?"

"In one of the holes in the rocks."

"But that theer dorg 'll be sure to smell us, an' 'ell 'unt us hout like rats out of our 'oles."

"It's our only chance," said James.

His dark eye kindled as he spoke, and he picked up a piece of tough wood that lay near.

Ikey stood watching him, and stimulated by his companion's example, imitated him, he seizing upon a log almost as big as himself.

"Hi knows vot yer picked hup that bit o' wood for, Jem," he said—"it's to keep hoff th' dorg."

"It's to try to," answered James, quietly.

"This is to try, too," said he—"if 'e tries to bite me, Hi'll drop this 'ere on 'his nob."

This was a magnificent idea on the part of Ikey, if the dog could have been induced to stand still and submit quietly to the operation, but as that was more than doubtful, it did not seem to James's mind to be likely to be of much practical utility.

"That piece of wood's too heavy," he remarked. "There's a lighter piece—take that."

He pointed as he spoke to a remnant of a spar on the ground.

"Theer's a sharp pint at vun hend," cried Ikey, as he seized upon it. "That 'ere dorg 'ad better look hout for 'isself, or 'e'll 'ave this in 'is heye."

At this moment footsteps were heard approaching.

James, grasping his companion by the arm, drew him rapidly away.

They were only just in time to wedge themselves into the narrow cleft, where they had on a former occasion concealed themselves.

It was then a matter of no great difficulty, on account of the lightness of their clothing; but now, wrapped up as they were in thick frieze, it was a very tight fit indeed.

They had hardly disappeared, when Octavius, with evident caution, looked into the cavern.

The boys held their breath for a tremendous time— it seemed to them quite ten minutes—whilst the dreaded new-comer ran his eye round the cavern.

They could not divest themselves of the idea that

that sinister, evil eye could penetrate even through rock, and might at that moment be regarding them during that dead silence as they sat quaking in their place of concealment.

"So!" he exclaimed, at length, "the place deserted—all gone!"

He entered the cave, the dog following at his heels, not barking, but evidently ill at ease, and whining impatiently, as though he had some information he wished to deliver, had he not been commanded to be quiet.

Octavius marched deliberately to the other end of the cavern, and contemplated the entrance, now blocked up by the mass of rock, charred and blackened by the explosion.

The news of the catastrophe had already reached him, and he stood gazing silently at its results.

"Who would have imagined," he at length exclaimed, "that these scoundrels should have been so well prepared for an attack? The consequences have been disastrous to the assailants, the only advantage being that the pirates have taken their departure."

His soliloquy was interrupted by the continued whining of the hound, that exhibited a restlessness which forced itself upon his master's notice.

"Something disturbs the brute," he said to himself. "What is it, Ranger?" he cried, addressing himself to the dog.

Ranger looked up in his master's face, and gave several short but expressive barks.

"He seems to have something to communicate," said Octavius, thoughtfully; "what can it be?"

The dog barked and whined again, and looked wistfully towards the other end of the cavern.

Ikey, who was watching the proceedings from his place of concealment with all the eager vigilance of fear, felt highly indignant at the conduct of the hound, which he considered as almost certain to lead to their detection.

"If that beast of a dorg 'ud be quiet, Mr. Hotty" (he had caught that abbreviation from Augustus) "wouldn't know nothin' about our bein 'ere," he remarked, in a low tone to James.

"Perhaps it's not our being here that makes him bark," James replied, in a whisper.

"Oh yes, it his," maintained Ikey. "See 'ow th' beast keeps a lookin' 'ere, jest as if 'e know'd wheer ve vos!"

"There must be something more than common to make the dog keep up this incessant whining. Come, boy," he cried to the hound, "we'll search."

He approached the fire, and took from it one of the smouldering logs.

Holding this in his hand, he went into the outer cave.

Waving it to and fro for a few seconds, it burst into a flame.

The scrutiny this enabled him to make only showed him that the place was empty.

He had hardly come to this conclusion, when his eye was once more attracted by the body of the dead boy, shrouded with its dark drapery.

He approached and examined it.

"So they have forgotten in their hasty flight to carry off their dead," he said.

He remained gazing at the dead face earnestly for some time.

Some latent idea in connection with the corpse appeared to strike him.

He bent down, and by the light of the blazing ember scrutinised the features intently.

"About the same size and complexion; the colour of the hair too, dark, like his," he murmured to himself; "the difference could not possibly be detected."

The two boys, with a kind of desperate curiosity, had crept from their retreat, and advanced to the aperture leading from one cavern to the other.

Octavius little thought how closely he was watched as he stood gazing at the dead body, or that the words that fell slowly and thoughtfully from his lips were heard and treasured up in the memory of the listeners.

He still remained motionless before the corpse.

Presently he started as from a reverie.

"Yes," he cried, "this may assist me materially."

"Vot does 'e mean?" whispered Ikey to James.

"Sh!" ejaculated his companion; "I don't know quite."

The boys were very much astonished to see Octavius slide his hands under the dead body, and, raising it from the rock on which it reposed, carry it to the darkest corner of the cavern, and place it on the ground, afterwards covering it carefully with the dark drapery.

When he had done this, it would not have been noticed at all without the closest scrutiny.

"There," he exclaimed, "it will rest quietly there; and should I require it, I shall know exactly where to find it."

At this moment the loud barking of Ranger startled him.

"What can be the matter with that confounded dog?" he cried. "I fancied that it was this body that excited him. There must be something that I am ignorant of that causes him to bark so vociferously."

Our readers, not being so much in the dark as the last speaker, will know that it was the presence of the two boys that aroused the instinct of the animal.

Ranger had discovered them at his first entrance into the cavern, and he had been in a restless state after their disappearance.

When, however, with more curiosity than prudence, James and Ikey had crept forward to watch the motions of Octavius, the dog caught a glimpse of them.

They were aware of the fact that the animal had seen them, and retreated precipitately.

This measure, though perfectly excusable under the circumstance, was perhaps the most imprudent one they could have adopted, since it excited the fretted dog to rush after them.

Our little heroes, we may be sure, used their legs to the greatest advantage.

But they were sorely impeded in their retreat by their new costume.

It was something like running packed up in two hampers, with holes at the bottoms to let out their legs.

Besides, under any circumstances, four-legged animals can always overtake animals with two.

The consequence was that Ranger was up with them in a moment.

James was hindmost in the flight.

Consequently the dog seized the first part of him that offered itself.

This happened to be a mouthful of frieze.

On this the dog fastened with angry growls, and commenced shaking his prey in the usual canine fashion.

James, though alarmed, was still able to congratulate himself that his assailant's teeth were fastened in his coat instead of his arm or his leg.

His self-possession did not desert him, but, feeling that the dog had no right or title to him whatever, and that he was justified in attempting self-defence, he swung his hand behind him, and astonished Ranger with such a smart rap on the nose from the piece of wood he carried that he immediately released his hold.

It was, however, only to return to the charge; but this time Ikey was the assailed.

The boy struggled manfully, but the dog's teeth were too firmly fixed in his loose sleeve to be shaken off.

Not wishing to be devoured, he grasped his pointed stick with all the force and nervous energy his ten years could supply, and, using the weapon spear-fashion, lunged at the animal till sundry red spots showed he had drawn blood, and the irritated beast unclosed his jaws.

In an instant they had wedged themselves once more into the rocky recess, and for the present were safe from their opponent's teeth."

Now all this had taken place in very much less time than it has occupied to describe it, so that when Octavius, roused by the barking of the dog, re-entered the large cavern, all that he could see was Ranger, with ears erect, in a wrathful, rigid attitude, lashing the air with his tail, intently regarding a cleft in the rock, with several jets of blood trickling from his body.

Ikey caught sight of Octavius.

"Oh lor', Jem, it's hall over wi' us!" he exclaimed; "'ere's Mr. Hotty!"

Mr. Hotty was at first puzzled to account for what appeared to be some strange phenomenon.

A rat could not have inflicted such wounds as it was evident the dog had received.

[CAUGHT AT LAST.]

A fox might; but it was an unlikely place in which to look for such an animal.

"What can it be?" he muttered, as he drew nearer, and peered into the cleft.

He discerned a dark mass of something that had the appearance of a pilot coat.

And more than this, he perceived a pair of shining black eyes open to their fullest extent, gazing at him in a very fixed and earnest manner.

"The dog was right!" he cried; "there's some one there!"

He clutched his pistol as he spoke, and exclaimed:

"Who's here?"

There was no answer.

"Who are you? Speak, or I'll try if a bullet can unlock your tongues!"

Octavius had a suspicion that one, or perhaps more, of the pirates were lurking there, and he spoke fiercely.

"Who are you?" he repeated.

"We're only two boys, sir," answered the mild voice of James.

"What boys?" asked Octavius, with less fierceness, but still sternly.

"*Poor* boys," returned Ikey, emphasizing the "poor" as a means of paving the way for a little sympathy.

"What are you doing there?"

"Nothin' pertickler," said Ikey

"Then come out!" cried Octavius.

"A dog flew at us just now, sir," explained James, "and we got in here to get out of his way."

"Nonsense! but he won't fly at you now I'm here. Come out."

"Ve'd rayther stay vheer ve hare," said Ikey, "if it's hall th' same to you."

"But it's not all the same to me—I wish you to come out," returned Octavius, impatiently.

"But ve'd rather stay 'ere," Ikey replied, unwilling

to leave the snug retreat ; " ve don't vant to be flew'd at by that theer dorg, an' 'e can't get hat us wheer ve hare."

"I tell you he won't fly at you," cried Octavius, with increasing petulance ; " he wouldn't have touched you before if you hadn't struck him first."

"We didn't, sir," replied James; " he caught hold of me first, and I hit him to make him leave go."

"Oh, you did, did you ?" exclaimed Octavius, savagely.

" 'E caught 'old o' me, too," followed up Ikey, " an' Hi progged 'im with a bit o' sharp stick till Hi got away."

"Come out, you young vagabonds !" shouted Octavius. " If you trifle any longer with me, I'll break every bone in your bodies, and throw you to the dog to be devoured."

This awful threat, instead of drawing them forth, only made them resolve to keep inside the sanctuary as long as they possibly could.

This persistent disobedience to his orders did not suit the overbearing brutal temper of Octavius.

He could not brook opposition even from a child, and it roused all his most angry passions.

"Ranger !" he cried, " good dog ! out with 'em !"

He patted the animal and urged him on.

But the animal was puzzled.

He no longer saw his prey that appeared to have escaped him, whilst at the same time his sense of smell informed him that it was near at hand.

He looked suspiciously at the impervious surface of the frieze jacket as it filled up the cavity in the rock, behind which crouched the bodies he longed to get at.

Urged by his master he barked and growled, and at length, wound up to the proper pitch of fury, bounded forward, opening his wide jaws, and snapping at, without being able to make any impression on, the woollen barricade.

Non-success seemed only to stimulate the irritated animal.

With savage perseverance he renewed the assault, endeavouring with all his might to get a hold with his teeth, whilst the saliva dropped from his jaws in angry drops.

Suddenly he bounded back with a howl.

Ikey had contrived to thrust out his only defensive weapon—the sharp-pointed stick—through a rent in the seam of the coat.

The lunge was given at a venture, but the result was highly effective, as the dog found to his cost, for the wooden instrument passed into his open mouth, and came in violent contact with the back of his throat, which it pierced, sending the unlucky animal howling back, vomiting blood, and for the present out of fighting condition, at least, if nothing worse.

In plain English, he had had enough of it.

One animal being disabled, it was now the other's turn to begin.

Furious at the audacity that presumed to wound his dog before his face, Octavius sprang forward.

"You young scoundrels !" he shouted, " if you don't come out I'll murder you !"

As he spoke he made a dash at the frieze, that nearly knocked the breath out of Ikey's body, and as the sudden shrinking of the latter at the rough assault into the smallest possible compass allowed the garment to bag a little, Octavius was enabled to grasp it.

Escape was now impossible.

With one venomous wrench the merciless gentleman (ruffian would be the more appropriate term) emptied the recess of its contents.

James and Ikey lay prostrate on the ground.

Octavius Challoner stood glaring down upon them like an infuriated savage, whilst the discomfited Ranger sat at a respectable distance, not seeming to care about venturing upon a nearer approach.

Chapter XV.

CONFRONTING THE FOE.

I HAVE just now said James and Ikey lay on the ground; I may now remark that, although they were actually there, their dearest and most intimate friends—had they been possessed of any —would have been utterly unconscious of the fact.

They had, during the wedging process they had undergone, and urged probably by their strong desire to get as far as possible out of the dog's reach, so buried themselves in the thick garments they wore, that nothing but the latter were to be seen at all.

Their heads were tucked in, and their legs were drawn up, and they looked like a couple of human periwinkles coiled in their shells, nose and knees together.

They presented an appearance that would have rejoiced the heart of an " old clothes " man.

Nothing but coats, sleeves, and buttons were visible.

This state of things was not to be endured ; and in order to render it unendurable to the parties most interested, Octavius Challoner commenced by giving the *coats* a kick apiece.

It seemed as though these kicks imparted an immediate vitality to the aforesaid garments, since they rolled out of the way in a most lively manner.

But the affair was not to be adjusted, or the wrath of Octavius averted, by any playful little acts on the part of the coats.

"Now, then, you two boys ! do you intend to come out of your sacks, or must I fetch you out ?" inquired Mr. Challoner, in a quieter but by no means an agreeable tone of voice.

This summons was immediately responded to by Ikey, who thrust out his head.

" 'Ere I ham, sir," he exclaimed. " But where's th' dorg ?" he added, glancing round suspiciously.

"You may well ask that, when you've nearly killed the poor brute !" returned his indignant master.

This intelligence was received with heartfelt satisfaction by Ikey, who rejoiced at it, on the equitable principle, that if he had not nearly killed the dog, it was more than probable the dog would have quite killed him.

On this ground, therefore, his conscience acquitted him.

James had by this time contrived to unbury his head, and look out over his coat collar at the ferocious personage, of whose tender mercies he had had not many hours before so excellent a specimen.

Octavius recognised him immediately.

"Oh, it's you, is it ?" he remarked, with a sardonic smile ; " well, look out for yourself, that's all ! There's no old gentleman with white hair to help you now."

He clutched his riding whip expressively, as he spoke, as though he felt a malignant pleasure in exciting the fears of the poor children.

"Come ! I've had enough of this nonsense !" he cried. " Get up, I want to ask you a few questions."

The two pilot jackets, after several abortive efforts, contrived to stand upon their feet.

The appearance they presented would have been highly comic, had not the associations connected with their position, and the circumstances that surrounded them, thrown a halo of sadness over their pale, wan faces, that forbade mirth.

But Octavius Challoner was in no facetious mood ; his thoughts like the expression of his features, were dark, and full of evil.

He seated himself deliberately on a piece of rock, like a stern magistrate taking his seat on the bench.

"What are you doing here, you two ?" was the first question he asked.

There was a hesitating pause at this question.

After the murderous proposal the poor boys had heard issue from the lips of their questioner to the pirates, they could only regard him as a monster of cruelty, and they naturally hesitated before replying, lest by that reply they should draw down upon their heads some signal vengeance.

As Octavius addressed them both, not singly, neither answered.

" Now then, you James Cook, and you Ikey Mangles," he said, seeing they did not reply, " you are neither of you troubled with deafness, are you ?"

He casually tightened the lash of his whip, and drew the whipcord at the end through his lips, as he spoke.

" No, sir!" answered the boys, quickly.

" Ah! I thought not; what brings you here ?"

" We were brought here, sir," said James.

" By whom ?"

" A gentleman, sir."

" What gentleman ?"

" Genl'man hin a vhite vig," answered Ikey, readily.

" Oh, indeed! What was the gentleman's name ?"

" Mr. Crew," Ikey replied.

" Where is he now ?"

" I don't know, sir," said James. " He left us in this cave, and told us to wait here till he came back."

" Have you any idea when that will be ?"

The boys at that instant recollected the white, deathly face of their friend as it floated past them.

Ikey, with his usual volubility, that would not be content with simply answering the questions, said :

" I don't think as 'e'll hever come back."

" Why not ?"

" Because ve saw 'im floatin' in the sea, an' 'e looked so vhite an' orful! I thinks as 'e vos dead, an' so does Jem. Don't yer, Jem ?" he asked, turning to his companion.

" I'm afraid so," James assented.

" Floating in the sea ?" remarked Octavius, with assumed surprise. " When did you see him floating in the sea ?"

" To-night, vhen ve vos in th——"

Receiving a slight nudge from James's elbow, he paused.

This movement did not escape the watchful eye of the grand inquisitor.

" Go on!" he said, in a quiet but particularly unpleasant tone. " When you were in the *what* ?"

It was too late to recall his words, so Ikey said :

" In the boat."

He was now extremely sorry that he had let his tongue run so fast.

He foresaw in the distance question after question rapidly advancing, until the terrible catastrophe of the boat would be arrived at, and then !

" What were you doing in a boat on such a night as this ?" asked Octavius, with well-feigned surprise.

Ikey hesitated and fidgeted, and at length replied, in an embarrassed manner :

" Ve vos a-sailin' hin it."

" I suppose so," remarked the questioner, sarcastically ; " but you must have had some *strong motive* to induce you to go out for a sail in such weather as it was last night."

" It vosn't last night : it vos this night !" said Ikey, glad to turn the argument, if possible, from any subject but the boat, and unconscious he had slept for many hours, and that the next day had almost passed.

" I tell you it was last night !" exclaimed Mr. Challoner. " Don't contradict ! but tell me why you went into that boat ?"

" Becos—a—a—becos ve——"

" Go on !"

" Vos—a—a——"

" Well you *was* ? Speak !"

" Afeard !"

" Of what ?"

" As we should be heaten alive !" Ikey contrived to jerk out.

" Eaten alive ! Who was to eat you ?"

James, who saw his companion nervously floundering through the mire, into which his own imprudence had led him, stepped in to the rescue.

" We heard the men in this cavern say they were pirates," explained James.

" Yes, sir," interrupted Ikey, " that they did, an' vun on 'em said as ven 'e vos 'ungry, and vanted a boy to heat, 'e'd devour me fust !"

Octavius gazed sternly at the boy's eager look of terror, from under his eyebrows, but not a shadow of a smile appeared on his morose features, even at this piece of information.

" And did *you* labour under this apprehension ?" he asked, addressing himself particularly to James.

" I—I thought we were in danger here, sir," he answered, with some little hesitation ; " and when we saw the dead body of a boy in the other cavern, we were all the more frightened."

" I suppose you thought it would be your turn next ?" Octavius remarked, with for the first time a grim smile.

" Yes sir," said James, " and that was what made us go in the boat."

" Umph !" exclaimed Octavius, fastening his eyes steadily on the boys ; " and pray who was in the boat besides yourselves—of course, you were not alone ?"

The eyes of the questioner never wavered as he asked this, and the sensations of the unhappy boys may be easily imagined.

They felt they were drawing nearer and nearer to the brink of the dreadful truth.

As for Ikey, he almost wished he had been safe at the bottom of the sea, with the crabs and shrimps—anywhere, rather than under the scrunity of the cruel eyes, that pierced him through and through, in spite of his thick frieze jacket with the large buttons.

" N—o, sir," answered James, in as firm a voice as he could muster, but which faltered palpably in spite of his efforts ; " there was some one else in the boat with us."

" Who was it ?"

" Another young gen'l'man," interposed Ikey, hoping that would set the matter at rest without further inquiries.

Alas, vain hope !

" What young gentleman ?" inquired the inquisitive Octavius.

" A young gen'l'man as vos vith us," Ikey replied.

" Don't prevaricate !" shouted the questioner, in a voice so loud and abrupt, that it nearly shook the poor little fellows out of their wrappers. " Of course you knew his name : what was it ?"

He clutched the terrible whip tightly as he spoke.

" Are you going to speak ?" he cried.

" Yes, sir ; it was Master Augustus Markham !" exclaimed James, with a desperate effort.

The first crisis had now arrived.

Octavius Challoner started to his feet, as though in a paroxysm of the extremest consternation.

" Augustus Markham !" he cried ; " Augustus, my cousin !" Then he continued, as though talking to himself : " How could he possibly have wandered here ?—who could have brought him ?"

Ikey thought that Mr. Challoner, in his alarm and excitement, must for the time have lost his memory, so he obligingly assisted him by replying :

" You did, sir."

Octavius stopped his mutterings suddenly, and glaring at Ikey, exclaimed :

" I !—I brought him ?"

" Y—es, sir," returned Ikey, once more painfully conscious that he had—to use a common expression—" put his foot in it;" " Jemmy an' me see you come hinter th' cave a 'oldin' 'im by th' 'and."

It would have made a good picture, if a skilful artist had been able to have pourtrayed the expression of the three countenances of our *dramatis personæ* at this moment.

They formed a combination of fear, expectation, and suspicion.

The boys feared the whip of Octavius, and expected to receive a receipt in full for what had passed.

Octavius suspected that, as they had seen him enter the cavern with his young cousin, they might also have heard his cold-blooded offer to the pirates.

If this was the case, his designs must be known to them.

Young as they were, he felt their faculties were sharpened beyond their years, and he almost trembled —so cowardly is guilt—that his secret guilt should be in the keeping even of two children.

The result of these thoughts passing rapidly through his mind was to make him suddenly calm.

At the very moment when the two culprits were fully prepared for a knock-down blow with the butt end of the heavy whip, the voice of their formidable interrogator suddenly changed to a tone of quietness—nay more, of kindness.

" Don't be frightened at my manner," he said, " the fact is, I am so agitated at the loss of my cousin, that I entirely forgot at the moment he came with me to the cavern. I remember now, he did accompany me. We lost our way, and wandered hither quite by chance."

" Ho, vot a crammer !" muttered Ikey, to himself.

"But tell me," continued Octavius, in a conciliatory tone, "since you all went together in the boat, you must all have returned together; but I do not see my cousin. How is that?"

This was another dreadful question to answer, but there was no alternative.

"It was very rough, sir," said James, in a faltering voice, "and after we had been tossed about by the waves for a long time, at last, all in a moment, the boat upset, and—and we were thrown into the sea."

"Yes, yes!" ejaculated the eager and excited listener, "but you were saved?"

"Yes, sir. We held on to the boat, and it was dashed on to the shore."

"But, my cousin! Was not he saved as well?"

"N—o, sir!" cried the boys with one breath; "*he was drowned!*"

And having reached this grand climax, their overwrought nerves could endure no longer, and they burst into a flood of tears.

But Octavius heeded not their sobs.

He clasped his hands with a report like the cracking of a whip, and buried his face in them.

Not with remorse, but joy.

His end was accomplished.

But those two boys knew more than they dare confess, he felt certain.

At that moment, he resolved to have no witnesses.

He started up suddenly, and addressing himself to the boys, exclaimed, with serious earnestness:

"It is through you my poor cousin has met his death. Had you not persuaded him to enter the boat, he would have been still alive. I do not blame you, but the law will hold you accountable for his death, as though you had murdered him."

The poor little innocent culprits shuddered from head to foot, as the wretch played upon their fears.

"Hide yourselves—keep out of sight—or you will be hunted down and sent to prison—hung, perhaps!" cried Octavius.

"Where shall we hide—where?" groaned the terrified boys.

"Anywhere!—in there!" exclaimed their remorseless adviser, pointing to the cleft in the rock which had before contained them.

In a moment they plunged in for dear life, trembling like aspens, seeking to hide themselves in that dark recess from the hands of justice.

No sooner were they safely in, than a mass of rock, rolled forward by an unseen hand, blocked up the opening, and the poor boys were entombed.

It is almost needless to say that the hand that propelled the rock forward was that of Octavius Challoner.

There was a fiendish smile on his face as he contemplated the trap, in which he had secured his unsuspecting victims.

"'E's shet us in, I think," said Ikey.

Before James had time to reply, Octavius bent down his head and hissed out:

"You will be quite safe now!—no one can see you—no one will hear you, if you remain quiet. When the danger is over, I will come myself and let you out."

Having thus expressed himself, he called his dog, who still appeared moody and suffering from the effects of his recent encounter.

He approached the animal and examined his wounds, which, though not very perceptible outwardly, were more serious than they appeared; especially the one at the back of his throat.

Octavius coaxed the hound, which was at length induced to make an effort to follow his master, though it was evident it was a painful one.

In a few moments after the cave was silent, and deserted by all but the two prisoners.

Octavius mounted his horse, and rode slowly along the shore under the shadow of the cliffs, his dog Ranger, with his head hanging down, and in evident bodily distress, limping after him

Chapter XVI.

VOICES IN THE ROCK.

AFTER the occurrences of the previous night, it took some time to remove the dead of the unfortunate Coastguard blockade, and to attend to the requirements of the wounded.

Medical and surgical assistance had to be summoned.

There were no electric telegraphs in those days, and all intelligence had to be conveyed by messengers.

At first the dire catastrophe, as awful as it was unexpected, threw the whole body of the survivors into a state of confusion.

After a time, however, notices were sent off to different parts for surgeons and physicians, and in a few hours several had arrived at the Coastguard *depot*.

Amongst these was our previous acquaintance, with the shirt frill and the gold watch and seals, Dr. Julep, M.D., M.R.C.S.

By the exertions of these practitioners, wounds were bound up, shattered limbs amputated, and everything done that could be performed under the painful circumstances.

It being perfectly apparent that the pirates had effected their retreat and pursuit in the darkness, and the storm being impracticable, those who were unwounded were able to bestow all their attention upon their injured comrades.

Amongst those who rendered good service as messengers to carry the news of the disaster to the surrounding members of the medical profession was a gipsy tinker, who perambulated the country, carrying his stock in trade in a box at his back, and his pan of coals in his hand, and who went by the name of Tinker Morgan.

He did not always follow his trade, being given to periodical fits of vagrancy, during which he bade adieu for a time to his box, and his coals, and his tinkering; and consorted with his tribe, who were always glad to see him, as Tinker Morgan was a stalwart, cheerful fellow, and very skilful at snaring game and catching fish, to say nothing of a peculiar adroitness he possessed of transferring any plump pullets that came in his way into his capacious pockets.

It was not *all fish* that came into his net.

He was not particular what he laid hands upon; but while he was with his tribe, whatever he picked up was sure to be honourably contributed to the common stock.

Fowls, hares, pheasants, rabbits, trout, or what not, invariably found their way into the gipsies' kettle.

There was no denying the fact that many a hearty meal had come out of the pockets of Tinker Morgan.

The *sobriquet* Tinker had originated from the calling he occasionally followed, but his Christian name was Ishmael. But it mattered little to him by which title he was called, as he answered alike to both.

This man had had several narrow escapes of conviction for poaching in Squire Markham's woods; and a short time previous to the commencement of our story he had been brought before Octavius in the justice-room up at the hall, who, in the absence of the old squire, had given him, on suspicion, a fortnight on bread and water in the cage.

On account of this, Ishmael owed Octavius a bitter grudge, and had been heard to mutter some ominous threats, to the effect that if ever he had the chance, he would wring that gentleman's neck with as little remorse as he would a chicken's.

It will be remembered that, after the attack upon George Carew, and his precipitation from the cliff, his assailant had turned his steed loose, to wander whithersoever it pleased.

Without owner or guide, therefore, the animal, thus turned adrift, trotted off any way, and that happened to be precisely the road along which Tinker Morgan was travelling.

He had been prowling in a neighbouring wood, and was returning from his expedition with his pockets laden with spoil, with which he was hastening to the gipsy encampment, when he heard the hoofs of a horse behind him.

Visions of pursuit, mounted gamekeepers—the cage

and the stocks—flitted before him instantaneously, and, quick as lightning, he dropped into the ditch at the road side, and peering cautiously out, prepared to reconnoitre the advancing traveller.

No traveller, however, appeared; but instead, a magnificent gray steed, harnessed with all his trappings, but riderless.

"Oho!" said Ishmael to himself, "what's the meaning of this? Horses do not usually harness themselves, or come out for a gallop on the high road with no one to back them!"

The gray steed, quite unconscious of the remarks he was eliciting, came trotting on.

Tinker Morgan, just as the animal drew near, glided out of the ditch and noiselessly grasped the bridle.

There was a momentary plunge and a slight struggle, when the horse found himself checked.

But it lasted but for a moment.

The gipsy, who was acquainted with most of the arts of a rambling, predatory life, amongst other accomplishments, knew something of the management of horses.

He used no violence with the startled gray, but, by dint of giving him his way as much as possible without letting him go, and patting his neck, and whispering a few coaxing words, he soon had him under his command.

"A fine fellow this!" soliloquized Ishmael, as he contemplated the graceful and powerful limbs of the noble animal by the side of which he stood; "broad chest, small head!—but where's his master?"

Some strange ideas seemed to suggest themselves to the gipsy, as he asked himself this question.

"It seems he has no master now but myself," he exclaimed; "so, my noble friend, I shall take the liberty of mounting your broad back, riding to the camp, and emptying my pockets. After which I'll return and see if I can find the owner, whom I'm inclined to think is lying on his back somewhere, either drunk or dead, I don't know which."

Having come to this determination, he put his foot in the stirrup and vaulted lightly into the saddle.

A short ride brought Ishmael to the tents of his brethren.

There was no little surprise at his appearance, mounted as he was on a splendid charger, and many were the surmises set on foot as to the means by which he had become possessed of it.

The common impression—which amongst these pilfering people must by no means be considered as disgraceful—quite the reverse—was that Tinker Morgan had taken to a line of business in addition to his other handicrafts, and turned horse-stealer.

However, to all the supposititious questions, direct and indirect, put to him by his companions, he answered indefinitely, and having made a hasty supper, departed, mounted on his gray prize, to see if he could discover its owner.

If he should be fortunate enough to do so, there was a certainty of a handsome reward for his trouble.

If not, the next cattle fair would enable him to dispose of the animal, and so remunerate himself.

"Take care of yourself, Ishmael!" cried a pretty, dark-eyed gipsy woman, just before he mounted.

"Depend upon that, Zita," he replied; "that's one of the cares I never forget."

He hugged his wife to his breast, and in a moment was gone.

Very careful did the gipsy search as he rode along, looking on either side of the road, expecting every moment to see a prostrate, senseless body lying there.

But nothing of the kind met his gaze.

Neither were there any tracks to guide him. Though it was moonlight.

A sudden and rapid thaw had set in, and the slushy road did not retain the marks of the horse's footprints.

After proceeding some distance, he came to a standstill.

"I may go on travelling all night at this rate," he thought, "to no purpose."

His eye happened to light upon a gate at a short distance: it was partially open.

He approached, and almost mechanically entered.

He discerned marks of a horse's hoofs on the grass.

On dismounting and comparing the size of the impressions with the hoofs of the gray steed, he found they corresponded exactly.

This was a clue, at all events, and this decided him to continue his present route.

In course of time he came to another gate.

Through this he passed, and observed the same marks on the grass on the other side.

It was a singular fact that he was now on the very track that George Carew had travelled a few days before.

Continuing his journey over the fields he came, in course of time, to the foot of the cliffs.

Here he paused again.

He was entirely off the scent, and the search appeared hopeless.

"I shall have to sell the horse after all," he cogitated. "Well, it will be more in my pocket."

He had hardly delivered this remark when the hurried tramp of a horse arrested his attention.

It was rapidly drawing near, and he had hardly time to get on the right side of the road, when a horseman dashed down the descent from the cliff at a breakneck pace, and flew past him like a dark meteor. Not so dark, however, but that the keen eye of Ishmael Morgan recognized him.

"So, so, Mr. Octavius Challoner!" he ejaculated. "Had I known it had been you, I'd have given you a trip up, in return for the fortnight's caging and starving on bread and water you gave me. Never mind!" he added, "you can go your way for this time; we shall meet again one of these days."

While he was still looking in the direction of the retreating horseman to whom these words applied, and wondering whether he would reach the hill without breaking his horse's knees or his own neck, the bright glare from the beacon light suddenly burst forth.

"There's a fire somewhere!" he exclaimed.

He looked round, but being in a hollow he could see no habitation.

He walked the horse up the acclivity, and gradually reached the top of the cliff.

"It's in the coast-guard *depot*!" he cried suddenly, as he neared the summit.

He was glad to find he was mistaken, and that it was only the beacon light that blazed through the gloom.

He could discern small dark forms moving hither and thither like insects, and he fancied he heard shouts borne indistinctly by the wind.

Something must have happened, he thought.

He resolved to ride forward and see.

He was the more anxious, because he was on good terms with most of the men there, who did not trouble themselves about land depredators, provided the *coast was clear*.

Many a chat did he have with the brave fellows as he passed on his peregrinations, and many a tinkering job fell to his lot, from the repairing of culinary utensils for the use of the *depot*.

It was natural, therefore, he should be anxious.

It was just as he had resolved to proceed there when the terrible explosion previously recorded took place.

The very ground seemed to quiver beneath his feet, as if with the shock of an earthquake.

The terrified animal he bestrode came to a dead stop, as though suddenly deprived of the power of motion.

Then the next moment it darted madly forward, in a state of almost uncontrollable terror, right towards the edge of the cliff.

It required all the gipsy's nerve and strength of arm to restrain his headlong flight.

But he did this at length by turning the horse's head, so that, instead of plunging over the dark abyss of the cliff, he ran along its brow.

It was in the midst of the first horror and confusion of the calamity that the panting, scared steed came tearing up to the scene of slaughter.

Ishmael, having speedily gathered the particulars of what had occurred, and which grieved him, vagabond as he was, more than anyone would have supposed, lent his assistance in removing the wounded, the dying, and the dead.

He then set off as rapidly as possible to Marton.

In this journey the gray steed did him good service, carrying him over the ground in half the time any ordinary horse would have done.

Ishmael did not, however, return by the same route as that by which he had come.

There was another way that shortened the journey

nearly one half, but it was a dangerous way, as the path lay along the edge of a deep morass, into which the traveller, unless well acquainted with the road, was liable to wander.

Many had perished there, and Ishmael had a faint idea that the owner of the horse might have added one more to their number.

He performed the journey safely, but without discerning any traveller struggling in the slough, as he passed by the dangerous brink.

Dr. Julep was comfortably tucked up in bed, snoring loudly enough for a whole college of doctors, when Ishmael grasped the handle of the gate-bell, and pulled incessantly, until not only the M.D., M.R.C.S. had started from his sleep in a panic, but the entire household were *rung* out of their beds by the continuous peals of the remorseless alarum.

"What's the matter?" shouted the little doctor, opening his bedroom window, and swallowing a mouthful of 'night mist that set him coughing furiously. "What's the matter?" he repeated.

"There's been a desperate explosion on the Beacon Cliff!" cried the gipsy: "twenty men altogether dead and wounded! You're wanted, sir, directly!"

"Good gracious!" exclaimed the little doctor, "Twenty men! I'll be there as soon as possible!" he called out.

The M.D. withdrew his head and closed his window, and proceeded to dress himself with all possible expedition.

The doctor was an enthusiast in his profession, and this was a case that aroused his sympathies.

To measles, or croup, or whooping-cough, he was adamant, but the prospect of a surgical operation was meat and drink to his soul.

"Quick, John!" he cried, to his man, who was coachman, valet—everything to him. "Tell Simon to put the saddle on the brown mare. I'll ride over; I can go quicker on horseback than in the chaise. You'd better come with me, John; you can mount the cob: he's a good one to get over the ground."

The little doctor was soon equipped, and John came speedily to inform him the horses were ready.

"Now, let me see: have I got everything?" he asked himself, thoughtfully—"my case of instruments, lint strapping. John," he cried, "be sure to take plenty of lint and strapping!"

John, who was used to these preparations, assured his master he had packed up a sufficient quantity.

At the gate, waiting, the doctor and his man found Ishmael Morgan.

"Are you coming with us?" asked the M.D. of the latter.

"Yes, sir," replied the gipsy; "we must ride quickly. You'll have plenty of work to do, doctor: there's some terrible cases amongst the poor fellows."

"We'll see what can be done!" cried Doctor Julep, as the trio galloped off.

As Ishmael stated, the doctor found on his arrival there *was* plenty of work.

Several professional brethren arrived in due course, and they had such a night of cutting, slashing, and strapping as they had hardly ever encountered in the whole of their experience.

At length, however, their duties were accomplished, and having done all they could to alleviate the terrible suffering by which they were surrounded, they returned to their respective homes.

Tinker Tom, however, did not depart.

He was a useful fellow to have handy in case a messenger was needed, and he stopped willingly.

A body of men were also to be despatched the next day to examine the cavern, and he was to be one of the number.

It was as Octavius Challoner left the cave, accompanied by his wounded dog, this party descended the rocky path towards the scene of the previous night's catastrophe.

They were supplied with strong crowbars and levers, and at length, after great exertions, they succeeded in raising the mass of rock, and rolling it back to its former position. On their entrance, they, of course, found the cavern empty, save from a few small tubs, and sundry miscellaneous articles scattered about here and there. Amongst these may be mentioned the discarded rags of James and Ikey that were still perched up on the wooden framework the boys had erected near the now extinct fire.

Sad were the thoughts that filled the breasts of the men as they looked round the vast cavern.

Some of them had lost relatives by the explosion—a brother, a father, or a son—but all comrades and friends.

Bitter and angry were the feelings with which they looked out across the troubled sea, on whose bosom the pirates had effected their escape.

How ardently they wished they had been there, that they might have inflicted a righteous retribution hand to hand; but wishes were unavailing.

The execrations of the wrathful survivors reached not the ears of the lawless men at whom they were levelled, and at length they ascended once more to the summit of the cliff.

Ishmael Morgan was slowly about to follow, when his eye fell on a small mass of congealed blood. He was standing near to where the wounded dog had been crouching, and it was the blood of the animal he was looking at.

Of this, however, he was ignorant.

He saw blood, and it set him wondering whose it might be.

It was a very wide field for conjecture, since the slaughter took place outside the cave.

Had it been inside, he would not have thought it at all strange.

He stood perfectly silent, looking down upon the dark crimson clots in a kind of reverie, when he was aroused by the sound of voices near at hand.

He looked round but saw nothing.

"Surely my ears didn't deceive me?" he thought.

The voices had ceased suddenly.

He listened intently, and again the sounds were repeated. It appeared to him as though two persons were conversing together almost at his elbow, and yet these persons, whoever they were, were invisible.

"Where can they be? In the next cavern, perhaps," he thought.

He was about hastily to advance towards it, when, from the sound of one of the voices, he was convinced the speaker was somewhere in the cavern where he then was.

Guided by his ear, he looked on his right hand, but he saw no cavity that seemed to promise any adjacent cells.

Nothing but a moderately large slab of rock, that jutted out from the side of the cave, and which in his mind he set down as a fixture.

Still the voices seemed to come from thence, as it appeared, out of the solid rock.

With the utmost caution he drew near.

The conversation, whatever and between whomsoever it might be, was carried on in such low tones as to be almost indistinct.

He held his breath and strained his ears to listen.

Again he heard the voices. There was no doubt about it. And they—surely they came from the very depths of the rocky walls.

It was too much for him; he could not understand it.

He was about to regard it as some curious echo, when three words distinctly fell on his ear.

Those words were: "*Starved to Death!*"

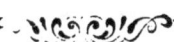

Chapter XVII.

A TERRIBLE POSITION.

A VERY peculiar and horrible dread had seized upon poor James and Ikey when they ensconced themselves in the narrow cleft, where they now lay closely packed.

They resembled two little unfortunate mice in a trap. But they looked upon themselves as atrocious criminals, for whom the keen-eyed law would search with unremitting scrutiny, as being guilty of the death of Augustus. There was in their own minds no loophole for escape—no extenuating circumstances.

They had, by their own persuasions, induced the unfortunate young gentleman to embark with them on board the boat; the boat had capsized, and the poor young gentleman was drowned, whilst, in aggravation of their guilt, *they*—poor ragged little rascals as they were—were saved.

What right had *they* to have been thrown on shore more than *he*?

Why did not they bring him to shore with them; or, at least, if that was impracticable, why did they not, as they ought to have done, accompany him to the bottom?

That would have been a redeeming point at least.

But, no! they lived, and the very fact of their living whilst he was drowned was a proof of selfish, reckless indifference, that none but two such hardened outcasts of society as themselves could have been guilty of.

This was the light in which their fears painted themselves to themselves.

If ever any two poor boys felt themselves particularly guilty and condemned, and richly deserving the tender mercies of Jack Ketch, those two boys were James Cook and Ikey Mangles.

Of course, we all know that their fears were groundless.

It was not the fashion then in England, any more than it is now, to hang boys of ten years old under any circumstances.

But then these two poor children did not know this.

Their fears had been worked upon by a heartless and cruel man to a pitch of unbearable terror.

Every one knows how easy it is to work upon the credulity of childhood, that believes all it is told.

It was just this that the villain Octavius Challoner had done, and he had succeeded so effectually in his vile efforts that the poor boys would have remained there in their rocky prison and have died there rather than have called for help.

What did it matter to them, they thought.

They might as well be *starved* as *hung*.

For a long time after the footsteps of their evil genius had ceased to echo through the cavern they remained silent, trembling.

Their hearts beat so palpably against their ribs that they felt certain if any one were in the cave they would infallibly hear them.

But they dared not clothe their thoughts in words.

At length, however, the silence being so unbroken as to make it quite certain no one was near, Ikey ventured to ask his friend in affliction, "'ow 'e felt?"

"I feel so cramped up I can hardly bear myself," was the reply.

"So do hi;" said Ikey, "an' hi'm afeard to stretch out my legs 'cos I might push down th' stone at the hentrance, an' then if hany vun vas to come in they'd see us, and ve should be took to pris'n an' 'ung."

At this horrible idea they shuddered violently.

It was at the same time rather a good idea on the part of Ikey, that of supposing his feeble strength was sufficient to displace the stony mass that shut them in.

The dread, however, that such a casualty might possibly occur had the effect of making him keep his legs particularly quiet.

"It vouldn't be good for us, when Mr. Hotty comes to let us hout if 'e found th' stone down, vould it?" he observed.

"No," said James, with a weary sigh, caused partly by his cramped limbs, and partly by sad recollections.

"It vos kind on 'im though to 'ide us avay here, vasn't it!" Ikey continued.

"Yes," replied James, rather mechanically.

"I thought e'd a killed us houtright vhen ve told 'im as Master Augustus vos drownded; instead o' vich 'e seemed kinder than e' did afore," Ikey continued.

"So he did," answered James; "but he wished his cousin dead, and I think most likely he was glad to hear that he *was* drowned."

"Oh, ah, I forgot that! Hi dessay 'e vos," responded Ikey. "Hi s'pose e' vos obliged to us, and that's th' raisin vhy 'es 'id us 'ere."

"I hardly know what to think," said James; "but it seems to me a strange sort of kindness shutting us up in a place like this."

"Vhy, don't yer see, it's to keep us hout o' sight!" exclaimed Ikey, a little impatiently at his companion's dulness.

"I feel as if I should never be able to walk again!" James remarked, in a tone of irritability that was not natural to him.

The poor boy's limbs were so jammed and cramped that he hardly knew how to bear himself.

He made, however, a desperate sort of effort, and contrived to shift his position a little.

Slight as the change was, it was a relief to him; and he was able to speak in his usual manner.

He did not, however, seem to be so much impressed by the belief of Octavius's kindness.

He had been pondering the matter in his mind, and he had formed his own conclusions.

"Do you know what I think was the reason Mr. Challoner hid us away here?" he asked.

"Not 'xac'ly; hi can't make it hout," said Ikey.

"I think I can!" continued James. "I fancy he thinks we heard what he said to the pirates, about killing his cousin!"

"Vell, but that vouldn't make 'im hinclined to do us a good turn, vould it?"

"No; quite the contrary, because he might think we'd tell the squire about it."

"Hi don't think as 'e thought that, cos if 'e 'ad, 'e'd a knock'd our brains hout with 'is vhip 'andle," said Ikey; "besides if 'e'd vanted to kill us 'e'd never a put us hout o' sight hinto this snug place."

"I don't like to think bad of anybody," answered James, earnestly; "but I can't help thinking, now the first fright's over, that he shut us up here *on purpose to get rid of us!*"

"Oh! that can't be!" exclaimed Ikey incredulously. "Don't go hon talkin' in that vay, Jem."

"I can't help thinking so."

"But didn't 'e say as this 'ere vas the honly place ve could 'ide in from th' law? An' didn't 'e give us advice, as ve vos to be qviet an' 'old our tongues for fear hany vun should 'ear us?"

"Yes; because if any one heard us p'raps they might let us out, and I don't think he wants us to get out."

"Then vhy did 'e say 'e'd come an' let us hout 'isself?"

"To deceive us, and keep us quiet, I think," said James.

It was astonishing how accurately the boy's mind had translated the dark designs of Octavius Challoner with respect to himself and his companion.

"An' do yow mean to say, then, as yow thinks 'e von't come an' let us hout?" asked Ikey, eagerly.

"I don't think he will," answered James.

"Vot! not never?"

"Never!"

There was a pause.

This was putting matters in quite a new light to poor Ikey, who now became suddenly conscious that his limbs were becoming permanently fixed in dreadfully cramped positions. Then it suddenly flashed before him that he was being suffocated.

"I vish I vos hout o' this 'ole," he cried, dolefully; "'ere goes: I shall down vith the stone."

Suiting the action to the words he made a desperate lunge against the rock with his feet.

He might as well have tried to swallow it.

As if in mockery of his puny strength, the rock remained perfectly firm and unmoved.

He tried again, but with no better result.

The stony mass laughed to scorn his impotent efforts.

He began to grow desperate.

"I von't stop in 'ere!" he cried. "I shall call hout, Jem! Come hon, let's both call hout!"

The boys were both about to cry out desperately, when the murmurings of many voices and heavy blows were heard at the entrance of the cavern.

This was the men without endeavouring to roll back the rock from the entrance.

These sounds revived all the poor boys' imaginary fears, and banished for the time from their minds the real horrors of their situation, which had been gradually dawning upon them.

In a moment cramp, suffocation, and all such minor inconveniences were forgotten, and their terrified imaginations pictured a formidable host of constables, loaded with chains and handcuffs, hastening on the wings of outraged justice to seize them, malefactors as they were.

Bang—bang—crunch—crunch went the hammers as

they struck against the wedges, in the operation of raising the rock.

The poor boys' hearts died within them.

"They're a comin' arter us, Jemmy!" groaned Ikey, "they knows ve're here—perhaps Mr. Hotty's told 'em."

"Let's be quiet," said James. "Pray be quiet!" he repeated, with desperate intensity, "an' p'r'aps they won't find us."

There was no need to repeat this warning.

Both the boys were still as death.

The knocking was continued, to their inexpressible dismay, and presently a loud ringing shout informed them that they—the constables, of course—had effected an entrance into the cavern.

If they had had any lingering doubts as to whom the new-comers were in search of, the exclamations they distinctly heard on all sides speedily dispelled them.

"Villains — miscreants! — inhuman scoundrels!— bloodthirsty murderers!—dastardly assassins!—unhung wretches!" were the fierce expressions ejaculated from burning, wrathful tongues on all sides, mingled with groans and execrations.

"They means hus!" whispered the terrified Ikey. "I vunder vhether they'll 'ang us at vonce, as soon as they finds hus?"

The men, having given the first vent to their indignation, rushed into the outer cavern.

"Theer a-lookin' for hus in the hother place now," said Ikey. "Oh, 'ow I vishes I vos hout!"

They did not remain long there, but as has been before stated, having vented their burning indignation in vain words, returned to the large cave and departed by the now open entrance.

The boys were still safe.

Their hiding-place had not been discovered.

Silence once more reigned around.

Again the fear of the constables died away, and the terrible cramp pains revived with renewed force.

The poor boys groaned again with the anguish of their confined position.

Once more they contrived to screw out a very slight movement of their limbs.

Even this was a little alleviation of their miseries.

It struck James that, after all, it was not they the party in the cavern had been in search of.

"I don't think they meant us, Ikey," he said, in a low voice, to his companion.

"Hi dunno, an' Hi don't care!" groaned the latter. "I vishes they 'ad a found hus! My back's a breakin' in 'alf, an' my legs is—oh, oh!"

"Hush!" whispered James: "remember the gentleman told us to be quiet."

"Hi can't be quiet!" returned the tortured Ikey. "Hi've got th' cramp in both legs, an' pins an' needles in my feet—oh, oh!"

The pain of these accumulated afflictions was so unbearable that Ikey thrust his tortured legs out in a species of desperation, when, to his great astonishment and still greater delight, the portion of the rock against which he pressed his feet seemed to yield to his efforts, and to allow him to stretch out his cramped limbs to their full extent—no great stretch either.

But it was like Paradise to him.

"Jem, Jem!" he whispered eagerly, "put yer legs theer, close to mine, hi've bored an 'ole in th' rock with my 'eel. 'Ave a good stretch!"

James, thinking his companion was losing his senses with pain and fright, nevertheless, to humour him, did as he was requested, and, to his great surprise, found that he, too, could stretch himself to his heart's content, and by so doing get rid of his miserable sensations.

They were now once more able to converse calmly.

"An' so yer don't think as the men as vos in the cavern jest now come arter hus?" he said.

"No, I don't!" answered James. "We're not scoundrels and bloodthirsty murderers, are we?"

"I don't think as ve is," Ikey responded. "I never killed nothin' but an 'are, an' I von't kill them no more," he added, "hif I ever gits out o' 'ere!"

"If we wait for Mr. Octavius, I'm afraid we never shall," said James.

"I'm afeard ve never shall hany 'ow!" cried Ikey, with a wail of despair. "Hi can't move th' stone as blocks hup th' 'ole, an' if ve can't do that, vot are ve to do?"

"We must wait here quietly till Mr. Octavius comes to let us out," James said, quietly.

"But s'pose 'e never comes?"

There was a pause. James did not reply: the question almost answered itself.

"Hi knows!" exclaimed Ikey, in a freezing tone of horror. "Ve shall both on us be starved to death!"

It was these words, uttered in a thrilling accent of terrible conviction, that fell so distinctly upon the ear of Ishmael Morgan.

After the first shock he experienced on hearing these ominous words, uttered by the invisible speaker, had subsided, the gipsy, whose nerves were a compound of iron and steel, wisely concluded that they were spoken by some one who needed help, and not at present seeing his way clear to render any assistance without some further information, he placed himself as close to the rock as possible, and putting his hand to the side of his mouth, after his customary manner when he bawled "Pots and kettles to mend, oh!" he cried:

"Who's there?"

His voice sounded deep and sonorous, and echoed hollowly through the cavern.

It also fell with full force upon the ears of the youthful prisoners.

Had a thunderbolt descended and riven the stone that covered the entrance of their narrow cell, it could not have produced a greater or more sudden shock than did this simple question, pronounced by that deep, hollow voice in the midst of the dead silence of the cavern.

Neither answered.

There was no doubt their pursuers had artfully left one of their number behind to discover their retreat.

And now it was discovered.

Ikey wriggled himself in a most extraordinary manner *somewhere.*

Where that was neither he nor his companion had the remotest conception.

James had a sort of impression that he was losing him, and the only information he received was a hasty whisper:

"Come on, Jem, 'ere's an 'ole!"

No other word was spoken.

Tinker Morgan, having proposed his question, waited patiently for a reply.

None came, however.

He therefore exclaimed again:

"Who's starved to death?"

Still there was no answer.

He grew impatient.

"I could take my oath the voice came from here," he exclaimed, impatiently. "Can't you speak, whoever you are?" he shouted.

The silence still continuing he grew desperate, and without any very definite idea of what he wished to accomplish, he spurned the piece of rock before him with all his force.

It fell over, and disclosed a dark, narrow cavity.

He looked eagerly in.

It was perfectly empty

Chapter XVIII.

TRAVELLING IN THE DARK.

THIS may appear to our readers very strange and mysterious; but, like many other mysteries, it will turn out perfectly simple and natural when explained.

The cleft or recess in the rock in which James and Ikey had lain crouched was to a casual observer barely large enough to contain even their small bodies.

But this old cavern had from time immemorial been the resort of smugglers and other nautical desperadoes, who made this recess a receptacle for any miscellaneous articles it was capable of containing.

Amongst these was an old sail, that had got jammed

[JAMES COOK AND HIS COMPANION IN THE MORASS.]

into one corner, where it lay year after year in dark oblivion, till it seemed to form part of the solid rock itself.

However, that part where the old remnant of canvas lay damp and mildewed, was not solid, there being a cavity which the sail had filled up.

When, therefore, Ikey in his desperation stretched out his cramped legs, his feet were pressed with some force against this plug, which, gradually yielding, at last gave way entirely, and disclosed a cavity, which led to a kind of natural perforation in the rock.

It was through this cavity the boys, in the first instance, thrust their tortured limbs.

It was through this Ikey in the next place wriggled himself, and James followed, not knowing where they were going, and hardly caring, so long as they could escape the terrible constable, with the deep, hollow voice.

No. 7.—The Adventures of Captain Cook.

The passage along which they crept was not large enough to admit of their standing upright.

They were therefore compelled to advance on all-fours.

It was perfectly dark, but there was plenty of fresh air; and though their perpendicular motions were somewhat circumscribed, they could stretch themselves horizontally to any extent, which privilege was in itself, after the confinement they had been enduring, a perfect luxury.

But they were too anxious to get as far away as possible, to pause.

They heard the deep voice put the questions mentioned in the last chapter, and they went scrambling along, crawling on their hands and knees, wondering how long they would be able to travel in that fashion, and where the narrow path would terminate.

Ikey was presently seized with a terrible idea.

"Hi say, Jem," he said, "s'pose this 'ere vay don't lead nowheers, vot are ve to do then?"

"It must lead somewhere," answered James.

"Yes; but Hi mean som'eres vheer ve can get hout."

"Well, then, we shall have to stay where we are," returned James; "but even that would be better than the miserable, narrow little place in which we were cramped up."

"Hi don't think as th' constable could get up 'ere arter us," said Ikey, in a tone of self-congratulation; "th' 'ole hain't big enough to let 'im hin."

At this moment the rock, impelled by the strong hand of Ishmael, rolled over with a sharp crash that reverberated through the cavern.

"'E's pulled the stone down!" cried Ikey, eagerly; "come on, Jem."

The boys set off crawling faster than ever, each stimulated by a kind of apprehension that, in spite of the narrowness of the passage, they might at any moment feel a strong hand grasping their ankles and dragging them back.

Nothing, however, interposed to stay them, and their exertions were in a short time rewarded by a faint glimmer of light in the distance.

Their progress had for some time past been more difficult.

They had evidently been travelling up hill, though, in their excitement, they had not noticed it.

They were now, however, brought to that conclusion by feeling very tired and out of breath.

As they paused a moment to rest, James caught sight of the faint illumination, and pointed it out to Ikey.

"See!" he exclaimed, joyfully, "there's daylight!"

"So theer his!" cried his companion; "hooray!"

"Forward! forward!" urged James.

Escape—freedom—was before them, and the prospect gave them new strength.

They went clambering and groping on. The passage seemed to wind, but the streak of light before them increased in brightness.

Yes—there was no doubt about it now, for the fresh stream of air blowing upon them told them they were near some outlet.

In another moment their eyes were gladdened by a distinct revelation of the place they were in.

It was evidently a natural perforation in the chalky rock, that led, by a tortuous and gradual ascent, to the heights above.

"Look, Jem," cried Ikey; "there's an 'ole!"

He pointed as he spoke to a narrow fissure, at a few yards' distance.

It was so small that it had nearly the appearance of a crack on the surface of the ground, as though the earth had yawned slightly.

But, small as it was, it was sufficient to allow the prey to escape, though not for any hunter to follow.

How grateful the poor boys felt at that moment that they were so little!

Their task was accomplished.

One more slight effort, rendered necessary by the thick frieze jackets they wore, and James Cook and Ikey Mangles, covered from head to foot with the chalk they had accumulated in their journey, and looking more like two infant Polar bears than anything else, stood upon the summit of the Beacon Cliff.

They took a long breath, and were surprised to find that it was daylight, and how much milder the air was than when they had last stood beneath the canopy of heaven.

They looked ruefully at each other.

"Ve're as vhite as snowballs," remarked Ikey.

They made an effort to beat the chalk out of each other's coats, and raised such a dust that they were apprehensive the cloud would attract attention.

The question then proposed itself, what were they to do?

Poor James's thoughts flew back to the humble cottage where his dead mother lay, and his eyes filled with accusing tears as he reflected how he had forgotten her in the excitement of the scenes he had passed through.

"Poor dear mother!" he cried, bitterly; "if you could see me now leaving you all alone, you'd think I never loved you at all!"

The hot tears ran down his cheeks at this reflection, but he felt that that was not a place in which to indulge his grief, so he wiped his tears hastily away, and began to think what course would be the best to take.

Heaven help the poor boys! It would have puzzled a wiser head than theirs to have decided this point.

Ikey, as usual, had no particular idea on the subject.

He sat on the edge of the crevice from which he had just emerged, with his legs dangling down, rejoicing to a certain extent in his temporary freedom, and looking at his companion patiently, till he should offer some suggestion.

"We mustn't stop here," said James, at length. "But where can we go?"

"Hi dunno," answered Ikey. "Oh!" he exclaimed, suddenly, "s'pose ve vos to go to th' cottage: they von't 'xpec' to find us theer, and if hanyvun comes, ve can get hinto th' cupboard; besides, theer's some soup an' some vine left behind theer."

Ikey evidently had an eye to the corporeal comforts the humble cottage was likely to afford; but James thought of his mother.

"I should like to go there!" he exclaimed, with a longing, wistful earnestness, "and I think we will, Ikey. If they're hunting after us, they're sure to find us, and we may as well be caught at home as anywhere else; besides, I must see dear mother once more."

The poor little fellow sighed deeply, and Ikey remarked:

"Don't yer think ve'd better go back into our 'ole till it's dark, then no vun 'ud see us?"

"P'r'aps we had," replied James; "it won't be long before then. The clouds are gathering over the sky."

The boys looked up at the dark canopy over their heads, from which large drops of rain were beginning to fall.

"Hit's a going to be vet," remarked Ikey; "let's get hinside again—there's summat to heat down in th' cave, an' Hi'm gettin' 'ungry. Shall Hi go fust?"

"If you like, Ikey," James answered.

"'Ere goes, then!"

But before this could be accomplished a strong but not violent hand was laid upon their collars, and they were held fast.

"Where are you youngsters going—eh?—burrowing like a pair of rabbits!" demanded a hearty voice.

The boys were too scared to notice the speaker, though, had they looked up at his swarthy but not unkind face, fringed with its jetty beard, and lighted up by a pair of dark, keen eyes, that twinkled with suppressed mirth at their comical appearance, they would have recognised one that was more likely to prove a friend than an enemy.

Tinker Morgan was well known to all the boys in the country for miles round, and being himself fond of young people was, as a natural consequence, a favourite amongst them.

If anyone wanted a cricket-ball stitched or a cricket-bat spliced, Morgan could do either of these repairs.

Did any youthful angler require a fish-hook, or an artificial fly, Morgan's handy basket could invariably supply him; or, if not, his skilful hands would speedily manufacture the required articles.

He was besides an authority with respect to the keeping of pigeons, rabbits, dogs, &c., and was always ready and willing to give all the information possible upon any of these subjects whenever he was called upon.

It was not then to be wondered at that the tinker was known to and liked by all the youngsters.

He was perfectly familiar with poor little James Cook and Ikey Mangles, and they were equally so with him.

Hardly a week passed that he did not stop at the cottage of the former, to see if there was any odd job to be done.

In Ikey Mangles he found a willing pupil, to whom he had on more than one occasion given some private lessons as to the most successful plan for snaring rabbits. To the boys, therefore, he stood in the light of a mutual friend.

But just now their senses were so frightened and bewildered that everything seemed

"Out of time and harsh."

Every wind that blew carried with it a threat—every hand that touched them was the grasp of an enemy.

Had it not been so they would at once have recognised the tinker's voice.

Ishmael observed the marks of terror on their features and in their manner, and marvelled at the cause.

He had called the day before at Mrs. Cook's cottage and found it silent and deserted, save by the presence of death.

He was, therefore, prepared to sympathise in his rough way with the young orphan.

But the symptoms the boy expressed were not sorrow, but dread, and Tinker Morgan was once more mystified.

"What's the matter with you both?" he cried.

"Oh, if you please, sir, don't stop us!" said James, in a voice of earnest entreaty, "or they'll catch us!"

"Catch you?—who'll catch you?" asked Morgan, with surprise.

"Th' constables!" replied Ikey, vehemently.

The Gipsy laughed; he couldn't help it, their appearance tickled him.

"Well, you do look like a pair o' juvenile burglars," he said; "what have you been up to, eh? stealing a sack of flour by the look of you."

"Oh no, sir!" cried the boys.

"What then?—what can you two babies have been doing to be afraid of constables, eh?" he inquired; "if it was me, now, there might be some reason; but I don't fear 'em! What have you been doing, eh?"

"Ve're bin drownin' a boy!" gasped Ikey.

"What boy?" asked Morgan, opening his eyes to their fullest extent with surprise at this piece of information.

"Master 'Gustus Markham!"

"Where?"

"In the sea," James explained: "we went out in a boat—Ikey, Master Augustus and me, and the boat overturned, and poor Gus was drowned."

"And how was it you were not drowned as well?" asked the tinker.

This was such a home-thrust, that the boys fell on their knees, sobbing.

"We clung to the boat's keel, and were thrown ashore; we thought poor Master Gus would have held by it, too, but he didn't, and he was drowned. We're very sorry; don't take us to prison, and hang us! Let us go!"

Their grief and terror was so earnest, that Ishmael began to feel it was a great deal past a joke.

He fancied too, from their manner, they did not recognise him.

He was right in his conjecture.

It might be very strange, but they did not—they were stupefied with fear.

"Don't you know me, my boys?" he asked, kneeling down to bring himself to their level. "I'm Tinker Morgan."

At this well-known name the poor little sufferers looked up for the first time, and, seeing it was indeed their friend, their horror instantly subsided.

"Tinker Morgan!" they ejaculated, and then as though they felt certain they could trust him, they rushed forward simultaneously, and nestled like two frightened birds against the broad chest of the rough but kindly Gipsy.

After their first emotions had subsided, they related their adventures to their friend, omitting only their knowledge of the designs of Octavius against his cousin, which they feared to confess, and merely saying

that he came with him into the cavern, and that it was the dread of the pirates, and the sight of the dead boy, that induced them to go in the boat, and to persuade the young Augustus to accompany them.

"And so you're hiding away lest the constables should lay their hands on you, and drag you up for murder; are you?" asked the Gipsy.

"Yes, Morgan; we are!" cried James, with intensity, "and we're frightened to show ourselves, or they'll take us to prison and hang us!"

"Oh! no they won't," said the Gipsy, soothingly.

"Oh! but they vill though!" persisted Ikey; "th' gen'l'man said so."

"What gentleman?"

"Mr. Hotty—Master Gus's cousin.'

"Mr. Octavius Challoner, eh?"

"Yes, Morgan."

"He's been poking fun at you two boys," said the tinker, with a frown upon his features as he spoke.

"Hi don't think as 'e vos in fun," said Ikey; "'e vos in a dreadful vay vhen 'e 'eered as is cous'n vos drounded, an' said ve vos to 'ide, cos hif th' const'bles saw us ve should both be 'ung."

"Was it your voices then I heard in the cave?"

"Yes."

"What did you mean by the words, *starved to death?*"

"Why, I said to Jem if Mr. Hotty didn't come an' let us hout o' th' 'ole in th' rock, ve should be starved to death."

"What!" exclaimed Ishmael, with flashing eyes. "Was it he who shut you up in that recess, and rolled the stone before the opening?"

"Yes, that it vos," answered Ikey; "but 'e honly did it to keep us hout o' sight, an' 'e said as 'e'd come and let us hout—didn't 'e, Jem?"

"Yes," said James.

The tinker gave vent to a stifled execration.

He could give no reason for indulging such a dark supposition, but it seemed to him as though Octavius Challoner had contemplated the death of these poor boys.

Though why the destruction of two such obscure individuals should have been necessary to any schemes of his, he could not imagine.

Octavius was no friend of the tinker, who had always a very vivid recollection of his fortnight's imprisonment, but still the latter could hardly make up his mind to accuse Mr. Challoner of designing the deliberate murder of two children.

He began to think that their fears had to some extent unsettled their faculties, and he rather hoped it was so.

"Well, my boys," exclaimed Ishmael, "after being shut up as you have been in the bowels of the rock, I should think you'd like to see the sight of a good fire; wouldn't you?"

The boys offered no objection to this.

"And then, if you please, Morgan," said James, in a low tone, "I should like to go home. I want to see poor mother; she's dead, and lying there all alone."

"Ah, poor boy!" ejaculated Ishmael, affected by the deep sigh that followed these words. "Well, you shall see your mother, in spite of all the constables in Yorkshire!" he cried; "and now come to the fire."

Taking the two boys by the hand, he led them towards the Coastguard Watch House.

Chapter XIX.

OCTAVIUS MEETS WITH A SURPRISE.

TINKER MORGAN introduced his young charges to the rough but kindly men that were assembled at the *Depot*, as two poor friendless orphan boys, in whom he took an especial interest.

This was enough to interest everyone in their favour. They were installed in the warmest seat by the fire, and two good basins of bread and milk were set before them.

They were soon quite warm and comfortable again.

One of the men came down a flight of stairs from an upper compartment, and approached the superintendent of the *Depot*.

"Poor Willis is very bad, sir," he said; "he's afraid

his leg's mortifying, and if you could send for the doctor, he'd like very much to have it off."

"Poor lad!" exclaimed the superintendent, with a shake of the head and a melancholy smile. "He begs for amputation as though it were a luxury!"

"Life's sweet, sir, to everyone," observed the man.

"True, Tom," replied the superintendent. "The poor fellow shall be saved if possible; I'll send over for Dr. Julep. Here, Morgan," he cried to the Gipsy.

The tinker was at that moment giving James and Ikey an account of the disaster of the previous night, and the terrible results of the pirates' work.

He rose instantly at the sound of his name.

"I want you to ride over directly to Dr. Julep, and tell him from me to come over at once and amputate John Willis's leg—that is, if it's not too late."

"I'll be off directly, sir," said Ishmael, in reply to the superintendent's words.

The Gipsy went to the boys who were snugly seated by the blazing fire, and whispered:

"I've got to ride over to Merton for the doctor. I sha'n't be gone long."

"Are we to stop here till you come back, Morgan?" they asked.

"Yes."

Ishmael went to the stable, where the gray steed stood ready saddled and bridled for immediate service.

He led him out, mounted, and rode off.

As he journeyed along, he could not help thinking of the forlorn condition of the two poor boys he had left behind.

Then by a natural transition those thoughts shifted to Octavius Challoner, and then they became very misty indeed.

"What could he have wanted in the pirates' cavern at night?—accompanied by his young cousin, too!" he thought.

He little guessed how explicitly James Cook and Ikey Mangles could have answered that question had they dared.

As it was, it was a riddle he could not solve, and therefore, as many had done before him under similar circumstances, he gave it up, and galloped on as hard as he could.

He had not travelled far when he perceived a horseman coming towards him.

Strange! It was the object of his thoughts—Mr. Challoner himself.

Octavius seemed buried in his own reflections as he rode along, and did not appear to notice who it was that was advancing to meet him.

"I'll scan his features well as I pass," muttered Ishmael. "He shall see I'm not afraid to look at him, though he is a gentleman and I'm only a Gipsy."

The horses drew near each other.

Octavius suddenly started from his reverie and looked straight before him.

His eyes fell on the gray steed, and it appeared to magnetise him.

He slackened his speed, and finally pulled up.

Ishmael also slackened his, and advanced, looking Mr. Octavius, in anything but a respectful manner, full in the face, as though he had been quite an ordinary person.

In the Gipsy's gaze there was more than the absence of respect—there was defiance.

Octavius observed this, and bit his lip with rage.

He had recognised the steed as having belonged to George Carew, and though he was not concerned at seeing him bestride it, he envied the Gipsy its possession.

"Hullo, you Gipsy!" he shouted, as Ishmael passed him and made as though he would have gone on. "Stop!"

Morgan reined-in his horse, and turned his head round with the utmost nonchalance.

"Well, what do you want?" he asked, abruptly.

"That's a fine piece of horseflesh you mount," said Octavius, endeavouring to speak calmly.

"Yes," answered the Gipsy, coolly: "yours is nothing to compare with it."

"It is not usual for Gipsies to own such a valuable animal as that."

"No, that makes my good fortune all the more remarkable—doesn't it?" grinned the tinker, displaying his white teeth.

"How did you come possessed of it?"

"What is that to you?"

"You are a suspicious character, and I am justified in asking."

"I understand you, Mr. Octavius; but I didn't steal the horse or murder the rider."

This was said without any particular meaning being thrown into the words.

But they seemed very significant to the guilty conscience of Octavius.

He turned pale, and bit his lip.

"Who accused you of murder, or robbery either?" he asked, sternly.

"I thought from your words you seemed to think I'd stolen him," said Ishmael.

"It is not at all an unnatural supposition," returned Octavius. "But if not, where did you get him?"

"Well, if you must know, I found him last night trotting along the road, saddled and bridled, but with no one on his back. Not long after I had made this discovery I saw you pass, Mr. Challoner."

"I?"

"Yes, you!"

"Very likely—I was out last night," Octavius answered. "But what has that to do with the question?"

"Why, I thought perhaps that as I had accounted for the horse, you might be able to give some intelligence of the rider."

This was another unpremeditated dig in the ribs for Octavius, who, conscious of his guilt, felt almost inclined to believe the Gipsy suspected him.

And yet a moment's reflection convinced him that could not be the case.

He therefore collected himself, and, putting on a dignified, magisterial air, said:

"You admit you found the horse, consequently you will be prepared to admit it is not your property; I therefore feel myself justified in taking charge of the animal until the owner be discovered."

This idea, however correct it might have been on the part of Mr. Challoner, by no means coincided with the intentions of the Gipsy.

"Suppose the owner's never found, the horse will be mine," he said, somewhat doggedly.

"Such an event as that is not likely to happen," returned Octavius; "but if it does, and the steed remain unclaimed, it will be then time enough for you to take possession; for the present——"

"For the present, I'm on his back," said Ishmael, abruptly, "and I don't mean to give him up—they say possession's nine points of the law, and so——"

"What do you know about the law?" cried the irritated Octavius.

"About as much as you, if you were a magistrate, would know about justice!" answered the Gipsy, rather impertinently.

The indignant gentleman seemed inclined to make a dash forward, but Ishmael called out:

"I'm going for a doctor, sir, and while we're talking here about a runaway horse, a poor fellow may be dying for want of help."

"Go on then, but I will ride back with you," said Mr. Challoner, determined not to be set at naught by a travelling tinker. "When you have delivered your message to the doctor, you can resign the horse to me."

He touched his steed slightly with the spur, and was at the side of the Gipsy in a moment.

It was rather an imprudent act on his part, for no sooner was he alongside, than Ishmael, suddenly bending low in the saddle, grasped Octavius by the heel, and with a powerful and adroit muscular effort, hoisted him clean out of his saddle.

Before the astonished horseman had time to count two, he was measuring his length in the muddy road.

"Lie there, Mr. Busybody!" muttered the Gipsy, as he rode off. "That's one for the cage and the bread-and-water."

There being no one at hand to pick him up, Mr. Challoner picked himself up.

He was very much shaken, but not particularly hurt.

That is bodily—his spirit was, however, full of wrath against the Gipsy, and he breathed out some threats that we need not repeat here.

After an abortive attempt to remove some of the mud from his riding coat, he gave up the attempt, and slowly remounting his horse, that had remained perfectly quiet by his side, he trotted off towards the Coastguard *depot*.

He had not been there since the night of the explosion, and he now made his appearance with a face heavily laden with sympathy.

I may even go so far as to say that his eyes looked red and watery, but that might have been the result of the shaking he had experienced.

The superintendent scarcely recognised the mud-bespattered, rueful-looking individual for the dashing nephew of the squire.

But Octavius accounted for it satisfactorily.

"A fall from my horse, lieutenant," said Mr. Challoner, as he dismounted. "A very sad piece of business this," he continued—"very sad! I had no idea when I expressed my suspicions that smugglers were in the cave, that the consequences would have been so terrible."

"Terrible, indeed!" echoed Mr. Gray, the superintendent, with a sigh, "six brave fellows blown to atoms, and ten wounded more or less severely."

"Dear, dear!" sighed Mr. Challoner, with the utmost commiseration: "poor creatures!"

These words fell from his lips as he entered the house, and they fell upon the ears of two other *poor creatures*, who were sitting snugly enough by the side of the fire, walled in by a clothes-horse, on which hung sundry sheets and linen garments, airing for the use of the invalids above.

They were out of sight therefore, but the sound of that voice startled them like a sudden thunder-clap.

Ikey was possessed with a sudden idea of getting up the chimney, but as the fire was roaring up it like a furnace, he was compelled to remain where he was.

"Keep quiet," whispered James, "and perhaps he won't see us."

As this advice was being delivered, Octavius was ascending to the sick ward.

There he spoke a few words of sympathy to the wounded who were able to listen to them, and left a donation from his uncle, the squire, who, in the midst of his own grief for the loss of his child, sympathised with the sufferers.

What a master of hypocrisy was his nephew!

No one overhearing him speak so kindly up there, in the sick ward—nay, even administering words of religious consolation to the lacerated men—would have believed how black and hollow was the heart of the speaker.

Poor Tom Willis was in great pain, longing for the arrival of the doctor.

"We have sent for Dr. Julep," said the superintendent, as they descended the stairs. "I'm afraid the only chance for him is to lose his leg."

Octavius did not mention that he had encountered the messenger, for obvious reasons, but said instead:

"I think I will wait the arrival of the doctor. I am anxious to learn his opinion of the poor fellow."

"By all means, sir," answered the superintendent, who then went out to scan the expanse of waters with his telescope.

The evening was fast drawing on, and a drizzling rain falling.

A mist spread itself over the sea like a fleecy pall. Octavius was alone—at least, he thought he was, and stood moodily looking out into the darkening twilight.

His thoughts reverted to the Gipsy who had so unceremoniously unhorsed him, and he inwardly resolved to have his full revenge at the first opportunity.

That the horse the tinker rode was the property of the man he had hurled from the cliff he felt convinced, and that added to the annoying sensations he experienced.

"If the vagrant is ever brought up again, the squire shall transport him," he muttered between his teeth; "and if it ever falls to my lot to occupy my uncle's place, I'll hang the scoundrel if I can!"

With this charitable resolve, he turned from the cheerless prospect of the drizzling rain towards the fire, whose cheerful blaze glowed forth over the barricade that enclosed it.

Attracted by the genial sight, he approached and leant his arms upon the top rail, little expecting what he was destined to behold.

Nevertheless, there, snugly seated behind the screen, were the two boys he had left quite as snugly, though far less comfortably, incarcerated in the rocks.

To say he started and turned pale would not describe the effect produced.

Had not the fire warmed his features, they would have been perfectly ghastly.

Our young heroes were not so much taken aback.

They had received an intimation of his presence from the sound of his voice at his first entrance, and had been expecting to see him for some little time.

Consequently, their features did not express that terrified surprise they might have worn had Octavius appeared suddenly upon them.

As it was, they sat, with cheeks glowing with excitement and the fire-light, looking up in his face with speechless embarrassment.

Octavius quickly recovered himself.

It was marvellous how two such children could have so unnerved him even for a moment.

"You here?" he burst forth, at length.

"Y-es, sir," answered the boys, with considerable trepidation.

"What is the meaning of this?" Octavius continued. "How did you get out?"

"We—we found a way out in the rock," said James, with some hesitation.

"In the rock? What do you mean?"

"Theer vos a 'ole in vun corner o' th' place, wheer we vos shet up, an' this 'ole run into a narror passage, as led right hup to the top o' th' cliffs," explained Ikey.

Mr. Challoner looked searchingly and incredulously at the speaker.

"You are sure no one let you out?" he inquired.

"Quite sure, sir," answered James.

"How is it I find you here?"

"We met Tinker Morgan, and he brought us here, and told us to wait till he came back," James said.

"Of course you did not mention to him anything that happened in the cave?" Octavius inquired, hastily.

"Ve honly said as you vos kind enough to 'ide us avay in th' rock," answered Ikey.

"You did?"

"Yes, sir—ve did," Ikey repeated.

The eyes of their questioner blazed fiercely, and he frowned deeply as he exclaimed, in a tone of alarm:

"You've destroyed yourselves by your imprudence!"

"Oh no, sir!" replied Ikey, eagerly. "I'm sure he won't do us any harm. We know him wery vell. He's wery kind, and will take care of us."

"Take care of you?" scornfully repeated Octavius. "He's a pretty fellow to take care of anyone, when he can't take care of himself! Don't you know he's a very bad man—a vagrant, poaching thief, and that the constables are after him?"

The boys opened their eyes at this intelligence.

"When they find him they'll take him off to prison," continued Mr. Challoner, "and if you are found with him they'll most assuredly take you as well; and you know then what will happen to you."

This was sufficient to revive the apprehensions of the boys, though James still made an effort to argue the point.

"Morgan told us they wouldn't send us to prison for what we'd done," he said.

"An' 'e said besides as they didn' hang little boys," added Ikey.

"He's a fool and a liar!" exclaimed Octavius, wrathfully; "but if you choose to trust him, trust him, only, when you find yourselves locked up, don't expect any help from me!"

The boys were beginning to look very blank at this.

Octavius continued to heap up the pile of terrors.

"If you had waited quietly where I placed you," he said, "I was coming to let you out to-night, and I should have taken you to a place where you would have been safe. As it is now, you must shift for yourselves. You have disobeyed me, and must put up with the consequences!"

"Oh, sir, we didn't mean to disobey you," cried James. "We were only afraid you might forget to come for us. Please don't let them take us!"

"It is not my wish to do so; but you have been seen," replied Octavius. "Should inquiries be made at this place, they will of course say that you were brought here by this Gipsy, and that will all go against you; besides, should I be doing right to screen you, knowing, as I do, that it is through you my poor cousin lost his life?"

"Oh, pray—pray forgive us that!" cried the frightened boys. "We're very sorry, but we didn't think what we were doing when we got into the boat."

"Oh, I forgive you," coldly replied Octavius.

"But please tell us what we're to do?" they asked, eagerly.

"You must leave this place directly," Octavius answered.

The boys started up as though they would have run to the world's end, had they been ordered.

"Stay! Where are you going?"

"Anywhere, sir—wherever you tell us!" they answered.

"Ah, that's the difficulty!" said the designing man, in a half tone, as though talking to himself. "What is to be done must be done at once!"

He went to the door, and looked out.

No one was in sight.

The superintendent was housed from the weather in the small watch-box from which he made his observations.

The coast was perfectly clear.

"Come here!" he cried, hastily, to the boys.

They advanced with eager readiness.

"Do you see that small hut?" he asked, as he pointed to the building where George Carew, two nights before, had paused to stable his horse on his road to the cavern.

The hovel was barely visible in the deepening twilight; but this was sufficient for the boys.

"Yes, sir," they exclaimed, simultaneously.

"Make the best of your way there, and wait for me inside the building. I'll see what can be done for you. But mind you *do* wait this time," said Octavius.

"Oh yes, sir! Thank you, sir!" answered the boys, gratefully.

"Off with you, then!" he cried. "I'll follow you presently."

The little fellows darted off, unbuttoning and throwing open the thick jackets they wore to expedite their movements.

They heeded not the drizzling rain that fell, being at that moment as glad to depart as they had been a short time previously to remain.

Chapter XX.

FOOTPRINTS IN THE DARK.

THEY were not long reaching the hut, the door of which they easily opened, and, having entered, closed again very carefully.

The inside was damp and cheerless—in melancholy contrast with the comfortable habitation and the warm fire they had just quitted.

There was a gloomy silence of some minutes' duration. At length Ikey spoke.

"I vonder vot's a goin' to become on us?" he remarked.

"I don't know," said James; "but I suppose we shall find out by-and-by."

He spoke in a tone of sad resignation, as though he had almost made up his mind for the worst.

"I'm not certain after all whether it wouldn't have been better to have stayed where we were till Morgan came back," James observed, dubiously.

"Vell, but," returned Ikey, "if it's true vot Mr. Hotty said as th' const'bles is arter 'im, 'ow could 'e look arter hus?"

"I hardly know what to think," James continued; "but I can't help believing that Tinker Morgan's a better friend to us than Mr. Challoner."

"P'r'aps 'e his; at least, vhether or not, I likes 'im better, hever so much!" Ikey answered. "But the vust on it his, as Morgan's allus in th' voods a trappin' 'ares an' rabbits, an' if ve vos found vith 'im they'd say ve vos as bad as 'im."

At this moment the sound of horses' hoofs on the wet ground suddenly checked their conversation, and filled them with alarm.

Who could it be?

They were not long kept in suspense, for in a few moments three horsemen galloped past the hut in which they were concealed.

These were Dr. Julep, his factotum John, and Ishmael Morgan.

The doctor, on the strength of another surgical operation, was riding for dear life, and digging away with his spurs at his unfortunate pony's sides, as though he were running a race.

"Come on!" he cried, excitedly, "the progress of mortification is rapid, and if the limb isn't off before——"

Before another word could be uttered the pony slipped, and fell on his knees, and off went the doctor, over his head.

The stout little gentleman rolled over like a floored nine-pin, but, with wonderful energy, he was no sooner down than he was up again.

"All right!" exclaimed the enthusiastic Esculapius, as he staggered to his feet, puffing and blowing like a hippopotamus rising from a roll in its congenial mud— "no bones broken!"

He grasped the pony's bridle, and speedily remounted, and, in a few moments, the party reached the *Depot*.

The boys had recognised Morgan's voice inquiring if the doctor was hurt, and James felt half inclined to call out to his Gipsy friend, but Ikey entreated him to be silent, and to "*wait for Mr. Hotty.*"

And so they waited.

Not long, for in a very few moments the individual in question rode up to the hut, and bending down in his saddle, opened the door.

He dismounted, and looking down upon the boys—who had long since exchanged the temporary glow caused by the warm fire of the *Depot* for the pallor of anxiety and fear—he said:

"It's lucky for you, you departed as you did. Dr. Julep has just arrived at the Coastguard house; he's a great friend of the Squire's, and he would have been sure to have seen you had you stayed there."

James and Ikey, as they gazed up at his stern features, tried to feel glad that they were safely out of harm's way, but it was a failure.

The cold, remorseless eyes of their *friend*, the miserable solitude of the damp hovel, and the uncertainty of their future prospects, chilled them to their very marrow.

"What are we to do now, sir?" asked James.

"You must come with me," answered Octavius. "I must try and conceal you somewhere for a time; though, were it known I was saving the lives of those who had caused my poor little cousin's death, I am quite at a loss what reason I could give for so doing."

This speech set the boys wondering why he should speak in such regretful terms of his cousin, when, only a few hours before, he had been so anxious for his destruction. It did more than this—it caused the dim shadow of suspicion that they were in dangerous hands to increase in bulk, and then to wish that they were by the side of the Gipsy once more.

But it was now too late to wish.

"Couldn't we go home, sir?" asked James, wistfully. "Poor mother's lying dead there, and——"

"Ah, true!" interrupted Octavius, with a very poor attempt at sympathy in his tone. "Your mother! Well, don't fret about her; she will be decently buried by the parish; I have arranged that."

"But couldn't I see her once more?" cried the orphan boy, the tears running down his cheeks; "she's all I had to love——"

"Oh—nonsense!" coldly answered Mr. Challoner, all his assumed sympathy vanishing at once. "What good would it do you to see your mother: you can't bring her to life again, can you?"

"No sir; but I should like to see her face once more," sobbed the heart-broken boy.

"You'd like to see the inside of a prison, you mean, for most assuredly you'll be sent there if they find you," answered Octavius, emphatically.

The usual shudder followed this warning.

"Come, it's time we were off!" he continued, in a peremptory tone. "Give me your hands and let me hoist you up into the saddle."

He mounted his horse as he spoke.

The arms of the boys were timidly stretched forth, and grasped by the hand of Octavius, who drew them up into their seats.

"Now—hold on!" he cried, as he urged his horse onwards.

The poor boys thought of the time when they had occupied a similar position in the saddle of their friend, the President.

But then a pair of kindly arms had encircled them with a grasp that ensured their safety.

Now they were so loosely held, that they dreaded a fall at every movement of the steed that bore them.

Then, kind and encouraging words cheered them; now there was nothing but ominous silence, or portentous threats, even more depressing.

When Ishmael Morgan reached the *Depot*, his first thought was of his young charges.

Great was his dismay when he discovered they were missing.

He made instant inquiries, but without success.

His discovery of their absence was the first intimation that had been given that they were not still snugly stowed away in the chimney corner.

Ishmael was both amazed and bewildered.

No one had seen the boys depart.

It was a very mysterious affair altogether, he thought.

There must have been something more than ordinary to tempt them to quit that bright, warm fire for the damp, drizzling night without.

But he heard casually that Mr. Octavius Challoner had been there, and from what he had previously learnt from the lips of the boys themselves, his anxiety broadened and deepened into suspicions that the squire's nephew was at the bottom of their mysterious disappearance.

The more he reflected the more did his suspicions assume the form of certainties.

He did not, however, spend much time in surmises.

Tinker Morgan was a man of action.

He speedily resolved in his mind, that there was only one course to pursue, and that was to start at once in search of them.

Without saying a word, therefore, to anyone, he left the *depot*, and went out into the moist air.

Evening was now set in.

The temperature seemed to have changed by magic.

A slight rain was falling; a heavy mist floated overhead; whilst on the ground, instead of hard frost, there was nothing but mud and slush.

It was just the kind of night to suggest to the mind of an explorer every possible kind of difficulty and failure.

But Morgan did not yield to these fancies.

Many and many a night he had braved damp and wet and cold, in the dense woods, searching for forbidden game, and it appeared to him nothing uncommon that this particular night should be so dark and cheerless.

The principal things that grieved him were that the darkness would limit his powers of searching, and that he was entirely ignorant of the track our young adventurers were pursuing.

One thing, however, struck him as a fact, and that was that with several paths before them, the boys could go only *one* way at a time.

The task then to be accomplished, was to discover that one.

The first place of concealment that entered his imagination was the cavern.

It was possible they might have returned thither.

That he determined should be the starting point of his search.

He accordingly went at once to the stable, and led forth the gray steed, and making free to borrow a dark lantern he found there, he quietly took his departure.

He went at once to the cavern, and in the murky darkness, by the light he carried, which was very inadequate to the occasion, he thoroughly searched the rocky retreat, but utterly without success.

He ascended once more to the summit of the cliff, and proceeded almost mechanically in the direction of the hut.

Possibly, he thought, they might be crouched there.

He entered the small building, but here again he was disappointed.

No—not quite.

On the ground lay a button he recognised as belonging to one of the pilot jackets the boys wore.

That was a clue—they had been there, then.

He was now upon the trail, and being a keen hunter, he began to have some hope of running down the game.

As a preliminary step, he threw the light of his lantern on the ground, and examined the marks there with scrutinising attention.

There was a confusion of footprints.

It required an experienced eye to decide what they were. But Ishmael Morgan had that keenness of perception, and he speedily discerned that the feet of boy, man, and beast had lately pressed the soil on which he stood.

There was no doubt at all about it in his mind now. *He felt certain!*

It next became necessary to discover the track which the feet had taken.

He found, upon examination, that the confusion of footmarks soon ceased.

Following them carefully, he observed that, at merely a step or two from the hut, the only footprints visible were from the hoofs of a horse.

"He is carrying the boys in his saddle!" he said to himself.

He continued following these tracks in a direction with which he seemed perfectly well acquainted.

He paused suddenly with knitted brows and a thoughtful expression on his keen dark features.

"He has taken the road leading to the morass. Why has he gone there?"

Ah! why?

Chapter XXI.

IN THE MORASS.

DEATH is described in the figurative language of the inspired volume as mounted on a *pale horse*.

As Octavius Challoner rode along on this gloomy night, with the two orphan boys before him, he looked like a darker copy of the original picture.

Could his features have been revealed, and the deadly expression of his eyes translated as he proceeded on his journey, he would have been found to represent no exaggerated picture of the arch destroyer gloating over the destruction of innocence.

During the ride he took every possible care to enlarge upon the *crime* the poor children had committed.

He laboured most successfully to bring home a harrowing conviction of guilt to their childish hearts.

Again and again he stabbed them through and through with the terrible penalties the law had in store for them if it caught them.

Their hearts died within them as they contemplated the atrocity of their crime.

So far from their youth being any extenuation of their guilt, their remorseless accuser made it appear to them as enhancing its magnitude tenfold, proving them more than usually depraved.

To be only ten years old, and to have caused the death of a poor young gentleman not more than their own age, was an awful crime for all good folks to shudder at.

The poor children trembled like aspens in the dark, surrounded as they were by ghastly terrors that their arch enemy conjured up at every word.

They travelled on thus for some time.

They no longer stood on the summit of the lofty cliffs.

They had been descending gradually, though they knew it not, and were rapidly drawing near the spot that Ishmael Morgan had pictured to himself with so much dread.

This was a wild and lonely tract of country known as the EASTERN MORASS.

Into this the streams from the neighbouring mountains trickled incessantly.

Its treacherous bosom sucked in these constant supplies, and whilst outwardly it looked—at times especially—firm and solid, it was in reality a region of perpetual swamp.

Many an unsuspecting traveller had urged his steed onwards over its deceitful surface without discovering the fatal mistake until beyond the possibility of reparation.

Slowly but surely the slimy deposit sucked them in, until, entirely engulfed, both horse and rider perished miserably.

The traveller who essayed to journey along the sloping edge of this dangerous morass had need to be well acquainted with his path.

At night, too, the route would of course be trebly difficult.

But Octavius was intimately cognisant of its perils, and felt himself perfectly secure, having frequently travelled this road.

James and Ikey were utterly ignorant where they were.

As Mr. Challoner guided his horse along the edge of the morass, the rain which had been drizzling throughout the journey gradually ceased, and a sickly, yellow-looking moon peered down through the mist and partially lighted up the fatal marsh that spread out its treacherous surface at their feet.

But it did not impress the boys as terrible

It was simply inanimate nature, and as such had no horrors for them.

All the bogs and quagmires that had ever engulfed travellers, or bred agues, had not for them one tithe of the dread that a gamekeeper or a constable would have inspired.

They looked upon the widely-extending morass as they would have done on any other desolate tract of land.

It appeared solitary, certainly, but nothing more. Its surface was covered with herbage and peat, and they would not have hesitated a moment to run down the sloping bank and trust themselves to its deceitful bosom.

Its very loneliness was rather a recommendation to the self-convicted child-criminals, and the irregular clumps of rank weeds that rose up darkly from the surface seemed to offer places of concealment from two prying eyes.

But this was only because they, poor things, knew no better.

Those who were more experienced in the matter would have shuddered at the thought of trusting their feet on its apparently solid surface.

There were certain narrow paths intersecting it where the footing was secure, but these required the most accurate knowledge of the locality to venture over even in the daytime; but at night it was an utter impossibility.

The green rank verdure that flourished on the surface of this terrible abyss smiled on the passer-by with its tempting hues, only to betray: wooing him to venture, where to set his foot was destruction.

Perhaps for one or two steps all seemed safe, but at the third the foothold was lost, and the traveller's leg disappeared in the soft mud; at the fourth, the other leg followed.

Then came the terror, the sudden desperate effort to return—but all in vain !

Every succeeding struggle increased the peril.

The unfortunate sank to his waist, and could distinctly feel himself gradually sinking lower and lower.

Then came the horror of impending death:

The arms flung widely above the head—the desperate cry for help, where no help was.

And now, with all these agonising efforts, the victim has gradually been drawn in as though by some supernatural agency, till he is up to his neck in this terrible slough.

But he does not remain in this position long.

He sinks lower and lower.

The slimy surface touches his lips.

He recoils and throws back his head with heart loathing, to escape the muddy death draught.

All in vain !

Lower and lower still !

He utters a last dreadful shriek—his mouth is filled with the stagnant filth.

He essays one final desperate bound, but there is no place on which to rest his foot; the very effort sinks him still deeper.

One more faint struggle, one more bubbling, choking, gasping sigh, and the surface of the morass closes over the victim's head for ever.

Such, then, was the place at the edge of which Octavius Challoner stood, mounted on his horse, with the two boys before him, contemplating the region of destruction.

His thoughts were dark and deathlike as the scene around.

There lay the stagnant mass sweltering in the mild night, giving out its humid exhalations, which floated as they rose in the night mist.

There flickered and danced the lambent flame of the *Ignis Fatuus* or *Will-o'-the-wisp*, now floating on the surface of the swamp, and then darting playfully along with its lurid light, as though in spectral revelry. On these objects Octavius stood looking in an absorbed and moody manner.

The poor boys, too, also gazed silently, and found some food for speculation in the meteoric appearances that flitted before them.

Ikey seemed to be acquainted with these vaporous goblins.

"Do you know vot them lights is?" he asked his companion, in a whisper.

"No," said James; "I never saw them before."

"Theer Jack-o'-lanterns," Ikey explained; "theer good coves, too, on a dark night; they runs afore traw'llers vot's lost theer vay, an' shows 'em a light."

"That's very kind of them," remarked James.

The thoughts of Octavius were far different.

He rejoiced in the hope that his cousin was dead—drowned at sea; he had no doubt that such was the case, but he could not repel the suspicion that the boys, James Cook and Ikey Mangles, had heard his conversation with the pirates in the cavern.

He could not rest under this idea, and felt that their death was necessary to his safety.

How he had endeavoured to bring about this event, by enclosing them in the rock, and how his horrible design had been frustrated, the reader knows.

The boys still lived, and he had brought them deliberately to this lonely morass, to ensure for them a fate more certain.

Why, then, as he stood on the edge of this deadly slough, did he not coolly take them in his arms, and plunge them into its muddy depths?

It would have been but the work of an instant. They could not have resisted, and he would have been for ever free from their unwelcome presence. Why, then, did he not at once destroy them?

It was this that deterred him:

He knew well the commandment, *" Thou shalt do no murder;"* the words seemed to look him full in the face, written in large brazen letters, glaring at him from the gloomy sky.

He had made one attempt to take the lives of his victims, and they had been wonderfully preserved; but though he earnestly desired their death, to make a second attempt *he dared not.*

That is, not a direct attempt.

He would have stood by and watched their dying struggles with exultation, and yet he could not summon up resolution sufficient to take them up in his arms and deliberately cast them into the morass.

He now stood ruminating on the brink, as it were weapon in hand, but afraid to strike.

He bit his lips in a fearful state of indecision.

How were they to be got rid of ?

The Spirit of Evil was not long in coming to the assistance of so faithful a servant as Octavius Challoner.

The suggestions he offered were to this effect :

"If I were you," he whispered, "I don't think I should lay a finger on these children; murder has always an ugly sound, and is as well avoided, especially when the result may be arrived at by other means."

Octavius coincided in this idea, which at that moment was very congenial to him.

The fiend continued :

"Those means are entirely within your grasp. You

[FLOORING THE BEADLE.]

are now at the very brink of a morass, from which none who have the misfortune to fall into it, ever return alive. These children are unacquainted with the treacherous nature of the quagmire. You have very skilfully worked upon their imaginations, till they 'fear each bush an officer.' Why not go a step further, and lead them to imagine they are pursued at this very moment? The *ruse* could not possibly fail—you could advise them to fly for their lives: guided by you, they would, of course, run blindly into the morass—its capacious maw would receive them into its depths, and no questions would be asked or answered, since the dead can reveal nothing."

This plan was eagerly embraced by Octavius, and relieved him from every difficulty, since it promised him the result he desired, whilst his hand was not required directly to strike the blow.

Whilst he was thinking how to get up an alarm of pursuit, the means were, by a kind of fatality, placed in his hands.

No. 8.—The Adventures of Captain Cook.

A voice was heard shouting in the distance.

The boys, who were now tremblingly alive to every sight and sound, shivered again.

Their diseased imaginations distorted every object on which they fastened.

"What's that?" they cried, in dismay, clinging to Octavius, in their desperation, for protection.

Octavius himself pretended great anxiety.

"Sh—sh!" he cried, in a cautious tone, as though fearful that even the wind should waft his words to the advancing parties. "Let me listen!"

He strained his ear attentively, and murmured audibly as he did so:

"It sounds like a horse's hoofs—yes! I am not mistaken; who can it be?—surely not——"

He listened still more anxiously.

The boys could hear his heart throb and feel his limbs tremble.

"Alas, yes!" he cried, suddenly, "there's no doubt of it, *it is*——"

"Who? what?" inquired the anxious boys.

"The constables, *after you!*" returned the cruel Octavius, with crushing emphasis.

The boys uttered a cry of hopeless dismay.

"Oh, what shall we do?—where shall we go?" they exclaimed, with all the excitement of extreme terror.

"Run!—fly for your lives!" answered Octavius, vehemently, lowering them to the ground.

"Where?—which way?" they asked, eagerly.

"Anywhere—no matter whither!—see, straight before you are reeds and shrubs, behind which you may hide yourselves!"

The false guide pointed right across the morass.

"Come hon!" cried Ikey, desperately; and without an instant's hesitation, or even staying to thank their treacherous informant, they ran down the sloping bank into the pit of destruction.

It bore them on its bosom firmly.

But they were very light weights.

"Run on!" cried Octavius. "I'll put the constables off the scent, and when they've passed I'll call out."

But there was one who called out before him.

This was Ikey, who, making a hasty step forward, sank up to his knees in mud.

"Take care, Jem," he cried, but with no great alarm expressed in his tone, "Hi've got my leg in a 'ole; don't come this vay!"

But it was too late to pause.

James had already taken his step in the same direction as Ikey, and with a similar result.

"I've got mine in a hole, too," he cried.

Then immediately followed another exclamation. Their left legs had followed their right: both were now firmly imbedded in the slush. They felt they were by degrees sinking lower and lower.

"Hi say, Jem," said Ikey, "Hi don't like this; Hi'm stuck fast in the mud, and can't get hout any'ow?"

"So am I!" James exclaimed.

They were close together, and that was some consolation.

"Hi vonder 'ow far it his to th' bottom?" remarked Ikey, dubiously.

"It doesn't seem to have any bottom," returned James; "at least, I can't feel any."

"P'r'aps ve shall find a 'ard bit presently," Ikey said; "give us yer 'and, an' Hi'll feel about with my foot."

James grasped his companion's hand, whilst Ikey struck out in all directions with his legs, but without coming upon anything solid.

The only discovery he made was that his exertions had sunk him deeper in the mire, which now reached up to his waist.

James also found himself gradually going down.

"What did it mean?"

Up to this moment they had had no idea of the actual peril of their position; but as the cold, slimy filth gradually, almost imperceptibly enveloped them, they began to awake to the consciousness of danger.

"Ve shall be smothered in this 'ere," said Ikey, "if it comes over our 'eads."

"I can't make out where we are," James exclaimed, anxiously.

"Ve'd better ask Mr. Hotty to 'elp us hout. Mr. Hotty! Mr. Hotty! please come an' give us a 'and up!" Ikey cried.

The appeal was made in vain.

The boys could see their pretended friend mounted on his horse, standing on the brink of the morass, coolly looking down upon them.

"Help us, sir, please! help us!" fell distinctly on his ear.

The heartless wretch stirred not, but smiled with grim satisfaction as he watched the poor little victims struggling in the slough, and gradually becoming less and less as its greedy jaws sucked them in.

"Mr. Hotty! Mr. Hotty!" shrieked Ikey. "Help us!"

"Turn to the right!" cried the mocking brute, "and then you can't go wrong; you'll find a path there."

"There isn't any path, sir!" called out James; "and we're sinking deeper and deeper every moment."

"I'm werry nigh hup to my shoulders!" bawled Ikey, desperately.

"Have patience," returned Octavius, who could not resist the brutal jest; "it will be over your head shortly."

But poor Ikey, who found himself getting every moment deeper and deeper into the mire, could not be patient.

"Ve shall be smothered!" he shouted, in a voice of terror. "'Elp us—'elp us!"

The cry had hardly burst from his lips, when, as if in answer, a voice that the boys ought to have recognised rang out through the night air, at no great distance from them.

But, strange as it may seem, they did not so distinguish it.

Their senses must have been paralysed with terror, or they would surely have remembered the friendly tones of Tinker Morgan.

His voice was not raised in reply to their cry for help.

Probably he had not heard it.

He seemed rather to be shouting at random, in order that the boys, if they were within hearing, might know they had a friend at hand.

Both James and Ikey heard his voice but their bewildered senses translated it into the voice of an enemy.

The poor children were immediately silenced.

"It's the constables arter us!" gasped Ikey, in a low, quivering voice.

"They won't find us," answered James, gloomily, "nor anyone else, in a few moments more."

"I shall call hout at vonce, then," cried his companion, desperately. "I feels as I'd sooner be 'anged than smothered in this 'ere muck. 'Elp!—elp!" he shouted again.

At that moment James cried out, excitedly:

"Don't call, Ikey; I feel something hard under my feet."

"Hi don't; Hi'm a sinkin' as fast as Hi can. Hi can feel th' mud hunder my chin."

"Come this way; let me pull you."

Poor Ikey, too glad to see the smallest glimpse of a chance to be saved from suffocation, clung to his companion's hand, and floundered in the direction in which he was pulled.

The effort was successful, and suddenly he too cried out:

"Hi feels something 'ard!"

What it was that offered them a resting-place for their feet they knew not; but certain it was, they found themselves all on a sudden standing on some solid substance, just at the time when another instant would have seen them over their head and ears in the slough.

As it was, they were imbedded in the muddy quagmire up to their necks.

But that seemed as nothing.

They had, as it were, received a reprieve at the last moment; or, at least, sentence of death had been deferred.

"I don't mind this," said Ikey, in the first burst of his joy, "so long as th' muck don't come hinter my mouth."

Once more Ishmael's voice was heard shouting.

Octavius began to think it was time to withdraw.

He accordingly drew back from the edge of the path, and retreated into the gloom.

The boys' voices were no longer audible, and their heads alone being above the surface, they were barely visible in the uncertain light.

Octavius believed the brief struggle was over, and that they had perished.

But he felt curious to know who the approaching traveller might be.

He accordingly waited to see.

Shrouded in the misty obscurity that hung around, he remained perfectly secure from observation.

He had hardly vacated his post, when Ishmael Morgan came up, and stood upon the spot he had recently occupied.

The Gipsy paused upon his journey, providentially, just at the right spot.

There was no particular reason why he should have stopped just where he did.

He might as well have continued his course fifty or a hundred yards farther.

It seemed as though it was ordained he should halt there for a special purpose.

He glanced round anxiously.

All was silent; and yet, as he came along, he fancied he heard cries for help.

He strained his eyes over the dark, wide-spreading swamp at his feet.

A cold shudder ran through his stalwart frame, as his fears suggested that the two poor boys he was in search of might be lying buried in the stagnant mass, as far beyond the reach of assistance as the crime that hurried them to their early graves would be beyond the power of detection.

Casting the rays of his lanthorn downwards, he anxiously scanned the misty surface of the swamp so far as the light permitted.

"Surely he cannot have had the heart to destroy the poor orphans!" he murmured.

Jem and Ikey saw the dark figure on the brink, but they took it, as a matter of course, for Octavius.

Help from him they now felt to be a hopeless expectation.

Therefore they made no further appeal, but remained silent in their critical position, wishing earnestly that it was day, that they might form some idea of the extent of their danger.

Ishmael, disappointed in his fruitless search, thought he would try his voice again.

He therefore called aloud:

"Jem! Ikey! are you here?"

"It's Tinker Morgan!" exclaimed the boys, as they recognised the friendly tones.

The quick ears of the Gipsy caught his remarks.

"They are somewhere near, and they are alive, thank Heaven!" he joyfully exclaimed.

"I hear your voices," he continued, "but I can't see you. Where are you?"

"Here, Morgan!" cried James.

"An' ve're hup to hour necks in th' mud," added Ikey, impressively.

This intelligence, if not very satisfactory, was at least explicit.

Ishmael descended instantly from his saddle.

"How far are you from the bank—have you any idea?" he asked.

"We're not fur," answered Ikey; "if yer looks straight for'ards yer'll see our 'eads, vich is hall of us as his wisible."

By dint of the most earnest scrutiny, the Gipsy at length descried two round, white objects, that had the appearance of two toadstools sprouting up out of the mud.

"I see you, my boys!" he cried, joyfully; "but the difficulty now is how to get at you. I must think."

"This is the quickest way!" hissed a voice behind him.

He turned quickly at the familiar, but unpleasant sound, when a violent blow lighted on his forehead between his eyes, and he fell backwards with a heavy thud into the morass.

"You'll be able to get at them now!" the same mocking voice repeated.

There was a moment of silence, broken only by the retreat of Octavius, who, having mounted his horse, galloped off, leading with him the gray steed of his first victim.

Chapter XXII.

RESCUED!

THE squire's nephew rode along through the dark, with his head bent forward in the saddle, and in a hurried and anxious manner, as though some ugly monster were at his heels scaring him onwards.

Nothing, however, was to be seen but the occasional shadows of the horses and the rider, thrown by the faint moon athwart the road.

It may, therefore, be imagined that no uglier monster was at hand than the guilty conscience Mr. Challoner carried in his own breast.

But this of all the haunting spectres superstition has created, is the ugliest and the most terrible.

The guilty rider after galloping far away from the scene of his murderous acts, paused at length, to wipe the cold drops from his brow.

He then—not because he particularly desired such a retrospect, but simply because he couldn't help it—found himself briefly summing up his recent deeds.

His mental register briefly but distinctly noted them down as follows:

"*Imprimis*: GEORGE CAREW.—*A dangerous witness of a past deed of guilt. Got rid of by a cowardly stab in the dark, and a plunge over the cliff—dead!*

"AUGUSTUS MARKHAM.—*My nephew, whom I would have destroyed, but who saved me the trouble by getting drowned—dead!*

"JAMES COOK and IKEY MANGLES.—*Two poor boys for whom nobody cares. Suspected of knowing too much for my safety, and led by me into the morass, where they perished miserably—dead!*

"ISHMAEL MORGAN.—*A Gipsy vagabond, who intruded himself into my affairs, and has received his reward at my hands—dead!*

"Total—FIVE SOULS FOR WHICH I MUST GIVE AN ACCOUNT."

Five souls! This was the terrible summing up!

No wonder as this thought fastened on his mind, the guilty wretch felt the cold drops he had just wiped from his forehead oozing out again.

No wonder he shuddered, as though an ague fit had passed through his frame, or that he once more spurred on his horse, as though he would have flown to the world's end to get rid of the accusing voice within.

Onward he went, guilt-haunted, till he found himself drawing near to the Hall.

There were two ways by which he might approach the park.

One was by a narrow lane, the other by the main road, at an angle of which stood the ancient village church, looking very time-worn and hoary in the dim moonlight.

The yew trees reared themselves dark and majestic in the churchyard, defying the cold and wind to strip them of their sombre green, whilst their brethren were dismantled of their foliage, and stretched forth their bare, leafless branches, casting fantastic shadows on the bleached tombstones that covered the dead ashes that slept beneath them.

He paused as the church came in sight, as though hesitating which path to take.

The narrow lane was distasteful to him, in his present state of mind, and he almost hesitated to pass the sacred edifice blood-stained with murder as he was.

The dead silence of the hour, too, added to the peculiar awe that in spite of himself stole over him.

"Am I turned coward?" he murmured to himself. "Psha, courage!" he added, with a desperate attempt to regain his self-possession—"what have I to fear?"

He walked his horse forward, still leading the noble gray by his bridle, intending to pass the church humbly and quietly, and not at a gallop.

The unpretending but sacred edifice was surrounded by a low wall, so that the churchyard was distinctly visible from the road.

An aged trunk, completely covered with ivy, leant forward over the wall, as though by reason of age and infirmities it could no longer stand upright.

His eye fell upon this trunk, and though he had often seen it before, it seemed to him on this particular night to be endowed with life.

He could almost fancy it some old sylvan giant, keeping guard and nodding at his post.

He could almost see his drapery fluttering in the wind. It looked weird and strange.

Half ashamed of his own fancies, he continued to advance, when, just as he approached, a sudden and violent flapping was heard, and a pair of large owls, startled from their retreat, dashed out of a hollow in the trunk.

The fright was mutual.

Both steed and rider recoiled with a sudden terror.

"Phew!" ejaculated Octavius, whose mind was a little shaken off its balance by the overpowering weight of guilt. "I tremble like a child! yet why should I? There is no witness to my deeds but myself and my victims, and they are safe—*the dead tell no tales!*"

"No! they are reserved for the living!" returned a deep and solemn voice, that seemed to come from the old trunk.

The guilty horseman clutched his rein with such sudden violence, that his steed reared, and fell back almost on to his haunches.

The voice seemed familiar—terribly familiar.

Surely it was the voice of the dead speaking to him!

With trembling limbs, livid features, and lips that quivered with horror, Octavius remained rooted to the spot.

His wildly-glaring eyes strove to penetrate the dark recesses of that ivy-covered trunk.

By degrees a dark object seemed to detach itself, and to wear a human form.

A figure enveloped in a cloak stood slowly revealed.

His eyes, as though magnetised, scanned the shrouded form, till at length they fastened on the face, and then——

Oh, horror! could his guilt already have found him out?

Could the ocean have given up its dead, to convict him by that ghastly presence?

Yes; there could be no doubt that it was so.

There, precisely as he had appeared during his life, only paler and sterner, stood George Carew, the President of the Confederate Brothers.

The horror of that moment was too much to endure.

His overwrought imagination drove the blood from his brain.

He muttered a few gibbering, incoherent words, and fell forward on his horse's neck in a dead faint.

*   *   *   *   *   *

The blow that hurled Ishmael into the morass was so sudden and violent, that there was no resource but to yield to it.

Consequently, the good-natured Gipsy, instead of being able to assist his young friends, found himself lying on his back half stunned, in the jaws of the morass.

But Tinker Morgan had a good strong head of his own, and it was not a single blow from a clenched fist that could knock him out of time for long.

Besides, he had a very distinct knowledge of the place into which he had fallen.

He felt that it was a "toss up" whether he ever came out again alive.

This probably had the effect of bringing him rapidly to his perfect senses.

One great proof that he had all his wits about him was, that he made not the slightest attempt to struggle.

All he did was to extend his arms and legs very quietly, so as to make as much surface as possible to float upon the stagnant mass.

James and Ikey, who had witnessed the sudden and precipitate descent of their friend, without exactly knowing how it had been brought about, were somewhat surprised to see him lying with such apparent composure on his back.

As he neither moved nor spoke for a few moments, the boys began to be apprehensive.

They had heard the words of Octavius, and seen his retreating form as he rode off, and this was sufficient to lead them to suppose that he had done the Gipsy some kind of injury.

James, unable longer to repress his anxiety, spoke to him.

"Morgan—Morgan!" he exclaimed, cautiously.

"Yes, my boy?"

"Are you hurt?"

"No—nothing to speak of."

"Vot are yer doin' on?" inquired Ikey.

"Lying on my back," answered the Gipsy.

This seemed very wonderful to Ikey.

The idea of anyone lying on his back in that dangerous place was a little more than he could conceive.

"Yer hain't a goin' to sleep, hare yer?" he inquired, with some anxiety.

"I hope not," replied Ishmael, rather drily. "If I do, it strikes me I shall never wake again in this world."

"Vot're yer lyin' on yer back for, then?"

"I'm thinking how to save your lives, and my own," returned the Gipsy.

"Be as quick as yer can, theer's a good feller!" Ikey cried. "I feels so jolly huncomfortable!"

"How deep have you sunk in the mud?" asked Ishmael, quietly.

"We're both up to our necks," James answered.

"Poor boys—poor boys!" murmured the Gipsy, who felt his own legs beginning to sink, but who was still able to sympathise with the boys, who were so much nearer than himself to destruction.

James heard his friend's ejaculations, and wished to give him some hope that their case was not quite so bad as he seemed to think.

"I don't think we shall sink any lower, Morgan," he said.

"What makes you think so?" the Gipsy asked, with a melancholy smile of incredulity.

"Because it feels hard underfoot," replied James.

"Does it?" eagerly exclaimed Morgan.

"Yes," said Ikey. "Ve've bin a standin' just vhere ve hare now for hever so long, an' ve hain't sunk a hinch lower. If ve 'ad, ve should a' 'ad our mouths full long ago."

This intelligence was exceedingly gratifying to Ishmael, and it set him thinking how to account for it.

He soon came to a conclusion.

"They must either have got on to a clump of roots that have matted together from the bottom, or else they are standing on one of the solid paths that lie a little below the surface," he thought.

"Remain where you are! Don't move!" he added.

There was not much necessity for this injunction.

Both the boys set far too much value on the small portion of solid ground on which they stood to have any desire to venture from off it.

"Does it feel very solid where you are?" asked Morgan.

"Yes," said Ikey. "It seems as hif ve vos a standin' hon the top of a vall as vos kivered with moss."

"That's one of the sunken paths," soliloquised the Gipsy. "How fortunate!"

"If you could give us your hand, Morgan," said James, "I think we might be able to pull you on too."

"Or I might pull you off, I'm afraid," returned the Gipsy.

As he spoke he glanced round cautiously, and saw that a very short distance separated them. It then struck him if he could turn on his face, and contrive to reach one of the boy's hands, he would be easily able to draw himself forward to where they were posted.

Now, all this was to be managed with the greatest coolness.

There was to be no floundering or struggling, or kicking.

Any such acts would have been fatal to the success of the plan.

The boys, who were not strong, would have been dragged from their circumscribed place of refuge, and all would have perished.

All that Morgan wanted was one of their small hands outstretched, on which he could rest the tips of his fingers.

This would be sufficient to keep his head from being covered by the mire, and his body, as it sank, assuming the perpendicular, would be almost close to theirs.

Having thus made up his mind what to attempt, he said, in the same quiet tone that had characterised all his words:

"Hold fast to each other, and one of you stretch out one of your hands, keeping the palm upwards."

The boys planted their feet as firmly as they could in the concrete soil, or roots, or whatever it was on which they stood, and clasping each other, according to the Gipsy's direction, James extended his hand.

It was not visible, being beneath the surface, but the boy raised it gently.

It was begrimed with mud, but the Gipsy could see it.

"Are you ready?" he asked.

"Yes," replied the boys, who felt quite elated at the thought, that instead of Tinker Morgan helping them, they were going to help him.

It made them feel quite big and strong.

"Now, my boys," said the Gipsy, "remember this: as soon as my hand rests upon the one now stretched out towards me, you must both lean in the opposite direction, as though you were pulling away from me; by so doing you will counteract my weight, and be able to keep your balance."

The boys comprehended, and promised to obey.

All being ready, Ishmael exclaimed:

"Now for it!" And immediately, by an energetic motion, turned himself over in the same manner as he would have done had he been swimming.

At the same moment he extended his hand, and found that at full stretch the tips of his fingers could just touch those of James.

The pressure experienced by the boy was but slight, whilst it was sufficient to keep the head of the Gipsy out of the mire.

His body sank gradually in the slimy mud till, on its reaching the perpendicular, he found himself, as he expected, close to the boys.

How James and Ikey rejoiced to have their stanch friend once more by their sides!

How exultant they felt!

"There is now only one thing more to be done, and that is to get a footing on the same spot as that on which you stand," said Ishmael.

"Can't you mount up on to it?" asked James.

"That's just what I'm going to try," returned the Gipsy.

He raised his leg as he spoke; and after one or two efforts he found that his foot rested on a foundation considerably firmer than mud, though by no means so solid as he could have wished. However, having got foothold, he, by a strong muscular effort, sprang upwards, and to his joy found himself the next instant standing upon some substance, which, if not rock, appeared at least to him firm enough to support its burden.

The first congratulations having passed, Ishmael looked anxiously around him.

They were at this moment about twelve yards from the bank, and though rescued providentially from immediate peril, were by no means yet in a place of security.

Morgan stood upright, with the boys clinging to him, considering what would be the best next step to take.

It seemed more than probable they would have to remain in their present plight until morning dawned upon the desolate scene.

And even then it was a chance whether any traveller passed by to whom they could send any message for help.

The boys were up to their necks in mud, which only reached to the upper portion of the Gipsy's thighs.

He looked as pitifully down upon the two brave little fellows as they looked piteously up to him. He felt inclined to take them in his arms; but a moment's reflection convinced him that this was impracticable, since he could not have supported their weight hour after hour in the insecure position he then occupied, and in the event of any casualty occurring he would have been hampered beyond the possibility of extrication.

He therefore stifled his feelings, and after speaking a few words of encouragement, he looked once more around him.

Behind and on either side extended the monotonous surface of the swamp, whilst in front rose the shelving banks, only a few yards from them.

It was a cruel position.

Death was on all sides, and the only place of safety, though close at hand, they were utterly unable to reach.

It was like being wrecked in sight of port.

And now even while he was thus looking, Morgan fancied he could feel the foundation on which they stood becoming less firm.

Strong-nerved as he was, a cold sweat broke out upon him at the mere thought.

But it might have been fancy, and he paused before expressing an opinion which, however groundless, would have awakened the apprehensions of his young charges.

But even while he was trying to cheat himself into the belief that the motion he felt had been fancy, he experienced a repetition of the sensation. And if further proof had been wanting, the boys, in a tone of alarm, cried out:

"Oh, Morgan!—Morgan! the ground's moving under our feet!"

There was no doubt it was so, but the Gipsy strove to dissipate their fears.

"Oh, no!" he cried, "you must be mistaken!"

"No—no! we're not!" they exclaimed together, "we're sinking deeper; we're standing now on tiptoe, and holding on to you, and even then we can hardly keep our mouths out of the slush."

This was a painful but positive proof that Morgan could not dispute, though it was with a heavy heart he acknowledged it to himself.

"Lift us up in your arms, will you, please, Morgan?" asked James, "or we shall be smothered."

"Certainly I will, my poor boys," responded the kindly-hearted Gipsy. "I'll do all I can for you: that's why I came here, though," he murmured to himself, "I fear it's little good I can do now either for you or myself."

As he spoke he drew them up gently, dripping with the slippery mud in which they were encased, and supported them in his arms.

"You're very kind, dear Morgan," whispered James, pressing his besmeared lips against the Gipsy's cheek.

"Yes, that yer his!" warmly acquiesced Ikey, giving his friend a very muddy squeeze to express his gratitude.

The poor tinker, rough Gipsy, poacher, vagrant as he was, felt strangely moved at these tokens from these children, and the hot tears trickled from his eyes.

But there was little time for weeping.

He became suddenly aroused to the painful consciousness that the interwoven mass on which they stood was gradually and rapidly giving way beneath their feet.

He had already sunk in the mire up to his breast.

How he reproached himself at that moment for having, by the additional weight of his body, expedited this calamity!

But it was too late to repair the mistake now.

He was fettered too with the frightened boys, who in the dim moonlight saw the hungry swamp gradually but slowly drawing them into its inexorable jaws.

"Oh, Morgan! dear Morgan! can't you save us somehow?" they cried.

"Alas, my boys, I'm afraid not!" was the sad answer.

It seemed terrible to those young innocents to die like that, and not less formidable to the strong man appeared the King of Terrors as he scowled upon him face to face in that hideous swamp.

And now, with a sudden motion, their treacherous foothold sank a foot deeper.

The Gipsy's head was all that was above the surface.

With desperate energy he grasped the slender arms of the boys, and hoisted them in the air.

They were enabled to take a momentary gasp of breath.

In a wild tone that despair rendered almost unearthly, Ishmael shouted:

"Help! help! help!"

The cry echoed far and wide across the swamp, that seemed to absorb it, but no answer was returned.

"Help! help!" again rang through the air.

This was the last; for at that moment the mass suddenly broke from under them, and the Gipsy, still clasping his young friends tenaciously, was plunged headlong forwards.

Where?

Into the depths of the fatal slough, whose slimy filth was to be the grave of its unfortunate victims?

No! but, on the contrary, on to a solid path that extended—not more than a few inches beneath the surface—almost close to their side.

It was fortunate Ishmael had grasped the boys as firmly as he did, or the sudden shock of the fall would inevitably have shaken them from his hold.

But determined that if they must perish they would go together, he had held on with a grasp of iron.

The first impulse, at this wonderful preservation, was naturally a feeling of gratitude to Heaven.

"Thank God!" cried Ishmael, fervently, falling on his knees. "Thank God for this! Are you safe?" he asked, in an earnest and excited manner.

"Yes, Morgan!" answered James, with equal excitement. "Quite safe!"

"Let me feel your arms round me!" exclaimed the impetuous Gipsy, who, in his excited gratitude, felt quite paternal. "Embrace me!"

He threw his arms eagerly round the boys, or rather *boy*, for there was but *one*.

Ishmael paused aghast: one hand clasped James;

the other grasped—not Ikey, but *his coat*—the poor boy was not in it!

Where was he?

James shrieked in an agony of dismay, and would have thrown himself, in his eagerness to discover his comrade, after him, had not Ishmael restrained him.

The Gipsy started to his feet, and looked with eager eyes in the direction in which he supposed the poor boy had fallen.

To his great joy, he beheld a small object struggling desperately in the mud, within arm's-length, and almost simultaneously the half-stifled voice of the half-smothered unfortunate announced that he was still in the land of the living.

In an instant he was grasped by Morgan, and clasped in his arms, where, with beating heart and heaving breast, the poor child lay panting till the breath of life had returned to him again.

"You're better now, my man?" asked the Gipsy.

"Y—es," said Ikey; "but don't let me fall in there agin, please; Hi vas nearly smothered."

"No, no," returned Morgan, "we're safe now: the ground we're treading on's as firm as rock."

This was one of the intersecting paths before alluded to, which afforded a secure footway over the morass.

These paths were at certain seasons, principally in the summer, when, on account of the dryness of the weather the swamp was low, perfectly visible and safe to travel in the daytime; but at this season all were completely covered, the entire extent of the morass presenting nothing but one continuous unbroken muddy lake.

The spot on which the boys first, and subsequently Morgan, had set their feet, was a mass of alluvial deposit that had rested on some old roots springing up from the bottom, and which, increasing from time to time, had formed a kind of sunken mound, which,

though strong enough to support the light weight of James and Ikey, had gradually given way under the heavier tread of the Gipsy.

However, as the result of the catastrophe was so satisfactory, this was a matter of congratulation rather than regret.

They were all safe, and it now only remained for them to reach the bank as speedily as possible.

It was necessary, however, to proceed with the utmost caution.

One rash step on either side, since the path was barely three feet in width, would have plunged them again into the fatal slough.

An idea entered the Gipsy's head, upon which he immediately proceeded to act.

With some difficulty, he managed to fish up from his pockets, saturated as they were with slimy mud, a small bag of bullets and a coil of twine.

Having fastened the bag to the string, he proceeded on the principle of sounding.

Keeping the boys close together before him, and heaving the leaden weights on both sides of the pathway, so as not to step beyond the solid track, he was enabled gradually but safely, to approach the bank.

Once more they stood on the solid ground in safety.

Ishmael was a little chagrined to find the gray steed had disappeared, but he checked his regrets at the loss of the horse by reflecting how narrow an escape he had had of losing his life.

To repine would have been ungrateful.

"Come on, boys!" he exclaimed, in a cheerful tone, "we've a long pull before us, but I must carry you by turns. By the time we get to the camp we shall be baked dry in a crust of mud."

With these words he caught up the boys, and set off at a sharp pace, carrying one under each arm, as though they had been a pair of chickens.

Chapter XXIII.

THE GIPSY CAMP.

WHEN Octavius recovered consciousness, he found himself lying in the road, with his horse quietly standing by his side.

He slowly rose to his feet, fully expecting to encounter the cloaked figure that had so appalled him.

But it was gone.

The gray steed had also disappeared.

His mind was in a state of great confusion, and he shivered with cold from head to foot.

It was with some difficulty in his present unnerved state, he contrived to drag himself on his horse's back, and continue his journey towards the Hall.

However, he reached it at last, and utterly prostrate in body and mind, he sought his chamber.

He slept from sheer exhaustion, but on awakening the next morning, felt little better for the rest he had taken.

There was none of the buoyancy of spirits that follows upon sound and refreshing slumber.

But instead, a heavy languor weighed him down.

A terrible apprehension pressed like lead upon his heart as the cloaked figure of the President recurred to him.

He tried to argue himself into the belief that what he had seen proceeded from an over-excited imagination.

But then the gray steed had vanished.

But still even that was not conclusive.

The animal, finding itself at liberty, would naturally wander away, as it had done before.

He strove earnestly to rouse himself—to throw off the feelings that oppressed him—and with some success.

As the morning wore away, and nothing transpired, —no officers of justice appearing to arrest him—he began to be himself again.

By the time he had breakfasted, and drank several glasses of wine to steady his nerves, he was perfectly calm, and had almost made up his mind that the figure He had gazed upon was not reality, but merely a phantom of his brain.

Poor Squire Markham was still inconsolable at the loss of his son, and in the midst of the general grief and excitement that prevailed, any depression that Octavius might exhibit would be attributed to his sympathy with his bereaved uncle.

He endeavoured to soothe the sorrowing parent with the hope that the boy would be found.

He inwardly rejoiced at the conviction that this hope could never be realised; but he contrived to cheer up the old man with hope at last.

Then, to ease his conscience, he thought it would be an act of charity to bury poor Mrs. Cook, whose body lay in the desolate cottage, unnoticed and uncared for.

He accordingly gave the orders for her funeral. The conscience of Mr. Octavius Challoner must have been easily pacified, since everything was to be done in the humblest and cheapest manner possible. The coffin was not even to be covered with cloth, or studded with nails, but plain wood, such as a pauper might expect. Such useless additions were only for those who could afford to pay for them.

Having performed this magnanimous act, he sat down to dinner, congratulating himself that he had atoned for his crimes towards the living by his considerate treatment of the dead.

* * * * * * *

When Ishmael Morgan reached the camp, smothered in mud, with his charges in a similar state packed under each arm, he excited no little surprise.

As he had predicted, by the time they reached the tents the mud had dried, and they then presented an appearance more like three newly-discovered specimens of the crustaceous order of animals than human beings.

However, in course of time their dirt-encrusted garments were exchanged for others; and having been well warmed at the fire, and refreshed by a plentiful meal of steaming soup, the tired boys were packed away in a snug corner of Ishmael's tent, where they soon forgot all their troubles in a deep slumber.

Great was the indignation of the tribe when Ishmael recounted the events that had taken place, and in which he had taken so prominent a part.

Dark eyes flashed, and angry arms were raised threateningly, as they listened to the cowardly attempt against the life of one of their tribe.

A volley of fierce execrations drowned the voice of the narrator.

"Let's burn down the Hall!" cried a dozen furious voices, "and scorch the accursed Gentile in the flames!"

They started up with angry vehemence, rife for any violence, and had the object of their indignation shown himself at that moment, they would have infallibly have torn him limb from limb.

As it was, they shouted to Ishmael to lead them on to the work of retribution.

Their excited fury was arrested by the voice of a white-haired patriarch of their tribe.

"Stay—you are too hasty!" he cried.

Phares Darro had been a great man among them in his day, and even in his old age his voice had a constraining power.

They paused at his words, and turned towards him, but impatiently.

"Why should the innocent suffer for the guilty?" asked the old Gipsy.

"They are all alike—they are a cruel race—hard and unjust!" cried the impetuous men; "death to them!"

"No," returned the patriarch; "they are not all alike, neither are they all hard and unjust. Squire Markham has several times shown kindness to us wanderers."

This was a fact not to be denied, and several of the men softened down at once.

"It is not against the squire we owe any grudge," they answered; "but against the would-be squire, his nephew. Ask Morgan, and he will tell you that had the power of this Octavius been equal to his will, his hands would have been doubly dyed with innocent blood!"

A groan of execration followed these words.

"Is it not so, Ishmael?" they inquired, appealing to their comrade.

"It is," he replied.

"You hear, Phares!—you hear!" they shouted.

"I do; but the old man now mourns the loss of his child," returned the peace-maker, calmly. "Why, then, should we, by carrying strife and violence to his homestead, add bitterness to the grief that bows him to the earth?"

"We have said it is not against the squire we seek revenge, but against his nephew," replied the Gipsies, in more temperate tones. "You are old, Phares, and your blood is chilled, or you would not counsel us to pass over so quietly a cowardly attempt to assassinate one of our tribe."

The eye of the old man kindled, and a flush passed over his wrinkled features as he said:

"True, my blood is chilled, and my arm is feeble now, but I can still feel for the wrongs of my children; but even in the path of retribution, Justice should walk side by side with Vengeance."

"What, then, do you propose?" asked the Gipsies, impressed by the words of the old man.

"Raise no hand against the squire or the Hall; but for Octavius Challoner, when you meet him——"

"Ay—ay!" they cried eagerly; "what then?"

"Deal with him as he has dealt with others!" exclaimed the old man, firmly.

"Good—good! You counsel justly Phares!" they said, in reply; "we will abide by it; our brother Ishmael shall decree his fate, and we will see the sentence carried out. Speak, Ishmael!"

The Gipsy thus called upon to pronounce the doom of the man who would have destroyed him, glanced towards the tent where the tired children slumbered, and then said:

"In this case my voice is dumb! I cannot pronounce any sentence on this man—I mean any that our hands need inflict."

"What!" cried a score of voices, in great astonishment, "not pronounce sentence against him who, with his own hands, deliberately sought your life!"

"True, he did," returned Ishmael; "but I believe that was merely to silence my tongue from betraying his attempts against other lives, and not from any particular desire for my death. He thought I knew too much for his safety."

"By the bright stars," cried the deep voice of one of the tribe, "he has done too much for his safety!"

"What are we to do, Morgan? Speak!" they asked, unanimously.

"Nothing!"

"Nothing?"

"Leave him to himself," returned Morgan; "his plans against the innocent lives have failed, and the greatest punishment he can receive is to be allowed to live."

"To live?" ejaculated his hearers, in a tone of disappointment.

"Yes; his doom is in the future—let him wait for it; depend upon it, it will find him out!"

There was a dead pause.

This advice was highly uncongenial to the fierce, hot-blooded spirits by whom Ishmael was surrounded.

Still, as they all knew him to be a courageous and determined fellow when occasion required it, they could not attribute his present forbearance to fear.

Besides, rough and unlettered as he was, there was in his tone, as he finished his speech, something prophetic —something that led them to suppose he saw more clearly into the future than they did. They therefore yielded, though reluctantly, to his decision.

"Let him live then," exclaimed the same deep voice that had spoken before, "since our brother Ishmael wills it so; but the curse of blood is on him, and he will never prosper; it will eat away his life as rust consumes iron."

A general murmur of approval followed this brief harangue, and the Gipsies betook themselves to slumber.

The following day had partly advanced before the boys woke from their sleep.

At first they hardly remembered where they were, having latterly seen so many changes, but the pleasant recollection soon dawned upon them that they were not in the cave or the morass, but safe in the Gipsy camp.

They crawled, as soon as they were thoroughly awake, to the entrance of the tent, and ventured to look out.

It might have been expected that they would have been alarmed at the swarthy faces and curious flashing eyes that scrutinised them.

But the boys were not unused to see these wanderers of the roadside.

They did not, therefore, shrink from the eager looks, in which a rough kindliness was mingled with curiosity that told them they were among friends.

In a few moments Miriam, Morgan's wife, came to them, and after a few kind words brought them some breakfast.

It was some comfort to reflect that, with all their trials, they had not lost their appetites.

Indeed, as a kind of compensation balance to what they had endured, they had been fed considerably better than usual.

Their meal was roughly served, but the words that accompanied it were kind, and the poor boys thoroughly enjoyed it.

Before long Ishmael, who had been absent for some time, returned to the camp.

Their hearts rejoiced at the sight of him, and they felt, seated by his side, perfectly safe, in spite of his precarious condition from the pursuit of the constables.

After some conversation, poor little James, whose heart yearned to be once more by the side of his mother, and who could not fancy she was quite gone, so long as she lay there in the cottage, said in a low tone to his friend Ishmael:

"Morgan, I should like to see dear mother once more."

These words were spoken so intensely that the Gipsy looked down involuntarily upon the speaker.

"Should you?" he replied, gently.

"Oh, yes; very much! they haven't taken her away, have they?" James inquired, eagerly.

"No, not yet."

Morgan was able to speak positively upon this point, for he had just come from the cottage, where the sheeted dead lay still on the bed in her quiet sleep.

He had looked in several times, wondering who was going to consign the lifeless clay to its kindred dust. His active hands had repaired the door which the gamekeeper's heel had damaged. He felt it was a very slight service, but he performed it as a small tribute of respect to the poor woman, who had always a kind word for him while she lived.

He had besides a sort of indistinct idea that she

would somehow or other know what he had done, and this thought pleased him.

"It's only natural," Morgan said to James, "you should wish to see your mother, and you shall see her too."

"When, Morgan—when?" asked the little orphan.

"As soon as it gets dusk," answered the Gipsy; "we'd better wait till then."

"Yer'll let me go too, von't yer?" asked Ikey, who did not wish to be left behind.

"Oh yes; you shall go too," said Morgan.

This assurance perfectly satisfied the boys, who waited patiently till the day began to wane.

It being the month of January, the afternoon was but short; and as soon as it was sufficiently dark Morgan proposed starting.

To this the boys readily assented.

Once more they had changed their costume.

Miriam Morgan had washed their muddy garments, but there had been no time to dry them; their attire, therefore, was completed by voluntary contributions from the various members of the tribe, and was, consequently, of a very mixed description.

All that could be said of their garments was, they were better than none.

The evening was mild, and the sky clear for January; and as the boys trudged along they began to be conscious that they were approaching old familiar scenes.

In course of time they came to the narrow lane, and the old turnstile, the sight of which conjured up visions of Farmer Gripman and the gamekeepers.

All, however, was quiet enough now; no angry voices threatened, or angry faces frowned on them.

The narrow lane was passed through, and in a brief space they stood at the door of James's humble home.

"Home!" Sweet word! so full of joy to some, so fraught with sadness to those who have known its sweetness, and lost it.

All was very quiet there too.

Morgan paused reverently at the door, and waited a moment.

But while he did so he fancied he heard a sound within.

He listened, and said to the boys:

"Did you hear anything?"

"No," they replied.

"It must have been my fancy," said the Gipsy to himself.

He opened the door softly and entered, leading the boys, closing it after him.

They stood once more in silence with the dead.

Chapter XXIV.

AT HOME AGAIN.

IT seemed to James he had been away so long. He almost fancied to hear his mother's voice reproaching him, and that he could see her upbraiding eye fixed upon him for his neglect.

But he felt glad that he was at home once more.

It was very dark in the cottage, but James was not afraid.

He withdrew his hand from the grasp of the Gipsy, and went direct to the bed.

"Don't be angry, mother dear!" said the poor little fellow, pleadingly: "it wasn't my fault that I've been away so long."

He stretched out his arms towards the place where he expected to find his parent lying, but uttered a sudden and startling cry, that thrilled through the breast of Morgan, as he failed to find the beloved object he sought.

"She's gone!—she's gone!" he shrieked; "she's not here! they've taken her away, and I shall never see her any more!"

As he uttered these words, he threw himself forward upon the bed, sobbing bitterly, in a paroxysm of uncontrollable grief.

Ikey crept towards him in a state of considerable apprehension and concern at the emotion of his companion.

Besides, it was dark, and Ikey did not feel at all comfortable in his mind under the circumstances.

It was some relief to him when he reached James, and threw his arm round his neck.

"Don't cry so, Jemmy—don't, ole chap!" he whispered, nestling as closely as possible to the young mourner, who at that moment refused to be comforted.

"Mother! Dear mother! I shall never see her again!" wailed the orphan.

"Don't say that, Jemmy, my man!" said the comforting tones of Morgan, who was at that moment chipping away with a flint and steel, trying to get a light. "P'r'aps they've moved your mother upstairs."

This was enough to inspire the anxious boy with fresh hope.

"I'll go and see," he cried, hastily.

"Hi'll come vith yer," said Ikey.

The two boys ascended the stairs to the empty room above.

James entered unhesitatingly with Ikey at his heels.

Their eyes eagerly scanned the dark, desolate chamber.

Their search was vain.

There was nothing but the dull, cold plastered walls trying to be visible in the gloom.

No white outline shone forth of the form on which he so longed to fix his eyes.

But there was something else.

A dark shadow seemed to stand erect in a fixed, motionless attitude, as though observing them.

Ikey was the first to observe this.

"Jem—Jem!" he whispered, in a voice of terror. "D'ye see that?"

He pointed as he spoke.

"What?" inquired James. "Is it mother?"

He had no thought just then but of her.

"No!" returned Ikey, with quivering lips, "it hain't 'er—it's summat else; look!"

James looked in the direction in which his companion pulled him, and he then noticed the dark object that had so alarmed him.

"Let's call Morgan," whispered Ikey.

"No," said James; "he's lighting his lantern—don't call him. I'm not afraid, are you?"

"Vell, Hi ham a little," answered Ikey, in a tone that implied a great deal. "Hi don't like dark shadders."

"Let's go up to it and see what it is," said James.

"No, don't, Jem—don't!" entreated Ikey.

"Yes, I shall!" answered James, boldly. "Dear mother always told me, if I was afraid of anything in the dark, to go right up to it. I shall go! You needn't come, if you're afraid," he added.

This was a reproof Ikey couldn't bear.

"Hi hain't a-goin' to let yer go by yerself, Hi knows!" he exclaimed.

"Come on, then! Let's go together!" James said.

They advanced slowly but firmly towards the spot where the shadow stood.

It surely must be some one standing there wrapped in a cloak.

"Who's there?" asked James.

There was no reply.

The boy, with a kind of nervous impatience, advanced desperately and grasped—

A cloak, but that was all!

It fell to the ground with the tug he gave it.

It had been hung on a nail, and that had given way.

Ikey recoiled with affright as the garment fell down, fully impressed with the idea that it was some fierce constable or pirate, or gamekeeper, or some other deadly foe to naughty boys, about to pounce upon him.

"See!" said James, "it's nothing but a cloak after all."

This trivial event had for a time transformed the weeping boy into a heroic little philosopher.

Still it set him wondering how the cloak came there.

Some one must have been in the room to have left his cloak behind him.

"I wonder who it belongs to?" remarked James, thoughtfully.

[JAMES ENCOUNTERS THE GAMEKEEPER ONCE MORE.]

"P'r'aps it's Mr. Hotty's!" said Ikey, with a shudder. "Hi 'opes as 'e ain't a comin' 'ere."

"Morgan will take care of us, if he does," answered James, confidently.

"P'r'aps 'e knows summat about th' cloak."

"Perhaps he does; I'll ask him."

At this moment the voice of the Gipsy, who had been some time getting a light, on account of the tinder being damp, was heard calling eagerly from below.

"Jem! Jem!" he cried, "she's here!"

"Mother?" exclaimed James, with equal eagerness. "Yes!"

Cloak, shadows—all were forgotten in that word.

He flew down the stairs with as much eagerness as though he had been rushing to her embrace.

Nay, had he seen her on his descent, sitting as she used to do, ready to welcome him, he would, at that moment, have been more delighted than astonished.

So much did he yearn to gaze upon her once more—to be near her.

He paused, however, as he reached the room below, that was now lighted by the rays of the Gipsy's lantern, and recoiled in something like dismay, as his eye fell on a coffin that stood on one side of the room, supported on trestles.

He uttered an ejaculation at the same time, and then stood gazing at the dark, narrow tenement.

At length, he said, in a half whisper to Morgan:

"Is—is mother there?"

"Yes," replied the Gipsy, softly, wondering at the same time what kind friend had paid this last tribute of respect to the dead.

"Who put her in there?" asked James.

"I don't know," said Morgan; "but whoever it is, it's some one that means kindly."

"Hi think Hi knows," suddenly exclaimed Ikey, who

had followed James down stairs ; " Hi thinks as it's Mr. *Parish* 'as done this, 'cos Hi 'eerd Mr. Hotty say as Mr. *Parish* 'ud bury 'er decent."

" He means th' parish," murmured the Gipsy to himself ; " and yet," he added, " that's not like a parish coffin."

Morgan was perfectly right—it was not ; and though, on the other hand, there was nothing grand about it, it was all that decency and respect for its inmate could have demanded.

It was covered with black cloth, and studded with nails of the same colour, with a plate on the lid, on which was engraven the name of the deceased.

It was quite evident that it was Mr. Octavius Challoner's *conscience gift.*

Who then had sent it ?

The sight of the coffin, like the dark shadow in the room above, had caused a temporary suspension of the orphan's grief.

But it now began to resume its power.

" I don't like to see her shut in there," he said, at length, his tears beginning to flow afresh.

" She is warmer there, my boy," remarked Ishmael, trying to throw in a word of comfort.

" Let me look at her, Morgan," he said, wistfully ; " I want to see her."

The Gipsy raised the boy so that he could see his mother's features distinctly.

The stern rigidness had passed from them, and they had relaxed into a peaceful smile.

" Dear mother ! how pale and white she looks !" exclaimed the poor child, sadly, as he gazed with tearful eyes upon the placid face ; but he noticed the smile, and added :

" But she seems very happy though, doesn't she, Morgan ?"

" Yes, my boy," answered the Gipsy, " she's happy enough now. She's out of all her troubles ; she'll never know what it is to be cold or hungry again."

" No, never !—never !" answered the eager listener, catching joyfully at the idea that his dear mother was at peace.

He gazed at her silently for a few moments, and then said, as though talking to himself ;

" I think I'd rather see her lying like this than in pain, as she used to."

" I would if she was my mother," said Morgan, to cheer him.

" Let me kiss her, please."

The Gipsy supported him on his knee whilst the poor boy bent down and poured his last kisses on the pale lips and marble brow of his mother, whilst his tears fell fast over the senseless clay.

" There," said Morgan, gently, much affected at the grief of the little orphan, but not wishing to prolong a scene that was painful to all ; " let her sleep now, Jemmy."

" Yes, let her sleep," echoed James, quite entering into the idea of rest his friend meant to convey ; " good night, dear mother !"

He imprinted a farewell kiss upon her pale cheek ; and the Gipsy then lifted him to the ground, and replaced the lid of the coffin.

This had hardly been done when a murmuring of voices and the sound of approaching footsteps reached their ears.

Morgan darkened his lantern instantly.

" Who's that ?" whispered the boys, anxiously.

" I don't know," answered the Gipsy. " Oh !" he whispered, " they may be only passers by, and not coming here."

It was evident, however, from the increasing distinctness of the voices, that they were not chance passengers, but that they were approaching nearer and nearer to the cottage every moment.

It seemed evident that the parties, whoever they were, were coming there.

" This be the place !" cried one of them, in a hoarse voice, as though he had a cold.

" Then," exclaimed another, " it's given me a warning !"

The new-comers now stood on the threshold of the door.

It was time for those within to think of concealing themselves, if they did not wish to be seen, especially as the rays of a lantern might have been seen shining in from the bottom of the door.

There was a cupboard in the room, and into this Morgan and the two boys crept.

They had hardly been there an instant when the door opened with a rude bang.

Then followed a trampling of feet, and after that a sound as of a heavy weight set down on the floor.

Ishmael and the boys could from their retreat in the cupboard command a view of the whole room.

The sight that met their gaze surprised them exceedingly.

The party consisted of Peter Nails, the village undertaker, who was also the parish clerk, Jonas Clay, the sexton, and last, not least, Gurgles, the beadle.

The first of these worthies carried a lantern, the next a rudely-made shell, or apology for a coffin, and the last carried nothing but himself.

" I thought we'd never a' got here !" said Jonas, releasing himself from his burden by shooting it off his shoulder on to one end, in which position it stood upright.

" Take care !" cried Gurgles, " what 'ee be a doin' of, or yer'll 'ave them four bits o' wood a dissolvin' partnership !"

" No fear of that !" said Peter, somewhat indignantly. " When I makes a thing, I makes it ! This 'ere coffin ain't very 'igh finished, but I can answer for its oldin' together !"

He wiped the heat-drops from his forehead as he spoke with his red cotton pocket-handkerchief.

" It'd 'old you, Measter Gurgles, longer than you'd like to be shut up in it, I know !" he continued ; " that is, if yer could squeeze yerself into it !"

" Pooh—nonsense !" returned the beadle, with a smile of supreme contempt ; " it wouldn't 'old one o' my legs !"

" Well, never mind," said the undertaker, " I dessay as it'll 'old 'er as it's made for fast enough ; an' as it's Mr. Octavius's orders as she should be coffined and screwed down to-night, the sooner we does it the better, becos' I wants to get 'ome !"

As he spoke, Mr. Nails gave the shell a push with his hand, and shot it over from the perpendicular to the horizontal.

" Where's yer trestles ?" asked the satirical beadle. " You're a nice undertaker !"

" Haven't got none !" returned the undertaker, who was getting irritated. " Paupers can't expect luxuries !"

" Unless yer calls splinters luxuries : there's plenty o' them !" replied the remorseless Gurgles in allusion to the slovenly workmanship and the careless manner in which the pauper shell (it was nothing more) of four planks was tacked together.

" Well, never mind !" cried Peter, " let's get our work done an' joke arterwards—bis'ness is bis'ness ! Come on ! 'elp us in with th' body !"

He drew near the bed as he spoke, but looked in vain for what he sought.

There was nobody there.

" Why, where is it ?" he exclaimed.

" Hallo !" cried the beadle, at the same moment as his eye caught sight of the handsome black coffin, " what's that ?"

" What's what ?" asked Mr. Nails.

" Why, look !" answered the beadle ; " don't yer see ?"

The undertaker fixed his eyes upon the sable repository of mortality, and immediately conceived the idea that some rival in the same line of business had been there before him.

" This won't do !" he exclaimed. " My orders was ' no cloth an' no nails—quite plain !' This won't do ! It's against all rules o' the parish !"

At the idea of any such infringement, Gurgles suddenly woke up in defence of the parochial orders.

" Cert'nly !" he ejaculated ; " th' parish *did* say ' no cloth an' no nails,' and this 'ere coffin 'as got cloth an' nails too, consekently it won't do !"

" What's to be done ?" asked the undertaker.

" What's to be done ?" answered the beadle, vehemently. " Why we must take the body out o' the wrong box, an' put it into th' right 'un !"

This proposition, which promised to expedite matters, was joyfully acceded to by Mr. Nails.

" Come on !" he cried ; " bear a hand ! Come on, Jonas, don't go to sleep !"

The sexton woke up from a slight doze into which he had fallen, and the transfer was about to be made, when the indignant Ishmael, bursting from the cupboard, commanded them, in a voice of thunder, to forbear.

The three officials—who had no idea that there was anyone but themselves in the cottage—were so thoroughly taken aback that they almost thought the roof had fallen in.

The frightened undertaker clasped the beadle, who in his turn embraced the undertaker, whilst the sexton threw his arms round both.

In this very undignified position they stood, with open eyes and mouth, gazing at the sudden apparition.

"How dare you disturb the repose of the dead?" cried Morgan, clenching his fist fiercely.

"We—we wasn't aware we was disturbin' anything!" murmured the undertaker. "We was only doin' our duty; and the parish——"

"The parish!" scornfully repeated the Gipsy. "The parish let the poor creature, that's now resting there, lie an' starve an' die, without taking the least notice; an' now some good Christian would see her decently buried, the parish would interfere, and consign her to a trumpery deal box, that I wouldn't have a dog of mine buried in!"

Ishmael spoke excitedly, and the blood swelled in his veins with indignation, till his face was crimson.

But by this time all the parties present had recognised the speaker as a wandering tinker, of vagrant habits and disreputable character; just such a person as a virtuous and well-disposed parish would hold in particular contempt.

Gurgles felt his official dignity rising rapidly.

Visions of the cage and the stocks rushed before him.

"So it's you, Mister Ishmael Morgan, is it?" he exclaimed, in the most pompous tones he could possibly throw into his voice.

"Yes; it's me, Mr. Beadle!—me, myself!" answered the unabashed Gipsy.

"Beware! beware!" cried Gurgles, getting very red in the face. "Be warned by me: don't trifle with the law—don't interfere with us in our dooties! The parish says distinctly, 'no black cloth an' no nails,' therefore it's our dooty to see as there ain't no black cloth an' no nails."

"That for the parish, and you into the bargain!" exclaimed the Gipsy, snapping his fingers in the very face of its representative. "Heaven help the poor wretch who expects anything from the tender mercies he can find amongst any of you! You are not wanted here—begone!"

He pointed angrily to the door as he spoke.

"We are wanted 'ere!" cried Gurgles; "the parish wants us to——"

"Never mind th' parish—I object. You're intruding here. There's the door—get out!"

The attitude of the Gipsy was so decidedly pugilistic, that the beadle felt there was nothing to be done but to make an example of him at once.

Under this impression, he drew from his pocket a small staff with a brass crown at one end, which he flourished majestically for a moment before Ishmael's eyes.

"You have thought proper to interfere with me in th' execootion o' my dooty," he exclaimed; "therefore, in the name o' the law, I takes yer into custody, an' I calls upon you, Peter Nails an' Jonas Clay, as good an' loyal subjects, to assist me in the same!"

The valorous beadle grasped the Gipsy's coat with a very fat, puffy hand.

But the good and loyal subjects, I am sorry to say, hung back.

They were not beadles, nor in any way warlike or chivalrous, and they each had young families to support.

Therefore they very wisely left Mr. Gurgles to fight it out by himself.

But to their great surprise, the stalwart Gipsy used no violence whatever.

He simply glanced down at the beadle's fat knuckles, and laughed derisively and softly.

This quiet demeanour on the part of Ishmael was entirely misconstrued by the valiant trio.

They imagined it proceeded from fear, and this thought wound them up suddenly to such a pitch of dauntless courage, that Messrs. Nails and Clay redeemed their characters by laying violent hands on the Gipsy, in addition to the grasp already placed upon him by the beadle.

This was strong odds against one man.

But he, strange to say, seemed rather to enjoy it.

In the meantime, his captors, having seized their prey, began to feel somewhat embarrassed what to do with him. It was exceedingly awkward.

"If the stocks was only handy now," thought Gurgles; but, unfortunately, they were a mile off.

Ishmael having quietly suffered them to detain him as long as he thought proper, said, at length:

"Well, are you three almost tired of amusing yourselves?"

"Amusin' ourselves?" echoed the beadle—"amusin'!"

The idea seemed so deliciously simple, that Mr. Gurgles laughed till the tears rolled down his cheeks.

"Because," continued Ishmael, "I've had enough of your company; and if you don't take your hands off my coat, I shall astonish you by knocking your heads together."

The sexton and the undertaker immediately took the hint, and took their heads and themselves out of harm's reach.

But the portly Gurgles, trusting to the awe and terror of his coat, cocked hat, and buttons, still retained his grasp; nor could he be persuaded that these tremendous ensigns of authority could fail to be recognised, till he suddenly found himself lying on his back, with a peculiar stinging sensation about his nasal organ, as though he had received a violent punch from something hard.

Highly indignant at this treatment, he scrambled to his feet, and seizing upon his two timorous colleagues, he held them before him as a barricade, and addressed the Gipsy over their shoulders.

"For the last time, you vagrant," he cried, "do you mean to let us remove that body into th' other receptacle which th' parish 'as provided for it?"

The reply to this question came not from him to whom it was put, but from a deep voice behind them.

"No, I do not!" it said, distinctly.

The beadle swung round as if on a pivot, taking the undertaker and the sexton with him, when, to their great terror, they encountered a tall, dark figure, wrapped in a cloak, with features ghastly pale, and eyes fixed sternly upon them.

To reply was utterly impossible.

The power of articulation was gone.

They fell on their knees in abject terror.

"Rise and begone, fellows!" cried the voice, in a peremptory tone, "and tell the parish that the poor woman whose body you would desecrate needs not its help to consign her to her last resting place. And now begone!"

The stranger stamped his foot violently, and the three functionaries scrambled on to their feet like three emancipated "Jack in the Boxes," and rushed towards the door.

There was some tugging to open this, and when at last they succeeded, it came asunder so suddenly that they fell back and rolled upon each other.

Morgan, in order to expedite their movements, threw the shell they had brought on to the top of them.

"Take your rubbish with you!" he cried.

The command was obeyed with all possible speed, and the cottage was once more clear of the unwelcome intruders.

Chapter XXV.

LAID TO REST.

ISHMAEL MORGAN, stranger as he was to the new comer who now confronted him, was prepared to recognise him as a friend, from the words he had previously spoken.

There was something in the pale, handsome features that invited regard. The stranger, too, was favourably impressed by the acts of Ishmael, whom, unknown to him, he had watched almost from his first entrance with the boys into the cottage.

James and Ikey, who had been silent spectators of

the scenes that had lately transpired, ventured forth from their concealment.

But no sooner did their eyes fall upon the stranger's features than they uttered an exclamation, partly of joy, partly of alarm.

"Mr. Carew!" they cried.

"Yes, my boys!" answered the President, anxious to put them out of their suspense. "I am happy to say it is me, though I candidly confess I never expected to meet you again."

"No more did I, sir!" said James; "but I'm very glad to see you again!"

"So am Hi!" joined in Ikey; "though Hi can't make it hout, cos th' last time I see you, you vas drowned!"

"You mean you thought I was drowned," said the President. "My preservation was most extraordinary and providential. Some day I may relate it to you, but not now. But for you," he added, turning to Ishmael, and grasping his hand, "I cannot express how much I am gratified at your conduct towards these poor boys."

Ishmael looked somewhat surprised, and almost felt inclined to suspect his new friend of some supernatural power.

He was a stranger to him, and he yet appeared cognisant of his actions.

"How did you learn, sir?" he was about to inquire; but the President interrupted him.

"I can soon explain that to your satisfaction!" he answered. "It is sufficient that what I have learnt of you is such that I shall always be proud to shake you by the hand and call you my friend."

The honest Gipsy's dark face glowed with pleasure at these words.

A long conversation then took place between them, which being ended, the President took his departure.

Not long after, Ishmael and the boys left the cottage, and returned to the camp.

Two hours later the beadle, the undertaker, and the sexton, accompanied by a posse of auxiliaries, returned to take forcible possession of the body of Mrs. Cook.

Their schemes, however, were foiled.

The coffin and its inmate were no longer there.

*   *   *   *   *   *

On the second day following the night when these events took place, the bell of the small village church at Marton tolled for a funeral.

The sexton had been paid to dig a grave, and he had dug it.

The bell-ringer had been ordered to toll the bell, and he tolled it.

The beadle, Mr. Timothy Gurgles, was there in his professional capacity; and the aged minister was also there, ready to read the funeral service.

But who was to be buried?—no one knew.

At the appointed time, a small cavalcade, consisting of the coffin, borne by four men, strangers at Marton, appeared slowly advancing towards the churchyard.

Two mourners only followed.

One of these was George Carew, the other a little boy clad in black.

He was James Cook.

The funeral party drew near and entered the churchyard, and were met by the minister.

The service was read, the body lowered into the grave, the grave filled up, and the churchyard presently cleared.

By-and-by, however, a pretty, delicate boy, with dark, curling hair and dark eyes, might have been observed creeping cautiously along by the churchyard wall, as though fearful of being observed.

No one appeared near, and the child opened the small gate and entered the sacred precincts, wandering on till he came to the grave he had so lately quitted.

It was poor little James, who could not tear himself away from the spot where the sacred remains of his beloved mother lay buried.

Having arrived there, he threw himself upon the newly-raised mound, as though he would get as near as possible to the dear parent that slumbered beneath, and sobbed in the utter loneliness of his heart.

So absorbed was he in his grief, that he was quite unconscious of the presence of another besides himself.

Yet there was a person watching the weeping boy, whose countenance wore a somewhat perplexed expression, but withal a most unsympathetic frown.

This was no other than Mr. John Burnley, the squire's gamekeeper.

He had, in common with the rest of the lookers-on who had attended at the funeral, strolled down to see what was going on, and had been considerably astonished at the likeness between the well-dressed, genteel little boy, who stood weeping by the grave, and a certain ragged little delinquent whom he had looked up in the cage a few nights previously, and who had most audaciously *filed* his way out and escaped.

John Burnley looked, scratched his head, and looked again.

The two boys were wondrously alike, and yet he did not seem quite able to connect the one with the other.

He watched and waited till the ceremony was over, and followed the President with his eyes as he led the sorrowing orphan from the churchyard.

Had he been alone, he would have at once set his doubts at rest, by questioning the boy.

As it was, there was something in the appearance of George Carew that seemed to forbid anything like intrusive questioning.

He, therefore, allowed them to retire as they came without molestation, and still remained pondering on the strange resemblance long after the churchyard was deserted.

"It's very strange—uncommon strange!" he soliloquised. "I can't make it out! That boy must be James Cook; and yet he doesn't seem to be th' same boy at all! If he is, where did he get his suit o' black? an' who was that gentleman with him? It's a reg'ler puzzler!"

Had John Burnley known the share the gentleman alluded to had taken in the boy's escape from the cage, he might, perhaps, have spoken of him with less respect.

But he did not know it, and so he continued his meditations.

"I should like to know whether it really is the same," he said, talking to himself; "I'd soon have hold of him again. It ain't very likely as boys is to be allowed to trifle with the laws in this manner."

It was, therefore, with quite an exultant feeling that John Burnley, on raising his head indignantly, after uttering the above sentiments, perceived the object of his thoughts returning towards the churchyard.

Slowly he came on, as much lost in his own sad thoughts as the gamekeeper had been the moment before in his more rancorous ones.

Seeing him approaching, and surmising the spot to which his steps were directed, Mr. Burnley anticipated James by entering the churchyard, and keeping out of sight, by stooping down behind the tombstones, till the boy reached his mother's grave, over which we left him prostrate in the full indulgence of his grief.

The gamekeeper drew near quietly, and peeped over an adjacent tombstone at the young mourner.

"Oh! mother! mother!" were the pathetic words that burst from the boy's lips.

Certainly he had had a mother himself once, but she was dead long ago, and forgotten.

It will, therefore, be easily understood, that the wailing cry of the orphan awakened no answering echo in the gamekeeper's breast.

It was the tones of his voice that impressed him.

He was certain now it *was* James Cook, the young good-for-nought, who had added to his list of crimes the additional one of breaking from his prison.

If any portion of John Burnley's anatomy was visibly affected it was his fingers, and they worked nervously, as though itching to grasp their prey.

But he remained quite still, listening to whatever James in his grief might pour forth.

The poor boy, as it were, sobbed himself empty, and when he had no more tears left, he wiped his swollen eyes and knelt upon the grave.

It was time to depart he felt, and he must go, but oh! how hard it was to tear himself away.

If he could have had a little house close by, so that he could have lived always close to his dead mother, how nice that would have been, he thought.

But this he knew was impossible—he must go.

"Good-bye, dear mother!" he exclaimed, in an earnest, tender tone, as though quite sure she listened to his words, "I must leave you now in your cold bed; but I won't forget you. You will always be before me, your words will always live in my memory, to make me, if not a great man, at least a good one, which you have often told me is better still. Good-bye, darling mother!" he murmured, in a low voice of intense affection; "I shall come and see you in the summer if I can, when the grass will grow, and the sun will be shining on your grave. But I must be gone. For the last time, darling mother—good-bye!"

He rose slowly and lingeringly from the ground, and at the same moment a heavy hand fell on his shoulder.

He looked up with a startled cry, and beheld the red face and burly form of the gamekeeper.

"You've been sayin' 'good-bye' long enough, I should think," he said, "an' now, yer'll jest come along o' me."

"Oh, sir! please don't take me now; they expect me back—they do indeed!" said James, earnestly.

"Who expects yer?"

"The—the gentleman, and the—th——"

"Go on! The who?" exclaimed John, giving his victim a shake to assist the flow of words.

"Th—th—Gipsies," replied James.

"You're a nice article, you are!" cried the keeper. "You must think me precious green to let you off now I've got yer once more—to go back to the Gipsies, too! I should like to see myself doing such a thing. You broke out of the cage, too, didn't yer? I'll take precious good care yer don't do it again, though!"

John Burnley wound up this harangue with a shake that caused the seams of poor James's new black suit to crack audibly.

But James, in the stirring vicissitudes through which he had passed since he had last been honoured with a shaking from Mr. B., had acquired a certain amount of hardihood from his acquaintance with danger.

He did not feel so very much terrified as he thought he should be at this formidable personage.

His only desire was for a giant's strength for half-a-minute, that he might be able to lay his captor quietly on his back on the ground while he ran away.

Acting upon this desire, he, to John Burnley's great astonishment, gave himself a sudden jerk, and slipped out of his fingers as nimbly as an eel, and ran hastily towards the churchyard gate.

John, as soon as his surprise would allow him to move, followed in pursuit.

James burst through the gate, like a young greyhound, while Mr. Burnley followed like a good-sized elephant.

It was evident, however, that the gamekeeper, burly as he was, could run faster than the little boy he pursued.

James was scudding along by the side of the churchyard wall, the gamekeeper gaining upon him every second.

It seemed evident he would be caught before he could turn the corner leading into the high road.

James strained every nerve.

If he could but get round the corner, he thought.

Onwards he went, panting like a hunted hare; his pursuer close upon his heels, groaning and puffing like a steam-engine.

"Stop, you young villain!" he gasped; "it'll be the wus for yer when I catch yer!" He made a grab with his hand, but James popped round the corner and avoided him.

Round rolled the burly gamekeeper after him, and the chase continued along the road.

Suddenly poor James set his foot in a rut in the road, and fell.

John Burnley uttered a broken-winded gasp of triumph.

"Ha!—ha!—told yer I should ketch yer!"

His large hand was once more outstretched, and the prostrate boy would in another instant have been hoisted up a prisoner, when suddenly something dark leaped out from the hedge, and performed some mysterious act, that caused the gamekeeper to rebound instantaneously, and fall on his back in the middle of the road.

For the satisfaction of our readers we may state, the *something* dark was Ishmael Morgan, and that the act *mysterious* was a well-delivered blow on Mr. Burnley's forehead, that felled him like a bullock.

But the adventure had not yet arrived at its crisis.

The Gipsy had barely delivered the blow that had floored the ill-disposed keeper, when he found himself grasped by the back of the collar by a powerful hand from behind, whilst at the same time an angry voice exclaimed :

"You scoundrel! I'll teach you to assault the squire's agents!"

The Gipsy could hardly believe his ears.

It was the voice of Mr. Octavius Challoner.

In an instant Ishmael comprehended that he was unrecognised—the surprise was yet to come.

He simply turned his face over his shoulder, and looked at the man who held him.

He was free in an instant.

With a cry of dismay, Octavius dropped his hand from the collar of the Gipsy's coat, as though it had been red-hot.

At the same time he recoiled several paces, as from a serpent in his path, and then stood gazing almost helplessly at the man he had just before so rudely assaulted.

The fact was, as the Gipsy had divined, Octavius had not recognised him, owing to his having put off his mud-saturated garments, and being clad in others of an entirely different description.

James Cook, too, with his clean face, and glossy suit of black, had also escaped recognition.

All that Octavius saw as he reached the spot was John Burnley violently knocked over by—as he thought—some ruffianly tramp or other, and with the instinctive hate he bore to all such people, he hastened to prevent it.

He had now found out his mistake

He had recognised both Ishmael and James.

The last time he had looked upon them was as they struggled in the deadly depths of the morass.

Now they were safe and sound, confronting him on the king's highway.

He wished at that moment his hands had been cut off 'ere they had seized upon the Gipsy.

He wished himself at the world's end—anywhere—rather than there.

Some good genius seemed intent on thwarting all his murderous plans.

One by one his intended victims started up before him into life.

First the President—then Ishmael Morgan and James Cook. Who was to be the next?

These thoughts whirled through his excited brain with electric speed.

What to do—what to say—he knew not.

A thousand terrors seemed to haunt him.

Was it strange that he should feel thus?

Was it to be wondered at, that he should be speechless before those whom a moment before he could have sworn were numbered with the dead?

While he stood thus glaring upon the Gipsy and the boy, Ishmael, after enjoying his dismay in grim silence for a moment, gave a shrill whistle.

In a moment, in answer to this, from the hedges on each side of the road darted forth swarthy forms, and gathered round him. His vision was bewildered, and he seemed to look through a mist. A rope was thrown over his head, and his arms pinioned behind him.

But in the bewilderment of his thoughts, he was unconscious of it.

He had a dim idea that he was fettered in some way, but how he knew not.

He looked straight before him, and looked wildly at Ishmael, who then spoke.

"You may well look as though the Last Enemy had laid his icy hand upon your heart and stopped its motion!" cried the Gipsy. "You call me scoundrel, who never raised my hand against any life more precious than that of a few hares and pheasants. I never sought to destroy in cold blood a fellow-creature, much less one of my own flesh and blood!"

An ominous groan burst from the lips of the Gipsies, who crowded round the scarcely conscious Octavius like a swarm of bees.

"Away with him to the camp!" exclaimed a deep voice of command.

"Ay, ay!—away with him!" echoed the rest.

The guilty victim, incapable of resistance, was dragged rather than led from the spot.

Not that he was conscious of the rough manner in which he was unceremoniously hurried along.

He seemed to be in a dream, with angry, harsh voices shouting around him :

"To the camp! To the camp!"

Chapter XXVI.

ON THE BRINK.

IN course of time the camp was reached.

Gradually as the shock he had received wore off, he was enabled to comprehend his position. No very enviable one if he had but known it.

He was surrounded by fierce and angry men, who were there to judge him for a deliberate attempt to murder one of their tribe.

On one side sat his intended victim, with two others, James and Ikey.

Facing him was the old chief, Phares Darro, looking like some old Eastern patriarch, in whose stern eye, if he could discern justice, he might not expect mercy to disarm it.

The arms of Octavius Challoner were pinioned, and a Gipsy stood on each side of him, to arrest the slightest motion.

He was utterly powerless, and had no resource but to gaze upon those whom he had made his deadly foes, and to listen to his condemnation from their lips.

But by this time his full senses had returned, and with them his self-possession, and the audacity that was natural to him.

And with this he began to chafe at the position in which he found himself.

He forgot his own past acts, and thought just then only of the indignity offered to himself.

If the remembrance of his guilt crossed him, it was only to reflect that there were no witnesses, save his intended victims themselves.

This thought increased his audacity.

Bound as he was, and surrounded by men by no means scrupulous, he still did not consider himself in peril.

They would not dare to harm him, the pilfering, wandering vagrants.

Such was his opinion. Let us hear and judge.

The aged Phares, having surveyed their prisoner silently for some time, opened the proceedings:

"This man is brought before our tribunal to be judged according to the laws of right and justice, for attempting the life of one of our brethren?" said the old man, firmly, pointing with outstretched arm to Octavius.

"He is!" responded the Gipsies, with one voice.

"Who accuses him?" asked Phares.

"I do!" returned Ishmael; "I accuse Octavius Challoner of striking me a coward's blow when I was unprepared, that plunged me into the morass."

A low groan followed from the Gipsies.

"Nay, more," continued Ishmael, "I declare that he struck this blow at the time when he knew I was seeking to save the lives of these poor children, whom he had previously cast into the slough."

A groan still deeper passed through the tribe.

Octavius, who had previously listened to the charge with a smile of contempt, burst out passionately:

"You lying scoundrel!" he shouted, fixing his indignant eyes on Ishmael, as though he would have pierced him through with their fierce glance. "It is only to the vagrant set by whom you are surrounded you dare talk such preposterous rubbish: none else would believe you!"

"It is sufficient for us that we believe him—and for *you*!" exclaimed the deep voice of Esau Yahal.

"Though the lamb knows not its butcher by instinct," said Phares, "children, young as they are"—he pointed to James and Ikey as he spoke—"remember those who seek to harm them. Speak, children, and fear not," continued the old man, addressing himself to the boys. "Has Ishmael Morgan spoken truth? Did that man seek your life as he has said?"

The boys paused for a moment, and then replied:

"Yes; he did."

"'Tis utterly false!" returned Octavius, with flashing eyes. "The words of children are worth nothing. They speak under intimidation, and will say anything."

"They do not speak under intimidation!" replied Ishmael Morgan.

"I say they do!" shouted the furious Octavius. "Tell me, you two brats!" he called out to the boys, who felt some apprehensions lest, even coerced as he was, he should burst his bonds and annihilate them in presence of the whole company, "did you not walk into the morass of your own accord?"

There was a slight pause—the boys were silent.

Octavius spoke again.

"Did I throw you in?" he demanded, fiercely.

"No," answered the boys; and then James, having, as it were, broken the ice, continued:

"You did not throw us in; but you told us the constables were coming after us to take us to prison; and when we asked which way we were to go, you pointed right across the morass, and we went the way you told us and fell into it."

"Yes," joined in Ikey, "that yer did; an' vhen ve vos a sinkin' deeper an' deeper till ve vos almost choked in th' muck, yer vouldn't put hout a finger to 'elp us—yer know yer vouldn't!"

These words, warmly asserted by Ikey, who was inwardly resolved to give his enemy a lift while he had the chance, elicited another groan from the Gipsies.

"It is all absurd nonsense!" cried Octavius, who grew more and more annoyed in proportion as he saw his judges give credence to the assertions of the witnesses. "The boys foolishly wandered into the slough, in spite of my warnings; and once there, how was it possible for me or any one else to help them, save at the sacrifice of his own life?"

"You never tried!" said Morgan.

"You did," returned Octavius; "and in so doing narrowly escaped destruction. Even now, I am at a loss to know how you escaped; at the same time I deny that I hurled you into the morass."

"You are as full of falsehoods, Mr. Challoner, as the summer twilight is of gnats," answered Ishmael; "but I have spoken truth—it was the hand of Heaven alone that saved me and these poor orphans from an awful fate."

There was a moment's silence, and old Phares then continued, looking round at his brethren:

"We have heard the words of our brother Ishmael, and of these children; for my own part, I believe them to be true. Do you also believe them?" he asked, throwing a sweeping glance of inquiry around.

"We do!—we do!" burst from every lip.

"Is there any one of us who doubts? If so, let him speak."

There was a dead silence.

"You have also heard the words of the accused," the old man continued, pointing to Octavius, who stood with frowning brow, and cheek flushed with impotent and constrained rage, scowling upon him.

"We have!—we have!" shouted the Gipsies.

"What of them?" inquired Phares. "Do you discredit them?"

"We believe them to be lies—false and treacherous as himself!" was the stern reply.

"I believe so too," wound up Phares.

"What, then, is the sentence accorded to those who seek the destruction of one of our race?" asked the old man.

"Death!" was the ominous and appalling reply.

This one monosyllable, spoken in slow and solemn earnestness, as with one breath, fell like lead on the ears and heart of Octavius Challoner.

It was the first time the idea of capital punishment at the hands of these roadside wanderers had crossed him.

He drew himself up desperately.

"What are your laws to me?" he cried, fiercely.

"Nothing, and less than nothing," returned the aged patriarch; "but they are everything to us."

"But I do not own to them; neither will I be judged by them!" exclaimed Octavius.

"You have no alternative. You have been judged and condemned."

"Ay, ay!" shouted every voice in the assembly. "Death to him—death!"

"Scoundrels!—villains!—release me!" foamed Octavius, struggling to burst his bonds; "if you dare to offer any insult to me, the whole country will be up in arms against you!"

"That is nothing new to us," returned the calm, deep, impassible voice of Esau Yahal. "But that matters little; if they hunt us from one spot we can flee to another!"

The voice of Phares once more spoke.

"You have pronounced the sentence of the would-be murderer," he said, "but not the means of death. How shall he die?"

"The rope—the rope!" cried several voices; "let him die the death of a dog!"

A score of eager exclamations echoed this proposal. The position of Mr. Challoner was growing more and more critical.

It was in vain he struggled—he was held fast by the two stalwart men on either side of him.

It was in vain he raved or threatened.

His voice was drowned by the angry shouts of those who surrounded him.

At length a shout rose in the air.

Octavius turned desperately to ascertain the cause.

What he saw was terribly significant.

It was a rope dangling from the branch of the tree beneath which he stood, with a noose at the end.

Was this then really to be his end?

Nothing appeared more certain.

"Up with him!—hang the murderer!" rang through the air.

Octavius turned deadly pale.

With all his audacity, he could not, now his own time seemed to have arrived, face the grim monster to whom he had so remorselessly consigned others.

He entreated and besought mercy, but there was none.

He offered rewards—any amount of money—if his life could be spared; but in vain.

"Place the rope round his neck!" cried Esau.

The command was instantly obeyed.

"Now, who will be the executioners?" he asked.

"I will!" shouted twenty voices, as many hands grasping the rope.

"Gently," ejaculated Phares; "this is life and death!"

A dead silence instantly prevailed.

The rope was drawn tightly round the neck of the victim.

The executioners wanted only the final signal to hoist him into the air.

But ere that could be given, Ishmael Morgan, who had been speaking to Phares, advanced towards them.

"Stay!" he exclaimed.

His colleagues looked at him with mingled expressions of doubt and impatience.

Was he going to plead for the life of the murderer?

"I have been thinking," said Ishmael, "that the punishment of this man should be the same as that he intended to inflict on us."

The Gipsies looked at each other. Ishmael continued:

"He would have buried us in the morass; let that, therefore, be his grave."

"Good! good!" cried the Gipsies; "let it be so!—the morass!—the morass!"

The course of Gipsy justice being thus diverted from its intended channel, the noose was removed from the neck of Octavius.

He had given himself up for lost, and half dead from the fear of death, could scarcely stand.

However, even this brief respite restored him in some measure to himself.

He made no remark when ordered to accompany the Gipsies, and when he heard the fate to which he was destined, the prominent idea in his mind was that it was preferable to hanging like a dog.

It was some distance to the morass, but they walked quickly, and ere long the fatal swamp appeared in sight.

In a few moments the culprit, surrounded by his executioners, stood on the brink.

Ishmael Morgan was at his side.

James and Ikey, who had shuddered inwardly at the terrible preparations they had so lately beheld, were left behind in the camp.

When it came to the moment when the man who would have destroyed them was to suffer before their eyes, their hearts relented, and they would have given anything to have been able to have saved him from this doom.

They expressed their desire in a whisper to Morgan, and it may not be impossible that their appeal had some weight with the Gipsy in inducing him to suggest the alteration in the manner of the execution.

Perhaps he wished to spare the children so horrible a sight.

But whatever was his motive, the ultimate fate of Octavius seemed decreed.

There he stood on the edge of the shelving bank of the morass.

He had been led, in order to make his punishment as retributive as possible, to the very spot, where he had stood and gazed a few hours before, with a malignant smile on his features, exulting over terrors that were now to be experienced by himself.

Morgan detailed to his companions the events of his critical position and narrow escape, and by so doing stirred up their wrath to a still higher pitch.

"In with the murderer!—let us serve him as he would have served others!—let us see him drink the muddy waters of the swamp!" they shouted.

There was nothing to wait for.

Justice need no longer be delayed.

"Lead him to the brink!" cried the deep voice of Esau.

Two Gipsies led him forward.

The wretched, guilty man glanced despairingly round at his stern custodians, and then his eye wandered across the treacherous slough before him.

"Now, Octavius Challoner," Esau exclaimed, "say your last prayer—and quickly!"

But Octavius could not pray—he never had prayed; and now his thoughts were one wild chaos of horror and confusion.

But though he could not pray to Heaven, he could entreat men.

"A thousand guineas for my life!" he cried, despairingly—"two thousand!"

"Twenty thousand would not save you!" was the cold response from Esau's lips. "Your prayers—quickly! Ask mercy of Heaven; from us you will get none!"

The condemned cast up his terror-stricken, despairing eyes to the bright sky over his head; and if he uttered an entreaty, it was in thought, not in word.

"Now, Ishmael Morgan," said Esau, deliberately, "as his hand struck you from this bank into the depths below, so shall your hand administer the blow that shall send him there. Get ready! Nerve your arm, and, when I give the signal, strike with all your force!"

Octavius was turned round, so that he stood with his back to the morass, facing Ishmael.

At that terrible moment their eyes met—the eyes of the victim and his executioner; but no word was spoken.

There was a dead silence.

"Is your hand clenched?"

"It is."

"You are ready?"

"Yes."

Esau's tongue had already begun to speak the last fatal word of command, "Strike!" when the sound of a horse's hoofs, coming on at full speed, caught his ear.

He paused.

In another moment a gray steed, mounted by a Gipsy lad, was seen tearing along the edge of the morass.

It dashed up into the midst of the throng, and the rider called out, holding out a strip of paper as he spoke:

"For Ishmael Morgan!"

Ishmael instantly took the paper, and the gray horse and his rider departed as quickly as they had arrived.

The Gipsy glanced at the brief epistle, and then handed it to Esau, who read it in silence.

He then approached his companion, and said, in a low tone:

"He is in your hands. It is for you to decide."

"I have decided—to obey!" answered Ishmael.

"Good," replied Esau, with characteristic brevity.

Ishmael drew his clasp knife, and approached his fettered victim.

Octavius, with an inward shudder, closed his eyes, expecting to feel the keen blade buried in his heart.

Judge, then, his surprise when, instead of this, the voice of the Gipsy whispered in his ear:

"*You are free—to live—and to remember!*"

He then with one stroke severed the rope that bound the captive, and turned away from him without another word or look.

The revulsion of feeling was too strong—the transition from death to life too sudden—for the tortured mind of Octavius to endure.

He threw up his arms wildly in the first consciousness of his reprieve, and then, with an hysterical laugh, fell senseless to the ground. When he came once more to his senses, the sun was still shining; but the dark eyes of the Gipsy tribe no longer flashed vengeance on him.

He was alone—alone on the edge of the morass.

Chapter XXVII.

BURNING OUT THE VAGRANTS.

THE above proceedings, and the fact of a scrap of paper saving the life of Octavius Challoner, will doubtless appear mysterious to our readers. Let me, then, explain at once that it came from the President of the Confederate Brothers, and that it contained these words :

"*Release Octavius Challoner. Leave him to the judgment of Heaven, and the supervision of the Confederacy. His punishment must be to live.*—GEORGE CAREW, *President.*"

During the short interview that had taken place between Ishmael Morgan and the writer of the above, the latter had enrolled the Gipsy a member of the order.

It was, therefore, on the strength of this fraternity he demanded and obtained the release of Octavius, when heaps of gold would probably have failed to purchase it.

And what effect had the ordeal to which he had been submitted taken upon Octavius himself?

It had been severe and terrible—the very bitterness of death had passed over and through him.

One would have thought that the recollection of the horrible despair that had weighed him down would have made him from that hour a different man.

But, strange as it may appear, it was not so.

Though a short time before he would have given worlds for his life, had he possessed them, still, now that he had gained that life gratuitously, he seemed entirely to forget its former preciousness.

As he gazed up at the sun-lit sky, and no longer saw the dark forms of his enemies, his feelings turned completely round.

The joy he had felt at his unexpected preservation changed rapidly into indignation at the insults he considered he had received.

He was ashamed, too, at the fear—the deadly fear—he had betrayed.

Gratitude gave place to wrath, and, instead of thanking Heaven that his guilty life was spared, he cherished his evil thoughts until he was filled with nothing but the direst thoughts of vengeance against the whole of the Gipsy tribe.

Could he have exterminated them all at one blow, he would have done it.

It was with such feelings this evil-disposed man left the spot he never could have expected to depart from alive, brooding over the past, and meditating destruction to those who had caused him so much terror.

In the mean time the Gipsies had reached their camp.

Although they had fully resolved to glut their vengeance in their own way on him who had wronged their brother, they yielded immediately to the command to spare, and returned, quite satisfied that they had at least given the would-be murderer a lesson he would never forget.

Alas! they knew not Octavius. He had already forgotten it. He was himself again.

President Carew was at the camp on their return, and distributed largess among the tribe; nay, more, he enrolled them all as members of the Confederacy, and, having done this, he departed amid the hearty cheers, and carrying with him the firm devotion of the whole company.

The consequence of his donations was a great revel in the camp that night.

Ishmael Morgan did his share towards the entertainment, by shooting a brace of hares and several pairs of pheasants.

Various other contributions came in from other members of the tribe.

Liquors of various kinds were sent for, and the bright fires, as the day declined, lighted up the eyes and features of the Gitanas with a flush and a brilliancy they did not always wear.

The song and dance succeeded each other in rapid succession.

James and Ikey, who had never in their lives before witnessed anything like this wild revelry, were partly alarmed, partly amused.

But by degrees they grew accustomed to the din of voices and the shouts of laughter; and, as their friend Ishmael was close by them, they yielded to the novel excitement, and at length almost enjoyed it.

Still, ever and anon, when the mirth was loudest, poor James found his thoughts stealing away to the quiet churchyard where his dear mother lay.

He would rather have been sitting there quietly by the side of her grave.

"What would she say to me if she could see me here?" he murmured to himself.

Then he comforted himself with the thought that he was not in the midst of that scene of dissipation from choice.

"She knows I can't help myself," he thought, "and that, if I had my will, I would much rather be with her."

As for Ikey, who had no such sorrow at his heart, the entire proceedings afforded him unmingled delight.

If this was Gipsy life, he was resolved to be a Gipsy from that time henceforward.

The boy was in the highest state of exhilaration.

He sang so lustily, and hopped about so incessantly, that a parched pea was a fool to him.

The rough Gipsies felt quite flattered by the hearty way in which the little urchin entered into their festivities.

They fed him with eatables and drinkables till he was on the very verge of bursting.

He had never before tested what spirit he was of; and now he was putting his newly-discovered propensities to the proof he found himself playing the wildest pranks imaginable.

Of these, the most prominent, and one which caused the Gipsies most amusement, was an apparently uncontrollable desire on his part to stand on his head, with that important member of his body thrust into one of the soup kettles.

After numerous attempts at this wonderful feat, it was discovered that his head was wedged so tightly in the pot that it was necessary to extricate him by main force, and when, at length, his face was once more visible, it was found to have assumed a hue many shades darker than any of the complexions that surrounded him.

But, as all things come to an end in due time, so did this night revel of the Gipsies.

The last song was chorussed, the last bumper quaffed, and the tired revellers sought their pillows, such as they were, and silence once more reigned throughout the camp.

Ikey, in the highest possible spirits, sought his companion, who was by no means elated by the festivities he had witnessed, but, if anything, rather depressed, although the novelty of the scene had for a time excited him.

Ikey, still under the influence of the good things he had eaten and drank, having snapped like a young gudgeon at everything that was offered him, whether solid or liquid, was in a state of enraptured excitement.

The fluids he had imbibed—it must be confessed much too plentifully for a boy of his years—had had their effect, and the lad, to speak plainly, was, to use a nautical term, more than "half seas over."

[HID AWAY.]

It would be impossible to describe the unintelligible gibberish he talked to James, or the strange antics he performed in the tent.

I may only remark that the propensity to stand on his head again developed itself in full force.

He made repeated efforts to perform this feat for James's special edification, and as often fell on his back, and was much chagrined because his comrade declined following his example.

To speak the truth, James felt rather annoyed at his friend for the absurdities he was committing, and at the cause.

He could see plainly enough, young as he was, what was the matter with him, and it rather shocked than amused him.

He contented himself with watching Ikey's vagaries with a sad, thoughtful expression on his pale face, till,

quite tired out, Ikey gave in at last, and fell asleep, and snored like a dissipated young porker.

James had not upbraided him—it would have been useless, but he resolved to tell him what he thought at the first opportunity.

All being quiet, he knelt down in a corner of the tent, and said his prayers.

This done, he tried to compose himself to sleep. But the effort was vain.

His brain was excited by the strange and unusual scenes he had witnessed.

The Gipsy revellers still seemed to flash before his eyes in the whirling dance.

The Bacchanalian chorus still rang in his ears.

He closed his eyes and tried not to think.

But his thoughts were rebellious, and refused to be controlled.

He thought of his mother in her silent grave : he fancied himself tossing upon the stormy ocean in a tiny boat ; then he was struggling in the miry depths of the slough ; after that, battling with a great hungry hound, that seemed ready to devour him. From this foe he fancied he fled away, and was running at the top of his speed along the road. Suddenly a dark figure started up in his path, and grasped him. He recognised the face in a moment—it was Octavius Challoner.

He uttered a startled cry, and sprang to his feet, trembling violently.

Surely he must have dozed off into a dreamy slumber without being conscious of it, and had just awoke?

All was dark within the tent.

Ishmael slumbered at the further end ; Ikey close by his side, still making the most inharmonious sounds with his nose.

But beyond this all was silent.

Ashamed of his fears, James lay down again, and was at length dropping off to sleep, when a light footstep fell upon his ear.

Again he started up and listened, his heart beating audibly.

Who could it be?—what feet could be wandering at that silent hour?

He reflected for a moment.

It might be some chance traveller who had strayed inadvertently that way ; but he could not assure himself that such was the case.

Without knowing why, he seemed instinctively to recognise in that stealthy tread the approach of danger.

If it were so, and an enemy were approaching, the Gipsies were utterly unprepared to meet it.

Buried in profound sleep, deepened by their unusual libations that night, they would be difficult to arouse from their lethargy.

But perhaps, after all, his fears were groundless.

He resolved to reconnoitre.

He accordingly crept towards the entrance of the tent, and looked out.

It was a beautiful moonlight night, and quite mild for January.

There were the tents, peacefully covering their slumbering inmates, but no signs of living creature appeared.

"I must have been mistaken," he thought, and was about to return, much relieved that it was so, when the low murmuring of voices fell upon his ears.

He crouched down and listened eagerly.

"The vagabonds are all kennelcd for the night," he heard a voice say. "It would not be a bad idea to fire the tents, and singe them in their own burrows."

He looked towards the spot whence he fancied the sound proceeded, and perceived several dark forms under shadow of the trees.

The Gipsy camp stood in a hollow at some distance from the main road, on the borders of a wood.

It was at the entrance of this wood the speakers stood.

Full of anxiety and alarm, yet still anxious to learn who they were, James crept cautiously forward.

Presently one of the party emerged from the shadow into the moonlight, as he pointed out some particular spot to his companions.

James felt a cold shudder creep over him, as he recognised this one.

His dream seemed partly realised—it was the pale features of Octavius Challoner.

His presence was a guarantee of evil.

Without a moment's pause he retraced his steps.

The principal idea that fastened on his mind was that the object of his visit there was to seize upon Ikey and himself, and sacrifice them in revenge for the evidence they had given against him before the Gipsy tribe.

It did not strike him that the Gipsies themselves might have come in for a share of his resentment, although the suggestion to burn them in their tents looked something like it.

But even had he thus reflected, he would have looked upon the cruel step as only a certain means to frustrate any possibility of their escape.

He reached Ishmael's tent, and aroused him.

The Gipsy was soon wide awake, with all his faculties at his command, listening to James's recital of what he had seen and heard.

"Remain here !" he said to the boy, "till I return. I shall not be long."

He then glided from the tent.

James, in a state of great apprehension, attempted, as soon as he was gone, to arouse the inebriated urchin, Ikey, who still snored in a blissful unconsciousness.

"Ikey—Ikey !" he whispered, in a low tone, shaking him at the same time, "wake up ! We're in danger !"

"Ooray for th' merr' green vood !" murmured the slumbering good-for-nought, repeating in his sleep one of the Gipsy songs he had heard that night.

"Don't sing, Ikey, but wake !" cried James, shaking him more vigorously. "They're after us !"

"Vith 'is bloss'ms an' boughs," muttered Ikey, still asleep.

James was in despair at his companion's insensibility.

"Ikey—Ikey !" he cried, once more, desperately. "If you don't get up we shall be caught ! Here's Mr. Octavius and the constables."

As though there was a sort of magic in the word constable, Ikey sprang up.

"Where are they ?" he exclaimed, wildly, about to rush forth anywhere.

"Hush !" cried James, holding him, "not there, they'll see you !"

"Hi von't be took to pris'n ! Let me go !" roared Ikey, struggling violently, thinking, in the confusion of his stupified faculties, that he was in the grasp of one of these terrible functionaries.

"I'm not a constable," whispered James, soothingly, frightened to death lest they should be heard. "I'm Jemmy, your friend ! Don't you know me ?"

"O' course Hi does !" whimpered Ikey, who had arrived at a little more consciousness. "But I thought you said as th' const'bles vos 'ere and Mr. Hotty ?"

"So they are !"

"Where ?"

"There—outside ! Hush !"

Ikey, now that he was thoroughly awake, was as fully alive to the horror of such a propinquity as his companion.

"Let's run away !" he cried.

"Stay !" interposed James. "Ishmael knows they're here, and he has gone to look out. He told me to wait here till he came back."

"Hi 'opes 'e von't be long," murmured Ikey, with nervous fretfulness, "Hi've got such a horful 'eadache. Hi thinks ve'd better run, it'll do it good, th' cool hair."

"No, let's wait for Morgan," said James. "You shouldn't have eaten and drank so much ! that's what has made your head ache."

"Hi feels werry bad !" moaned Ikey—"oh ! oh !"

He put his hands to his aching forehead with an appearance of so much suffering that James relented.

"Never mind," he said, "you'll be better presently."

"Hi 'opes Hi shall," returned Ikey. "If Hi hain't, Hi knows Hi shall die !"

"Oh no you won't," James replied, in a consolatory tone ; "lie down if you like. I'm not sleepy—I'll keep watch."

"No, Hi von't lay down, cos Hi might drop hoff to sleep, an' then th' const'bles 'll ketch me."

"No they shan't, I'll wake you," said James.

But Ikey was too apprehensive to accept his companion's offer.

And so they both remained quietly in the tent, counting the moments till Ishmael should return.

The Gipsy, on leaving the tent, had cautiously glanced around, and observed the dark forms spoken of by James.

"So, so !" he murmured "he thinks to burn us in our nests, does he, the treacherous snake ! But that I am pledged to the Confederacy not to take his life, this night should be his last on earth !"

He hissed these words through his teeth, and then crawling along on the ground, approached the nearest tent and gave the alarm.

This he repeated till he had aroused the whole camp. He then returned to the boys, who thought he was never coming back.

In the meantime let us glance at the dark figures lurking in the entrance of the wood.

First and foremost among them was Octavius Challoner. He had already been recognised, though he was unconscious of it.

He felt himself perfectly secure.

The news of the grand revel the Gipsies had held that evening had been brought to him by spies he had proviously sent to reconnoitre, and he felt assured that they would be surfeited with strong liquors and be soundly wrapped in the slumber of intoxication.

One would have thought that after the experience he had that day had of their stern administration of justice, he would have paused ere he trusted himself so near them, within no shorter lapse of time than a few hours.

But Octavius Challoner was not contented with having escaped with his own life.

Precious as it had seemed to him at the time he seemed on the verge of losing it, he appeared to have entirely forgotten its value, as soon as the immediate peril was past.

It seemed as though some evil demon was urging him on from crime to crime—from injustice to injustice.

He would not be content till he had inflicted a terrible retribution on these Gipsy vagrants, for the daring insults they had heaped upon him.

He would bitterly resent the terrors they had inflicted upon him, by their mock trial, and the appalling sentence, which he was now convinced—not knowing to whose interference he owed his safety—they had never intended to carry out.

An inkling of the diabolical manner in which he proposed to revenge himself has been already gathered.

The tents were to be set on fire, and in the hurry and terror of the sudden alarm, Octavius and his colleagues, who accompanied him, numbering about forty stalwart countrymen, were to lay on to the unprepared Gipsies with their knotted cudgels, with particular orders to spare neither life nor limbs.

"Come !" said Octavius, who having remained in ambush long enough to assure himself that the whole camp was buried in sleep, was anxious to accomplish his cruel purpose. "It is time to make the attack."

You will perceive it was not a fair hand-to-hand contest Octavius desired; it was a bloodthirsty retribution he sought, what in savage warfare would be called a war of extermination.

If every man, woman, and child of the wandering tribe in the tents before him, had been scorched by the flames, or crushed and mangled by the cudgels of his party, he would have been well contented.

He should have been a wolf, not a man.

Everything was prepared.

Some of the party had lanterns, some had links, or torches of twisted yarn soaked in tar; some had pistols or guns; but all had cudgels.

"Now," said Octavius, in a low tone, "follow me, cautiously and silently."

The party slowly emerged from the dark wood, about forty in number, and in a crouching position approached the tents.

It seemed as they left their place of ambush, that their place was supplied by forty more. But this might have been fancy.

The countrymen, as they drew near the tents, divided into two parties, till they completely surrounded them.

They had advanced with the utmost caution.

No man spoke.

All within the tents was profound silence.

The Gipsies' sleep after their night's debauch was heavy indeed.

Truly their position was most defenceless.

Octavius raised a lantern aloft.

At this preconcerted signal, every man instantly lit the torch he carried.

Again Octavius raised—not a lantern, but a torch.

This second signal was to commence the work of destruction.

Thirty blazing torches were instantly placed against the canvas of the tents, and in a few seconds, as if by common consent, they burned into a flame simultaneously.

The assailants uttered no cry of triumph.

Each man grasped his cudgel, or his pistol—some both—and, with eyes fixed on the burning tents, waited.

The struggle would soon begin.

It was strange how quiet they all were within.

Were they dying of heat or suffocation without a struggle ?

It seemed incredible—even Octavius was perplexed.

Each man looked in his fellow's face in amazement.

"It's mortal strange !" they said.

It was strange ; but had the gallant crew looked over their shoulders, and seen dark, prostrate forms gliding towards them along the greensward, like gigantic lizards, it would perhaps have helped them to solve the mystery.

However, they soon understood all about it.

The intense heat of the flames soon demolished the frail coverings, and as they yielded to the devouring element, the interiors of the tents were laid open to inspection.

No calcined bones, no scorched bodies of dead men and women were to be seen—nothing at all.

The cause of the silence was now palpably explained —*the tents were empty.*

Chapter XXVIII.

A NARROW ESCAPE.

THIS was a poser—one surprise following on the heels of another—but the reign of astonishment was not yet over ; there was yet another to come.

The Gipsies were not there, that was certain.

This fact suggested another—they must be somewhere else. *Where ?*

This was a question mentally asked by everyone of the assailants.

The answer came instantly—unexpectedly—*awfully !* in the shape of a ringing yell close behind them.

It was then perceptible that the gigantic lizards were Gipsies.

Gipsies, who, warned by their comrade Ishmael, had crept out of their tents, and, by a short circuit entered the wood in the rear of their assailants, and quietly followed behind them, trailing their lengths along the grass up to the very scene of their operations.

It was indeed a thrilling, terrible moment.

The loud shout caused them to turn round with a start of terror.

Then they found themselves face to face with their indignant foes, whose angry features and flashing eyes told ominously against the panic-stricken assailants.

Without a word the attack began.

The Gipsies, stimulated by resentment and indignation, fought like wild wolves.

The countrymen, roused to the necessity of a strong effort, met the attack like a herd of baited bulls.

But they had been cowed by the suddenness of the assault, they were no longer the assailants but the assailed : they had lost heart—they were panic-struck ; but they were Englishmen, and still they fought.

They had no resource ; they were obliged to fight.

Their wild assailants, furious with the liquor they had drunk, were terrible foes.

They were, moreover, more accustomed to night work than the countrymen, who were entirely at a disadvantage.

Still the battle raged.

Shouts, groans, execrations, yells, and shrieks rang through the quiet night, mingled with the occasional report of firearms.

Octavius had made a good night's work of it.

But where was he ?—in the thickest of the fray cheering on those whom he had led thither ? Not he.

Events had fallen out very differently from the way he had anticipated.

Accordingly, acting upon the principle of " discretion being the better part of valour," he quietly withdrew out of harm's way, leaving his colleagues to fight *his* battle without him.

At length the contest, fierce as it was, began to slacken.

Each side had had enough of it.

The Gipsies were tired of striking, the countrymen of being struck.

Many were gashed, bruised, and wounded—two Herculean farming men were dead.

Gradually the Gipsies disappeared into the surrounding darkness.

The discomfited countrymen gathered together.

The two unfortunate victims of the fray in their midst.

Octavius then re-appeared, breathless and panting, as though he had been taking the whole weight of the battle upon his own shoulders.

"Well, my brave fellows," he cried, "how do we fare?"

The men who, in their confusion, did not know but that he had borne his full share of the peril, were glad to see their *gallant* leader.

"Eh, Maister Octavies," said one, "we've got soom oogly knocks amoong us; them Gipsies fout loike woild Injins!"

"The scoundrels!" exclaimed Octavius. "But we've sent them flying at last. I hope no one is seriously hurt?" pretending not to see the two bodies on the ground.

"Eh, sur, but theer be," answered the former speaker; "two of our best men be dead—John Moore an' Jem Sands. Oi dun know what poor Jem's old moother 'll say about it; it'll go noigh to breck t' poor creetur's 'eart!"

"It's very sad—very!" said Octavius, in a tone of the deepest sympathy. "We must break it to her gently, and I must do something for the bereaved mother. Come, my lads," he added, after a slight pause, "take up the dead, and let us be going. We've taught these rascals a lesson, and the sooner we are on the road back the better."

The bodies of the two unfortunates were raised, and slowly and sorrowfully the party moved off the ground.

Ishmael Morgan, previous to the contest, had conveyed James and Ikey to a safe retreat in the wood, admonishing them to remain there till he returned to them.

There they stayed in a state of great anxiety and suspense.

They saw the glare of the fire from the tents, and heard the shouts of the combatants, and felt quite certain the Gipsies were getting the worst of the affray.

Several bullets whizzed over their heads.

Ikey was beside himself with terror.

"It's no good hour a stayin' 'ere!" he cried. "Don't yer remember as Mr. Hotty said as Morgan couldn't take care of us, cos' th' const'bles vas arter 'im?"

"Yes, I do remember that," answered James.

"An' didn't 'e say as hif ve vos caught vith 'im ve should be sent to pris'n?"

"Yes, I remember that too."

"Yer don't vant to be sent to pris'n, does yer?"

"No, Ikey, indeed I don't!"

"No more do Hi! an' that's vhy Hi vants to get avay," wound up Ikey.

"But where are we to go to?"

"Hi don't know vheer—anyvheer's better nor stoppin' 'ere. Let's go hout on the vorld, an' make our fort'ns."

James smiled sadly to himself in the dark.

Fortune did not seem very favourably disposed either towards him or his companion, he thought.

"Ve're allus a gettin' hinter some trouble or nother 'ere," Ikey continued, "an' Hi don't think as our luck 'll hevver change till ve gets right clean avay."

At this moment, whiz! came a bullet about six inches above his head, and went crashing into the trunk of the tree against which he leant.

"Ere's the constables!" he cried, grasping James's arm. "Hoh, do let's come! Ve shall be sure to get along some'ows or another."

Ikey tugged hard at James, as he spoke, to try to get him to move.

James hung back without replying.

He was thinking—hesitating before he should take the final step—and, as Ikey suggested, run away.

It required some resolution to do it.

It was his native place.

All the pleasant associations of his life were connected with it.

But then, on the other hand, so were his unpleasant ones.

Then he would have to go away from the churchyard where his mother lay.

He would have to leave Morgan, to whom he was strongly attached, and who appeared to be the only friend he had.

But then, he being only a wandering Gipsy—not that James liked him the less on that account—a vagrant and a poacher, his friendship was rather likely to injure his prospects than advance them.

Still, if he left the neighbourhood of Marton, he would be free from the pursuit of Octavius Challoner, whom he had now, with good reason, learnt to look upon as the most formidable of all his foes.

Then, again, he thought if he tried to do his duty as his mother had taught him, Providence would take care of him wherever he went, and then if he prospered he could return one day to his native village, and place a marble slab over his mother's grave with the inscription engraven on it: "*Sacred to the memory of my dear mother.*"

Ikey wondered why he hesitated, but he was glad when James, breaking from his reverie, said at length:

"I think you're right, Ikey! There seems little good to be got by stopping here; so suppose we go?"

"Vot!" cried Ikey, in a tone of delighted surprise, "d'ye mean run right clean avay for good?"

"Yes, I hope so," answered James, "because——"

Crash! went another bullet into the trunk of the tree.

"I think this place is no longer safe for us!" he added, finishing the sentence the bullet had interrupted.

"Come hon!" urged Ikey, eagerly, "let's be hoff!"

And while the shouts of the strife echoed far and wide, the boys stole like two guilty fugitives from their place of concealment, and gradually got farther and farther from it.

After proceeding some distance along the edge of the wood, they branched off, and scudding across a field, came into the high-road.

"That's right!" exclaimed Ikey. "Now ve knows vheer ve hare."

They could still hear the indistinct murmur of the angry voices, but they were growing fainter and fainter.

"There's honly vun vay now to go," Ikey remarked, "and that's straight hon."

James looked back for the last time wistfully.

"Good-bye, old place!" he cried, sadly—"good-bye, dear home!—good-bye, darling mother! Some day, perhaps, I shall come back again!"

"Good-bye, how'rybody!" exclaimed Ikey, briefly, "an' hif Hi newer sees yer no more, Hi shan't cry my heyes hout."

These were the parting words of the boys, who therewith went forth to seek their fortunes on the wide and stormy ocean of the world.

* * * * * *

At the very earliest moment after the contest had terminated, Ishmael Morgan hastened to the spot where he had left the boys.

Great was his anxiety when he missed them.

He shouted their names—he went in search—he fretted himself, did this Gipsy vagrant, that he could not find them.

"They can't have fallen into *his* hands again!" he exclaimed, aloud. "Where can they be?"

The reader knows, though Ishmael did not.

* * * * * *

Some miles had been travelled over by the small feet of the young adventurers, James and Ikey, before they confessed to feeling tired.

The latter being filled with qualms, and all kinds of uncomfortable sensations from the effects of his recent dissipation, was the first to give in.

"Hi say, Jemmy," he said at length, beginning to walk very slowly, "Hi feels as sick as a dorg!"

"I'm very sorry," said James. "We'll rest a little."

"Hi should like to," remarked his indisposed companion.

They sat down for a moment on the bank by the roadside.

But Ikey could not escape the penalty of the gorge he had indulged in, or get rid of his uncomfortable sensations.

"It's horful to feel sick, hain't it, Jem?" he moaned, in a doleful voice.

"It isn't pleasant, certainly," said James, quietly.

Iky groaned, and doubled himself up expressively.

"Pleasant!" he murmured. "It's for all the vorld as

hif some'un vas a turnin' a 'andle and screwin' me round hinside.''

"I daresay it's very painful," James replied, in a sympathising tone ; "but you'll be better presently."

"Hi opes Hi shall," whined Ikey, groaning again. "Oh, Hi do feel bad!—oh—oh !"

He rolled over on the grass, and after sundry writhings and contortions, Dame Nature kindly came to his assistance, and he was violently sick.

But this painful operation entirely cured him. He rose from the ground quite restored.

"Hi'll never heat nor drink so much, never no more !" he asserted, vehemently. "Hi thought Hi vos a goin' to die."

"Eating and drinking kill a good many people, I've heard," said James.

"They sha'n't kill me," answered Ikey. "Hi shall remember to-night for a long time."

"I hope you will," said James, seriously.

Having rested themselves, they continued their journey.

But they could not go on walking all night.

They were both, by this time, thoroughly tired.

The hour was late, and there was no inn in sight, or any dwelling where they could seek a lodging.

"Hi'm so tired !" whimpered Ikey.

"So am I," said James.

They went on slowly a little farther.

"We must lie down by the road-side," James proposed.

There seemed no alternative, when Ikey suddenly pointed to a building on the other side of the hedge.

"There's a 'ouse !" he cried.

The boys clambered over a gate that was close at hand, and approached the structure.

It was a very small house, and from the fragrant odour that came from it, appeared to contain hay.

Ikey lifted the latch ; the door opened, and they entered.

They were not, however, able to proceed far into the interior, it being filled with hay.

They closed the door, and then, by dint of perseverance, contrived to scramble up and make their way over towards the back.

Here the hay seemed less tightly packed, and here they resolved to stop for the night.

Burrowing down for the sake of warmth as deeply as they could, they pulled as much hay as possible over them, and almost immediately afterwards fell asleep.

They slept soundly and sweetly, in every sense of the latter word, and, in course of time, they awoke.

They were perfectly rested and refreshed ; but they lay so snug and comfortable in their fragrant bed, that they felt inclined to linger there and enjoy it.

"Hain't it nice an' varm ?" murmured Ikey, in a tone of luxurious comfort.

"Beautiful !" responded James.

"Hi think ve may as vell stop 'ere for another night," Ikey suggested.

Before James had time to reply, their conversation was interrupted by voices outside.

"'Ere's somebody comin' !" whispered Ikey, apprehensively. "Theer seems to be allers somebody comin' vheerever ve goes !" he added, repiningly.

But he only spoke the truth : there did seem to be *always* somebody coming to disturb the poor boys.

"Sh !" whispered James—"lie still till they're gone."

No two little lifeless plaster figures ever remained more motionless than did James Cook and Ikey Mangles in their bed of hay.

They hardly dared to breathe for fear of discovery.

Presently there was a great creaking overhead.

It seemed to them as though some one was trying to batter down the roof upon them.

No such design, however, was meditated.

On the contrary, could they have seen what was going on outside, they would have known that an effort was being made by a short, stout, good-natured little red-faced man—evidently a farmer—and his assistant, to raise the roof—or rather the top—of the shed, which opened like a trap-door.

But they could see nothing, and as they lay there, nestled together, the knocking and banging to open the trap seemed terrific.

One thing comforted them ; the voice they heard speaking was a kind voice, and its tone was round and pleasant.

"Now, then, lad, oop wi' t' ladder !" it cried.

The ladder was placed as directed, and footsteps were heard ascending.

Then came another tremendous bang, as the trap was pushed open and fell over.

"Now, then, Sam, coom oop !" called out the pleasant voice.

Sam was on the top in a twinkling.

There was a little pause then.

The boys became conscious that some change had taken place by feeling the incoming of the fresh air.

The pleasant voice again spoke.

"Oi think we'll hae it oot 'ere," it said.

"Varry weel, measter," answered another voice, speaking with a very broad dialect.

Then followed a crisp, sharp sound, as if something was cutting the hay.

"What's that ?" whispered James.

"Dun know," answered Ikey ; and almost in the same breath he uttered a hideous yell :

"Oh, oh, oh—oh——h !" he roared.

"What's the matter, Ikey ?" exclaimed James, startled out of his silence.

"My 'ead's cut hoff !" he groaned. "Oh, oh !"

Could the boys have seen how the honest little farmer turned as pale as death, and how Sam suddenly dropped his cutting implement, and opened his mouth and turned up his eyes, as though he had cut off somebody's head instead of a truss of hay, they would have been quite assured that no harm was intended.

But Ikey could not see this, so he continued moaning.

The good-natured farmer and the lad with him were sorely perplexed to account for the cries and the groans that appeared to come from the middle of the hay.

"What be it, measter ?" asked the lad.

"Nay, lad, I doan't know what to make on it !" returned the master. "I ne'er 'eard th' loikes of it before."

There was a slight pause, and still the "Oh, oh, ohs !" continued, though fainter.

"'Ere," cried the farmer, in a sudden tone of energy, "let's lift out the bit o' hay you've cut, Sam. P'raps we shall see then."

After some little pulling and tugging, a large square, neatly-cut lump, or truss of hay, was lifted out from the mass, and placed on a portion of the roof.

It was then the cause of the unusual phenomenon was explained.

"Oh, lor', measter !" ejaculated Sam, opening his eyes and mouth once more with horror. "Look'ee theer !"

The worthy farmer looked, and, in his turn, uttered an exclamation of alarm.

"Odds boddikins !" he cried. "Is it possible ?—it can't be !"

The good man held up his hands in a state of amazement that would have been ludicrous, had not the cause of his excitement been so closely allied to the terrible.

Yes ; there in an exact line with the side of the cavity from which the hay had been removed, and at a right angle to, and barely beyond the reach of, the sharp, formidable scythe-like instrument that had swept at a hair's breadth past them, appeared side by side a *couple of human heads.*

Well might the honest farmer have turned pale.

Well might Sam have opened his mouth and turned up his eyes.

The least shade nearer, and he might have been the executioner of two boys.

As it was, the sharp blade of the instrument had merely shaved off a very thin slice from the top of Ikey's *cranium.*

It was sufficient, however, to cause a considerable effusion of blood.

The farmer first caught sight of the crimson fluid, and pointed it out to Sam, who, in the firm conviction that he was a murderer, began to howl piteously.

"Oh, oh, oh !" he roared, "'is 'ead be coot in arfe ! 'E be bleeding to death—Oi know 'e be !"

James involuntarily placed his hand upon his own head, thinking possibly there might be something wrong there, of which he was unconscious.

But he could discover nothing. He then manipulated Ikey's head, who winced and suddenly ejaculated, "Oh, oh !"

He noticed his companion's head felt wet and clogged, and on looking at his hand it was drenched in blood.

His heart sank with dread.

Most of us know when an accident has happened and blood flows, with what suspense and anxiety we watch the wiping away of the sanguinary fluid, that is to reveal the full extent of the injury.

We wish to know the worst, and yet we almost dread to learn it.

Our hearts seem to stand still as we watch, wondering whether it is merely a trifling scratch or a ghastly, dangerous, perhaps deadly wound.

Fortunately there was nothing serious, as far as Ikey was concerned, beyond the loss of a small piece of skin and a little blood.

But as yet this fact had not been ascertained, and the dismay and consternation were for a time general.

"Be Oi to roon for t' doctor?" asked Sam, excitedly.

"Eh! ees," returned the agitated farmer. "Tell 'im to coom at oonce, 'cos we ha' coot a boy's 'ead off!"

But Ikey, who didn't like doctors, contradicted this assertion by popping up his head, as the best possible proof that it was still on his shoulders.

"My 'ead hain't cut hoff!" he cried. "Don't send for no doctor."

With his hair dishevelled and matted together, with innumerable pieces of hay bristling out from it in all directions, and his face tattooed with thin streaks of blood that trickled down it, Ikey looked like a very small edition of an Indian warrior in his plumes and war paint.

This intelligence of his, however, greatly relieved the honest farmer, who there and then took upon himself to examine the wound, and who, finding there was nothing serious, flew suddenly into a violent passion, and demanded of the boys "what the dickens they were doing in his hay shed?"

James explained their case briefly; and the good man was mollified immediately.

Anger did not seem to suit him, and the genial smile once more overspread his good-natured face.

The idea of the doctor was dismissed, and James and Ikey were lifted down from their roost.

"You may as well coom wi me 'oop to farm. Dame 'll give 'ee soomat to yeat?" said the farmer, as he took them by the hand, and led them across the field.

The boys couldn't help thinking how different he was from stern Mr. Gripman.

"An' so you be goin' out on t' world to make your fort'ns, be 'ee?" he asked, in answer to James's relation of their intentions.

"Yes, sir, if we can!" answered James.

"An ye ha' gotten no feyther nor moother either on you—eh?"

"No, sir," they replied.

"Poor boys," murmured the kind-hearted man, "it be a hard world they ha' got to travel through."

They were not long in reaching the farm.

A very comfortable, snug dwelling it was, too; at least, so the boys thought.

Everything was bright and clean, and there was a cheerful fire burning in the grate.

"'Ere, dame," the farmer cried, to a comely, round-faced woman, with rosy cheeks, and a pleasant smile, "'ere be a coople of poor boys as want their breakfast. Joost look after 'em, will 'ee?"

The kind woman, who was the farmer's wife, willingly undertook this; and having first washed both their faces, and applied a piece of sticking-plaster to the abrasion on the top of Ikey's head, she set about preparing their meal. In a very short time our young adventurers were seated by the fire, before two plates of savoury eggs and bacon, and in addition, two bright pewter cups of clear, golden-coloured cider.

The farmer and his spouse stood and watched the boys, as they attacked these good things, with faces beaming with satisfaction.

But the farmer had to be off on business; so he whispered to his wife, and then taking leave of James and Ikey, departed.

They having finished their meal, and gratified the curiosity of their kind hostess, by a short account of their past adventures, began to think it was time to be gone.

James suggested this to Ikey.

"It's werry comfor'ble 'ere!" he replied, wistfully, looking at the bright fire.

"Very!" returned James, "and these good people are so kind, I feel as though I should like to stop; but you know we didn't run away to sit by the fire and be comfortable, did we?"

"No," answered Ikey, in a tone of conviction, "we run away to make hour fort'ns."

"Besides," James continued, "we want to get a long way from Marton, don't we?"

"Yes—yes!" acquiesced Ikey.

"And I don't think we're more than five or six miles off yet."

"Then let's be hoff hout o' reach o' them const'bles, an' hout o' th' vay o' that Mr. Hotty," suggested Ikey, eagerly.

This being determined on, they expressed their readiness to depart, thanking their good-natured hostess for her kindness and hospitality.

"Dont'ee go yet," urged the friendly woman; "you bean't in such a hurry, be 'ee?"

But they explained to her that it was better they should start as early as possible.

The dame therefore made no objection.

She did not, however, let them go away empty handed.

She first gave them a gigantic lump of bread and bacon and a shilling each, accompanied by her blessing. She then, with tears in her eyes, gave them a hearty mother's kiss apiece, and dismissed them.

The boys trudged along manfully, having resolved to carry their provision by turns so long as it lasted. They looked back as they reached the gate of the field, and took a last look at the comfortable farm.

The good dame still stood in the porch watching them. She waved her hand to them; they waved theirs in reply.

"God bless and keep th' poor things!" she exclaimed, fervently, as they disappeared. "It be a 'ard world for grown-oop folk to get along in, let alone two poor children wi' no feyther or moother to look after 'em."

"Now," said James, when they were fairly on the road, "we'll walk fast; we must get over a good many miles to-day."

"Yes," answered Ikey, "we'll see 'ow fur we can go. Let's try an' valk fifty miles. Hi'll race yer."

This was not a bad idea for keeping up their speed, and they journeyed along light-footed. and, considering all things, light-hearted.

Chapter XXIX.

THE BOUNDING BROTHERS

THE boys walked well this day, and although they could not keep up the speed at which they started, they had walked a good many miles before the day seemed to show signs of declining.

Quite far enough to digest the eggs and bacon, and to make them look forward to the demolition of the provision with which their kind hostess had supplied them, with much pleasure.

Neither, however, had as yet expressed any desire to come to a halt.

But at length Ikey, unable any longer to restrain his craving sensation, exclaimed:

"Hi say, Jem, Hi'm werry 'ungry!"

"So am I," replied James. "Suppose we stop and have our dinner?"

"Hi think it'd be the best thing we could do, an' then we can go on valkin' arterwards," remarked Ikey.

Just as they made these remarks they came up to a small spring that oozed forth from the bank at one side of the road, and trickled down.

"See," cried James, "there's a spring: we'll stop here."

This being agreed upon, they sat down and commenced their meal.

They were very hungry, and enjoyed their repast as only hungry people can do.

The bacon was so relishing, the bread was so sweet! Nay, even the water seemed to be endowed with unusually delightful properties, and to taste as water had never tasted before to their palates.

"Ah!" exclaimed Ikey, immediately after taking a good swig, "that's a great deal betterer nor all that muck as Hi drank last night!"

"I should think it was," returned James, "and I hope, Ikey, you'll always think as you do at this moment. Water quenches your thirst better than anything else, and never does you any harm."

"Hi've made hup my mind to stick to vater, any-how," Ikey answered, firmly.

They found that when their meal was finished, they had still about as much more remaining.

"We must take care of this," said James. "Tie it up in the paper: it will do for to-morrow."

"Vort is der use to provide for to-morrow, when to-morrow nevair coam?" exclaimed a sonorous voice, with a foreign accent.

The boys looked up with a start.

Ikey sat with the remains of the bread and bacon in the paper, on his knees, staring with all his might.

Before him stood a shabby-looking man, of somewhat foreign appearance, with a dark beard round his mouth and chin, wearing a dark blue blouse, and a broad-brimmed, sugar-loaf hat.

He stood between two other shabby-looking youths, who also wore dark blue blouses and sugar-loaf hats, but no beards.

"Yah—yah!" they ejaculated, as if in assent to their companion's remark.

The boys sat gazing at the trio in mute astonishment.

It seemed to them as though some one or other was continually interfering with them.

Were they never to be left to themselves?

What did these three curious men want?

The first speaker spoke again.

"You two yong jentlemans look soorprise," he remarked. "It is pair'aps der foorst time you evair see three soch illoostriose pairsons."

He waved his hand in the air, grandly, and then continued:

"No doubt you vondair vhot ve am?"

There was no doubt about this: the boys were full of wonder.

"I shall tell you," the speaker went on. "Me an' dese two jentlemans are broders—ve am de *Bounding Broders of Poland!*"

He leant his elbows on the shoulders of his brethren as he spoke, and looked under his eyebrows at James and Ikey to observe the effect of this announcement. However, as they still continued silent, the illustrious foreigner spoke again.

"I am a Pole, and so are my two broders. Ve are all Poles. My name is Karl Gingeritz Cheerivitzki; der names of my two broders is Johann an' Florio."

After all this explanation, the boys were as much in the dark as ever.

The Pole saw this, and proceeded:

"You would like to know vhat ve do for our——I mean," he added, checking himself, "our professiong?"

James and Ikey looked rather inquiringly at the "professiong," and the Pole continued:

"Ve are *artistes*, attached to the travelling caravan of Herr Splutzer Von Boomberisch, the renowned Dutch explorer! Of course, you have hear of him?"

The boys never had, and shook their heads in reply.

"Dear, dear!" ejaculated the Pole, shrugging his shoulders, and raising his eyebrows piteously. "Nevair hear of Splutzer Von Boomberisch!—nevair hear of der Bounding Broders! Poor tings—poor tings!"

Having thus given vent to his sorrow at their lamentable ignorance, the "Bounding Brother" approached the boys, and scrutinised them with one eye attentively.

He had two eyes, but the other was occupied in surveying the bacon and bread, that still lay uncovered on the paper in Ikey's lap.

"You eat your dinnair, I see?" he remarked.

"We've just done, sir," said James.

"Yah! I pairceive! Vot is it you eat?" he inquired, dexterously catching up the paper and its contents as he spoke.

"Bacon, sir," James replied.

"Ah! bacone, der flesh of svines," returned the "Bounding Brother," bringing the savoury meat into somewhat close proximity with his nose, and sniffing at it with evident relish. "Bacone," he continued—"pigs! I remembair I eat pig vonce, many year ago—it vos very goot! I vondair eef it's goot now?"

The illustrious foreigner drew out a clasp knife with much dignity, and divided the bacon and bread into three portions.

Reserving the centre piece for himself, which was twice as large as the others, he offered a share each to the juvenile Poles at his elbows, who accepted them with the utmost condescension.

Ikey watched these transactions somewhat ruefully, but when he saw the active motion of the jaws of the three strangers, he thought it was time to speak.

"Hi say, Jem," he exclaimed, nudging his comrade, "them 'ere Poles is a heatin' our bacon."

"Well, never mind," said James, soothingly, "perhaps they're a long way from home, and are hungry."

"Hi don't so much mind," returned Ikey, "honly Hi think as they might 'a hask'd fust."

"But they're foreigners, and perhaps it isn't their way to ask as we should," explained James.

By this time the bacon and bread had disappeared, and the Poles were looking as though they could have endured a second edition of the same.

But there was no more—not a crumb!

The eldest brother then closed his knife, and they all took a drink at the spring—did those illustrious individuals.

Then Karl exclaimed, in an entirely different tone, divested of everything foreign:

"I dessay these 'ere young gents 'ud like to see a little ground an' lofty tumblin' before we parts. I've no doubt they'll be able to scrape us together a few coppers."

James and Ikey were so much astounded at the sudden transition of tone and accent in the speaker's words, that they had hardly noticed the allusion to the "coppers."

And before they had time to recover from their surprise they received a still greater.

The senior brother exclaimed:

"Come on, cullies—peel—off with your kicksies, and show 'em your spangles."

In an instant, as if by magic, off flew the blue blouses and the heavy boots they wore, and the "Bounding Brothers" stood revealed in all the glory of flesh-coloured tights, crimson sandals, and breeches profusely spangled, with the addition of a crimson band encircling each of their foreheads.

They fell into position at once: Karl in the centre, his brothers on either side.

This was but for a moment.

The senior Pole uttered an exclamation that sounded something like "*Hoop-la!*" and immediately the performance began.

Without attempting to describe this minutely, we may remark it was very wonderful.

To James and Ikey more than that—it appeared too marvellous to be accredited by anyone but an eye-witness.

How the juvenile Poles tumbled over head-and-heels forwards and backwards; how they turned somersaults in the air without their hands touching the ground; how they bent their bodies backwards, as though they had no bones in them at all, and picked up objects on the ground with their teeth; how the elder Pole placed his hand under the backs of the younger Poles, and turned them round and round till it made the beholder quite giddy to look at them; and then how they formed a tower by standing on each other's shoulders, and finally dropped down all of a sudden into their first position, must be left to the imagination of the reader.

It will be sufficient to state that the audience—James and Ikey—for whose special amusement this performance was given, were electrified.

As for Ikey—he was enraptured.

He thought of his own crude, inartistic efforts of the previous night to perform even the simple feat of standing on his head, and blushed at his own miserable incapacity.

If *that* was so difficult to accomplish, how many years would it take to become a "Bounding Brother?

It seemed a hopeless case altogether, and Ikey breathed a sigh of despair.

What would he have given to have been able to throw even one somersault, or to be able to shoulder his leg as a soldier would his gun !

What a delightful thing it would have been to have had no joints, no spinal vertebræ, so that he could tie himself up in a knot whenever he pleased.

But, alas ! alas ! for poor Ikey ; he had all these encumbrances—joints, bones, spinal vertebræ—all complete, and he almost hid his face in shame before the illustrious individual under a sense of his defects.

In the meantime these elastic creatures had returned to their natural selves.

The blouses, boots, and sugar-loaf hats were resumed—all but one—that was Karl's.

The senior Pole advanced to the boys holding forth this last-named article.

He made a brief appeal in the usual manner.

"A few coppers, young gents, if yer please."

It was a very embarrassing position this for James and Ikey.

They would not have thought of insulting these wondrously gifted creatures with anything so paltry ; but, since "coppers" were particularly mentioned as the desired reward, and even they limited to a *few*, the boys hardly knew what to do.

James was suddenly struck with an idea.

"We haven't got a *few coppers*, sir," he said.

The countenance of the Bounding Pole became clouded at this.

James noticed it, and hastened to explain.

"We've got nothing less than a shilling," James continued, humbly.

The cloud vanished from the face of Herr Karl.

"But, if you can change it into coppers, you can take as few as you like," wound up James, as he handed the only shilling he possessed to the Bounding Brother.

To the donor's great delight, the Pole offered no objection ; on the contrary, he transferred it to his pocket, and appeared to forget the change entirely, whilst his countenance expressed the liveliest satisfaction.

"It's all right," thought James ; "he isn't angry."

Ikey, who had been a silent listener to what had passed, observing the gracious condescension of the great Karl, thought he might venture to offer his coin.

He was yearning for some means to express his admiration, and seeing that the gifted trio were lighting their pipes previous to departing, he resolved to make the proposal.

They were just off, and he had little time to lose.

"Good day, young gents !" cried Karl ; "see yer again some day, p'r'aps !"

The youthful Poles echoed their brother and said, "A good day !"

What condescension !

Ikey was desperate.

"'Ere ! 'eigh ! stay, Mr. Pole, if yer please !" he cried. "I vants t' ask yer a favour."

"Fire away !" answered the individual addressed, stopping.

"Hi've got a shillin', too, as well as Jem, an' if yer vouldn't be offended, Hi should like to hoffer it to yer, if yer'd be kind enough to accept it."

Ikey looked at the great man very dubiously, half afraid he would decline, but it was not so.

Quite the reverse ; the senior Pole screwed up his face in a manner decidedly comic, and then winked at the junior Poles, who screwed up their faces.

Eventually they indulged in a laugh of intense enjoyment.

"My boy," at length said Karl to Ikey, "I'm not in the habit of doing sich things, but, on this occasion, if it 'll pertic'larly oblige you, I don't mind takin' th' coin."

He held out his hand, into which Ikey, brimful of gratitude and admiration, placed the shilling.

The Bounding Brothers laughed again.

"I'm open to take as many of these as yer like to give me," observed Karl, still holding forth his hand.

But there were no more to come—the bank had stopped.

Ikey explained this, and the talented trio, wishing the boys once more good afternoon, proceeded on their way.

"'Ow wonderful kind !" murmured Ikey.

"How jolly green !" chuckled the Bounding Brothers.

Chapter XXX.

AN AWKWARD BEDFELLOW.

THE travelling establishment of Splutzer Von Boomerisch was of a mingled description.

The proprietor was said to have been a great traveller—he always said so himself—and that the animals which composed his *menagerie*, whether living or dead, had been captured by his own enterprising hand.

This he also frequently asserted.

Many believed in the Dutchman, many did not.

This is a very censorious world we live in, and there were not wanting some ill-natured people who went so far as to assert that Splutzer Von Boomerisch was an impostor—nay, they even asserted that he was no Dutchman at all—that he couldn't speak his own language, and that the jargon of broken English in which he was wont to speak was all humbug.

As much so as the assumed dialect of the posturer Gingeritz Cheerivitzki.

As for the great deserts, the African forests, the Arctic Regions, which Splutzer had explored, where he had undergone unheard-of perils, and captured tigers, monkeys, snakes, and white bears—though he never explained how he got them home—the above incredulous people pooh-poohed the idea altogether, and dared to affirm that he had never even been across the English Channel.

Certainly he did make extraordinary blunders and mistakes in the accounts he was accustomed to give of his adventures, and the places he had visited, and the animals incidental to those places.

He would mix up circumstances and events, men and animals, in such an extraordinary way, that those who knew nothing about anything, said "What a wonderful man !" whilst those who were better informed, exclaimed "What a fool !"

But they were wrong there—Splutzer was no fool.

Ignorant he might have been of the subjects he insisted upon talking of ; but he had sense enough to acknowledge his ignorance—to himself only—and it was this consciousness that made him so audacious and reckless in his assertions.

He would never allow himself to be brow-beaten or argued down.

The consequence was, that many believed in him to an unlimited extent.

His ideas certainly were very confused.

He would speak of his combat with a polar bear in the great desert of Sahara, and how a boa-constrictor twined round his body on the ice-bound shores of Greenland ; sharks he had been known to catch in the depths of an African forest, and monkeys in shoals in the Highlands of Scotland.

When taxed with these absurdities, he fell back upon his memory.

"It had never been good since he had been frostbitten while crossing the Equator," he asserted.

There was no getting over Herr Splutzer.

But whether anyone else believed in him or not, the public did.

The Dutchman made plenty of money.

When other exhibitions failed, his was always successful.

But Von Boomerisch was artful ; he seized upon the public in every possible way.

He not only invited them to witness his natural curiosities, but he had an unlimited quantity of *unnatural* ones, in the shape of a giant and a dwarf, a lady with a pig's face, and a dog with two heads.

And not only so ; but being sensible that the public grew tired of simple nature, whether monstrous or

[A WARM EMBRACE.]

otherwise, he brought forward, to render the attractions of his establishment perfectly unrivalled, the wonders of art, in the shape of Chinese jugglers, Persian fire-eaters, Indian snake-charmers, tumblers, and contortionists of all descriptions, and of any country—of the last of which the Bounding Brothers of Poland may be considered a fair specimen—and last, not least, a real English clown.

With all these magnets of attraction to draw them, it is not to be wondered at that Boomberisch's menagerie was always thronged with visitors.

Gorgeous oil paintings of the struggles of the proprietor with ferocious beasts, covered the exterior of the exhibition.

They, alone, were worth paying to see; many had been heard to say that they far exceeded anything that was to be witnessed inside.

But they must have belonged to the ill-natured class before alluded to.

There was one time of the year, however, when the menagerie was a dead-letter.

That was at Christmas and for some weeks after, when folks were too much intent upon domestic enjoyment and festivity to care for anything but roast beef and plum pudding, family parties, and good fires.

Consequently, at this period, and while the snow lay on the ground, the animals of the establishment, human and otherwise, had a holiday.

The only difference was the latter were fed as usual, the former were *not*.

It was very trying to the poor fire-eaters, jugglers, and tumblers to be thus thrown out, and to be earning nothing, just when everybody else was eating and drinking. And it was this that had induced the Bounding Brothers of Poland to take a stroll into the country to try and pick up an odd shilling or two.

This will account for the eagerness with which they devoured the bacon and bread, and the readiness with which they condescended to accept the donations of James Cook and Ikey Mangles.

From the sudden change that had taken place in the weather, from frost and cold to the warmth almost of spring, Von Boomberisch was thinking of commencing his campaign earlier than he was wont to do.

His entire stock of animals travelled in four-wheeled vans.

These, when they reached their place of destination, were arranged end to end in the form of a square.

One side of each van, composed after the fashion of shutters, was removed, and the bars of the cages became visible, together with the animals they contained, to the visitors.

The whole was then covered with a thick tarpaulin, and the structure was complete.

In front of this magnificent edifice was a platform, the ascent to which was by steps.

It was on this parade the jugglers, fire-eaters, tumblers, dwarfs, and giants, and the clown, went through their enticing performances, in order to attract customers to the interior.

It was, then, on this particular day, the menagerie had made a grand move towards a particular town, where it was going to make a temporary sojourn.

The vans had started with their respective loads, and the Bounding Brothers, when they left James and Ikey, hastened onwards, expecting to overtake one of these conveyances, and get a lift to their place of destination.

Having explained thus much, let us return to Ikey and James, whom we left seated by the roadside supperless and penniless.

They did not feel their hapless condition then.

They were too full of satisfaction at the condescending urbanity of the Bounding Poles to be depressed, and, having just finished their dinner, they were not hungry.

They sat there thinking over what they had seen, James thinking that a life passed in tumbling over head and heels was, on the whole, rather a strange and useless occupation; Ikey, on the other hand, impressed with the idea that to be a "Bounding Brother" was the great end of existence.

It was growing dusk, and they knew not as yet where they should pass the night.

"I think," James remarked, starting up, "we may as well be moving."

"So do Hi," returned Ikey, standing with his feet close together, and swinging his arms as though half inclined to try a somersault. He, however, relinquished the idea, and said to James, "Vot shall ve do for supper now ve've give avay both th' shillin's?"

This was the first time such a thought had crossed them, and now, for the first time, James thought he had been rash.

But he made the best of it.

"It won't matter much," he said; "we've had a good dinner, and we can do very well without supper."

So they started off once more, briskly.

The twilight faded into evening, the evening into night, yet still our young heroes trudged on.

But they were beginning to grow tired.

Their pace gradually slackened to a walk—they had had enough for that day.

"Hi vishes Hi vos in bed!" murmured Ikey.

"So do I; I feel very tired," said James, languidly.

But there was no bed but the damp road, so they walked on.

"Hadn'i ve better lie down hunder th' edge?" asked Ikey.

"We must if we can find no warmer place," returned James.

"Hi don't see much chance o' that!" Ikey said, with a tremendous yawn.

The words were scarcely out of his mouth, when James called out:

"See, there's a light straight before us."

Ikey shook the "dustman" out of his eyes and looked.

There certainly was a light—rather dim, certainly; but still a light.

It was not across the country, at the extremity of some distant field, but tolerably near, and in the very road they were travelling.

"Is it a 'ouse?" inquired Ikey.

"I can't say," answered James; "we shall see when we get up to it."

They increased their speed, and soon drew near the doubtful object.

It stood at one side of the road, and had the appearance of a small house at a little distance.

There was the chimney pot, and smoke issuing from the top.

However, as they got close up to it they found it had four wheels to it.

"It's a carriage, Hi think," said Ikey.

"No; I think they call it a caravan," corrected James; "they travel about the country and go to fairs."

James, if not entirely correct, was partially so. It was one of the vans belonging to Splutzer Von Boomberisch, and was the last on the road.

The horse had been detached and sent forward to assist the others, and it had been left at the road-side till it could be sent for.

This van, though the last, was by no means the least in the opinion of the proprietor.

It was in this he resided, as might be known by the bright green door and the brass knocker, with the steps with a hand-rail leading up to it.

The windows also had red curtains to them, which conveyed the idea of much warmth and comfort within.

It was in this domicile, too, the Dutchman kept his particular treasures: all his curiosities, his pet odds and ends, the best of his wardrobe, and his money till he banked it, which was once a week.

It was in this sanctuary he wrote his letters, transacted his business, and paid his people their salaries on the Saturdays.

He was there at this particular moment, in deep and earnest conversation with his most valued and confidential servant, Mr. Jeremiah Dowlas.

Both master and man appeared to be in much perplexity and distress.

They sat before the fire, a small table between them, and on the small table a large bottle and two capacious tumblers.

A small kettle was on the fire, and a golden-looking fluid floated in the glasses, that bore a great resemblance to rum and water.

James and Ikey, curious to discover what kind of a place it was, crept softly up the steps, and made the investigation we have been enabled to record, partly through the keyhole and partly by standing on the wheel and looking through the window, which the red curtains only partially covered.

They could see the two occupants of the small cabin quite distinctly.

Herr Splutzer was a massive, broad-shouldered man, with a red face, gray hair, and splendid beard.

He had a commanding countenance altogether; but in his eyes lurked an expression of low cunning that spoilt all the rest.

With Jeremiah Dowlas it was entirely different: he was a little spare man, with a placid, quiet expression of countenance, but with the brightest and pleasantest eye and the most genial smile in the world.

We shall, perhaps, speak more of him anon.

In the meantime both the proprietor and his factotum were in trouble from two causes.

A very fine African ape, answering to the name of Smuttee Smut, had died during the vacation—that was one grief.

Long Tommy, the boa constrictor, had bolted the blanket in which it lay, and was in a precarious condition—that was another.

The upper part of the window through which the boys were peeping opened on a hinge, and happened to be down at that moment, so that they could hear all that passed.

"It's a great loss—a awful loss—that there ape! I wouldn't 'a taken 'is weight in gold, that I wouldn't!" exclaimed the proprietor, who, when alone with his friend Jerry, spoke as good English as most people of his class.

It was only in public that he assumed the Dutch.

"It is a loss, guv'nor, but it's no good grievin' for what can't be helped," said Jerry.

"I shall never forget ketchin' that theer hape!" exclaimed Splutzer, dolefully. "'E wos peltin' a crocodile with snowballs, on a block of ice off the coast of Greenland——"

"Excuse me, guv'nor," interposed Jerry: "wasn't it in Africy you dropped on him?"

"Oh ah! so it was," cried the Dutchman. "I remember: I caught him by the tail."

"No, guv'nor; he had no tail."

"I know that—I pulled it off! Ha, ha!—had you there, Jerry, old boy!" he laughed; but it was only for a moment, for, having taken a good swig at the liquor before him—which good example Jerry followed—he relapsed into his former sadness.

"That was a wonderful animal, that ape!" he continued.

"So he was," assented Jerry.

"Such an attraction to the menagerie!"

"Immense!"

"So sagacious and tractable!"

"Sometimes."

"So full of tricks!"

"Very: he nearly throttled me once."

"Couldn't he drink his tea out of a tea-cup, and hold the saucer like a Christian?"

"So he could, guv'nor."

"Couldn't he smoke his pipe an' drink his grog just as nat'ral as we could?"

"There's no disputing it."

"And now he's dead! It's a clear loss of—I don't know how much a year, losing Smuttee Smut."

"Smuttee Smut!" echoed Ikey. "Vot a rum name, hain't it?"

"It's the name of an ape," replied James

"Vot's a hape?" Ikey inquired.

"I think it's a monkey."

"And then," continued Von Boomberisch, "there's the boa, Long Tommy."

"'Oo's 'e?" asked Ikey.

"That's a snake," explained James.

"Is there any chance for him, Jerry?" the proprietor went on, in a doleful voice.

"Well, guv'nor, I can't say as yet," replied Jerry, dubiously.

"What d'ye think?"

"Well, certainly, boas, as a rule, are very voracious."

"Very! When I caught him, with a bit of pork, in the Mediterranean——"

"You mean in a swamp in South America, guv'nor."

"Well, it's all th' same! Go on: they're very voracious. Well?"

"And I think could digest almost anything; but a blanket, guv'nor——"

"Well, why not a blanket?"

"It's so awful tough!"

"We must physic him."

"He's been physicked."

"Can't we get the blanket up anyhow?"

"Not without pulling poor Tommy's inside out with it."

The owner gave a melancholy grunt.

"I s'pose we shall know in a day or two."

"I think so," said Jerry. "You'll be able to get the blanket after he's dead: he'll never be able to digest it."

Herr Splutzer shook his head despondingly, emptied his glass, and mixed another.

Jerry also imbibed and replenished.

"Did yer 'ear that, Jem?" Ikey took this opportunity to inquire.

"Yes."

"The hidear o' a snake swallerin' a blanket! Mustn't 'e 'a bin 'ungry?" he remarked.

"There's one thing," said Jerry, in a hopeful tone, "with respect to Smuttee Smut."

"What?"

"Though he's dead, I've got his skin."

"No good!" mournfully exclaimed the explorer. "Stuffed animals are nothing to live ones."

"I wouldn't stuff Smuttee," said Jerry.

"What would you do, then?"

"I've got an idea, guv'nor, about that," answered Mr. Dowlas. "I think I can perform a miracle."

"How d'ye mean?"

"Why, resuscitate Smuttee—bring him to life."

"What! now you've skinned him?" asked Von Boomberisch, incredulously.

"I could never do it if I hadn't skinned him," Jerry replied.

"But how are you going to set about it?" demanded his master, eagerly.

"Don't ask me now, there's a good fellow," entreated Jerry; "I'll show you how before long."

"If you can do that, I'll raise your salary!" exclaimed the proprietor. "In the meantime, if you've got the skin handy, I should like to see it."

"You can do that at once," Jerry replied; and going to a cupboard in one corner of the van, he produced a long board, on which was nailed the skin that had formerly covered the body of poor Smuttee.

"It looks in good condition," remarked Herr Splutzer.

"It is, too, and as sweet as a nut," added Jerry. "Rather pleasanter than when it was on Smuttee's back; he was rather a powerfully-scented animal."

"See," said Jerry—"here are his teeth; I shall want to make use [of them, and—— Hollo! what's that?" they both exclaimed, starting up.

Ikey, in his anxiety to get a glimpse of the teeth, had thrust his head in at the open window.

In so doing, he loosened the string that supported it, and it fell forward suddenly.

In his hasty retreat, he overbalanced, and in his excitement, clutching hold of James, who was unprepared, they fell to the ground together.

The noise both of the window and the fall, were distinctly heard by the inmates of the van.

It was this had caused them to start up.

The proprietor was suspicious of thieves or footpads.

He strode to the door and opened it.

"Who ish dere?" he cried, in a gruff voice.

There was no answer; he looked out, but saw nothing. Jerry did the same, with a similar result.

But all was quiet again.

"It's nobody, guv'nor," said Jerry; "it must have been one of the shutters rattled."

"P'r'aps so!" returned his master; but as a gentle hint to all whom it might concern, he exclaimed, in a formidable tone:

"Now, mind, whoevair you are, don't let me to catch you do dat again!"

He then closed the door, and drank some more rum and water.

James and Ikey, who were pretty well shaken by the fall, were not in a running condition.

They accordingly, with much presence of mind, rolled themselves quietly under the van, where, fortunately, finding a soft, warm rug, they lay down upon it, hardly daring to breathe during the investigation that was taking place above.

Whether it was that they were very tired with their walk, or that the warm rug on which they lay had a composing influence, certain it is, that they, almost as soon as the door shut to, fell asleep.

They could not have slept long, when, from some cause or other, James awoke suddenly.

The cause was that he could not breathe

Ikey was strangling him.

His arm was pressing upon his chest like a screw.

"Oh!" he cried. "Ikey, don't squeeze me so!"

But the pressure still continuing, he was about to raise his arm to dislodge that of his companion.

But he found to his great distress that, in addition to being hardly able to breathe, he was entirely powerless to move.

He became alarmed.

Ikey, too, began to cry out that somebody was choking him.

James glanced down desperately towards his breast, and saw a dark object lying across it.

What was it?

Could it be Long Tommy, he thought, wildly, not satisfied with the blanket, come to bolt him, into the bargain?

His reflections were disturbed by Ikey suddenly crying in his ear, in a terrified tone:

"Jemmy—Jemmy! Help us! Somethin' alive's got 'old hof me. Hoh—hoh!"

The frightened boys struggled violently to release themselves, but in vain.

Their breath seemed to be being gradually pressed out of their bodies.

Their struggles became more and more violent, when suddenly they were answered, and their terrors redoubled, by an angry growl.

"Oh, lor'!" gasped Ikey, horrified and breathless, "it's Smuttee S——"

Before he could finish the word, poor James gave a wild shriek, for as by a desperate effort he turned himself a little round, he heard the deep panting and felt the hot breath of some animal puffing in his face.

The next moment he understood the position of his companion and himself.

He saw the round eyes and formidable fangs of a large brown bear.

And there they were clasped in his terrible paws.

This was the *warm rug* they had lain upon !

No wonder they could not breathe.

Their condition now was desperate—appalling.

They shrieked wildly for help !

The bear, too, growing more and more irritated, growled louder, and hugged stronger.

It was fortunate he was muzzled, or the consequences might have been dreadfully serious.

As it was, they were nearly breathless.

The struggle going on beneath, the growlings of the bear, and the shrieks of the boys, had aroused the occupants of the van above.

"It's that rascal Bruno !" cried Von Boomberisch. "Has he got loose ?"

He started up as he spoke, and lighted a lantern.

"I think not," said Jerry ; "I tied him up myself."

"We'll go and see," returned the proprietor.

He opened the door and descended the steps.

Jerry followed.

"Look under the van, will you ?" said Herr Splutzer, who was a stout man, and not well adapted for stooping.

Jerry, taking the lantern, looked under obediently, but instantly uttered a loud cry of alarm, and in his excitement started up, forgetting where he was, and nearly splitting his skull against the bottom of the van.

He dropped the lantern, too, in his confusion.

"Murder !" he roared.

"What's the matter ?" shouted the Dutchman. "Has the bear got hold of you ?"

"No—no ! not me, but two poor boys ! They're black in the face !"

"Dead ?" gasped Herr Splutzer.

"I don't know ! I hope not ! Leave go, you brute !" shouted Jerry, raining such a volley of blows with his clenched fist on the nose of the unlucky Bruno, that in utter bewilderment he unloosed his paws, and allowed the boys to fall to the ground perfectly senseless.

In a moment Jerry had dragged them from beneath the carriage, and laid them *pro. tem.* upon the grass. There they contemplated them with looks of considerable apprehension.

As for Herr Splutzer, he began to speak Dutch, or rather broken English, immediately. He always did so on important occasions, and in situations of emergency, and this appeared to be somewhat critical.

"Mein Gott—Mein Gott, Jerree ! dis ish bad—very bad ! Vot do you tink of dish—eh ?" he inquired.

Jerry answered by screwing up his mouth and shaking his head ominously.

It certainly appeared a bad case.

The poor boys lay motionless, without showing any signs of life, whilst their swollen and purple features, together with a slight, frothy foam upon the lips, seemed to indicate all the agonies of suffocation.

"Ah, vell," said Herr Splutzer, "it'sh no use letting dem lie here."

"Not a bit," assented Jerry.

"Let us carry dem into de van," said his master.

Jerry obediently lifted Ikey Mangles from the ground, and Herr Splutzer performed the same good office for James Cook, and after a few severe words of reprimand to the bear, which did not appear to affect the latter in any way whatever, the pair with their several burdens, ascended the steps, and were once more in the sanctuary of the van.

Chapter XXXI.

JUST THE BOYS WE WANTED.

THE first step they took in the way of reviving the sufferers was to place them on the ground with their heads raised.

Then they opened the small window, and bathed their foreheads and temples with vinegar and rum.

These ablutions being interspersed with sundry rubbings on the chest and extremities.

After some little time had passed, the operators were delighted to observe the swollen appearance of the features and the purple hue gradually decrease.

Presently a faint sigh was heard, to the great relief of both master and man.

"It's all right, Jerry ; they'll do now !" cried Herr Splutzer, dropping his Dutch now the danger was over, and speaking English. "Give 'em a spoonful of rum."

"Yes, guv'nor," answered Jerry, obediently.

The spirit was administered at short intervals, and seemed to have the most beneficial effect.

The boys began to take deep inspirations, and to breathe freely, at the same time recovering with their breath their full consciousness.

They appeared a little mystified at the place in which they found themselves ; but they had by this time become so accustomed to adventurous vicissitudes, dangers and difficulties, that they had come to the conclusion that life was one long succession of scrapes to be got *into*, and to get *out of*, and so they took their present position as a matter of course, and quietly waited to see what would come of it.

As a natural act, they looked at the living occupants of the carriage, whose respective appearances by no means indicated anything to be feared.

On the contrary, both the proprietor and the factotum had sundry points in their faces that seemed to assure the boys—and they had particularly keen perceptions on this point from past experience—that they were more likely to be friends to them than foes.

They also suddenly remembered where they were, and recognised the interior, and recollected also how they had looked through the little window, and heard and seen what was going on, until they experienced their sudden drop.

Their memory carried them up to the time when they settled down under the van—as they thought, on a comfortable rug ; after that it was very dim and confused. Misty terrors, compounded of a confused jumble of dog-nosed apes, long Tommies, and live rugs, with terrible strong arms and claws, seemed to fill up the background of their brief mental retrospect.

The fact was, they were hardly conscious what it was they had escaped from.

Their reveries were interrupted by the proprietor.

"You are pettair, ain't you ?" he asked.

There was a pause : neither answered ; the manner in which he spoke was new to them.

"Can't you shpeak ?" he continued. "I ask you, are you pettair ?"

"No, sir," answered Ikey, briskly, "we're not pepper—we're boys."

Herr Splutzer opened his eyes very wide, and looked at Ikey, who in his turn looked at him.

The former then turned to his confidant, Jerry, and a peculiar stifled laugh passed between them.

He, however, checked it, and once more fastening his gaze on Ikey, he asked :

"Vot do you mean, eh ?"

Ikey perceived at once by the manner of the questioner, that he (Ikey) had made a mistake somewhere, so he replied :

"Hi thought yer ax'd if ve vas 'pepper,' and Hi said no, ve vas boys."

"Oh, oh—I see, mein boy—I see !" returned the good-natured Dutch English, English Dutchman, with a smile. "You do nort undairstand my tong ! You must learn it ; of all der tongs, der Dutch tong is der best."

Ikey received this information in silence, simply glancing in the grate, probably to ascertain whether there was any of that particular species of fire iron to be seen there.

Again the showman laughed, and then the proprietor, still smiling, said, bluntly, in plain English :

"Are you better?"

"Oh, yes, thank'ee, sir!" answered Ikey, quickly.

"D'ye feel inclined to eat anything?"

"Yes, sir, please," both the boys replied, eagerly.

"I suppose you're not very particular, eh?"

"Not at all, sir."

Herr Splutzer whispered to Jerry, who went to the cupboard. Through the half open door of this receptacle, Ikey's curious eyes caught a glimpse, in its distant recesses, of something that looked like the *head of a monkey*.

Ikey was at that moment—in fact, as he usually was—very hungry; but a kind of inward qualm passed through him, caused by certain ideas which this head suggested.

He remembered hearing of the death of the dog-nosed ape; he had seen the dog-nosed ape's skin—but where was the body?

Surely they did not eat such ugly-looking animals?

Ikey was perhaps of all mortals the least fastidious in the article of food.

He got what he could, and was very glad even to get that, but the idea of a monkey's ribs, or a monkey's leg, or arm, or tail, or any other joint, however temptingly cooked, seemed to make him shudder all over.

"Hi shall never be hable to svallow it; Hi knows Hi shan't," he inwardly cogitated.

In the meantime, Jerry had produced from the cupboard the repast destined for the boys, and placed it on the table.

During this, Herr Splutzer said a few words in a low tone to James, who had lain perfectly quiet, and hardly opened his mouth from the first moment of his recovery. What he did say, however, during the brief interchange of words that had just passed, seemed to please the proprietor, and convinced him—as it did all who had the opportunity of noticing the difference between the two boys—that though Ikey was the most forward and demonstrative, the sharpest and the readiest to reply, James had the most valuable qualities in himself.

"Now," said Jerry, who had by this time completed his preparations, "there's your supper, my boys, and all you have to do is to eat it."

A very savoury supper it was, too, consisting of the remains of a stew of Ostend rabbit and pork, which had been cooked for dinner.

The odour of the seasoning dispersed its powerful fragrance throughout the small chamber, inviting the hungry boys to a delicious treat.

But the distempered imagination of poor Ikey distorted everything, and for the first time in his life he couldn't eat.

James, who had no such misgivings, ate his supper and enjoyed it.

"'Owever he can heat monkey, Hi can't think!" cogitated Ikey, as he glanced ruefully at his comrade, who was quite engrossed with his knife and fork.

"'E dunno vhat 'e's heating of," he continued to himself; "an' p'raps e'll go an' p'ison isself. 'E shan't, if Hi can help it. Hi'll tell him. Hi say, Jem—Jem!" he whispered, to his friend.

"What?" inquired James, with his mouth full.

"D' you know vot you're a heating?" he inquired, in a tone of alarming earnestness.

"No," replied James, innocently; "but whatever it is, it's very nice."

"Ugh!" shudded Ikey. "When Hi tell yer vot yer've bin a swallerin' yer'll be ready to 'eave yer 'eart up!"

James paused at the evident horror expressed on his companion's features, and said:

"What is it I've been eating?"

"Vy," replied Ikey, in a harrowing whisper, "yer've been a eatin' a dead monkey!"

Now, to be told this in the middle of one's dinner is not altogether pleasant, especially at first sight.

Calmly reviewed, however, after the first start at the announcement—provided we have enjoyed our dinner, and that the monkey has proved a well-flavoured, tender monkey—we don't see, after all, that any great harm would result from such a repast.

James seemed to be a little of this opinion, but his countenance wore a puzzled expression.

"I don't think, somehow, it *can* be monkey, after all," he said.

"Oh, yes, it is!" persisted Ikey. "Hi see 'is 'ead theer in th' cupboard!"

Herr Splutzer and his confidential man-of-all-work had turned to the fire, but had been attracted by the profound discussion in which James and Ikey were engaged.

As they looked round towards the table, they saw the two engrossed boys in earnest conversation.

They observed also that Ikey had left his plate entirely.

This appeared somewhat inexplicable, since he had declared himself to be hungry.

The shortest way to arrive at an explanation would be to ask the reason.

This the proprietor resolved to do at once.

"I say, my lad," said Herr Splutzer, "I thought you said you were hungry?"

"So Hi did, sir."

"Then, now you are supplied with food, why don't you eat?"

"Don't want any, sir: thank'ee all the same," Ikey replied.

"That's strange!"

"No, it ain't, sir. It's a p'int o' taste, an' Hi can't abear 'em."

"What can't you bear?"

"Monkeys, sir!" exclaimed Ikey, with a shudder.

"Monkeys!" echoed Herr Splutzer and Jerry, in the most profound surprise.

"Oh, Hi dessay has they're all werry well in cages, but when yer comes to cookin' 'em for dinner—ugh!"

He suddered at the awful prospect of the perils of such uncongenial food.

"And do you really imagine that you have been offered a slice of monkey?" asked Herr Splutzer.

"Hi feels sure on it. Hi see 'is 'ead in th' cupboard, there," he said, pointing with the most rueful look and the wryest of faces to that receptacle.

This was too much for Herr Splutzer.

The great explorer who had travelled all round the world, and brought home a piece of the North Pole—so it was said—in his pocket, gave in at this, and throwing himself back in his chair, began to roar with laughter, till he had nearly choked himself.

Jerry, seeing his master so convulsed, felt he could not do less than follow his example, and he roared in concert.

"Oh! Mein Gott!—mein Gott!" gasped the Dutchman, falling back in the vehemence of his mirth upon his Dutch jargon. "Vot shall I do? Oh—oh! dis vill kill me! Vhy, you stupid leetel donce, dat vat you haf on your plate ish not monkey, but rabbits—rabbits mixsht mit pork. Ah! dunder unt blitzen! You don't know vort ish good for yourself!"

Poor Ikey felt very much ashamed of himself, and was heartily sorry he had made any allusion to the monkey.

He was afraid he should be deprived of his supper as a punishment; and now that his doubts were allayed, his appetite suddenly returned in all its pristine vigour.

However, the showman was a good-natured man, and did not evince any displeasure, treating the affair rather as a joke than anything else, merely remarking:

"Don't be sillee: eat your supper vhile you can get it."

Ikey needed no further invitation, and speedily redeemed the time he had lost.

When the appetites of the boys were fully satisfied, Jerry, at a sign from the Dutchman, drew from a recess a small bottle of ale, which he uncorked, and having poured the contents equally into two glasses, he placed one before each of the lads, and said:

"Drink!"

The glasses were quickly raised to their thirsty lips and drained to the dregs.

What delicious nectar it appeared to them!

The effects of the draught soon became apparent on the young wanderers.

They began to nod in their seats.

"Poor boys!" exclaimed the proprietor, sympathisingly; "they've had enough for to-day. They want to go to bed."

"Ah, yes!" said the factotum, meditatively scratching his head. "That's the point; where's the bed to come from?"

"Oh! they won't be particular," cried Splutzer. "Throw your great-coat on the floor, and cover them with mine. They'll have a better bed then than I've had half my life."

Jerry did as he was ordered, and then lifted the boys —who had fallen fast asleep where they sat—into their place of repose, where, having covered them snugly up, he left them to their dreams.

Herr Splutzer mixed himself some more rum and water, and having taken a tolerable gulp, smoked his pipe in silent meditation, looking into the red-hot embers of the grate, until he fancied himself in the torrid deserts of Africa.

Jerry, who strictly imitated his respected superior in everything, had also replenished his pipe and his glass, taken one long and strong pull at the latter, and settled down also into deep contemplation.

The only difference between the meditations of master and man being that, whilst those of the former rested upon difficulties, and went on imaginary rambles to impossible places to obviate them, the mind of the latter fastened upon plans within his reach and possible to be accomplished.

For a considerable time silence reigned in the van.

Silence broken only by the monotonous puff—puff— puff of the absorbed smokers, and a periodical snore from Ikey.

At length the thoughts of Herr Splutzer found vent in words—Dutch jargon, of course, this time; he was in a difficulty.

"Dere ish no doubt I am unfortunate—verree! I haf pad luck" he soliloquized. "Foorst dere vash der boa-constrictor Tommee—he die, den der vash der dog-nosed ape, Smuttee Smut—he die, an' last der infant crocodile, dat I expect from der banks of der Nile ish not arrive', an' I have announce him to appear at my exhibition next week, an' he vill not be dere. I must break my vord to der pooblic. Oh! no, on vos evair so unfortunate ash me!"

This melancholy summing up so affected the perplexed Dutchman, that he emptied his glass at a draught. Jerry, having imitated his master in the performance of a similar feat, and knocked out the ash from the top of his pipe, turned to the Dutchman, and said:

"I've been thinkin', guv'nor."

"So have I, Jerry," interrupted his master, "and I foresee a great deal of disappointment and difficulty from our losses during the recess. A boa-constrictor like Tommy, and a monkey like Smuttee Smut, are not to be picked up every day."

"No, guv'nor, I know they're not!" returned Jerry; "but, if you'll just listen to me, I think I've got hold of a good idea."

"Have you?—out with it! What is it?" eagerly inquired the proprietor, leaning on the arm of his chair, and looking with great expectation in the hopeful face of Jerry.

"Why," answered the other, "I think I see my way clear to get ourselves out of all our difficulties, and keep faith with the public."

"Well, but how can we do that without Smuttee Smut and the crocodile?"

"I'm coming to that, guv'nor now. I think I can provide you with another dog-nosed ape, so like poor Smuttee, that even you wouldn't know the difference."

"My dear fellow—my invaluable Jerry!" exclaimed the delighted Dutchman, "are you in earnest?"

"Never was more in earnest in my life," returned the other, assuringly.

"And will this new monkey have all poor Smuttee's accomplishments? Will he be able to pour his tea into a tea-cup, and drink it like a Christian? Will he be able to crack nuts with nutcrackers, smoke a pipe, make his bed, put on his nightgown and nightcap, put the extinguisher on the light, and get between the sheets, like a human being?—eh?—eh?" demanded Herr Splutzer, excitedly.

"He shall do all this, and more!" replied Jerry, in a tone of confident assurance, that was balm to the anxious soul of the proprietor.

"But where is he to be found—such a treasure?"

"There!" exclaimed Jerry, triumphantly, pointing as he spoke where Ikey, with his hair dishevelled and his mouth open, lay blissfully unconscious of the enormous responsibilities that were so soon to fall upon him.

"That boy?" cried Herr Splutzer, in a tone of evident disappointment. "Oh, teifel!"

"Only wait, guv'nor, you'll see. I don't generally say things without meaning 'em."

"No, you do not, Jerry; that's true."

"Out of evil comes good!" continued the factotum. "When we found those boys half smothered in the paws of Bruno, we thought it was evil; yet now we find that they're just precisely the two boys we wanted!"

Jerry spoke in a tone of great exhilaration; but his master by no means appeared to share in this feeling.

"I don't see clearly at present what you mean, Jerry," he remarked, lugubriously.

"Well, then, you know my business, before I joined you, was that of a preserver and stuffer of birds, beasts, and fishes?

"Well, after Smuttee's death, I very carefully removed his skin and his teeth."

"Yes, you showed them to me."

"I also preserved his head, so that at any time I can reproduce his likeness. Very well, then, I've fixed my eye on that little knowing coon there, with the large eyes"—he pointed to the slumbering Ikey as he spoke—"and if I can't disguise him in Smuttee's skin, and paint him up artistically to the life, say I know nothing at all about natural history."

Having thus delivered himself, the little man threw himself back in his chair and nursed his leg, screwed up his face till one eye was entirely closed, and having thus focussed his master, looked at him scrutinisingly with his other eye to watch the effect of his oration.

That it had taken an effect was undeniable, for the Dutchman applied once more to the bottle, and mixed himself and—this time—his skilful admirer a tumbler each.

He then lit his pipe, and then, after a few profound puffs, said:

"It might do—yes, I think it might, certainly!"

"*Might do!*" echoed the sanguine Jerry. "It *will* do —it *must*—it *shall!*"

"Well, you're a very clever man!" exclaimed his master, in a strong tone of thorough confidence, "and when a really clever man tells me he *will* do a thing, I invariably notice he *does* it. I believe it will succeed admirably!"

"That's right, guv'nor; I'm glad to hear you talk so," replied Jerry. "Now we shall get along."

"And can you teach this boy all the habits of a monkey so as not to betray the deception?" inquired the explorer.

"I'll turn him out in the course of the next fortnight such a genuine specimen of the monkey tribe, guv'nor," Jerry answered, "that if Smuttee's own mother were to come over from the coast of Africa to see her son, she wouldn't recognise the difference."

"I'm satisfied," said Herr Splutzer, quaffing a draught of Jamaica. "But about the other?"

"Of course we can't deputize for snakes, guv'nor, we——"

"I didn't mean Long Tommy—I was thinking of the infant crocodile, now supposed by the public to be just arrived from the banks of the Nile," explained the proprietor. "What's to be done about him?"

"I can manage the crocodile as well as the monkey," replied Jerry—"in fact, he's far easier than the other."

"But where's the skin to be got?" inquired the Dutchman.

"Fortunately, I have a young one preserved at home which I can send for. It is just the size for the other youngster to encase himself in."

"Capital!"

"All I shall have to do will be to remove the stuffing, moisten and revarnish the skin, and make the jaw work by means of spring and a wire fastened skilfully inside."

"Upon my word, Jerry, you're an invaluable fellow, that you are!" exclaimed the delighted Splutzer.

"I hope this isn't the first time you've found that out, guv'nor?" observed the confidant.

"Oh no, no," eagerly replied his grateful master. "I always said you were unrivalled! You're worth your weight in gold, *you* are, everyone knows that!" He made no mention, considering the preciousness of the estimable Jerry, how little of the said gold had fallen to his share; but this was probably an oversight on the part of Herr Splutzer. "And when shall you commence your preparations?" he inquired, eagerly.

"The very first thing to-morrow," answered Jerry.

"Good! then now unroll the rug, and let us have a few hours' sleep—I begin to want it!"

Jerry spread the rug on the floor, having first removed

the tables and chairs into the remotest corner. The tired and somewhat fuddled proprietor threw himself on the shake-down, and was asleep almost before his head touched his pillow.

Jerry also tired, and also somewhat fuddled, locked the door, made up the fire, and replenished the kettle, ready for the morrow's breakfast, and then threw himself beside his master, and there and then slept with an intensity of purpose that would have driven a bad sleeper mad with envy.

Chapter XXXII.

A NEW PROSPECT.

THOUGH Jeremiah Dowlas was the last to go to rest, he was the first to awake in the morning. The cold, gray light of day had scarcely spread itself over the earth's face when he, full of the work he had to accomplish—no less a feat than transforming one boy into a monkey and another into a crocodile—started from his recumbent position and glided into his small-clothes.

This was his first move. His next was to the door, which he unlocked, and emerged from, standing for a few moments on the steps in the chill morning air, to get what he called a freshener, having, for the furtherance of the said freshening, nothing on but the garment before mentioned and his shirt.

This being accomplished, he performed his toilet in a very expeditious manner, raked the embers of the fire together, and replenished it with coals, put on the kettle, and, in a marvellous short time, a clean white cloth covered the small table, and a rattling of cups and saucers proclaimed the advent of breakfast time.

While the kettle was boiling, Jerry made toast perseveringly, so that by the time that event took place, he had prepared quite a pyramid, which stood in a plate on an iron footman before the fire.

The water having declared itself in a proper condition by boiling over, the indefatigable little man made tea.

He then fried some ham and eggs for the master's breakfast, who was a bit of an epicure in his way, and now all things were prepared, and he only waited for the milk, which a boy from an adjacent farm was accustomed to supply them with while they remained there. During the pause that ensued, Jerry had a few moments' leisure to ask himself how he felt, and the answer he returned to himself was that if anybody else experienced at that moment similiar sensations to those he experienced, that person would decidedly accuse himself of having slightly overstepped the strict bounds of temperance on the previous night.

If the truth must be told, Jeremiah had the headache, but he braced himself up, washed his face, combed what scanty hair there was on his head, and felt better.

At this juncture the milk-boy's steps were heard, and the next moment the well-known "Milk-oh!" was chanted without vociferously.

Jerry did not keep the lad waiting, and having now all the materials, he made himself a good, strong cup of tea, which, to use his own words, "set him on his legs, and made him a man again."

And now, the proper time having arrived, he aroused his master, informing him that breakfast was ready, and that, as there was much work to be done in a little time, the earlier it was commenced the better.

Herr Splutzer was drowsy that morning, owing to his unusually copious libations of the previous night.

His factotum had considerable difficulty in arousing him to the conviction that it was time to rise.

Von Boomberisch grunted, and "psha'd!" and talked Dutch, and ended by declaring he would not be disturbed in the middle of the night for anybody.

It was in vain Jerry informed him the ham and eggs were spoiling.

He only got in a passion, and consigned ham and eggs to certain remote torrid regions, the precise locality of which need not be designated.

It was only when, as a last resource, his patient man-of-all-work whispered the "dog-nosed ape," and "infant crocodile" in his ear, that he woke up to the necessity for action.

"You're quite right, Jerry," he said; "but I don't ever remember feeling so sleepy as I do this morning, and my head is like a pan of hot coals. Ugh! I think I must have had a little too much rum-and-water last night."

Jerry at this crisis came to his relief with a strong cup of tea.

The Dutchman received it eagerly, and drank it greedily.

"Ah!" said he, as he dipped into the reviving beverage, "we didn't get this in South Africa! What a blessing tea is!"

The tea strung up Herr Splutzer's nerves, and enabled him to dress himself.

Having performed his ablutions, he sat down to the bacon and eggs, and altogether contrived to make a breakfast that completely effected his cure.

It was then thought expedient that our young heroes, James and Ikey, should be awakened.

The slumbers of childhood are light, and there was no difficulty in arousing them.

Especially as Jerry had the tact to inform them that breakfast was ready.

This was enough for Ikey, who sniffed the savoury odour of ham, tea, and toast, all blended in delightful harmony, and sprang up at once, followed by James. Having never removed their clothes, they were already dressed.

Jerry, however, insisted on their washing their hands and faces, and restoring their tangled locks to something like order.

This was entered into heartily by James, and not objected to by Ikey, though it is more than probable the perspective breakfast was the secret of his ready obedience.

At length, however, they were seated with a plentiful supply of tea and toast before them, and the remains of the ham and eggs left by the proprietor at their disposal.

It is needless to say neither of the boys rejected these luxuries.

They ate as those might be supposed to eat who would never have the opportunity of eating another breakfast as long as they lived.

Herr Splutzer and Jerry amused themselves by watching them.

"Well, my lads," said the Dutchman, when they had tired themselves, "are you satisfied?"

They both replied in the affirmative.

"Then come and sit down and listen to me," returned the Dutchman.

Jerry placed a couple of stools for the boys, the Dutchman lit his pipe—he always smoked after breakfast—and the audience commenced.

"Now," said Herr Splutzer, "I want you to tell me the truth!"

He fixed his eyes scrutinisingly upon them, as much as to say it was an idle hope to attempt any tricks upon a person of his penetration.

The boys also fixed their eyes on him, and listened patiently for what was to follow.

They were not kept long in suspense.

"The first thing I want you to tell me," said Herr Splutzer, "is whether you two boys have run away from home?"

"No, sir," answered Ikey, boldly, "that's kimpossible. Ve couldn't run avay from 'ome, 'cos ve ain't got no 'ome to run avay from."

"Oh!" ejaculated the explorer. "Very good. And now your parents—where are they?"

"Hi never 'ad none," said Ikey.

"You're one of the wonders of creation," remarked his questioner, laughing. "And you?" he added, inquiringly, to James—"I suppose you had such necessary articles as parents, eh?"

"Y-es, sir," faltered James, the tears coming into his eyes; "but they're both dead."

"Poor boys!" exclaimed Herr Splutzer. "Well, I suppose you have relatives of some kind living, haven't you?—uncles, aunts, cousins, or——"

"No, sir," interrupted James, mournfully, "we have not a single one!"

"Then you've no one to guide or check you, or, in fact, to care whether you come or go, or live or die?"

"No one, sir," answered James; "we've started together to try and make our way in the world honestly."

"Yes, sir," joined in Ikey, "ve're svorn pals, an' ve're a goin' to stick together hall our lives."

The Dutchman smiled.

"And how are you going to live?" he asked.

"The best way we can, sir," said James. "Heaven is kind to poor orphans and won't let us want!"

"But still you must do something for your living. Wouldn't you like to earn your own bread?" the showman inquired.

"Oh, yes, sir," answered James, eagerly. "There is nothing I should like so much."

"Very well, then, here's a chance for you!" said Herr Splutzer. "I am the proprietor of one of the largest collections of animals in the world, and of course I employ a great many auxiliaries in my establishment. Now if it suits you to remain with me, and make yourselves useful to the extent of your ability, and be good, well-behaved, obedient boys, you'll have an opportunity of acquiring a perfect knowledge of natural history. You'll be able to study the habits of the animals of the torrid and arctic regions, from personal observation, and, in addition to these gigantic advantages, I'll feed, clothe, and lodge you, and give you a trifle for pocket-money into the bargain. What do you say?"

Having finished this harangue, the Dutchman paused upon the dazzling offer he had made, and waited to let it work its effects upon his listeners.

It was not an offer to be slighted in their critical condition, and though they could not gather from Herr Splutzer's speech the slightest inkling as to what they would be expected to perform in his employ, still, it seemed to them anything was better than nothing, and that food, clothes, and shelter were infinitely preferable to hunger, cold, and rags.

"I am willing to stop, sir," said James, "if Ikey is."

"Hi should think Hi ham!" answered Ikey, determinately. "Ketch me a givin' hup a chance like this! Hi'm fond o' hanimals, 'specially 'orses. 'Ave you got any 'orses, sir?"

"We have a very fine zebra, or striped horse of the desert," replied the showman, grandly. "Then I s'pose I may consider the matter settled? You agree to stop with me—eh?"

"Yes, sir," replied the boys.

"Very good," returned the Dutchman. "Mr. Dowlas, you'll enter these boys on the list of my company. No salary till I see what they're worth."

"Very good, sir!" said Mr. Dowlas.

"And now I'll go and send the horses back for this caravan, that we may join the rest of the party. If I don't show myself among them, I know what it will be —all play and no work!"

Having uttered these remarks, he glanced significantly at Jerry, threw a meaning look across to the boys, which was perfectly understandable, and went out.

Jerry was now alone with the youngsters. There was something in the plain, unvarnished, simple story the poor little fellows had declared, that touched his heart, and Jerry Dowlas was far from being the most hard-hearted man in the world.

He was one of those characters frequently met with in most unlikely places, who, without being held up as perfect models of virtue, have, nevertheless, served their masters for too often a miserable pittance, with all their heart and strength; and, having grown gray and worn quite out in that service, have died as poor as they lived, unheeded and forgotten.

Jerry being with them alone, began his little plan of making the assumption of the monkey character appear to Ikey to be an enormous proof of the confidence his employer had in him, and a great privilege for which many sighed in vain, but which only a favoured few were ever destined to attain.

The confidential servant had taken rather a fancy to James and Ikey, and fancied he saw in them two valuable boys.

"Well, my lads," he cried, in a bland, cheerful tone, smiling out of his bright, kind eyes, till the boys both quite loved him, and felt they could have done anything for him, "I hope we shall be comfortable together, and I'm sure I don't see why we shouldn't. You've come to the right place here to get on. I only wish I'd been so fortunate as to get such a place when I was a boy, but there was no such luck. Times were different then."

"Ah, this *is* a place!"

Jerry nodded his head so significantly, and rubbed his hands so cheeringly as he spoke, that the boys were inspired with the most lively expectations.

"His it sich a *nice* place, though, 'ere, Mr. Jerry?" Ikey inquired.

"It is indeed!" returned Mr. J., "and if a boy's clever, and pleases the guv'nor, it's as good as a fortune to him."

"An' there's lots o' beastes, hain't theer?"

"Quantities!"

"Wild beastes?"

"Yes, besides birds, fishes, and reptiles."

"Vot's reptiles?" inquired Ikey.

"Snakes belong to that class," said Jerry.

"Hany monkeys?"

"Plenty!"

"I likes to see monkeys. I see vun vonce; hain't they full o' tricks?"

"Very, and so sagacious too," replied Mr. Dowlas, rejoicing in his inmost heart that Ikey had led the way to the subject voluntarily.

"What monkey was that that died?" inquired James.

"That was the guv'nor's favourite, Smuttee Smut."

"Vot a rum name: Smuttee Smut," remarked Ikey. "Vos 'e a black 'un?"

"Very dark indeed," said Jerry, "and wonderfully intelligent: there was positively nothing he couldn't do."

"Could he talk?"

"Oh, no! speech is always excepted; but he could do everything else. Herr Splutzer prized him more than all the other monkeys—he had so much trouble in catching and bringing him over to this country."

"Lor!" ejaculated Ikey. "Did 'e catch 'im 'isself?"

"Undoubtedly!"

"Vot a clever gen'l'man 'e must be!"

"I assure you the loss of this monkey distresses him greatly," continued Mr. Dowlas, "not merely on account of the loss itself, but because the animal is announced to appear at the re-opening of our establishment."

"Hi 'spose 'e can't come hif 'e's dead?" Ikey inquired, innocently.

"Not very easily," answered Jerry, drily, "and that's just where the botheration of it is. You see, Smuttee Smut was an extraordinary animal, that could perform all kinds of curious tricks. The public are accustomed to see Smuttee, and Smuttee's an enormous favourite. Smuttee's announced to appear on our opening night, and if he doesn't appear, the public will be disappointed and indignant, and when the public—the British public —are disappointed and indignant, do you know what they do?"

"No," answered the boys. "What?"

"Why, they'd think no more of setting fire to the menagerie, and hanging me and the proprietor, or tearing us to pieces, than they'd think of scratching their noses."

This seemed to the boys to imply a very unjust and sanguinary temper on the part of the British public. But it also had the effect of suggesting some sort of plan to Ikey's simple mind by which the outraged monster might be appeased, or at least gulled into quiescence.

"'Aven't yer got some hother monkey as yer could paint th' same colour, an' as'd do the same tricks as Smuttee, so as the publics vouldn't know the difference?" he asked, inquiringly.

Jeremiah Dowlas's heart fairly bounded within him at these words.

It was strange that in the mind of this boy the very same kind of idea was floating as that which filled his own brain.

There was, however, still a slight difference between them, which Jerry proceeded to reconcile.

"Well," said he, thoughtfully, as though he had been impressed by the boy's words, "I don't think we

[JAMES COOK VISITS SQUIRE MARKHAM.]

could substitute any other *monkey* for poor Smuttee, because, you see, he was so different in appearance; but I think, perhaps——"

Here he paused, and looked in a peculiarly scrutinizing and meditative manner at Ikey, as though he were contemplating something in connection with *him*.

Ikey was fully aware of what the other intended to convey, and thought to himself:

"'Ow 'e looks at me! Does he vant to make *me* into a monkey?"

"Yes—yes," at length oozed out slowly and thoughtfully from the lips of Mr. Dowlas, as though he were quite alone, and buried in a profound reverie, "I think it would do—I feel *sure* it would!" Here he stopped abruptly, and contemplated Ikey for some moments.

"He looks like a sharp boy," he murmured, as though utterly unconscious of the propinquity of the object of whom he spoke. "I think we could trust him—I'm sure we could!"

Mr. Dowlas started from his temporary absorption, and approaching Ikey quickly, as though a great idea had just dawned on him, said, in a hasty manner:

"Do you think you could perform the character of a monkey?"

"Hi dunno," Ikey answered. "Hi never tried."

"Would you like to try?"

"Vell, Hi shouldn't mind, if you'd teach me vot Hi'm to do."

"I'll teach you!" exclaimed Jerry, who now saw all his difficulties vanish.

"But the British public 'll be sure to know as Hi hain't Smuttee, an' p'raps they'll tear me to pieces," suggested Ikey, apprehensively.

"I'll answer for your safety," said Jerry.

"But Hi hain't a bit like a monkey, ham Hi?" asked the boy.

"Not at present," returned Jerry; "but I'll see about that. I've got Smuttee's skin, and when I fit that on you, and trim you up as I mean to do, you'll fancy you are a monkey."

Ikey grinned all over his face at the idea, and Jerry Dowlas laughed, too, as he said:

"But, you know, there's more in imitating a monkey than simply wearing his skin."

"Hi should think so," answered Ikey.

"I shall have to instruct you," continued Jerry, "in the habits of the animal."

Ikey acquiesced with a nod.

"Are you pretty active?"

"Uncommon."

"Can you jump?"

"Like an 'are."

"Can you climb?"

"Can't Hi?—like vinkin'—hup trees arter birds' nestes!"

"That's a very important faculty," said Jerry; "all monkeys are good climbers. I suppose, also, you can crack nuts?" continued Mr. D., with a smile.

"Crack 'em?—Hi believe yer—an' heat 'em, too," grinned Ikey, "when Hi gets the chance."

"You'll have the chance now, then, of cracking as many as you like, and eating them, too."

Ikey's eyes sparkled with joy: he was very fond of nuts—often he had had nothing else to eat.

"Well then, Ikey," said Mr. D., "I'll see what we can do with you. We shall be moving away from here this morning to join the rest of the caravans; but as soon as we're settled, I'll take you in hand, and in less than a fortnight I'll teach you more natural history than ever you heard of in your whole life."

Ikey received this intelligence obediently, and in course of time two strong horses came from the next town to convey the solitary carriage to join its companions.

There were very few preparations to be made.

Bruno's muzzle had to be tightened, and his chain looked to previous to starting.

While these operations were being performed, the boys had an opportunity of contemplating their affectionate friend of the previous night.

Bruno, who did not seem to recognise them in any way, lay very composedly under the carriage, which was oftener than not the post assigned him.

James and Ikey could not forbear a shudder, as they reflected on what they had escaped.

"Th' hidear o' goin' an' layin' down on 'is body, an' thinkin' it vas a rug—hoh my heye!" He shuddered at the thought of their reckless imprudence.

Their imagination was suddenly checked by the voice of the factotum.

The horses were harnessed and everything ready for departure.

"Now, boys," cried Jerry, "will you ride in the van er on the horses' backs?"

He put this question to test their adventurous qualities.

With much satisfaction he received from both the unhesitating reply:

"The horses' backs, please sir!"

"Up with you, then!"

Now, though Jerry gave this injunction, he offered them no assistance in mounting, wishing to see how they would manage to accomplish this feat.

The horses were large, strong animals, lusty and well fed, and as the boys stood by their sides looking up towards the region whither they sought to aspire, they might have reminded the beholder of two small Trojans looking up in amazement at the colossal proportions of the *Giant Horse.*

Jerry smiled to himself as he watched the thoughtful expressions on the countenances of the would-be equestrians.

They did not, however, waste much time in thought — James Cook grasping the leather trace with one hand, sprang up, and by dint of an energetic kind of struggling, scrambling effort, succeeded in mounting to the position he sought.

Ikey, on the other side, had taken a run and a jump, and by dint of a similar scramble, contrived somehow to meet his comrade at the top of the horses' backs.

Jerry was perfectly satisfied at the manner in which the boys had performed this feat, and inwardly chuckled over the energy they had displayed.

"Very good—very good!" he cried, smilingly. "I see I shall be able to make a monkey of you yet."

This was especially addressed to Ikey; but James, perhaps wondering what was in store for him, said:

"What am I to be, sir?"

"Well, I don't know yet," replied Jerry, "but I daresay we shall be able to find something for you."

And with this piece of information, Mr. Dowlas shouted to the man in charge of the horses:

"All right!" and the ponderous machine commenced its not very rapid journey towards the next town.

Chapter XXXIII.

BUILDING THE SHOW.

NOT very rapid—still by continually plodding on in the right direction, the distance gradually but surely decreased, and the town at length was reached.

Might not our young readers take a useful hint from this slow journey?

It is not always the strongest, the cleverest, or the quickest travellers who show the best at the end of a journey—nay, these not unfrequently never arrive at the end at all; whilst, at the same time, one neither strong, nor swift, nor clever, may have one quality—*determination,* or if you like, *perseverance.* Armed with this, he has kept steadily on, often assailed and hindered on his road, sometimes stopped, now and then driven back. But never turning aside either on the right hand or the left, by degrees he tires out his opponents, overtakes and outstrips numerous aspiring and boastful competitors, and reaches the goal at last, slowly, but surely, like the van in our history.

Having gained the town, they were not long in arriving at the plot of ground hired by Herr Splutzer, as the temporary site of his world-renowned menagerie.

The work of erecting this magnificent fabric had been in progress for some days, and the arrival of the proprietor that morning had given a stimulus to the operations of the labourers.

Herr Splutzer, the renowned explorer, had a very keen eye for profit and loss.

On his establishment he did not keep a single cat that had not its proper quantity of mice to catch.

Neither did the proprietor see the propriety of paying talent for doing nothing; therefore whenever he engaged a fresh hand, whether some Continental celebrity (which general turned out to be an importation from Lambeth, Whitechapel, or Bethnal Green) or otherwise, he made it an invariable clause in the agreement, in order to keep them in healthy exercise during idle hours, that they should assist in taking down or putting up the Mammoth establishment, whenever he deemed it advisable to adjourn to some fresh locality.

Accordingly, when the van arrived, the whole *corps gymnastique* were as busy as bees.

Tumblers, posturers, jugglers, fire-eaters, snake charmers, &c., &c., were rushing about with their coats off, and their sleeves tucked up, in a state of intense perspiration, hurrying on the completion of the gigantic structure.

It was quite a novel scene to the boys, who, having slid from the backs of the horses on to the ground, contemplated the scene with great interest.

The vans were ranged in order, end to end, in the form of an oblong, at the open end of which they were erecting the platform, or *parade,* as it was termed.

This was raised some eight feet from the ground, and it was upon this platform the strength of Von Boomberisch's attractions were displayed.

Here it was he threw away sprats to ensure a good netful of mackerel.

Here his whole body of tumblers, contortionists, conjurers, fire-eaters, giants, and dwarfs went through the mysteries of their various crafts.

This was the secret of the great explorer's success.

The public was astounded, dazzled, bewildered.

"If," said the beholders, with one voice, "it is so delightful outside, what must it be within?"

Ah! what?

To arrive at that it was necessary to pay for admission, and then it invariably proved that the entertainment they had witnessed externally was by far the most attractive part of the performance.

Von Boomberisch, whip in hand, perched on an elevation, looked down upon the busy swarm, and directed their labours like an experienced supervisor, as he undoubtedly was.

"Now, den," he called out, "you Mistair Hocus-pocus conjurair"—he always used broken English on these occasions — "do you go to vork mit your eyes shut?"

This was addressed to the renowned "Wizard of Bagdad," who was struggling to keep his equilibrium under the weight of three long planks.

Anyone who had witnessed the marvellous facility with which this individual could transform eggs into plum-puddings, peppermint drops into half-crowns, catch bullets in the palm of his hand, and bolt a handful of table-knives at a meal, might have wondered why, for the sake of his own convenience, he did not, *pro tem.*, transform the heavy planks he carried into paper or feathers, till he had reached his destination, and then cause them to reassume their natural appearance.

James and Ikey wandered about in a kind of flutter of delight, getting in people's way, and getting out again as quickly.

As they were thus roaming here and there, they encountered, to their unbounded amazement, the very last person they would ever have expected to meet there.

This was no less than the Bounding Pole, the renowned Karl Gingeritz Cheerivitzki.

The boys positively recoiled with amazement.

"Vell, Hi declare!" said Ikey, "if it hain't Mr. Ginger-beer-an'-vhisky! Oo'd hever a' thought o' seein' 'im 'ere, an' doin' this sort o' vork, too?"

It was, indeed, a sinking in poetry.

The Pole had certainly, as when the boys had met him previously, something balanced on his shoulder; but this time it was not either of his illustrious relatives.

It was a pole of another description—a scaffold-pole.

This renowned individual caught sight of the boys, and paused as he drew near.

James and Ikey pulled off their caps, and felt quite abashed in the presence of such transcendent talent.

As for Ikey, he felt as if, could he have been permitted to grovel in the earth at the feet of the gifted and noble foreigner, it would have been but a poor expression of the nothingness he felt in his presence.

The renowned Karl, however, was blissfully unconscious of the profound sentiments of respect he had inspired.

The only thought he had, was, whether the boys might "kick up a dust about the bob."

He, however, smiled in the blandest and most unembarrassed of manners, as he said:

"Ah, cullies, there yer are! Come to see some more ground and lofty tumbling—or, do yer want yer change, eh?"

The boys never thought of taking such a liberty, and felt quite shocked that the illustrious Karl should imagine them capable of such dreadful disrespect.

They endeavoured to express as much.

The noble foreigner condescended to accept their apologies.

After a little desultory conversation, the Bounding Pole took the opportunity of inquiring into the state of their funds, as he required change (so he said) for half a guinea.

Poor James and Ikey would, if they could, have chopped themselves up into shillings or sixpences—or, in fact, any coin that had been required—rather than have had to confess their inability to oblige the noble foreigner.

But the other received their humble and earnest apologies with a haughty grandeur that suggested some offence.

They were quite cut up.

"Oh, it don't make no odds—not in th' least!" remarked the august Karl. "I might ha' been able to a' done you a good turn one o' these fine days. No matter!"

"Hi'm werry sorry, sir!" exclaimed Ikey; "but if yer doesn't mind trustin' me vith th' 'alf-guinea, Hi'll go an' get change for yer."

The Bounding Brother looked at Ikey, gave a short laugh, and said:

"No, thank'ee, verdant—never mind. I shall be goin' to the bank myself presently."

At this juncture, the voice of Von Boomberisch was heard in very forcible tones.

"Now, then, you Mistair Gingair Pop, how much longer vill you stand to talk and vaste your time? I dorn't pay you to talk—I pay you to verk!"

"All right, guv'nor!" cried the illustrious foreigner, humbly—"I'm with yer!"

And shouldering the scaffold-pole he had set down, he hurried off to his work.

James and Ikey were once more astonished.

"Don't Mr. Broomsticks make 'em all vork!" remarked Ikey. "Hi say, Jem, ve must try an' get on at nat'ral 'istry, or ve shall get in for it, sha'n't ve?"

"I shall do my best, as soon as I know what I am to do," returned James.

At this moment Jeremiah Dowlas advanced.

"Ah, there you are!" he said, with a kind smile that comforted the boys greatly. "I thought I'd let you have to-day to yourselves, as it's a broken day, and to-morrow we can begin in earnest. If you like to come with me, I'll take you to the monkey-cages, and there you'll be able to judge what their habits are to some extent."

The boys were delighted at this, and followed their conductor, who led them to a part of the square that was already covered over.

Here he removed the shutters, and disclosed the interior of the cage; he then drove out a whole tribe of monkeys, gibbering and chattering.

Jerry then, by dint of teasing and other little knacks, contrived to show off these peculiar animals under as many aspects of their mischievous, spiteful, and cunning nature as possible.

He took out an empty box and pretended to take snuff, and then, holding the same box to the side of the cage, a troup of monkeys came clustering to the spot to imitate Jerry by taking a pinch.

It was very amusing to see one solemn-looking old monkey sniffing at his finger and thumb with the most profound gravity, as though he was enjoying the imaginary luxury.

James and Ikey enjoyed the sight amazingly, and laughed till the tears ran down their cheeks, at the curious antics and the comical faces of the various monkeys.

Ikey was almost beside himself with admiration and wonder.

The tricks of these active animals had an especial attraction for him, since he would, in all probability, in a short time be called upon to personate one.

"Don't they look like hold men?" Ikey remarked. "Oh, look," he cried, suddenly—"look at that vun!" pointing, as he spoke, to a venerable old monkey, who sat winking, and blinking, and looking the picture of wisdom, periodically scratching his head—probably to assist his meditations—and evidently finding something there at each time, which he conveyed to his mouth, and nibbled with much apparent satisfaction.

"Hain't he like hole Gurgles, th' beadle at Marton?"

James laughed—he could not help it, for there was in the monkey's face a certain expression that did recall the cross-grained functionary alluded to.

Gurgles himself probably would not have perceived it, but anyone else who knew him could easily have done so.

Mr. Dowlas watched the eager interest Ikey took in the monkeys with intense satisfaction.

He could see he would at least have an apt and willing pupil.

Having locked up these animals once more snugly in their cage, and replaced the shutter-door, he gave the boys a kind of general lecture as to their future conduct.

The main point of this was, that they were not to mix up too much with the *artistes* of the troupe, or to allow themselves to be converted into fetchers of beer and tobacco for those talented individuals, and that they were to do their duty, and look to him, and he'd be a friend to them.

The lads slept that night in the van, and the next day Jerry began his instructions to Ikey in earnest.

He showed him how to walk on all-fours, monkey fashion; he initiated him into certain monkey actions, and showed him how to produce with his mouth a peculiar sharp, chirping noise that these animals frequently make.

All these instructions Ikey swallowed with avidity.

Mr. Dowlas then tried him with some nuts, and, it is almost needless to state, he swallowed them with equal readiness.

But then boys eat nuts in one way, monkeys in another.

Jerry had to teach him the true monkey mode, and this Ikey acquired as if by instinct.

When he had been at this peculiar species of drill for a couple of hours, his master paused.

"Now," said he, "we'll see whether you remember what I've told you. Now, mind, you must fancy yourself a monkey, and whatever I tell you to do, you must do like a monkey."

Ikey expressed himself perfectly ready.

"Go into the corner, Smut," said Jerry.

Ikey hopped to the end of the van as artistically as possible.

"Now, then, won't you take a chair?"

Ikey made a spring, and mounted on to the piece of furniture indicated, on which he squatted in a manner that gratified his instructor exceedingly.

"Good, Smuttee!" he cried. "You deserve a few nuts for that."

Ikey thought that a few expressions of gratitude might not be out of place here, he therefore uttered two or three sharp chirps.

"Very good—very good, indeed!" exclaimed the gratified Jerry. "In a fortnight you'll be perfect!"

This was very encouraging, and, as Mr. Dowlas continued his instructions daily, Ikey's progress was wonderfully rapid; indeed, so heartily did the latter go in for practice, that he was now rarely to be seen in an attitude of repose, or walking in the usual manner.

Hanging on to every available door-handle he encountered, swinging on iron rails, hopping about on all-fours, hunting imaginary fleas, and chirping instead of whistling, were his constant avocations.

In the meantime the Mammoth Menagerie reared its colossal head, and gradually drew near completion.

At length the last plank was adjusted.

The gorgeous oil paintings were unrolled in the front of the building, and displayed to the eager eyes of the admiring multitude; and amidst the flourish of trumpets from Von Boomberisch's brass band, it was publicly announced by the great explorer himself, through a speaking-trumpet, that the exhibition was open.

To say the public came in answer to this appeal, was to say nothing.

Never, in the whole course of Herr Splutzer's professional experience—or Jerry's either—had there been such an overpowering influx of visitors.

The crowd struggled, and pushed, and fought, and tore one another's coats in their desperation, lest they should be left outside.

It was a scene of wild excitement.

As to the money-taker, he positively groaned under the weight of coppers.

The Bounding Poles, the Indian jugglers, the Persian fire-eaters, were all in full feather, delighting the gaping crowd from the platform, whilst Signor Wilhelm Mullini (Bill Mullins), the clown, ate yards and yards of real pork sausages for the amusement and edification of the beholders.

So much for the exterior; but what of the inside?

How was Smuttee Smut, the dog-nosed ape, getting on all this time?

Had the deception been seen through, and exposed? Not a whit.

To set any doubts on this point at once aside, I may inform my readers that Ikey's assumption of animal life was a complete success.

Those who had never before seen the wonderful ape, Smuttee Smut, were perfectly astounded at his almost human sagacity, whilst those who had, only remarked that he was cleverer and more wonderful than ever.

Neither is it particularly strange that such a result should have attended Jerry's efforts.

It must be remembered that Ikey was completely enveloped in the skin of the deceased ape, and that the portion of the face of Smuttee's representative that was visible, was so artfully painted by Jerry himself, that he bore a resemblance to the original that defied the closest scrutiny.

James, also, had not been neglected, though his position was somewhat subordinate, and more passive than active.

Mr. Dowlas introduced him to the interior of a young crocodile's skin, that encased him like a suit of armour, and had an odour very like a stale fish shop.

However, there was nothing to be done but to make the best of his peculiar position.

In fact, it was the only thing to do, since, once fastened up in the scaly monster's hide, there was no possibility of getting out again without assistance, so James, as the "Infant Crocodile," waddled about, occasionally snapping his jaws, and giving as much sign of being interested in the general proceedings as a crocodile of such tender years could reasonably be expected to give.

Von Boomberisch was in ecstasies with the public, Jerry, Ikey, James—in short, with everything and everybody.

Neither was this a transient gleam of success.

On the contrary, the tide of prosperity having fairly set in, continued to flow in with unabated vigour.

There was not the least doubt that in Ikey and James (the former in this case especially) Herr Splutzer had found a treasure.

The showman seemed to think so from the fact of his putting them down in his list of expenses at the munificent salary of five shillings per week each.

The boys were now permanently attached to the caravan, and wherever that travelled there were to be found the Dog-nosed Ape, Smuttee Smut, *alias* Ikey Mangles, and the Infant Crocodile, *alias* James Cook.

Leaving, then, for a time, the Mammoth Exhibition, to its wanderings, let us return to the old Hall up at Marton.

Chapter XXXIV.

AN UNEXPECTED MEETING.

TWO months had now passed away since the mysterious disappearance of the young Augustus.

The chill mantle of winter had disappeared from the earth, and Spring, with her robe of green and early buds, was beginning to deck the fields with vernal beauty.

But old Squire Markham, who had in past times taken so much delight in watching the successive changes of the seasons, appeared now to heed their flight no longer.

With his young son, the light of the old man's life and home had departed.

So long as there remained a doubt of the boy's fate, the squire had borne up manfully; but when the dread certainty, in the shape of the body itself, was brought before the sorrowing parent, he sank down, as though prostrated by an overwhelming blow.

The body was washed ashore by the waves, and brought to the Hall.

The features, from being long saturated in the sea water, were so decomposed as to be utterly undiscernible; but the long, dark curls, and the well-known garments the young gentleman wore, too fatally, in the squire's mind, established his identity.

I say in the squire's mind, because the whole affair was actually an entire deception.

The body the agonised father gazed upon was not the body of his son, but that of the dead sailor-boy our readers will remember being left behind in the cavern, and which the ruthless Octavius—a sufficient time having elapsed—had enveloped in a suit of his cousin's clothes.

It was a plot worthy of the evil mind that planned it, and which now exulted darkly over its prospects of success.

The old man drooped from day to day.

In vain the bright April sun shone forth, and the birds hopped and twittered joyfully from branch to branch.

He heeded neither the brightness of the one, nor the music of the other.

Life had lost its charm—there was nothing further to live for.

Octavius, more assiduous than ever, was the most exemplary of nephews.

There was not a wish of his uncle he did not anticipate—not a solitary fragment of consolation that he did not essay to administer.

But all in vain.

"Give me back my son!" was the old man's cry.

But this was beyond his nephew's power, and the mourner refused to be comforted.

But still, though the squire's grief was beyond human power to assuage, he was not insensible to the efforts of Octavius to that end.

Though he could not appropriate the consolation, his heart warmed towards the would-be consoler,

Having now no son to inherit his name and estates, he began, in his own mind, to look upon Octavius as his heir, and Octavius, who foresaw what was coming, waited with what patience he could, heaping hypocritical kindnesses and condolements upon his unsuspecting uncle, and heartily wishing, at the same time, that he would make the will that should consign the property over to himself, and die as soon as possible afterwards.

This seemed to be in the old man's mind, for one day, when they were alone, the squire said to his nephew:

"Octavius."

"Sir?"

"I feel I shall not last long."

"Oh, sir," cried his nephew, "do not say that. You will, really—you must!"

"Never, Octavius—never!" said the old man, shaking his head sadly. "I shall never recover this loss. I feel I have received a wound from which I cannot rally. It bleeds inwardly, and drains my life away slowly but surely, drop by drop! I shall never live to see another spring. Long before that the old squire's seat will be empty."

The old man spoke in a tone of such sad foreboding, that even the hopeful Octavius did not hazard a contrary opinion.

"Yes," the old man continued—"I shall die. Death to me will be no evil, for it will unite me to my son. 'I shall go to him, but he will not return to me!'"

He paused for a moment on the words of the royal Psalmist, and then took Octavius by the hand.

"I shall leave you my heir," he said. "You will be squire in my place when I am gone."

The hypocrite bowed his head with well-assumed reverence, and the old man continued:

"I trust you will endeavour to do your duty, as I have done before you."

"I will, sir," murmured Octavius.

"Never act unjustly—judge impartially between man and man—do not oppress the poor, or decide harshly against such on account of their poverty. Be kind, charitable, and easy of approach, so that you may be loved as well as honoured by your fellow-men, and so that, when your part in life is played out, and you are called upon to render an account of your actions, you may have good reason to hope that you will not be found an unprofitable servant."

"I will endeavour, sir, to live in a manner worthy of your great kindness, and, that I may do so, I need no better example than your own exemplary and well-spent life."

As he spoke, Octavius bent down and pressed his lips to his uncle's hand, squeezing out, by a prodigious effort, a solitary tear, which he was particularly careful to let fall on the spot he had previously kissed.

This significant act touched the squire, and convinced him that his nephew was worthy to be his successor.

"I have written to my lawyer," said the old man, "and I expect him here in the course of the day, to assist me in drawing up my will in your favour."

Octavius bowed.

At this moment a servant entered with a note, to which no answer was required.

Octavius, in a whirl of joy at the prospects before him, went to the window and looked out upon the bright face of Nature, that seemed to smile upon him.

The squire after glancing at the note, which was addressed in a strange hand, proceeded, with trembling fingers, to unfasten it, and read its contents, which were as follows:—

"*Pause before making a will, assigning your property to Octavius Challoner.*—A Friend."

Had not the subject of this brief epistle been at that moment revelling in a gorgeous day-dream of future wealth, he would have noticed that the old invalid squire was much excited.

As it was, he stood in the recess of the window, looking out, lost in a world of his own creating.

"'Tis strange—very strange!" murmured the old man. "Who could have written this! What can it mean? Why should I pause?"

He looked again at the note. It was certainly *not* the handwriting of his lawyer.

It was very brief, and very indefinite; but it placed the squire on a rack of anxiety.

Had he been equal to the effort, he would have hastened at once to Mr. Probate's, to consult him about this mysterious warning.

But, as this was impossible, he would write to the lawyer at once.

In a short time the letter was written, and despatched, with strict injunctions to the messenger to use all possible haste, and to bring back an answer.

During the interim of waiting, the squire was so evidently disturbed, that Octavius could not forbear remarking on it.

The squire excused himself at first, but at length, unable to control the anxiety that oppressed him, revealed the cause to his prospective heir.

Octavius, on hearing it, felt as though a sharp sting had been driven through him.

He mastered his emotion, however, and tried to reason away the fears that were ready to rush in from every quarter, and overwhelm him.

Since the note was evidently not written by Mr. Probate, what motive could anyone else have in counselling the squire to delay the making of his will in his then delicate state of health.

The more he reflected the more perplexed he became.

After all, it might be nothing—some officious busybody, perhaps, had taken upon himself to suggest some ridiculous objection that would prove upon discussion utterly untenable.

This thought had hardly crossed his mind, when the messenger returned with the intelligence that Mr. Probate had been away from home on business for upwards of a fortnight, and was not expected back again for a similar term.

The mystery to the squire appeared more complicated the more he reflected on it, whilst, to Octavius, a thousand fears presented themselves, none the less terrible because they hung looming, indistinctly at present, in the distance.

He saw, frowning at him through the dark future, hideous spectres of his guilt—ministering agents of retribution starting up to oppose him, and to snatch from him his coveted inheritance just as it seemed on the eve of falling into his hand.

"It is very strange—very mysterious, this brief caution," thought the old squire. "Well, there is nothing to be done till Mr. Probate returns at the expiration of a fortnight. He will then, perhaps, be able to help us to solve this difficulty."

Octavius ground his teeth, and clenched his hands at the delay.

A fortnight seemed an age to wait. What might not occur in such a space of time?

* * * * * * *

During the last two months, Von Boomberisch's Royal Travelling Menagerie had been taken down, and put up, and had shifted its quarters twice.

It was now opening its colossal portals, and offering its numerous attractions to the usual crowd assembled at the Spring Fair held in one of the seaport towns on the coast of Yorkshire.

Its popularity was in no way diminished.

If some shows in the fair had reason to complain of want of patronage, the Mammoth Establishment was a triumphant exception to the rule.

Splutzer Von Boomberisch grew broader, and more red-faced, and talked more broken Dutch than ever.

Jerry Dowlas was also beginning to make flesh, and as for James and Ikey, no one would have known them.

Good living and kind treatment—for Jerry was like a parent to them, and petted them to their hearts' content—were rapidly effacing the premature lines, and the sad, scared expression that had marked their wan faces.

Their limbs were becoming round and symmetrical, and a healthy glow now tinged their cheeks.

Ikey was now so thoroughly at home in his character, that he would venture into the cage in the midst of the whole troupe of monkeys, who appeared to look upon him as a kind of big brother, who was to be treated with deference, but never to express any suspicion that he was not one of themselves.

James, too, grew accustomed to his crocodile's skin, and contrived to pass a certain number of hours in it every day without inconvenience.

It was a bright spring morning.

The sun shone out in all its radiance, and crowds of pleasure-seekers, dressed in their best, thronged the fair, and, of course, congregated round the Mammoth Establishment.

There was, however, on this particular morning a counter attraction at a rival show that stood hard by Von Boomberisch's.

This was a giant nine feet high, who flourished his club, and was declared to eat two men and a boy every day for dinner, the aforesaid meal being shortly about to take place.

The crowd, always fickle, wavered between the two, and remained in a state of indecision, uncertain which to patronise, and in the meantime going to neither.

Herr Splutzer's keen eye observed this, and he saw that a strong effort must be made to turn the tide in his favour.

He said as much to his factotum, Jerry, who was ready with an idea immediately.

" We'll have Smuttee on the platform, and let him go through his performances. He'll annihilate the giant, I know."

" Aha, yes," cried Von Boomberisch, " dat ish a goot idea—dat vill do !"

In a moment the gong sounded, the cymbals clashed, and the stentorian voice of the great explorer was heard addressing the wondering crowd.

" Oigh—oigh—oigh ! der greatest vondair in der vorld ! Der renowned Dog-nosed ape, Smuttee Smut, from der coast of Africa, vill go through his vondairful performance ! Dis ish a sight dat ash nevair yet been seen in der memory of man, an' vill nevair be seen again ! Oigh—oigh—oigh !"

The proprietor wound up this harangue by ringing an enormous bell, which served completely to stun the entire body of spectators.

Before they had time to recover their auricular faculties, up skipped Smuttee Smut on to the platform, and commenced his antics.

From the moment he appeared, the giant was no-where.

In vain the monster declared till he was hoarse that he was the biggest giant that had ever appeared since the days of Goliah.

It was to no purpose he protested to the public that the two men and the boy were served up to table, and only waiting their presence to be eaten.

No one took any notice, so, after bawling till he was black in the face, he gave up in despair, and retired to the interior of his booth to drown his disappointment in beer and a pipe.

In the meantime Smuttee's efforts were received with loud shouts of approbation.

Just as the performance was about to commence, a handsome man, with delicate aquiline features and fair hair, clad in a costume that bespoke him a naval captain, and bearing on his features the bronzed hue, common to the sons of the wave, drew near.

He was leading by the hand, or rather being led by a pretty, dark-haired boy, of about ten years of age, who endeavoured to drag his elder companion forward.

" Oh, do let's come, dear Captain Palmer !" said the child, eagerly. " I should so like to see the monkey !"

" Should you ?" said his friend, good-naturedly. " Then you shall see him ; and in order that you may have a better view, I'll mount you up aloft."

With these words, he swung the child up on to his shoulder, and supported him there.

Smuttee commenced his performance by calling up his friend by a succession of sharp chirps.

In answer to this summons, forth waddled the Infant Crocodile, to the great amusement of the crowd.

Jerry explained that they had been brought up to-gether and suckled out of the same bottle, and that they were bound together in the strictest terms of friendship.

This having been explained, Jerry suggested it was time for breakfast.

On this, Smuttee, who was attired in a little coat and small clothes, took a key from his pocket with great gravity, and proceeded to unlock a small buffet, brought there for the purpose.

From this he brought out two cups and saucers, and, having first spread a cloth upon the table, he placed the various articles in order.

He then made the tea, cut slices of bread and butter, poured out the tea in the cups, and invited his infant friend, the crocodile, to share his meal.

The latter being rather embarrassed for want of hands, Smuttee assisted him, by emptying the contents of one of the cups into his capacious jaws.

All this was received by the spectators with great satisfaction ; but when, on Jerry's suggestion that it was bedtime, Smuttee dragged forward a small bed, which he commenced making with the most profound gravity, the applause was unbounded.

Then there was the operation of putting on his night-gown and nightcap, and then, as a sort of final act previous to retiring to rest, he deliberately filled a short pipe, after which, jumping into bed, he pulled the clothes up round him to his chin, and lay winking and blinking at the spectators, looking like some old Gipsy crone.

The plaudits were long and loud, but by no one were the feats of Smuttee more thoroughly appreciated than by the young gentleman with the curls perched on the captain's shoulder.

He clapped his hands and literally shrieked with glee.

Being raised up above the crowd, he was a conspicuous object as he gave way to his exultations.

So much so that, at last, he attracted the attention of Smuttee Smut himself.

It was remarkable to observe what a sudden and violent effect the sight of the excited child took upon the monkey.

He started up in the bed, keeping his eyes riveted upon the child, and feeling as though he had turned red-hot and cold in the same moment.

He forgot entirely the assumed part he was performing, and shouted to the Infant Crocodile, excitedly :

" Hi say, Jem—Jem ! theer's Master Gus ! Open yer mouth and look !"

James pulled the string that opened the jaws of the animal, and distinctly saw the well-known features of the boy he had thought he should never see again.

" Then he vorn't drownded arter all !" cried Ikey, utterly unconscious of the effect he was producing. " Hooray ! Come on, Jem ! Let's let 'im know ve're alive !"

Without the least hesitation he bounded down the steps, the people hurry-scurrying hither and thither to get out of the way, thinking the animal might have gone mad.

James essaying to follow, but being very much encumbered by the case he wore, missed the top step, and went clattering to the bottom, where after a moment's pause to recover his breath, he got up and waddled after his companion.

It is needless to say Ikey was the first to reach Augustus.

Captain Palmer was somewhat surprised to see an ape clinging to him on one side, and an Infant Crocodile on the other, and would, probably, have astonished the animals in question, had he not shrewdly formed his own opinion, that the feats they performed were rather too good to be true.

This idea was instantly confirmed when Ikey shouted out at the top of his voice:

"Master Gus!—Master Gus! Hit's me an' Jem! Don't yer remember us?"

If Augustus did not, Paul Jones—or rather Captain Palmer, as we shall now call him—did.

A smile of gratification passed over his sunburnt features, whilst Augustus eagerly asked to be set down, when he embraced his companions with the utmost affection.

"Oh! how glad I am to see you both again!" he cried. "I'm sure I never expected to."

"No more didn't ve!" exclaimed Ikey. "Hi felt certain as yer'd gone to the bottom. An' 'ow vell yer looks!"

"I can't see how you look, either of you, in those strange dresses," said the young gentleman. "Why do you wear them?" he inquired.

"Ve vears 'em," returned Ikey, "because they vos put hon us, an' vhen once they're hon, there's no gettin' 'em hoff agin till Mr. Dowlas takes 'em hoff."

Captain Palmer laughed at the grotesque appearance Ikey presented, and the crowd having by this time ventured to approach, it soon got rumoured about that the wonderful ape was endowed with the faculty of speech, in addition to his other accomplishments.

Von Boomberisch and Jerry, utterly at a loss to divine the cause of the extraordinary behaviour of Smuttee and the Infant Crocodile, came, as soon as they had recovered from their surprise, hurrying to the spot in a state of considerable anxiety.

They were naturally fearful that the imposition should be discovered, and, accordingly, they did all in their power to keep the crowd from coming too near.

"Stand avay!—stand avay, good peoples!" shouted Herr Splutzer, with well-feigned anxiety. "Dey are verree dangerous animals to come close to! Mein Gott! if der crocodile vos to get 'ole of von of your legs, you should nevair forget it."

This was received by a shout of derisive laughter.

"Ee, ee!" cried one, "'e bean't no crocodile; Oi' see th' boy's head inside 'un!"

This was the signal for sundry groans.

In proportion as the crowd had been astounded at the extraordinary feats of the animals, so was their indignation at the idea that they had been imposed upon.

Matters were becoming decidedly unpleasant.

"This won't do!" whispered Von Boomberisch to Jerry. "We must get them inside."

"All right, guv'nor," Jerry answered.

"You look after the monkey, I'll attend to the crocodile."

"Now, then, come on!" he exclaimed; and, as he spoke, he hoisted up the fictitious reptile under his arm, while Jerry took possession of Ikey; and thus loaded, master and man, as hastily as possible, sought the interior of the show.

Augustus was very much chagrined at the sudden disappearance of his companions, and looked up somewhat ruefully in Captain Palmer's face.

"Oh!" he said, in a tone of disappointment, "I wanted to have had a nice long talk with them. I feel quite anxious to know how they escaped."

"I daresay you do," returned the captain; "and so you shall. I wish to ask them a few questions myself. Let us ascend these steps. I must speak to the proprietor of this exhibition."

So saying, Captain Palmer mounted to the platform and made his way to the money-taker's box. Through the medium of this individual he despatched a note to Herr Splutzer Von Boomberisch, to the effect that he must see him immediately.

After some little delay he was admitted to the presence of the great explorer.

It was with considerable misgivings the Dutchman listened to the captain's expressed intention of taking away James and Ikey with him.

It seemed like being called upon to part with his most valuable property, and he did not feel inclined to relinquish that.

"I don't see, sair," he said, to Captain Palmer, after a great deal of "hum"-ing and "ha"-ing, "how I can spare dese boys. You see, I have mit moch trobel teach dem, an', derefore——"

Captain Palmer interrupted the proprietor somewhat abruptly.

"You can spare yourself any further explanation, as my time is precious; and with respect to these boys, let them be taken out of the masquerade attire in which they at present figure, and clad in their own clothes as soon as possible."

The captain spoke in a tone of decision, that left no room to doubt he meant what he said.

Von Boomberisch looked at him intently, and the captain looked at Von Boomberisch out of his pale gray eyes with an expression that seemed to say: "It is for me to command, you to obey."

So the Dutchman gave up the point, and ordered Jerry to take them out of harness, and wash and dress them in their own habiliments.

This operation Jerry performed as speedily as possible; and when the boys were introduced to the captain with clean faces, glossy hair, and clad in a respectable suit of clothes, the latter was at once struck with their improved appearance, and did not hesitate to express his satisfaction.

"One thing I can plainly see," he said. "These boys have been kindly treated and well fed since they have been with you."

This was addressed to the proprietor, who bowed in acknowledgment.

"We have been very kindly treated here, sir," said James to the captain, "both by the master and by Mr. Dowlas."

Poor Jerry stood by with the tears in his eyes at the thought of losing his young *proteges*.

"You're not going to take 'em away for good, sir, are you?" he inquired, anxiously—"two such promising boys as they are too!"

"Oh, no!" answered Captain Palmer; "they will be at liberty to return to you, if they wish it, though I should think they might find some better employment than counterfeiting monkeys and crocodiles."

"Oh, sir!" exclaimed Jerry, in a tone of expostulation, "but consider what a fine study natural history is for——"

"Yes, I daresay it is," abruptly interrupted Captain Palmer, rising; "but when I find a lad burying himself in the carcass of a crocodile, or walking about with the skin of a monkey on his back, I consider he goes far too deeply into the subject. Now, my lads!"

Beckoning them as he spoke, and seeing them out first, the captain followed them, leaving Von Boomberisch and Jerry Dowlas to sundry speculations as to whether they should ever see their two valuable actors again.

Chapter XXXV.

HOME AGAIN.

CAPTAIN PALMER having got clear of the noise and hubbub of the fair, conducted his young charges to a comfortable inn on the outskirts of the town.

Here he established his quarters, and after dinner prepared himself to listen to the accounts Ikey and James had to deliver of the various vicissitudes that had befallen them, and of the almost miraculous manner in which they had been preserved.

The captain listened with evident interest, whilst now and then a grim smile stole over his features as he traced the evil hand of Octavius Challoner in more than one of the poor boys' perils.

"Well, my lads," he said, as they concluded, "you've

passed safely through all your perils, and it will be your own faults if you have to encounter any such again."

The account Augustus gave of his rescue was simple enough.

When the boat capsized, he had grasped an oar, to which he clung, and which kept him from sinking.

Drenched and half drowned by the surging waves, he still held firmly to his only support.

But his limbs were numbed with the cold, and he felt that he would not be able to retain his grasp upon the oar much longer.

His senses were fast deserting him.

He remembered uttering one last faint cry for help, and then no more until he found himself in Captain Palmer's comfortable cabin on board his vessel.

The captain, whom our readers will remember going in search of the boys in a boat, came up to the spot just as the unconscious Augustus was about to relax his grasp, and in time to stretch forth his hand and snatch him from destruction.

The captain had to go out on business, and the boys were left alone in the snug room at the inn.

There was an immense deal of curiosity in the minds of James and Ikey respecting Captain Palmer.

They expressed their doubts and misgivings to Augustus, who hastened to set them right on certain points, and with perfect success.

"Then Captain Palmer is not a pirate, after all?" asked James.

"I don't believe he is," said Augustus; "but, whether or not, he saved my life; and he's a kind, good man, and I won't hear a word against him."

"Hi thinks as 'e his too," Ikey assented, "honly, why did 'e call 'isself Paul Jones in the cave, and Captain Palmer 'ere?"

"I don't know, I'm sure," answered Gus; "but people do change their names sometimes, without being bad either."

"Does they?"

"Yes. Didn't you change your name to Smuttee when you had the monkey's dress on?"

"Vell, so Hi did, certinly," Ikey responded.

"Well, but you don't think any worse of yourself for doing so, do you?"

"No, Hi don't," answered Ikey; "'cos Hi was erbliged to."

"Then I daresay Captain Palmer was obliged to change his, and he needn't be any the worse for it," argued Gus.

"Hi dessay as ye're right," returned Ikey; "but theer's summat else," he added.

"What else?"

"Vhy, th' boys as 'im an' Mr. Blackbeard heats."

Augustus laughed.

"Who told you he eats boys, you silly fellow?" said Augustus.

"Vell," returned Ikey, "all Hi knows is, as 'e said 'e'd heat me."

"It's all nonsense, Ikey," said Gus. "If you're never eaten till Captain Palmer eats you, you may consider yourself perfectly safe. I'm very fond of the captain; I'm sure if I had been his own son, he couldn't have been kinder to me than he has been."

"And have you been with him all this time?" asked James.

"Yes, I've been all the way to America and back," Augustus answered.

"And did you like the sea?"

"Very much."

"And I suppose you've come back now for good?"

"I suppose so."

"You're not sorry to come back?"

"Oh, no. I long to see dear papa once more."

"Don't yer vant to see yer cousin Hotty, Master Gus?" inquired Ikey, in a peculiar tone.

A flush rose in the cheek of the young Augustus, and a slight frown passed over his features.

"Don't speak of him," he said, in a low tone; "I'm afraid he's a very wicked man."

"So am Hi," acquiesced Ikey—"in fact, Hi'm sure on it."

"I did not think so once," Gus continued; "but I think now that he did take me to that cavern to get rid of me."

The return of Captain Palmer put a stop to further conversation.

He had made up his mind how to proceed, and he explained his plans, so far as it was necessary for them to know, to his young friends.

Could Octavius Challoner have heard what those plans were, he would have been ready to sink into the earth with terror and dismay.

* * * * * *

A week had passed since the squire had received the note that appeared to him so inexplicable.

It would be another week, perhaps more, before the lawyer would be at home to consult on the matter.

It was on a beautiful April afternoon that the squire sat in his library, the large window of which was partially open, to admit the mild genial air. The old man sat in his easy-chair, and appeared to be lost in thought.

His eyes were closed, and a casual observer might have fancied he was asleep.

But he was not so. From time to time he murmured indistinctly, as though addressing some invisible listener.

Everything was profoundly still, the only signs of life being the quivering shadows of the boughs, as they danced in the embrasure of the window.

Suddenly *another* shadow darkened the threshold, which, as it gave place to the substance, revealed the form of James Cook.

His manner was cautious and quiet; but, from his behaviour, it was evident that he did not expect to find the room empty.

The boy looked in as if for a moment reconnoitring the interior, and his eye fell upon the squire in his easy-chair, as he sat in his waking reverie.

The old man's thoughts were afar; perhaps roaming in those wide regions of space—those evergreen Elysian fields, where the emancipated spirits of the blessed wander.

Or perhaps the distant strains of some heavenly choir reached his enraptured ear, the sweet voice of his boy forming part of the harmony.

Whatever it was that enthralled his fancy, his manner seemed entirely absorbed.

James wished to attract his attention, but was somewhat at a loss how to do so.

He had proceeded no further into the room than the embrasure of the window, and he now sought to attract the squire's attention by gently scraping his foot upon the window-sill.

The plan succeeded; for the old man, aroused from his meditations by the sound, turned towards the window, where the first sight that met his eyes was the fair, delicate features of our hero, James.

This unexpected appearance did not appear in any way displeasing to the squire.

Always fond of children, he had since the loss of his own son evinced a peculiar regard for such, and he now contemplated James, who stood somewhat timidly on the threshold of the window, with a benign and paternal smile.

Seeing that James waited to be addressed, he said to him, kindly:

"My child, what do you want?"

"I wish to see the squire, if you please, sir," answered James, respectfully.

"I am the squire. Come in; don't be afraid; I am fond of good boys," said the old gentleman.

James, thus encouraged, advanced towards him.

The squire fixed his eyes on him with an earnest gaze, and then remarked:

"I think I remember your face—I am sure I do; but my memory has not been so good of late. I cannot recollect your name; what is it?"

"James Cook, sir," answered the boy.

"James Cook—James," repeated the old man, closing his eyes, the better to collect his thoughts, "the son of Widow Cook, are you not?"

"Yes, sir," replied James.

"Your mother lives in one of the cottages on my estate, does she not?"

"She did, sir, when she was alive; but she's dead now," replied James, sadly.

"Dead!" echoed the squire, in a dreamy tone. "Ah! yes! death will come! And so your mother is dead?"

"Yes, sir."

"Poor boy!—poor boy! Yes, I remember now—I remember. And you are an orphan, then?"

"Yes, sir."

"Are you in want?"

[THE FACE AT THE WINDOW.]

"No, sir, thank you."

"Then why do you come to me?"

"I came to tell you something I thought you'd like to know."

"Have you, child?" said the old man, eagerly. "Then bring a chair close to me, and sit down, and I will listen."

James did as he was ordered, and dragged one of the massive, old-fashioned chairs till it almost touched the squire's, and then seated himself.

"And now," inquired the old man, "what is it you have to tell me?"

"If you please, sir, it's about Master Augustus," answered James.

The sudden light that blazed up in the dim eyes of the bereaved parent, and the vehemence with which he raised himself in his chair, and looked eagerly at the boy, quite startled him.

"Augustus—my son!" exclaimed the old man, excitedly, "is it of him you speak?"

"Yes, sir."

"Go on, then—quickly!—quickly!"

"We were in the cavern with Master Augustus, sir, on *that* night——"

The squire looked at the boy in a bewildered manner.

"Of what are you speaking?" he asked. "What cavern?"

"The cavern in the Beacon Rock near the Coast-guard House," James replied.

The squire pressed his hands to his head as though striving to collect his thoughts.

"Cavern!—Beacon Rock!" he ejaculated, in a disjointed manner. "How is it possible he could have been there? Are you sure you are speaking the truth?" he added, inquiringly.

"I am sure I am, sir," affirmed James, "for I saw him and spoke to him."

"And what night do you allude to?"

"The night when we went in the boat, sir."

Our readers will readily understand that James was

talking perfect Greek to the old man, who was in utter ignorance of all that had transpired in the cavern.

He murmured to himself incoherently and excitedly, as he tried to set James's words into something like order in his mind, but he failed.

Suddenly, however, the improbability of the story seemed to fasten on his mind; for once more he sat upright in his chair, and said to James, somewhat sharply:

"How could my poor boy have been in the cavern on the night you speak of? Who could have taken him there?"

"I know, sir," answered James, firmly.

"Give me his name, quickly!" the old man cried, excitedly.

"It was Mr. Octavius Challoner who took him there."

"What?" almost gasped the squire. "Boy, do you know what you are saying? Do you mean to affirm that Octavius Challoner, my nephew, took my poor Augustus to that cavern?"

"I do, sir," returned James. "There were pirates in the cavern."

"Pirates!" exclaimed the old man, almost incredulously. "It seems a story impossible to believe! What could my nephew have to do with pirates? But, even admitting that, why should he have taken his cousin—a mere child—amongst such lawless characters?"

"You won't be angry, sir, if I tell you the truth?" asked James.

"No—no, my boy. I wish you to tell me the truth—the entire truth."

"The reason, then, why Mr. Challoner took Master Gus to the cavern," said James, deliberately, "was to ask the pirates to *drown* him!"

"Good Heaven!" almost shrieked the squire, in a voice of agony. "Oh! it is too horrible! It cannot be true!"

"I heard him ask them, sir," said James, persistently.

"But what motive could Octavius have had for so unnatural, so horrible an act?"

"I heard him say he wished his cousin dead, that he might have all your money, sir."

The poor squire clenched his hands with horror, and heavy drops bedewed his pallid features, as the first intelligence of his nephew's guilt was thus forced upon him.

"Would I had been in my grave," he cried, "rather than have heard this! And was it these wretches—urged by my, by a wretch greater than themselves—who thrust my poor darling into an open boat at night, and drove it forth upon the stormy sea?"

"No, sir; it was me persuaded him. When we heard what Mr. Octavius said to the pirates, we pressed your son to get into the boat, thinking it was the only chance of escape. We all went together, and the boat overturned."

"And my poor boy was lost!" cried the anguished father, clasping his hands despairingly.

"We thought so, sir; but *we* were saved, and——"

"Then my son alone perished!" the squire continued, in bitter accents of grief. "His dead body was found cast ashore by the waves! I looked upon it with my own eyes! I recognised the clothes he wore! Oh! yes—yes, there is no doubt my son is dead!"

"Excuse me, sir," said James, "but are you quite positive the body you looked upon was really your son's body?"

The question was asked so searchingly that the old man turned his eyes full upon the boy. He remembered how utterly undiscernible the features of the dead had been, and at the same moment a wild hope darted like lightning through his brain—a hope that he almost feared to indulge—that his beloved Augustus might be alive.

"You mean something by these questions, boy," he said, eagerly, to James.

"Yes, sir; I mean that I believe you have been deceived, and that you have not seen your son's dead body at all, but another dressed in his clothes."

"But have you any proof of what you say?" he asked, wildly.

"Yes, sir; the best of all proofs—my own eyes."

The old man's lips moved convulsively, as though he would have spoken, but no sounds issued forth.

"I saw your son, Augustus, yesterday and to-day, alive and well."

The old man burst into an hysterical laugh, and sank back in his chair.

"Thank Heaven—thank Heaven," he ejaculated, presently, "for this great mercy!"

He covered his eyes with his hands, and wept silently for a few moments.

Then, looking up, he said, in a yearning tone of supplication:

"If he be alive, where is he?"

"He is quite safe, sir," answered James; "but the gentleman who picked him up, was afraid the shock of seeing him suddenly might be too much for you, so he told me to come and break it to you as well as I could by degrees."

The old man smiled as the great joy that his son lived stole over his heart.

"My son—my son!" he cried, fondly. "Who but a monster could have had the heart to injure him?"

As he spoke, footsteps were heard without.

The light elastic tread caught the rejoicing father's ear.

"It is his step!" he cried, eagerly, starting up just at the moment when Augustus, alive, and glowing with ruddy health, bounded through the open window, and ran to the arms of his enraptured father.

"Papa—dear papa! I'm alive and well! See!" cried the child.

The squire, with almost childish delight, could do nothing for the first few moments but clasp his boy to his breast, and then holding him from him at arm's length, devour him with his eyes, and draw him again to his embrace.

Truly, the old man felt vividly his son had been "dead and was alive again."

It was not until the first transports of joy had, in some measure, exhausted themselves, that the squire became conscious of the presence of Captain Palmer.

A slight exclamation from the latter, however, caused him to turn towards the spot where the captain, accompanied by James and Ikey, was waiting for his cue to speak.

As if by instinct the squire, as the delicate but bronzed features and the naval uniform of this gentleman met his gaze, divined that he looked upon the preserver of his child.

But in order to put this beyond a doubt, Augustus grasped Captain Palmer by the hand, and led him eagerly forward to his father.

The old man, with trembling earnestness arose, and warmly pressed the outstretched palm of the mariner.

"A father's blessing rest upon your head for the precious treasure you have restored me!" he cried, with emotion, tears of joy and gratitude trickling down his cheeks.

"And this gentleman not only saved my life, papa," said Augustus, "but he has been so kind to me—I couldn't tell you half his kindness."

"I shall ever look upon him as my dearest friend," exclaimed the grateful old man. "As long as I live, my heart and my home are his!"

Captain Palmer, in a few words, expressed the joy it gave him to have been the instrument of causing so much happiness; but, at the same time, entreated the squire not to magnify his services beyond their desert.

"I am only too happy," he said, "to have been able to rescue your son from a position of imminent peril; and, also, that the opportunity is afforded me of opening your eyes to the dastardly villany of one in whom you have hitherto placed implicit confidence."

"My nephew! the wretch! the ingrate!" exclaimed the squire, with strong indignation. "It might have been too late. I might have made my will; and, in my present weak state, have died long since, and then my poor boy would have been a beggar; whilst that viper—— But there, thank Heaven! my eyes are opened in time; it is not yet too late."

"No," warmly returned Captain Palmer; "the evil schemer will be foiled yet."

"One question, and one only, I would ask you," said the squire, earnestly—"since the terrible revelation of my—I cannot call him nephew—of Octavius Challoner's guilt has reached me through the lips of James Cook: do you endorse the accusation?"

"I do," firmly replied the captain.

"You swear solemnly that this bad man sought the life of my son?"

"I swear solemnly that Octavius Challoner, mistaking my character, and believing me to be a pirate, offered me and a brother captain a large sum of money to destroy that child."

He pointed to Augustus as he spoke.

"Hi'll swear it, too," asserted Ikey, warmly, "'cos Hi 'eerd 'im."

A stern frown overspread the features of the old man, as the conviction of his nephew's heartlessness forced itself upon him—

A heartlessness all the more glaring, because exhibited in the face of paternal kindness and long years of almost filial adoption.

But the mine was ready to explode; the storm hung suspended, waiting only the fitting moment to burst upon the head of the guilty Octavius.

The mysterious warning that started his fears, that were becoming quieter, and aroused his conscience that the prospect of a speedy triumph had, like a sweet opiate, lulled to repose; but he was not prepared for the full rush of the torrent that, at a moment when he least expected it, burst upon him with overwhelming force.

Just as Ikey's protestation escaped from his lips, Octavius, deeming the squire entirely alone, as he almost invariably was, entered the library hastily.

He was so buried in his own thoughts, that he had almost reached his uncle's chair before he became conscious of the fact that there were others in the room besides his uncle and himself.

He raised his head quickly, and looked.

Such a look!

We have heard of the fabled Gorgons, gazing on whom the beholder became stone.

Some such an effect passed over Octavius.

Not that he did actually become petrified into that hardened mass; but as he gazed on the features of Captain Palmer and his boy cousin, a convulsion like that of a violent electric shock passed through his frame, a shriek of deadly horror burst from his lips; and then, fixed, rigid, and ghastly as a marble effigy, he remained motionless and speechless, a tremulous quivering of the jaw, and a restless fluttering of the strained eye-balls alone proclaiming him a living man, and not a statue or a corpse.

It was one of those sudden surprises when artifice or self-possession could avail nothing.

It was that terrible moment when guilt came full butt against conviction.

There was no time to frame an excuse.

The power to dare a lie was gone.

The appalled criminal felt that it would have been a mocking absurdity to attempt it.

Therefore he uttered not a word, but stood, silently glaring at his accusers, self-convicted, certain of the verdict that would be pronounced—ghastly, horror-struck, guilty, and condemned.

Chapter XXXVI.

FACE TO FACE.

THE old squire was the first to speak, and the sound of his voice fell upon his guilty nephew's ear like the thunder of an earthquake.

"You may well be silent!" he cried—"you may well be covered with speechless horror and confusion, as your crime starts forth as from the grave itself, in which you thought it buried, to confront and accuse you! Villain—villain! the frozen snake warmed into life, and stinging the breast that cherished it, is an emblem of charity compared with you. Monster! ingrate! I have no words to express the loathing with which I regard your monstrous crime! Leave me, and never again pollute my threshold with your presence! I cast you off—I disown you! Begone!"

But even at this desperate moment, the natural audacity of Octavius Challoner, having recovered the first shock, did not entirely desert him.

His cheek became a little less ghastly, and he seemed to awake in some degree from the stony rigidity in which he had first fallen.

"You—you are deceived, sir!" he murmured, in an unsteady, faltering voice. "I—I do not understand this sudden and unjust attack!"

"You do—you do!" almost shrieked the old man, "you understand it all too well! Your quivering lips, your agitation, your bloodless cheeks, all rise up in judgment against you, and proclaim you the guilty wretch you are!"

"Of what crime am I accused?" Octavius contrived to inquire, desperately.

"Of seeking my child's life!" returned the indignant squire.

"I? Never! it is not true!" his nephew had the effrontery to declare; "did I ever in any way attempt to injure you, Gus?" he asked, appealing to his cousin.

"From what I have heard," answered Augustus, "I am obliged to believe you have tried to kill me. I do not say with your own hands, but that you wished me dead, I believe, that you might have all my father's money."

A bitter frown darkened the countenance of Octavius at these words.

"You have been taught to say these words—they have been *parrotted* into your mind by those who have got up this vile charge against me!" sneered Octavius, between his teeth.

"But you cannot deny that you took me from my bed on the night you carried me with you to the pirate's cave. Did you not come and wake me after I had been asleep, and tell me to be quiet because you did not wish anyone to know that I was not asleep?"

"I did," returned Octavius, sullenly, "but it was only to avoid the fuss your nurse would have made had she known you were going out with me at night; what proof of guilt is there in this?"

Ikey burst in at this juncture, as though unable to restrain himself any longer.

"D'yer mean to say as yer didn't hoffer hever so many thousan's o' poun's to Capting Jones to dround Mast'r Gus?" he asked, bluntly.

Octavius cast a look of such vindictive hatred at the speaker, that if looks could have slain, Ikey would most surely have been annihilated by the withering power of that glance.

But beyond this he vouchsafed no reply.

Captain Palmer then spoke.

"It is not on the evidence of a few poor boys the crimes with which you are charged rest," he said, sternly; "there are men, to confront whom your coward heart and guilty, self-accusing conscience would shrink, as you well know—who could by one word set aside every plea you have to offer, and cause you to stand forth revealed to the world as you are—a dastardly traitor and murderer."

Octavius turned deadly white; he clenched his hands with fierce despair, and his lips moved as though breathing forth imprecations that were, however, inaudible.

The old squire, who had never removed his eyes from him, lost all patience, being now more than ever convinced of his guilt.

He rose from his seat.

"Octavius Challoner," he said, in a firm, stern tone of condemnation, "I blush that I cannot disclaim all affinity with one so utterly lost as you are to the common humanity that should bind all men together. But though you are my sister's son and bound to me by ties of kindred, from this moment I cast you off, and wipe you from my heart and memory as though you had never existed! Begone, miscreant! Never let the shadow of your evil presence darken my doors again, for in that moment I shall treat you as a common felon, and set the ministers of justice on your track without one atom of remorse or resolution! I have nothing more to say to you! there is the door—begone! and never let me look on you again!"

The squire pointed imperiously as he spoke to the solid oak portal, and the guilty Octavius—his last faint hope utterly shivered into dust—slunk from it like a baffled fiend—hopeless, despairing, mad with rage, remorse, and every evil passion; but still withal lacking one grace—*repentance.*

The evil spirit having departed, the home atmosphere seemed to become light, genial, and joyous, as though relieved of a heavy weight.

The squire, in the newly-awakened joy of his son's

return, whom he had mourned as dead, seemed to revive to all his former heartiness. He would not hear of any separation of the party.

James and Ikey, humble as were their positions, and boys as they were themselves, were still demanded by the warm-hearted squire, to gather round his hospitable board.

Rarely had a happier party met together than that assembled in Squire Markham's dining-room on the evening of this particular day.

It was very small, consisting only of the squire, Captain Palmer, James, Ikey, and Augustus; yet never did the former sit down to eat with a company that appeared so entirely congenial to his taste as this.

The old man's heart seemed so thoroughly opened and expanded with the gratitude that glowed there that the innocent hilarity of his young guests was more acceptable than the most refined sallies of wit, or the most polished treasures of intellectual conversation would have been.

As he sat there, with his silvery white hair glistening in the light, and his venerable features relaxed into a happy, peaceful smile, he formed a perfect illustration of a "fine old English gentleman," one whose heart, speaking in his kindly beaming eye, was full of those generous emotions that were wont to make the squires of yore beloved in their lives and regretted in their deaths.

During the evening Captain Palmer gave the squire a complete account of the manner in which he had rescued his son from destruction, together with certain reasons that had compelled him to take the boy with him to America instead of restoring him at once.

The squire was perfectly satisfied with the captain's explanations, and the evening passed rapidly and joyfully away.

The old man, although the excitement and joy that possessed him for a time gave him a false strength, became wearied; and at a comparatively early hour he returned thanks to Heaven for the mercies he had experienced, and the happy party broke up before the church clock had struck ten.

James and Ikey were lodged with Augustus, who would not be separated from his young friends, whilst Captain Palmer occupied the bed-chamber, rendered vacant by the departure of Octavius Challoner. It was quite an event in the lives of James Cook and Ikey Mangles this night, on which, for the first time in their lives, they stretched their limbs on a down bed. It was a night of thorough enjoyment in every way, for not only did Augustus insist on having a bed prepared for his friends in his own room, but that being accomplished, he vacated his own couch and established his quarters in that of his companions, who were perfectly willing to receive him.

It will be easy to imagine that the boys went to bed full of joy and excitement.

Even when snugly tucked between the sheets by the careful hands of Mrs. Wilson herself, with strict injunctions to "shut their eyes and go to sleep instanter," they were so far disobedient as not only not to shut their eyes as directed, but also to open their mouths and talk over past events long after the worthy nurse was in the land of dreams.

"What a beautiful soft bed!" said James, with a burst of involuntary admiration.

"Hain't it?" echoed Ikey; "it's jest like bein' berried in hever sich a lot o' feathers. D'yer allus sleep hin a bed like this, Master Gus?" he inquired, of the squire's son.

"I always have ever since I can remember," answered Augustus.

"Lor! 'ow you must a' felt it that night as ve vas in th' boat!" observed Ikey. "It didn't come so 'ard upon hus, 'cos ve vas used to it like; but you, as 'ad bein nuss'd up in this 'ere lux'ry—yer must a' felt it horful!"

"I did feel it," said Augustus, with a sigh of pleasure, as he contrasted his present warmth and comfort with the misery and horror of the night in question, "but that's all over now, and I hope we shall never be in such a plight again."

"I suppose," remarked James, "your cousin, Mr. Octavius Challoner, will never live here any more?"

"Never!" replied Gus. "Didn't you hear what papa said?"

"Yes."

"I never heard him speak like that in my life before," he continued. "You may be sure after papa saying what he did, he would never forgive my cousin."

"Sarve 'im right, too!" exclaimed Ikey, warmly. "People as does sich vicked things houghtn't to be forgiv'n!"

"Who would have thought anyone could have been so cruel, and so kind as papa has been to him, too! He always treated him as though he had been his own son."

"Hi looks upon 'im as a hout-an'-hout bad 'un!" said Ikey, vehemently; "an' as sure as 'is name's Hotty, 'e von't come to no good!"

"I was just wondering," remarked Augustus, "how he'll live now he's sent away from the Hall."

"E'll know vot it is to be cold an' 'ungry 'isself, now, p'r'aps," Ikey observed, and in a tone which seemed to imply that a little acquaintance with these cheerless companions would be, on the whole, decidedly beneficial.

"I hope he won't take to poaching or stealing," said Augustus. "It would be so shocking for one who has been brought up as a gentleman to come to that."

"Hi believes many a vun 'as," returned Ikey, sententiously. "Ven gentlemens gets cold an' 'ungry, they hoften furgits vot's right an' vot's wrong, jest like poor people, an' vhen they feels like that an' anything nice comes hin the vay, Hi don't s'pose as they'd stand pertickler who hit belonged to as long as they got a bit on hit."

"But a real gentleman," remarked James, "would bear cold and hunger, or even death itself, rather than do anything dishonest."

"Yes," said Augustus. "I have read in books that many good men have preferred to sacrifice their lives rather than their characters."

"Vell," replied Ikey, rather dubiously, "Hi dessay thee're quite right to do so—that is, them as can—but some'ow or hother, hit don't seem hin my natur' to do hit; an' vhen a poor chap's werry nigh starvin' hit don't seem to me the wust crime in th' vorld hif 'e prigs a loaf, or a bit o' cheese, or meat."

"I don't think it is myself," assented Augustus; "but still, if a man was caught stealing, the magistrate wouldn't let him off because he put in the plea of hunger in extenuation of his guilt."

"Hi knows that," answered Ikey, "but Hi should jest like to keep th' magistrate vithout vittals as long as th' poor thief 'ad bin, an' then ask 'im 'ow 'e felt."

"Well, but if a magistrate was to let every thief go unpunished who declared he was hungry," James argued, "he would never have to punish any, because they'd all very soon learn the same story by heart, and for every robbery that was committed the excuse would be 'I was hungry, and therefore you mustn't punish me.'"

"Well," said Augustus, "I hope Otty will be sorry for what he's done. I don't wish him any harm, though he did try to kill me. I hope he'll try to live honestly, and not sink lower by becoming a thief."

"Hi 'opes 'e vill, Master Gus, but Hi doesn't think so; hit's too much t' expec' hall at vonce."

The conversation now began to flag, and drowsiness rapidly stole over the young debaters.

An occasional sleepy remark oozed out, and was as sleepily answered, and the boys were almost asleep when Ikey suddenly sat up in the bed, ejaculating, in a startled whisper:

"What's that?"

His hasty action and the tone of alarm in which he spoke, aroused his companions immediately, who instantly followed his example and leant up in their beds.

"What's the matter?" they asked.

"See there—there on the wall!"

Ikey pointed as he spoke to that portion of the wainscot of the room that was lit up by the bright moonlight that came in in a slanting direction from the window.

It reflected the fantastic and elongated figures of the diamond-shaped panes on the wall, but it was not that that had attracted Ikey's attention.

The cause was that over and above these quaint and

natural appearances there was reflected on the wall in unmistakable distinctness—

The figure of a man!

For a moment the shadow oscillated, as though the original without was trying to make good his footing—on the balcony perhaps.

The following instant this point seemed to have been gained, and the shadow stood still.

The man, whoever he was, had evidently paused to listen and assure himself that he was not observed.

During this pause the boys spoke:

"It's a man, hain't it?"

"The shadow of one, I am sure."

"The man himself, then, cannot be far off."

"No 'e must be close alongside by th' vinder."

"D'ye think he's coming here?" asked Gus, in a hurried whisper. "I hope not."

"Hi dunno!" said Ikey. "Let's lay down a little more. Ve can peep over th' top o' th' close jest as vell, an' then, if 'e looks in at th' vinder 'e von't be hable to see us."

The boys, acting on this prudent suggestion, suddenly dropped down in the bed, shrouding themselves under the clothes, three heads, three pairs of eyes, and a portion of three noses being all that was visible, peering cautiously over the top of the coverlet.

It was well they took this precaution, for the next moment the man himself appeared cautiously looking in at the window.

His features were effectually concealed by a crape mask, but from the contour of his figure, there was little difficulty in recognising the squire's banished nephew, Octavius Challoner.

Augustus was the first to express this opinion.

"It's Cousin Otty!" he whispered. "What does he want?"

"'E's a lookin' through th' vinder as though he vanted to get hinside!"

"But he ought not to come here when papa told him not to come any more, ought he?"

"O' course not; besides, 'e can't be 'ungry yet."

At this moment Octavius pressed his hand against the window lightly, but, finding it quite firmly fastened within, he paused an instant as if in thought.

"'E'd get in hif 'e could, Hi knows," observed Ikey.

"See—see!" whispered Augustus, "he's looking in again!"

The six eyes were instantly fixed upon the nocturnal intruder, who was utterly unconscious that he was so closely watched.

His gaze this time was evidently directed to the bed.

After an earnest scrutiny of several moments, the better to assist which he shaded one side of his face from the moon's rays with his hand, he withdrew from the window.

"'E's gorn now," said Ikey, in a tone of relief; "an' a good job too!"

"But where has he gone to?" asked Augustus, apprehensively. "Although he has left the window, it may only be to try some other part. If he wishes to get in, I don't believe he'd be so easily turned from his purpose."

"Nor I," said James.

"I'm afraid he might make his way to papa's room, and——"

The bare idea of what might possibly occur in the event of such an occurrence, desperate as his cousin would then be, and reckless from despair, caused the poor boy to shudder violently.

His agitation was not lost upon James and Ikey.

"If you think he would dare to enter your papa's bedroom," said James, "p'raps the best thing to do would be to arouse the house."

"I am not yet certain that he means to enter the house, and I should not like to alarm papa, especially now that his health is so delicate," answered Augustus.

"Well, then, let us get up and watch," proposed James. "You know every part of the house, and could show us the parts most easy of entrance. Don't you think that would be the best way?"

"I think so," replied Gus. "Let us dress ourselves."

This operation they performed as rapidly as possible. Being dressed, they opened the door of their room and went out.

All was profoundly still.

It was a beautiful moonlight night.

The rays of the bright luminary shone in at the windows, basked on the staircases, and flooded the landings of the old Hall with silvery light.

"It's so bright," remarked Ikey, apprehensively, "that if 'e vos to come hin hunavares 'e'd be sure to see us."

"We must listen, and be as quiet as mice," whispered Augustus.

Accordingly they crept along, having removed their shoes, for the better imitation of the little animals in question, and at length reached the dining-room, where they had passed so delightful an evening.

The shutters were closed, and the only light visible was from a small space at the top.

As they stood there, in an undecided manner, they fancied they heard stealthy footsteps on the gravel.

"Hi wishes as Hi'd got a pistol," said Ikey, chivalrously—"Hi vouldn't be afeard o' nothin' then."

"Do you know how to fire pistols?" asked Augustus, in a tone very much approaching admiration.

"Yes," replied Ikey; "an' Hi knows 'ow to load 'em too."

"There are no pistols," continued Gus, "but there's a gun in the corner yonder, that papa always keeps loaded. Will you have that?"

"Von't Hi, jest!" exclaimed the boy, eagerly. "Get us th' gun an' then ve shall be all right."

Augustus, who knew exactly where to put his hands upon the weapon, crossed the room hastily, and quickly returned with it in his hands.

"Here it is," he cried, as he delivered it to Ikey Mangles.

"That's right!" ejaculated the latter, as he received it with all the confidence imaginable. "Jest vait a minnit," he said. "Hi'm a goin' houtside for a hinstant, to see if it's loaded."

Ikey eagerly went out into the hall, where the moonlight revelled in full profusion, and soon returned in a state of considerable elation.

"It's hall right!" he exclaimed. "It's loaded an' primed as vell. Now, then, if hanyvun puts 'is nob in th' vay, 'e'd better look hout, i' case it should go hoff by accident."

"Be careful, Ikey!" said James to him, quietly.

"Oh, Hi'll be werry careful!" returned Ikey, assuringly.

"Hark!" whispered Augustus. "Don't you hear something?"

He laid his hand on James's arm as he spoke.

"Yes!" replied James. "I hear the same sound as before—footsteps on the gravel outside!"

"Then he is still seeking for a place by which to enter?"

"Yes; no doubt on it. In my erpinion 'e means to get in by 'ook or by crook," remarked Ikey, deliberately. "Vell, Hi don't vant to 'urt him pertickler, but, hif 'e does hanythink hobstrop'lus, Hi'm afeard th' popper 'll 'ave to go hoff."

As he uttered these words, the footsteps drew near the window of the dining-room, and paused there.

The boys were breathlessly silent.

They could hear a hand tampering with the window-hasp.

But it appeared to resist the efforts made to open it, and in a few moments the footsteps moved away and were heard no more at that particular spot.

"He has gone!" exclaimed James and Augustus.

"To try some'eres else, Hi suppose," said Ikey. "Vhich d'ye think 'd be the next place as 'e wisits? 'cos vheerever that his, Hi should like to be has near has possorble with th' popper."

This seemed to be a matter of some doubt, and while they were considering which would be the most available post to occupy, any further deliberation was at once abruptly stopped by a loud cry that fell upon the silence of the night with startling distinctness.

Chapter XXXVII.

A MIDNIGHT INTRUDER.

CAPTAIN PALMER, on retiring to his room—the same apartment, as has been explained to the reader, usually occupied by Octavius, while he had been an inmate at the Hall—having no inclination to sleep, did not at once seek his pillow.

The hospitality of the squire did not leave him at the mercy of the four walls of a strange bedchamber for company.

A cheerful fire blazed on the hearth, and on the table stood silver cruets, containing spirits and liquours of various kinds, to comfort the heart of the guest, if he were disposed to taste them.

A steaming kettle of hot water sung merrily over the fire.

This last might have been in compliment to the captain's profession, a glass of grog being usually considered the natural nightcap of a sailor.

The captain glanced at these luxuries, and smiled brightly, and felt gratefully towards their venerable suggester.

Nor was he by any means tardy in availing himself of the comforts that surrounded him on every side.

Throwing off his naval coat, he replaced it by a brocade dressing-gown, and then mixing himself a glass of hollands-and-water, he lighted a cigar, and drawing the cosy arm-chair up to the fire, resigned himself to a blissful state of smoke and reflection.

He thought of the benevolent squire—of the joy it had been his happy lot to be the means of restoring to his kindly heart.

He thought of the squire's son—of the two orphan boys, James and Ikey, wondering what would be the best course to adopt towards them.

Of course, being a sailor himself, the sea appeared to stand forth most prominently in the mental picture he was forming as the home that promised them the most favourable fosterage.

As sailors, if they did their duty, they might advance themselves to posts of honourable distinction.

At any rate, he thought serving their country afloat was infinitely preferable to playing the fool or the mountebank—for so he denominated the occupation at which he discovered them—ashore. Then his reflections rested on Octavius, and there they seemed to linger.

All that he could ever imagine of baseness and cruelty seemed to be summed up and concentrated in his character.

He sat quietly puffing his cigar and looking into the red-hot embers of the fire, occasionally sipping his grog, till at last he seemed to yield to the combined lethargic influences, and dozed off into a gentle slumber.

How long he lay in this state he could not have told; but he suddenly started from his doze, and sitting up in his arm-chair, listened.

Why did he listen? Had he been dreaming? and was he, now that he was awake, continuing some event that had occurred to him in his dream?

No.

He listened, because he felt conscious that the sound that had awakened him from sleep was caused by some one without endeavouring, without noise, to undo the fastening of the window.

Captain Palmer was a man of strong nerve; he was, moreover, a sailor, and accustomed to face those perils which almost hourly start up in the watery waste where the sons of the ocean make their home.

The idea, therefore, of being startled, or timid, or anxious, never for a moment entered the captain's mind.

He merely listened a few moments, as he might have done had he fancied he heard a mouse nibbling a cheese in the cupboard, just to assure himself that it was a mouse; and then, having satisfied his own mind as to this fact, he coolly picked up the cigar which had fallen from his lips, relighted it, and, quietly raking the embers together, sat listening as at first to the scratchings of the *mouse* without.

The shutters were closely fastened, therefore there were no means of reconnoitring the midnight intruder.

All that he could do was to remain quiet and patient until the nocturnal visitor, whoever he was, should—if

he were able to accomplish a breach in the shutter—put in an appearance.

Captain Palmer little knew that his three young friends, James, Ikey, and Augustus, were at the same moment, with far more anxiety and excitement, awaiting the appearance of the midnight intruder.

As far as he was concerned himself, it seemed to him a matter of so little importance that he would have been strongly tempted to dismiss the trifling incident from his mind, and after another glass of grog and a cigar retire to rest in the fullest sense of security.

But as he was in a strange house, he thought, for the sake of the worthy squire, he would keep watch for another hour at least, so as to be in immediate readiness for action in case of alarm.

As a means to an end, he lighted another cigar, mixed another glass of hollands, and opened his ears to their fullest extent, ready to catch any sounds that might come in the way.

None such came, however.

The window-scraper seemed to have grown tired of his unprofitable efforts, and to have departed.

At all events the sounds had ceased, and Captain Palmer began to ask himself serious questions as to whether they had not existed in his imagination only.

"Yes, yes," he cried—"it must have been fancy; nothing more. I dreamt it, undoubtedly; ha, ha! yes."

And, with a laugh at his own credulity, he emptied his glass, and prepared to retire to rest.

This occupied him but a very short time, and almost as soon as his head touched the pillow the captain was asleep.

His dreams were of a curious character.

He fancied himself wandering in strange places he had never seen before.

He fancied himself the inhabitant of extraordinary and eccentric chambers, such as the most quaint invention could never have conceived.

He found himself wandering from one old room to another, each one seeming to grow smaller and narrower than the last.

This prospect had an unpleasant effect upon the captain's mind, and jarred upon his sense of freedom even in his dreams, and he essayed to return.

But this was impossible; the door had closed firmly behind him, and there was no resource but to walk forward into the room beyond.

The door of this, in the same manner as the rest, closed behind him with a bang, and in this way he was lured on till he found himself enclosed in a little sentry-box of an apartment, where he could barely stand upright, and had no room to extend his arms.

While he was marvelling at this strange treatment, he observed, to his horror, that, small as the chamber was in which he was placed, it was rapidly becoming *smaller*.

He could no longer stand upright, but was compelled to bend to avoid being crushed.

But here a new difficulty presented itself; the sides contracted as gradually as the height decreased.

There was no longer room to bend his knees.

The ceiling of the collapsing prison pressed with stony hardness upon his skull.

For a moment, by a strong effort, he seemed to be able to resist it; but only for a moment.

The steady, crushing weight overpowered him, and he gave way beneath it.

He could feel himself being palpably jammed closer and closer together.

In a few seconds he would be crushed into a shapeless mass.

A deadly horror seized upon him.

He gave one wild, desperate plunge to escape from his terrible dungeon, and in that struggle he *awoke from his dream*.

Yes, he awoke to find himself in bed.

But where? Was it the same in which he had retired to rest?

It might have been, but the room seemed different. There was no glowing, red-hot, comfortable fire. The lamp had gone out; and, instead of the cosy, snug appearance the apartment had formerly presented, there was a large, chilly-looking latticed window, that seemed to occupy almost one side of the room, through which the chill, ghastly moonlight intruded itself in a manner that was exceedingly unpleasant to contemplate.

To crown all, a dark figure, the captain did not at once recognise, was standing with his back to him, doing something to the fastening of the window.

The whole affair partook of the strange weird character of a dream, and would have made an excellent companion to the little romance of the collapsing chamber.

The captain sat leaning up in his bed, in a kind of dreamy wonderment, gazing with all his eyes at the mysterious figure, which, opposed to the moonlight, came out in black and startling distinctness.

The window fastenings, which it was evidently endeavouring to unloose, were refractory, and the sable figure uttered a muttered execration.

But that ejaculation, brief as it was, brought the captain to his senses, and gave him the key-note to the whole affair.

The dark figure was Octavius Challoner, who had gained the interior by some entrance—the door, perhaps, —for some purpose, of which he was better informed than anyone else.

His object in seeking to unfasten the window, was that he might have a quick and ready means of escape, in case he required it.

Having come to this conclusion, Captain Palmer, without an instant's pause, slipped quietly from the bed, drew up the clothes, and shrouded himself in the curtains at the head of the bedstead.

This act was not performed a moment too soon; for, the next instant Octavius, having loosened the window fastenings, and cautiously opened the window—a fact that was unpleasantly manifest to the captain's bare legs—gazed for a moment at the bed where he imagined the unconscious sleeper slumbered, and, drawing a poniard from his breast, drew near.

"You have crossed my path, and sought to ruin me," he murmured, "and this is your reward!"

With these words, he raised the dagger, and struck it with all his force into what he supposed would be the slumbering Captain Palmer.

Instead of this, however, the keen weapon buried itself in the down of the luxurious bed, and before the assassin could repeat the blow, or even withdraw the weapon, a strong arm dashed over his shoulder, his wrist was seized with a nervous iron grip, the dagger wrenched from his grasp, and he himself hurled backwards on to the ground.

The shock was so sudden and unexpected, that the baffled murderer uttered a startled cry of terror.

It was this cry that reached the ears of the boys.

His retreat was cut off by the way he had entered, which had been through a masked entrance in the panelling of the wall, leading by a narrow passage to the exterior. Neither could he escape by the window, for the captain rushed to it and fastened it before Octavius could regain his feet.

There was only once chance—the door.

He would not hazard a second struggle; he was anxious only to make good his retreat.

With a desperate bound, therefore, he sprang over the bed, and reached the door before Captain Palmer was aware of his intention.

Snatching the key from the lock, Octavius rushed out, slamming the door to, and locking it on the outside. Without pausing an instant, he hurried forward, and

would have entered the dining-room, and made good his escape by the window there, had not the sound of voices —those of James, Ikey, and Augustus—caused him to change his intention, and hastily ascend the stairs.

Just as he was disappearing at the end of the first flight, Ikey emerged from the dining-room, gun in hand, ready to do battle in the cause of right, and if necessary, fire off the ponderous weapon he carried, though he was by no means strong enough to raise it to his shoulder.

The boy recognised Octavius, who disappeared immediately.

While he was hesitating whether to follow upstairs in pursuit, or fire the gun as a kind of general alarm, a loud knocking was heard in Captain Palmer's room.

This was caused by the captain, who was locked in, and was anxious to be released.

He added his voice to his knocks.

"That's the captain's voice!" exclaimed Augustus, as he ran forward to release his friend.

At this juncture a shrill female screech was heard in the direction in which Octavius had fled.

Ikey's chivalrous soul was up in arms immediately.

"'E's a murd'rin' that ole nuss!" he cried. "'Ere goes!" Cocking the gun and hugging it under his arm, he ascended the stairs.

The voice of the nurse was still heard in accents of terror, and then an execration from Octavius.

Ikey, who was wound up to boiling point, could resist no longer.

Bang! went the gun, and away went Ikey with the rebound of the clumsy weapon into some remote corner, whilst the unfortunate nurse, Mrs. Wilson—fortunate, I should rather have said, in this case, since she narrowly escaped being blown to pieces—made her appearance, minus her two side-curl papers, which Ikey, in the excitement, had shot away, and with her somewhat voluminous night-cap smoking like a volcano, the wadding of the discharged weapon having buried itself in its ample folds.

There is but one step from the sublime to the ridiculous, and when the worthy nurse began to inhale the odours of her own smouldering nightcap, and sniffing gravely, remarked that she was sure there was something on fire, the ridiculous predominated.

Ikey, who had picked himself up after the gun had knocked him over, was the first to explain her condition to the old lady.

"If yer please, ma'am," said he, "your nightcap's a smokin' like hanythink."

"My nightcap!" gasped Mrs. W., in a terrible fright —"good gracious me! I thought I smelt——Here, boy! —quick, quick!—pull it off!" she cried, hastily; and untying the strings, she bent down her head to Ikey.

The latter obeyed with such alacrity, that he not only pulled off what the worthy lady desired, but a great deal that she did not desire should be removed.

Yes, alas! with the nightcap was ruthlessly dragged away poor Mrs. Wilson's flaxen wig with the natural curls, and the afflicted dame, who had prided herself in not having a gray hair in her head at the age of sixty-nine, retired in dire confusion, under bare poles, to the seclusion of her own apartment, till the damaged flaxen should be brought her to enable her to appear once more in public.

The venerable squire was aroused from his sleep by the midnight disturbance, and it took some time before order was once more restored.

It is almost needless to add that in the confusion, the cause of all, Octavius Challoner, had effected his escape.

Chapter XXXVIII.

HEMMED IN.

THE next morning the accounts given of the previous night's events by the boys and Captain Palmer, were listened to with patience and calmness by the squire, until his nephew's base attempt to assassinate the captain, forced from him a burst of involuntary indignation.

"Is it possible?" he cried. "How can I have been so blindly duped and deceived, as to have ever believed in the goodness of such a wretch?"

It was almost in vain Captain Palmer suggested that a man so lost to generous feeling, was unworthy even of indignation.

The outraged old man could not suppress his wrath. "The viper!—the cold-blooded, heartless wretch!" he exclaimed, fiercely. "But let him beware! he has gone too far! For the honour and credit of my name and family, I would have avoided, if possible, the disgrace of a public exposure, but after this renewed outrage, I will no longer screen him. The law shall expend its full rigour on the murderous villain. No false sense of shame shall hinder me from bearing full witness to his monstrous guilt!"

It was long before the squire could recover his equanimity.

By degrees, however, the friendly efforts of Captain Palmer, and the joy of his son's society, removed the dark cloud from the brow of the good old man, who, from the very benevolence of his nature, felt his nephew's unnatural malevolence all the more acutely.

Once more the serene calm light shone tranquilly in his eye, and he appeared to have forgotten all that had so lately troubled him.

And what, in the meantime, had become of his graceless nephew?

He contrived to escape in the confusion, and, in the hurry and disorder of his mind, not knowing at the moment where better to go, he fled like a demoniac into the darkest recesses of the wood on the estate.

Here he wandered up and down like a lost spirit, "seeking rest and finding none," equally tormenting to himself as to others.

He was truly possessed with the very spirit of the Evil One.

Not one faint spark of sorrow for the past glimmered in his darkened soul.

No gleam of penitence gave the faintest light to give the tenderest angel hope that there might dawn a better day yet for the misguided man.

He was like the stormy, troubled sea that could not rest, and as each fresh wave of passion rolled within, he cursed and execrated his bungling hand that had allowed his victim to escape his vengeance.

Yes! if ever guilty man had plotted evil to its full extent, and found his diabolical schemes one by one palpably frustrated, that man was Octavius Challoner.

If he could only have revenged himself in some way—if he could have poisoned the cup of happiness for others, he was forbidden to taste himself—he would have been comparatively happy.

He would not shrink from the punishments, provided he could have seen his guilty schemes of revenge accomplished.

But that he—he, the artful schemer, the daring plotter, who had laid his plans so carefully that he would unhesitatingly have staked his life upon their successful issue, that he should now find them all shivered like so much glass—swept away like sand before the wind—that he should see all those whom he would have annihilated happy and joyous, whilst he alone was baffled and miserable, and without the least hope of retrieving his lost ground! Oh, this was gall and wormwood!

This was indeed the bitterness of death!

In the dark recesses of the wood, he paced to and fro like some furious tiger.

He groaned and gnashed his teeth in his fierce despair, and clenched his hands with such terrible intensity that the nails were almost buried in the flesh.

During one of these paroxysms, two of the squire's gamekeepers came upon him.

They, ignorant of what had befallen, still looked upon Octavius as their master's heir.

So little did they expect to find him in the woods at that hour of the night, they did not even recognise him, but thought he was some poacher — drunk, perhaps.

They seized him roughly, and turned their lanterns on to his face.

They started as his features met their gaze, not so much as they recognised the features of Octavius, as at the terrible expression those features wore.

"Mr. Octavius!" exclaimed the scared men, with one voice.

Almost before the words had escaped their lips, the demoniac had dashed the poor fellows with desperate violence to the earth, as though they had been mere infants, and had fled still farther into the recesses of the wood.

Here he threw himself madly on to the ground, and, heedless of the heavy falling dew that drenched his clothes, and saturated his dishevelled locks, lay there in sullen despair, till the gray light of morning peered down even into that dark recess, and told him another day of wretchedness had dawned for him.

The violence of his raging fit had exhausted itself, and in a kind of desperate moody determination, he set himself to ponder on some plan that might bring him at least a part of the revenge for which he thirsted.

His meditations seemed to be attended with some success, for, as the sun began to show his face, he started up, and with a lurid, malignant smile in his dark eyes, he shook the drops from his drenched garments, wrung out his saturated hair, and quitted the wood by an unfrequented by-path.

He strode along, heeding nothing, looking neither to the right hand nor to the left, and not noticing, much less acknowledging, the respectful salutations of the rustic labourers who met him on their road to their daily toil, and who inwardly marvelled " What was the matter wi' Measter Otty to make 'un look so scared loike?"

As for the object of their wonder, he kept on until he came to a small roadside inn, that did not bear the best of reputations.

He had often found this a convenient place of concealment when he wanted to keep out of the way for a day or two, and he now entered the yard with careless haste.

The landlord, who was by no means a temperance advocate, was putting his head under the pump to bring his brains to a proper state of steadiness after the potations of the previous night.

"Ullo, Mr. O'tavius!" he said, in a tone of surprise, gasping from the effects of the cold water, "'as anything 'appened to 'ee? You seem all sixes and sevens loike."

"Ask no questions!" growled Octavius, like a surly lion. "Show me to my room. Let me have pen, ink, and paper, and brandy directly!"

Octavius Challoner was a customer it would not do to neglect; accordingly, a fire was immediately lighted, in the room he was accustomed to occupy when he stayed there, and the articles he ordered were instantly placed before him.

Octavius, as soon as he was alone, commenced writing a letter.

The epistle was but brief, and as soon as it was finished, sealed, and addressed, the landlord was summoned.

" Let this be conveyed in the course of the morning according to the address."

The landlord having departed, Octavius, who was exhausted and worn out by the violence of conflicting and stormy passions, and from having had no rest the previous night, threw himself on the bed, and assisted by the brandy, of which he drank abundantly, slept heavily for some hours. When he awoke, if he did not feel greatly refreshed, he was at all events less weary.

Again he summoned the landlord.

"You despatched my letter?" he inquired.

"Oh, yes, sir," answered the host. "A gentleman passed by that was going past the Coastguard Blockade, and he promised to deliver it. That'll be all right."

Octavius seemed gratified at this intelligence, and ordered the landlord to bring him dinner.

Having despatched this meal, he passed the day in smoking and drinking the somewhat questionable wine of the landlord.

As the day progressed his anxiety increased.

Several times he inquired whether he (the landlord) had heard any news from the Hall that day. The man was obliged to confess that he had not.

It was not till at a later hour, in answer to the thrice-repeated question of Octavius, the host was enabled to say "he had heard something."

"What?" eagerly demanded Octavius.

" Young Measter Gus, as wur thou't drownded, be coom to loife," was the reply.

Octavius uttered such a sharp, vindictive bark of rage at this announcement that the man instinctively started back to prevent being bitten.

"Begone, fellow!" he cried, savagely, in a tone of bitter scorn.

The landlord left the room as quickly as possible, the prevailing impression on his mind being that " young Measter O'tavius were goin' off 'is brains."

Octavius could do nothing but surmise and speculate as to the result of the letter he had despatched.

"It will succeed!" he cried, in a tone of suppressed exultation—"it must! Ha, ha, they haven't yet forgotten the suffering and loss of life caused by the explosion! Their duty will be stimulated by the desire of vengeance. Yes, yes, he will pay for it yet with his life!—with his life!"

The letter, on the result of which the evil Octavius was so sanguine, had been duly delivered to the superintendent of the Coastguard, and its contents had created an extraordinary excitement.

The fearful carnage caused by the explosion in the

[THE ATTEMPTED ASSASSINATION OF CAPTAIN PALMER.]

cavern of the Beacon Rock was, as Octavius rejoiced to know, still fresh in the minds of the Blockade-men.

It had only to be mentioned to rouse them all to a man to a pitch of indignant fury, and now the very man who had caused the calamity was a guest beneath the roof of Squire Markham.

It required all the power of discipline to restrain the men from rushing down in a body to the Hall and demanding the body of Paul Jones, the pirate.

The note of warning, however, received by the super-intendent stating that night would be the surest time to find him, they restrained their impatience till day should have departed and the night be come. Little did the squire and Captain Palmer dream, as they sat in the comfortable dining-room, the meal being just finished, of the storm that was brewing.

The captain had amused the old man greatly by his various anecdotes of naval service, and was just re-lating a particularly interesting incident of his early life, when a prolonged and violent ringing of the large

bell at the gate in front of the Hall caused the captain to pause in his narration.

"Who can it be in such haste?" said the squire. "Such a summons should imply a message of life and death importance. What can it mean?"

Surmise was speedily set at rest by the hasty entrance of one of the servants with a note.

"For Captain Palmer," said the domestic. "It was left by a man on horseback, who, as soon as he had delivered it, galloped off at full speed."

When the door closed upon the servant, Captain Palmer broke the seal, and read as follows:—

"Beware! Your present residence is known to the Superintendent of the Coastguard Blockade. You are betrayed by that snake in the grass, Octavius Challoner, who has written, informing the superintendent that Paul Jones, the Pirate, the cause of the fatal explosion in the Beacon Rock Cave, is now on a visit to Squire Markham under an assumed name, the squire being ignorant of the deception. They are now on their way

to the Hall. Fly while you have yet time to escape!

"A Friend."

The captain bit his lip and looked for a moment somewhat agitated and perplexed.

He knew what the wrath of a multitude meant, and he had every reason to fear the worst from the indignant wrath of the men whose comrades and relatives had suffered so bitterly from the terrible catastrophe.

The squire saw that something was wrong, and said:

"What is it, captain? May I know?"

Captain Palmer, without a word, handed the anonymous letter to the squire.

The old man read it deliberately, and, having done, an expression of surprise and pain passed over his face.

The cause of his surprise was, that in this anonymous epistle, the handwriting was identical with that of the warning he had received a week previous respecting Octavius.

The cause of his pain would be obvious. It was that the man to whom he was so greatly indebted and for whom he felt so strong an esteem, should be, after all, unworthy the friendship of a gentleman and an honest man, being more than an abandoned outlaw.

The squire thought this, but did not express as much.

He was evidently affected, nor was Captain Palmer unmoved.

"Oh! captain!" cried the old man, in a tone of deep disappointment, "am I never to meet a man whom I can trust?"

"You may trust me, my respected sir," replied Captain Palmer, earnestly, "with your life, or anything else you deem as precious, and when I ever betray that trust, may my name be consigned to eternal infamy as belonging to a coward and a traitor!"

"I do believe—I must believe you an honourable man!" exclaimed the squire, eagerly.

"Without wishing to boast, or ascribe to myself virtues I do not possess, I think I may say I am that at least," said the captain.

"You surely are no pirate?"

"I am not."

"And your name is not Paul Jones?"

"No; my name is John Palmer."

"But this explosion of which this letter says you were the cause—what of that?" the squire asked.

"It was a fatal mistake that no one more deeply regretted than myself. I wished simply to hinder the Coastguard-men from entering the cavern; but Heaven knows I little contemplated the result of the order I gave!"

"What was that?"

"Close to the mouth of the cavern stood a mass of rock so nicely poised, that though the pressure of a child's hand upon it would cause it to oscillate, a giant's strength could not dislodge it. Noticing this, I had several times thought that the force of a small portion of gunpowder applied to this would cause it to fall forward. Accordingly, when the Blockade were advancing, I ordered a barrel containing a very small quantity of powder to be rolled beneath the base of the rock.

"By some fatal mistake my orders were misunderstood.

"A barrel more than half full was placed there, and when I fired the train and the explosion took place, instead of the shock being merely sufficient to dislodge the rock and close the aperture of the cavern, its disastrous violence spread death and destruction on all sides; but believe me no one more regretted the fatal catastrophe than I did, when the news reached me of its terrible extent."

"I am truly thankful, captain, to hear you say this," said the squire. "I would not willingly renounce the good opinion I had formed of you. But what is to be done? You must not remain here. If these men find you here, they will listen to no explanation: your life would be sacrificed."

"I shall have time to effect my escape," remarked the captain, in a tone that evinced no particular anxiety.

At the same time Matthew, the squire's steward, entered hastily with an expression of consternation on his features.

"Oh, your honour!" he faltered.

"How now, good Matthew? What has happened?"

"A crowd of men are approaching the gate, and we hear they are come to demand the person of your guest!" returned the domestic.

"Oh, this is old news," said Captain Palmer, with a smile; "we have known that some time. Which way are they coming?"

"By the road in front of the Hall——"

At this moment a dull tramp of footsteps and the murmuring of many voices was heard ominously distinct in the direction indicated.

Captain Palmer did not evince any particular anxiety.

"Well," he said, smilingly, "since the way of escape is blockaded in front, we must be thankful the road at the back is still clear."

"Alas, sir!" exclaimed Matthew, clasping his hands nervously, "there are two distinct bodies. The back as well as the front of the Hall is surrounded!"

"Ha!" exclaimed the captain, but without in any way losing his presence of mind—"environed! Well, don't despair, my friend," he added, cheerfully. "I have managed to slip through a host of enemies before now in the course of my life. Let us hope that Providence will guide me safely this time!"

At this moment a ringing shout from the blockaders announced that the Hall was surrounded.

The squire started up.

"There is the secret subterranean passage!" he cried, hurriedly. "Matthew knows it, and will guide you. Farewell, my friend—Heaven preserve you!"

"Farewell, squire!" cried the captain. "We shall meet again, I trust, under happier auspices! Goodbye, my boys; I sha'n't forget you!"

These words were addressed to James, Ikey, and Augustus, who were squatted down on the hearth rug before the fire, in some consternation at what they had heard, and at the deafening shouts of the Coastguard-men without.

"Now, my friend, I am ready," said Captain Palmer to the old steward.

"Follow me, then," replied the old man.

Matthew went out at the door, with the captain close at his heels.

Chapter XXXIX.

AT THE GATE.

THE boys looked wistfully after them.

They had learned to look upon Captain Palmer as a stanch friend, and they now felt apprehensive for his safety.

"They won't catch him, will they?" asked Augustus, in an anxious tone.

"I hope not, I'm sure," answered James.

"They von't ketch 'im if they don't see 'im, vill they?" Ikey added.

"Perhaps as Matthew is going to take him out by the underground passage, they won't see him," said Augustus.

"Hi shouldn't think they vould, as it's dark," remarked Ikey, hopefully.

"I should like to go and see," whispered Augustus.

"So should I!" assented James and Ikey in a breath.

"Ve might p'r'aps be hable to 'elp 'im," added the latter, eagerly. "Shall us go?"

Augustus glanced towards the squire, whose attention seemed to be occupied with the confused murmur of voices without the gates.

"Yes, we will," answered Augustus; "we can slip out quietly. Come on."

In an instant the trio made their exit.

Their light tread on the soft carpet was entirely unnoticed by Squire Markham, whose mind was a little bewildered by the circumstances that were transpiring,

and that were so unexpected and unusual. He sat listening to the hoarse murmurs that rose upon the air like an angry wind, or a rushing tide.

In the meantime, James and Ikey, following Augustus, who acted as guide, had reached the subterranean passage.

The old steward had left the doors open so that the boys had nothing to do but to follow their leader

"Hain't it dark?" exclaimed Ikey.

"All the better," said James; "no one can see us."

"Sh!" ejaculated Augustus; "we are getting near the other end, I can feel the wind blowing through the door."

"So can Hi!" acquiesced Ikey, with a shiver. "It feels werry breezy indeed jest 'ere."

At this moment they reached the door that was ajar.

Augustus pushed it gently, and it opened, but grated slightly on its hinges.

The boys paused an instant as though fearful the sound would betray them.

No notice, however, was taken, and they ascended the narrow steps that led them out at the rear of the Hall.

Here they paused again and listened, hoping to hear the retreating footsteps of Matthew and the captain

But no such sound seemed to reach their ears.

Suddenly, however, as they stood there, they fancied they heard a stealthy footstep creep past them.

"What was that!" exclaimed Gus, in a startled whisper; "I heard something, didn't you?"

"Yes," returned his companions; "some one passed us."

"Who could it be?"

"'Ooever it was, 'e creeped past as sly as a cat as 'ad bin a stealin' summat," Ikey remarked.

"I think I know where Captain Palmer's gone," said Augustus.

"Where?" asked his companions.

"To the stables," answered the young gentleman. "Matthew will give him one of papa's horses to carry him away.'"

"S'pose ve goes to th' stables, hey?" asked Ikey.

"I think we will," returned his companions.

Accordingly they set off in that direction.

In the meantime, the bell had been violently rung, and the demand to open the gate vociferously urged.

But this demand had not been complied with.

Of course the irritation of those without was increased by the delay.

From ringing they proceeded to hammering at the massive portals, as though they would have battered them down.

So strong was the indignation of the men, that even the respect due to the white-haired owner of the Hall was forgotten.

"Down with the gates!" shouted the incensed men. "Burst them from their hinges!"

Then came a fresh outburst of fierce ejaculations, and an increased torrent of crashing blows.

It was well the gates of the old mansion were strong—

It was well the object of their vengeance was on the road to flight.

At a moment like that the maddened throng would have listened to no explanations—no assertions of innocence.

The victim would have been torn to pieces first, the explanation must have come afterwards when it would have been too late.

The squire, as he sat in his dining-room, listening to the Babel of sounds without, felt no apprehension on his own account.

His conscience accused him of no crime.

He was indeed a man *sans peur et sans reproche.*

Had he consulted his own inclinations only, he would at the first approach of the angry mob, have thrown open his gates, and bid them enter.

But the knowledge that the life of another—one, too, who had restored him his beloved son—depended on the ministers of vengeance being kept at bay for a time, had the effect of keeping the old gentleman still seated in his arm-chair, as though he heard nothing.

The alarmed domestics, some of whom had grown as white-haired in their master's service as the squire himself, was almost beside themselves.

Never had such a dire commotion been heard from the first moment they had entered the Hall until then.

Nothing of the real facts of the case was known to them.

They had made up their minds that the French had landed, and that they were to be all massacred without mercy the moment the foreign barbarians got footing within the walls.

Under these appalling circumstances, the scared household had congregated like a herd of frightened sheep in the spacious kitchen, looking as they supposed their last at the bright fire that glowed cheerfully in the ample grate.

Here they consoled one another by suggesting every possible mode of torture which a conquering foe might be supposed to inflict upon the unhappy prisoners that should fall into their hands.

At length, however, as the shouts grew louder, some of the more timid, unable longer to endure the horrors of suspense, suggested an appeal to their venerable master.

This was eagerly adopted by the entire body, who forthwith, huddled together in great alarm, almost clinging to each other, ascended the stairs leading from the kitchen.

It was at the end of a deafening shout from the Coastguard, that the squire became conscious of the approach of footsteps.

Raising his eyes, he perceived a crowd of domestics with blanched features and trembling limbs, crowded together in the doorway.

The old gentleman was almost tempted to smile at the extreme dread that was manifest in the entire body, but he was obliged to admit to himself that affairs were somewhat critical, and he, therefore, checked the smile, and said, gently:

"Well, my friends, what is the matter?"

The reply to this inquiry was a confused murmur of hysterical sobs from the females, and broken ejaculations from the men.

"Oh, your honour—oh! Th' French!—all be massacred! What shall we do?" And similar expressions came out confusedly.

The squire hastened to assure them that the noisy visitors were not French but English, and that, so far as they were concerned, they were in no peril whatever.

The squire also hinted that the men that surrounded his gates were labouring under a mistake.

This assurance of their respected master had the effect of allaying their fears to a considerable extent, though not perhaps of entirely dissipating them.

At all events, they returned to the kitchen, where it being suggested by the gardener that the ladies' nerves having been strongly *raked,* they might possibly require a slight stimulant, and the proposal being seconded by the under-keeper, and carried *nem. con.* by the rest, two colossal earthenware tankards of the squire's sparkling ale were drawn, and in a short time the colour lived again in every cheek—nay, in some it extended even to the tips of their noses: under the influence of the potent English liquor the hares became lions.

It would have been a poor look-out for any unfortunate *mounseer* who would have ventured to show his nose in Squire Markham's kitchen at that moment.

Let us leave this region for a moment, and ascend once more to the dining-room where the squire still lingered, listening to the storm that beat upon his time-worn gates.

Matthew had not yet returned with the assurance of the captain's safety; but calculating the probabilities, the squire felt that, from the time which had elapsed, he must have effected his retreat.

"I cannot keep them longer at my gate," the old man reasoned with himself. "It almost looks like guilty fear, or connivance with guilt."

He rose from his seat.

The restoration of his child had exercised a wonderfully restorative influence upon him, but still he was not the hale man he had been previous to that child's disappearance.

His manner was that of an old man, his step tottering and feeble.

Still, he did not, on that account, shrink from the duty that had suggested itself to him.

He went out into the corridor, and, taking his hat from the stand where it reposed, called to one of his domestics.

The gardener was, at that precise moment, comforting himself with a prolonged draught of ale.

Hearing the voice of his master, he paused abruptly, and hastily setting down the tankard—and wiping his lips with the cuff of his coat—went upstairs in obedience to the summons.

He found the squire with his three-cornered laced hat on his head, standing near the door.

"Draw the bolts, James, and unlock it," said the squire, pointing as he spoke.

James, not without some slight misgivings, in spite of the potent liquor he had imbibed, did as he was directed, but no more.

"Open the door!" said the squire.

"Open it, your honour?" gasped James.

"Yes! I am going out to speak to our friends at the gates, before they batter them off their hinges," he replied. "Don't be alarmed," the squire continued; "the sight of these white hairs may help to appease them."

James upon this opened the door.

This entrance was visible from the gates, and the venerable form of the squire was distinctly seen as he stood in the portal.

His appearance was greeted with a vociferous cheer.

"The squire—the squire!" shouted the entire body.

The tone of the shout seemed to imply that now the squire had made his appearance, justice would be immediately done.

The old gentleman advanced, the moonlight playing full upon his venerable features.

As the noise and clamour of voices hushed into a respectful silence, the squire said, in a pleasant voice:

"Well, my friends, what is it you require?"

"Justice! Revenge on a dastardly murderer!" cried out thirty voices.

"The squire doesn't know who he's got under his roof!" exclaimed a solitary voice.

"No—no!" echoed several of the others, eagerly— "he doesn't—he doesn't! or he'd be the first to give him up!"

"Who is it you seek?" inquired the squire, who thought by temporising a little to slacken the fury of the assembly.

"We want the man who caused the explosion up at Beacon Rock Cavern, that cost the lives and limbs of many of our comrades! We know he is here, and we demand him!"

These words were spoken in a tone of earnest determination, that seemed to admit of no contradiction.

"I think you are mistaken, my friends," said the squire.

"No—no!" they vociferated, impatiently. "We're not mistaken! It is you who are deceived, squire. This man has imposed upon you—he is Paul Jones the Pirate!"

A distant background of heads peering from the doorway, this announcement caught their ears, and filled them with renewed apprehensions.

The squire replied:

"There is no such person as Paul Jones here!"

This assertion revived the temporarily-suspended fury of the men.

"There is—there is!" they shouted. "He has imposed upon you by an assumed name; but he is here, nevertheless, and we are determined to have him. If you refuse us, we are desperate, and will burst in the gate, rather than be disappointed of our prey!"

A loud burst of determination followed upon this.

The timid crew in the entrance-hall yielded to the suggestions of prudence, and hastily sought the calm retreat of the kitchen once more.

The squire perceived from the excited manner of the Coastguard that it would be impossible to oppose directly.

He, therefore, as soon as he could make himself audible, said:

"Is the superintendent—is Lieutenant Grey here?"

"I am, squire!" cried the lieutenant, who had just arrived, and who now pushed through the crowd.

It was a fortunate circumstance that he appeared at that juncture, in time to exercise his authority, and restore somewhat of the discipline that had all but entirely disappeared.

"Back, men—back!" he cried, in a tone of command.

The men at these orders made way for their superior, who approached the gate.

"Lieutenant," said the squire, "let me speak to you a moment alone."

"With pleasure," returned the lieutenant.

The squire raised his voice.

"Bring the keys hither!" he cried.

This command reached the interior, from whence slowly issued the gardener, who advanced, with somewhat shaky legs and a head dizzy with draughts of home-brewed, bearing the keys.

On reaching the gate, there was some little delay in fitting the key in the lock, owing to the nervous anxiety of the temporary porter.

But this at last was accomplished. The gate was opened, the lieutenant entered, and the iron barrier closed again upon the men without.

The squire led the superintendent into the Hall, and as briefly as possible explained the circumstances in which he was placed, and detailed the account of the explosion, and the mistake that had been productive of such dire results.

The undoubted honour and unblemished reputation of Squire Markham were more than sufficient to impress Lieutenant Grey with the truth of what he revealed to him.

But the difficulty was to inspire the indignant crowd outside the gates with a similar faith.

"They are so exasperated," said the lieutenant, "against the perpetrator of this outrage, that any attempt to turn them from their purpose would, I fear, be only exasperating them beyond the verge of control."

"But," replied the squire, "Captain Palmer has been gone some time; and, surely, they would not wish, in default of finding him, to wreak their vengeance on me or my property?"

"Not in their sober senses, squire, I am sure!" exclaimed the lieutenant; "for there is not a man amongst them who does not respect you, in common with all who know you. But they have assembled here burning with indignant rage, and thirsting to retaliate upon the man who has robbed many of them of relatives, and inflicted on a large proportion injuries they will carry with them to their graves!"

"It is very terrible, certainly!" admitted the squire; "but even now, perhaps, a few conciliatory words from you might have the effect of pacifying them."

"I am seriously afraid my influence will be insufficient in the present instance," replied the lieutenant. "Their excitement borders upon mutiny; and when that is the case, what can one man do opposed to fifty? However, I will try," he added, out of compliment to the worthy squire.

He was about to leave the dining-room, where the above conversation had taken place, when a yell, louder and fiercer than any that had yet been raised, fell upon their ears.

The expression of the sounds, too, was different.

Hitherto it had been the hoarse murmurs of a body of avengers, threatening stern retribution; now, it was quite sharp and exultant, like the cry of a pack of hounds as they recover the scent of their prey.

It seemed to imply to the lieutenant that something had happened.

He turned slightly pale, as he murmured between his teeth:

"What does that mean? Can they have caught him? If so, they will infallibly tear him to pieces!"

Having uttered these words, he hastily opened the door in the entrance-hall, and looked anxiously towards the gate.

Strange! all was silent and deserted—not a soul was to be seen!

Chapter XL.

THE CAPTAIN'S FLIGHT.

IT did not take the steward long to conduct Captain Palmer through the subterranean passage to the exterior.

The spot where this secret entrance emerged into the open air was at the rear of the Hall, and at no great distance from the stables.

Towards these the captain and his guide proceeded as hastily as possible, utterly unconscious that a dark form followed them like a messenger of evil, evidently watching, and ready to frustrate the captain's escape.

Our readers will be at once ready to designate this cloaked figure as the arch traitor, Octavius Challoner.

Nor will they be wrong in their supposition. It was indeed he.

He had taken his precautions well.

Bringing the incensed Coastguard up to the very gates, not only in front but at the back, the Hall was, as it were, beleaguered.

At least, if escape was to be tried it must be from some outlet at the side that he could easily watch.

We may be sure that to a man of Octavius's habits he had not allowed so convenient a mode of ingress and egress as the subterranean passage to remain unused.

Quite the contrary, many a night he might have been seen cautiously emerging from its narrow doorway after the family had retired to rest, and returning thither after a night spent in feverish dissipation, in the dim gray dawn of morning.

It was by this he passed out with his young cousin, when he conveyed him to the Beacon Rock Cavern on that one eventful night.

He felt certain that when the alarm was raised this would be the spot by which the fugitive would attempt to make good his retreat.

Accordingly it was here he directed his particular vigilance.

He gloated darkly as he saw the captain, conducted by old Matthew, emerge from the passage. He felt then that his prey was in his power, and that he should infallibly hunt it down.

He glided after them spectre-like in the gloom, as equally unconscious in his eagerness that he was watched as they were whom he tracked so closely.

However, it so happened that his stealthy tread aroused the boys as they came out of the subterranean passage.

As Octavius cautiously followed, watching the movements of Captain Palmer, so James, Ikey, and Augustus followed with equal care, watching the actions—so far as they could see them—of Octavius.

A horse was speedily selected and saddled; and this having been done, the captain led him away over the greensward to where a side door opened into a lane.

Here they paused a moment.

The hoarse clamours of the men shouting for admission, both in front and at the back of the Hall, were distinctly audible.

To a person well acquainted with the locality it would have been easy, favoured by the darkness, to elude those who waited for him, and get clear off.

But Captain Palmer was on somewhat strange ground, where a wrong turn might bring him face to face with those he wished to avoid, or where a sudden scrape of his horse's heel on the gravel might set the whole body in pursuit.

He paused, therefore, listening to the shouts that rose in the air.

The captain smiled, not by any means attaching to his position the danger old Matthew thought it merited.

"They seemed to be so very well amused," he said, "barking round the trap, that I think the rat may venture forth without any fear of being taken the least notice of."

"I am going to let you out, captain, by a small door in the wall," Matthew informed him, as he put the key in the lock.

At this moment Octavius, confident in the security of the darkness, drew still nearer.

So near that he quite interposed between the boys and the captain, whom they wished to warn.

They felt inclined in their excitement to rush forward at any risk and upset the treacherous villain.

But they feared such an attempt would induce him to raise an alarm that might have been fatal.

So they were silent.

The gate swung open silently on its hinges.

All was quiet and admirably adapted for the escape of a prisoner.

Captain Palmer having led out the horse into the lane, mounted at once.

"Good night, my friend!" he said, cheerfully, to the old steward. "You'll hear of me again, I've no doubt, before long!"

The boys hardly dared breathe for anxiety.

They were expecting every moment to hear the loud voice of Octavius ringing the alarm, or that he would dart forward in the gloom and seize the horse's bridle.

They were very much surprised that nothing of this sort took place.

Old Matthew seemed anxious that his charge should be safe out of harm's way.

"Good night, captain! and a safe journey to you!" said the steward. "If you were acquainted with this locality I should advise you to keep straight on, but as you are not, you had better keep the lane till you come to a turning on the left about fifty yards hence, take that, and keep on till you come into the main road—there your path is clear enough."

"Thank you, my worthy old pilot," returned the captain. "Here goes, then, to set sail."

As he spoke he urged the horse forward at a walking pace.

The boys cautiously crept along, longing to call to the captain, but not daring to do so from the fact that they heard a stealthy tread also following on the other side of the road.

"Come!" they heard the captain cry, suddenly, "this is no better than drifting with the tide. I must crowd all sail on, or my friends yonder will blockade me after all. Ya ho!" he cried with energy, giving the horse a kick with his heel as he spoke. "Forward!"

At the same moment a dark figure plunged forward and seized the animal's bridle, and a sharp, ringing report rang through the air.

The horse reared upwards with a snort of agony, and fell backwards with a crash to the ground, bearing his rider with him.

At the same moment a loud voice cried:

"Help here! help! Paul Jones is here! help me to secure him!"

The shock of the fall was so sudden and unexpected, that it took Captain Palmer a moment or two to realise his position.

Fortunately none of his limbs were broken, but his brain was dizzy with the violence of the fall, and he gasped for breath.

Staggering, rather than rising to his feet, he was about to look round him to see what new peril waited him, when he found himself suddenly pinioned from behind, whilst a voice, which he recognized as that of Octavius, shouted vociferously for help.

It was this cry that had reached the ears of the assembled men at the gates, and caused them to proceed in the direction of the voice.

Half stunned as Captain Palmer was, escape seemed nigh impossible, for his vindictive assailant, stimulated by hatred and revenge, clung to him with the tenacity of a snake.

The struggle was unequal, and already the shouts of the advancing men answered in response to the cry of Octavius.

Captain Palmer himself began to look upon his case as hopeless.

"I'm trapped," he thought, "and I shall most certainly be torn to ribbons."

But just then a very unexpected event took place.

Four small arms encircled the legs of the traitor Octavius, and two others grasped the collar of his coat behind, and by a sudden and vigorous effort, they completely capsized him.

Yes, flat on his back in the middle of the road sprawled Octavius Challoner, whilst suddenly there appeared upon the spot, as if by magic, a horseman, mounted on a magnificent gray steed.

He dismounted with the rapidity of lightning, whispered a hasty word in Captain Palmer's ear, and in a manner that seemed little short of conjuration, hoisted him into the saddle.

Then leading the horse in a contrary direction to that he had been pursuing, he turned him hastily through a gap of the hedge into a field.

"Now," said he, "my friend, off with you like the wind! and if they catch you I'll forgive them! When you have reached a place of safety you can send the horse back to the care of Squire Markham. Now then! right across the two fields before you, and then into the road as soon as you please. Forward, boy!"

He gave the noble steed a farewell pat, and the animal darted forward like an arrow from a bow, and as though it were conscious that it carried on its back some treasure that was to be borne beyond the reach of peril.

All this occupied only a few seconds.

It was done quietly and so rapidly that no one had the least idea what *had* been done.

Octavius Challoner had been in his turn considerably startled by his fall, more especially as he struck the back of his head violently upon the ground.

Feeling, however, the necessity for immediate action, he scrambled on to his feet to find himself in the grasp of, and face to face with, the President of the Confederates, George Carew.

Though the light that surrounded them was indistinct, it was sufficient to reveal the pale features to the guilty Octavius.

This was the second time the President had appeared to him since the night when he thought he had for ever rid himself of his enemy.

So sudden and unexpected was his appearance that Octavius could hardly persuade himself that he did not look upon a being from another world. A deadly horror seemed to paralyse his limbs, his arms dropped nerveless by his side, as the calm, deep voice of the President fell upon his ear.

"What should prevent me now from taking your worthless life?" he said; "one reason only—that I would not take your punishment out of the hands of fate! Go on!" he continued, with ominous distinctness, "fill up the measure of your crimes! Rush on blindly to the doom that awaits you, and die the death of a dog at last! In your last moments you shall have no friends near you but the dark shadow of your past deeds—these, like avenging spectres, shall herald your guilty soul into eternity!"

The President threw the trembling Octavius from him as he finished his denunciation, and with a cry of terror and despair the guilty wretch fled away in the darkness, henceforth to be like Cain—a wanderer and a vagabond on the face of the earth.

When the Coastguard reached the spot they found nothing but the prostrate body of the dead horse.

This gave rise to a variety of surmises.

But one fact seemed to present itself to them very distinctly, and that was that the man they sought had escaped.

A great deal of their rage had vented itself in shouts and threats and the wild excitement with which they had hurried to the spot where they were now congregated, in answer to the summons of Octavius, who was now nowhere to be found.

They began to be undecided, and to think that after all they had been only on a wild-goose chase.

The appearance of their superintendent at this moment seemed to confirm their opinion.

"Come, my men," he said, "I am inclined to think there is some little mistake here. We had better return, for to-night, at least, and to-morrow I think I shall be able to explain to you that this disastrous explosion was the result of an error rather than a design ruthlessly to destroy life. At all events, the man you seek is, I am well informed, far beyond your reach."

The words of the lieutenant had an evident effect upon the men, and those who half an hour before were ready to have torn the gates of the Hall from their hinges now quietly formed into rank, and accompanied the superintendent back to the depôt.

Old Matthew, the steward, as he lingered at the gate in the wall, looking after the retreating form of Captain Palmer, had heard the report of the pistol; and although his age prevented him from taking any active part in the affray, he had quietly crept forward near enough to witness the escape of the captain and the discomfiture of Octavius.

He had also been an unseen spectator of the departure of the men—a circumstance that relieved him of a load of anxiety.

All, therefore, being once more quiet, he slowly entered the gate, which having locked he returned once more to the Hall.

The boys had already preceded him thither.

Great joy spread itself through the household of the squire when the steward informed them that the besiegers had departed.

The squire himself, too, listened to the intelligence with a feeling of relief.

The sentiment of anger had at one time appeared so strong that he had began to apprehend the worst consequences. And all this had been fomented and instigated by that worthless nephew to whom he had acted a father's part.

It was no wonder that the old gentleman felt strongly indignant against the heartless villany that had yielded so vile a return for all his care and kindness.

It was evident that the good squire had received a shock which, in his present state of health, he was in no condition to withstand.

Now that the tumult had subsided, and he could sit quietly and reflect, his thoughts were very painful.

James, Ikey, and Augustus having performed their part—no unimportant one either—in the events that had recently transpired, had quietly crept back to their station on the hearth-rug, the squire having been so absorbed one way and another as not to have noticed either their departure or their return.

His eye suddenly fell upon them, and a benevolent smile lighted up his features.

But there was much sadness mingled with the smile.

"Poor boys!" he murmured to himself. "Two of them orphans, and the other—how soon may he be alone in the world!"

He covered his eyes with his hand thoughtfully for a few moments, and then called his young son to him.

The child ran to his father, and climbed up on to his knees.

The old man pressed him fondly to his bosom, and passed his trembling hands through his glossy curls

"My darling!" he exclaimed, in an earnest tone of affection, "I still have you spared to me; I shall still be able to rejoice in the thought that you will live to fill my place when I am gone!"

The boy looked at the pale features of the speaker and his tear-dimmed eyes, and nestled closer to his bosom.

"Oh, yes!" the squire continued, "I feel that my prayers in your behalf, my darling child, will be heard. I have prayed earnestly that you may not only live to arrive at man's estate, but that you may grow up to be a good man—a good man, my child!" he repeated, earnestly, "without which distinction far better is it to die young in the pure springtime of life."

The old man paused an instant, and then added:

"You will listen to your father's words, and remember them, will you not, Augustus?"

"Yes, papa," answered the child.

"I believe you will, my boy—I believe you will!" returned the squire, in a tone of confidence, "and in that belief I shall die in peace."

These words were spoken as though to himself, but Augustus heard them.

"Papa, dear," he said, anxiously, "you're not going to die, are you?"

The squire almost started at this question.

Was it that he felt such an event was nearer than even he himself was willing to acknowledge?

At all events, not willing to distress his child, he answered more cheeringly:

"Not at present, I trust, my boy. I would fain be spared a few years longer to watch over you and guide your conduct; still, I am an old man, and life is always uncertain. We never know when the summons may come. The all-important point, therefore, both for young and old, is to live so that we may always be in readiness."

The squire was evidently weary after the excitement of the evening, and when Matthew came, according to his usual custom, to inform him it was ten o'clock, he could see that his master was weaker than usual.

"Yes, Matthew," said the old man, in reply to the steward's inquiry whether he was ready for repose, "quite ready. I feel tired out. To-night's excitement has been too much for me."

As the squire rose to leave the room, he quite staggered, and Matthew was apprehensive that he should have to summon the assistance of a stronger arm than his own to support him.

But the squire would not permit it.

"No, no, Matthew!" he said. "I shall do very well with your arm."

With that assistance, therefore, the old gentleman, with more than usual difficulty, reached his bed-chamber—

That chamber which he was never more to leave alive.

As though he seemed to have a forewarning of his approaching end, he sent for his son to his bedside, and blessed him with solemn and affectionate earnestness.

He then fell into a calm and tranquil slumber.

The worthy old steward felt happy to see his master enjoying such peaceful repose, and left him, trusting that a night's rest would restore him.

In the middle of the night Matthew awoke, and his first thoughts were of the squire.

"I will go and see that all is well," he said.

He accordingly proceeded to the squire's bed-chamber. On arriving there he found that all *was* well.

The squire lay exactly in the same position in which the steward had left him.

There was a gentle smile on the lips, and the eyes were closed.

Matthew looked at him earnestly for a moment, and then placed his hand upon his old master's heart.

It beat no longer.

Squire Markham was dead !

Chapter XLI.

HOMELESS AGAIN.

THE usual gloom that seems to cloud the atmosphere where the presence of death is felt, hung over the Hall after the breath had left the body of its old master.

Everything looked dark and gloomy.

Shutters were closed, blinds were drawn down, and the domestics glided to and fro like ghosts, with sad countenances, and speaking with bated breath in harmony with the general depression.

Indeed, they might well do so.

The death of the good old squire depressed the entire household of the happy home in which they had lived so many years, where many of them had grown gray, and some even white-haired. Now all was over.

The squire was dead, and the young Augustus, then a child, would not require an establishment for some years.

The Hall, in the interim, whilst the future squire was away at school or college, would most probably be shut up in grim and mouldy silence, and the old domestics would be scattered hither and thither.

It was these thoughts that depressed them and made them feel bitterly that in the death of Squire Markham they had lost master, friend, and home.

Poor Augustus was deeply grieved at his father's loss, more so than boys of his age usually are.

James and Ikey crept about silently, feeling themselves rather in the way, their position at the Hall being somewhat indefinite.

In course of time mysterious people in black, with pale, solemn faces, came to and fro.

These were the undertakers, whose business it was to perform the last sad office to the deceased, and consign him to the narrow cell in which he was henceforth to sleep in peace.

The domestics crowded round to take a last, sad look at the placid features of their old master, whom they were to see no more upon this earth.

But time flew on.

The funeral was over—there had been an assembly of a few people in the dining-room, to hear the squire's will read by Mr. Probate, the lawyer.

At this meeting it was discovered that, with the exception of a few trifling legacies, and pensions to old servants, the entire property and estates were bequeathed to his son.

This being ascertained, the Hall was once more free from visitors.

Mr. Probate, who had looked very searchingly at James and Ikey, at last inquired who they were.

On being informed by Ikey that "they 'ad come to th' 'all vith young Mast'r Gus," the lawyer gave a peculiar shrug.

"Master Augustus," said Mr. P., "has left the Hall to prosecute his studies, and as there seems no provision made for you in any way, I think the sooner you take your departure the better."

As this was Mr. Probate's matter-of-fact view of the case, and as there was no reason to be given why they should remain, they prepared to obey.

Certainly there was some sympathy expressed by the servants for the poor boys.

The cook supplied them with a plentiful supply of food, and a general subscription secured them a little money, and then with the good wishes of the entire household following them, our young heroes once more trudged forward to look the world in the face.

James bore his position philosophically, uttering no complaints, but only wondering what strange adventure was next to befall them.

Ikey was not quite so contented.

He seemed to be somewhat chagrined at his sudden dismissal, and expressed his disappointment in very doleful tones.

"Hi did think as ve vas hall right hup at th' 'all, and then th' 'ole gen'l'man goes an' dies hall on a sudding, jest as hif it vur done o' purpose, an' 'ere ve hare turned hout agin, to go vich hever vay the vind blows us."

"No, Ikey," James said, in a tone of correction; "whichever way Heaven guides."

Ikey gave a somewhat impatient grunt.

"Hi knows vot Hi shall do : Hi shall go back to Mr. Boombrick's an' do the monkey agin. Shall ve, Jim ?" he asked.

"No, Ikey," replied James, "I think we can do something better than that. I think Captain Palmer was quite right when he said that going about in the skins of animals was a very useless way of spending our lives."

"Vell, but ve must do summat," argued Ikey; "an' Mr. Jerry was werry kind to us, an' ve us'd to get plenty to heat."

"I don't like the life," said James, firmly, "and I don't intend to go back to it."

"Yer means to say as yer'd part rather ?" snivelled Ikey.

"I should be sorry to part from you, Ikey," said James, very kindly, taking his hand. "I'm sure I don't wish to, and I don't see that there's any more reason why we should part now than before."

"Vell, but 'ow can ve 'elp partin' if you goes vun vay an' Hi goes another ?" asked Ikey, vehemently.

"Ah, then, certainly," acquiesced James; "but the only way to keep together is for both to go the same way."

"Vell, so it his," coincided Ikey, with reluctance; "but it's horful to be a vanderin' about like two stray pigs, not knowin' vheer ve're agoin', or vheer ve're to get any wittals."

"But you forget," remarked James, "that we've never been without food or friends yet since we started, and, since that has been the case, we must try and trust Providence that it will be so again."

"Vell, that's hall true enough, Jem; but Hi don't think as H'im quite so trustin', as the sayin' is, as you hare."

"We ought to try to be so," replied James; "after having been helped out of dangers as we have been, it seems quite ungrateful to be full of fears and discontent."

"Vell, theer, then, Hi von't grumble no moor!" exclaimed Ikey, with a laudable endeavour to control his discontent. "Hi von't go back to the show; an' ve'll stick together has ve said ve vould."

This being settled, the boys trudged along in the same road as they had formerly travelled.

They passed the hospitable farm where they had been so kindly received, but they did not stop at it.

Onward they went, until they drew near the spot where the caravan had stood the last time they had passed that way.

Now, however, no cheery light shone out of the little window with the bright red curtain.

All was dark, cheerless, and desolate.

"Vot d'yer think of this, Jem?" Ikey asked, in a desponding tone.

"I think we must go on till we come to some place where we can stop for the night," James replied. "We have got some money, you know."

On calculating the bequests of the domestics, the boys had found themselves the possessors of six shillings and sixpence—a sum which, to Ikey, appeared magnificent and inexhaustible.

"Oh, yes, Hi knows ve've got money!" he said. "That's vhy it's sich a noosance as ve don't come to some 'ouse or hother."

However, all Ikey's complaints by no means mended his condition, and his impatience increased in proportion as he grew more and more fatigued.

He was about to give way to a lamentable expression of his misery, when suddenly James drew his attention to a dark object at some short distance in the middle of the road.

"Vot his it?" exclaimed Ikey.

"It looks like a vehicle of some kind."

"Vot's hit a stoppin' for?"

"I can't tell at present," James replied.

"P'r'aps it's run avay an' broke down," Ikey suggested.

"I suppose you mean the horse?" said James, smiling.

By this time they drew near the dark object, which proved to be a two-wheeled gig, one of the wheels of which had come off, and deposited its load in the middle of the road.

This was a tradesman and his wife, of the name of Sanderson, who had been to visit a friend, and who had thus come to grief at some distance from any habitation.

They seemed to be, however, making the best of a bad job, and not increasing the unpleasantness by useless lamentations.

"My dear Mary," they heard the man say, in a consolatory tone, "John can't be long now, and we shall soon have him here with Rob the blacksmith."

"Oh, I don't mind waiting at all, William," replied the lady; "I am only too thankful that we are not injured, and that the poor horse stands so quietly."

The poor horse in question was one of those plethoric animals, that found it quite as much as it cared to do to drag the chaise along when it had its proper complement of wheels—to have attempted to move it in its present loggish condition, would have been a feat utterly beyond its powers of imagination even to contemplate.

But the equanimity of the overturned couple was a useful lesson to Ikey.

By this time they had approached quite close.

"Who's there?" asked Mrs. S., as she heard the footsteps.

"It's only hus, mum," responded Ikey; "two poor boys as is qvite tired hout a valking hall day."

"Yes, ma'am," added James, "we're strange in this part of the country, and we don't know where we can get a bed."

"Poor boys!—poor boys!" ejaculated Mrs. Sanderson, who was a very kind-hearted woman, "that's very hard; but we're almost in the same predicament ourselves. But there, we shall have the blacksmith here presently to replace the wheel, and then I daresay we can pack you in some corner, and give you a lift."

The boys expressed their gratitude, and in a very few moments footsteps were heard rapidly drawing near.

The light of a lantern flashed through the dark, and Robin, accompanied by John, came up.

"Better late than never," cried Mr. Sanderson, cheerfully.

"Now, then!" said Rob, "where be th' wheel?"

After some little investigation, it was found to have rolled into the ditch by the roadside.

The runaway being secured, the chaise was by the united efforts of the party raised, and the wheel properly adjusted.

The linch-pin was then fixed, and the old chaise stood erect in all its pristine firmness.

"There, that will do nicely!" exclaimed Mrs. Sanderson, approvingly, "and now, as we're going to give these poor boys a lift, you can walk back with Robin, John; it will be company for him."

There was no objection made to this arrangement, and the worthy couple having entered the gig, James and Ikey were hoisted into it, with a friendly admonition to take as little room as possible, and the vehicle drove off.

"Now," whispered James, "see how wrong you were to complain!"

"So Hi vas," replied Ikey. "Hi von't complain never no moor."

After riding several miles at a jog-trot pace, Mr. Sanderson stopped, and said, as he pointed down the road:

"There, my lads, you'll find a bed there. There's an inn a few yards onwards; and we're going to turn off here."

Accordingly James and Ikey were lowered to the ground.

Mrs. S. whispered to her spouse, who called out:

"Heigh, boys! have you got any brass?"

"Yes, thank you, sir," said James, "enough to pay for a bed!"

"Well, here's a crown for you; now you'll have more than enough," said Mr. Sanderson, as he bent down and placed the coin in James's hand. "There, good night—the inn's right before you."

"Good night, my boys," chirped Mrs. S., and the chaise turned off to the left, and was seen no more.

"Hi 'opes hit hain't fur to th' hinn," exclaimed Ikey, in an anxious tone.

"No, it can't be; the gentleman said it was right before us," said James.

"Come hon, then; let's valk as fast as ve can," cried Ikey, taking his companion by the arm, and hurrying him along as fast as he could.

In a very few minutes the lights from the windows of the roadside inn were distinctly visible.

This welcome sight incited them to fresh exertions, and a few moments more brought them to the very door of the inn.

It was not a building of gigantic size, or of any particularly imposing appearance, but it seemed to hold out signs of comfort to the weary traveller.

The red curtains were closely drawn, and the bright light within gave such a warm and glowing reflection on the darkness without, that it was hardly possible to resist the appeal.

The tired boys looked longingly at the windows and the red curtains.

"Don't hit look comf'able!" remarked Ikey.

"Very," said James. "Shall we go in?"

"Yes."

Without any further hesitation, therefore, the boys opened the door and went in.

It was very warm and snug inside.

Nobody seemed to take any particular notice of them.

While they were looking about asking themselves mental questions where two such insignificant individuals as they were would be allowed to bestow themselves, they caught sight of an open door, which led into a kind of kitchen, and in which a bright fire burnt.

This seemed to them just the kind of apartment that two tired boys might enter.

In, therefore, they went.

It was by no means an uncomfortable place after all.

Though there was no carpet, and though the floor was stone, still, it was clean and white, and sprinkled

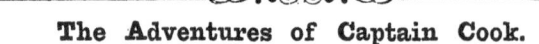

[OCTAVIUS CHALLONER'S NOCTURNAL VISIT TO THE BOYS.]

with sand, and the clear, red glow of the fire lighted it up, and made it quite cheering to look upon.

There were several parties of labouring men at the different tables smoking their pipes, and drinking their ale.

Dan, the ostler, waiter, boots, et cætera, et cætera, was there also.

The boys, when they entered, noticed a countryman in a smock-frock, with a bushy head of very red hair.

This man seemed to be either drunk or worn out with fatigue, since he had fallen forward in his seat, and was now fast asleep, his face buried in his hands.

Dan, on the contrary, was wide awake, and fixed his eyes upon the juvenile visitors with considerable earnestness.

The lads began to feel uncomfortable.

They could not divest themselves of the unpleasant idea that they were intruding.

James expressed his fears to Dan.

"I beg your pardon, sir," he said, humbly: "I hope we're not in the way here."

"Ee, ee !" laughed Dan. "Oi s'pose thee'll be wantin' soommat to yeat and drink, won't thee ?"

"Yes, sir, if you please," answered James. "We should like to have some bread and cheese, and——"

"Yale," added Dan, as a matter of course.

"Thank you, sir," said James, "but we're used to drink water."

"Eh, boot we don't sell water 'ere 'excep' for th' 'orses, soa yow must order yale, or yow won't get noa bread an' cheese," Dan informed them.

The boys thanked him for acquainting them with the rules of the establishment, and ordered ale instead of water.

The waiter considerately informed them that they were not compelled to drink the ale unless they so desired it, the custom of the place extending merely to the ordering and paying for it.

"Oi'll 'elp 'ee drink it," he said, in a private and confidential tone, that quite cheered James and Ikey, who were beginning to wonder how they should dispose of the ale they were compelled to order.

Dan disappeared, and soon returned with two gigantic slices of bread and cheese, and a large jug of ale.

"Theer," he said, as he placed the refreshment on the table, "theer you be. Oi s'pose thee'st gotten brass enough to pay for 'un?"

"Oh! yes," answered Ikey, "'ve've got lots o' money."

Just at this moment the drowsy countryman with the red hair might have been seen to shift his position, and, as he did so, glance drowsily at the boys, who were too much engaged with their bread and cheese to notice anything else.

"'Ave yer, though?" said the waiter, in reply to Ikey's remark about their wealth; "well, I 'ope you may always 'ave lots, it be varry convenient. Good health!"

Taking up the jug of ale, Dan took a draught that seemed interminable.

"That be rale good stuff," he said, smacking his lips and taking a long breath after the draught.

Ikey gazed rather wistfully at the bulky jug.

An idea crossed his mind, that as they were to pay for the contents it might not be unreasonable to taste a very small portion.

"Jem," he whispered, "Hi thinks Hi should like a little drop er hale."

"Very well, then, have some," said James; "there it is."

Ikey, without further hesitation, seized upon the portly flagon with both hands, and took a good drink. He then handed it to James, who also drank, but very slightly.

But this proceeding seemed to be quite irregular in the eyes of the thirsty waiter.

"Oi thout yow boys said yow couldna drink yale!" he said, in a tone slightly indignant.

"We don't usually drink it," James answered; "but as it was ordered, and as we shall have to pay for it, we thought we might just taste it."

"Oi don't think yale be a good thing for boys as a rool," remarked Dan; and in order to preserve them from any evil consequences that might ensue from a repetition of the draught, he raised the jug to his lips, and never removed it till it was empty.

After they had finished their supper, the boys sat looking at the fire, and feeling particularly drowsy. However, their attention was attracted by the arrival of two new guests.

These seemed to belong to the same class as the rest, having the appearance of agricultural labourers.

They entered hastily, and with some excitement, as though loaded with important news.

"Eh, lads!" they said, on entering. "What d'ye think?"

"What?" inquired everybody.

"Th' pressgang be oot! an' they ha' catch'd hold o' Jock Smith, an' Jem Barnes, an' Tom Barclay, an' taken 'em off to make sailors of 'em."

At this startling announcement more than one cheek grew pale.

The honest rustics who had, like their forefathers, been in the habit of toiling in the fields from morning till night, year after year, and who went on in the same jog-trot, monotonous manner from January to December, and from December to January, neither seeking nor desiring any change in the nature of their occupation, were quite aghast at the thought of being carried away by force to fight the *mounseers*.

"Oi wouldna go, Oi know!" said one.

"No; more'd Oi I" affirmed another.

"Oi'd loike to catch 'em alayin' 'ands on me!" exclaimed a third. "Oi wunder what my 'oud 'ooman 'ud say!"

"Eh, mon! they care not what 'oud women say, or young 'uns either," explained one of the newcomers; "if ye're at all refractory they just give yer a toppor on the head to stun yer, an' by the time you comes to your senses yer finds yerself on board ship."

This intelligence seemed to produce a kind of panic amongst the assembled parties.

They grew timid and uneasy, and glanced nervously at every sound towards the door, as though they almost expected to see the terrible pressgang rush in and lay violent hands on the entire body.

Dan, the boots, seemed to maintain his self-possession in a remarkable manner.

The cause of this was a firm conviction that waiters were a privileged class, and that, whoever else might be ruthlessly seized upon, they as a body would be exempted, inasmuch as they could render as efficient service to their country at home as ever they could abroad.

But as the rest of the company could not "lay that flattering unction to their souls," they began to fidget in their seats, and, by degrees, to go out.

In a very short time the room was empty, saving the presence of Dan, the sleeping countryman, and the two boys.

These last were very sleepy, and, in fact, had closed their eyes, and fallen into that drowsy state that is all but sleep.

They were aroused by a heavy footstep, and opened their eyes just in time to see the red-haired countryman go slouching out of the room.

Drowsy as they were, their faculties were sufficiently awake to enable them to come to the conclusion that they had *met that man before!*

This was strange, too.

They had not seen his face—they had not heard his voice, and yet they felt they knew him.

The waiter had left the room at the same time as the countryman, so that James and Ikey were now alone.

They looked at one another, as though each expected the other would speak, but they were silent.

The next moment the waiter's voice was heard.

"They be all gone but the two boys," it said, and the speaker then entered.

"Now, then, you boys! we be goin' to lock oop; soa you mun turn oot!" cried Dan.

"But we want to sleep here to-night," explained James, in a tone of some anxiety.

"Sleep 'ere!" echoed the waiter. "Why didn't thee say soa afoor?"

He spoke in a tone that implied the seriousness of the omission—nay, more, that seemed to say "you can't stop."

The boys looked at the boots very wistfully.

The boots appeared to be reflecting—calculating the number of beds in the house, perhaps.

"It's varry orkard—varry," he said to himself. "Oi doesn't know how it can be managed. P'r'aps Oi moight be able to——"

He scratched his head profoundly, and then said:

"Oi tell 'ee what—yow'd better order another quart o' yale, an' while yow be drinkin' it, Oi'll see what Oi can do aboot the bed."

Of course, the tired boys had no alternative but to submit to these petty extortions, especially as on that submission hung the only prospect they had of having a bed that night.

The waiter disappeared, and after some little delay returned, carrying a lighted candle.

"Oi've managed it for thee," he said, with a knowing wink at the boys. "Yow mun thank yowr stars that Oi wur 'ere to look after yow, or yer'd never ha' got it."

"Hi s'pose," said Ikey, "you forgot to horder the hale?"

"No I didn't," returned the waiter, with honest pride. "Oi never forgets noot. Oi ordered it, an' drank it, so as it shouldn't do yow no harm."

After this expression of his disinterested benevolence, Dan informed them that if they would come with him he would show them to their dormitory.

The boys, nothing loath, rose instantly, and went after Dan, who led the way up an old-fashioned flight of stairs, and along an old-fashioned kind of passage or gallery, with a great many doors on either side. Through one of these doors at the further end, the waiter led them.

"Theer yow be," he said, "an' a varry comfortable room it be too. Good neet!"

And with these words he went out

Chapter XLII.

THE BED-ROOM.

THE room, considering the earnest panegyric passed upon it by the boots, looked anything *but* comfortable. But then, probably, Dan looked at it through the cheering medium of strong ale, which magnified its advantages.

The walls were destitute of paper, and instead, covered by an unpleasant cream-coloured sort of wash.

The bedstead was a rickety apology for a very spindle limbed four-poster, whilst the bed, which was too small, was carefully spread out so as to cover the surface of the sacking.

There was a damp, unpleasant odour that pervaded the apartment, strongly suggestive of rheumatic fever for any unfortunate victim who ventured between the not over clean sheets that covered the rickety apparatus.

Ikey looked round scrutinisingly at the four walls with their creamy hue, and having inspected them silently and deliberately, dropped his eyes rather disconsolately on the patchwork quilt, and from thence allowed them to glide on to the floor, that might have been interesting to a curious observer, if only from the quantities of worm-holes that dotted it in every direction.

"Vell," said he, at length, "hif that vaiter calls this 'ere a comfor'ble bed-room, Hi doesn't think much on it myself. Vot do you think, Jem?"

"It isn't such a nice room as we had up at the Hall," said James, with an involuntary sigh at the contrast; "but," he added, with an effort at cheerfulness, "we can't expect always to get such a place as that to sleep in."

"Vell, no, Hi s'pose not," Ikey acquiesced, "honly this does seem sich a mouldy sort of a place."

"Well, we must make the best of it," answered James, "so suppose we say our prayers, and jump into bed before the light goes out."

The *brief* candle was flickering in its socket as the boys knelt down to pray.

James had taught his friend Ikey to pray, and the two poor orphans now offered up their evening petition together.

Before they had finished the light went out, and they were left in darkness, save a faint light from the moon through the window pane.

It did not take the boys long to undress themselves, and that being accomplished, they, with a certain amount of resolution, plunged beneath the bed-clothes.

The sensation was anything but inspiring.

For some time they lay huddled close together, shivering, without being able either to impart any heat to, or to imbibe any heat from, the things that covered them.

"Jem," said Ikey, at length, his teeth chattering as he spoke, "they've bin a vashin' these 'ere things, an' forgot to dry 'em."

This was by no means a weak description of the sensation caused by the damp bed-clothes.

James replied:

"They do, certainly, feel very damp. Suppose we get next to the blanket?"

"Or," suggested Ikey, "suppose ve puts hon hour close fust, and then, p'raps, ve shall get varm."

This being agreed to, our young adventurers glided from their *water-bed*, and reassumed their garments.

After this, they once more laid themselves down, the blanket (such a one as it was) this time being next to them.

This seemed to have a calorific effect.

Ikey welcomed the sensation of increasing heat with enthusiasm, and even went so far as to give his undisguised opinion that it was "prime."

James said little, being very tired.

Could they have seen the steamy vapour that rose from the bed, they might have been a little apprehensive of the consequences.

But the seductive heat drew them to sleep, and they slumbered on as soundly as though they had lain upon a bed of roses.

This blissful state of things had continued for some time—how long they of course had no idea—when suddenly, without being able to attach any reason for the sudden bursting of the bonds of sleep, the boys, as if by mutual consent, started from their slumbers.

It was a sort of start such as an ugly dream is apt to produce.

The boys instinctively clasped each other.

So far all was well; they were together.

"All right, Jem," said Ikey, drowsily.

But a circumstance at that moment occurred, that seemed to imply it wasn't all right.

From the bottom of a small portion of the wall streamed a bright light.

"Look theer, Jem!" cried Ikey, in a hasty whisper, "d'yer see hanythink?"

"Yes," replied James, "a light."

"'Oo is it theer vith a light, at this time o' night, Hi vunder?"

"I can't guess; perhaps we shall know presently."

"It's a comin' from hunder th' door as ve come hin by, hain't it?"

"No; for I noticed the door was opposite the window; and where we see the light shining, is at the side of the window."

"'Oo hever can it be?" murmured Ikey, apprehensively.

"I don't suppose, whoever it is, they want to hurt us."

"Hi 'opes they doesn't; but ve're bin through sich a lot, that vhenever Hi sees hanythink hout o' th' common, Hi allus smells danger."

"It may very likely be some one going to bed in the next room."

"It might be that vaiter," Ikey suggested; and then, as though one idea gave birth to another, he suddenly exclaimed, but in a very low tone under the clothes:

"Don't yer remember as ve told 'em ve'd got lots o' money: 'ow do ve know as 'e ain't a comin' to rob us, or p'r'aps to cut our throttles?"

There was a deal of horror in the manner in which these words were delivered, and even James himself was not quite free from some apprehensions, but he endeavoured to control his fears for the sake of his friend, and to reason with him.

"He wouldn't dare to come into our room to try to rob us, when there are lots of people in the house," James said; "he'd be sure to be found out."

"P'r'aps 'e vould," Ikey admitted; "but 'e'd 'ave time to cut our vizz'ns fust, if ve vas to call hout."

"Well, then," said James, "in that case, we'd better hold our tongues and pretend to be asleep."

"But Hi don't like th' hidear o' losin' all our fortin," Ikey remarked.

"But after all," returned James, "remember this is only your own fancy. We've been looking at that light now for some time, and we have neither seen nor heard anything to give us cause for fear. Do you know, Ikey, I fancy some one has gone to sleep and forgotten to put his candle out."

"An' p'r'aps 'o'll set th' 'ouse o' fire, an' ve shall be roasted as vell as biled."

Ikey was full of horrors, and could not be appeased.

"S'pose ve vos to knock at th' door, an' ask 'im vot 'e's a doing hof?" he continued.

"I think we'd better be quiet," returned James.

"Hi feels as hif Hi couldn't be quiet, so it's no good a askin' me," was the reply.

"Hi vonder vether theer's hany crack as ve could see through," Ikey remarked.

"Very likely there is," said James, "Hi thinks as Hi shall 'ave a peep."

The boy was worked up to a pitch of nervous excitement, that seemed beyond his control.

He paused for a few moments in a state of indecision, and then, as noiselessly as an eel, he slipped from the bed.

After searching for a few moments, he discovered an aperture that commanded a view of the chamber from which the light proceeded.

Of course, in the bright light of candle and fire, everything was distinctly visible.

To Ikey's great surprise, there was the countryman's

smock-frock thrown carelessly over the back of a chair, and, to his still greater surprise, there was his shaggy head of red hair thrown on the counterpane.

Ikey had once before had a little experience in the article of wigs, and he at once became horribly suspicious.

Another strange circumstance was that the countryman was neither in bed nor anywhere else in the room.

Certainly, it struck Ikey that, as the man had had so much sleep in the earlier part of the evening, he, perhaps, found it impossible to sleep during the night.

All these ideas passed through his mind instantaneously.

His mind, however, appeared to be made up.

He crept back to James.

"Well," asked the latter, "did you see anything?"

"Hi jest did," he replied: "there's a smock-frock on th' cheer, an' that shaggy red 'ead o' 'air on th' bed, honly theer hain't no 'ead hinside on hit. Hi don't believe hin vigs vithout 'eads. Let's jest go hout o' our door quietly, an' vake somebody."

But James still was not so impressed as his companion with the horrors of the circumstances he had heard, and hesitated before alarming the whole house, probably for no cause at all.

But Ikey still persisted.

"Come vith us, Jem," he said; "ve needn't make much noise. Ve'll tap gently at vun o' th' doors at t'other hend o' th' passage. Do come!"

Thus urged, James yielded, but with a kind of presentiment that they would be very unceremoniously bundled out of doors for making a disturbance.

"Tread has light has yer can!" whispered Ikey.

With gossamer steps, and hardly breathing, the boys drew near the door, when, just as James was about to extend his hand to open it, the key was very quietly turned in the lock on the outside.

They were locked in.

There was some reason now for a panic, and panic enough there was in the breasts of the startled boys.

Never in the whole range of human experience had keys been known to turn in locks by themselves.

And, as if to inspire an additional reason for fear, a stealthy footstep was heard cautiously stealing away.

"Hark!" ejaculated Ikey; "don't you 'ear it?"

"Yes, quite distinctly."

"Listen! It's a-stoppin' at the next door! Sh! now e's a op'nin' it! Now he's gorn in—now hit's shet agin! Phew! Hi feels has hif Hi vos a meltin' avay!"

"Don't make a noise now, Ikey," James begged, "especially as there's no way of escape."

But Ikey, who seemed to grow more desperate in proportion as the danger increased, once more, as by an uncontrollable impulse, looked through the cranny in the wall.

Some terrible sight must have met his gaze, for his features turned deadly pale, and he staggered back to the bed, clasping his friend in the extremity of terror.

"Ikey—dear Ikey!" murmured James, seriously alarmed at the deadly horror he could feel his companion suffered, "what is the matter?—who is it?"

"Hit's 'im—hit's 'im!" groaned the poor boy—"hit's Mister Hotty!"

This formidable announcement was enough to dissipate even James's calmness.

There was a moment's silence.

"There's the window!" said James, suddenly.

Ikey revived instantaneously.

Any way of escape was preferable to remaining there to be quietly put out of the way by Mr. Hotty.

A broken neck, or a dislocated spine, seemed very minor evils in comparison.

They both approached the window.

Alas! fate was against them.

Their progress was utterly hindered by a row of iron bars.

Despair settled down upon them.

To add to their dismay, there was a peculiar, quiet sound at the door—not as of a man endeavouring to break it open, but as though that had been done already, and the door was actually opening.

Quietly as ghosts, the poor lads—with great presence of mind, though half scared with terror—slipped once more into bed, and, huddling close to one another, feigned sleep.

The door silently opened, and the ghastly, ominous face of Octavius Challoner looked in.

He remained in this position for a few moments, in order to grow accustomed to the gloom.

"I wonder how much these young, beggarly whelps have got," he muttered, between his teeth; "whatever it is, I must have it."

James, fortunately, having his clothes on, had his money in a small purse close to him.

Octavius, ignorant that they had gone to bed thus accoutred, was groping about the room, searching, in vain, for two small suits of wearing apparel.

While he was thus fruitlessly engaged, James very quietly removed the purse from his pocket, and thrust it as far down in the bed as was possible with his hand, and then, bringing his feet to bear upon it, he pushed it completely to the bottom, where it lay unobtrusively enough—entirely unsuspected.

Octavius, baffled in his search after the money, gave vent to some muttered execrations, mingled with wonder where the boys had concealed their clothes.

James and Ikey, in the meantime—though their hearts seemed to them to be beating audibly—lay perfectly still, as though they had been asleep.

It was the only chance they had—so they thought.

If they had raised any alarm they felt it would have cost them their lives.

Therefore, by a desperate effort, they were silent.

At length, they heard Octavius mutter, angrily:

"They must be in bed with their clothes on."

And almost immediately after his deep breathing, as he leant over them, reached their ears.

That sensation was horrible, but it was nothing to the shuddering, sick feeling that passed over them as they felt a stealthy hand like some ugly insect creeping about their bodies and diving successively into each of their pockets.

Of course, this search was utterly unavailing.

Octavius was perplexed, and at a standstill.

Suddenly it struck him the boys might, before going to sleep, have placed the money beneath the pillow.

Cautiously the guilty hand—the crawling ugly insect—glided under the pillow, and searched very carefully for the desired treasure.

But no such thing was to be found.

The edges of the sacking were next investigated, but not a solitary coin could be discovered.

The scoundrel was baffled.

He did not, for certain reasons, desire to awake the boys and extort the money from them by threats, but he had counted most certainly on robbing them of every farthing they possessed, while they slept.

He was baffled and disappointed.

The boys could see through their partially open eyelids, the dark scowl upon the evil features of Octavius.

They knew that he was glancing at them malignantly, and saying by his looks as plainly as looks could speak:

"I should like to destroy you both, if I dared."

But he did not dare; and after another lingering pause of indecision, he went into his own room again, and closed the door after him.

His departure was like a reprieve.

The boys breathed again.

They heard Octavius pacing the room to and fro, like an unquiet spirit that could find no rest.

He spoke also in disjointed, broken sentences.

"I must have money—must! This sudden demolition of all my schemes—all my hopes—has left me in the lowest pit of ruin! Could I have expected this? Just when my hopes seemed so bright—so triumphant! Oh!" he groaned, hoarsely, "if ever mortal was justified in cursing his fate, and yielding to despair, surely I should be! Psha! I have no time for that: I have work to do. I must visit the Hall; though the squire may have cast me off, disinherited me, and left me a beggar, I have still the opportunity of helping myself. Yes; I must—I will!"

As though his mind was made up, he threw on the smock-frock, thrust his head into the tangled red wig, and went to the window in his own room.

James and Ikey heard him undo the fastening, and they quietly left their bed and looked cautiously from between the bars of their own window.

They could see nothing of Octavius, but they fancied they descried some figures below, standing in the shadow.

They could hear Octavius open the window, and could gather from the sounds they heard that he was by some means lowering himself to the ground.

His intention was evidently to proceed to Markham Hall that night, and in that disguise to effect an entrance, lay hands on all the money he could, and return unsuspected, by the window, to his chamber in the inn.

Presently there was a sharp sound of feet on the gravel beneath.

Octavius had dropped, and reached the ground in safety; and this was all the boys heard or saw of him.

Evidently this "bad man" had been away, and had only just returned.

The news of his uncle's death could not have reached him, or he would have known his visit to the lonely dwelling would be worse than useless.

"'E'll 'ave 'is journey for nothink," said Ikey, in a tone of much satisfaction; "an' it'll take 'im all night to go to th' 'all an' come back 'ere."

"Well," said James, "he didn't find our money, did he?"

As he uttered these words he drew the purse from out the bottom of the bed and once more restored it to his pocket.

Feeling now, from the departure of Octavius, a sense of security, they looked forward to being able to rest in peace.

But as Mr. Challoner had not been able to close the window after him, the chill night air blew in and insinuated itself through the crevices of the door in the partition in a manner rather too keen to be pleasant.

Suddenly Ikey said:

"Jem, Hi thinks as Hi'll go an' shet that vinder hin th' nex' room. Ve shall be ever so much varmer, an' Hi'll keep that vicked wiper, Mr. Hotty, from gettin' back agin."

James coincided in this arrangement, and Ikey jumped out of bed, opened the door, and went into the adjoining apartment.

Here he closed the window, and, having done so, stood contemplating the appearance of the chamber.

It was decidedly more comfortable than the one appropriated to the boys.

It was papered, and there was a fire burning in the grate.

The bed, too, seemed to be something more worthy of being called by that name than the unhappy apparatus in the next room.

There was, moreover, a piece of carpet spread over a portion of the floor, and two or three gaudily-painted pictures hanging over the mantelpiece.

Ikey evidently liked the contemplation of this chamber better than that he had just quitted.

James wondered what detained him so long, as he had heard him close the window some time previously.

He called out presently:

" Are you not coming to bed?"

" Not jest yet. Come 'ere, Jem; Hi vant yer!"

James made his appearance at the summons.

" What do you want?" he asked.

" Vot d'yer think of this 'ere room, Jem?" Ikey asked.

" It looks nice and comfortable," replied James— " with the fire, too!"

" Yes; don't it? Vell, Hi vas a thinkin' as ve've got rid o' Mr. Hotty, s'pose ve vas to come an' sleep in 'ere instead of in our hown room? Vot d'yer think?"

" Well," answered James, " I don't know whether we've a right to go into another person's room."

"'E hain't a person! 'es a wiper!" cried Ikey, in a tone of horror and contempt. " Let's stop 'ere—'o wouldn't a minded robbin' hus; vhy should ve mind goin' in 'is room? 'specially vhen 'e can't get back, 'cos ve've fastened 'im hout."

James considered for a moment, and as the room did look very comfortable, and as the circumstances of their case seemed perfectly to justify any little attempt at comfort, he gave in.

" Well, Ikey, then, suppose we stop here," he said.

" That's right; Hi thought yer vouldn't say 'no.'"

" Stay!" said James, with a sudden thought, going to the door, and unlocking it.

" Vot's yer goin' to do? asked Ikey.

" Get the key from the outside of the door of our room," said James.

He went out, but soon returned.

" It's gone already," he said.

" That Mr. Hotty's got it, of course," said Ikey. "'E's allus a takin' vot don't belong to 'im."

At this moment his eyes fell on the key, peeping over the edge of the mantelshelf.

" Theer it is," he cried.

It proved to be the right key on trying it in the lock; and now, with the window securely fastened, and the shutters closed, both doors locked, and the keys inside, they felt themselves at last secure.

The only thing now to do was to turn into bed, and this was very rapidly performed.

The cheerful warmth and pleasant glow of the fire gradually drew them into a sweet sleep.

But, as though it seemed to be the order of events, that the tired boys were to get no sleep at all that night, hardly had they closed their eyes, and sunk into forgetfulness, when a loud and prolonged knocking was heard at the door of the inn

Chapter XLIII.

THE PRESSGANG.

OUR readers were informed in the last chapter that, from the time our young heroes heard Mr. Octavius Challoner drop from the window, and alight on the gravel beneath, they neither saw nor heard any more of him.

For the general satisfaction, therefore, of those who peruse these pages, I will enlighten them on this particular point.

The pressgang, the report of whom had caused so much apprehension amongst the simple countrymen assembled in the tap-room of the inn that evening, had been scouring the country, hunting up and knocking down such able-bodied men as they could, for the purpose of hurrying them on board ship, or in other words, pressing them into the service of his Most Excellent Majesty, King George.

It need scarcely be added that these compulsory measures were looked upon with the greatest abhorrence by the population generally, the mass of whom infinitely preferred digging the ground to ploughing the sea.

But the parties employed in these man-hunting expeditions were not very considerate of the feelings of those they attacked.

It was with them "all fish that came to their net."

It so happened, then, they had an idea that certain persons calculated to adorn the navy were concealed in the inn on that particular evening.

They approached with the most cat-like caution, and quietly surrounded the house.

With much chuckling and suppressed mirth, they saw the unsuspicious Octavius descend from the window.

His feet had hardly pressed *terra firma* when he was pounced upon by his eager friends, who surrounded him like a swarm of bees.

He put out all his strength, and resisted furiously; but he was at once quieted by a smart tap from a cutlass in the region of the skull, which laid him prostrate and senseless on the gravel.

Not content with the one prize they had secured, they determined to knock up the slumbering landlord, to ascertain whether there were any others on the premises who would be fitting candidates for naval glory.

The knocking was so loud and prolonged that James and Ikey were completely aroused.

The first idea suggested by the clamour was that Mr. Octavius Challoner had returned, and, being deprived of the means of entrance at the window, was now indignantly hammering at the door for admission that way.

Then came the natural impression that it would be as well to return to their rightful apartment, and, accordingly, they rolled out of bed with considerable precipitation, and scudded, like two startled hares, into the next room.

They closed the door, and placed a dilapidated chair against it, and once more sought refuge beneath the bedclothes.

Still the knocking had kept up till the landlord, who was a very heavy sleeper, began to fancy he heard something.

On appealing to his better half, who was also a very heavy sleeper, that worthy female murmured, drowsily:

"She thought it wur soom 'un at t'door."

"Where be that lazy rascal, Dan?" grunted the sleepy host.

As might naturally be expected at that particular time, the "lazy rascal" was buried in the oblivion of profound slumber, sleeping off the narcotic effects of vast imbibings of ale.

But the increasing clamour was so vigorously maintained, that even the waiter began to have an idea something unusual was taking place.

His brains were, of course, muddled, and it took him some time to get them into something like order.

"It can't be t' brewer?" he thought, in his imbecility. "Noa, he doan't coom in t' middle o' t' neet."

Here the knocking grew louder than ever.

"Why doan't master go t' th' door?"

At this crisis, loud voices were heard.

"Is anybody going to open this door, or are we to break it in?"

After this the landlord's voice was heard.

"Daniel!—Dan!" he cried.

"Dan!" shrieked the landlady.

Dan argued the point with himself very briefly, whether he should get up and open the door, or whether he should allow the visitors, whoever they were, to put their feet through the panels.

Sad to relate, his faculties appeared warped.

The bed was warm, the waiter drowsy and leadenheaded.

"Noa," he grunted, "Oi bean't a goin' to toorn out o' bed for no one. If they mun coom in, let 'em boorst t' door oppen as they said."

"Dan—Dan—Dan!" cried the landlord and landlady together, "they'll knock the door down!"

Dan was fast asleep again.

The knocking ceased for a moment, and the anxious couple began to think the abominable noise was over at last.

But in the next there came one grand united effort, and a tremendous crash attested the fact that one of the panels had given way.

"Good gracious!" exclaimed the landlord, "they've knocked in one of the panels."

Hereupon there was a sound of bolts being withdrawn and chains removed.

"They be coomin' in to rob t' hoose, Samuel!" shrieked the little landlady, in a tone of horror. "Get up an' see what be t' matter."

Samuel, exceedingly loath to turn out, did, however, contrive to roll himself from his bed, and commenced hunting nervously for his garments.

After a distracted effort to dress himself, and several abortive struggles to insert his fat legs in the sleeves of his coat, and to wear his knee-breeches on his head, he contrived to be a little presentable.

In the meantime the pressgang, with their lieutenant at their head, came clattering up the stairs in a body.

"Here! heigh! Landlord ahoy!" they shouted. "Where are you?"

"Here I am, gentlemen," answered that individual, in a mild and humble little voice, as he appeared, taper in hand, at the door of his bed-room. "What do you want?"

"All the able-bodied men you've got in the house," replied the lieutenant, abruptly; "and then, something that's fit for honest sailors to drink."

The landlord's bowels had performed a complete revolution at the former part of this announcement.

A horrible suspicion seized him that he might be considered as answering to the description of able-bodied, and that they might take him.

However, anxious to mollify his imperious visitors, he said:

"P'r'aps thou'lt tak' a drop o' sommat foorst."

This was agreed to, and the landlord descended to the bar, where corks flew out and ale foamed in corpulent mugs, and a sirloin of beef made its appear-

ance, to the great joy and satisfaction of the whole party.

The landlord took his opportunity when he thought the lieutenant was a little mollified by his good cheer to suggest that, though he looked so rosy and corpulent, he hadn't the strength of a mouse.

"I could have told you that, my hearty!" answered the robust sailor, giving him a slap on the back that nearly annihilated him. "You're no good! The only use we could put you to would be to stuff you in a hole to stop a leak."

The men laughed at this, and the landlord rejoiced at the joke, even though it was against himself.

The sailors then routed out some drowsy commercial gentlemen, who did not promise anything for his Majesty.

They looked at lazy Dan, who was curled up in his nest like a dormouse.

"This lubber will do!" cried the lieutenant. "Here, tumble out, my fresh-water shrimp, we'll give you a taste of the salt."

As he spoke, the lieutenant gave the horrified Dan a smart slash with his rattan, that sent him howling from his bed.

"Oi doan't want to goa to sea—Oi won't go!" he roared.

"Won't you?" said the facetious lieutenant, quietly. "Very well. His Majesty is very indulgent to obstinate subjects: if you won't go, you must be carried."

At a slight motion of his head, away went Dan's heels from under him, and in a few moments he found himself trussed as neatly as a chicken.

In his dismay he bawled aloud:

"Measter!—measter!"

These were the last two ejaculations no aa power to utter.

A gag was thrust into his mouth, a bandage tied over it, and Dan was not only motionless, but voiceless.

The next room the men visited was that which Octavius had occupied.

Finding this empty, they passed through the door in the partition, and came upon James and Ikey,

The poor boys were very much scared at the noise and confusion, and the number of faces.

"Who have we here?" exclaimed the lieutenant, holding up the light so as to fall full on their faces.

The appearance James and Ikey presented at this moment was that of a pair of pretty, rather startled boys.

But there was a sharp, sensible look about them that attracted the lieutenant.

"These boys will do for something: they'll make a couple of first class powder-monkeys."

"More monkeys!" thought the boys, but they dared not object.

"Come, youngsters, turn out!" cried the lieutenant; "you're going to serve his Majesty on the high seas—quick!"

In a very bewildered state of mind, the sleepy boys disentangled themselves from their bed.

But in spite of the excited alacrity with which they obeyed, an involuntary yawn betrayed the state of their feelings to the lieutenant of the pressgang.

He began to feel a little sympathy for the youngsters; and, besides, this yawning was infectious, and he began to follow the boys' example.

The men also joined in, and it struck the officer suddenly that they must all be very tired.

He accordingly changed his mind at once.

"Here, boys!" he cried, "tumble into your hammocks again; we sha'n't start till morning!"

With unspeakable delight, James and Ikey again laid themselves down—this time to sleep soundly and peaceably.

Octavius and Dan were drafted off under an escort to a place of security, and the lieutenant and the remainder of the gang found sleeping accommodation wherever they could.

Morning came at last, as morning always will come; but the lieutenant did not hurry himself in rising from his pillow.

He had had a hard day's work the day before, and he felt knocked up and needed rest.

It was a great boon for our young heroes that it was so.

They lay luxuriously coiled up in a state of dreamy

comfort that it would have been almost cruel to disturb.

At length, however, they awoke.

Rested and refreshed, their first thoughts naturally reverted to the words of the lieutenant.

"Vot are ve a goin' to do, Jem?" said Ikey; "serve 'is Maj'sty on th' 'igh seas, an' powder-monkeys? Hi don't think as Hi shall like that."

James was silent a moment—he was evidently reflecting.

"Do you like it, Jem?" asked Ikey again.

"I don't quite understand what it means," answered James—"at least about the monkeys; but I think the gentlemen that came in here looked like sailors, so I fancy they must be goin' to take us on to the sea."

"Oh! Hi 'opes not!" exclaimed Ikey, in a tone of dismay; "hever since Hi vos hupset an' nearly drownded, Hi've got an 'orror o' the vater."

"Well, but we shouldn't go in a little boat like that, but in a large ship," James explained; "and then every one there would know how to manage it. I don't think I should mind that at all."

"Vell, Hi dunno has Hi should myself if Hi could be sure as Hi shouldn't be drownded."

"Oh, you mustn't be so afraid as that; look at Captain Palmer; he was out that night when our boat was upset, and he wasn't drownded; and besides that he's been at sea almost all his life, and yet he's alive now."

"Oh, yes!" said Ikey. "Hit's all werry well vhen it's like that; an' hif Hi vos sure it'd be so vith me, Hi shouldn't mind."

At this moment there was a tap at the door, and the chambermaid's voice was heard.

"Now, yoong gentlemen, yow be to get oop, an' coom an' 'ave yer 'an's and feaces washed before yow do go to breakfast."

The boys jumped up, and, having said their prayers —a habit James never omitted, or Ikey either, while he was with his companion—they left their room, and found a rosy-faced country-looking girl, with gigantic red arms, waiting to seize upon them.

They were immediately conducted to the kitchen, where they went through a liberal process of purification.

After this operation, their skins shone under the influence of yellow soap and hot water, like the coats of polished apples.

The girl then applied an oleaginous fragrant pomade to their hair, and they made their appearance in the breakfast-room, looking as bright as an April morning, and smelling almost as sweet.

The lieutenant smiled as they entered.

"Ah! that's right!" he cried. "I always like to see boys clean: it's a great passport in their favour. Cleanliness is a proof of delicacy of mind—in fact, no no man who is *not clean* in his person can be a *gentleman*."

The boys felt encouraged at his words.

"You haven't had breakfast, I suppose?" asked the lieutenant.

"No, sir," they answered.

"I suppose you eat breakfasts?"

"Yes, sir," James replied.

"Vhen ve can get 'em, sir," added Ikey.

"Ah, yes, of course! Well, and who are you? What are your names? Where do you live? Who are your parents?" asked the nautical gentleman, in a breath.

"My name is James Cook, sir," James replied.

"An' mine's Ikey Mangles," added his comrade.

"We lived at Marton, sir," continued James. "Our parents are both dead, and we've come out to do the best we can to earn an honest living."

"Well," said the lieutenant, encouragingly, "if I'm any judge, you seem to me just the two sort of youngsters likely to get on aboard ship."

"Do you mean that we're to be sailors, sir?" asked James.

"Of course I do," answered the lieutenant, "when you're big enough. At present you're nothing better than a couple of tiny cockle-shells."

"Never mind; that's a fault that will mend itself. You'll grow bigger.

"And now sit down and eat while I look at the paper."

There were two ample basins of bread and milk, followed by bread and butter, if they required it, but the former was sufficient.

By the time they had finished, the lieutenant had read his newspaper, and, having paid his bill and sundry other expenses incurred, he drafted his men before him on to Whitby—a seaport town about ten miles distant.

He then ordered a chaise to be got ready, and lifting the boys into it, he drove in the same direction.

They reached Whitby without any mishap, the lieutenant remarking, with much complacency, that he thought he had brought his craft to her moorings in a very seaman-like manner.

He appealed to the boys if they didn't think so.

They were, of course, entirely ignorant of what he meant, but they coincided obediently, and answered "yes."

Having arrived at the town, he found some one to take charge of the chaise, and drive it back to its legitimate proprietor, and then, having an hour or two to spare, he strolled leisurely round, paying short visits to many there with whom he was well acquainted.

Amongst these were two worthy men, Messrs. Charles and Richard Walker, coal merchants, of Whitby.

These gentlemen had been old schoolmates of the lieutenant, and a very warm friendship existed between them.

In fact, the Walker brothers were universally respected in the town in which they dwelt.

Lieutenant Samphire never came to Whitby without paying his old friends a visit.

It so happened this morning that there was a little something that appeared to have to a certain degree disturbed the usual calm equanimity of Charles Walker, the elder brother.

He sat in his office at his desk, with his spectacles stuck upright and resting against his bald forehead, looking earnestly at a man respectably attired, who held by the hand a snivelling gawky of a boy, who whimpered and so bored at his unhappy eyes with his large knuckles, that they seemed in a high state of inflammation.

Mr. Richard Walker stood with his back to the fire, nursing the ample tails of his coat under each arm.

The man who owned the boy was the first to speak.

"It isn't that I wish to behave in any kind o' way un'ansome, Mr. Walker," he said, "in taking my son away after binding him to you."

"I certainly think, myself," exclaimed the worthy Charles, "that the proceeding is highly irregular."

"Well, sir," the man (Mr. Jones, by name) replied, "I can't say but what it does seem so myself; but you know, sir, a father's feelin's is a father's feelin's, an' when his only boy——"

Here the *only boy* gave a despairing kind of subdued howl.

"I repeat," continued Mr. Jones, rubbing his knuckles together nervously, "when that only boy goes an' takes a disgust agin' th' perfession as he's bound to, an' says it's a shortenin' 'is days, an' sendin' him to a early tomb, what's an affect'nate parent to do?"

"Well, I tell you what I think I should do," said Mr. Charles, decidedly," and I'm not the most hard-hearted man in the world—I think I should be likely to expedite his departure out of the world with a good, sound caning!"

"Oh! Mister Charles!" expostulated the parental Jones.

"Oo!—oo!" gurgled Master J.

"Boys can't help their feelin's, Mr. Walker, any more than grown people," said Mr. Jones, somewhat positively.

"Stuff, sir!" cried the indignant coal merchant; "boys ought to have no feelings, they should accept the position their parents or guardians find for them. I did so, when I started in life."

"Yes, sir; but you're different, sir," pleaded Jones: "some men, even as boys, are remarkable for strong nerves; my Tom isn't strong nerved, never was —took after his mother, poor boy. She used to faint away at the sight of a tabby cat."

"I tell you what I think," said Mr. Charles, "you are very weak-minded, Mr. Jones, and I think you'll regret listening to your son's complaints. When he was bound to us, he came with the utmost willingness, and, now, at the end of a month, he discovers the life is killing him."

"I didn't know what sort of life it was," blubbered the watery-headed Tom. "I didn't like the sea-sickness, or the smell o' the tar, or the beastly dirty coals, or anything else—and I won't go in th' collier any more, that I won't," the spoilt youth exclaimed, firmly.

"There, sir !" exclaimed his parent, "you see 'ow I'm sitivated ; don't be hard, Mr. Charles : consider a father's feelin's ; 'e'll never take to it, I'm sure, so I vants yer to let 'im off—cancel 'is indenturs, and not make it a law bisness."

Mr. Jones clasped his hands and looked appealingly at the coal merchant, with hypocritical, moist eyes.

"Law !" echoed Mr. Charles, with contempt. "I am not so fond of law as you seem to imagine ; and, besides, even if I were, what would be the use of going to law with you ?"

"I'm very grateful, sir—very !" gasped Mr. Jones, spasmodically.

"You're exceedingly welcome, sir. If your son wishes to go, let him. He is not one of that class likely to be missed. He is at liberty from this moment."

As he spoke, the coal merchant opened his desk, and from one of the numerous small drawers drew out a paper tied with a piece of red tape.

"Here are his indentures," he said, as he handed them to Mr. Jones, who was profuse in his gratitude for such unheard-of generosity.

Master Jones, also, beamed suddenly up like the sun looking out of a fog.

"And now, I believe, our business is settled," Mr. Charles remarked, suggestively pointing to the door.

The grateful Jones backed towards the door, performing a succession of bows and scrapes, and finishing by catching his heel in the mat, and disappearing very suddenly through the spring door, dragging the interesting Tom with him.

"I think, brother," said Richard, as soon as the father and son were out of sight, "the loss of that boy is not much to be regretted."

"Regretted ! Not he, the great baby," said Charles. "He'll never be fit for anything but to be tied to his mother's apron-string."

"I thought you seemed annoyed, Charles," remarked his brother, quietly.

"So I am," replied his brother, rather tartly ; "but I assure you, Richard, it is more on the young simpleton's account than my own. I believe that a few years with us would have cured him of those whims and fancies he seems so full of ; but, there, the father is worse than the son. He has encouraged him in his follies, instead of using his authority, and compelling him to adhere to the business he had chosen."

"Well, Charles, you'll have to take another apprentice ; and I hope when you do, you'll be more fortunate than you were with the last. I confess I never particularly liked Master Jones."

"It's awkward," Charles replied. "We want a boy in our trade, and on board our vessels, and I was in hopes that this youngster was becoming used to the sea, and——"

"My dear Charles," interrupted his brother, "you may be sure such a puling, whining, watery-eyed baby as your late apprentice would never have made a sailor, if he'd been at sea for a century."

"Perhaps not—perhaps not, Richard ! Well, as we've lost one, I suppose we shall pick up another somewhere."

Suddenly Richard, who had strolled across the office, and was now looking from the window, which commanded a view of the street, uttered an exclamation :

"How strange !" he cried.

"What ?" his brother inquired.

"That, just as we were talking on the subject of boys,

there should be two smart-looking lads in front of our very door."

Charles Walker left his desk, and, approaching the window, arranged his spectacles, and looked out.

Yes ! there, as his brother Richard had declared, were two lads standing in front of his very door ; two smart lads too.

It was very singular. It would almost seem as though they divined what had passed within, and were waiting to offer themselves as apprentices.

There was, however, one peculiarity the brothers noticed, and that was, that, though there was a large plate on the gate in front of their house, with their names and trade boldly displayed on it, the two boys never once looked towards it, or noticed it in the least.

Their attention seemed to be directed down the street, and they stood looking as though they expected the arrival of some one.

The two brothers regarded the lads for some moments in silence.

At length Charles spoke.

"Very nice boys ! brother Richard—very nice, sharp boys !" he said. "I should be very glad to have such an one for an apprentice. I wonder whether they've fixed upon——"

Whatever Mr. Charles Walker might have been going to say was abruptly stopped by the sudden moving off of the boys.

They seemed to have caught sight of the person they were waiting for, and had evidently run to join him.

"Ah," said Mr. Charles, as he left the window and took a pinch of snuff—"Um !—very nice boys, one especially."

The old gentleman returned to his desk and sat down.

Presently a brisk, quick footstep was heard approaching.

"That's Jack Samphire's step, I know," cried Charles ; and sure enough, before the words were off his tongue, the lieutenant's voice was distinctly audible.

"I'm just going to pay a short visit to an old friend here," it cried. "You youngsters can wait outside ; don't get into mischief."

The next moment the lieutenant burst in in such a hurry as threatened to carry the swing door from its hinges.

"Ah, my dear boys ! How are you, Charley ? How are you, Dick ? How are you both ?"

The brothers were very well indeed—in proof of which after the first salutations were over, the bell was rung and certain orders given.

Then, shortly after, a domestic entered with something substantial in the way of food, and a flagon of sparkling ale, whilst from a private and confidential cupboard in the office were brought forth sundry bottles.

There was the usual popping of corks, and a very delightful odour of port wine pervaded the apartment.

After drinking each other's healths very cordially, Charles Walker said to the lieutenant :

"Jack, who is it you have left waiting for you outside ?"

"Oh," answered the officer, "only two young recruits I've picked up. They'll do very well there for half an hour."

"Well, but," replied the good-natured merchant, "let the youngsters come in—perhaps they'll like to pick a bit, or take a glass of wine."

"Oh, by all means," answered the jolly sailor, "let them come. I've no objection."

Now the fact is, Lieutenant Samphire was rather inclined to be proud of his two young recruits, as he called them, so he went hastily out, and shouted :

"James Cook and Ikey Mangles ahoy !"

Thus summoned, the two boys hastily advanced, and the next moment were ushered into the presence of the brothers Walker.

[THE NEW APPRENTICE.]

Chapter XLIV.

ALTERED PROSPECTS.

CONSIDERABLE astonishment was expressed in the features of the worthy merchants, as they recognised in James and Ikey the two nice sharp boys they had observed a short time before standing in front of their house.

Charles Walker, the senior, had to take several pinches of snuff before he could recover himself, whilst his brother Richard indulged in various ejaculatory remarks as a kind of outlet for his surprise.

Lieutenant Samphire, in the meantime, taking the license of an old friend, and a natural proclivity that usually attaches itself to seafaring men, lit a cigar, and puffed away, looking out of the window, thus leaving the worthy brothers to get rid of a little of their first astonishment.

"Dear me!" said Charles, at length, "this is really very singular—quite a little event, isn't it, Richard?" he inquired of his brother.

"Quite," answered Richard. "I look upon it in that light, I must say I do."

The lads stood quietly waiting to be addressed by the merchants, and in their turn wondering what there could be about them to excite so much attention.

The expression in the boys' faces seemed to say as much, and the kind-hearted brothers began to think they were submitting the youngsters to somewhat too severe a scrutiny.

"We're staring these two poor lads quite out of countenance, brother Richard," said Charles, "and that's not right, though I declare I had no intention of so doing. Come here, my boys," he continued, addressing himself to James and Ikey in a voice whose round mellow tones made them feel quite at home immediately.

How much there is in the sound of a voice!

We can almost predict whether or not we shall like a person before we have seen him, from his tone and manner of speaking.

It is almost needless to state that our young friends were greatly prepossessed in favour of the brothers Walker.

They advanced towards the merchants with the utmost confidence.

"Well, my boys," said Charles, with a kind smile, "I daresay you could drink a glass of wine if you tried, couldn't you?"

"They don't look as if they could," returned Mr. Richard, his eyes twinkling mischievously through his spectacles, at the bare idea of the fiction he was concocting.

"Well, at all events, we'll see," said Charles, as he poured out a couple of glasses of port wine, which he placed before the boys, accompanied by several biscuits.

The impression produced on the lads by these luxuries seemed to be decidedly agreeable, and on being heartily invited by the worthy brothers not to stand upon ceremony, but to make themselves at home, they at once commenced upon the biscuits, which they moistened with the fragrant liquor, to their hearts' content.

It was excellent wine, and its spirit seemed to run through their veins, and warm and cheer them.

"It's very nasty, isn't it?" inquired Charles Walker, with a beaming smile—"quite like physic, eh?"

It was the boys' turn now to smile.

The idea of that beautiful ruby-coloured liquid, with its fragrant perfume, being likened to physic, was in their opinion, going a little too far.

They therefore shook their heads in utter renunciation of the idea of anything *physical* appertaining to such nectar.

"What! you like it, then?" inquired the brothers, with well-feigned surprise.

"Yes, gentlemen, thank you—very much indeed!" the boys answered.

"Hif Hi never 'ad to take no wuss physic than that, Hi shouldn't care 'ow hoften Hi 'ad to swallow it," Ikey remarked.

The brothers smiled, and then turned away towards Lieutenant Samphire, who was blowing his cloud, and looking out of the window at the same time.

James and Ikey sat by the fire, and noticed that when the brothers joined the lieutenant at the window, the attention of all three was from time to time directed towards themselves, in such a marked manner, that it was evident they were the subject of conversation.

"Hi vonder vot hit his they're a-sayin' about hus," remarked Ikey.

"I can't hear," returned James.

Now what passed between the lieutenant and the merchants was as follows:—

After Jack Samphire had turned away from the window, and refreshed his faculties with another glass of port, Charles Walker remarked to him:

"Those seem two very nice boys you have with you."

"Yes," said the lieutenant. "So far as appearances go, they do seem very nice boys. I hope they'll turn out so."

"Who are they?" inquired Mr. Charles.

"Ah, now," returned the lieutenant, "you're asking me rather more than I can tell you, old friend."

"What! have they no friends—no name?" asked the merchants.

"They have the latter, but not the former," replied their schoolfellow; "the taller of the two tells me his name is James Cook, the other calls himself Ikey Mangles."

"And have they no relatives or parents?" Charles Walker inquired.

"None, according to their own account: they tell me they are orphans."

"Orphans?" ejaculated the brothers, in a tone of commiseration. "Poor boys!"

The snuff-box was called into requisition, and after several sniffs, the conversation was resumed.

"I dropped across them quite accidentally last night," stated the lieutenant, "while I was hunting up hands to serve his Majesty; and finding them likely lads, and hearing from their own account that they were drifting on the ocean of life without rudder or compass, I thought it would be but a friendly act to take them in tow."

"So it was a friendly act, Jack—a very friendly act!" exclaimed the merchants—"one, too, that will not be forgotten by Him who watches over the destiny of the orphan. And so you're going to make sailors of these lads—eh, Jack?"

"Such is my present intention," answered the lieutenant.

"Of course you'll place them in the navy?" inquired Charles.

"Yes."

"Don't you think *one* of these boys might be sufficient for his Majesty? God bless him!" asked Charles Walker.

Lieutenant Samphire smiled at the seriousness and simplicity with which this question was proposed.

"To tell you the truth, my dear fellow," he replied, "I daresay, for the matter of that, his Majesty might spare them both, and not be conscious of any loss. It is not what they are now—two small fry fresh from their mothers' apron-strings—but what they may hereafter become; and I fancy I can see in them a pair of true sailors—captains, who knows?—if they live."

"Ay, ay!" echoed Charles, "I quite agree with you. There's something about them lively and intelligent—something that I like, in short, and—and brother Dick's of the same opinion."

"I am, indeed," asserted brother Dick. "I never saw two boys that prepossessed me more strongly—never!"

Once more there was a clinking of glasses, and a sniffing of snuff, and then Charles and Richard drew the lieutenant towards the window in a private and confidential manner.

"You see, Jack," said Charles, "in our trade we want a sharp, active lad as an apprentice. We have always had one; but our last had served his time, and shipped on board a vessel in the East India service. We then took another, but he found out after a few months that a seafaring life didn't suit him. He came here crying this morning with his father, begging us to cancel his indentures, which, under the circumstances, we did; but now it leaves us without any apprentice at all, and we thought, if you could spare us one of those boys, he would be just the very sort of lad to suit us."

"Well, if you think so," returned the lieutenant, "and have really set your heart on one of those youngsters, I'm sure you're very welcome so far as I am concerned."

"That's very kind of you, Jack—very," exclaimed Mr. Charles Walker, warmly, grasping his friend's hand. "But before we go any further, of course, I shouldn't wish in any way to coerce either of the boys' inclinations, I should prefer leaving it entirely to their own will."

"Well," said the lieutenant, "there's one thing: they seem to be sworn friends, and to be much attached to each other. I don't know how they'll relish the separation."

"Ah, true!—um! yes!" ejaculated the brothers, thoughtfully.

"Perhaps," suggested Charles, "the shortest way of getting at the state of their feelings would be to ask."

"I think so," said the lieutenant; "but, by-the-by, which of the two boys do you prefer?"

"The taller, I think," replied Mr. Charles.

"No bad judge, either," returned the officer. "If I had to predict the career of those two boys, I should most decidedly mark out the highest post for James Cook."

"James Cook—oh, yes, that's his name," said Mr. Walker, thoughtfully.

"There's a great deal of intellect in his face," the lieutenant replied, "and much decision in his eye, and although at present he looks delicate, I feel confident that he has within him the material from whence springs a *great man*."

"I think with you, Jack; and if this be the case, and he is destined by Providence to become one of those whose names shall be recorded honourably in the annals of their country, he is just as certain to arrive at this distinction if he starts as an apprentice to a Whitby coal merchant, making his first voyage on board a collier, as though he placed his foot on the deck of a man-o'-war, under the auspices of the admiral himself. You know, my dear Jack, in these matters *man proposes*, but GOD *disposes*."

"Then it is your intention, if the lad be willing, to article him to you as your apprentice?" inquired the lieutenant.

"Exactly," answered Charles; "and then if he behaves himself well, he will in time become mate or master. But one thing you may be certain : if he does his duty to me, he shall receive the treatment a son would receive from a parent. I have taken a liking to that boy, and my heart seems to warm towards the poor orphan : it will be his own fault if this feeling does not ripen."

Now such words as these from such a man as Charles Walker were highly significant.

From some men they might have meant nothing.

They would have been simply so many words spoken over so many glasses of port wine.

But from kind-hearted, honest, benevolent Charles Walker they meant neither more nor less than this :—

"*Do your duty as a son to me, and I will do my duty as a father to you.*"

"Well, then," said the lieutenant, "suppose we put the question at once ?"

"With all my heart," answered Charles.

"Come here, boys !" exclaimed Lieutenant Samphire, good naturedly.

James and Ikey, who had an idea there was something *in the wind*, and who were momentarily expecting a summons, rose at once and came forward.

"Since I last spoke to you, my boys," the lieutenant commenced, "there has been a slight change in our anticipated course."

The boys looked earnestly at the speaker, then at the brothers Walker, and finally at each other.

"I told you I should take you both to sea, and that henceforth your lives would be on the ocean, and my word will be kept, only, that instead of your both entering the navy, which implies serving the king, and fighting under his flag against the enemies of your country, one of you will enter the civil service, which means a more peaceable employment in a merchant vessel, where there will be no fighting, but where, nevertheless, if you do your duty, you will have ample opportunities of distinguishing yourselves as honest men and good sailors."

There was a pause after this, during which the boys looked somewhat puzzled at what they had heard, as though not quite certain in what light to regard it.

One fact, however, seemed to present itself, and that was, that since one was destined for the navy, and the other for the merchant service, their separation seemed inevitable.

The merchants and the lieutenant seemed to comprehend these thoughts that oppressed the lads, and the officer at once proceeded to touch upon this point.

"Of course you are aware that you will have to part company."

The boys' countenances fell, and a cloud stole over their young features, whilst the tears neither could repress filled their eyes.

At length, after a slight pause, James said :

"Must we really be separated, sir ?"

"You must, indeed, my boy," returned the lieutenant.

James dropped his head sadly and made no reply.

Ikey was more demonstrative.

"Yer hisn't a goin' to sep'rate hus from each hother, hare yer, sir ?" he asked, eagerly.

The lieutenant shrugged his shoulders slightly, but remained silent.

"Vo'd rayther do hanythink than be sep'rated," Ikey continued. "Vhen ve started hout hin th' vorld to make hour fortins, ve agreed as ve'd stick together vherever ve vent, an' Hi thinks hif ve can't go to sea and be sailors vithout separatin', ve'd rayther not be sailors at hall."

The three friends glanced at each other rapidly.

The lieutenant's look implying distinctly :

"I thought as much !"

But he did not give up the effort of persuading his young charges.

"Listen to me, my boys," he said, in a firm but kind tone : "there are plenty of boys in the world—plenty who are boys no longer, having now grown to manhood ; but there is not one who either has not been, or will not be obliged at some time of his life to part from home and friends, when he starts upon the voyage of life. I had to do so, and these gentlemen, my worthy friends"—he pointed to the brothers as he spoke—"had to do the same."

"We did, indeed !" they replied. "We began life with hardly a penny between us, but by industry and integrity, and God's blessing on our efforts, we have acquired a very ample share of this world's good."

"So, my boys," the lieutenant continued, "you must not think your case different from that of hundreds—nay, thousands of other boys ; neither must you decide upon a wandering vagabond life, in order that you may not be parted. Why, how do you know, even if you reject your present opportunity, that the first turn in the wheel of fortune, or the first contrary wind that blows, may not drive you into totally opposite paths, where you may wander on and on and never see each other again as long as you live ?"

There was a dead silence.

The boys were evidently impressed with the words of the lieutenant.

There was strong common sense and truth in them, and they were uttered with a serious earnestness that carried conviction home to the hearts of the young listeners.

They began to look upon life with different eyes than heretofore.

Ikey suddenly inquired :

"Hif Jem an' me vos to sep'rate now, Hi s'pose ve should see heach other sometimes, shouldn't ve, sir ?"

"Undoubtedly," replied Lieutenant Samphire ; "you in the navy, and your friend James in the merchant service, you could meet, of course, if you wished it, as often as you came ashore."

"That'd be nice, vouldn't it ?" exclaimed Ikey, hopefully.

"But you must learn to write," continued the officer, "and then you can let each other know all you are doing, and that is almost equal to speaking face to face."

"So hit his ! Hi'll learn to write—see hif Hi don't !" Ikey said, in a tone of determination.

"Well, then, sir, what is it you wish us to do ?" asked James, appealing to the lieutenant.

"These gentlemen will explain," answered the lieutenant, referring him to the brothers Walker, towards whom James looked inquiringly.

"The fact is," said Charles, whose kindly, beaming, benevolent features shed a glow of sunshine over the boy's heart, "I've taken a great liking to you, James, and, having just lost our apprentice, my brother—this is my brother Richard"—indicating his relative by a nod of the head—"and I thought you would be just the kind of lad to fill his place. Therefore, if you are willing, you have only to say so, and we will article you to us for a term of years as our apprentice."

"Thank you, gentlemen, I am quite willing if the captain gives me leave," James answered.

The officer whom James had suddenly promoted was Lieutenant Samphire, who seemed perfectly satisfied at the turn matters were taking.

"You have my full permission," he said, "and I am sure you will have no reason to regret entering the service of these gentlemen ; neither, on the other hand, though I know but little of you at present, do I think they will have cause to be sorry that their choice has fallen upon you."

"Then, gentlemen," said James, to the brothers Walker, whose faces were quite glowing with satisfaction, "if you please, I will stop with you."

"That's right—that's just as I would have wished it. I think you've spoken very sensibly—very," exclaimed Mr. Charles.

"Very much so, indeed !" echoed Mr. Richard.

The gratified merchants patted James's curly head, and as it was such a very important occasion, Mr. Charles poured out another glass of wine slily, and intimated by a confidential nod that it was for his especial benefit.

"An' please vot ham Hi to do, sir ?" asked Ikey, who somehow or other felt rather forlorn.

"You'll go with me, my man," answered Lieutenant

Samphire; "and if you behave yourself, you'll be an admiral some day, I've no doubt."

"Vot!" exclaimed Ikey, "an' vear a cock'd 'at an' a feather, an' gold things hon my harms?"

"Certainly," returned the lieutenant, "and go to Court and kiss his Majesty's hand."

"Oh!" cried Ikey, much elated, "von't Hi make 'aste an' get to be a hadmiral! Hi s'pose hit'll take some time, von't hit, sir?"

"Yes," returned the lieutenant, drily, "a year or two. The first thing you must do is to learn to speak correctly."

"Hi'll learn hev'rythink as theer his to be learnt," said, Ikey, with the utmost confidence.

"Oh! I've no doubt we shall make something of you," answered Lieutenant Samphire.

Ikey's temporal affairs being thus settled, he glanced round and saw his friend, James, who beckoned him to share his second glass of wine. The brothers noticed this action on his part, and interposed.

"Come, come!" cried Charles, "that's not fair!

Share and share alike is my maxim. Here my lad: though we've chosen your companion, you mustn't feel yourself slighted; and though you will be in the navy, and he in the merchant service, there's no reason why we shouldn't be all friends; so drink this to your—I may say *our*—mutual friendship and prosperity."

As he spoke, the worthy old gentleman handed Ikey a glass of port wine.

Ikey expressed a wish that everybody might have "good 'ealth," and consoled himself with a pretty good sip.

The business being thus amicably settled, the brothers and the lieutenant remained chatting for some time longer, whilst the boys, conscious that they would soon be separated, but wonderfully cheered under the influence of the generous wine they were sipping, sat close to each other, wondering what kind of a life they were going to lead henceforth, and indulging in those vague surmises that youth and inexperience always indulge in when they try to paint from out their crude imagination pictures of the untried future.

Chapter XLV.

THE NEW HOME.

"VHICH do you think as you'd like best?" asked, Ikey, "bein' hin a man-o'-var an' fighting for yer country, or bein' as you're going to be without hany fightin' at all?"

"I really don't know, Ikey," said James. "It all seems so new to me that I hardly know which I should like, but I shall try to do my duty, and then, whatever I am engaged in, or wherever I go, I shall be happy at least."

"Hi've made hup my mind hon vun pint," Ikey said, "han that his to be a hadmiral, an' vear a cock'd hat an' feather, an' 'ave gold things hon my shoulders."

James smiled.

"I think, Ikey, it will be a good many years before you arrive at that, but then it's no reason you never should."

"No. Didn't Mr. Valker say as 'e began vith a penny between 'im an' 'is brother? Hi der'say hit took a good many 'ears a'foor they got to be rich men as they hare now."

"It does take a great many years," James answered. "Some never succeed after all, but I think it is generally owing to some fault of their own. I feel quite sure of one thing: that if we wish to succeed in anything, we must be quite sure that whatever we are trying after is something right."

"Vell, hit's right to fight for the king hain't hit, Jem?" asked Ikey, eagerly.

"I suppose it is," James replied, "though I don't regret being in the merchant service where there is no fighting. I shouldn't like to be killed myself——"

"No more should Hi!" eagerly acquiesced Ikey.

"And I shouldn't like to kill anyone else," added James.

"But you've a right to kill th' henemies o' yer country, hain't yer?" asked his companion.

"I don't know," said James. "I hardly know what to say to that. I remember reading in the Bible that we must 'love our enemies,' and killing them doesn't seem at all like loving them."

"No more hit does; hits seems jest hexactly th' hopposite. But vot should Hi do in a battle? Hi thinks as Hi should feel regler bothered. Vat should you do, Jem?"

James looked somewhat perplexed.

"I think," he said, at length, "we might, perhaps, do our duty in battle when we were obliged to fight, without allowing ourselves to feel hatred against our enemies, and I think we ought to show them all the kindness we could, instead of being glad to see them wounded or in pain."

"Hi know vot Hi'll do hif hever Hi'm hin a battle. Hi'll look fierce an' pertend to be hin a passion jest to frighten th' henemy, an' hall th' time Hi von't be in a passion at hall. Von't that do?"

"I think that would be deceitful," returned James.

"You would be pretending to be what you were not, and is not that something like telling stories?"

"Vell, Jem, Hi think Hi must give hit hup," said Ikey. "Hi don't seem as hif Hi could make hit hout."

"The best way—the only way to do," answered James, "is to trust in God to teach you to do your duty. Never forget to pray to Him, and He will guide you in the most difficult circumstances, and you will never be allowed to go into the wrong path."

Ikey looked very thoughtful.

James also spoke in a low but earnest tone.

He felt that they were about to be separated, perhaps for years, and he was anxious to impress his poor ignorant friend with those truths he had learned from his mother.

"You must promise me, dear Ikey," he said, taking his friend's hand in his, "never to neglect saying your prayers; let no ridicule or sneers from your companions tempt you to be ashamed of this duty. If you do, you will fall into all kinds of sin, and never rise or succeed in anything you undertake; but if you pray for help, you are sure to receive it, and you will be a good boy and grow up to be a good man, and have God for your friend always, whether you are on land or sea. Will you promise me you will always say your prayers?"

The voice of the lad was low but intense, his head was bent forward, and his hands clasped those of his friend with nervous intensity, as he pleaded with him.

"You will promise me, won't you, dear Ikey?"

"Yes, Jemmy dear, Hi vill promise," answered Ikey, with tears in his eyes.

"And you'll keep your promise? You won't forget when we've been separated for some time?"

"No—no, Hi von't, Jem—Hi vont!"

"You must keep this promise as long as you live, and when you come to die, you'll be glad that you have kept it."

"Hi vill!—Hi vill! has long has Hi live!"

"I shall never forget to pray for you, Ikey," said James, "and you must do the same by me."

"You may be sure o' that," Ikey answered, eagerly. "Hif Hi vos to forget to pray for myself Hi'm sure Hi never should for you."

The poor boy's heart was full, and the tears trickled down his cheeks.

Nor was James less affected.

"We will pray for each other," he murmured.

"So ve vill, Jemmy dear," faltered Ikey, as he threw his arms round his companion's neck, and in that loving attitude the sorrowing friends wept in silence.

This outpouring of affection had in some degree subsided, when the cheery voice of the lieutenant was heard.

"Hallo, youngsters! What cheer! Are you asleep? I see, the port wine has mounted into your upper rigging, eh? Come, rouse up, young tars, we're going down to the harbour ; you'll see there a few specimens of your future homes."

It took only an instant for the boys to wipe the tears from their faces, and to rise from their seats.

The brothers Walker took their hats from the pegs in the office, and expressed their intention of accompanying them to the harbour.

James and Ikey, at the prospect of seeing the vessels, cheered up, and natural curiosity for a time dispelled the sorrow that had a few moments before clouded their hearts.

Accordingly, as they left the office, every one of the party might have been looked upon as in a state of considerable intense satisfaction.

Happy privilege of childhood ! Is it that the clouds are but transient—that the rain drops in the path soon dry, and the sunbeams shine through the temporary gloom, and scatter it ere the darkness has reached the young heart ?

The party walked through the town of Whitby, and many a greeting met the handsome, white-haired merchants, whose very appearance bespoke the respect their well-known respectability demanded.

Lieutenant Samphire also appeared to have many acquaintances in the town, but especially as they drew near the harbour, when he was frequently hailed by some brother sailor.

James and Ikey had eyes and ears for everything, and as they stood upon the quay and gazed forth upon the various vessels of different sorts and sizes, and watched the hardy weather-bronzed sailors, and inhaled the wholesome tarry odour that proceeded from the rigging of the numerous craft, they began to think that, after all, a ship did not appear such an uncomfortable place to live in.

"Well, my lads !" cried the lieutenant, "what do you think of a three months' cruise in one of those floating houses ?"

The boys never having experienced the invigorating sensations usually attendant upon a first voyage, were at a loss how to reply.

However, they took the pleasantest aspect of the affair, and said, after a little hesitation : "They thought it would be very comfortable."

"So it is very comfortable—*very !*" echoed Lieutenant Samphire, "when you're used to it ; but, of course, everything must have a beginning."

To this truth the boys readily assented.

They observed the crews of the different vessels variously employed.

Some were washing the decks of their respective ships—some were engaged in splicing and mending those portions of the rigging that had been damaged in their recent voyage, whilst others were scraping the sides of the vessels previous to repainting.

Here and there might be seen craft thoroughly repaired, and ready for sailing, on board of which there appeared nothing to do, and where the crew—men and boys—leant idly over the sides, as though simply waiting for orders.

The town of Whitby stands on the banks of the river Eske, which divides it into two parts, and which forms the harbour.

The medium of communication between these two portions of the town is a drawbridge.

This bridge attracted the attention of the boys particularly.

It was evident that all vessels entering the harbour must pass under this bridge.

But they observed that the masts of most of the vessels were considerably higher than the bridge itself.

This puzzled them exceedingly.

They wondered what the vessels did with their lofty masts when they passed beneath the bridge.

"P'r'aps they takes 'em down vhen they goes hunder," suggested Ikey.

"I don't think they could do that," James replied.

The curiosity of the boys being excited, James asked Lieutenant Samphire by what wonderful manœuvre the entrance of vessels into the harbour was effected.

At this moment a Dutch trader, just arrived from Holland, was about to enter the dock.

The lieutenant pointed out this craft to the boys.

"See, boys," he cried, "you will now have an opportunity of arriving at a solution of what appears to you a mystery. Watch that Dutchman, and you will soon discover how she will make her way under the bridge."

James and Ikey needed no second inducement to watch.

Their eyes were riveted upon the heavy, clumsy-looking vessel, whose broad build, and broadly-rounded bows, bespoke the country from whence she came.

There was a good deal of shouting as the Dutchman drew near, and the wonder of the boys had reached its climax as they noticed the tapering masts of the vessel rising far above the arch of the bridge.

"Hit'll never be hable to go hunder theer !" Ikey exclaimed. "Hit's a great deal too tall."

He had hardly uttered these words, when a sound, as of a chain being wound up with a "clank—clank !" arrested their attention, and informed them that some operation was taking place, of which they were at present ignorant.

They were not, however, long suffered to remain so, for, as they looked, they perceived that portion of the bridge which spanned the arch gradually rise, as on a hinge.

At each clank of the chain, the iron mass became more and more inclined towards the perpendicular, until, at length, it stood perfectly upright, and, the obstruction being now cleared away, the vessel, with her towering masts, passed through, and the bridge was gradually lowered to its former position.

The boys were astonished and delighted at this mechanical contrivance.

"Isn't it clever ?" asked James of his companion.

"Hit jest his !" returned Ikey, in a tone of admiration.

"And it seems so simple and easy when we see it done, doesn't it ?"

"Werry. Hi vonder as ve never thought o' that vay. Vhy, arter hall, hit's no more than hopenin' a door, only hit seems to be wrong side huppards."

"And see now the ship's inside, and the bridge is down just as it was before."

"An' hit looks as hif nothin' could move hit."

"What a curious-looking vessel it is !" James remarked, with evident interest.

"Hain't hit a fat 'un ?" observed Ikey.

The boy was struck with the rotundity of the Dutchman's build, so different in appearance from the surrounding craft.

"That's not an English ship," said James.

"No," replied Ikey ; "an' they hain't Henglishmen vot's on board of 'er—they're furreners."

At this moment the lieutenant, who had been watching the Dutchman's entrance into the harbour, came up to them.

"Well, youngsters," he said, "I think you've witnessed a sight to-day you never saw before, haven't you ?"

"Yes, sir," they answered.

"You'll find you've many such in store for you," the lieutenant continued. "Why, before you've been at sea a twelvemonth, you'll have learnt more than you possibly could if you were to stay ashore till your hairs are gray."

"What ship is that, sir ?" inquired James.

"That is a Dutch lugger," answered the lieutenant. "She is just arrived from Amsterdam, freighted with cheese."

"I don't think I like her shape so well as the other ones," James remarked.

"No more do Hi," said Ikey. "She looks as hif the cheeses vos a rushin' hout o' 'er sides."

Lieutenant Samphire laughed.

"You are not singular in your opinions respecting Dutch built vessels," he said. "They cannot compare with ours in symmetry ; but, from their roundess and breadth, they are supposed to be able to endure rough weather ; so that must be looked upon as counterbalancing the clumsiness of their appearance."

The brothers Walker now came up, and proposed that they stroll to that portion of the dock where their own vessels lay.

They had four employed in the coal trade, two of which were then at sea, and the remaining two waiting to take in their cargoes.

These two were the "Charles" and "Richard," so christened after the proprietors.

They were of moderate size, being each of about three hundred and fifty tons burden.

Like all vessels engaged in the coal trade, they partook of the character of the merchandise they carried, being dark, and not particularly clean.

The merchants made their way along the gangboard which extended from the nearest vessel to the edge of the quay, and so reached the deck.

Lieutenant Samphire and the boys followed.

They were now standing on board the "Charles."

"Now, my lad," said the merchant, after whom it was named, "this is the vessel in which you will make your first voyage."

These words were addressed to James, who, after receiving this information, felt himself doubly interested in the craft that was to bear him for the first time upon the bosom of the ocean, and in which he was to take his first lesson in seamanship.

Mr. Walker beckoned to a man who was looking over the vessel's stern.

"Mr. Rushworth," he called.

The person addressed advanced.

He was the master of the vessel—that is, he acted in the capacity of master or captain on board the "Charles."

He was a good-natured looking man of about forty years old, who had been in the employ of the brothers for some years, and in whose skill and integrity they reposed implicit confidence.

He was attired in a rough pilot jacket, a cap covered his thickly-curling hair, and he had altogether that frank, open, sailor-like aspect and bearing that was in itself a recommendation before a word had been spoken of his character, which his employers could testify was strict, honest, and unimpeachable.

Allan Rushworth touched his cap in a manner of mingled respect and friendship, and awaited his orders.

"Allan," said Mr. Charles, "I fancy you had no great opinion of that boy Jones?"

"No, sir, I never had any opinion of him, but one, and that was, that the sooner he was sent back to his mother the better for him and for us."

"Well then, that opinion has been acted upon. He has gone back to his mother, and I have taken another apprentice," said Mr. Charles.

The master's countenance brightened at this information.

"I'm glad to hear it," he replied—"very glad! Is one of those lads your new apprentice?" he inquired.

"Yes, Allan. Here, James!" he called, to his new charge, who was making his first essay at climbing, accompanied by Ikey, and who was now clambering up the rattlins with much glee.

The party on the deck smiled as they gazed on the efforts of the youngsters, who were so engrossed with their new pastime, that they did not hear the summons.

Ikey was mounting as fast as he could.

"Hi'll race yer to th' top," he cried to James, who was before him.

"Very well," replied his companion, who redoubled his efforts and won easily, having seated himself on the yardarm before Ikey had reached him.

"You've beat me this time," cried Ikey. "Never mind, ve'll try agin presintly."

At this juncture the voice of the lieutenant was heard.

"James Cook a-hoy!" he shouted.

"You're vanted," said Ikey.

James instantly swung himself from his perch, and descended as rapidly as possible.

Altogether, considering it was his first attempt, he seemed to give general satisfaction.

As he stood on the deck with his cheeks flushed with the unusual excitement, and his dark curls clustering over his forehead, it would have been difficult to have found a prettier boy, or one more calculated to ingratiate the beholder in his favour.

"Is this the boy, sir?" whispered Mr. Rushworth to his employer as he glanced at James.

"Yes, Allan," replied Mr. Charles. "What do you think of him? Doesn't he do credit to my choice?"

"He'll do, sir," answered the master, in a tone of perfect confidence; "he's worth a hundred such whining young spoonies as Master Tom Jones. This lad will make a sailor if he lives whoever lives to see him."

"Well, then, Allen, I shall leave him to your care: you will look after him," said Mr. Charles; "and I may tell you that as I've taken a very strong liking to him, I shall consider any pains you take to instruct him in his duties and encourage him in his first attempts, as a personal favour to myself."

"You may depend upon me, sir; I like the look of him, and I'll do all I can to make a sailor of him."

"Thank you, Allan—thank you," warmly exclaimed Charles Walker, as he shook the honest sailor by the hand. "I have every confidence in you—every confidence."

The boys having received permission to ramble about the vessel, they were soon busily engaged in investigating every available hole and corner.

Whilst they were thus individually prosecuting their researches, suddenly there was a cry heard. It was neither violent nor piercing—in fact, those in the fore part of the vessel did not even hear it.

It, however, reached the ears of James.

It proceeded from Ikey, who, in the eagerness of his investigations, forgetting to use his eyes, had pitched very suddenly and unexpectedly headforemost down the hatchway.

Many boys under similar circumstances would have broken their necks, but Ikey was not one of these.

He seemed to have a capability of enduring an unlimited quantity of hard knocks without being much the worse for them.

The only result of this tumble was a good shaking, and much surprise at the expeditious manner in which he had arrived at the bottom.

Not less surprised were a party of three who were seated in a small cabin on one side of the foot of the steep steps, or rather ladder, down which Ikey had made such a precipitate descent.

This party consisted of John Marsh and James Bowers, the first and second mate, and one of the crew, named Michael Bossy, who, for the sake of brevity, went by the title of Boss.

These three were engaged, it might have been surmised, in a confidential tête-à-tête, since there were no visible means of occupation. Certainly there was a spirituous odour hanging about the cabin, mingled with another perfume, that strongly suggested the combined fragrance of rum and pigtail tobacco, the latter not being smoked but chewed.

It is not at all strange, then, that the sudden appearance of a small boy falling with a crash at the very door of the narrow apartment in which they were located should have caused them to start from their seats with a mutual exclamation of astonishment.

Ikey was not long in recovering his breath and his tongue.

"Hi begs yer parding, gen'l'men; but Hi didn't mean to do Hit, 'pon my word Hi didn't!" he said.

"I suppose," answered the first mate, in a surly tone that proved he by no means relished the interruption, "you've clambered over the ship's side from the quay, and have been larking on deck like a young monkey, till you've got your deserts. It'd served you right if you'd broken your neck."

Ikey thought the speaker was particularly hard upon boys, and was about to explain how it was he came to be there, when James, who had traced him by the sound of his voice, glided down the steps and stood at his elbow.

He had overheard the angry remark of the mate, and wished to set him right.

"We didn't clamber over the ship's side," he said; "we came on board with Mr. Walker and Lieutenant Samphire, and had leave to go about the vessel where we liked."

"Oh, indeed!" ejaculated the mate, in a tone not a whit more agreeable than before. "And pray who are you?"

"My name is James Cook," James answered, "and I'm Mr. Walker's new apprentice."

"Apprentice!" exclaimed the mate. "Come, now, we don't want any of those lies! Mr. Walker's got an apprentice already, and he doesn't want two at a time."

"I'm not telling lies," James answered, firmly. "I'm speaking the truth. Mr. Walker had an apprentice this morning, but he has left, and he has taken me in his place."

This intelligence did not seem at all to please the mate—in fact, nothing the boys could say did appear to please him.

Why this should have been so, or what difference

it could possibly have made to John Marsh whether James Cook or Tom Jones was Mr. Walker's apprentice, did not just then very distinctly appear.

Certain, however, it was that the mate looked upon James's fair young face with a very evil eye, as though he would have done him an injury if he could.

But of this ominous expression directed towards himself James was quite ignorant.

It was Ikey who noticed the scowling look the mate cast upon his unsuspicious companion.

John Marsh, who finished his inquiries of James, turned to Ikey.

"And who are you?" he asked, curtly, looking down at the boy from under his bushy eyebrows.

"Hi'm nobody 'ere," answered Ikey, looking up in his questioner's face with perfect *nonchalance*. "Hi don't belong to this 'ere ship: Hi belongs to th' navy, an' Hi'm goin' to be a hadmiral, an' vear a cocked 'at an' feather."

The first mate looked at the second mate, and the second mate looked at Boss; but it seemed as though there was not enough of good nature amongst the three even to admit a laugh.

They gave instead, however, a contemptuous scowl.

"You're a pretty article for an admiral!" exclaimed John Marsh, scornfully. "You might do to bait a hook for a shark, but an admiral—ho! ho!" and this was the most mirthful expression in which John Marsh indulged.

"Hi s'pose," remarked Ikey, "as this is Mr. Valker's ship; an' as e's give us leave to go vheer ve likes, ve may look hover it, downstairs as vell as hupstairs?"

"Oh, certainly," replied the mate, with a sneer; "but don't disturb us again, that's all."

The men returned once more to their conversation, their pigtail, and their rum, whilst James and Ikey wandered about the lower regions of the vessel, and at length found themselves in the hold.

"Vot a great, big, dark place, hain't hit?" said Ikey, with some apprehension.

"Yes," replied James, "that's where they put the coals, I think."

"Hi vonder vhether there's hany sich place has this o', board a man-o'-var," remarked Ikey, musingly.

As there was no one present able to give him any information on the subject, he made up his mind to wait until he should be able to receive ocular demonstration.

"Hi shall know all about hit afore long," he thought.

There being little of interest to be discovered below, and the vicinity of the three disagreeable sailors being anything but pleasant, the boys resolved to return once more to the deck.

As they passed the cabin-door, Ikey's quick eye noticed the glance the first mate threw upon James, and young as he was, its peculiarly sardonic expression fastened upon his memory.

"Hi say, Jem," he said to his companion, as they gained the deck, "did you see 'ow that man with the thick heyebrows looked at you?"

"No," answered James.

"Hi did. Hi see 'im tvice, an' vonce jest now as ve passed. Hi don't like 'im. 'E looked jest for all th' vorld as though 'e could 'a' stuck a knife hin yer, or chuck'd yor overboard."

"Oh," said James, smiling, "you must have fancied it. Why should he dislike me? I never saw him before."

"Hi dunno vhy, but hif Hi vos to see a man look at me as 'e looked at you, Hi should take good care to keep has fur hout of 'is reach as Hi could."

Ikey spoke very earnestly; and though at this moment the brothers and the lieutenant calling them to accompany them for a time banished those thoughts from his memory, still several times in the course of the day that dark malignant look rose up before the eye of his mind, and made him wish that his friend and John Marsh were not going to sail in the same ship.

Chapter XLVI.

THE HURRICANE.

IF it appeared mysterious to Ikey Mangles that a sailor in the employ of men so kind and benevolent in word and act as the brothers Walker should, without any apparent cause have regarded his friend James, who was far more calculated to win esteem and love than to cause repugnance, with looks of such deadly hostility, it will also seem equally strange to our readers.

Why was it?

There must have been a cause.

James Cook and John Marsh were utter strangers. Neither of them had ever seen the other before. The one was a strong, powerful man—the other a delicate, slightly-limbed boy.

What, then, could it be?

Evidently one of the causes of dislike sprang from the fact that James had superseded Tom Jones as Mr. Walker's apprentice.

But how could such a change affect John Marsh?

Or if it did, it would surely be a beneficial change to get rid of a dull, stupid, crying booby, and in his place to have a smart, active, handsome boy, with an intellect beyond his years.

But stop!

Perhaps in this last fact we have some clue to the mystery—some key to unlock the riddle of this otherwise unaccountable dislike.

Perhaps there was something wrong going on amongst these men.

Some plot at work which the dull, thick-headed Master Jones, who never could and never would have been able to see an inch beyond his nose, had he lived to the age of Methuselah, never dreamt of, but which this sharp, lively, bright-eyed boy might be keen enough to suspect.

Ah, John Marsh! I think it must be some such cause as this that has raised the bitter blood in your heart against the new apprentice.

The trio sat together chewing, drinking, and cogi-

tating long after the Messrs. Walker and party and honest Allan Rushworth had left the vessel.

They were evidently planning some evil.

Their conversation, though not leading directly to anything tangible, nevertheless betrayed a plot that had been previously contemplated and was now in the course of development.

"I suppose," said the mate at length, "we are still in the same mind?"

"We are," replied his companions.

"I'm tired and heart-sick of this beggarly life I'm leading, and am determined to bear it no longer. One bold stroke, and we may be rich men—at least, rich for us, who have never known what it is to have more than a pound or two in our pockets since we were born."

"I'm with you!" said the second mate.

"And I!" added Boss.

"It may be done the next voyage, I suppose?" asked James Bowers.

"Of course it may!—it must!—it shall!" cried the first mate, under his breath.

"It's unfortunate Tom Jones leaving, though, isn't it?" said Bowers.

"Yes," returned John Marsh; "I've been thinking of that. He was half an idiot, and understood nothing. But this new apprentice looks as though he could read everything at a glance."

"But then he's only a boy after all," suggested the second mate.

"True! only a boy; but he's not an ordinary boy, I can see that," replied his companion. "We shall have to be very cautious. There's that in his face which speaks of truth. He's slight and delicate certainly; but his eye betokens intelligence and daring. I wish Tom Jones had remained, and this new-comer at the bottom of the sea."

"It wouldn't take long to send him there, would it?" asked the second mate, with a sinister frown, "if he made himself too busy in matters that didn't concern him."

"Much better manage our affairs without bloodshed," replied John Marsh. "Murder's an ugly word when you come to consider it."

"So it is," returned his comrade. "Of course, I was only speaking of a desperate case."

"We must manage so carefully that our ends shall be accomplished without the least suspicion," said the first mate, decidedly. "Since the vessel has been laid up here, I have taken an impression in wax of the key of Allan Rushworth's locker."

"Have you, Jack?" exclaimed his companion, eagerly.

"I have! Allan is cautious, but I managed to slip into his cabin one day when he had left his keys dangling from the keyhole, and, from the impression I then took, I can get a counterpart made as soon as we reach London that shall put us in possession of our prize."

"Capital!" they exclaimed.

"But," inquired the second mate, "will the cargo of coals be paid for on delivery in cash?"

"Yes. I heard Mr. Walker speaking to Allan Rushworth about it only the day before yesterday."

"Then I don't see how we can fail."

"Not if we stick together and act with prudence, caution, and decision," replied the first mate. "And now we've been together long enough, let's separate," he added; "too long conferences may breed suspicion."

With these words they went on deck.

Enough has been said in this conversation to prove that there was a plot hatching between the first and second mate and Boss.

It is also sufficiently explicit that the nature of the plot was robbery.

How this was to be accomplished, together with other matters concerning it, the future will bring to light.

In the meantime Ikey and James, after taking an affectionate farewell, and shedding many tears over their parting, were separated at length.

Ikey going with Lieutenant Samphire, and James, of course, remaining in the house of the brothers Walker.

The worthy merchants had bound him in the usual legal manner, and he was now duly installed as their articled apprentice for five years, Mr. Charles assuring him that if he did his duty, he should regard him in a much nearer light than such a bond would seem to imply.

From all appearances, James and these worthy gentlemen seemed very likely to grow in each other's esteem.

The more they saw of their apprentice, the more he ingratiated himself in their favour.

His honesty, truthfulness, and integrity were so manifest, that the brothers congratulated themselves on their good fortune in finding such a treasure; while James, in serving two such kind-hearted, and benevolent men, found his inclinations and his sense of duty go hand in hand together.

The vessel, named the "Charles," was taking in the cargo of coal, with which she was to proceed to London, and in which James Cook was to make his first voyage.

The boy was in a mingled state of exultation and expectation.

He was already on excellent terms with Allan Rushworth, the master, who had, so far as he could in the time, explained many things on board the vessel that were useful for him to know.

John Marsh, too, from motives of policy, had thrown aside all his evil looks, and lost no opportunity of ingratiating himself in the good graces of the new and favourite apprentice.

James, altogether, began to feel quite comfortable and at home in his new profession before ever the vessel left the harbour, and began to think that poor Ikey had magnified dangers when he spoke so ominously of the first mate.

He had, however, reason to alter his opinion of the correctness of his friend's suspicions before he returned from his voyage.

It took some time to load the vessel; but at length, everything was ready for sailing.

The day before they started, the brothers sent for James into their private office, when Charles Walker, in a kind and fatherly manner, thus addressed him:

"Now, my dear boy," said the old gentleman, "this being your first voyage, I thought I would say a few words before starting, in order to encourage you on the one hand, and to prepare you for what you may have to encounter on the other. I am sure you are too sensible to expect to go through the world without experiencing a few knocks, and I am equally certain you are too much of a man to be daunted by the first wind that blows against you. You will, of course, find a sailor's life not the easiest in the world. You will have to bear cold and rough weather, wind and storm; but these will make you hardy, and teach you to look up to and trust in that Providence beneath whose care you are as safe at sea as on land, in the storm as in the calm. You will by degrees become inured to the haps and hazards of a sailor's life, and as you become more acquainted with the duties that belong to your calling, you will find your interest in that calling increase daily. Allan Rushworth will teach you all that it is necessary you should know, and I am sure he will find in you a willing and obedient pupil. Your first voyage will be to London, and while the vessel lies in the docks, you will have an opportunity of visiting some of the principal places of that great city. I have directed Allan to show you everything that may tend to amuse and instruct you while you stay there. In short, it is the wish both of my brother Richard and myself, that you should be treated in every way more as a relative than an apprentice. And now, having said thus much, I can only wish you a pleasant and prosperous voyage, and a safe return. Good-bye, my dear boy!"

The worthy merchants shook James cordially by the hand.

They could read in his face that his heart was full of gratitude, and they considered that far better than any professions his lips could have uttered.

Having thus taken leave of his employers, and all being now ready for departure, there was nothing further to be done but for James to go on board.

It was on a fine afternoon early in May, that the "Charles," coal brig, slowly made her way out of Whitby Harbour.

There was not much wind, and the vessel made her way somewhat sluggishly.

The sensation, however, of being on the water, and the gradual rising and falling of the ship as she got further and further from the land, together with the occasional shifting of the sails in order that they might catch the wind, were all new to James, and filled him with delight.

By degrees the sun set, and the shades of night began to cast their veil over the ocean.

The breeze, too, began to quicken, and as the sails caught the welcome gale and swelled out to their full extent, the heavily-laden brig seemed to awake to new life, and careered through the opposing waves as though she had been built of cork.

Gradually the lights in the distant town disappeared, and then, slowly and almost imperceptibly, they faded away, and they were out of sight of land.

The wind rose, too, and came in long, fierce gusts across the bosom of the sea.

The waves under the influence of the gale began to rise, and curl their crested heads with gradually increasing vehemence.

James remained on deck watching the foaming billows in silence.

He did not feel afraid, but he remembered one night when he had been exposed to a rougher sea than this, half-frozen, and in a small boat, and it made him thoughtful.

He was not cold, for he had on a warm, thick pilot-jacket, and the vessel he was in seemed in his eyes of such magnitude, that no storm would have been able to sink her.

At least, that was his opinion.

Allan Rushworth came to him as he was leaning against the ship's side, looking out over the troubled waters.

"Well, my boy," he said, cheerfully, "what do you think of this?"

"I think it looks grand and beautiful," James replied; "but it seems to be getting rather rough; we're not going to have a storm, are we?"

"A storm?" laughed Allan. "I hope not. This is just the weather we want. If this wind holds, it will make a difference of many hours in our favour in the course of the voyage."

[JAMES COOK'S FIRST LESSON IN CLIMBING.]

"You mean that if the wind blows as it does now we shall get to London many hours sooner than if it was to stop?"

"Exactly."

"Then I hope it will keep on. I shall be glad to see London: I've often heard such wonderful accounts of it," said James.

"Well, when we're safely there and our business is transacted, I shall take you to see as many of the sights as I can. It was Mr. Walker's wish that I should do so."

"Yes," answered James, "he told me so before we started. How kind of him!"

"He is one of the kindest men in the world," said Allan; "you may consider yourself a very fortunate boy to have found such a master: he's one in a thousand."

"I do think myself fortunate," answered James, "and I am very thankful to be where I am, and I wish to do all I can to prove that I am grateful."

"I am sure you do," returned Allan, "and we must

try how much of a sailor we can make you by the time we get back to Whitby."

The brig was now plunging through the waves, and rolling and pitching considerably.

"This is very different from standing still and quiet, as the ship did in the harbour, isn't it?" remarked James.

"Very," returned the master. "You could scramble up the ratlins readily enough then; do you think you would dare to venture now?"

James glanced upwards at the shrouds, and then rather doubtfully at the rolling waves on every side, to meet which the labouring vessel seemed to incline herself.

"If I were to get giddy and fall," thought James, "while the ship is lying on her side like that, nothing could save me from being drowned."

Poor James's trust in Providence failed him here; but his case was not a solitary one. Many a heart—a bold heart, too—has shrunk appalled before the stern aspect of the mighty ocean and the roaring of the blast,

that rocked the frail bark that alone interposed between life and death as though it had been a feather.

James Cook, however, though intimidated, was not cowed.

His was but the natural hesitation of inexperience and the timidity of youth.

But he reflected thus:

"If I am to be a sailor I must make a beginning or I shall never advance at all. It will never do to be a coward! besides, I am just as safe there as here."

Allan Rushworth stood by watching him.

The honest sailor divined what was passing in the boy's mind.

"It strikes me," he said, "you are feeling exactly as I did when I first mounted the ratlins in a gale of wind, the only difference being, that in my case it blew a hurricane, and a terrific sea was running, and that I was not asked whether 'I *thought* I could climb,' but ordered to 'go up at once.'"

"That was very cruel, wasn't it?" asked James.

"Well, I don't know; I daresay I thought so at the time," answered Allan; "but sailors are not generally very particular. Most of them as boys have had to endure hardships themselves, and they think as a matter of course that the boys of the next generation must do the same as they have done before."

"I daresay they're right," said James; "and I've made up my mind not to shrink from any duty I am called upon to perform; I'll go up the ratlins."

The boy spoke firmly and decidedly.

"That's a brave lad!" cried the master. "You are going the right way to conquer fear; there's no danger, the rigging is firm and strong; brace up your nerves, and as you mount look upwards."

James no longer hesitated; he grasped the shrouds, and in a moment was ascending the rope-ladder.

The ropes being wet with spray, were slippery, and the rolling of the vessel caused the most unpleasant sensations.

More than once James felt as though he must return; but he prayed a simple prayer for strength, and he received it.

He was enabled to persevere.

By degrees the uncomfortable feelings decreased.

His head felt steadier, his nerves stronger, and he proceeded with more confidence.

Struggling, slipping, and recovering his foothold, he at length reached the yardarm, where the sails, bellied out by the wind, strained and groaned as though they would have burst from their fastenings.

He could now, by entwining his arm and leg through the interstices of the shrouds, command a secure hold, and from the elevation at which he was placed, look down into the dark waters.

More than once as he hung there, when the careening of the vessel brought him completely over the foaming surface, he fancied the ship was about to capsize with all her freight, and that his first voyage would be his last.

But still the "Charles" kept on her way, pitching tossing, and rolling, but without the least idea of sinking.

James, too, began to grow more and more accustomed to his position, and felt that it was by no means so terrible as it appeared. As he clung there, he suddenly saw lights on the starboard quarter.

"What place is that where I see the lights, Mr. Allan?" he called,

"Scarborough!" cried the master, in return. "You can come down if you like now," he added.

James, permission being given him to descend, lost no time in reaching the deck.

Here he could distinctly see the cliffs of Scarborough and the numerous lights from the windows of the buildings in the town.

Gradually, however, these became more and more indistinct, until once more the vessel rolled on her way in darkness and solitude.

The wind, too, had shifted, and all hands were called up to trim the sails.

The vessel laboured more than she had previously done.

The breeze that had hitherto expedited her passage now seemed to oppose it.

The roughness of the sea increased.

It was necessary to keep a vigilant eye upon the sails.

Towards morning the wind increased to a gale, and as day broke, and they passed Flamborough Head, it blew a hurricane.

James had been in his hammock for some hours.

When, however, he turned out in the morning, the sea presented a very different aspect from that of the night before.

As far as his eye could reach, there seemed nothing but a boiling surface of white foam. The ship, too, no longer cut her path through the waves, but rose and fell sluggishly as though at the mercy of the winds and waters.

He noticed, too, the countenances of the sailors.

They seemed particularly serious.

They went about their duties in a quiet, steady manner, but so silently that one would have imagined it was a dumb crew.

James particularly scrutinised the face of Allan Rushworth, the master.

He fancied he looked a little pale, but that might have been fatigue—since he had been up all night—but he noticed him looking somewhat anxiously through his telescope, and heard him express a hope that the hurricane would exhaust itself with its own violence.

"We are so heavily loaded," James heard him say to the first mate, "that we can make but little way against a head-wind like this."

John Marsh, the mate, looked particularly downcast.

It almost seemed that not only certain plans he had formed would never be realised, but that his own life was in jeopardy.

As the day advanced, it by no means altered its stormy character.

The wind still blew dead against the ship's course.

The sky was dark and threatening, and heavy rain fell.

Not the smallest glimpse remained of the bright May afternoon of the preceding day.

As they struggled heavily onwards, they passed several craft that were more or less sufferers from the violence of the hurricane.

But the sea was running so high, and the wind was so furious, that they could neither help those they passed nor receive help from them.

And so another day dragged its heavy length along, and the semi-obscurity that had hung over the sky during the last twelve hours was once more obscured by the blacker darkness of night, with neither moon nor stars to afford a solitary ray to cheer them.

It was about eight o'clock in the evening when a somewhat singular event happened.

A cry of terror was suddenly raised by one of the crew.

Everyone heard it. It was one of those shrill piercing shrieks that evinced a sudden and violent horror.

Louder than the wind and storm this solitary cry burst forth, and then was silent.

At first it seemed like "a man overboard!" but this was not the case.

"What can it be?" thought the master.

He had never left the deck, neither did he intend to do so until the gale had in some measure abated.

It was of far more importance at such a crisis, to devote his entire attention to the labouring vessel than to consult his own sensations of weariness.

As to the startling cry that had reached his ears, he had forgotten it almost as soon as it had died away.

Whatever it might have been he presumed he should know before long.

James was standing near, as he generally did when he was permitted, feeling a sense of security in the company of the vigilant master.

Since the storm had so much increased, Allan Rushworth had hardly spoken, save to give his orders to the men.

James, seeing that his mind was preoccupied, forbore questioning him.

But after that sudden and piercing shriek the boy could not restrain his desire to address him.

He therefore said at length:

"Are we in danger, Mr. Rushworth?"

He spoke in a very calm, quiet voice; so quiet, that the master turned and fixed his eyes upon him, as though, even in the dark, he could read his features.

"What makes you ask that question?" he inquired, in a kind tone.

"That scream we heard just now," returned James, "seemed so startling and terrible."

"Was it that that made you think we are in danger?" asked the master.

"Yes, sir."

"That cry had nothing at all to do with any peril that may threaten us," Allan said: "it was uttered by one of the crew."

"Then we are not in danger?" asked James, who felt assured by the master's words.

"I did not say that," he answered.

"You think we are, then?"

"Yes, my boy," returned Allan, in a low tone. "This is your first voyage, but you may be at sea all your life and never encounter such a gale as we are now enduring. Hark! How the groaning timbers creak! If the vessel we are in were not in sound, good condition she would, in all probability, have sprung a leak before this."

James's head drooped, and his heart sank within him at these words.

The master hastened to cheer him.

"Come, my boy, don't be down-hearted," he said. "You asked me a plain question, and I've given you a plain answer, because I think you're a brave boy and deserve confidence. I've told you more than I would to any man in the ship, so mind and keep your own counsel."

James, even at that moment, felt flattered by this proof of the master's confidence, and Allan continued:

"You must not think, however, that because we are in danger we must, of necessity, be lost. A sailor is, to a certain extent, always in peril; at any moment, even in the calmest weather, some casualty may occur that may doom vessel and all aboard her to instant destruction; while, on the other hand, the greatest apparent dangers may be surmounted, and vessel and crew reach the port in safety."

"Then you think there is a chance of our getting to London?" asked James.

"Oh yes!" replied the master. "I trust by the blessing of Providence, that we may be safely moored in the London Docks by the end of the week."

As he finished speaking, John Marsh, the first mate, drew near.

"Can I speak a word to you, sir?" he asked of the master.

"Yes; what is it?"

"You heard that scream not long ago?"

"Yes; what was it?"

"It was Michael Bossy, sir, that shrieked."

"What made him shriek?"

"He's had a warning."

"What warning?"

"He's seen his wife!"

"What nonsense!— is he mad?" exclaimed the master, in a tone of ridicule.

"Mad or not sir," answered the mate, "he's below, as pale as death."

"And has the sight of his wife produced this effect?"

"Yes, sir."

"He must be labouring under a delusion."

"He declares it to be true, sir. He says he was just going on deck when his wife stood before him suddenly, just as in life, and held up her hand as though to warn him back. She said to him: 'Michael, Michael, don't go!' It was then he shrieked out, and fell to the ground in a fit. When he came to, he told me exactly what I've related to you."

"But of course you do not attach any importance to such a relation?" inquired the master.

"Well, as to that, I don't think it's right to slight warnings," the mate replied. "I was aboard a vessel once, when exactly the same thing occurred to the carpenter as has just happened to Boss. He came upon us suddenly, looking very pale, and said he'd just seen his wife, and when we asked what it portended, he replied 'we should be wrecked;' and, sure enough, that very night we were wrecked."

"Then do you mean to imply that from the appearance of Michael Bossy's wife to him we shall be wrecked?" asked the master.

"What else can I imply?" said the mate.

"I am surprised you can be so superstitious!" exclaimed Allan, with some contempt.

"Oh, it's not I alone," returned the mate, sullenly; "there's not one of the crew that doesn't think the same."

The master made a gesture of impatience.

"Look here, Mr. Rushworth, it's no use your getting out of temper over this," said the mate; "if a body of men have a fixed belief in any particular thing, it's more than one man can do to shake it out of 'em."

"But this appears to me so childish and absurd," argued Allan.

"Well, I don't know about that," returned the mate; "but when a man sees his wife, as it might be, yesterday afternoon at Whitby, and then finds her suddenly standing face to face with him at the foot of the cabin stairs, when he's far out at sea in the midst of a violent gale, I don't see anything childish, or absurd either, in looking upon it as something out of the common—in short, as a warning that something's going to happen."

Allan Rushworth shrugged his shoulders with some contempt.

"I thought you were a more sensible man, John Marsh," he said, "than to give credence to such idle superstitions. However, since you persist in doing so, as you say, it is impossible for me to alter your opinion. We are all in the hands of Providence, and the future will prove which of us is right."

"Yes," murmured the mate, sullenly; "but that's not exactly all. We're tired to death; and, as we're convinced we shall never outlive this gale, we think we may as well have something to comfort us for the short time we shall be together."

The master turned indignantly, and looked full in the mate's face, that was clouded with fear and sullen gloom.

As he did so, he saw gradually drawing round the rest of the crew.

His quick eye took them all in at a glance.

"What is it you mean?—what is it you require?" he asked, sternly.

"We want something to drink," sullenly answered the mate.

"Ay, ay!" joined in his misguided companions, "hand over the rum."

"Harkye, one and all," exclaimed Allan Rushworth, as he gently drew James behind him. "Since the commencement of this gale, save a mouthful of hard biscuit, I have tasted nothing, and I have never left my post. Now because one of your mates has distracted your minds with this idle chimera, you have made up your minds that the ship must inevitably be lost, and so resolve to act in such a manner as to do away with every chance of saving her. I am aware you require some stimulant to support you under your extra fatigue, and was about to distribute a double allowance of rum, but no more. This is all I shall allow myself, and this is sufficient. But whatever may betide—whatever be the result of this night's storm—whether we live to see to-morrow's light, or go down into the depths ere it break upon us, I will never, while I have the power to resist, allow any crew over which I hold command to add to their sins by going in a state of worse than brutal insensibility into the presence of their Maker!"

The master spoke firmly but solemnly, and the crew seemed impressed with his words.

One or two murmured something indistinctly; but there was no longer any actual demand.

At this moment there came a violent blast of wind that made the ship reel and groan again.

It was so sudden and powerful that it brought the crew to their senses.

"All hands aloft!" from the master was promptly obeyed.

It was necessary to shift the sails.

Mutual interest and mutual danger prompted them to mutual exertion.

While this was going on, there came another furious gust of wind.

There was a crash aloft and a cry.

One of the spars had snapped and gone overboard, but not alone—there was a man clinging to it.

Instantaneously rose the sickening alarm—

"A man overboard!"

But the roar of the winds and waves drowned it, and the poor wretch perforce was left to his fate.

In such a gale as was then blowing, to have saved him would have been an impossibility.

The sails were shifted and the broken spar replaced, and then the crew assembled upon deck.

In calling over their names to ascertain who was missing, one only returned no answer.

It was MICHAEL BOSSY!

A cold shudder ran through the limbs of the crew.

No class of men are so proverbially superstitious as sailors; and the fate of their messmate seemed in their eyes to realise all the importance they had attributed to the vision poor Boss had either seen or fancied he had looked upon.

"Now, sir!" exclaimed the first mate, "wasn't I and my messmates right?—didn't the appearance of poor Michael's wife foretell danger?"

But the master turned the melancholy accident to good account.

"If it did," he answered, "it was a warning for Michael himself, and it has been fulfilled; and, though I am sorry to lose one of my crew, I think, nevertheless, it is better that one life should be sacrificed than that all should perish."

No one appeared anxious to dispute this, and Allan continued:

"I think the gale is decreasing in violence, and I have hopes that, before morning, the danger will have passed away, and that the ship will ride easier than she does at present."

A kind of self-congratulatory murmur ran through the crew at these cheering words.

"Come," added the master, "do your duties like good fellows, and by the help of Providence we shall weather the storm yet. In the meantime, you all need something to invigorate you, and you shall have it."

Double allowances of rum and biscuit were served out, and under its influence, the spirits of the crew revived.

The gale, too, as Allan predicted, began to lull, and although the ocean was still turgid and angry from the fury of the wind that had swept over it, when the morning dawned the sky was brighter and clearer, and in the course of the day the sun broke forth and lighted up the crested waves with his bright beams.

"There," said the master to James the next day, "you have had an adventurous first voyage; you have narrowly escaped a wreck; you have seen the first outbreak of a mutiny, happily quelled, and with all this, you will find yourself safe in London in less than four days."

Allan Rushworth was right.

On the fourth afternoon after he had spoken, the "Charles" was making her way up the Thames, and long before nightfall, was anchored in the London Docks.

Chapter XLVII.

THE SHABBY MAN IN BLACK.

IT took some time to unload the vessel, but in due course this was accomplished.

The coals were consigned to the purchaser, and the money paid to Allan Rushworth for his employers.

A few days' grace were given, in order that James might have an opportunity of seeing some of the wonders of the metropolis.

The master took him to such places as he thought would interest him, and as time permitted.

St. Paul's Cathedral, Westminster Abbey, the Tower of London, Greenwich Hospital, and Drury Lane Theatre were the principal national establishments he visited.

One peculiar incident connected with the last-named place greatly surprised James.

Mr. Rushworth and his charge rode from the inn where they lodged in the Borough to the theatre.

As they drew near, the coach-door was besieged by dirty, squalid-looking men offering bills of the night's performance for sale.

There was a considerable din of voices, but one, of all the rest, struck on James's ear as familiar.

He leant forward and looked from the window, and there, with a bundle of playbills flapping in his hand, and clothes that looked wretched, and tattered, and hollow ghastly cheeks, he recognised, to his great astonishment—not to say horror—the well-known features of his old and cruel persecutor, Octavius Challoner.

Whether or not Octavius recognised him he could not say; but he fancied he did, inasmuch as he suddenly disappeared, and was seen no more.

The brilliantly-lighted theatre, and the novelty of the performance—that surpassed everything that James's imagination could possibly have conceived—banished everything else from his mind, and Octavius Challoner, together with all his own past dangers and vicissitudes, were alike forgotten.

The gorgeous entertainment at length, however, drew to a close, and James returned with his guardian to the George Inn to supper and bed.

As Octavius was an entire stranger to Mr. Rushworth, James, even if he thought of him, did not mention him to that gentleman.

However, it is possible that he did not enter his mind; and it was not long before James was snugly tucked between the sheets, and dreaming of the splendid scenes that had passed that night before his eyes.

The loss of Michael Bossy, who was blown overboard in the gale, rendered it necessary that another hand should be engaged to supply his place.

This was entrusted to John Marsh, the first mate, who had expressed himself sorry for his conduct on the night of the gale, and whom Allan, in full confidence, had believed to be sincere.

The worthy master, judging of others by himself, was particularly unsuspecting, and considered the attempted mutiny as originating more in superstitious fears than from a spirit of rebellion.

He little dreamt of the desperate resolve that was formed in the breasts of the first and second mates, or that the man who had met such an untimely fate had been their accomplice, and that it was necessary to the success of their plans that they should find another kindred spirit.

In this it was imperative to act cautiously, and feel their way gradually.

It would not have done to have opened their designs at once to a stranger.

They might have lighted upon an honest man who would not only have refused their guilty alliance with indignation, but have exposed the whole transaction.

They therefore proceeded with the utmost circumspection.

It happened that on the very night when Allan Rushworth and James Cook visited the pit of Drury Lane Theatre, John Marsh, and James Bowers were snugly packed up aloft in the gallery.

Each party, however, were ignorant of the propinquity of the other.

The mates—scoundrels as they were—inherited the usual fondness of sailors for theatrical entertainments; and, in proportion as they became interested in what they saw, so did they covet the means of indulging themselves more frequently in such amusements.

The performance over, they repaired—sailor-like—to refresh themselves at a not very reputable tavern in the neighbourhood.

While they were drinking at the bar, and wondering whether they should be able to pick up a messmate who would join them in carrying out their plot, their eyes fell on a man, whose appearance denoted not only poverty, but a certain desperate recklessness that seemed to imply anything but a submissive spirit in the endurance of his adverse circumstances.

This man had a pallid face, was particularly shabby, and was drinking misery's own peculiar beverage—gin—which he accompanied with copious whiffs from a short black pipe.

There was a certain *nonchalance* in his manner; yet he nevertheless glanced with a kind of suspicious nervousness at every new-comer as he entered.

We may presume that it never crossed the minds of

either of the sailors that this individual was exactly the man they needed.

In fact it did not. They glanced at him for an instant, and he at them, and then they returned to their grog, and he to his gin and short pipe.

But though this shabby individual withdrew his gaze from the sailors for an instant, it was only to fasten his eyes on them again the next moment.

He did not, however, look boldly at them, so as to excite their attention, but furtively, from under the rim of his battered hat, which he pulled very forward over his eyes.

John Marsh and James Bowers, having been confined in the heated air of Drury Lane gallery, were in a humour for drinking, and as they had nothing better to do with the money they earned afloat than to spend it ashore, they had plenty to gratify their inclinations in that particular.

The man who watched them so narrowly heard the silver jingling in their pockets, and enviously eyed the rapid emptying and re-filling of their glasses.

Sailors, as a body, are not remarkable for caution or skill in plotting.

These two men were not exceptions to this rule.

The more they drank, the less cautious they became, and the louder they spoke.

Not that their tones were sufficiently distinct to be audible to an uninterested spectator : it was only when a pair of ears were set to listen intently to what they were saying—like those of the shabby, pale-faced man —that anything particular could have been gathered.

Now this was what he heard, and from which he drew his own inferences :

"You're sure he has received the cash?" said the second mate.

"Yes," replied his comrade. "I heard him say so yesterday."

"Well, I'm determined to have it!"

"A fair share of it, of course you mean?"

"Of course!"

"How unfortunate it was poor Boss being blown overboard, wasn't it?"

"Yes! Everything was so well arranged, and, besides, he wouldn't have wanted an equal share. Twenty pounds or so would have satisfied him!"

"It was unfortunate, indeed! You see, there must be three of us to manage the job."

"Certainly—two to watch and one to act."

"Have you got a key made from the wax impression?"

"Here it is."

At this juncture the first mate took a bright, new-looking key from his pocket, and showed it to his companion, who eyed it with considerable exultation; but a moment after his countenance fell, as he remarked :

"I think the whole affair 'll come to nothing after all!"

"Come to nothing!" exclaimed his messmate—"it mustn't come to nothing!—it sha'n't come to nothing! not while my name's John Marsh. I've made up my mind to do it, though I have to take a dive from the cabin window, and swim for it!"

"Well, I don't see how your going to the bottom with the money in your pocket—as you'd be sure to do—could benefit anybody," remarked the second mate, sulkily.

"Well, I'm inclined to agree with you there," acquiesced the other; "and, to come to the point, I don't see how we're to succeed unless we can pick up an accomplice."

"Nor I; and there's the difficulty. It's rather awkward to make a proposal to a man that may, perhaps, win him a hundred pounds; but which, on the other hand—in the event of a failure—may cost him his life."

"Psha! You seem to anticipate nothing but failures! I prefer looking on the bright side of the question. I've no desire, I assure you, to see my neck in the hangman's noose."

"Well, whatever we do must be done quickly. We shall be starting again in two or three days."

"Yes, and unfortunately this is a kind of thing that can't be done quickly. It requires care and caution."

"I've watched the faces of a hundred men since I've been ashore to see if I could pick out one that looked as if it belonged to a scoundrel; but, for a wonder, they all seem so particularly *honest*."

The first mate laughed, for at that moment he happened to look towards the shabby man with the short pipe, who, seeing the sailor's eye turned upon him, immediately became intensely absorbed in the contemplation of his thumb-nail.

"What d'ye think of that face there?" the sailor whispered to his mate.

"Well, he looks as if he wouldn't object to a hundred pounds, or be very particular how he earned it."

"But he's no sailor; what could we do with a raw land lubber aboard?"

"Oh, we could manage that if he was willing to row in with us."

At this juncture their glasses were empty, and it was found necessary to replenish them.

The shabby man so contrived just then to catch their eyes.

He smiled a kind of sickly smile, that had in it a mixture of humility and good-fellowship.

A kind of smile that seemed to say in reply to their last remark :

"*If you have no objection to me, I'm willing to row in with you.*"

He, however, said no more than this :

"Good health, gentlemen."

And with these words, he drank off the very smallest possible drain of liquor that remained at the bottom of his glass, and which he had evidently economised for that purpose.

Without any definite purpose in so doing, the sailors invited him to indulge in another glass.

The man immediately assented, and having refilled his pipe, and the liquor being placed before him, he, without any further hesitation, carried his glass and himself to that part of the bar where the sailors were standing, and at once opened a conversation.

"It's something," he said, "to meet a friend in times like these."

"Do you find them hard?" they inquired.

"Hard!" replied the man. "What can be harder than to have sunk so low as to have neither friends, home, nor food?"

"It isn't a very pleasant look-out," answered the sailors.

"I should think not. I've been more than once about to throw myself over London Bridge, and put an end to my life and misery together."

"Oh, don't do that," said the first mate; "never throw *yourself* overboard : wait till a strong breeze takes you, as it did our messmate in our last voyage."

"Was he blown overboard?"

"Yes, worse luck!"

"Then, I suppose you want some one in his place?"

"That's just what we do want."

"Should I do?"

"You! But you're not a sailor."

"No matter; I suppose, like others, I must have a beginning."

"Do you wish to go to sea, then?"

"There is nothing I should like so much. In fact, I don't care where I go, or what I do, to put a little money in my pocket."

The first and second mates looked at each other.

It was strange, but here seemed to be the very man they were seeking.

Poor, half-starved, reckless, ready for anything.

"I think he'd do!" whispered the first mate to his companion.

"I think so too!" was the reply.

"We'd better not be too confident. We'll get away from here, and if he seems willing to accompany us, we can sound him as we go along."

The two plotters little guessed that not one word they had uttered had escaped the eager ears of the listener.

They would have been very much astounded if the shabby man had turned round upon them and demanded peremptorily, not only to join their plot, but to have the lion's share of the spoil under penalty of unmasking the whole transaction; yet he could have done so.

But of this they knew nothing.

As a preliminary step to departure, they emptied their glasses.

Their shabby companion emptied his, and buttoned his coat across his chest, as though he intended to accompany them as a matter of course.

"We're steering some distance from here," they said.

"No matter the distance: all places are alike to him who has no home. I'll follow in your wake—that is, if you like to take me in tow."

"Certainly, mate," replied the sailors. "We'll sail in company, and if you like to come to our lodging at Tower Hill, we may be able to give you a hammock for to-night; and to-morrow, if you're in the same mind, we'll talk over matters."

This being eagerly acceded to by the man, they went out together.

The conversation that took place during their walk home still further impressed the sailors that their new acquaintance, whose name he informed them was Oliver Armstrong, was the very man to suit their purpose in every way.

The place where these worthies located themselves was a low public-house in the neighbourhood of Tower Street, where seamen were wont to congregate, and where, when their funds ran short, they could be boarded and lodged on credit, in consideration of their being satisfied with eatables and drinkables of the worst possible description, at prices more than treble their value. However, sailors are not generally over nice or particular so long as they have something to eat and drink. They rarely quarrel either about the quality of their food or the price.

On reaching this nautical retreat they soon made arrangements for the reception of their friend.

Neither of the party was inclined to go to bed; accordingly sundry vile compounds that went by the name of grog, and something in a large yellow dish that luxuriated in the title of a sea-pie, were placed upon the table.

The mates assaulted the latter with evident relish; the shabby man simply tasted a very small portion.

It might have been also observed that he held aloof from the liquors.

This caution the sailors, who were more than "half seas over," did not notice.

It is a common proverb that "as wine enters the brain the wit departs."

What must it be then with those poor heads into which the fumes of strongly adulterated poison mounts?

The two sailors had entirely lost their caution, and informed Oliver Armstrong in confidence that there was £350 on board the vessel in which they were about to sail, to be had without risk or difficulty; that the master of the ship suspected nothing; and that they had a key made from an impression in wax, that would open the locker, and place the golden prize in their hands.

To all this their listener paid profound attention, and when the sailors—no longer able to keep their equilibrium, reeled from their seats to the floor, where they lay in a profound state of torpor—he quietly requested to be shown to his bed, where he lay till a reasonable hour the next morning.

He had been up an hour before his companions of the previous night made their appearance.

When they did, however, it was in a state of much mental and bodily prostration.

It took them a long time to collect their bewildered faculties that were all in a maze.

As to their friend and future messmate, they gazed at him out of their heavy bloodshot eyes, as they would have done upon an utter stranger.

It was only by very slow degrees some faint recollections of the previous night began to dawn upon them.

They remembered the theatre, and the public-house, and the shabby man at the bar.

Then, by a great effort, they dragged their memory forward to grasp the fact that they had brought their friend home to supper.

After this their minds became a blank.

It was not till they had swallowed some copious draughts of cold water and hot coffee, that they began to recollect certain points in their overnight's conversation, that they seemed anxious to ignore altogether in the morning.

But their new messmate was not to be shaken off so easily.

He went over the whole of the words they had spoken, as though he had learned them by heart; recapitulating everything: the sum to be secured, £350, and the means by which it was to be got posses-

sion of, not forgetting the key made from the wax impression.

These assertions were all made so coolly and deliberately, that from a state of bewilderment the sailors rapidly glided into a state of alarm, and appeared resolved to repudiate the affair altogether.

As to the key, they could not be brought to entertain the idea for a moment.

This being the state of things, the shabby man, after breakfast, commenced the task of allaying their apprehensions and restoring them to a proper state of mind.

"I'm rather inclined to think you doubt me—that you're afraid to trust me," he said.

"Doubt? Afraid?" they replied. "Oh, no; why should they doubt? What had they to be afraid of?"

"It seems to me," answered Oliver Armstrong, "that you are afraid to acknowledge this morning what you said last night."

"Oh, no!" they exclaimed, "we said nothing to be afraid of."

"Certainly not; that's exactly what I wish to convince you," returned Oliver. "Surely amongst friends and messmates there should be no fear; why should there be? Is there not a mutual understanding between us? Haven't you informed me that you are John Marsh and James Bowers, first and second mates of the 'Charles,' coal brig, bound to Whitby—haven't you told me that the master's name is Allan Rushworth, and that he carries back with him the sum of £350? of which we are to possess ourselves during the voyage home, and share equally; and in order to do this, haven't you had a duplicate key made that will open the master's locker?"

Oliver paused and looked in the faces of the sailors, who sat gazing at him in speechless astonishment.

"Why," he continued, "I'm surprised that you should be so suspicious of a messmate to whom you have yourselves given all the information he possesses. If," he continued, "I really did not mean fair towards you, what more easy than for me to expose the whole plot, and hand him over this as evidence?"

As he uttered these words, he coolly drew from his pocket the duplicate key, and held it up before them.

This was a clincher.

There was no longer a loophole to escape from.

"Why," murmured the astonished mates, "who—where did you get that key?"

"It dropped from one of your pockets when you fell off your seats on the floor, and thinking it would be safer in my keeping than a stranger's I picked it up, and I think as you are so careless of such an important accessory to the success of our little scheme, I'd better take charge of it until the time arrives to make use of it."

Having said this, he restored it to his pocket.

The sailors felt particularly uncomfortable.

They could see plainly enough, in spite of the soaking their brains had had on the previous night, that they were perfectly in the power of their new friend.

However, there was no resource but to make the best of it, and to accommodate themselves to circumstances with as good a grace as possible.

"The fact is," said the first mate, "I had rather too much drink aboard last night, and my head's only just coming to its natural senses. Of course, I remember everything perfectly now, and we go in together in this affair, sink or swim."

"Swim!" remarked Oliver—"swim by all means; I don't believe in sinking."

"No, more do we," replied the sailors.

"There's £350 to divide between us," Oliver continued.

"Equally?"

"Well, suppose we say a hundred each, but the odd fifty to be given in addition to the man who actually gets possession of the money?"

"Well, that's fair enough."

"Leave it to me, then—I'll manage that; the extra risk is well worth the extra fifty."

"Decidedly! then I consider you now as one of the crew of the 'Charles.'"

"In place of Michael Bossy, who was blown overboard?"

"Yes."

"Well, then, you must fit me out with some nautical rigging; I shall never pass current in these rags."

"You shall be supplied."

"And as sailors are not generally seen with smooth

faces, I think I must trouble a masquerade emporium for a pair of false whiskers."

"That's not a bad idea; we can't be too particular to avoid suspicion."

"No, this is a suspicious world."

"Then you prefer taking charge of the key?"

"Undoubtedly, after the specimen you gave me last night of your caution."

"As you please. It matters little who keeps it since we all row in together."

And this being settled, John Marsh went out to seek for a suit of sailor's clothes for his new hand, whilst the new hand walked westward, and bought a prolific pair of black whiskers, which, with the assistance of a little colour, entirely altered his appearance.

When he had assumed his nautical gear, no one would have recognised the smart-looking sailor as the shabby man in black of the previous night, drinking gin and smoking a short pipe at the bar of a public-house in Drury Lane.

Chapter XLVIII.

THE NEW HAND.

ALLAN RUSHWORTH was glad to hear from the first mate that he had engaged a new hand in the place of Michael Bossy.

But he was more than satisfied when he saw Oliver Armstrong for the first time.

He looked taller and stronger, and more sailor-like than the drowned man, who had always a weakly and unhappy appearance.

The vessel had remained in the docks a fortnight, and it was now time to return to Whitby.

A proper quantity of ballast had been stowed away in the hold, and everything was ready for sailing.

The crew were all on board.

The master and James arrived last.

The tide being favourable, the "Charles" threaded her way through the crowd of vessels, and was soon retracing her watery path to the haven from which she had started.

Allan had, of course, written to the Brothers Walker a full account of the voyage, and named the time when he should start for his return, so that there was no anxiety in the minds of the worthy merchants.

It was a beautiful morning in May as, with a favourable wind, the coal brig passed Greenwich.

She was not so heavily-laden on her homeward voyage, and consequently her course was much more rapid.

The wind still continued favourable.

No dark clouds or fierce gales opposed, either to depress their spirits or delay their progress.

All was smooth-sailing, and everyone appeared in excellent spirits.

By noon the next day they were well out at sea, not a vestige of land was to be seen.

James lost no opportunity of making himself acquainted with every part of the vessel, and had already acquired a knowledge of many of the technical terms peculiar to nautical phraseology. He also applied himself to the acquisition of practical skill, and would climb from rope to rope with an ease and celerity that delighted the worthy master, whose great desire was that James should turn out a pupil worthy of the pains he took with him.

This wish had every prospect of being realised.

When the boy was not actually engaged in some manual occupation, it was his constant practice to watch the crew, who, from long habit and experience, appeared to be just as secure, and as much at home perched up aloft, as when they were standing on the deck.

Sometimes he fancied they seemed even more at their ease in the former position than in the latter.

But amongst the sailors, one thing struck him as peculiar, and that was, that whilst all the rest were active and agile, *one* man only appeared to do nothing.

James Cook was a very close observer, and few matters worth noticing escaped his vigilant eye.

It seemed very strange to him, therefore, that a man who seemed to be of stronger build than the rest, should never set foot in the shrouds, never take a turn at the wheel, never lend a hand at reefing a sail; in short, never, so far as he could perceive, do anything that sailors were usually expected to do.

This struck the boy as so singular that he would have liked to inquire the reason.

But he shrank from asking either of the mates or any of the crew from the fear that it might reach the ears of the man himself. He thought also if he mentioned the circumstance to Mr. Rushworth he might be looked upon as prying and inquisitive, and this consideration sealed his lips.

Another thing struck him with reference to Oliver Armstrong, and that was that John Marsh and James Bowers evidently shielded his incompetency. If any order was given either of these would hasten to execute it rather than that he should be exposed to blame.

Indeed, so well was his evident ignorance of nautical matters masked by his friends that Allan Rushworth himself was blinded to the perfect inutility of the new hand.

Now all this was to James Cook a profound mystery.

But whenever anything occurred to set the boy's brain thinking, he seldom rested till he had, by following out his train of thought, arrived at a solution of his doubts.

Since this sailor, then, had by his peculiarity fixed himself firmly in the boy's thoughts, he had been more quietly observant of him than ever.

At the same time, he fancied the man shunned his glance and avoided looking at him, so that he could never have a distinct view of his features, which nevertheless, from the transient and imperfect glimpses he could take, appeared to him not unfamiliar.

His voice he had never heard: had the man been dumb he could not have been more silent.

The more James Cook contemplated and considered this man, the more restless he became, without being able to account for the peculiar sensations that oppressed him.

He felt conscious of a depression of spirits, and a certain sinking at the heart, and yet he could not tell why.

Perhaps he hardly realised the connection between his state of feeling and the presence of this strange man, or imagined that the one had anything to do with the other.

There was nothing on board to cause any anxiety; everything was going on smoothly—prosperously.

The weather was fine, the wind fair; all the elements combined to promise a safe return to Whitby in a few days.

James's feelings were therefore to himself utterly inexplicable.

But it was not long ere the mystery was unravelled in a very unexpected and startling manner.

Whether it was that the unusual excitement that had pervaded the boy's thoughts had extended from the mind to the body, and predisposed him to indisposition, certain it is that after having passed through all the gales and storms of his first voyage without the slightest qualms, he now, in comparatively calm weather, began to feel the approaches of that most prostrating of all sensations—sea-sickness.

Most of us who have been on salt water know something of this sensation, and to those who do not, we may say in this case "ignorance is bliss."

It will be sufficient to remark, then, when this dreaded sea malady attacks the voyager, there is no resistance.

Under such circumstances, the most resolute will, the most redoubtable hero, becomes at once prostrate and has no resource but to succumb until the terrible nausea has passed away.

James Cook tried manfully for one so young to shake off the remorseless foe, but he was unable to conquer that which the great Admiral Nelson could not overcome, and in a very short time after the first qualm had seized him he was utterly prostrate.

All the gales and storms that had ever blown had no terrors for him then : he would have listened to them all with perfect indifference, not seeming to care an atom what became of him.

It was a bright, fresh morning, with a stiff breeze blowing and plenty of sea, when James Cook quietly collapsed, and was carried by Allan Rushworth, who treated him as a son, to his hammock.

Here he had no resource but to lay quietly until the violence of the attack had subsided.

This took place in the course of a few hours, when the master visited his young charge, and having administered a little brandy and hard biscuit—which restoratives seemed to agree with the patient very well—left him to repose.

James accordingly fell into a sound sleep, during which happy state of oblivion Nature kindly performed her work of restoration.

The slumber in which the boy was wrapt was long and profound.

When he awoke it was night.

All was very quiet and very dark.

His awakening was accompanied by the pleasing consciousness that the horrible qualms from which he had suffered had entirely disappeared, and that save a slight sense of weakness, which was not enough to be painful, he was as well as usual.

But at the same time that his bodily sensations were those of perfect comfort and tranquillity, there was still that unaccountable mental depression hanging over him.

It was particularly strange, too, in his case.

We can understand men, who are enduring the wear-and-tear struggle of life, with their aspirations and ambitions often leading them out of the strict path of right, to find at their journey's end disappointment, and often remorse, suffering from such depressions, as they journey onwards.

But for this boy, whose career had only just begun—begun, too, so auspiciously—after all his earlier vicissitudes, on whose head rested neither care nor responsibility, and who was regarded with fatherly care by his employers—for *him* to feel as he did, was something out of the usual course of events.

Nevertheless, it was a fact he *did* feel as perhaps no boy of ten years and a half had ever felt before.

He would have closed his eyes and slumbered on as the readiest means of getting rid of his thoughts, but he found it impossible to sleep again—he had already slept some hours.

He could only lay awake and *think.*

Nothing reached his ears but the sound of the waves as they dashed against the vessel's side, and the gusts of wind as they flew hurrying and whistling through the rigging.

But there was nothing unusual in this.

He knew well enough by this time that these were perfectly natural sounds to expect at sea, and there was nothing in such to awaken any apprehension.

But even whilst he was thus reflecting, a murmuring sound of voices fell upon his ear.

At first indistinctly—but gradually he became certain they were the voices of men speaking.

This circumstance on board a vessel need not have been considered particularly remarkable.

Neither, perhaps, would James have thought it so, had not *one* voice in particular arrested his attention.

Yes—*that one voice!*

It seemed to rise suddenly above the rest for the express purpose of catching his ear, after which it died away in the general murmur.

That voice, so unpleasantly familiar.

Without a moment's further hesitation, he lowered himself from his hammock to the ground and listened.

Yes, surely there could be no mistaking those tones, and yet so strangely and startlingly did they fall upon his ear, that he was almost inclined to imagine he must be dreaming.

He accordingly gave himself a vigorous shake, and an energetic rubbing of the head with both his hands, in order to dispel any nightmareish illusions that might be disposed to hang about him, and listened again.

He strained his ear to catch, if possible, some of the words uttered.

But his efforts were unsuccessful.

The sounds were muffled, as though proceeding from some closely-shut chamber, and from the confused murmurs that reached him nothing could be gathered.

He went out of the small box—it was scarcely worth calling a cabin—in which his hammock was slung, and following the sounds, traced them until he came to a spot, beneath which it was evident enough the speakers were concealed.

All was profoundly dark.

It was, perhaps, on this account that James, being unable to see, felt his other senses more vividly acute.

He felt certain that the party, whoever they were, were beneath him.

Kneeling down, and passing his hand softly over the floor, he soon traced the square aperture of a trap.

The door was closed, and it was this circumstance that so deadened the sounds within.

As he moved his hand, he felt a ring that lay flat in the trap lid.

He longed to grasp this ring and raise it; his hand already touched it for thât purpose, but he paused ere he did so.

Should he be seen—as he most likely would be—by those beneath, what excuse could he make for being there?

Would it not seem despicably mean to be prying about in the dark, and eavesdropping, without any excuse to assign for being there?

Would he not bring on him the hatred of the whole crew?

He felt at a standstill.

Nothing was further from James Cook's disposition than meanness or artifice, and he could not bear the idea of even a suspicion of such attributes clinging to him.

"What right have I to be here at all listening to their conversation, when after all they may be engaged in some business necessary to the safety of the ship?"

True, it was night; but what of that? Sailors' hours were any hours—at any moment, night or day, they were liable to be called upon, so there was nothing extraordinary in the hour.

He was beginning to feel ashamed of his suspicions when the *voice* which he had forgotten suddenly darted again with full vividness into his memory.

That one voice!

It was speaking again.

James placed his ear to the ground with uncontrollable eagerness, and listened as though his very life depended upon his catching the words spoken.

This time he was more successful.

He did succeed in hearing the two last—

"*Done to-night!*"

Now these words appeared to James Cook sufficiently significant to whet his appetite to learn more.

His suspicions began once more to gallop along at full speed.

"What is to be done to-night?" he thought.

Not being able to see the speakers, he could not judge from the expression of their features whether the deed in contemplation was some act of duty, or some nefarious plot that demanded darkness and secrecy to mature it.

The trap-door was at his feet.

He once more grasped the iron ring.

It might prove a hazardous experiment, but he felt he could not resist the impulse that prompted him to raise the trap softly, and look down into the cavity below.

He paused an instant in indecision, but the intense desire he experienced could not be controlled.

He raised the trap very softly a few inches, and through the aperture he beheld, by the light of a lamp that hung suspended from above, and shed its rays upon their features, John Marsh, James Bowers, and last, not least, the *new hand*, whose utter incapacity had so perplexed him.

The mystery was now a mystery no longer; for this man had laid aside his false whiskers, and now, with the light of the lantern falling upon his head and face, James Cook recognised the wandering reprobate, Octavius Challoner.

[JAMES COOK AT THE CABIN WINDOW.]

Chapter XLIX.

MOMENTS OF PERIL.

IT seemed hardly credible that it could be he, yet in opposition to incredibility, there he was.

It was with the utmost difficulty James restrained himself from uttering an exclamation of horror.

His first impulse was to feel for the bolt of the trap to fasten them down, but there was none. His next was to dash down the trap, and fly from the spot.

At one time of his life he would perhaps have done so, but experience had taught him self-control and caution.

Besides, at that moment, there was a strong necessity that his presence should not be suspected.

The presence of Octavius on board that boat he at once instinctively accepted as an evil omen—a presage of danger.

The ominous words " done to-night !" flashed before him in the dark in warning characters, though to what peril the warning pointed he was at a loss to guess, and mystery and doubt still reigned triumphant.

James remained in the same kneeling position he had assumed, like one suddenly petrified, scarcely daring to move or breathe, lest he should betray his presence.

Was he for ever to be haunted by this evil spirit ?

Was there no place where he could be free from his presence ?

Did he follow him by sea, as well as by land ?

It was inexplicable—almost supernal.

The three men who were shrouded in the hold at James's feet were too much occupied with the immediate subject of their conversation to heed aught besides.

Otherwise, they might have noticed that the trap-door over their heads was partially raised, and that a pair of bright and intensely anxious eyes were looking down upon them, as though eager to read their very thoughts.

But of this fact they had no suspicion.

They continued their conversation, and their eager and unsuspected listener could now hear every syllable that fell from their lips.

"Well," said the first mate, addressing himself to the counterfeit Oliver Armstrong, "we've managed pretty well with you altogether in having blinded the master's eyes to the fact that you're as rank a land-lubber as ever stepped on board good oak."

"Umph!" replied Octavius, with a sneer, "you sailors are always complimentary to the rest of the world when you're on salt water; but you're a poor helpless set of victims on *terra firma*. No landsman can be ever so utterly helpless at sea as a sailor amongst the shoals and quicksands ashore. The shark is the terror of the seas he inhabits; but roll him over high and dry upon the beach and he is a shark no longer. Be good enough in your conversation to keep to the point, and do not indulge in remarks that may prove offensive; and now go on."

Octavius was nettled at the contemptuous manner in which the first mate alluded to his ignorance of nautical matters; and as he had a profound contempt for John Marsh and James Bowers, whom he looked upon merely as his tools, he thus endeavoured to bring them to a sense of inferiority.

Perhaps they saw that their new companion was out of humour, and did not wish to create any ill-feeling; at all events, John Marsh said in a tone calculated to conciliate:

"I didn't mean any offence, friend Oliver; but what I was going to say is, that the master's pretty sharp, and I think we'd better manage this job before his eyes are opened and his suspicions aroused."

"I agree with you there; the sooner the better," answered Octavius; "and I think, at the same time, you ought to thank your lucky stars that threw a man like myself in the way to help you in your difficulty, especially since from what I can judge of you two, you could never possibly have managed it without."

The two mates murmured something that was inaudible, but beyond that made no reply.

"And now, then," continued Octavius, "since you are for immediate action, what's your plan?" he inquired.

"To wait patiently," said John Marsh, to whom the question was put, "till Mr. Rushworth comes on deck, which he's sure to do in the course of half an hour; then to descend the hatchway, slip into his cabin, unlock the locker with the duplicate key I had made, and which ——"

"Is in my possession." Octavius could not forbear reminding his comrades of the coolness with which he had obtained and kept possession of this important implement from the commencement of their acquaintance.

"And then," continued the first mate, in rather a surly tone (the matter of the key annoyed him), "all you have to do is to clap your hand upon the gold, slip it into your pocket, re-lock the locker, and get off as quickly as possible, leaving everything as you found it."

"And you're quite sure," asked Octavius, "that the £350, the price of the shipload of coal, is in this locker? Let's have no mistake about that."

"Certain," returned the mate, "he always keeps his money in the locker in a canvas bag. I've seen him stow it away there often, when he hasn't suspected I was looking. It was that first put it into my mind to get hold of a little."

"A very good idea, too. Well, and after I've got the gold what then?" Octavius inquired, as if desiring to be guided implicitly by his instructor.

"You'll come up on deck as soon as possible, but keep out of the master's way," directed the mate; "as soon as he's made his observations, he'll retire to rest again, suspecting nothing, and we can then lower the boat and be off with the booty, leaving the vessel to shift for herself."

"I comprehend perfectly," said Octavius.

"If this affair is managed properly we shall have no difficulty in getting off, and with a nice little sum each in our possession, without trouble and bloodshed."

This last reflection seemed to be a great comfort to the first mate, and to act as a sort of moral equipoise, by means of which he counterbalanced his deed and his conscience.

But all this time we must not forget that our friend James had been listening to the foregoing conversation.

We may imagine the shock this intelligence conveyed to the boy's mind, coming as it did at that moment, and for the first time upon him.

It was like one blow following another in rapid succession.

First he had discovered that a remorseless, wicked man, who had proved himself a most dangerous and determined foe, was within a few yards of him, at a time when he could have been certain hundreds of miles interposed between them.

Next he had learnt that this man, in conjunction with others, was in league to rob and then desert the ship.

Certainly the plot was to be carried out without bloodshed, and so far the crime would have amounted only to robbery, unless the desertion, being followed by the loss of the vessel, with what lives were on her, attached to it a more awful title.

James Cook had acquired a sufficient knowledge of Allan Rushworth's character to judge of probable results.

He had seen enough of the master under trying circumstances, to know that he was not the sort of man to suffer his employer's money to be wrested from him by a gang of scoundrels without resistance.

And in case it came to this, what then?

It was such an unequal struggle, he pictured in his own mind, and naturally enough dreaded.

Though he had only overheard three actually discussing the contemplated robbery, how did he know but that the rest of the crew (they were only five in all besides the master and himself) were implicated in this design?

If so, what possible hope of escape could there be for one man opposed to five?

All these thoughts rushed tumultuously through his brain, as he still knelt there in the dark, holding the door of the trap a little open.

He was recalled to himself by the voice of the first mate.

"You'd better get on deck, hadn't you?" he said to Octavius; "it will look like vigilance when the master makes his appearance."

"Vigilance!" sneered Octavius, with a scorn he could not repress. "You're not more than half awake. The briny exhalations have obscured your faculties, or you would see the impolicy of a *land lubber* like myself getting into the master's way, especially after the efforts I have made since we started to keep out of it."

The mates saw at once that their sarcastic companion was right, and John Marsh replied:

"True, true; I forgot myself. On second thoughts, keep below—don't show yourself. If the master ordered you to shift a sail, or haul a rope, your inability to do either might lead him to suspect, and perhaps, cause a hitch at the last moment."

The mate said this with some gusto. It was a little retaliation for some of Octavius's spiteful remarks.

"It's settled, then, that you'll stay below, and I'll let you know as soon as Mr. Rushworth leaves his cabin."

"Don't forget!" said Octavius, with his usual sneer.

"Trust me!" returned John Marsh, with a grin.

This was too good a joke to be lightly passed over.

The second mate, James Bowers, joined his companion, and indulged in a slight ebullition of mirth.

The idea of forgetting anything that would lead to the possession of a hundred pounds was simply ridiculous.

"I don't think there's anything else to settle, is there?" asked the second mate, when their mirth had fully subsided.

There was a momentary pause, and then Octavius, fixing his dark eyes upon his companions, said, with marked emphasis:

" There's *one* other thing I should like to settle !"

" What ?" they both inquired.

" That boy you call James Cook !" he replied, sinking his voice, but with savage intensity.

" Ah !" echoed the two mates, " that boy !"

" I doubt him," continued Octavius, " and I advise you to be on your guard. I've noticed his eyes fixed upon me since the moment we left London. He suspects something, I'm certain."

" So I fancy," joined in the second mate, nervously.

" Let him suspect !" added John Marsh ; " he can prove nothing. But even if he could, he's down to-night ill—sick as a dog. He's been having brandy and hard biscuit, pretty dear, and he'll be fast asleep, for certain. We take care of our apprentices, I can tell you, mate. I wonder if *we* should have brandy, if we turned a little qualmish ?"

The second mate laughed, as he usually did at the first mate's jokes.

" No, no," John Marsh went on, in a tone of much assurance, " before he wakes we shall be miles off. To tell you the truth, since you've touched upon the subject," he continued, " I never liked that boy from the first minute I clapped eyes on him, and I've been particularly careful what I did before him ; his eyes are like two gimlets. But on one point I've made up my mind, if,"—he emphasized the little word vengefully—" he thrusts his nose in the way, or comes with his sharp eyes prying into our affairs, I'll give him a quick fling to the fishes before he has time to say Jack Robinson !"

As this cold-blooded determination reached James's ears, he thought of his friend Ikey' s warning, and how his suspicions had fastened upon the first mate.

" Dear Ikey was right," he murmured to himself, a cold shudder passing through his frame.

" To make sure, as I go on deck," said John Marsh, " I'll look in and see that Allan Rushworth's pet's safe in his hammock."

There was a general move at this.

James had only just time to close the trap and retreat hastily, before it was raised again and a glimmering light appeared through the aperture.

The boy cautiously crept back to his hammock, and scrambled into it, as it was absolutely necessary he should be found in it, in order to avoid suspicion.

With a beating heart he listened to the approaching footsteps.

He lay perfectly still, as the first mate looked in and held up the lantern to reconnoitre the sleeper.

The result of the investigation seemed perfectly satisfactory.

" All right !" he heard the man say, " sound as a church."

The light disappeared, the footsteps moved away, and all was dark again.

James heard the first mate say in a low tone :

" Wait there till I give the signal."

To which the voice of Octavius answered in a tone of acquiescence, " Ay, ay !"

The mates then ascended to the deck, and James Cook felt painfully conscious that the plot was going on, and that he was in close proximity to his enemy.

He knew that that enemy was lounging on the steps in the dark, waiting his summons ; he could hear his deep, regular breathing.

The thought then crossed James's mind what would be his best course to pursue ?

His obvious duty was to warn the master of the nefarious design in contemplation.

But it was easier to feel that he ought to do this than to do it.

There were almost insurmountable difficulties in the way.

First, his retreat was cut off, there being no way of gaining the deck but by passing Octavius, who would inevitably have seen him ; and from the opinions he had heard expressed both by him and the mates, he was fully conscious of the fate that awaited him, had he attempted to thwart their plans.

What could he do ? He, a mere boy !

He lay in a state of mingled apprehension and indecision, and could feel his heart throbbing violently against his ribs, as he thought how the occurrences of that night *might* terminate.

But with all this inward excitement, it was not alone the fear of personal danger that so oppressed him.

Of course the idea of a violent death had in it, as it always has, something terrible.

But only for a moment.

James Cook had always endeavoured to do his duty, and in this emergency he offered a brief but earnest prayer to Heaven for guidance and protection.

He did not therefore feel alone ; he realised an outstretched, powerful arm over his head, that could, if it so willed, ward off every danger that threatened him.

His position, trying as it was, did not overpower him.

But his principal anxiety was for his friend, Allan Rushworth.

The kindness he had shown towards James during their short acquaintanceship had won the boy's heart, and he felt far more solicitous on the master's account than on his own.

He would have given the world to be able to warn him.

But then that such warning should be of service it was necessary it should be conveyed secretly.

The plotters should know nothing of it.

To reach the master's cabin, he would have to ascend to the deck and go down another hatchway.

But how was this to be accomplished when the man he had most cause to dread was lounging across the only way by which the deck could be reached ?

Yes ! there was Octavius Challoner, once more disguised in his black whiskers, whistling in a whisper, in a somewhat impatient and nervous manner, waiting for the signal from his comrades.

As this did not appear to arrive immediately, he " phew'd !" and " psha'd !" and gave other indications of growing impatience.

His fingers were itching to touch the money.

He longed to feel the canvas bag containing the £350 in his grasp.

The sensation increased with every instant, until at last, unable longer to endure the suspense, he ascended the steps gradually.

First his head peered up cautiously, then his shoulders, and gradually his body, until he was all but on deck.

James could hear him crawling up the stairs, and could almost interpret the feelings that prompted him.

" Now or never," he felt, was the time.

In an instant he had lowered himself from his hammock, and was cautiously looking from the door.

He watched the dark form of Octavius disappear as it stepped forth on to the deck.

James followed instantly, but in spite of his haste, when he reached the top, Octavius had disappeared.

This circumstance was a matter of congratulation, and as it was his plan to reach Mr. Rushworth's cabin, he darted to the ship's side and crept along under the shadow of the bulwarks.

Thus far he had succeeded beyond his most sanguine expectations, and was congratulating himself on being able to accomplish the design he had in view, when he came full butt against some one, who was, like himself, crouching at the ship's side.

The man immediately seized him roughly, and in an angry whisper, which James recognised at once as the voice of Octavius, demanded, with savage haste :

" What are you doing here ?"

It was indeed a moment of peril.

James knew he was in the grasp of his enemy, and in his excitement answered—not, perhaps, over wisely —by a similar question :

" What are *you* doing here ?"

He was sorry the moment the words had passed his lips, but they were past recall.

The man whom he had thus questioned, replied in a harsh whisper :

" What's that to you, and what do you mean by sneaking about here, you prying young hound, eh ?"

" I'm not sneaking about, neither am I a prying hound," returned James, boldly, trying, but vainly, to disengage himself from the grasp of his antagonist.

" I've noticed you watching me ever since I joined the ship," hissed the fictitious sailor, under his breath, " and I'm glad I've got hold of you at last just to ask you why ?"

He tightened his grip of the boy's collar venomously as he spoke.

" Why ?" he repeated.

" You needn't tear my coat off my back," cried

James, indignant at the assault, and still struggling to release himself, but disdaining to cry out.

"Stand still!" growled his brutal assailant, "or I'll not only tear your coat off your back, but your heart out of your body."

He held him to the spot by main force as he spoke.

"Go to your hammock at once, and remain there," came forth gratingly from between his closed teeth; "and, harkye," he continued, "if I see your eyes fixed on me again, look out for yourself. I'm not in the habit of being scrutinized by coal heavers' apprentice boys, and if I catch you at it from this time, I'll cure you of the habit as sure as my name's Oliver Armstrong!"

This caution, fiercely delivered, was wound up by a furious shaking.

James, irritated at the unprovoked assault, was roused rather than subdued.

"Take care what you do," he gasped, excitedly, "or I may prove that your name is *not* Oliver Armstrong!"

"What do you mean, whelp? Do you dare to say it is not?"

"Yes! I dare to say it is not!" James replied, boldly—"I dare to say you're no sailor at all, but an impostor—instead of being Oliver Armstrong, you are Squire Markham's nephew, Octavius Challoner!"

As the excited boy concluded, he made a snatch at the false whiskers his prosecutor wore, and tore them from his face.

There was not much surprise in the mind of Octavius at James's words.

He had felt convinced at the first that he had been recognised.

But that this poor boy, whom he had been accustomed to treat as the very dregs of humanity, should dare to oppose him, to threaten, and to strip him of his disguise, roused all the bad blood in his bad nature.

As the scoundrel's eye flashed down upon the lad in the dark, it wore a murderous gleam.

Could James Cook have seen that bitter glance, he might have said "farewell" to hope.

The wretch bent forward and hissed like a venomous snake in the boy's ear:

"From this moment it shall be out of your power to babble any of your wonderful secrets into human ear! What you have, keep—keep till doomsday!"

He sprang up as he spoke with the savage fury of a wild beast, and wound his arms around his victim.

There was a slight scuffle of feet heard, a faint cry, a splash, and Octavius Challoner stood alone leaning against the ship's side.

The next moment he was skulking back in the shadow to his former post.

Chapter L.

STARTLING INTELLIGENCE.

THE first mate began to be anxious for the captain's appearance on deck.

He paced to and fro, and at length, looking down the steps, at the bottom of which he had left Octavius, said in a low voice:

"The master's late to night."

"So it seems," was the reply.

"Is that boy quiet, still?" he asked.

"Oh, yes, he's quiet enough, he'll never trouble anyone any more," answered Octavius, in a peculiar tone.

Indeed, so strangely were the words uttered, that it caused John Marsh to open his eyes.

"What d'ye mean?" he asked, "you haven't——"

"Never mind what I *haven't*—bend your head down, and I'll you what I *have* done."

"What?" inquired the mate, in a tone of some apprehension.

"I've done what you promised to do, given him a quick fling to the fishes."

Had it not been dark, John Marsh might have been observed to turn very pale.

He was one of those men who was fond of talking, but his words were ever in advance of his deeds.

To speak the truth, the first mate coveted the gold, but shrank from purchasing it at the price of blood.

"Haven't you been hasty?" he asked, in a faltering voice.

"Yes, I have," answered Octavius, candidly. "The young spy dogged my steps; I met him on deck, close to the ship's side, he was insolent, and I hurled him over; I never performed any act more hastily."

Whatever John Marsh might have thought of his cold-blooded accomplice, he said but little; the new hand, however, appeared to him the sort of man he would not care to sail with a second time.

"It's not unlikely," he remarked, after a pause, "that Mr. Rushworth may want to see the boy, as he's been ill, before he turns in for the night; should he do so, what's to be done?"

"Why, he won't be able to find him, that's all," replied Octavius, coolly.

"But he'll make inquiries of us."

"Well, we shall know nothing, of course."

"You're the coolest hand I ever met in my life!"

"For a land lubber, eh?"

"For any lubber, land or sea," returned the mate. "I never heard a man talk like you, just after committing a——" He paused, for the thought struck him, that the word he had intended using might prove offensive, and he had in a brief space of time learned to look upon Octavius as a desperate character.

"Well," he continued, branching off suddenly in another direction, "if Mr. Rushworth should want to see the apprentice, we must make the best of it; but it's very awkward and——"

"Psha!" interrupted Octavius, irritably, "tell him the boy's all snug and sound asleep, he'll not wish to disturb him. Throw something into the empty hammock and cover it with a jacket; you've no brains at all."

The mate did not venture to dispute this fact, and went off to perform some duty at the other end of the vessel, leaving Octavius still on the watch for the signal.

Very early in the evening on which the events just narrated transpired, Allan Rushworth sat in his cabin.

The business that had taken him to London on his employer's behalf had been satisfactorily concluded, the cargo landed and paid for.

The ship had withstood the fury of a violent gale that had threatened destruction, and was now making her homeward voyage steadily and pleasantly.

Allan Rushworth lived at Whitby, and though a sailor, was sufficiently domesticated for a landsman.

He was married, but had no family; but he nevertheless rejoiced when from time to time his duties permitted him to spend a few days at home in the society of his wife, to whom he was fondly attached.

Allan was, on this particular evening, in that complacent humour which men experience when for some brief halcyon interval care and anxiety seem to disappear, and the affairs of life go on just as they would have them.

The master was occupying himself in drawing up a written plan for James's improvement; a programme of the course of study, which, in his opinion, was best adapted to the boy's future.

In this benevolent task, time flew on, but he continued very pleasantly at his work, until he had made his arrangements to his satisfaction.

Then he arose, opened his locker in which he placed his papers and writing materials, and in which snugly reposed the canvas bag containing the £350.

After this he drew forth a bottle of Hollands and a glass, which he partly filled.

He then took down from a nail on the wall an old-fashioned Dutch pipe of carved wood, that had been given him years back by a worthy citizen of Amsterdam, and which had been his constant companion at home and abroad ever since.

Having filled this, he lit a small spirit lamp, from one of oil that hung from the ceiling, and placed it in a groove on the table before him.

The next moment the fragrant odour of the Virginian weed floated through the cabin, and Allan Rushworth settled himself in his chair for a smoke and a think—aided and abetted by an occasional sip at the Hollands.

It was not often he thus indulged himself; but the best of men have their weakness, and it was in one of these moods that Allan found himself on this particular evening.

As he thus sat, his thoughts naturally at the onset roamed to his sunny little cottage at Whitby, with its white walls and trim garden, and its quickset hedges; and then his imagination went on to picture a pretty dark-eyed woman, who sat in the parlour at work, ever and anon pausing to listen to the passing breeze, that reminded her of her husband at sea.

"Ah, well!" he ejaculated, "I shall see my old girl again in a couple more days."

Then his thoughts wandered to James.

"Strange," he said to himself, "so well as he was through all that storm, that he should have knocked up in this fine weather. Ah, well," he continued, as he puffed his pipe and sipped his Hollands, "we must all have a taste of it sooner or later. Ugh! I remember making its acquaintance myself. It's an ugly visitor!"

Allan took an extra sip to wash down the unpleasant recollection.

"The boy will be better to-morrow," he said, cheerfully, "the sickness once stopped, as it has, with a little sleep and quiet, 'Richard will be himself again'. I dare say he's as sound as a church now, I shall look in at him when I go on deck."

He puffed a few seconds at his Dutch pipe, and took another sip at the Hollands, and then soliloquized again.

"He's a good boy! a fine boy!" exclaimed the master, in a tone of enthusiasm; "how proud I should be if I could call him my son; he's fit for something better than a grimy coal brig. Yes, yes, he and his companion ought to have changed places."

"The navy should have been his destination—not that I want to part with him. I like the boy! I love him! and I'm only speaking as respects his interests. Ah, well! five years rambling about with coals will teach him to navigate the channel, and that's something, and in the meantime he can study mathematics, so that if a chance does come in his way, he'll be able to take advantage of it; I'm sure the Brothers Walker wouldn't stand in the way of his advancement, I'm sure they wouldn't!"

The good master became so absorbed in his contemplations, that as the smoke rose from his pipe, he could almost fancy James in an admiral's uniform, standing on the deck of a frigate in the heat of an engagement.

"I said so—I said so!" he murmured.

Gradually, however, the vision became more indistinct.

The quaint old Dutch pipe slipped from the master's lips on to the floor; the master's head sank upon his broad chest, and he slept.

It was a very unusual thing for him to sleep out of his regular hours, but who can account for the variations of this most complicated and variable machine, the human body.

Perhaps it was the happy state of mind in which Allan Rushworth then happened to be, that thus wafted him to the land of dreams.

Perhaps the old Dutch pipe, and the small quantum of Hollands he had sipped, helped to produce this effect.

No matter what it was, the master of the "Charles" not only slept, but slept, as the saying is, like a top.

The hours passed on, and still the placid slumber continued.

Suddenly, however, the spell was broken.

Allan broke the chains that held him, and started from his sleep.

He listened for an instant as though he had heard some unusual sound.

Was it fancy, or was it a cry and a splash in the waves, that had roused him?

He rubbed his eyes, stretched himself, turned up the lamp, and was by that time wide awake, and in full possession of all his faculties.

He smiled as the old-fashioned brown face of his pipe looked up at him from the floor.

"Ah! I see," he exclaimed, as he stooped to raise it, "I've been asleep and dreaming."

He placed it on the table, drained his last sip of Hollands, and looked at his watch.

It was near midnight.

"So late!" he ejaculated. "It's time to go on deck and see after my boy, though I'll be bound he's right enough."

As he spoke he went to the door and placed his hand upon the handle, merely throwing his eye round the cabin previous to going out.

He was half way out at the door, when a slight noise at the window caused him to pause.

It was a strange noise—particularly strange, or it would not have arrested his attention.

It was no uncommon occurrence for the waves to dash up against this window, but the sounds that caused him to stop so abruptly were different.

"What can that be?" he ejaculated, hurriedly.

He re-entered the cabin and stood listening, holding the handle of the door in his hand.

The next moment the sounds came again.

This time they were like some one tapping at the window.

Allan hastily closed the door, and was about to advance, but started back suddenly ere he was half way across the cabin, with a scared look upon his features, as he caught sight of a white face looking in at him from without the window.

There are certain times and seasons when, from circumstances, we are all more or less inclined to yield to the influence of the terrible and the marvellous.

It was so with Allan Rushworth at this moment.

He was usually a brave and determined man; yet now he felt inclined to yield to the very superstition he had lately condemned, and to tremble at the supposed presence of some incorporeal visitant.

He could feel the drops standing on his forehead.

It must be Michael Bossy's spirit, restless and wandering in space, that he gazed upon.

These were, of course, only the first thoughts that attacked the master, and these passed through his distempered brain with the rapidity of lightning.

But they as quickly disappeared.

The healthy tone of his mind returned, and he was able to scout the idea of supernatural visitants.

"It is absurd! ridiculous!" he exclaimed, and advancing towards the window, he threw it open.

A startled cry broke from his lips at the sight that met his gaze.

 A spirit direct from the immaterial world could not have more utterly astounded Allan Rushworth than did the dripping form of James Cook, as it clung to the framework of the window.

"Good Heavens!" cried the startled man, "it is impossible! it can't be James!"

The gasping cry of the poor boy went straight to Allan's heart, as he darted forward and drew him in, drenched and shivering with cold, to the hospitable shelter of the cabin.

"My dear, dear boy!" he exclaimed, "am I dreaming still, or is it really you I hold in my arms?"

"It is I," said James. "I never thought I should see you, or anyone else again," and the poor boy burst into tears.

"You are alive, safe, unhurt?" eagerly inquired the master.

"Yes," answered James.

"Thank Heaven for that!" exclaimed Allan, fervently; "but you are shivering, you are cold!"

"I am," James replied, his teeth chattering as he essayed to speak.

"You shall soon be warm, I'll call——"

"No one, dear Allan," cried James—"call no one; bolt the door, I have much to tell you."

The boy's words were so earnest, that the master walked at once to the door, carrying him in his arms, and bolted it.

"And now, before you say another word, these drenched things must be taken off," cried Allan.

He placed James for a moment in his chair, and took from his locker a bottle of brandy.

He made him drink a small quantity, and then rubbed his neck and chest with the spirit.

After this, he stripped off his dripping garments, and dried him with a coarse towel.

He then hurried him into a dry suit of clothes, with the addition of a thick jacket of his own.

All this had been but the work of a few moments, but James felt the benefit of his kind attentions.

A sensation of warmth spread over all his limbs, and as Allen took him in his arms and nursed him there as he would have done an infant, the boy was in a genial glow, and feeling like a child safe in his father's embrace.

"And now," inquired the master, as he looked down upon him with kind solicitude, "let me hear what you have to tell me—that is, if you feel strong enough."

"Quite!" James answered. "There's a plot on board!"

"A plot?" echoed the astonished master.

"Yes, sir, to rob you and desert the ship."

"My dear boy!" exclaimed Allan; "are you certain of this—are you sure you're not dreaming?"

"I am certain, quite certain—I am speaking the truth," affirmed James.

Mr. Rushworth looked at him in a bewildered manner, as though he could not quite make up his mind that the boy's attack, or disaster, had not in some way deranged his faculties.

"I do not doubt for a moment," said Allan, "that you believe what you are saying to be true—but are you sure you are not yourself deceived?"

"I am positive I am not, sir; I overheard all from the lips of the men themselves. I was roused by voices as I lay in my hammock, and one voice in particular, that I fancied I recognised, made me get up and listen."

The master grew intensely interested.

"What did you hear?" he asked, eagerly.

"You know the new hand that joined the ship in the place of Michael Bossy?"

"Yes, perfectly—Oliver Armstrong."

"He is not Oliver Armstrong, but a very cruel, wicked man. He is here on board under an assumed name, and is no sailor at all; the whiskers he wears are false, as false as his name, which, instead of being Oliver Armstrong, is Octavius Challoner."

"Is it possible?" cried the master.

"He and some others know that you have £350 in gold in your locker there," James continued, "and they mean to steal it."

The master's cheek turned slightly pale for an instant, and his heart beat quicker at this unpalatable intelligence, but he restrained his emotion.

"Go on, my boy," he said, calmly.

"The first mate has taken an impression of your key in wax, and had one made in London exactly like it."

"The scoundrel!" muttered Allan.

"As soon as you go on deck," James continued, "this new hand, that calls himself Oliver Armstrong, is to enter this cabin, open the locker with the duplicate key, and remove the bag of gold."

The captain clenched his hands fiercely, as though he fancied himself at that instant struggling for his master's property.

Had the conspirators seen the determined expression of his features, they would have been, perhaps, a little anxious as to the result in case of detection.

"And when they have the gold, what then?" asked the master, with nervous intensity.

"They'll wait till you go to rest, and then they'll go off with it in the boat," answered James.

"And how many are there in this plot?" inquired Allan.

"The first and second mate and the new hand were all I heard."

"But Jackson and Blake may be implicated," soliloquised rather than answered the master. "Yes, I'm afraid they're all in it, and five to one is long odds."

He remained silent a moment, and then suddenly, as though with a fresh recollection, said to James:

"But you have not told me yet about yourself: how was it I found you clinging to the rail outside this cabin window? Did you fall overboard?"

"No, sir," replied James, in a low voice, that betrayed a shudder, "I was *thrown* overboard!"

"Thrown!" ejaculated the master, "by whom?"

"The new hand, Octavius Challoner," answered James.

"By him?"

"Yes. I was coming to warn you of what I had heard, when he stopped me, and almost tore the clothes from my back. He hated me, and had tried to kill me once before; he knew that I recognised him then, and when I threatened to expose him, he caught me up in his arms like a fury, and dashed me over the ship's side into the sea."

"The murderous, cowardly wretch!" exclaimed the master; "but by what miracle were you preserved?" he inquired, looking with eyes of wonder at the boy.

"I hardly know," replied James. "I suppose when I was caught up, I stretched out my hands to cling to anything that might be in the way. Providentially I must have grasped a piece of loose rope, for when I plunged into the waves, I remember feeling something in my grasp, and that I was being dragged quickly through the water. I pulled myself along with all the strength I had till I came to the surface, and was able to breathe. I then found myself close to the ship's side, and under the window of your cabin; I saw a light there, and when I felt I had recovered my strength a little, I pulled myself up till I reached the railing, through which I thrust one arm, whilst I twisted the rope round the wrist of the other. You heard me tapping, and opened the window just in time to save me, for I could not have held on much longer."

"Poor boy—poor boy!" murmured the master, whose voice was hoarse with indignation and emotion, "and this inhuman monster would have murdered you in cold blood!"

His voice failed him as he pressed James to his heart, whilst the tears trickled down his cheeks.

"Heaven has preserved you, my dear lad," said Allan at length, "and the same Power can, and I believe will exert itself to preserve us still and the property of my employers, which these cowardly thieves seek to possess."

"But there are so many against you," James remarked.

"True, there are. But tell me, were any of my crew, besides that rascally new hand, concerned in the attempt against your life?"

"None! they were not near at the time; that was entirely the work of Octavius Challoner," James replied.

"It will come home to the ruffian!" said the indignant man, "no shedder of innocent blood ever escapes."

"Don't think of me!" urged James eagerly; "think of yourself and the ship."

"Yes—yes, my boy," murmured Allan, thoughtfully, "I—I am thinking."

The captain was hastily calculating chances — his position.

He had his master's vessel and property to protect. This was the first consideration.

Open resistance against five men, desperate and eager for plunder, would have been in all probability to sacrifice all.

That would have been worse than madness.

There was only one course of procedure that promised success.

The plotters sought only plunder.

The canvas bag with its contents, was the extent of their desires. That secured they would depart.

Allan Rushworth's mind was made up, he resolved to give them the length of their tether.

They should have the canvas bag.

As for the vessel, he would trust to Providence for its safety.

The master having thus decided upon his course of action immediately began to carry it out

Chapter LI.

AN UNEXPECTED RESULT.

HE opened his locker and removed from it whatever spirits it contained.

This did not amount to more than a bottle of brandy, and a case containing four bottles of schiedam, the master's favourite liquor.

These he placed in a chest fastened by an iron staple to the wall.

Several empty bottles he left untouched.

He remained some time at the locker preparing for the reception of his visitors.

At length all his arrangements were completed.

Whatever he had taken out of the locker he locked up securely in the chest, placing the key in a secret corner of the cabin, where no one but himself could find it.

He then turned to James.

"Now, my boy," said he, "as you are supposed to be dead, you must be kept out of sight."

He pointed to a kind of recess, or bunk, in the wall of the cabin, saying, at the same time:

"That is my bed; I think you cannot do better than stow yourself away there; your presence in such a place will be entirely unsuspected."

He held open the curtain with one hand, and giving James a friendly squeeze of the shoulder, the boy sprang in, and nestled down in its remotest recesses.

"You have nothing to fear now," said Allan; "I shall not be long away. Should, however, anything occur to render it necessary, if you call, I shall hear your voice."

The master then examined the primings of his pistols, which he had recently loaded, and turning down the oil lamp till it gave only a faint light, went on deck.

James was now alone.

As he lay coiled up in his snug retreat he could hardly realize his situation.

But a short time before struggling with suffocating waves, now once more snatched as it were from the jaws of death, and enjoying the luxurious consciousness of warmth and security.

He lay in momentary expectation of the entrance of the man who had sought his life, but he felt no fear of him.

So conscious must Octavius have been of his destruction, that even had he seen him, he would have believed him to be a spirit rather than an inhabitant of this world.

With this assurance he waited with curiosity, rather than apprehension, for the approach of him at whose footstep he had once shuddered with horror.

He was not long kept in suspense.

Allan Rushworth had not left the cabin more than a few moments, when a stealthy step was heard rapidly approaching.

It drew near the door of the cabin.

The door opened—the person entered without the least hesitation.

It was Octavius Challoner.

James could not forbear creeping forward and looking at him through the curtain.

He had evidently reconnoitred the scene of action previously, since he went direct to the locker and applied the key.

On the door opening, an exclamation of joy escaped him as the canvas bag met his gaze, standing upright in one of the compartments.

He seized it eagerly and transferred it to his pocket. The bottles next attracted his attention.

He tried them successively, but to his chagrin found them all empty.

Allan Rushworth had taken good care of that.

He uttered an angry imprecation, and then closed and relocked the locker.

Having thus performed his task, he left the cabin as guilty and rapidly as he had entered it, bearing the plunder with him.

Had he known who had been watching him all the time, had the pale face of James Cook quietly protruded itself from behind the drapery, and his voice once more breathed the question, "*what do you want here?*" it is probable the guilty wretch would have uttered a cry of horror that would have roused the whole ship.

But James kept perfectly still and silent, being willing to let his would-be murderer go his way, and fill up the measure of his guilt, until the hour of retribution should overtake him.

Octavius watched his opportunity to sneak up on deck, and to communicate to the first mate, that his task had been successfully accomplished.

This was a source of much exultation to John Marsh, who was now only anxious to see the master retire once more to his cabin.

But Allan Rushworth appeared in no hurry to retire on this particular night.

He strolled up and down the deck with his hands behind him, and tortured the anxious mates by stopping suddenly as though with some particular idea, and then again continuing his walk.

Each time he stopped, the conscience-troubled sailors felt certain he was going to pay the apprentice a visit.

But this was not the case.

The night was fine and the master seemed to enjoy it.

He had on, too, his heavy pilot coat, with large pockets at the sides—they did not see the pistols nestling snugly inside—which seemed to imply a longer stay on deck than usual.

He lighted a cigar from one of the ship's lanterns, and continued his perambulations, smoking with the utmost complacency.

John Marsh and James Bowers groaned inwardly.

They had scarcely ever known him to do as he was doing that night.

Why he should select that particular occasion for such an unusual amount of pedestrian exercise, save for their particular annoyance, they could not imagine.

But this was exactly the state of the case.

Allan Rushworth was a brave man, and had the vessel and the money on board her been his own, he would have placed his back against his cabin door, and with a pistol in each hand have dared the conspirators to desert the one or touch the other.

His stern command would have been: "Return to your duty!"

Those who refused must have abided the result.

But as it was his hands were fettered.

He felt himself responsible to his employers for the ship and their money, and to secure these, he had to pursue a course that chafed him, and wounded his pride.

"The sneaking curs!" he murmured to himself, "it's fortunate for them I only act for others!"

The only revenge he could take was that which he was taking, and it rather pleased his indignation to walk up and down puffing furiously at his cigar, knowing that all the time he was keeping the guilty sailors on the rack.

At length, however, he became tired himself, and resolved to leave them to their own devices.

One last feint he reserved as a *bonne bouche*.

Throwing away the end of his cigar, he went towards the hatchway, as though he would have descended to his cabin.

The first and second mates exulted as he departed.  Octavius watched with apparent indifference.

Suddenly the master stopped.

"Stay!" he ejaculated, "I haven't seen my boy; I must look at him before I turn in."

By dint of a great effort the first mate said:

"I looked at him, sir, about ten minutes ago; he's quite comfortable and sound asleep."

"You lying rascal!" muttered Allan; but he subdued his anger and said:

"I'm glad to hear it, but I'll just look in upon him."

There was no evading this, and the men made up their minds for the worst.

"Hold the lantern, Marsh," cried Allan as he descended the steps.

The first mate followed in dire apprehension, and held the lantern so that Mr. Rushworth could just see the hammock, in which, by the advice of Octavius, something had been placed, and a jacket thrown over.

To the great delight of the whole party the master seemed satisfied.

"He seems all right," he said, "there's no occasion to disturb him, he'll be all right to-morrow."

To-morrow! how they chuckled at the word.

To-morrow they would be far away.

Allan Rushworth retired to his cabin.

They had now only to wait till Jackson and Blake turned in for the night.

These men were perfectly unconscious of the plot in hand.

Had the master but known that he would have acted differently.

He imagined, and perhaps with reason, the whole crew were accomplices; it was that impression which made him control his own impulses, and act cautiously as he did.

"All seems smooth and quiet," remarked Jackson, with a yawn, to the first mate.

"Ay, ay," answered John Marsh, "everything's as right as it can be; you can turn in if you like—you and

Blake; we can manage the ship for the next four hours."

Nothing loath to be released, the two men took the hint and disappeared, and in five minutes were snoring in their hammocks.

The coast was now clear.

For the first time since the robbery had been effected the accomplices had the opportunity of exchanging words.

"Is it all right?" eagerly asked the first mate of Octavius.

The latter replied by dragging the canvas bag from his pocket and holding it up before his companions.

Their eyes glistened with pleasure.

"There was not the least difficulty," said Octavius; "the key opened the locker at the first attempt; nothing could have been managed more expeditiously."

He restored the bag to his pocket as he spoke.

"Decidedly!" echoed his companions.

They had moved towards the end of the vessel.

The second mate had taken the helm from Blake, and was steering the ship.

Allan Rushworth had left his cabin, and, shrouded in darkness, was, with James by his side, keeping a strict and vigilant watch upon their actions.

They little thought themselves the objects of so keen a supervision.

It was now time to make preparations for their departure.

The ship's boat hung athwart the stern.

"Now, then," said the first mate, "I'll make the helm fast; the wind blows so steadily from one point, the craft could steer herself."

This having been done, Octavius inquired:

"How are we to lower this boat?"

"We must cut her away with our knives," answered John Marsh; "but first I must secure her from drifting away before we're all on board; that would be a sorry wind up to our successful undertaking."

As he spoke, he threw a coil of loose rope into the boat.

One end of this he made fast to the boat's head, whilst the other end he attached to the ship's stern.

The rope was sufficiently long to allow her to float, whilst it still kept her tethered to the vessel.

All being so far ready, John Marsh cried to Octavius:

"Now, then, jump in!"

Octavius obeyed, and stood alone in the boat that hung oscillating over the waves.

The first and second mates stood on the stern of the brig at either end of the boat, with their clasp knives open in their hands.

"Are you not coming?" Octavius inquired.

"Of course we are," answered the first mate; "when we've cut away the boat, we shall follow you by the rope, then all we have to do will be to give that one slash with the knife, and we shall be clear of the ship for good, d'ye see?" he inquired.

"Oh, yes, perfectly," answered Octavius, drily, as a peculiar sneering smile stole over his features.

"Come, then, Jem," cried John Marsh, flourishing his knife, "are you ready?"

"Ay, ay!" was the reply.

"Cut away, then," said the first mate.

One stroke of the knives was given, and the boat, with Octavius, fell steadily into the sea.

"All right?" they inquired.

"Now, then!" cried the first mate to his companion, "in with you, quick!"

James Bowers, grasping the rope, launched himself over the vessel's stern, and descended hand over hand.

John Marsh followed instantly, and found his heels coming into collision with his messmate's head.

"Go on!" shouted the first mate—"why don't you go on?"

"There's nowhere to go to!" shouted Bowers in return.

"Where's the boat?"

"Gone!"

This was a fact. The unprincipled Octavius, thinking the whole better than a third of the booty, had taken advantage of his position and cut the rope, and was already some distance from the brig.

To describe the chagrin and rage of the bamboozled mates would be well-nigh impossible.

There they were, dangling by the rope over the vessel's stern, as full of wrath as it was possible for two men to be.

They each felt a strong desire to annihilate something or somebody, and expressed their feelings by frantic and vindictive demonstrations with the only limbs they had at liberty, their legs.

It will readily be conceived, that the second mate being underneath, and receiving the full benefit of his messmate's heels on his devoted head, began to grow slightly bewildered.

"Avast there, Jack!" he cried, "you're knocking my brains out."

The first mate fiercely consigned his companion's brains to—no matter where—and then growled out:

"We'd better come aboard again!"

This was in decided accordance with the feelings of the second mate, whose wrists were beginning to ache as well as his head.

He accordingly hauled himself up the rope after his companion.

Having reached the stern railing, they rolled themselves on deck, where, to their horror, they beheld the master, Allan Rushworth, looking down upon them with a countenance of calm severity.

Blake, instead of being in the hammock to which he had retired a short time before, had been evidently summoned thence, and was now at his former post, the wheel, steering the ship.

There was too great a confusion prevailing just at this moment in the minds of Messrs. Marsh and Bowers to enable them to enter very clearly into their precise position.

There was something in the expression of the master's face dreadfully ominous.

His lips were compressed, his features pale, and his gray eyes gleamed with a concentrated brightness that bewildered the two men more than a flash of lightning.

To speak comprehensively, John Marsh and James Bowers were at that moment in that state of mental fog, when they could not have distinguished a great A from a chest of drawers.

Not only had they lost the gold they had so eagerly plotted to obtain, but the loss had come upon them in so sudden and unlooked-for a manner, just at the very instant when they, as it were, felt it in their grasp—just when their itching fingers seemed to be clutching the coins.

And worst of all, it had been snatched from them by the very man they had been at so much trouble to secure as an accomplice.

It was too much for their faculties to endure, and as the keen eyes of the master pierced them through and through, they swayed to and fro—the joints of their knees failing to yield their usual support—lolling against each other, and looking at Allan with the most vacant and imbecile of expressions.

Their sensations were not improved, nor their wits sharpened by observing two unpleasant-looking instruments glistening in the master's hands.

Everything seemed calculated to hold them up in their true colours—a pair of baffled detected criminals.

The voice of Mr. Rushworth fell upon their ears like a deep bell.

"What were you doing over the ship's side?" he asked.

No answer.

"Who was that left in the boat?"

Still no answer.

The master made an impatient gesture, and clutched the unpleasant-looking instruments forcibly in his hands.

"Speak!" he cried, sharply.

A faint gurgling was heard in the throats of the two men, but no definite sounds came forth.

"Are you dumb?" he shouted. "Answer me at once, or——"

The mates opened their mouths with a simultaneous promptness that proved that it was the power, not the will to speak that was lacking.

"Tell me," said the master, still keeping his eyes fixed on them intently, "who was it departed in that boat?"

"O-O-O-Oliver Armstrong!" the men contrived, after a considerable deal of stammering, to ejaculate.

"Why did he so?"

"D-d-don't know!" answered the first mate.

[OCTAVIUS CHALLONER OUTWITS THE MATES.]

"W-we—that is, me and Jem, saw him get into the boat, and—and——"

Here his invention failed him, and he fished helplessly for words, without being able to find any.

"Go on!" urged Allan.

"We asked him what he was doing," dropped in the second mate, coming to his companion's assistance with a falsehood.

"And what reply did he make?" was the stolid rejoinder.

"He said, a—he said, he—he was—going!" jerked out the first mate, spasmodically, as though the words had been shaken from his lips.

"Where?" shouted the master, with such startling abruptness, that the sailors had the greatest difficulty to prevent themselves falling on their knees.

"He—he didn't know; he wanted to leave the ship," gasped the second mate.

"Well? go on!"

"W-we t-told him th-the boat belonged to the—the vessel, and that he must stop where he was. He said

he wouldn't stop another minute; and I said to Jem—didn't I Jem?"

"Ye——"

"Don't ask questions, but go on!" cried the incensed master.

"I said," continued the first mate, "we must hold him back; so we let ourselves down by the rope; but when we got to where we expected to find the boat, we found there was no boat at all, so we had to haul ourselves up again, and it was just as we'd pulled ourselves on board, you found us."

Under all the circumstances, this agitated account might have been looked upon as a specimen of a certain amount of presence of mind.

Perhaps, had Allan not been previously aware of the facts of the case, he might—being of an unsuspicious temper—have been induced to believe it, but knowing, as he did, the whole history beforehand, it only increased his indignation.

He had no fear of these two shrinking pilferers; there was no reason why he should have any.

He had caught them just at that precise moment, when what might, under some circumstances, have produced desperation and made them dangerous, but which now acted as a moral paralysis, and left them maudlin and powerless.

Allan Rushworth stood before them, firm as a giant or a rock, whilst they, cowed and trembling, tacitly admitted his power.

After regarding them, at the conclusion of the first mate's lucid explanation, for a moment in silence, he said, in a peculiarly dry tone:

"Oh, indeed! So, then, you mean to affirm that what you have told me is the truth?"

"Every word!" answered John Marsh, feeling at the same time, however, the most unpleasant internal convictions that the master did not quite regard it in that light.

"And have you no suspicion as to the cause that induced Oliver Armstrong to quit the ship?" asked Allan, searchingly.

This was a home question—both the sailors felt it so—and the manner in which it was dug into them made it still more probing.

Their eyes wandered up and down and askant—here, there, and everywhere—to avoid the dreaded gaze of their questioner.

Allan repeated the question.

"Have you no suspicion?"

No; they had no suspicion—they supposed the new hand had shipped in a hurry, having nothing better to do, and had found out, upon trial, that he didn't like the sea, and that his sudden departure in the boat was, in his opinion, the readiest way to get ashore again.

The master listened, with a very stolid countenance, to this supposition.

"And this you really think to be the reason of Oliver Armstrong's departure, do you?" he asked.

"Yes, we do; we can't imagine anything else," they replied.

"Can't you, indeed," returned Allan. "Then I'll assist your imaginations, that just now appear to be in a terribly disordered state. The reason why Oliver Armstrong deserted this vessel, is because he has *committed a robbery!*"

An inward shudder, like a galvanic shock, passed through the two human frames at these terrible words.

The deed, then, was known.

"And," continued Allan, "the reason why you were dangling at the end of that rope, was not to prevent the thief from escaping, but to drop into the boat and accompany him!"

The two men trembled; how was it the master had thus discovered their intentions?

He went on:

"You would have been with him at this moment, only being fools as well as knaves, you gave your accomplice the opportunity of which he has taken the advantage. Having used you two thickheads as his cat's paw to extract his chestnuts from the fire, like the monkey in the fable, he enjoys the fruit, leaving you to taste only the smart of the burns."

The mates were utterly speechless.

"You see I am perfectly acquainted with all your plans," the master continued. "The wax impression and the duplicate key were very skilful contrivances, such as anyone would have thought must have been successful, and yet you see how signally you have failed in your expected results—you have been foiled and baffled by your own accomplice!"

These words were gall and wormwood to the disappointed sailors.

They bit their lips, and clenched their hands till the nails almost pierced their flesh, in the bitterness of their defeat.

But Allan had not done yet.

He suddenly changed his tone from the sarcasm it had assumed, to that of solemn earnestness.

Looking down upon them with those keen, gray eyes full of condemnation, he said:

"Robbery on the high seas is a crime the law punishes by death! what penalty, then, think you, should be inflicted for the darker and deeper sin of *murder?*"

As he uttered these words, the terrified men raised a cry of terror, and fell on their knees at his feet.

"We didn't murder the poor boy! it was not our hands that threw him over the ship's side!" exclaimed the men, in a tone of extreme horror.

"You are unworthy of belief," said Allan Rushworth, sternly.

"A man may want money," cried the first mate, in an agitated voice, "and when he's in a fix such as we were just now, he may say what isn't exactly true, but there's no reason he should be a murderer. I'm no murderer—I swear I'm not!"

"No more am I!" protested James Bowers.

The men were now thoroughly prostrate.

All their feverish anticipations of the luxuries their stolen booty was to have purchased, had faded into the thin vapour of non-realisation, and the conviction of their guilt alone remained.

They felt they had forfeited their claim to the character of honest men, and that there was nothing left them to expect but disgrace and punishment.

"Don't be hard upon us, master!" said the first mate, in a voice of humble entreaty.

"We were never mixed up in such a piece of work before," added his companion, in a like tone of submission.

"I am very sorry to find that you have so far forgotten yourselves now," replied Allan, in a voice which, while it expressed regret, had in it neither weakness nor indecision.

The men could gather from it that, while he regretted their deviation from the path of honesty, no false emotions of pity would screen them from the hand of justice.

"You should have considered the consequences of your deed before you committed it," said the master.

"We ought to have done so," admitted the first mate, in a penitent tone, "but when the devil tempts, it's just the time when we don't consider; but we hope you'll give us another chance."

"I give you another chance," said Allan. "You speak as though you had robbed me; you forget that what has been taken is the property of my employers and yours, the Brothers Walker, of Whitby, and that I am responsible to them for it. When the hue and cry is posted after this Oliver Armstrong, and when he is taken, do you not think he will name his accomplices?"

The sailors ground their teeth in a simultaneous execration of their treacherous ally.

They felt certain that this would be the very first thing he would do; and they heaped reproaches on themselves for having trusted him to the extent they did.

"You have done wrong," said Allan Rushworth, in a calm, clear voice, "and you must abide the penalty. Go forward!"

He pointed with the barrel of the pistol his right hand grasped, as he spoke, and the mates, who had nothing more to say for themselves, or the energy to offer the least resistance, went as they were directed.

The master followed.

They went on until they stood by the trap door, where James had once stood to gain his information.

"Open the trap!" said the master, pointing to it with his pistol.

The trap was instantly raised.

"Now, descend!" he cried.

The cowed men glanced hopelessly at the brace of weapons the master held, and without a word dropped into the hold.

The trap was shut, and the conspirators caged.

A strong brace of iron staples was driven into the floor, and all means of exit was thus effectually cut off.

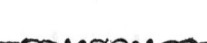

Chapter LII.

ALONE IN THE BOAT.

OCTAVIUS, when taken by the pressgang, had been carried off with some other unfortunates similarly circumstanced, and lodged under a guard of marines at a public-house used for such purposes.

The blow that felled him to the ground as he dropped from the window was not of a serious nature, and he soon recovered from its effects, but, from motives of his own, feigned to be much worse than he actually was.

The sergeant of marines seeing he did not regain his consciousness, began to think his skull was fractured.

Under these circumstances, it was deemed advisable to make his an exceptional case, and to accommodate him with a bed apart from the rest, where he lay with eyes closed, without any signs of life save his heavy, stertorous breathing.

The sergeant and landlord looked at him the last thing before going to bed, and the latter shook his head ominously.

"I think, Mr. Sergeant," said he, "you've given it this poor chap a little too strong; it strikes me he'll not be here in the morning."

This prediction was literally fulfilled, he was *not* there in the morning, having suddenly recovered in the night, and dropped from the window under cover of the darkness more successfully than on his former attempt, and got clear off.

With what money he had he made his way to London, where his cash being exhausted, want and privation stared him in the face.

How he was existing there by selling play-bills at the doors of one of the theatres, the reader knows.

This slight digression must be excused, being explanatory of the means by which Octavius got clear of the pressgang.

He was now in the boat, tossing to and fro, alone.

Alone with the coveted canvas bag—the booty that had cost so much planning to secure—alone with his thoughts in the dark, with the spray dashing in his face.

Terrible, one would have imagined, must have been those thoughts; as each wave yawned, his guilty conscience might have been supposed to look for the dead body of his victim.

But these ideas did not oppress him.

He had got rid of something he hated, and there were no lurking superstitious fears remaining behind.

But even had there been, one touch of his hand upon his weighty pocket, one thought of the booty he had acquired, would have been sufficient to put them to flight.

He, however, grew heartily sick of the ceaseless motion of the boat.

Day broke gradually, but too slowly for him; and the scoundrel chuckled to himself as the majestic sun tinged the Eastern horizon with its beams.

It was pleasant to see daylight once again.

Still daylight brought no change to him.

Still the same monotonous rocking up and down, that seemed to threaten an upset at every buffet.

He had expected to have speedily passed a vessel, but his expectations were not realized.

He saw vessels certainly, but they were distant, and looked like specks on the ocean.

There was nothing in the boat either, which he could hoist as a signal.

There were a pair of oars, and to relieve the monotony of his situation, he essayed to row.

But he soon grew tired of the exercise he performed in so unskilful a manner, and which only resulted in blistered hands.

He laid aside the oars, and suffered the boat to drift as before.

He was entirely ignorant where he was, or whither he was drifting.

Slowly the hours passed, and he began to feel awfully hungry.

The fresh sea breeze created an intense appetite, but there was nothing to eat.

Gradually this day also began to decline, the sky became overcast—the stars shone forth—it was night once more.

No prospect now of relief till the morning.

He began to grow apprehensive. The hours seemed to wing their flight more tardily than ever.

He shivered with cold, he grumbled and complained. "Am I to go on tossing for ever on this watery waste?" he growled through his teeth.

He began to think that the small boat he was in might fail to attract attention, and in that case what was he to expect—starvation—a retributive punishment for the sins he had committed.

Hunger gnawed at his entrails; he felt he would have given half the contents of the canvas bag for a loaf of bread.

He became drowsy, and between dozing, dreaming, and starting, the second night wore away.

He had fallen asleep at the bottom of the boat, and when he awoke the sun was shining down upon him.

He dreamed he was about sitting down to a magnificent banquet.

The mockery of the dream irritated him.

"Am I to starve?" he cried, fiercely,"and with £350 in my pocket? No!—no! there are vessels yonder—they will see me."

He looked eagerly to where, in the distance, several craft were perceptible.

"Yes!—yes!" he cried, excitedly,"one of them must see me."

It seemed more than probable such would be the case, since one of them seemed to be coming directly towards him.

He watched it with riveted eyes, and there was in a short time no doubt on that score, from the increasing size of the vessel.

How eagerly he watched it, how wildly he shouted, and as it drew nearer, how he exulted as he heard his shout returned!

In a short time he was alongside the welcome craft, which proved to be nothing more than a fishing smack.

No matter, however, what it was, the opportuneness of its arrival magnified it into the most peerless of vessels.

"Hallo, mate! what cheer?" hailed one of the rough fishermen.

Octavius was prepared with his answer:

The boat had broken adrift on the previous night and left him as they found him.

He was welcomed on board the smack.

"Where are we?" asked Octavius.

"Off Yarmouth," was the answer.

"Do you belong there?"

"Yes. You've boarded us at the right time; we're homeward bound," they said.

Octavius, on consideration, was not sorry to hear this. He was a stranger to Yarmouth—he would know no one there, and no one would know him—a very strong recommendation in his eyes.

On reaching shore he parted with the fishermen, who, believing him to be an honest jack tar, wished him good luck, without expecting any remuneration for the service rendered.

The only thing he left behind was the boat, and that only because it was impossible he could take it with him.

Having then got clear of his friends, he entered the town of Yarmouth.

He was weary and ravenously hungry, and having for some time past experienced the miseries of poverty, he resolved now to indulge himself in some of the luxuries that money can always purchase.

He accordingly advanced boldly and entered the best inn in the town with the confident assurance of a man who had been accustomed to hold a good rank in society.

His manner and bearing were those of a gentleman.

Desperately evil as he was at heart, he could, when he wished it, gloss all over with a fair exterior.

It was no wonder, then, that the landlord of the "Spread Eagle" hotel believed Octavius, when he asserted that he had been wrecked off the coast, and escaped only with life and the sailor's suit on his back.

There was an air of confidence and truthfulness in his assertions that gave them credit.

The landlord believed them implicitly.

Octavius, with his handsome face—though it was then pale from recent trials—and commanding figure, looked a man to be believed.

The host of the "Spread Eagle" was strongly prepossessed in his favour; and when he spoke of remittances that were to arrive from his banker in London, the worthy man begged his visitor to draw upon him for any immediate sum he might require until such remittances should arrive.

This offer was very acceptable to Octavius, since a plentiful supply of ready cash would not have been quite compatible with the condition of a shipwrecked passenger.

He, therefore, accepted the offer of the friendly landlord, and, moreover, requested him to recommend him such tradesmen as might, by their good offices, enable a gentleman to appear in public.

These were readily found; and in a few days Octavius Challoner appeared in all the glory of his former position—that is, as far as dress was concerned.

On the fourth day after his arrival at Yarmouth, he had dined luxuriously, and was sitting in his private apartment (for cogent reasons he did not use the ordinary dining-room of the hotel) in a state of epicurean enjoyment.

A couple of bottles of wine stood on the table, and he had drunk himself into that condition when caution is forgotten, and when the present moment, tinged with the roseate draught, seems the whole of existence, unsaddened by past regrets, unclouded by future apprehensions.

Octavius began to grow tired of solitude, and to long to hear the voices of his fellow-men.

He resolved to descend into the dining-room below.

There he could listen to the conversation of the diners, or at least to the rattle of their knives and forks, and the jingling of their glasses, and that would be preferable to the solitude and silence he felt so irksome.

He accordingly left his chamber and descended into the dining-room.

There were not many visitors there; but he found the landlord—a busy, civil, cheerful little man, bustling about, making as much business as he could out of a little.

"Ah, Mr. Rolleston!" (Octavius had adopted this alias since his arrival at the "Spread Eagle") he said, cheerfully, "come to pay us a visit downstairs? That's right; you'll find this a very comfortable room."

"I felt rather tired of sitting alone, and have strolled in here for a change," Octavius replied.

"Perhaps you'll like to look at the newspaper," said the landlord, handing his visitor one of the daily journals.

Octavius took the paper, and went to the further end of the room.

The apartment was partitioned off into small, snug compartments, and in the most remote of these he placed himself.

Although this was not particularly lively, there was more light in it than in the room above.

He had not been there long when the door opened, and the landlord entered with two gentlemen.

"You can let us have dinner," said one of the gentlemen; "our friend will be here, I have no doubt, by the time it's on the table."

"Yes, gentlemen, this instant," replied the landlord, as he hurried away to give the necessary orders. But, in the meantime, what effect had these harmless words, uttered by the new-comer, produced upon the solitary occupant of the furthermost compartment?

They had caused him to clutch the paper he was feigning to read, rather than reading, convulsively in his hands, and turn deadly pale.

Not an ordinary pallor, but a ghastly, livid hue, like that of death itself, whilst his brow and hands were bathed in a cold sweat. The voice seemed to act as a spell upon Octavius, for although it appeared to strike him with such deadly terror, it seemed also to fill him

with an irresistible desire to look upon the face of the speaker.

The two gentlemen had not seated themselves, but stood conversing in the middle of the room, waiting the serving of their repast.

Octavius, with extreme caution, glanced round from his box, and took a keen but rapid survey of their features

It was more than sufficient. There, within a few yards of him, stood George Carew, the President of the Confederate Brothers, and Captain Palmer. He rapidly withdrew his head, and with a sinking of the spirit, that he was ashamed to acknowledge even to himself, sank back against the wall, deadly faint.

He felt at that moment that if the floor could have yawned beneath his feet and engulfed him it would have been far preferable to the agony he was then enduring.

It seemed to him that he, a living man, sat in the presence of the long since dead—of those whom he had sent to their account—and that they must be conscious of his presence.

This idea was, of course, preposterous; but the sudden shock had unnerved him, and he was the sport of terrible fancies.

A universal tremor pervaded his limbs, and he looked like a man stricken suddenly with the ague.

He could hear the cheerful clatter of the dishes as the waiters placed them on the table, and the voice of the landlord as he gave directions; and it was some slight relief to think that the two men whose presence he dreaded had taken their seats.

Then there came the lively sound of the uncorking of bottles; but all these things brought no pleasant associations to the conscience-stricken Octavius.

He sat still, faint and heart-sick, lolling back against the wall, feeling as though at any moment he might fall prostrate on the ground; longing to groan, but not daring to utter a sound.

Presently a hearty, genial voice was heard in the distance.

"What!" it cried, "are they here, and dinner on the table? Go ahead, Master Ikey; never let it be said that Jack Samphire fails to keeps his appointments with his friends."

A hasty step followed these words, the door was quickly opened, and Lieutenant Samphire, closely followed by a good-looking lad, with large dark eyes, entered the dining-room. There was a hearty greeting between the two gentlemen and the new-comer, such a greeting as almost filled Octavius Challoner with despair.

It seemed to him that all the world possessed friends save himself.

"You're just in time, Jack," exclaimed George Carew; "but who have you with you?" he inquired, as he looked scrutinizingly, but with some appearance of recognition at the boy with the large dark eyes, whom the reader will readily guess was no other than our young friend, Ikey Mangles.

Yes, the boy had found a friend at last, having ingratiated himself so far into the good graces of Lieutenant Samphire, that he had resolved to take upon himself the charge of the boy's future.

"This is a young protégé of mine," he said, "and having neither kith nor kin of any description, I've promised, if he behaves himself, to make a man of him."

"Why, surely!" exclaimed George Carew, looking earnestly at Ikey, "we have met before."

The boy looked intensely at the President from out of his black eyes for an instant, and then cried:

"O' course ve 'as; you're the gen'l'man vith the vite vig!"

George Carew laughed, and replied:

"You're perfectly right, my lad; you have a very excellent memory. I congratulate you on having fallen into such good hands."

Captain Palmer then addressed the surprised boy:

"And haven't you a word to throw away upon an old friend?" he said.

"Vot!" cried Ikey, "Captain Palmer! Oh, Hi ham glad to see you! Oh, vouldn't poor Jem be 'appy if 'e vos 'ere."

The captain shook hands with him cordially, and inquired kindly after James Cook, and dinner being now the paramount object of consideration, talking for the present gave place to eating—Ikey, as he feasted, noting it down, as a fact worthy of remembrance, that he had never been amongst so many kind friends in his life before.

Octavius recognised Ikey's voice at once, and felt that there were two more eyes whose glance he must endeavour to avoid.

Never in his life had he realised the misery of suspense so vividly, as at the present moment.

His experience whilst tossing upon the dark ocean in a frail boat, was almost happiness in comparison.

Oh, what would he have given for the seclusion of his private room once more! How he execrated his folly for leaving it! It was impossible to retreat, until the party he wished to avoid had retired; and there he must sit, a prisoner, not daring to speak or even to give an order, lest he should betray his presence.

But his friend, the landlord, who had taken a particular liking to his handsome, pale-faced, ship-wrecked guest, did not leave him alone long.

Having seen his new visitors attended to, he came up to the partition in which Octavius was enduring tortures no one could have conceived but himself, and added to them by a cheerful account of the party in the box near at hand.

After dinner they would make a social circle in the billiard-room, being pleasant, convivial people, just the kind that become friends immediately.

The horror of such an idea was so great, that but for the stern necessity of retaining his senses, Octavius would have swooned at once.

As it was, he sat swaying backwards and forwards so helplessly, that at last the landlord perceived there was something wrong.

"Good gracious!" he cried, as the ghastly face of his visitor met his view. "My dear sir, you're ill!—very ill! Good Heavens!" he said to himself, "he looks as if he was dying! I must call——"

With a sudden energy that sent the worthy landlord's shirt-button flying yards off, Octavius clutched his wrist and held him firmly to the spot.

"Call no one!" he whispered, hoarsely — "it is nothing. Since I had the brain fever in India I am subject to these attacks; take no notice of them—let me be quiet—bring me some brandy."

The sympathising landlord, with his torn shirt-cuff and aching wrist, on which the nervous fingers of Octavius had left their impression, hurried off for the spirit.

This was speedily procured, and never did the parched traveller in the desert more eagerly welcome the reviving draught of nature's pure element, than did Octavius Challoner the glass of cognac the landlord held to his quivering lips.

By dint of several applications to the bottle, he became more composed; the faintness disappeared—he grew stronger—better.

The dinner was over at last, and the gentlemen quitted the dining for the billiard-room.

At the very earliest possible moment after their departure, consistent with safety, Octavius rose, and with the utmost caution sought once more the retirement of his own apartment.

Here the feelings that had so fearfully oppressed him disappeared rapidly, and in order to expedite his restoration, he drank glass after glass of the landlord's choice old port.

This, acting in concert with the brandy he had previously taken, had the effect of producing drowsiness.

Octavius fell asleep.

The landlord entered.

He had missed his guest from the dining-room below, and felt anxious to see how he was progressing.

The tradespeople, too, had left their bills, in accordance with Mr. Rolleston's request, and he brought them up at the same time.

Seeing, however, that Octavius was asleep, he placed the bills on the table, made up the fire, and departed without disturbing him.

In the meantime, the party below were playing a very cheerful game at billiards.

Ikey accompanied the gentlemen into the billiard-room; but, in course of time, growing tired of seeing the white balls knocked about, without the slightest prospect of getting a blow at them himself, he contrived to slip out unobserved, and with the curiosity that was

strongly developed in his disposition, commenced a desultory ramble over the length, breadth, and height of the hotel.

He wandered into the kitchen, where the cook and her fellow-servant wondered what the "young gentleman with the large eyes" wanted.

He strolled into the stable, where he narrowly escaped sudden annihilation from the heels of a vicious horse, and then, directing his course once more into the interior, he crept upstairs, and honoured some of the bedrooms with a personal inspection, indulging in vague surmises as to which one he was destined to occupy.

As he descended, a door stood ajar, and a sound, as of some one snoring slightly, was distinctly heard.

He looked in—the room seemed uncommonly warm and comfortable, and smelt of port wine, which smell Ikey liked particularly—it seemed to him highly suggestive of comfort.

No one appeared to be there, so he entered very quietly.

Suddenly he stopped short—there *was some one there.*

The light of the freshly stirred fire shone brightly on the features of a sleeping man; on features never to be forgotten by Ikey Mangles, since they belonged to one who, before all others in the world, he had learned to look upon with abhorrence.

He stood stock still, as though paralysed; the predominant idea in his mind being to call "murder" as loudly as he could.

But as his tongue clove to the roof of his mouth, he found this a matter of difficulty.

So he stood motionless, gazing at Octavius, as he lay slumbering in the firelight.

"Certinly," he said, to himself, "'e dunno as Hi'm 'ere, cos 'e's asleep, an' hif 'e vos to vake, Hi could be hoff like a shot afore 'e know'd 'oo Hi vos; besides, hif 'e did, Hi've got frien's now as vouldn't let 'im knock me about."

These reflections seemed to give him more confidence.

Then the thought came over him how strange it was he should be there, and then that perhaps he had been mistaken after all.

He approached nearer, with the utmost caution, quite astonished at his own boldness, and examined the features of the sleeper more scrutinizingly.

Yes, there was no doubt as to his identity.

Just at that moment, to his extreme horror and without the slightest previous intimation, Octavius awoke from his sleep and sat up in his arm-chair.

Ikey had no time to reach the door; all he was able to accomplish was to drop on to his knees and creep behind the back of the arm chair.

"Who's there?" demanded the deep voice of Octavius, husky from past excitement and port wine.

My readers may be sure Ikey did not gratify his curiosity by informing him of his propinquity.

He remained, on the contrary, perfectly silent.

"I thought I heard some one in the room. It must have been fancy," he said to himself.

He poured out a glass of wine and drank it, during which operation Ikey, cautiously taking a step back to get as far as possible from his terrible companion, trod on a wooden instrument used for the pulling off of boots, overbalanced, and fell on his back.

"Who's there?" shouted Octavius, in a startled manner, turning round suddenly in his seat.

There was no reply. Ikey had managed to reach the shelter of the window curtains, behind which he crouched.

"I certainly heard something," muttered Mr. Challoner, who, in spite of the wine and brandy he had drunk, was nervous, and averse to strange noises of any description. "Do they keep cats here?" he continued. "I hate cats; they're treacherous."

"You houghter a bin a cat," murmured Ikey, behind the curtain.

As Octavius spoke he rose drowsily from his seat, and stood with his back to the fire.

Ikey could see his shadow on the wall and ceiling, like the shadow of a giant.

He could see that Octavius was peering from where he stood into the corners of the room, as if he expected to see something unpleasant.

"I can't bear the idea of being watched," he muttered. "I'd stab my own brother to the heart if I found him watching me. It was that prying, sneaking habit of his that cost that young fool James Cook his life!"

What words for poor Ikey to listen to!

His blood seemed to curdle in his veins.

Nor were his sensations in any way alleviated when Octavius, looking very heavy-eyed and sullen, commenced a kind of drowsy rambling search about the room. He pulled the arm-chair forward and looked behind it; he opened a chiffionier and examined its recesses; he tapped the mirror, as though he half expected to find a trap-door concealed behind it; he raised the table-cover and glanced beneath it, but he found nothing to excite his apprehensions. There was only one place he had not examined, and that was the very spot where Ikey lay concealed behind the curtains. He fixed his eyes on them—Ikey, who was watching, fancied timorously—as though half afraid to look behind them.

However, after a few moments, he advanced with a not over steady step, and flung one-half of the curtain aside.

He then repeated the same process with the other.

He was rather clumsy in these operations, and Ikey had time to shift his position from one half to the other, and from that to beneath the table. He was now half way across the room, and by so much nearer to the door.

Octavius repeated his search at the curtains of the other window, during which Ikey, with noiseless steps, contrived to make his escape.

Mr. Challoner having satisfied himself that the room was free from intruders, drank another glass of wine, and slept again.

Chapter LIII.

STRANGE REVELATIONS

QUITE cured of his wandering propensities for that night, at least, Ikey crept downstairs, congratulating himself that he was still alive, and slipped into the billiard-room, his absence from whence had not been noticed.

What revelations Ikey made to his guardian, Lieutenant Samphire, relative to the vision he had seen above-stairs, may be gathered from the fact that, in less than ten minutes from the time of his descent, the lieutenant and his friends, George Carew and Captain Palmer, were standing by the chair of the slumbering Octavius eagerly inspecting his features.

To these gentlemen, the countenance of the villain was perfectly familiar.

Lieutenant Samphire was the only one of the party to whom they were strange.

They descended once more to the billiard-room, of which they were the only occupants, and summoned the landlord.

The little man entered in his usual brisk, cheerful way, and stood awaiting the orders of his guests. But no orders came. He noticed, too, that they all looked unusually grave.

He wondered what it meant, and began to fear that something had displeased them.

"Sit down, my friend," said George Carew, in a serious tone, pointing to a chair.

The landlord seated himself obediently, and then went on to wonder what was coming next.

"I wish to ask you a few questions, Mr. Plummer," the President went on.

Mr. Plummer inclined his head in tacit acknowledgment that he was ready to answer any questions that might be put to him, and the President continued, inquiringly:

"What gentleman is it you have occupying your suite of apartments above-stairs?"

"Mr. Arthur Rolleston," returned the landlord, promptly. "He is a gentleman from London, who was wrecked off the coast, and is stopping here for a short time, until he is ready to start for the metropolis."

"You are sure he *is* a gentleman?" inquired the President.

"Oh, quite sure, from his manner, and—and from other circumstances," answered the landlord, confidently.

"You are also sure he comes from London?"

"Oh, dear, yes—at least he says so—and he banks there."

"Are you sure he banks there?"

"He tells me so."

"Ah! but are you sure he banks *anywhere*?"

It was very annoying to the worthy little landlord to have these questions so quietly and persistently put, and in so grave a manner, by a gentleman of such undoubted respectability as the questioner appeared to be.

"I believe," he said in reply, "that we cannot be quite certain of anything in this world; but so far as appearances can justify belief, I think I may say that I am sure what Mr. Rolleston has told me of himself is correct."

"My good friend," answered George Carew, "this is only one more instance how easily we may be deceived. There is no such person as Mr. Arthur Rolleston."

The little landlord opened his eyes to their fullest extent at this assertion of the President, and at the same moment the waiter entered with a printed bill in his hand.

"'Hue an' Cry,' gentlemen," he said, as he affixed the bill to the wall.

"What a singular combination of circumstances," remarked the President, thoughtfully. "It is wonderful!—it seems as though all the crimes he has committed were gradually enclosing him, until no loop-hole being left for escape, the crisis of retribution will arrive, and he will meet the fate he so richly merits."

This was spoken by the President in a low voice to himself, rather than to those around him; but the few words Mr. Plummer was able to gather seemed to him particularly incomprehensible and mysterious.

Could it be his handsome guest, Mr. Rolleston, at whom these ominous expressions pointed? Was it possible that he could be a man for whom there was such an accumulation of retribution in store?

The worthy landlord felt bewildered; his eyes glanced towards the bill on the wall.

"Be good enough to read that bill?" said the President, seeing his looks were in that direction.

Mr. Plummer took out his silver-rimmed spectacles, and, adjusting them carefully on his nose, proceeded to read the printed form with due emphasis and discretion:

"£50 REWARD!

"Whereas, on Wednesday night, May 25th, 1736, OCTAVIUS CHALLONER, *alias* OLIVER ARMSTRONG, did, on board the CHARLES Coal-brig, of Whitby, maliciously and wilfully seek to destroy James Cook by throwing him overboard. The above reward will be paid to any person or persons who shall deliver the above OCTAVIUS CHALLONER, *alias* OLIVER ARMSTRONG, to the hands of justice, or give such information as shall lead to his detection. He is tall, and dark, with a pale complexion; will most probably be dressed in sea-faring costume.

"WALPOLE."

"Well, my friend, what think you of that?" asked George Carew, as the landlord finished.

The latter removed his spectacles, and remarked it was very shocking that a man should raise his hands against the life of a fellow-creature.

"What should you say, then," repeated the President, "if the Octavius Challoner, *alias* Oliver Armstrong, whose life is here declared forfeit to the law," pointing to the bill as he spoke, "was identical with your Mr. Arthur Rolleston?"

"W—hat?" exclaimed the landlord, in a faltering voice, "do you mean to assert that the criminal described in that bill, and my visitor, are one and the same person?"

"I do," answered the President.

"Impossible !" returned Mr. Plummer, with energy—"it *must* be impossible !"

"My dear sir," calmly replied George Carew, "nothing is impossible; but this happens to be an indisputable fact. I could not have spoken so positively had I not seen the man."

"Oh !" exclaimed the landlord, "then you have seen him ?"

"I have, not a quarter of an hour since. He was asleep, and I had the opportunity of scrutinising his features closely. He is well known both to this gentleman and myself; we recognised him at once."

"Yes," said Captain Palmer, "we have each good reason to remember him."

"You say, gentlemen," the landlord remarked, in a disturbed tone, "that this gent—I mean person's—name is not Rolleston, what *is* his name ?"

"His name is Octavius Challoner," replied the President; "Armstrong and Rolleston are both *aliases*,"

"But, believing him to be a gentleman, I have advanced him money, until he receives his remittances from London."

"Um !" ejaculated the President, doubtfully.

"Under the same belief," continued the landlord, growing more and more distressed in his tone, "I introduced him to tradespeople, who have supplied him with goods, for which I am responsible !"

"I am sorry to hear it," replied George Carew; "because you may take my word for it, he'll never pay a farthing."

"Then the story of his London banker ?"

"A mere fiction."

"He must be a complete swindler, then !" cried the landlord.

"He's one of the greatest scoundrels unhung !" wound up the President.

This was a death blow to the flattering opinions Mr. Plummer had formed of his dashing visitor.

"I'm very much obliged to you, gentlemen, for this warning," he said; "but what do you advise me to do ?"

"Keep quiet; seem to take no notice," answered the President; "do nothing to lead him to think you suspect him, and the natural course of events will most certainly prove the truth of what we have told you. We shall be here."

"But since he is acquainted with you, if you should meet here, what then ?" asked the landlord.

"He has not the least suspicion that we are so near," replied the President, "and we must keep out of his way. But of one thing be certain, there is a fate hanging over this man's head that we need not seek to expedite, and from which he cannot escape."

The landlord retired from this conference, comforted with the reflection that the two gentlemen would remain at his hotel, but much troubled and perplexed at the character he had received of Octavius.

"However, I am to take no notice of anything I've heard," he soliloquised; "but let matters take their course, so I can't go wrong there."

This being established in Mr. Plummer's mind as his course of action, he became calmer, and thought he would go upstairs and see whether his visitor were awake.

On his entering the room he found his visitor quite roused from his slumbers, the lamp turned full up, and the fire burning brightly. Octavius had been indulging in a plentiful ablution, and now appeared quite revived and lively.

"Ah, my friend !" he exclaimed, in a cheerful tone, as the landlord's good-natured face showed itself, "got rid of your visitors yet ?"

He asked this question carelessly. But Mr. Plummer was not the Mr. Plummer of an hour ago; he had grown suspicious, and he fancied that his questioner had a motive in asking.

"Oh, yes," answered the artful landlord, "all gone now."

"What a relief it must be to you, old fellow, to have a moment to yourself."

Yesterday the landlord would have thought himself too highly flattered at being called by the affectionate title "old fellow ;" now it fell lifeless on his ear.

"To tell you the truth," continued Octavius, "your excellent wine drew me to sleep; what delightful dreams it gave me !"

This praise of his wine affected the landlord deeply. He was a sensitive man, and if he had a peculiar weakness, it was especially touching his wine.

"I think your port is, without exception, the finest I ever tasted."

This was another dig at the host's weak part; he began to waver in the opinion he had been compelled to form of the gentleman before him.

"Could it be possible," he thought, "that so amiable a person, and such an excellent judge of wine, should be a rascal ?"

He glanced at Octavius, and in contemplating his clear pale face and dark eyes, he again began to feel his kindly feelings revive within him. But he made an effort to stifle such pusillanimous sentiments, and tried very hard to steel his heart against the handsome scoundrel.

"These bills were left to-night, sir," he said, in his usual tone of voice, "so I thought I'd better bring them up as you wished it."

"Ah, yes—the bills," repeated Octavius, in a mellifluous tone of voice, and, with a pleasant smile, taking up the papers at the same time and looking over them, as though it was quite a pleasure, "quite right, Mr. Plummer. I shall receive my remittances from London to-morrow, and will discharge them, together with the amount with which you have kindly supplied me."

Here was another blow at the landlord's suspicions. Could this courteous acknowledgment of his debts, and his ready promise to pay to-morrow justify the assertion that Mr. Rolleston was a swindler ? It was impossible ! there must be some mistake.

Octavius, having run through the items of the bills, tossed them on to the table.

"I don't want to be bothered with them to-night," he said, "you can take charge of them till to-morrow, when they shall be all paid ; you can let me have them after breakfast."

The landlord collected the bills and put them into his pocket.

"And now, my worthy host," exclaimed Octavius, throwing himself back luxuriously in his arm-chair, "as your customers have all gone, and as I feel inclined for a little pleasant society, suppose you go and fetch another bottle of your unrivalled wine and some cigars, and favour me with your company for an hour ?"

What was to be done ? The idea of drinking and smoking with a criminal did not seem at all correct to Mr. Plummer's moral perceptions, but he remembered the words of the gentleman, that he was to take no notice or to do anything to excite his visitor's suspicions that his real character was known ; he therefore expressed himself willing to accept his visitor's invitation.

He accordingly left the room to procure the wine, and at the same time took the opportunity to inform the President and his friends of all that had taken place.

George Carew comforted the worthy host with the assurance that he was adopting the right course.

Mr. Plummer, accordingly, went with a clear conscience direct to the cellar, and brought thence another bottle of port, encrusted with cobwebs and sawdust, and having decanted it, proceeded with that and a box of Havannahs to the apartment of Octavius.

Here, in this very questionable society, did the good man assist in drinking his own wine and smoking his own cigars, and, alas ! for frail human nature, in spite of the surrounding circumstances under which these acts were performed, enjoyed himself extremely.

Octavius was lively, and the wine was good, and when Mr. Plummer went to bed, it was with the impression that if Mr.—whatever his name was—*was* a rascal, he was one of the most agreeable of the species he had ever encountered.

Chapter LIV.

OLD FRIENDS.

ON the second day after the departure of Octavius from the "Charles," that vessel entered Whitby harbour.

The drawbridge was raised, and ship and crew were once more snugly moored amongst the numerous craft that lay there.

Allan Rushworth, the master, went direct to the house of his employers, accompanied by James, to report the result of the voyage.

The good merchants expressed themselves highly gratified at the accounts they received from Allan of their apprentice's diligence and obedience; and the narrow escape he had experienced seemed to enhance his value in the eyes of the brothers.

Of course they were informed of the plot that had been concocted by the mates, John Marsh and James Bowers, and the piece of treachery by which Octavius effected his escape from the ship alone.

It became a question with the Brothers Walker as to what should be done with these men.

They had been in their employ for some time, and had always done their duty, until this last voyage.

The merchants were benevolent men, and in any case like the present the natural feelings of their hearts inclined to the side of mercy.

But then there was the other side of the question, justice.

As for the mates themselves, they expected nothing less than to be immediately handed over to the authorities on their arrival at Whitby, and, in that belief, had, in the short space of two days, grown quite thin and haggard.

The Brothers Walker had been on board the brig and had an interview with the culprits, who had pleaded earnestly for mercy.

"Give us another chance, gentlemen," they begged, "and we'll be different men from this moment."

Allan Rushworth, having performed his duty, not screening them in the least, now put in a word in their behalf.

"These men have yielded to a temptation to dishonesty," he said; "but I think the lesson they have received will keep them from such an act in future."

James also added his entreaties, and eventually the Brothers Walker consented not only to overlook their transgression, but, at Allan Rushworth's entreaty, to retain them in their service.

But with Octavius Challoner it was different.

They could not overlook the cold-blooded attempt on the life of their apprentice.

Information was immediately despatched to the proper authorities; no expense was spared to ensure expedition; and in a very short time printed bills, offering a reward of £50 for the apprehension of Octavius, were circulated in every seaport town.

In addition to this, private detectives, paid from the purses of the merchants, were set to work to arrest the criminal.

It was, however, early yet, and no tidings of the culprit had been heard.

The affair had got wind in the town of Whitby, and James Cook became quite an object of interest whenever he appeared abroad.

There was a good deal of excitement also, in the office of the Messrs. Walker.

Many letters were received from the various police stations, which had to be answered at once; and several mysterious individuals came and went, the sight of whom would have made a guilty person shiver in his boots.

In the midst of all this there came two visitors whom they little expected to see.

These were none other than Lieutenant Samphire and Ikey Mangles, whom he now took with him wherever he went.

The lieutenant had some weeks at liberty before he would have to join his ship, and he now threw himself heart and soul into the plan the President of the Con-federates had devised with respect to Octavius Challoner.

Lieutenant Samphire travelled post haste, neither money nor horse-flesh had been spared; and not many hours had elapsed between the time when he was playing his game at billiards in the hotel at Yarmouth and when he stood at the door of the brothers Walker, at Whitby.

The intelligence he brought was electric.

Such a combination of circumstances, all tending to one end, seemed scarcely possible.

What this intelligence was our readers may possibly divine; but we will not here stop to detail that which the progress of events will rapidly eliminate.

James and Ikey met with intense pleasure.

They had fancied themselves severed for many long months, if not years, and now to be together again so soon was a joy the greater because so perfectly unanticipated.

They had each, too, passed through certain adventures which had to be related; they had each lived apart from the other, and made the discovery that it was possible to exist under such circumstances.

They were, however, together again now, and they resolved to make the most of it.

Having nothing to do while the lieutenant was closeted with the Brothers Walker and Allan Rushworth, the boys, as if by a natural instinct, left the town with its quaint old houses behind them, and wandered into the country.

It was a beautiful May day, the sun was shining, and the birds were singing, and everything transpired to make them feel happy.

Now they were not wandering tired and footsore, hungry and forlorn; but as two young hearts full of life and hope, with a bright world before them, and a good dinner awaiting them when they got home.

They talked of their past experiences, of their future prospects—in short, they talked of everything, not forgetting Octavius Challoner.

It was a marvel to them, up to that moment, what two poor boys, as they were, could have done to provoke such deadly enmity in his mind against them.

"Vell," said Ikey, "I vouldn't like to stand in 'is shoes jest now, any'ow. Vhen 'e shied you overboard, Jem, 'e did a bad thing for 'isself, didn't he?"

"I'm afraid he did," replied James. "I forgive him, and I hope he'll live to come to a better mind towards one who never did him any wrong."

The boys had now come to a turn in the road, and a little to the right, through a clump of trees, they saw smoke rising.

"'Ullo!" said Ikey, who caught sight of it, "is that th' smoke of a gipsy's fire?"

"It looks like it," answered James.

"Shall ve go an' see?" asked his companion.

"I think," replied James, "it's hardly worth while, especially as we must be get'ing back."

"Don't you remember that night vhen ve vas hin th' gipsies' camp, an' they vas goin' to 'ang Mr. Hotty fust, an' throw 'im hinter th' svamp hartervards?" Ikey asked.

"I do," James answered.

"An' don't you remember the gipsy tents bein' set fire to, an' tinker Morgan 'idin' us avay in th' trees vhile th' fight vas goin' hon?"

"I remember it very well."

"So do I. Didn't the bullets keep comin' an' crashin' among th' trees!"

"Well, we're out of all those dangers now," said James.

"I vonder vot's come o' Ishmael? Hi should like to see 'im."

At this moment a loud shout of exultation burst from behind the trees where the boys had seen the smoke.

"Vot's goin' on there?" remarked Ikey, curiously. "I should like to see. Do let's come!"

[MORGAN RESCUING JAMES COOK FROM THE MANIAC.]

" Well, then, for a minute; but we'd better keep out of sight. If they're gipsies, they won't care about intruders."

James and Ikey clambered over the hedge, and ran hastily forward.

The ground which led to the trees, and which was covered with green, fresh grass, was on the incline, and the boys panted for breath as they reached the coppice.

They pressed forward, and making their way through a tolerably thick undergrowth of bushes, they perceived in a hollow, seated round a blazing fire, the whole gipsy tribe, the centre figure of which was their old friend, of whom they had just been speaking, Ishmael Morgan.

They all seemed excited and exultant, and the cause appeared to be a printed bill which Ishmael held in his hand, and which he had evidently just been reading.

The gipsy tinker had just returned from one of his pedestrian excursions, and brought back the document he held for the especial benefit and satisfaction of the tribe.

It was the official offer of fifty pounds' reward for the apprehension of Octavius Challoner.

It was the execration in which he was held by the gipsies that awakened the shouts of triumph.

There was not one of the tribe who would not have walked a hundred miles to see him hung.

Ikey recognised the " Hue and Cry " bill, and informed James of its contents.

" That's hall on your account, Jem," he said. " Don't they 'ate 'im like pison?"

This was evident, from the various remarks the gipsies made.

" Didn't I say," cried Ishmael, " that his deeds 'ud come home to the cowardly hound?"

" You did, Morgan—you did!" vociferated his pals.

" Ay," said the patriarch. Phares Darro, " the moment I first set my eyes on that man's face, I prophesied there was a fate in it. What that is," the old man continued, with something of solemnity, " I know not; one thing only I know, Octavius Challoner will never die in his bed, nor in any ordinary way of justice; his destiny will find him out, and his doom will meet him at the appointed time, face to face."

"Confusion to the cur! Death to him! May he die like a dog, and his memory be accursed!" shouted the gipsies.

"I should like to speak to Morgan." said Ikey, eagerly.

"So should I," echoed James.

"Vouldn't 'e be surprised to see us?"

"Very much, I should think."

"Let's call hout, vithout showin' ourselves, an' see if he remembers our woices," suggested Ikey.

This was an innocent little practical joke, that James could offer no objection to; they therefore, at a signal, called out:

"Ishmael Morgan!—Ishmael Morgan!"

The boys hardly anticipated the effect these exclamations would have.

There was a dead silence instantly, whilst the colour went from Ishmael's bronzed cheek, as though he were listening to a voice from another world.

It suddenly struck James that that was the idea prevailing in the gipsy's mind, and he was anxious to dispel it.

"I fancy he thinks we're dead," he said to Ikey.

"Vell, but 'ow could ve 'a called hout if ve vos dead?" Ikey argued.

This was a question James could not answer very satisfactorily, but he said in reply:

"Suppose I call out to him by myself?"

"Call away," returned Ikey, "p'r'aps 'e'll remember your voice."

James immediately cried out:

"Ishmael, are you there?"

The tone of the boy's voice seemed to impress the gipsy as more natural this time, for he answered:

"Yes, I'm here. Who calls?"

"Here are two friends of yours, Ishmael, waiting to see you," James replied.

"Where are you, then?" cried the gipsy.

"Here!" returned James; and as he spoke, he and Ikey burst from the bushes, and stood before the tribe.

Nothing could exceed the joy and astonishment of the rough, but impulsive children of the greensward at this sudden appearance of the boys.

At first there was a dead pause of silence, and then a deafening shout, whilst Morgan, with tears in his eyes, rushed forward and threw his arms round them.

"My dear boys!" he cried, "you won't wonder at me and my brethren being a little scared at the sound of your voices, when I tell you that we all thought you were in Heaven long ago. None of us ever again expected to look on your faces again in this world."

James and Ikey, having been welcomed warmly by the whole tribe, they informed Ishmael of their good fortune, and of the happy change in their circumstances.

The warm-hearted gipsy rejoiced to hear this good news, and triumphantly displayed the bill offering the reward for Octavius.

But Ikey told him he had known all about that long ago, and gave him other information that made his dark cheek flush, and threw him into a state of strong nervous excitement.

"He's at Yarmouth, is he?" he cried.

"Yes, that he is," answered Ikey. "He changed his name, and he's living at the 'Spread Eagle' hotel, the same hotel as we're stoppin' at."

"What, then, are you living at Yarmouth as well?" asked the gipsy, with surprise.

"Vell, ve're not livin' there, only stoppin'," Ikey informed him. "Lieutenant Samphire vent there to pay a visit to some frien's o' 'is, an' it vos me as found out Mr. Hotty was there. Ve're a goin' back almost directly. Ve travels vith post 'osses, ve does."

"Travel on, my boy!" cried Ishmael, with enthusiasm; "post horses, camels, ostriches, if you like! you won't be long in advance of me. Hark'ye, brothers!" he exclaimed, turning to his companions, "this murderous snake's at Yarmouth. Would you not like to hear his last death-rattle?"

Thirty gleaming dark eyes looked the answer.

"Who goes with me to Yarmouth?" shouted Ishmael.

"All!" they shouted in reply.

Chapter XLV.

THE END.

OCTAVIUS CHALLONER, little dreaming of the storm that was preparing to burst over his head, slept very soundly.

He did not wake very early the next morning, and when he opened his eyes, he was conscious that his head was somewhat heavy with the fumes of port wine and cigar smoke.

But he was not in bad spirits by any means.

He rejoiced in the landlord's mendacious information that the visitors, so dangerous to his peace, had departed, and he felt he could breathe again.

By the time he had shampooed his head with an enormous sponge that lay on the washstand, and completed his toilet, he felt quite revived and ready for breakfast.

Mr. Plummer, who had been up for some hours, was becoming, with the matutinal aspect of affairs, quite nervous and fidgety that his visitor did not ring for breakfast.

He almost began to suspect the possibility of his having taken an abrupt departure by the chimney, when, to his great joy, the long expected sound of the bell was heard.

Up went the landlord with all possible expedition to find his visitor ready dressed and smiling, seated cosily by the fire.

"Good morning, Mr. Plummer," he said, sweetly. "I have again to plead your magnificent port as my excuse for lying so late this morning. Let me have breakfast, if you please."

The landlord thrust his hand into his waistcoat pocket, and fingered the tradesmen's bills, his own account included; but as Octavius made no mention of them, he left the room without alluding to them.

"I will wait till after breakfast," he thought within himself.

Octavius sat looking into the bright fire, in a pleasant reverie, till the waiter entered with the breakfast and the newspaper.

Octavius, divided between these luxuries, contrived to keep his worthy host on thorns for nearly another hour.

At length, however, the meal was finished and removed, and then once more Mr. Plummer presented himself.

He came in ready loaded and primed this time, and when Octavius would have indulged in a little desultory chat, went off at once by suddenly producing the bills from his pocket—so suddenly, that they flew out of his hand, and scattered themselves on the floor.

"Oh, ah, those bills," said Octavius, as he observed them on the carpet.

"You desired me to bring them to you in the morning," said the landlord, as he stooped to collect them, with a very red face, the intensity of which was probably increased by the idea that he had been a little premature.

"Quite right," replied his affable visitor, who did not appear to notice Mr. Plummer's eagerness. "You can leave them on the table. I shall be going to the post-office shortly for my letters: when I return I will attend to them. Is your own account—— Oh, yes, I see it is among them."

"Yes, sir," answered the landlord, again staggered by the confident and courteous manner of his visitor, and feeling sundry throes of penitence and remorse for his unworthy suspicions. "If you remember, you told me to make out my account, and——"

"Certainly, my dear fellow." (His dear fellow! Was there ever heard anything like it?) "I remember telling you to do so perfectly well," interrupted Octavius, in the most assuring manner possible. "We will talk about dinner when I return from my walk; I suppose you can get me some fish?"

Never was Mr. Plummer so completely floored. He murmured something in reply, but whether it had reference to *fish* or *flesh*, for the life of him he couldn't have told.

He effected his retreat from the room in a state of mental distraction that was perfectly overwhelming.

Octavius, once more alone, prepared for his stroll.

This he did in a somewhat strange manner.

It was a windy morning, and to protect his eyes, he put on a pair of green glass spectacles.

To secure his chest from the breeze, having lived long in hot climates, and being susceptible to cold, he muffled himself as far as his nose in an ample wrapper. Then, pulling his low-crowned, broad-brimmed hat well over his forehead, and securing that by an additional silk handkerchief passed over and tied under his chin, Octavius pronounced himself ready.

A suspicious person, seeing him thus strangely transmogrified, might have been tempted either to indulge in unworthy surmises, or to make unpleasant remarks.

But whatever may have been the motive that prompted Octavius Challoner to this extraordinary transformation, one thing is certain—if *disguise* was the object, it was certainly attained—his most intimate acquaintance wouldn't have recognised him.

Of course, Octavius knew very well that he had no letters to receive at the post-office, but it was necessary that he should do matters in a business-like manner, in order to account for the receipt of the gold which the canvas bag was to furnish him.

He met the landlord—he was always meeting him now—at the foot of the stairs; and that worthy, but inwardly-agitated individual, nearly fell on his back with surprise at the alteration in his handsome guest's appearance.

"Why, good gracious, heart alive! my dear Mr. —a-h'm—Rolleston, is that really you?"

"I believe so," returned that gentleman, smiling at his host's surprise.

"But you're surely not going out so—so disguised as that?"

"It looks very much like it, my friend, doesn't it?" replied his visitor, smiling more vividly than ever, as he walked towards the swing door.

He turned as he reached it, and holding it partly open in his hand, said:

"As regards fish, if there is any turbot to be got, I should prefer it."

He then went out.

"Turbot!" echoed the landlord out of the depths of his perplexity. "Well, of all the extraordinary—turbot, too!"

He was aroused from his distracted soliloquy by a touch on his shoulder, and, turning round, he found George Carew standing at his elbow.

"Well, my friend, what do you think now?" he asked.

"What do I think?" echoed the landlord, in a bewildered tone. "All sorts of things. I think this thing, and that thing, and the other thing, and—and, in short, it just amounts to this: I don't know what to think."

"You will find that what I have told you is the truth," said the President; "but with respect to yourself—I mean the money you have advanced to this impostor, and the expense he has incurred during his stay at your hotel—be under no apprehension, you shall be no loser; I will discharge the entire debt."

This was a joyful piece of intelligence, and went far to restore the landlord's mind to its proper balance.

He was very grateful—most grateful—could never sufficiently thank Mr. Carew for his advice and assistance; if he must speak the truth, had always suspected his visitor from the first, &c., &c., was about the sum and substance of Mr. Plummer's reply to the President of the Confederates.

In the meantime, Octavius had strolled into a cigar shop, and was at that precise moment strolling along the quay, causing much remark by the oddity of his appearance, but feeling in that very oddity his security from recognition.

He wandered round the Town Hall, and directed his course to the post-office, which he entered.

He looked about him there for a moment, and having amused the clerks by the absurdity of his appearance, inquired in a muffled voice if there were any letters for Mr. Arthur Rolleston.

There were none, of course.

The curious questioner having received this intelligence, departed as he came.

As he left the post-office, a poor, shabby-looking man touched his hat respectfully.

Octavius bowed in return, and, moved with a fit of generosity, gave the shabby man sixpence.

Had he known he was a detective from Norwich, the probability is he would not have been so liberal.

But of this interesting fact Octavius was utterly unconscious, and went on puffing his cigar, and contemplating a journey to Germany, until, in a pleasant vista of plans and arrangements for the future, he once more reached the hospitable threshold of the "Spread Eagle," holding a fictitious letter in his hand.

The landlord was, of course, quite accidentally fluttering about, so that Octavius could not avoid seeing him.

"I shall be ready for you before long, Mr. Plummer," said Octavius, as he went upstairs. "What a fine bracing morning—rather too keen, though, for me after the tropics," he added, with a real or assumed shiver.

The landlord gave up any further reasoning upon what appeared to him such a profound enigma as his guest, and went to decant some wine.

Octavius, having removed his encumbrances, examined the bills, and with a pencil made a memorandum of the total.

Thirty-six pounds fifteen shillings exactly.

Octavius smiled.

What was that to a man possessing £350.

Owing to the landlord's kindness, Octavius had had no occasion to make use of any of the contents of the canvas bag.

Satisfied with the consciousness that he had it close at hand, he had not even opened it, but kept it in the pocket of his jacket, just as he had taken it off, locked up securely in a bureau that stood in his bed-chamber.

The moment had now arrived when he was to draw it forth from its place of concealment, and feast his eyes with the sight of its contents.

He first took the precaution to lock the door, and then unfastening the bureau, took from thence the jacket.

After some tugging he extricated the canvas bag from its retreat, and taking it into the next room placed it on the table.

His eyes gleamed exultingly, as he contemplated it for a moment with a gloating eagerness, such as the giant in the story book might have been supposed to have done his money bags.

Opening his pocket knife, he severed the string that tied up the mouth of the bag, not hastily, but cautiously, to prevent any sudden out-pouring of the glittering coin.

But none came; and, eager to regale his sight with the golden treasure, he held the bag open and looked in.

What horrid mockery was this?

No gold—no glitter—not a solitary coin of the realm met his gaze; but leaden pellets, bullets, nails, and all kinds of sordid rubbish, seemed to sneer in his face.

He sat motionless, gazing at it with haggard face and distended eyes, and then, with a bitter groan of heart-felt disappointment, he sank back in his chair.

Allan Rushworth knew what he was about when he allowed him to remove the canvas bag, and had wisely substituted another for the original; and Octavius Challoner at that moment awoke to the consciousness that he, clever, cunning schemer as he was, had been himself the dupe.

The shock was so great that it was some time before he could collect himself sufficiently to consider his position.

But there was a great necessity that he should do so.

He could not go on day after day trespassing upon the generosity of his host—a reasonable time having transpired to enable his remittances to arrive from London.

Besides, there were bills waiting to be paid, and he without a solitary farthing in the wide world.

He clenched his hands and ground his teeth in the fury of his despair, and then sat moodily looking at the fire.

What could he do? Was ever discomfiture so complete?

His reflections would not have been rendered more agreeable could he have seen his benevolent landlord on the other side of the door, risking a violent cold in his eye, by his persistent efforts to watch everything that was going on within.

He could see the canvas bag, and his visitor's ghastly face, that looked in a few moments years older, and he guessed that something was wrong somewhere—what it was he knew not.

Octavius rose at length suddenly, and paced the room with rapid strides.

Mr. Plummer, who was possessed with the idea that his visitor had caught sight of his eye through the key-hole, retreated with such precipitation that he narrowly escaped pitching head first down the stairs.

However, he recovered himself and descended in safety.

But Octavius was thinking of matters far more important to himself than the landlord's eye, or any other member of his body.

He was reflecting how he should get out of his immediate difficulty, and what plea he could offer for requesting a further advance from Mr. Plummer.

There was only one plan to adopt, and that was to put a good face upon the matter.

His mind was soon made up. By a strong effort he swept the traces of annoyance from his face, hurriedly consigned the vile bag and its sordid contents to the bureau, unlocked his room door, and rang the bell.

The waiter entered.

"I have been taken suddenly unwell, Richard," he said, as the man entered, "let me have some brandy directly."

The liquor was brought; and, by means of a copious draught, he began to recover, in some measure, from the blow he had received.

As soon as he felt equal to the task, he sent for the landlord, who had been detailing all he had seen through the keyhole to the President, George Carew.

In a few moments Mr. Plummer, quite restored to his self-possession, and quite convinced now that his visitor was everything that was bad, made his appearance.

He still wore his genial smile, and Octavius remarked within himself:

"I am safe here; this man, at least, does not suspect me."

"Oh, Mr. Plummer," he said, in an off-hand manner, "I find I shall have to wait for my remittances from town longer than I expected."

"Oh, indeed!" remarked the landlord.

"Yes, my property is invested," Octavius continued, "and my agent writes me word that stocks are at present very low, and that if I sell out now I must do so at a great disadvantage, therefore for a week or two I must remain in your debt."

"Oh, certainly! with pleasure!" exclaimed the landlord, "as long as you like; pray don't mention it, it's not of the slightest consequence; it would have been a thousand pities to have sold out at a loss!"

It was a great consolation to Octavius to find Mr. Plummer so full of confidence; the discovery fell like balm on his wounded spirit.

"I suppose," he remarked, alluding to the bills, "your word will be sufficient for these good people?"

"Oh, dear, yes, quite—quite sufficient!"

"I will give them my note of hand if you wish it!"

"Not the least occasion, my dear sir, I assure you!"

"I shall have to draw upon you for some ready cash, if you will oblige me," Octavius went on to say, emboldened by the perfect acquiescence of the landlord to all his requests.

"I shall be most happy," returned Mr. Plummer, with the most willing readiness. "What sum do you require?"

"Thirty pounds will be sufficient," answered Octavius. "I happened this morning to run against a very fine horse that I should like to purchase; twenty pounds will be sufficient to bind the bargain."

"I can let you have that sum," the landlord said, "I'll fetch it for you."

Octavius could hardly suppress a smile of exultation till his supposed victim had quitted the room, and then he drank another glass of brandy, and chuckled audibly.

Mr. Plummer, be it remarked, witnessed the disappearance of the brandy, and heard the chuckle through the keyhole, and went away chuckling in return, not to fetch the thirty pounds, but to report the state of affairs to the President.

"Am I to let him have the money?" asked the ductile Plummer.

"No!" counselled George Carew, "you can promise it, but make some excuse for not handing it over; the necessity for any evasion will not be for long."

Octavius had resolved on the course he should pursue, and that was, that having got the thirty pounds in his possession, he should keep that as a reserve fund. The comfortable lodging and good living of the "Spread Eagle" would be appropriated as long as they possibly could be without suspicion; and when that was no longer feasible, he would quietly take himself off under cover of night, never more to show his face there.

He had hardly settled this programme, when the landlord returned.

Of course Octavius looked for the cash, but there was none forthcoming.

Mr. Plummer was very sorry, but on referring to his cash box, he found he had miscalculated his ready money, and that, having paid his wine merchant's bill only the day before, he should not be able to oblige him till the end of the week.

Octavius, who believed in the proverb of the "bird in the hand being worth two in the bush," did not quite like this announcement, but as there was no resource, he was compelled to submit with a good grace.

"The end of the week will do very well for me," he remarked.

Accordingly, Octavius went on as before, eating and drinking the best the hotel afforded, and putting the host through a course of enforced dissipation by insisting on his company to help him drink his own wine.

He had already dismissed from his mind the loss of the £350, and now began to look forward to the thirty, with which the landlord was to supply him, as a very comfortable little sum under all the circumstances.

Three days passed, and on the third morning of the third day, after Octavius had finished his breakfast, the landlord, with a radiant smile on his features, entered the room.

"A person below wants to see you, Mr. Rolleston," he said.

"Who is it?" inquired Octavius, with some apprehension. "I know no one here."

"It's no one of any consequence," returned the treacherous Plummer. "Some begging-letter imposter, I imagine, by her appearance."

"Oh, it's a woman, is it?" said Octavius, his anxiety at once subsiding.

"Yes," answered the landlord; "but they're worse than the men—don't allow her to impose upon you."

"Trust me, I will not."

"Am I to show her up?"

"Oh, yes."

The landlord departed, and in a few moments ushered in a female, closely veiled, who appeared very modest and retiring in manner,

"Pray be seated, madam," said Octavius, in a bland voice, as he pointed to a chair.

The retiring female, before complying with this request, conducted herself in a very strange manner.

She first locked the door, and took possession of the key.

Having done this, she seated herself opposite and almost close to Octavius, and raised her veil.

Was it fancy, or did the fictitious Mr. Rolleston recognise in the features of this peculiar female the face of the shabby individual who had a few mornings previously touched his hat and received sixpence in acknowledgment?

Before Octavius had time to argue with himself, the lady said:

"Your name is Rolleston, I believe?"

"It is I."

"You are quite sure?"

"Quite; why do you doubt me?"

Without answering to this, the female produced a printed bill, headed "£50 reward!" and held it up before him.

"Do you know anything of that?" she demanded.

Octavius grasped the bill mechanically, and his eyebrows contracted as he ran over its contents.

"What should I know of it?" he exclaimed, in a voice husky with agitation.

"As your name happens to be Challoner instead of Rolleston, I thought perhaps it might refer to you," replied the lady, coolly.

"My name is Rolleston, not Challoner!" returned Octavius, more and more agitated.

"Your name *is* Challoner — Octavius Challoner!" cried the strange female, springing up with great energy as she spoke.

In an instant, bonnet, curls, and the entire feminine paraphernalia were thrown aside, and the startled criminal found himself confronted by a man—the identical begger he had relieved—ungratefully pointing a pistol at his breast.

"I am a detective officer," said the man, sternly, "and I arrest you, Octavius Challoner, *alias* Oliver Armstrong, as the man named in this bill, on the charge of attempted murder!"

"'Tis false! utterly false!" cried Octavius, starting up, and preparing for a struggle.

"'Tis true! perfectly true!" exclaimed a deep voice from the adjoining room, and at the same moment the door leading to the bedroom opened, and George Carew, the President of the Confederates, accompanied by Captain Palmer, entered.

Uttering a yell of horror, the conscience-stricken Octavius recoiled, and the detective took advantage of his agitation to slip the handcuffs on to his wrists.

Octavius, with blanched cheeks, and eyes that seemed ready to start from their sockets, stood glaring upon the men he knew so well.

"You can swear to the person of this man?" inquired the detective of the new-comers.

"We can," they replied, simultaneously.

"Of what am I accused?" fiercely demanded the guilty man, who was beginning to grow reckless with despair.

"The attempted murder of a poor boy!" answered the President. "Nor is this the first time you have raised your coward hand against his life. Look, also, upon us, and say whether, if Providence had not interposed to save us, you would not have had our blood to answer for."

"I know not what you mean!" cried Octavius, desperately. "I am no sailor, but a gentleman. As for this boy, whose life you accuse me of attempting, I know not what you mean!"

"Let the boy himself, then, convict you!"

As the President uttered these words, the folding-doors were thrown open, and James Cook, with his friend Ikey, accompanied by the brothers Walker and Allan Rushworth, with Lieutenant Samphire, and the first and second mates of the "Charles," came slowly forward.

Octavius regarded them with an expression almost of insanity.

The President addressed James:

"You know the nature of an oath, my lad," he said.

"Yes, sir," James replied.

"Can you not swear, then," continued George Carew, "that that man," pointing, as he spoke, to Octavius, "sought to destroy you by throwing you from the deck of the 'Charles' coal brig into the sea?"

"Yes, sir," answered James, firmly, "I swear he did."

Octavius staggered and sunk into the arm chair by which he stood.

He appeared convulsed, and gasped for breath.

"He is dying!" cried Charles Walker, pouring out a glass of brandy, and holding it to the lips of Octavius.

The wretched man drained it eagerly, and craved for more, which was given him.

The fiery spirit gave him the sudden strength of a maniac.

Starting up, with a yell like that of a wild beast, he, with a desperate wrench, snapped the link of the handcuffs as though it had been glass.

Then, before anyone had time to arrest him, he dashed forward to where James stood, snatched him up in his arms as though he had been an infant, and rushed from the room.

Up the stairs he flew, burst wildly into one of the top rooms, and closing the door after him, locked it inside.

There was a dense crowd in the passage below, and amongst them many dark, gipsy faces.

The detective followed in pursuit of his prisoner, and dashed in the door in time to see him drag his prey from the window.

"Good Heavens!" cried Charles Walker, in an agony of terror, "that monster will destroy the poor boy! Will no one save him?" he exclaimed, frantically—"a hundred guineas to the man who rescues him!"

The news of James's peril spread like lightning, ladders were procured, but, alas! none were long enough to reach the top of the house.

One dark, gipsy form was seen on the summit of one of the ladders, looking up despairingly at the intervening distance that separated him from the roof.

It was Ishmael Morgan.

Suddenly a shout of terror was raised by the masses congregated below.

Octavius, with the fury of a demon in his looks and gestures, had appeared on the roof, dragging with him his defenceless victim.

His malignant intentions were too evident.

With a maniacal shout of triumph he answered the shouts of the crowd, who returned it with a groan of indignant horror and disgust.

"Oh, save him! save the poor boy!" shrieked a hundred excited voices.

Ishmael heard the shouts, and he heard what the crowd could not hear, the piteous appeal the hapless victim made to his remorseless assailant for mercy.

Another moment, and it might be too late.

It would have been too late, had not the detective, who had followed, gained the roof, and advanced to the rescue.

But the man, though powerful, was no match for the raging maniac with whom he had to cope.

Though he had only one hand at liberty, he met the attack of the detective like a rock.

Grasping his throat, he whirled the unhappy officer to and fro like a reed in the stormy hurricane.

The man grew black in the face with suffocation, and was past resistance.

Maddened beyond endurance at the horrible suspense he was suffering, Ishmael had caught sight of a waterspout at about a yard distant to the right of the ladder on which he stood.

It was a desperate resource, but the only one.

He bent over from the ladder, and clasping the pipe firmly with his hands, allowed himself to swing from the ladder to that, to which he clung by his hands and feet.

By a desperate effort of strength, at that giddy height from the ground, he managed to work himself up the wall, hand over hand and step by step, amid the deafening "hurrahs" of the crowd, and reached the coping-stone of the parapet, when another moment would have sealed the fate of the unfortunate detective.

With a last grand effort he dragged himself over on to the roof.

Panting, but not waiting to breathe (there was no time), he staggered forward, and grasped the insane wretch, as he was wringing almost the last breath out of the body of the officer.

Seizing him in his strong grasp, Ishmael compelled him to release his hold of the detective, who fell a dead heap on the roof, though still alive.

But the maniac still held poor James, who had been dragged to and fro in the fierce struggle, till he was almost senseless.

But it was not for long: seizing the wrist of Octavius in his teeth, the gipsy bit the wrist that grasped the boy to the bone.

With a yell of pain he released his hold, and James was free.

It now became a struggle for life and death between the gipsy and the mad Octavius, who seemed to have more than a giant's strength.

How the contest would terminate was doubtful; for Morgan, wearied with the tremendous effort of ascending the waterspout, was all but exhausted.

Nearer and nearer the combatants, who had fallen in their struggle, rolled to the edge of the roof, when a loud shout was raised, and a body of gipsies came crowding hurriedly from the windows.

Octavius, in his semi-insanity heard the shout, and seeing numbers approaching, suddenly released his opponent, and starting up erect, with a wild, discordant laugh, threw himself headlong into the street beneath.

He fell with a sickening crash on to the stones beneath, and his guilty career was ended at last.

"No one destroyed him," said a deep voice, "his doom followed him—it has found him."

It was George Carew who spoke those words.

*   *   *   *   *   *   *

James Cook, thus rescued by Ishmael Morgan, was restored to his friends, to their great joy.

Mr. Charles Walker pressed upon the gipsy the hundred guineas he had promised, but the brave fellow resolutely refusing to accept them, the sum was divided amongst the tribe.

Little now remains to be said, save that James Cook served his apprenticeship with the worthy merchants, and in course of time entered the navy, where his talents became so remarked, that he was selected to conduct the exploring expedition, that has ever since been recognised by the title of " Captain Cook's Voyages."

Ikey Mangles, under the guardianship of Lieutenant Samphire, who was promoted to the rank of admiral, in time, became himself the captain of a war sloop.

Here, then, we leave our heroes, with the brief remark, that with honesty and integrity for a motto, the most unpromising commencement of life may have the brightest finish.

[END OF THE VICISSITUDES OF CAPTAIN COOK'S BOYHOOD.]

www.ingramcontent.com/pod-product-compliance
Lightning Source LLC
Chambersburg PA
CBHW080831250626
47160CB00008B/2898